JAMES BALDWIN

Just Above My Head

"Moralistic fervor, a high literary seriousness, the authority of the survivor, of the witness—these qualities made Baldwin unique."
—*The New York Review of Books*

"Some of the finest scenes in recent American literature. Baldwin expands the territory of the black novel."
—*The Village Voice*

"In this monolithic, turbulent novel of black families caught in thirty years of a murderous century, the power of love redeems the dead as well as the living."
—Paul Bowles, *The Atlanta Journal & Constitution*

"Baldwin is at his earthy best. Deliberately shocking and writing as brilliantly as ever about 'how it was and how it is.' "
—*The Kansas City Star*

"In Baldwin's work . . . race and sex are the arenas in which we fight for love."
—*The Nation*

"This is familiar Baldwin territory—that unique mixture of black family life and religious experience, of anger and frank sexuality that stimulated the American conscience . . . always interesting, occasionally powerful."
—*Library Journal*

Books by

JAMES BALDWIN

JAMES BALDWIN

Just Above My Head

Delta Trade Paperbacks

A Delta Book
Published by
Dell Publishing
a division of
Random House, Inc.
New York, New York

ISBN: 978-0-385-33456-3

Reprinted by arrangement with The Dial Press

Manufactured in the United States of America

Published simultaneously in Canada

For

My brothers,
George
Wilmer
and
David

and my sisters,
Barbara
Gloria
Ruth
Elizabeth
and
Paula Maria

and
Bernard Hassell
and
Max Petrus

BOOK ONE

Have Mercy

Work: for the night is coming.

TRADITIONAL

Daniel
  saw the stone
that was
  hewed out the mountain.
Daniel
  saw the stone
that was
  rolled into Babylon.
Daniel
  saw the stone
that was
  hewed out the mountain,
tearing down
  the kingdom of this world!

TRADITIONAL

THE DAMN'D BLOOD BURST, first through his nostrils, then pounded through the veins in his neck, the scarlet torrent exploded through his mouth, it reached his eyes and blinded him, and brought Arthur down, down, down, down, down.

The telephone call did not go into these details, neither did the telegram: urgently demanding my arrival because my brother was dead. The laconic British press merely noted that a "nearly forgotten Negro moaner and groaner" (this is how the British press described my brother) had been found dead in a men's room in the basement of a London pub. No one told me how he died. The American press noted the passing of an "emotion-filled" gospel singer, dead at the untidy age of thirty-nine.

He had been losing his hair, that rain forest of Senegalese hair, I knew that. Jimmy had not been with him; Jimmy had been waiting for him in Paris, to bring him home. Julia had been clearing up their rooms in her house in Yonkers.

I: sat by the telephone. I looked at the marvel of human effort, the telephone. The telephone beside my bed was black—like me, I think I thought, God knows why I thought it, if I did. The telephone in the bathroom was gray. The telephone in the kitchen was blue, light blue.

The sun was shining that morning, like I've never known the sun to shine before.

He had been found lying in a pool of blood—why does one say a pool?—a storm, a violence, a miracle of blood: his blood, my brother's blood, my brother's blood, my brother's blood! *My* blood, my brother's blood, *my* blood, Arthur's blood, soaking into the sawdust of some grimy men's room in the filthy basement of some filthy London pub.

Oh. No. Arthur. I think I laughed. I think I couldn't cry. My brother.

The house was empty. Ruth was out shopping, Tony and Odessa were at school: it was a Thursday morning.

My brother. Do you know, friend, how a brother loves his brother, how mighty, how unanswerable it is to be confronted with the truth beneath that simple word? Simple. Word. Yes. No. Everything becomes unanswerable, unreadable, in the face of an event yet more unimaginable than one's own death. It *is* one's death, occurring far beyond the confines of one's imagination. Or, surely, far beyond the confines of my imagination. And do you know, do you know, how much my brother loved me? how much he loved me! And do you know I did not know it? did not dare to know it: do *you* know? No. No. No.

I looked and looked and looked at the telephone: I looked at the telephone and I looked at the telephone. The telephone was silent. This was the black telephone. I stumbled to the gray telephone, in the bathroom. Perhaps I thought that it might have mercy on me if I humbled myself on the toilet. Nothing came out of me, not even water, and the phone did not ring. I walked to the light-blue telephone in the kitchen, and looked at it and looked at it: it looked at me, from somewhere over the light-blue rainbow, and it did not ring, it did not ring, it did not ring! It did not ring. *How* can you do this to me, *how* can you tell me what you have just told me, and now, sit there like that, *over the motherfucking goddamn rainbow!* and hold your peace? Oh. If you were a man, like me. Oh. Oh. Oh. Arthur. Speak. Speak. Speak. I know, I know. I wasn't always nice to you, I yelled when I shouldn't have yelled, I was often absent when I should have been present, I know, I know; and sometimes you bored the shit out of me, and I heard your stories too often, and I knew all your fucking little ways, man, and how you jived the people—but that's not really true, you didn't really jive the people, you sang, you sang, and if there was any jiving done, the people jived you, my brother, because they didn't know that *they* were the song and the price of the song and the glory of the song: you sang. Oh, my God my God my God my God my God, oh my God my God my God oh no no no, my God my God my God my God, forsake me if you will and I don't give a shit but give me back my brother, my God my God my God my God my God!

I did not cry. Nothing came out of me, not even water. I stood, as dumb and naked as a horse, under the shower. I dried myself, and I shaved—very very slowly, very very carefully: I was shaving someone else. I looked into my eyes: they were someone else's eyes. I combed my hair. The phone did not ring. Soon I would have to pick it up and dial a number and get on a plane. London Bridge is falling down. My fair lady.

Ruth found me naked, flat on my back, on the bathroom floor, my razor in my hand: and the phone was ringing.

Two years ago: if Arthur were alive now, he would be approaching forty-one. I am the older brother, and I will be forty-eight this year.

My name is Hall: Hall Montana. I was born in California, but Arthur was born in New York and we grew up in New York.

Our father, Paul, died several years back—died, I think, from having crossed a continent to find himself in New York. He had been born in Tallahassee, grew up in New Orleans, and had had a rough, rough time in California. He died, anyway, while Arthur was still Arthur, thank God; he split the scene before Arthur started down. Florence, our mother, once Arthur was in the ground, went back to New Orleans—where she and Paul had met—and she's staying there now, with one of her younger sisters. Ruth, and myself, and the kids try to make it down there for a couple of weeks every summer, and sometimes I bring Mama up here, for Christmas. But she doesn't like it up here. Maybe she never did—but now, when she visits, I can feel her flinching. She doesn't say anything, the pain is at the very bottom of her eyes. I catch it sometimes, when she's just sitting still, looking at television or looking out of the window, or sometimes, when she's walking along the street. She doesn't like to go to church up here. She says that the people don't have any spirit, that their religion ain't nothing but noise and show: they've lost the true religion. That may be true. I don't go to church myself. But even if what she says is true, and I remember, too, how these people treated Arthur when he branched out from gospel, that's not the reason. Any church up here might have Jesus on the main line all day and all night long, and Mama would never so lower herself as to go anywhere near that phone. No, never. She doesn't like this city because it robbed her of her son, and she feels that the people in the church, when they turned against him, became directly responsible for his death. She goes to church down home, though, where she can grieve and pray, away from all the spiteful people whose tongues so lacerated her boy. She can sing to herself, without fear of being mocked, and find strength and solace in the song that says, *They didn't know who you were.* And she's not singing about Jesus, then, she's singing about her son. Maybe all gospel songs begin out of blasphemy and presumption—what the church would call blasphemy and presumption: out of entering God's suffering and challenging God Almighty to have or to give or to withhold mercy. There will be two of us at the mercy seat: *my Lord, and I!*

Two years ago: and I have never really talked about it: not to Ruth, not to my children, Tony and Odessa (who love their uncle), not to Julia, not to Jimmy: and they can't talk about it until I can talk.

I know I'm wrong to trap them in my silence. Maybe it's partly because I was Arthur's manager. I had to talk about him for years, living, and then, dead, as a property, as a star: I had to protect him because Lord have mercy that nappy-headed mother did not know how to protect himself. That made me afraid that I'd lose him as my brother: that he would think that I also thought of him as the can of beans anybody could buy and which everybody sold—and down the river, baby, at a mighty handsome profit.

I don't think that he thought of me that way. I know he didn't. If he had, he would have died much sooner. I know it because I know that he never tried to hide anything from me, though sometimes, he tried to protect me, too. I know I loved him, and he knew it; with all my heart, I loved him; even when he made me so mad sometimes that I felt like I wanted to beat his brains out. He made his life so hard! Well. That's not true, either. He lived the life he lived, like anybody, I guess, and he paid his dues, like everybody. Maybe what I mean when I say he made his life so hard was that he always tried to pay his dues in front. That isn't always possible: it can even be called a bad habit. Maybe some dues are paid. Some dues may be just a bad memory; but you can't really take that for granted unless you can trust your memory. The truth, anyway, is that I wouldn't really give a shit about all these abstract speculations if I weren't trying to talk about my brother. He was on stage. He caught the light, and so I saw him: more clearly than I will ever see myself.

I had this dream this morning, this Sunday morning, just as I was beginning to come up out of the cave of sleep, just at the moment, down in that cave, I heard Ruth sigh and turn toward me and, in my sleep, but beginning to rise up out of it, I turned toward her.

But the dream still held me. Me and Arthur and Jimmy and Julia were all someplace together, some insane place, like Disneyland, or Coney Island. But the children weren't with us. It was night, and Jimmy said something to Arthur, something funny, which I didn't catch, because, at that exact moment, I felt Ruth move.

I kind of shifted my weight, so that Ruth could move as she pleased, closer to me, closer: I was waiting. Waiting. Arthur answered

Jimmy, and Julia held between them a doughnut covered with white icing, and Ruth put her head on my chest, and my hand got tangled in Ruth's hair. Julia threw the doughnut way up in the air and then my mother came along—she was carrying some breakfast dishes—and she said, *You better let that doughnut stay up yonder, where it belongs. You don't know doughnuts like I know doughnuts.* Then we all went away to the country. I was in a wagon, going up a hill. There were lots of trees on the hill. Arthur was in the road, with his big shoes flapping in the dust. He was running to catch up with the wagon. He was just a little boy, about five, and he was crying, and snot was coming out his nose. I was trying to stop the wagon, but I didn't know how. I couldn't make the driver hear me. Every time I tried to crawl to the back of the wagon to bang on the window of the cab and beg the driver to stop and let me pick up my brother, the truck shook and zigzagged all over the road and it threw me from side to side.

Arthur was still running and crying and the trees were moving right behind him: some trees had moved right up close beside him and a few trees were a little bit ahead of him. I decided to jump off the wagon and grabbed for a tree to break my fall, but the tree moved aside. I grabbed for another tree, but this tree knocked me back against the cab window. I was determined to jump and I crawled forward on my face and belly to the front of the wagon, but then, the truck leaped upward, starting down a steep hill, throwing me all the way back again. The trees were laughing: I could still hear Arthur screaming. I crawled up, up, up to the very edge of the wagon and the wagon rushed down this hill and then water rose over my head, gray, salty water. My mother measured some baking soda into a cup. She said, *No. Not like I know,* and lowered the heat on the biscuit in the oven. I ran and ran and got into the subway train just before the doors slammed. A whole crowd of people just stared at me, most of them were white, but there were a couple of brothers in the car, too, I didn't know them, and I said to myself, *Well, hell, if you all going to be like that, I'll just be my own bartender* and I walked over and poured myself a big vodka martini. Then, I poured another one because I figured Arthur needed a drink and Arthur was waiting for me in the next car. I started pushing through the crowd, trying not to spill the two big cold drinks I had and Arthur started singing "Precious Lord, Take My Hand," and I thought he was in the next car but a woman said, *No, he's home, honey. He's home.* I was so happy to hear my brother's voice, a voice that could go high enough to make you shiver and growl low enough to make you moan, that I almost pissed my pants, and, just then, the subway stopped on my rooftop and I ran out of the subway and down the steps, with these two big dry martinis in my hands. But I didn't know which door Arthur was behind. I wanted to knock, but I couldn't knock with a glass in each of my hands. The floor was so crooked, I was afraid the drinks would spill if I set them down. I kicked a door and it opened suddenly; all of a sudden the door just flew open, on the sky. I couldn't catch my balance. I arched myself back but my feet began slipping off the edge, into space. Then Ruth moved, and put her lips on my chest. Then in my sleep, I moved toward her, I turned to her, I clung to her, catching my balance; somewhere between sleep and waking, I began to caress my wife. With my eyes still tight closed, I clung to my woman, and her sigh, her moan, dragged me up from the deep. I was trembling. Her fingers on my back began to stroke the trembling out of me. My arms tightened around her, her thighs encircled me, her feet tickled my ass, the hairs in the crack of my ass. She opened, I entered; I entered and she opened. She stroked the dream out of me, she brought me to her, she brought me awake, she stroked me into a waking torment, and, slowly, slowly, as though preparing herself to carry it safely and spill not a single drop (*I thought of the two dry martinis!*) she dragged the dream upward from the base of my belly to the edge of my sex. I was so grateful, grateful, I felt such a gratitude, and I clung to my wife, who held me tight and waited for me, and then, after a pause, a mighty pause, I shot it all into her, shot the grief and the terror and the journey into her, and lay on her breast, held like a man and cradled like a child, released.

———

Ruth got out of bed, and I watched her move away from me, into the bathroom. Ruth's a big chick, heavy, with a color somewhere between mahogany and copper, with a lot of steel-wool hair, just beginning to turn gray. I always watch her buttocks when she moves—she says I'm an ass freak. Her buttocks are big, but firm and heavy and beautiful—*juicy*, I say, sometimes, and that's when she calls me an ass freak.

I didn't know what time of morning it was. Then I remembered that I didn't have to get up today, it was Sunday. Tony and Odessa had spent the night at Julia's house. Ruth was going to pick them up. She'd call me from there, later.

She would say, "How you feeling, babe?"

"I damn sure don't feel like driving."

"You never do. That's why I took the station wagon, just in case. But, come on, baby, Julia'd love to see you, and the kids always dig it when you come get them. Tony gets to ride with you and Odessa gets to ride with me and then, they feel, you know, like they got real grown-up secrets from each other."

She would laugh.

"Actually, Odessa would much rather ride with you, but Tony's getting big now and he don't want to have nothing to do with girls, neither his mama, and certainly *not* his sister."

Tony is fifteen. It certainly doesn't look to me like he'll ever get to be heavy, like Ruth; but Ruth says that he will. Ruth isn't fat. She's big-boned, and solid. She says that she looked even worse than Tony when she had been Tony's age and there hadn't been enough flesh for the bones. Right now Tony looks like an Erector set, waiting for someone to put it together. Like, he might turn into a train or a train station or a skyscraper or a truck or a tractor or a steam shovel, it all depends on whose hands touch it. The poor boy's ankles are raw from the war going on between them, and, every once in a while, the ankles seem, somehow, to attack his knees, which are in a pitiful state. Tony's knuckles and wrist bones and elbows and shoulder blades are simply an immense magnetic field for all of the most brutal inanimate objects of this world. I've seen tables and table legs leap at him; open windows, when he touches them, turn themselves into guillotines; doorways just grin when they see him coming; he is most eagerly awaited by stairs. I hurt for that child almost every time I see him move. He's got no flesh on his ass yet, either; in fact he's got no behind at all, and floors, especially old ones, with splinters, won't let his behind alone.

Yet he can dance—very, very beautifully, I think; it's strange to see all that awkwardness transformed, transcended, by something my son is hearing in the music, beneath the bone. He has enormous dark eyes—like his uncle Arthur—and hair somewhere between the Africa of Mississippi, where Ruth comes from, and the Indian-stained Africa of California, where I come from. He looks more like his mother than his father. He has Ruth's high cheekbones and her wide mouth, but he has my nostrils and my chin.

I have the uneasy feeling that I am probably a rotten father—my son is made of mercury, but I am not—but I hope that Tony does not feel that. I don't know if my son loves me—you always feel that you must have made some really bad mistakes—but I know that I love my son. I know this, somehow, because I loved my father; I know the two things don't necessarily have anything to do with each other. I tried to be a good son to him, but—I don't know: he was formed in a world I never really saw. I tried to be a good brother to my brother, too— but—I don't know. Arthur lived in a world I only glimpsed, sometimes, through him: I didn't really pay my dues in that world, not the way he did. But I'm not sure that the people who live in Arthur's world were really very good to him, either. I always felt that there was something about Arthur that frightened them.

Tony's not very nice to his sister, either, as far as I can tell. Odessa is thirteen. She and Tony agree on nothing, except that each agrees that the sex of the other is loathsome: if that can be called agreement. *Odessa, I'm going to kill you!* I once heard Tony shout this from the kitchen, while Ruth and I sat in the living room. I looked up. Ruth looked at me. She yelled, "If you two don't come out of that kitchen,

I'm going to come in there and kill both of you! And *I* got the butcher knife. Now come on. If you can't be quiet, go to bed. Lord!" And she went back to her book.

But sometimes they seem to get on very well, especially if they are both mad at us. Odessa is going to be beautiful. I've always thought so, though I have never been sure what my son will look like. For me, my son takes more after his mother. Odessa takes after nobody, really—well, maybe *my* mother, a little bit. My Indian ancestors have gracefully bent Odessa's nose, and slanted, slightly, her eyes. It can be said that she's got my high forehead. And I'm taller than Ruth, but not as heavy; people probably take me as a pleasant-enough-looking dude, dark-brown-skinned, built a little on the lightweight side, and just beginning to pick up some weight. Odessa is going to be beautiful, and she is going to be tall, like me. As I've said, I'm forty-eight. Ruth is forty-two. We married each other when she was twenty-seven, and pregnant with Tony. I was then thirty-three.

Ruth is the first real commitment I have ever made, outside of my commitment to Arthur, and this commitment was possible only because, loving me, she knew how much I loved my brother, and, loving me, she loved Arthur, too.

Now, not awake, not asleep, I listened as she finished in the bathroom. Not awake, not asleep, I was aware of her getting dressed in the adjoining room.

We live in a fairly old stone house, on the edge of The Bronx, near Yonkers; and Julia lives in Yonkers. I was my brother's manager and I'm still in show business. I bought the house during one of Arthur's more spectacular years; one of the very last spectacular years, before I had to face the beginning of the end of my brother. Arthur had been talking about buying a house in Istanbul—he had been there a few times, sometimes to work and sometimes to rest, and he liked it there. It was a nutty idea, which I neither encouraged nor discouraged. Luckily, he had hooked up with Jimmy by this time, and Jimmy agreed with me: this particular American citizen wouldn't long be able to get to his grits in the principal city of an American satellite, with borders on both Greece and Russia: to name but two of the borders. He would be squeezed to a lonely death there; his song would cease. I didn't really give a shit if Arthur bought a house in East Hell, Tahiti, or Lower Switchblade, Iceland. My role was just to make sure that he had the bread to pay for the house—he'd never live in it, anyway—because he damn sure worked hard enough to pay for whatever the fuck he wanted to do. I once heard myself shouting at some asshole white producer, who was giving me some mealy-mouthed crap about my brother's private life being a problem, *If he likes boys, then buy him a bathtubful, you hear? Buy him a* boatload! *What the fuck do* you *like?* I'll never forget that cat's face: some people look at you like you've farted when you try to tell them the truth, or when they know you mean what you say. And I remember, saying to him, in simple fairness to Arthur, *Anyway, that's not exactly my brother's problem:* and it wasn't. I bought this house with Arthur in mind, it was supposed to be the place where Arthur could always crash. He didn't see it that way, though, he didn't want his sorrow to corrode my life, or menace my children's lives.

I say, it's funny how we never talk about it, but that's not true. Ruth can't talk about it, nobody can really talk about it until *I* can talk about it. It's nearly two years ago. I've been so busy, covering up for Arthur, strong-arming the press, flying half over the goddamn globe—I was so busy getting my brother into the ground right that I've hardly had time to cry, much less talk.

Ruth comes into the room, dressed, her Sunday high-heeled shoes clicking lightly.

She leans over me. She has on her green fall suit, and a light-gray topcoat. She is bare-headed—that beautiful, spinning, black-gray hair seems to be a gift she is offering to me. She has put on a little makeup, and a little perfume. I like the smell. I like the way she looks.

"There's hot stuff in the oven," she says. "It'll stay warm. All you got to do is plug in the coffeepot. Coffee's all made."

I kiss her. She tugs at my hair, lightly, and straightens.

"You go on back to sleep," she says. "I'll call you in plenty of time."

"Okay, mama."

I watch her face, and there stirs in me, again, the overwhelming gratitude I had felt in her arms in the morning.

"Okay. But, you know, I might not really feel like driving over to Julia's. I might just lie around the house."

"We'll see. I'll call, anyway. Okay?"

"Okay, babe."

"Later," she says, and kisses me again, and leaves me. I hear the door close lightly behind her.

I lay there, in a torpor which was not physical—a charged torpor, in the depths of which something slowly gathered, to crouch, to spring. *Ruth.* Sometimes, especially when we were younger, but even now, I wake up while she is still sleeping, and stare at her; at all that I can, physically, with my eyes, see of her; which is her body. Yet, invisible antennae register something deeper than my eyes can see. I am happy with her, simply. I never knew that I could be happy. It never occurred to me; I had never seen it. I knew no one who was happy, God knows, in that world of the gospel singer: the musicians, the buses, the costumes, the theater owners, the churches, the pastors, the deacons, the backing choir, booking agents, the hotel rooms, the cars, the buses, sometimes the trains, eventually the planes, the fucked-up schedules, the fucked-up nerves, Red and Crunch and Peanut and Arthur, in their early quartet days when Arthur, at fifteen, was lead singer. *Jesus is all this world to me motherfucker hold on this little light of mine oo-ba shit man oo-ba oo-ba if I don't get my money hal-ay-lyu-yah! I don't want to hear that noise Jesus I'll never forget you going to have you a brand-new asshole you can't crown him till I oo-ba oo-ba boom-boom-boom yeah and how would you like till I get there a brand-new cock and when the roll is why? you don't like called up yonder oo-ba oo-ba swinging on sweet hour of prayer my old one no hiding place! No more? Jesus I'll never forget man dig them oh they tell me titties man oo-ba oo-ba oh shake*

*it off Mama an uncloudy cat's digging day you down below how did you
man feel when you yeah baby keep digging come it ain't half hard yet out
the wilderness oh baby! leaning don't go nowhere leaning yeah sister fox
oo-ba oo-ba yeah leaning oh you precious freak you leaning on oh don't it
look good to leaning you now on the Lord come on back here 'tis the old
yeah you stay ship right there of Zion it going be beautiful my soul I'm
going let you have looks up a little taste to Thee.*

Lord. And yet: they walked by faith.

I lit a cigarette, and turned on my side, inhaling the memory of
Ruth's odor, staring at the place her body had lain—I'm happy with
her. Every inch of her body is a miracle for me; maybe because her
body has taught me so much about the miracle of my own. Sometimes, when I wake before she wakes, I lay as I lie now, and watch her:
the square feet, which love walking the naked earth, the blunt stubborn, patient toes. And I kiss them. Kneeling, I kiss her legs, her
thighs, my lips, my tongue, move upward to her sex, her belly button,
her breasts, her neck, her lips, and I hold her in my arms, like some
immense, unwieldly treasure. I, at least, thank God that I come out
the wilderness. My soul shouts hallelujah, and I do thank God.

I put out my cigarette. I fall to sleep.

A thunder rolled inside my head, a stunning thunder, and I woke up.
My whitewashed ceiling, with the heavy, exposed, unpainted beams,
had dropped to crush me—was not more than two inches, just above
my head. This weight crushed, stifled, the howl in my chest. I closed
my eyes: a reflex. Then I opened my eyes. The ceiling had lifted itself,
and was where it had always been. I blinked. The ceiling did not
move, neither up nor down. It looked like it was fixed there, forever,
like the sky outside, fixed, forever, just above my head.

And I trembled, as I had never trembled before. My ceiling will not
succeed forever in holding out this sky. That sky will be there just
above my head, forever, long after my ceiling crashes, and long after I
descend beneath that darker sky, the earth, which has borne my
weight until this hour. That darker sky, the earth, will scour me to

bone, then powder: powder in the bowels of the earth. For pure terror now, my bowels rumbled, and I got up. My piss and shit were already a part of the earth, dropping into it daily. Every day a little bit of one-self drops into that darkness, accumulating patiently there the terms of an ultimate rendezvous: one day, one's shit will hit the earth an hour or so before one joins it, or, maybe, less.

Arthur had sometimes sung a takeoff on an old church song,

> *Went to the gypsy*
> *and she said*
> *rejoice*
> *you'll know your lover*
> *by the sound of his voice*
> *she said, hush hush*
> *somebody's calling*
> *your name?*

Well, down yonder, you'll know yourself by your stink, and keep your rendezvous by following your nose. This rendezvous had been made in the womb, with your mother's shit and piss, before that, with the food your father ate, which gave his sperm its texture and its taste, and long, long before that, and the dread, the mighty, the unavoidable rendezvous continues long, long, long thereafter, forever. I thought, wiping myself, flushing the toilet, watching my dark messengers being whirled under by the tide, turning on the water to wash my hands and to prepare to shave, watching myself in the mirror, of Arthur's favorite verse from the Bible: *Oh, Lord,* Arthur said often, sometimes smiling, sometimes weeping, *we are fearfully and wonderfully made. Such knowledge is too wonderful for me.*

I have a cold, still feeling that that moment when my ceiling had seemed to descend to crush me—will never leave me. I do not trust my ceiling anymore, I will never trust it again, and I, consciously, do not look up at it when I walk back into the bedroom. I do not even try to laugh at myself about this. I am far too frightened to try to laugh. I am too frightened to take consolation from the fact that the descent of the ceiling was nothing more than an optical illusion, produced by fatigue, by failing eyesight.

I come out of streets where life itself—life itself!—depends on timing more infinitesimal than the split second, where apprehension must be swifter than the speed of light. I have spent a lot of my life on rooftops. I do not dare go back to bed. Reluctantly, I begin to get dressed, and face what is left of this Sunday: and the phone has yet to ring: it is two thirty in the afternoon: Ruth is giving me all my time: I think, *Shit. Suppose I'd been lying on my belly on the roof, and the street had seemed that close and I'd tried to snuggle up to it?* I heard my cry, and saw my fall, as, too late, I awakened—in the middle of the air; and the palms of my hands, my armpits, my balls, and my asshole are wet as I begin dragging myself into my clothes.

By and by, I sat sipping coffee in the kitchen, staring through the kitchen windows at the exiled trees which lined the sad streets of a despairing void. It's better than the city—that's what we say; it's good for the children—my royal black ass. It's one of the blood-soaked outposts of hell. The day is coming, swiftly, when we will be forced to pack our things, and go. Nothing can live here, life has abandoned this place. The immensely calculated existence of this place reveals a total betrayal of life.

So the trees, daily, with their expiring breath, warn me. They, too, are about to be cut down, will soon go to join their ancestors in the happy hunting grounds.

I see Arthur standing in this kitchen, looking through the windows.

"I know," he said, "that you think I ain't never satisfied with nothing, and—I guess—that's true. In a way."

Then he stopped, and looked at me. I was sitting where I'm sitting now.

"You don't know, and I don't know what *that* means—never to be satisfied with nothing. But man"—then he had laughed; he had been drinking Scotch and milk; all of the landscape's waning colors turned to fire in his glass—"this place *sucks*. With a straw. You ever look into the faces of these people? Oh, baby. Shit. How did *that* happen?"

"We just want to be free," I said. "We couldn't all make it to Canada. Some of us had to stop here."

Arthur laughed, walking up and down this kitchen, but the sound was not the sound of release. Then he stood still before the window, his glass in one hand, his back to me, as still and as astonished as a prisoner.

The failing sun abruptly burned him, then, into what I would come to call my memory.

"Nobody," Arthur said, "is happy here." He sounded, really, like a child. I wanted to say—I think I wanted to say, *Oh, shit, man, get over that:* but I didn't say anything. "I wonder what goes on behind all these careful shutters. It *can't* be—*nothing*. But"—he finished his drink and turned to face me—"it sure don't seem to be *something*. It would show." He raised his eyes to mine. "Wouldn't it?"

"*I* show," I said. "*I'm* something."

He grinned a dry grin, and poured himself another drink.

"I'll fucking well give you *that*," he said. "You a mother*fucker's* motherfucker."

Beams of heaven, as I go.

That was Arthur's favorite song, the first song he ever sang in public, in Julia's church. Our parents, Paul and Florence, had been there, though they were not members of this church. But Julia was the granddaughter of a neighbor, a friend of our mother's from New Orleans. Julia was a child evangelist, about eleven years old, and this was her home church. Her younger brother, Jimmy, was then about nine.

Our father, Paul, played the piano behind Arthur.

Through this wilderness below.

Pentecost Sunday: Arthur, at thirteen.

Guide my feet in peaceful ways,
Turn my midnights
Into days.

Julia's church had then been located in a dilapidated brownstone
on 129th Street and Park Avenue, in the shadow of the elevated New
York Central Railroad tracks: and a train roared by as Arthur was singing.

When in the darkness
I would grope,
Faith always sees
A star of hope;
And soon from all life's grief
And danger, I shall be free,
Someday.

It was a very grown-up song for such a tiny figure. I remember him
as wearing a dark-blue suit, and a white shirt, and a blue bow tie, and
he was wearing highly polished black pumps with pointed toes, and
he had waves in his hair. The waves were very grown-up, too, for a boy
so young, but it was the fashion dictated by his peers, and no one
knew on what grounds to dissuade him from wearing his hair that
way.

For that matter, our father, Paul, who was sturdy and attentive at
the piano, wore *his* graying hair after the fashion of *his* peers, slicked
down flat with Vaseline, seeming, almost, to be straightened.

But I do not know
How long it will be

Or what the future may hold
For me:
But this I know,
If Jesus leads me,
I shall get home,
Someday.

This was Arthur's debut, and it was a great success; the women's hats moved like breakers on the sea; the church was filled with the thunder of adoration. I was older, I was uneasy, I did not know why I was happy for my father and mother, because they were happy. I told my brother that the way he wore his hair made him look like a sissy, and that may be the first time I ever really looked at my brother. He cracked up, and started doing imitations of all the most broken-down queens we knew, and he kept saying, just before each imitation, "But I *am* a sissy." He scared me—I hadn't known he was so sharp, that he saw so much—so much despair, so clearly. But he made me laugh until tears rolled down my face, and I ended up on the floor, both arms wrapped around my belly.

Perhaps then we really began to be friends.

Arthur wore his hair that way for a while, but then, abruptly, he cut it, and he never conked it: during his professional heyday, he looked, with his rough rain forest of Senegalese hair, like a good-natured basketball player.

HALL MONTANA PRESENTS:
(*limited engagement*)

and here was Arthur's picture, full face, close-up, my baby brother's long, lean face, singing, the nostrils quivering like a stallion's nostrils, the big teeth faintly gleaming, the short upper lip, the wide lower lip, the cleft chin, the enormous eyes, looking upward—*my faith looks up to Thee!*—I always saw the sweat pearling, curling, making a splendor of the hairline, I always see, beneath the unanswerable glory, the unanswerable fatigue—Arthur loathed his photographs, and always insisted, because he did not want to be dishonest—that's what he said—on being photographed as he looked *now* and not as he had looked *then*, and I always did as he insisted, at least in the public domain: but the photograph, though Arthur never seemed to realize this, was always, somehow, the same.

Time attacked my brother's face, as time attacks all faces; but it was wonderful indeed for me, and strange, to be forced to see (since publicity was my department) how the enemy, time, could also be an ally, a friend, and a witness. Arthur was photographed endlessly for more than ten years, but whatever held the face together held, changing all the time, yet never changing; and, insofar as Arthur, eventually, was forced to suspect this, he was made mightily uneasy. Time could not attack the song. Time was allied with the song, amen'd in the amen corner with the song, inconceivably filled Arthur as Arthur sang, bringing Arthur, and many thousands, over. Time was proud of Arthur, so I dared whisper to myself, in the deepest and deadliest of the midnight hours; a mighty work was being worked, in time, through the vessel of my brother, who, then, was no longer my brother, belonging to me no longer, and who was yet, and more than ever, forever, my brother, my brother still.

Indeed: for I had to make certain that Arthur got out of his wringing wet clothes and took a bath or a shower and had a stiff drink, Scotch or vodka, depending on the night and the city, and got something to eat, and crashed somewhere. Until Jimmy came along—or, I guess I should say, until he came back into our lives—this had been an enormous problem for me, for Arthur was capable of picking up anybody, and I, after all, couldn't sleep in the same room. Many times I didn't sleep at all and many times it was very rough, since Arthur had to be up around showtime: but I had to be up in the morning, the same morning.

Yet in spite of all the shit, we always loved each other. I was always able to make Arthur listen to me because Arthur always trusted me. I miss him, miss, miss, miss, miss him, miss him worse than you miss a toothache, worse than you miss the missing tooth, worse than you miss the missing leg, even worse than you miss the stillborn baby. His voice is everywhere, but not even the voice can fill that space in which Arthur moved and walked and moaned and talked and belched and farted and pissed and shit and wept and wept and wept and wept and wept and cried sometimes and laughed sometimes and sometimes—making me know he loved me—put his big hand upside my head and tangled his fingers in my hair and said, *Shit, man, we don't get to hang out together most often, have another one! On me. Come on, now:* striding, striding, striding, in his big, flapping traveling shoes, all, all over my heaven.

HALL MONTANA ENTERPRISES
IS PROUD TO PRESENT

THE SOUL EMPEROR
ARTHUR MONTANA

Ladies and gentlemen, it is a great delight and a mighty privilege to bring on The Soul Emperor, Mr. Arthur Montana!

And the theme which brought Arthur on, however disguised, was always the same:

> *Let the church say*
> *Amen*
> *Let the brothers say*
> *Amen*
> *Let the sisters say*
> *Amen*
> *—And, all together, now!*
> *Amen*
> *Amen*
> *Amen!*

And, yes, the church, wherever it was, whatever it was, a football field in Montgomery, Alabama, a stadium in Tokyo, a music hall in Paris, Albert Hall in London, or as far away as Sydney: rocked.

It was nearly four o'clock when I finally got into the car and started driving toward Julia's house. I might have got into the car by that time only because Ruth hadn't called me—or because I was afraid to sit in the house. I suddenly wanted to see Ruth and my children.

From my house to Julia's house takes about half an hour, through a placid and terrifying landscape. It's terrifying because it isn't true. It's here, but it's not; it's present, but it's gone. Some people, some faces, make you feel this, like the face of a woman who knows that she is beautiful. If she knows that, then you wonder what else she knows, or if she knows anything else; for it is not easy to know that you are beautiful. And she can be beautiful, really, smiling with you in the evening, or crying beneath you at night, or naked, in the morning, with no makeup on: she can get your dick hard, she's got your nose wide open. And yet, and still, at the very bottom of the clear and candid eyes, something lives which gives the lie to the beauty of the surface, and which, when you really must deal with it, troubles the beauty of the deep. You begin to sense, dimly, but powerfully, a lack of coherence— a smile on the wrong line, a cigarette awkwardly relit, an earring which should not be on *that* ear, one chewed fingernail—and only one—and you wonder what this incoherence hides and begin to be frightened of what it may reveal. Finally, you begin to recognize that there is nothing you can do with this absolutely sincere incoherence; it is a desperate sincerity. Sincerity is so cheap a virtue, haggled over, daily, in every public square, written on walls, in toilets, on flags—so cheap a virtue that, mainly, it is not a virtue at all, but an abject re- flex—that one finally looks hard at the person who bought this partic- ular consumer item at so extravagant a price. There is something un- real, then, about the reality of this beauty, something profoundly willed. Anything brought into existence by so powerful an act of the will is nothing less than a mask, a disguise, a lie, is hiding some-thing—from itself: this suspicion fucks with the mind, and leads to terror. Or, for example, I remember a white boy Arthur knew once—briefly, thank God—a boy named Faulkner, who was as beautiful and limpid as a Viking saga, and as ruthless as the Russian steppes. He could not help it. He was a liar and a thief and a cock-teaser; he was searching for the prison in which he could be raped forever by an army of black studs. Rape does not come naturally, and that child was hell unloosed. The only times I ever knew him not to be smiling was when he was sobbing out his innocence, and begging not to be beaten to death. At least, I thought that's what he was begging for. I once had to beat the living shit out of him, turned him upside down, and shook Arthur's money out of his pockets; but now, I think that he was maybe begging me to kill him. Life in death, or death in life: but a change is got to come.

The streets I am driving through to Julia's house are, somehow, something like that. They frighten me like that, because nothing I am seeing is true. These houses, these penny-pinched lawns, the angular streets; for one thing, it was never intended that *we* should live here. This is not yet forgotten. The trees and the houses and the grass re-member; the stoplights remember, the fire station, the churches, and the courthouse. The people do not seem to remember—very few are out—but, then, they have had to remember so little for so long, that one simply awaits, now, numbly, their next convulsion—and indeed, the smiles of the few people out walking, or riding, reveal clenched teeth and leaping jaw muscles. Their placid eyes reflect their placid surroundings (the church spire wavering at the bottom of the cheerful eye) and, by this time, for me in any case, are capable of reflecting nothing more.

There was a time when I found this sad. Perhaps I still do, but pity is a dead-end street, a useless doom; sympathy, repudiated, turns to bile: forget it. Some hale and hearty white people walking around to-day are going to be butchered corpses soon—like tomorrow, but it is utterly absurd to pity them. The song asks, *Sinner man, where you go-*

ing to run to? and advises against heading for burning rock or boiling sea, and wonders, from a distance, *Who shall be able to stand?*

The car ahead of me has a bumper sticker reading, AMERICA: LOVE IT OR LEAVE IT, and I want to get as far away from that car as I can. (Peanut's body was never found, after that trip to Georgia.) I want to see my wife and my children. Each stoplight takes forever; I cannot shake the car with the bumper sticker, it is traveling in my direction. I am ridiculously aware of the Sunday policemen, scattered sparsely over the landscape. I do not look at them. But I know that they see me. I know that they never expected to, never intended to, and are smoldering with the need to be revenged for this violation. *Up yours, mac, and I hope it puts a hurting on you:* but I do not usually feel this way.

I park the car in Julia's front yard, and stumble up her steps—red brick steps, which I hate, but Julia's very fond of them. I ring the bell, but the record player's going—Esther Phillips, *From A Whisper To A Scream*—and I stumble down the steps, and go around to Julia's backyard.

It's early spring, a little after five in the afternoon, it's beginning to be chilly but it's not really cold yet.

Julia's standing alone in the back yard, at the Bar-b-q range, turning the ribs over. The hot, funky smell of the meat is marvelous, and Julia, standing alone, head down, in profile to me, studying the meat, judiciously adding her spices and sauce, a drink—gin—standing on the edge of the Bar-b-q range, a cigarette burning in an ashtray next to the glass; Julia, dressed in a loose, vaguely African robe, her hair tied up in a gaudy cloth, one talismanic bronze earring dangling, eyes narrowed against the smoke from the cigarette and the smoke from the fire, standing in the shadow of the menaced trees of her backyard, platform sandals on her feet, picking up her cigarette, dragging on it, putting it back in the ashtray, picking up her drink and sipping from it, and turning over about three or four more ribs, was marvelous, too, and I said, "I guess I got here just in time."

She turned, with that smile, a child's smile, which had made her so moving a child evangelist, and, later on, so moving. "Ruth's just been on the phone to you," she said. "She figured you were on your way. How you keeping?" And she laughed. "You *look* all right."

"So do you," I said, and I went over to her, and kissed her.

Julia and I had a big thing, a brief thing, a big thing, a long time ago, long, long after she had left the church, and both of us were wandering, a long time ago. It gave us something which we'll never lose, a genuine freedom with each other, a genuine love, born of the fire and sorrow of our long ago. *Be seeing you, baby. Please take care.*

Then I was much older than she; now I'm not. If Arthur were living, he would be forty-one. Julia is thirty-nine.

She doesn't look it. If she looked her real age, whatever it is, she'd turn to dust.

"Come on in the house," she said. "These be ready soon." She turned over a couple more ribs, picked up her drink, and stubbed out her cigarette. She took my arm.

Billy Preston has, at last, thank heaven, dethroned James Brown in Tony's soul- or value-system—not that I ever insisted—for it is certainly Tony who has put on the Billy Preston record which greets Julia and I as we enter the house. Tony is dancing with his mother, doing a bump to Billy's "Nothing From Nothing."

"Hi, Dad," says Tony, not missing a beat, and, "Hi, Dad," says Ruth, grinning, and not missing a step, and bumping Tony's fleshless behind. Odessa runs over, and throws herself into my arms. "Come on, dance with me, Daddy," she says, and "Why not?" I say, and so we join Ruth and Tony, clapping and bumping, while Julia lights another cigarette, and stands watching us, at the door. How strange and beautiful—it must be one of the few real reasons for remaining alive, of desiring to—to dance with your daughter, your son, and your wife; touching, really digging it, laughing, and keeping the beat, free. Odessa is a very aggressive dancer, or so, at least, she is with her father, whom she is using as rehearsal for an event of which she, as yet, knows nothing. Ruth is very gentle with her son, who is at once very mocking and gentle with her—he, too, is involved in a rehearsal. Yesterday, we were the children, Ruth and I and Julia: we're the old folks now, and this is what will happen to Tony and Odessa, please God be willing. Oh, life may look very like another: but I'd a whole lot rather dig it as a cornfield than lie about it as a crock.

The number ended; Julia clapped. Tony said thank you to his mother, and I said thank you to Odessa. I sat down on one of Julia's cushions. Julia's house is dominated by cushions and pallets and low tables and African sculpture: genuine. I said that I needed a drink, and Ruth brought me a Scotch on the rocks.

"Ruth," says Julia, "I think we better eat inside, don't you?" and Ruth and Julia immediately disappear, followed after a moment by Odessa, leaving Tony and I alone.

And, in the split second before Tony had actually said, "I want to talk to you, Daddy," I realize that this is a moment which Tony has been attempting for a long time: and I have been avoiding it.

I sip my drink, and look into his eyes and say, "Okay."

Tony looks down at his enormous hands, and then wraps them around his enormous feet; and I feel a rush of helpless love for my growing boy.

But then, there are sounds from the kitchen, and, just like a man, Tony stands and looks at me, and says, "Let's go outside a minute."

We walk to the door, and I yell, "Tony and me taking a walk in the yard," and we step outside. The air carries the sound of the growling meat, of spices, and dimly, beneath all, the odor of the earth after the rain has fallen.

We walk around the house to the front yard. We have not spoken. We pass the brick steps and stop at the car, and we look at each other.

"What was my uncle—Arthur—like?"

"Well—why do you ask? *You* knew him."

"Come on. I was a baby. What did *I* know?"

"Well—what are you asking?"

"A lot of the kids at school—they talk about him."

I wish I had thought to bring my drink with me.

"What do they say?"

"They say—he was a faggot."

And Tony looks at me. I think I hear a dog bark somewhere. A woman screams at her child. A motorcycle farts monstrously down the street, into infinity.

"Well—you're going to hear a lot of things about your uncle."

"Yeah. That's why I'm asking you."

"Your uncle—a lot of people—"

"No. I'm asking *you*."

"Okay. Your uncle was my brother, right? And I loved him. Okay? He was a very—lonely—man. He had a very strange—life. I think that—he was a very great singer."

Tony's eyes do not leave my face. I talk into his eyes.

"Yes. I know a lot of men who loved my brother—your uncle—or who thought they did. I know two men—your uncle—Arthur—loved—"

"Was one of those men Jimmy?"

Lord. "You mean—Julia's brother?"

"Yes."

Good Lord. "Yes."

Tony nods.

"I know—before Jimmy—Arthur slept with a lot of people—mostly men, but not always. He was young, Tony. Before your mother, *I* slept with a lot of women"—I do not believe I can say this, his eyes do not leave my face—"mostly women, but—in the army—I was young, too—not always. You want the truth, I'm trying to tell you the truth—anyway, let me tell you, baby, I'm proud of my brother, your uncle, and I'll be proud of him until the day I die. You should be, too. Whatever the fuck your uncle was, and he was a whole lot of things, he was nobody's faggot."

Tony leans on the car, watching me.

"Tony—didn't me and your mother raise you right? didn't I—we—tell you, a long time ago, not to believe in labels?"

He looks away from me. Then, "Yes. You did."

"Can I ask *you* a question?"

"Sure."

"What did *you* think of your uncle?"

He looks down; unwillingly, he smiles.

"I thought he was a crazy, beautiful cat." He looks at me. "I loved him—that's why—" Tears drip from his nose; he throws his head back. "I just wanted you to tell me," he says.

I do not dare to touch him, for fear that I will weep. Odessa calls, "Come in you all—food's getting cold!" We hear the door slam. We stand there. Tony is nearly as tall as I.

"Well," I say, "thank you for asking me," and we walk on back around the house.

We enter the room, which is now very different. The hi-fi is silent. Julia has placed two tall white candles on the low table, but she has not lit them yet. The table is a darkly varnished, gleaming board, with dark placemats—seeds of some kind, dried and polished, and tightly woven together—copper mugs, heavy wooden pepper-and-salt containers, two great wooden bowls with wooden spoons and forks, one flat wooden platter. There is a salad of raw spinach, lettuce, tomatoes, and radishes in one bowl, a fiery pale potato salad in the other bowl. The mahogany ribs are on the mahogany platter. There is a small bowl of very hot African peppers, smoldering green and red, a wicker basket full of hot buttered rolls, and Coca-Cola, red wine, and beer.

The table is in the center of the room, with bright cushions all around it. One wall is a bookcase. The facing wall is mainly a great picture window, overlooking the small space of shrubs and gravel which separates Julia's house from her neighbors'. There is a wooden African deity standing in a corner near the door; on either side of the door are two small windows—which had once been too high for the children to see out of—overlooking the yard. The room leads, two steps down, to a long hall which leads to two bedrooms, and the bathroom, the kitchen, the den, the front door, the front porch (of the red brick steps) and the basement. The rooms which Arthur and Jimmy occupied are upstairs.

Julia is seated at the bottom of the table, her back to the door, and to the small, upright piano in the corner opposite the African deity. On top of this piano are photographs of Arthur, Julia, and myself, and smaller photographs of Ruth, and of Tony and Odessa—when they were five and seven—and a photograph of Jimmy.

I sit at the head of the table, Ruth on my left, the children on my right. The cushion next to Julia is empty.

"Let us say grace," says Julia, "silently, each in his own way," and we bow our heads. "Amen," she says, after a moment. "Now let's get it on, kids!" and we laugh.

The room is different because Tony and I have talked, and the burden which has weighed on me so heavily and so long has begun, almost imperceptibly, to lift. I hardly know that this is what I feel; but this is what I feel. I almost want to sing, and the salads and the ribs and the peppers and the bread and the wine are delicious. The light coming through the window begins to be a kind of fiery mother-of-pearl. Except for the eating sounds and the sound of wood striking lightly against wood—a somehow breathless sound—the room is silent.

Odessa has tied a yellow ribbon in her hair, and knotted it in the hair at the nape of her neck, allowing the ribbon to fall down her back. And she is wearing a pale blue jump suit. Tony is wearing brown corduroys and scuffed shitkickers and an outsize gray sweater, and he could use a haircut—I think, I have no idea what his plans are for his hair. Anyway, I'm certainly not much of an example, in my old black turtleneck and old blue jeans.

Tony looks at me for a moment, and smiles; a different smile than he has ever smiled before.

"Guess who I ran into the other day," says Julia. Then, "No. You'll never guess—old Red! You remember Red!"

"You're kidding."

Red was part of the quartet years ago: Red, Peanut, Crunch, and Arthur.

"Yes. I was just coming out of Bloomingdale's. I had to go there to get something for one of my nephews—I was standing at the corner, waiting for the light to change, and here come this dude, wearing that same old stingy brim—I swear it's the same one—and he stops in front of me. My mind was somewhere else, I knew somebody was standing in front of me, but I didn't even notice him until he called my name. So low, like he was saying it to himself—'Sister Julia?' Why, whoever says *Sister,* now, except the radicals? and he didn't look like that. I don't know what I started to say, but I looked into his eyes, and suddenly, there he was—old Red!"

Arthur had been fifteen-sixteen, Red had been seventeen-eighteen, when they sang together. Their quartet—The Trumpets of Zion—didn't get too far before the hammer of Korea smashed it; but it had been a good quartet, very heavy in the churches, and in battles of song; and they were, really, very nice boys, crazy though they were.

Red was built close to the ground—square; with hair that turned sandy in the summertime; and with freckles, like the pricks of needles, dotting his copper skin. He had big square teeth, and a nice grin—and, if I remember correctly—since I am now approaching that head-on collision between not daring to remember and hoping to remember—unwillingly, remembering: he sang bass. That was, certainly, his quality, not low, but deep.

The quartet broke up, the boys scattered. Arthur went solo, *Arthur became a star!* Crunch went mad, Peanut was murdered, and Red: became a junkie. To spell it out a little, he was thrown into prison for a crime he hadn't committed, then was thrown into the army, and then his ass was hustled to Korea, and he got hooked, as one of the more esteemed of the American lyricists would put it, over there. I saw him just after he came back from over there. He had barely had time to learn to wipe himself, and was already on his way over yonder. His doom, and, still more, his pretense that it was nothing more than a heavy cold, made me despise him. It was many years ago; watching Red was like watching a one-armed man on the basketball court. I hope I've learned since then, and I hope I'll be forgiven.

"Who's Red?" asks Odessa.

"Your uncle Arthur used to sing with him," says Julia. "They were part of a quartet—a long time ago, before you got here, baby."

"Before I met your father," Ruth says.

But Odessa has very little interest in whatever is rumored to have happened on the other side of the flood. She accepts Ruth's *before I met your father* without flinching, armed with her knowledge of biology. Obviously, she is thinking, as I gather from an impatient movement of the yellow ribbon, her father and her mother must have met somewhere, or she—nor, of course, her brother, whom she now stares at rather disdainfully—would not be here.

"How *is* Red?" I ask.

"Oh." The one earring moves briefly, like a tear thrown backward, out of the corner of the eye. "He is *trying*, honey, he is *trying*. He walked me to the Automat close by. I didn't really have the time, except, sometimes, you *better* have the time, and he sat me down. We had a cup of coffee."

She chews on a rib, her dark eyes seeing something.

"He's just come out of jail—armed robbery, not the first time—and now he's on that methadone program and he's trying to work with children in the streets. But no matter what you do, they're still in the streets. And methadone kills you, too, you're still a junkie—just maybe a little more lobotomized, a *good* junkie, and they can do whatever the fuck they want with you—I mean, Red knows it's a bullshit trip. But, it's just like he said to me—'what *else* you going to do?' He's *trying*." She pauses again, and sips her wine. "His wife, Lorna, she's gone, and she took the two boys. He says he *knows* she was right—but you can see how bad it hurt him. He says he don't really have no reason to live—just keeping on because he's afraid to die. Or because there are so many people he'd like to kill—slowly, so they suffer, and so they'll have the time to *know* why you killing them—looking in their eyes the whole time, while death comes closer and they find out why. Yes. Now, he says, he understands the songs he was singing, way back there—but he can't sing no more, and he don't want to, anyway." She looks at Tony and Odessa. "He was a real good friend of your uncle's," she says, in quite another tone of voice, a tone of voice which makes it all real for them suddenly, "when we were all children, when I was a preacher." She grins at me, that child's grin. "Don't believe I understood my sermons, either; might just be beginning to understand them now. Lord. Have mercy."

"How old were you when you were a preacher?" Odessa asks.

"*You* knew she was a preacher," says Tony impatiently.

"Yes," says Odessa—not to Tony—"but how *old* were you?"

"Well," says Julia, sounding very dry, "I was—*called*—when I was seven, and I stayed in the pulpit until I was almost fourteen."

"What made you leave?" asks Tony.

"The passage of time," says Julia, and laughs. "The natural passage of time." Then, "No. I found out something about love. Or *I* might have turned into a junkie." She looks at Ruth, and me. "But one of the reasons I didn't—maybe the only one—was that I was so afraid that Jimmy would. He had a bad enough time, being the *little* brother of a child evangelist." She grins at Tony and Odessa. "Oh. Honey, in *my* heyday, Billy Graham wouldn't of come nowhere near the town *I* was going to preach in. Who?" Then she grins at me. "We had it locked up there for a while, now didn't we? And it had *us* locked up, too."

"I didn't want to say that."

"Oh, come on, Hall—you grinning now just like you used to grin back then." She turns to Tony and Odessa again: Tony is delighted. "Only then, we didn't call him Hall. We didn't say it, because we didn't dare—I don't know why—but we *thought* of him as *Ha!* We used to say, 'You see Mister Ha back there with his Ha? Just wait till the *Lord, He* puts a *ha!* on him'—because that's the way he always looked at you—like he just couldn't understand none of this foolishness at all!"

"I was much older than all of you," I say.

"Ha!" says Julia, and Ruth and the children laugh. "I got pictures of that quartet," Julia says. "I'll get them after supper."

Julia's den is her secret place—in the biblical sense; and no one enters it without being asked. I have been there a few times. Arthur was there more often. It is a meditation room, says Julia, and that's not bullshit. You feel a concentration of human passion in the room; which holds, otherwise, two tape recorders, many books, all kinds of books, from *Foxe's Martyrs* to *Valley of the Dolls*—"they're connected," says Julia—several Bibles, hymnbooks. On one wall above a baby grand piano: a tambourine, a desk, a typewriter, a chair, and a cot.

But we do not go into the den tonight, perhaps out of consideration for the children. After we have had hot apple pie with ice cream, and after Julia and Ruth and I have had coffee—and Tony and Odessa abstractedly play a game of cards which they appear to be inventing—Julia goes into the den alone, and comes back with two large folders. I have seen many of these photographs already, but not for many years: perhaps I have half hoped, knowing the hope to be futile, never to see them again.

We make ourselves comfortable on the cushions, on the floor. Julia sits with one knee up, a cigarette in one hand. She is at once present and very far away, and with a beauty I have seen only in those who have been forced to suffer into, and beyond, astonishment. This beauty is terrifying because it cannot be denied and it cannot be possessed; while utterly at the mercy of the human being, it is beyond all human help.

Julia opens one folder. "Some of these are just me," she says, "but your daddy will remember some of them. Some, I hardly remember myself. The people who take the pictures, sometimes they remember better than you do. But The Trumpets and me, we used to work a lot of churches together." She looks up, and smiles. "Because we was all so young. Had we had us a decent manager, we might have got a contract with Metro-Goldwyn-Mayer." She laughs. "I'm glad we didn't, though."

"But then, Red might not have turned into a junkie," Tony says. Then, after a moment, looking briefly at me, as though willing himself to test everything, awaiting the reaction to what is, in fact, a question: "And my uncle might not have died."

Julia looks at him, and does not attempt to evade the unspoken accusation. "There are lots of ways to be a junkie. At least, Red *knows* he's a junkie. And, since he *knows* it, he *might* recover."

Tony and Julia watch each other very carefully, and Odessa watches them both. Ruth leans against the wall, watching Julia, a faint smile on her face.

"It's like we used to say in the church, and it's still true—the sinner can't be saved unless he *knows* he's a sinner. And you surrounded by junkies, child. This is a nation of sleepwalkers, and they *can't* wake up." She reaches out, and touches Tony's face, lightly. "And death comes, baby, that's all. It's best, when death comes, that he wrap his arms around you, and take you with him. Death *can* strike you, and leave you grinning where you are—like a skeleton with clothes on. It's happening around us every day. You just look around you, when you walk out tomorrow morning."

Tony and Odessa are still, hypnotized, not so much by what she is saying as they are by the passion in her tobacco voice. "Your uncle and death walked off together, arm in arm. Death didn't despise your uncle, because your uncle never despised life. Don't grieve." She taps a page. "Look."

We look down at the child Julia in her long robe, her crocheted white cap on her head—how well I remember!—standing in the pulpit, before an enormous open Bible. Behind her is a window on which a crucifix is painted; on either side of the child tower vases holding lillies of the valley. The child's eyes stare upward, her tiny hands flat on the Scriptures.

"That was one Easter, in Reverend Kelsey's church, in Brooklyn. I still remember my text, *the fairest among ten thousand*—and, do you know, that man's still there? pimping just as bad as ever. But you hardly ever come that far with us."

."Oh, come on, Julia! I drove to Philadelphia, and to Washington, lots of times."

"Yes. But that was later."

"How old were you then?" asks Odessa.

"Then? Oh, I was about nine years old. There I am, again, with my mother and daddy, and Jimmy—but these ain't the pictures we want to be looking at—"

"Wait a minute," Tony asks, and holds the page, forcing us to look at a very pretty woman—and, yes, I remember, Julia's mother looked like that—wearing a hat perched forward over one eye, in the fashion of the forties, wearing a bolero jacket over a white blouse, and a tight-fitting skirt. She is holding a proud, grinning Julia by the hand, and here, Julia is bareheaded, with her hair curled, and with a ribbon in her hair, wearing a white middy blouse and a black pleated skirt, and those flat patent-leather shoes which button on the side. She looks happy enough to burst, and her joy is so intense that it blazes up at us—and especially at me—from thirty years away, causing Tony to mutter "Wow," and Odessa to look quickly from the photograph to Julia, and say nothing. Julia's father and mother stand hand in hand, and I remember this very handsome dude, his wide grin, open-necked shirt. He is holding Jimmy by the hand. Jimmy is about three years old, on sturdy legs, in short pants. His father is holding him by the hand, but Jimmy seems to be leaning forward, willing them out of the frame; his eyes are huge, and he is smiling.

"Jimmy and his father never really got along," Julia says, and turns the page. "No more than me and my mother," and she looks at Ruth, and both women smile.

Julia keeps turning pages, ruthlessly, and yet with a certain tenderness, shuffling beyond the images of her family, her relatives, the hieroglyphics spelling out the root, and the beginning, of her sorrow. We come to a photograph of Red, Peanut, Crunch, and Arthur, singing somewhere, incredibly young, uplifted, Crunch grinning, and holding the guitar. Their hair is slicked and curly, their foreheads, noses, teeth, gleam. *The fairest among ten thousand.* "Look at them," Julia murmurs. "I always think they're singing 'Sweet Hour of Prayer.' " I have no idea what song they're singing, on their way to glory; nothing has yet hit them hard enough to flatten the nose, close the eye, turn the lips into hamburger and ketchup. Crunch had all his teeth then; but for years before he was carried away, the two front teeth were missing. A cop had kicked them out, a black cop; and because it was a black cop who had attempted to destroy him, Crunch never had his teeth replaced. He could have; he was into every hustle, he was smart, and he was ruthless. But, no: he wanted black people to see what black people did to black people: *White man couldn't touch us if we'd just learn to love each other!*

This didn't help him to love either his women, or his woman.

One morning, fucking, he realized that the devil had got inside his woman, and was pulling on his prick, and he tried to beat the devil out of her. He didn't reach the devil, neighbors broke down the door and pulled him off and out of her, and carried him away. They had to carry her away, too, poor girl, nobody's ever seen her since, not, anyway, to recognize. Crunch is still alive, somewhere upstate.

Now, on facing pages, we come across two photographs of Arthur and Julia together. The first photograph is long ago. Julia is in her white robe and her white cap. Arthur is in a black suit and white shirt and black tie, and his hair is shining and curly.

The second photograph is much later, of Arthur and Julia at a party somewhere. Arthur's hair has gone back to natural, he is wearing a tight blue suit with a Chinese collar, and a heavy gold chain around his neck, and a heavy gold ring on the middle finger of his right hand. I know that Jimmy has the ring now, and that anyone who wants the ring will have to take the finger; I don't know what happened to the chain. This photograph was taken when Arthur was riding high. I remember the suit and I recognize the gold, and, still more, Arthur's proud and carefree grin, his head so high. He holds Julia around the waist; Julia, with her hair piled high, silver flashing at her ears and neck, wearing a low-cut, flaring evening gown, a cigarette in one hand and a champagne glass in the other, laughing, and very, very beautiful.

"I put these side by side," Julia says, "because both times, I'd asked Arthur to do me a favor. And, both times, he did." She taps the first photograph. "This time, I'd asked him to do me a kind of"—she laughs—"professional favor. He was singing with the quartet then, but I asked him to come sing, solo, for me, at the funeral of a real old lady who had just died. She'd asked for me, not long before she died, to preach her funeral sermon. And I promised that I would." She looks at me. "It was at Reverend Parker's church, you know, up there on Madison Avenue. It's gone, now."

"I think I remember," I say. But, if I do, I remember very dimly, and only because Arthur told me about it, much later. Or, maybe, he told me about it then. I'm not sure. When Arthur was sixteen, I was twenty-three. I avoided funerals, and, except for driving the quartet—and sometimes Julia—here and there, I didn't go to church.

Still, Julia and the photograph make me dimly recall—something. I listen to her, and, at the same time, I am trying to place—more precisely—the second photograph.

"I needed Arthur," Julia says, "because this old, blind lady—Miss Bessie, her name was Bessie Green—had had trouble with Reverend Parker. I was only fourteen then—almost fourteen—but I never could stand him, he always looked to me like a fat round bug, with a mustache. And, later on—or, maybe, even then, because he was *repulsive* to me—I used to wonder how any woman could ever look at him naked, and not throw up. I mean it. Making love to him had to be like mixing a chocolate cake for a couple of weeks. His wife was always sick, said the Lord had afflicted her body. He damn sure had!"

Ruth laughs, and Tony is silently howling, his big feet beating on the floor. Odessa, watching Julia, puts her head on Ruth's shoulder. Julia lights a cigarette.

"Anyway, I got to be part of the trouble between Reverend Parker and Mother Bessie. Reverend Parker didn't have no sense, nor no real manhood—and it was, really, almost right after her funeral that I left the pulpit—and, just because he was really nothing, he was always making pronouncements—issuing decrees—like the goddamn Pope. And the reason for the trouble between him and Miss Bessie was that the Lord had just told Reverend Parker that it was a sin for women to have earrings in their ears. Well, it was just that kind of bullshit—you remember, Hall—that got me most upset. I mean, why in the world should the great God Almighty even *notice* you wore earrings? Especially if you were past eighty years old, and blind—that woman had to have been born during slavery—and couldn't nobody *see* the damn earrings, which you didn't go out to the store and *buy:* somebody put them in your ears when you were a baby. God knows, Mother Bessie couldn't see them, she couldn't *see.* Well. I was just a traveling evangelist, I wasn't a member of that church, but, after Reverend Parker had run down all this nonsense, I used to go and pick up Mother Bessie and bring her out to church. And this was terrible, because two of Reverend Parker's church members had been bringing Mother Bessie out and Reverend Parker had made them stop. But *I* was the fire-baptized child evangelist, Little Sister Julia—he couldn't make *me* stop. So I climbed the stairs, Sunday after Sunday, to Mother Bessie's room and helped her get herself together and brought her out to church, earrings and all.

"Reverend Parker got after my parents; but Reverend Parker wasn't putting no bread on their table—*I* was. And I just said that I was acting as the Lord led me—and, I guess, really, that was about as close to the truth as I could get. I couldn't turn back. I just did not think it was right to let this poor old blind black lady, who smelled like old people smell sometimes, you know? and who was exasperating like old people can be, I just did not believe it was *right* to leave her alone with all those rats and roaches, and let her die alone like that. I did not *believe* that I had been called to the ministry to be a party to that.

"And maybe I enjoyed watching Reverend Parker every Sunday.

He couldn't throw me—us—out. After all, he wanted me to keep on preaching in his church, at least from time to time—I put bread on *his* table, too.

"Anyway. Mother Bessie testified one afternoon—she prophesied on Reverend Parker's head, really, she *told* him what was going to happen to that daughter—and she said that she would soon be gone and she wanted me to preach her funeral sermon. And I promised that I would.

"But then, Arthur pointed out to me that in order for me to keep my promise and preach the funeral sermon, there had to *be* a funeral: and who was going to pay for it? *How* was the woman to be buried? She'd been paying insurance, a dime a week, since the Emancipation Proclamation—but let's not go into that, if I start talking about the life insurance companies, I'll blow what little cool I have left. Anyway. Between your brother and the quartet and my parents, and a few extra sermons I preached, and a nephew Arthur somehow managed to track down—between some heavy sweat and some light blackmail—we had got some change together by the time Mother Bessie died. The nephew even managed to get some money from those life insurance thieves. Mother Bessie had been dying a long time, and I knew it, and yet, she died all of a sudden. I don't believe she suffered; she died in her sleep. It was strange. I had felt closer to her than I'd ever felt to my own mother, or my own father, and I didn't, really, even know her. And then, I thought—for the first time—that maybe that was why I'd entered the pulpit in the first place. Because I was so far from God in my own house, so far from anyone who loved me. The love of God was the first love I knew anything about. I *will* say: it brought me from a long ways off."

The room is completely silent, still: night fell long ago. Tony has his arms wrapped around his knees. He is watching Julia with an intensity of wonder which I have never seen in his face before; his eyes are, more than ever, like Arthur's eyes. Odessa leans against her mother, in an attitude too tense to be described as shrinking, too eager to be described as fear. Ruth is watching Julia, I press my back against the wall. I see Ruth's face without looking at it: she and I are connected by all the other presences in the room.

"So I asked Arthur to come up and sing at the funeral for me, and he did. He sang two songs—one, just before my sermon, and then, one at the end." She looks at me, looking, again, like a little girl. "I never told you?"

"You never told me all *this*—what you've just told me."

"Well. I guess it takes time—more time than anybody wants to imagine—to sort things out, inside, and then try to put them together, and then try—not so much to make *sense* out of it all—as to *see*. Maybe that's why what seems to be past begins to be clearer than what seems to be present. Anyway." Julia smiles, and silence comes again; briefly, for Odessa asks, "What was the text of your sermon?"

"Why did you ask me that?"

"I don't know—I just had a—feeling—"

Tony says, "Odessa just figures that since you and Uncle Arthur got into all this heavy shit together, whatever you was doing must have had an effect on him—like, dig, Julia, if you two were two trapeze artists, working together up there, his timing and your timing would have to be impeccable right?"

"How well you put it," Julia murmurs. Then, "I took my text from Isaiah: *Set thine house in order, for thou shalt die, and not live.* But he hadn't heard the sermon when he sang his first song."

"No. But he knew the text."

"Yes. I told him the text."

"Yeah. And he *knew* that you were going to take that text way out." Tony grins, hugging his knees. "I can dig it."

Julia watches him, smiling; then, she looks at Ruth and me. "I wasn't really preaching it for Mother Bessie—she was beyond all that, now. I was preaching to Reverend Parker—and," she says, after a moment, glancing at Tony and Odessa, "to myself."

"What two songs did Arthur sing?" I ask.

Julia smiles. "I'll never forget. That afternoon made a great difference in my life. I'll never forget that afternoon. I sensed—I guess I *knew*—that I had come to the end of my ministry—of *that* part of my ministry, anyway—and that it was *my* house that I would have to set in order. If I was to live. I was preaching Mother Bessie's funeral. But you don't always get carried to the graveyard when you die. Reverend Parker proved *that*. Mother Bessie smelled of age—of sour clothes, sour food, sour stomach—I could deal with that, I could even accept that I might smell that way one day, just like I know I'm going to die one day. But Reverend Parker, and almost all the other ministers, they smelled—of corruption. It was in their hands, in all that self-righteous lust—you can see it when they're eating the Sunday chicken dinner. Hell, I could see it when they looked at me, like I was the breast and the wing and the stuffing. And the Lord wouldn't mind if two of His faithful and weary servants gave each other solace and comfort for a little while, under the stairs. And I couldn't deal with that." She is silent, then she laughs. "They still talk about that sermon, some people do, until today. One thing, I never topped it, not in *that* pulpit. Like old Dinah might have said, that's all there was to *that!*"

She stands up, kicking her feet back into her platform sandals.

"I'll try to play it for you, I can't describe it. That church was packed. Anyone who was there still remembers it, even if they don't *know* that they remember it." She walks to the piano. "You got to remember how young he was. And hadn't nobody he ever loved yet died. And he wasn't, you know, saved, like me." She laughs, and sits down at the upright piano. "Arthur was kind of off and on, about salvation." She strums her fingers over the keys. "I can't sing, don't know why I'm doing this—but, Hall, you'll get the picture, I know."

She plays the opening bars—the opening beat—both solemn and honky-tonk, too calmly determined to be called aggressive—absolutely undeniable: you listen or you run. The church sits, waiting, and exhales, at last, with the singer, a moan, distant, like a muffled, subterranean roar, like the first faint warning of an earthquake.

I'm thinking of friends whom I used to know

Not yet, he couldn't be thinking of friends he used to know; but he might be singing of the swiftly approaching hour which would carry away the people before whom he now sang; or he, on the other hand, simply because of the sacred fragility of his youth, might be forced to make the journey on without them.

Who lived, and suffered, in this world below.

Yes, say the sea of women's hats, the rocks of men's shoulders: a slow wind ruffles the sea, and breathes on the rocks, drops, then rises.

They've gone up to heaven,

and some raise their faces, as into the wind, and some cover their faces with their hands,

And I want to know

Everything is still. Only the voice is rising, like a lone bird against the coming storm.

What are they doing there now?
Oh, thunders the piano, and *Yes,* breathes the wind,
What

and the voice, the lone bird, mounts,

are they doing in heaven today?
Where sin and sorrow are all washed away,
Where peace abides, like a river, they say.
Oh, what are they doing there now?

I watch Sister Julia's fingers decipher the text in the keyboard. It is a strange wind that rises, from so far away, and the lone voice rises above the wind.

> *There were some*
> Yes
> *Whose hearts*
> Yes
> *Were burdened with care.*
> *They passed every moment*
> Yes
> *In sorrow and tears*

The sea moves back and forth, and rocks move from side to side, the lone voice rises, approaching a hard triumph,

> *They clung!*

the piano bearing witness, the wind slowly dropping

> *to the cross*
> Yes
> *with trembling and fears,*
> *Oh, what*
> *are they doing there now?*

Julia stops, and the room seems suspended, changed, by the passion of that far-off afternoon.

"And then," says Ruth, "you preached your sermon."

"Yes. And then we drove Mother Bessie to the graveyard."

Tony is framing his face to ask a question. The front doorbell rings.

"This time of night?" says Julia; for it is a little past ten o'clock.

"It's all right," I say. "I've been dying to meet your secret lover."

Julia rises from the piano stool, as the doorbell rings again, and strides across the room. "Come on with me, Hall, if it's not my secret lover, it might be some other kind of nut."

She walks before me, down the hall, and puts her eye to that small hole in the door, which shows you who's outside. Then, she screams with joy, *"Oh, shucks!"* She turns to me, laughing. "You wanted to meet my secret lover—here he is!" and she opens the door. "Come on in the house, Jimmy!"

And here he is, too, very sharp. I haven't seen him in almost two years; and he wasn't sharp the last time I saw him. Neither was I. I like Jimmy very much—I guess I love him, really. He's kind of a stocky dude, gingerbread colored, very, very quiet, with great big brown eyes in a square and chiseled face. He's got a grin like a lantern, and a voice like Saturday nights: somehow, I always see him when he'll be an old man, sitting somewhere with lots of kids around him, telling them the tallest stories they'll ever hear, and with laughter crackling around him like a fire.

He surprised me, Jimmy did, very much, especially during those last months with Arthur. Not many people are present in time of trouble—if you doubt me, I dare you: to get in trouble—and Jimmy was present. In many ways, in ways he couldn't speak of, not even to me, his trouble had to have been even worse than mine. And he looked it, at the funeral, gray: bone-dry, thinned by an acid eating from within. Then he disappeared, upstairs, in this house where he and Arthur had sometimes lived. I was still on the road, but even if I hadn't been, I was the last person in the world who would have been able to help him.

Julia wanted to help him, she wanted her brother in her house; but he wasn't really *in* her house, he was weeping at the grave of his lover. She prevailed upon him, at last, to move, and I last saw him just before he took a boat to go, he said, "somewhere." He looked very young that day.

He seems, now, to have got himself together: black boots, blue slacks, dark tan raincoat. He drops his bags on the porch, and grabs

Julia in his arms. Julia pulls back, at last, holding him by the shoulders.

"Why didn't you let me know you were coming? and where you coming *from?*"

"I just come in from Rome, honey." Jimmy's speech has always been a little breathless; he sounds as though he's improvising, one step ahead of disaster. Before his improvisation can continue, he raises his eyes, and sees me, and we step into each other's arms. "Hey, *brother,*" says Jimmy, and we cling to each other for a moment. It is mightily reassuring to hold him for a moment, to feel myself held. Tears are behind his eyes, and behind my own, and we kiss each other on the cheek. We grin, I move to the porch and pick up his bags, and close the door. "I was hoping you'd be here," Jimmy says.

"How'd you know *I'd* be here?" Julia asks.

Jimmy laughs, and kisses her again. "Your phone's been busy, honey," he says. He turns to me. "She forgets she gave me a key."

"I might have changed the lock," Julia says.

"And without telling nobody, naturally, just to make sure little brother's ass was out in the cold." He laughs again, very happy. It is astonishing. "Come on, you all have a party? Can I have a drink? You got anything to eat? Or you want me to haul my ass off to the nearest Chinese restaurant?" He pauses, with that grin on his face, that light, his coat half on, half off.

"Give me that coat," says Julia, taking it, and slapping his lean behind, "and go on inside. Take him inside, Hall. Jimmy, you just going to have to take potluck—how'd you *get* here?"

"Rented a car, and I drove, sister." He and I walk down the hall. Ruth is standing at the entrance to the living room, Tony and Odessa behind her. *"Hey!"* cried Jimmy. "We got the whole family tonight! Come here, mama!" and he and Ruth grab each other, laughing, and almost crying. Ruth pulls him into the living room, I can scarcely make out what they are saying to each other, but they are beautiful to see. Jimmy kneels on one knee before Odessa, holding both her hands in his, and Tony towers above them. Julia comes, and stands beside me, one foot on one step, and Jimmy rises, and grabs Tony around the neck. Tony is both uneasy and delighted, I can see it in his face, but delight, and a natural affection conquer, and he grins, and says to Jimmy, "I was thinking about you. I knew you were coming tonight, I swear I knew it! It was the song that brought you—it was the song!"

Swiftly, unconsciously, Jimmy touches the gold ring on his finger, and stares at Tony.

"What song?" He is half smiling, half frowning.

Julia steps into the room. "I was singing one of the songs Arthur used to sing, a long time ago, when I was a preacher."

Jimmy looks at Tony, and smiles. Something seems to relax between them. "Well—I can believe you, man. I can believe the song brought me here." He walks to the table. "Looks like you all had a *feast*."

But Ruth, Julia, and Odessa are already taking the plates away. "Give him a drink, Hall," Julia says, "while we heat the food up," and, "So sorry," says Ruth sweetly, as she carries away the ribs, and, "We'll be right back," says Odessa, who is carrying the potato salad and the rolls. Tony carries out the glasses.

I pour Jimmy and I a drink. Jimmy sits down, and takes off his boots, puts his head on one cushion, and his feet on the other, takes his drink from my hand, and sits up.

I sit down next to him, and he raises his glass.

"I'm mighty glad to see you, brother."

"I am, too."

We touch glasses, and drink. Odessa comes in, and wipes down the table. There is a silence between Jimmy and I—not uncomfortable, but tense. With our first words, whatever they may be, we will have begun a journey. But we smile. Odessa swings out of the room.

"Well—what were you doing in Rome?"

"Man—what was I doing anywhere? I hardly know. Well, I *do* know." He finds his cigarettes, and I light his cigarette, and mine.

Maybe what I mean when I say Jimmy's quiet, is that Jimmy can go out on you in a second, and still be there, as motionless, and as private, as a cat. He smiles. "I went on a kind of pilgrimage. I was in Istanbul. I was in London, and Berlin, and Geneva. I was in Venice. I was in Paris—places where Arthur and I had hung out together, or just places where I knew he'd been. I was in Barcelona—we'd been very happy in Barcelona." He grins, and sips his drink. "The Stations of the Cross." Then, "Don't misunderstand me. I discovered how much I'd loved him—love him still. And then—I began to be able to swallow without hurting. It—began to be all right. Hell, maybe nothing's ever all *right*, but you know what I mean. I stopped hating God—or whatever. Whatever had hurt us so. Whatever smashed him." He leans back on one cushion. "You know, I'll tell you all about it, soon."

Tony comes in. "You guys mind if I come in here? I mean, you know, I'm in the way in the kitchen, but I can always go upstairs and read a book." He smiles, but he's worried just the same.

Jimmy pats a cushion. "Sit down, Tony. I ain't dumb enough to think I got any secrets from you. Hell, I ain't got no secrets, period," and the three of us laugh, and Tony sits down; or rather, he rearranges his sharp angles into what can roughly be called a sitting position; he isn't standing up.

"What were you doing in Rome?" Tony asks.

"Some lardheads had some wild idea of doing a movie about your uncle's life. I told them"—turning to me—"that you were the man to talk to, but, after one session with them, I wouldn't even give them your address. I'll tell you about it. *Bloody Pentecost Sunday,* in black-face, or *Porgy and Crown.*" He makes a retching sound. "The *end,* baby. Otherwise," he says to Tony, "I was playing piano. I played piano everywhere I went. That's how I kept myself alive. It was a rough gig." He sips his drink. "Don't believe I'm going to do it no more. It wasn't the same, it didn't mean the same thing to me. I began to understand, better than I had—" Jimmy stops, and finishes his drink, and hands his glass to Tony. "Do the old man a favor? Put some more Scotch in there with a couple more rocks?"

"Right," says Tony, and looks at me, but I signify, No. I'm terri-

fied of drinking when I'm driving, and, also, on the drive home tonight, Tony and I will be alone, and Tony will be full of questions.

"What did you begin to understand?" I ask.

"How Arthur had to feel, after a while. It wasn't him singing, anymore." Jimmy sighed. "That's what he felt, I know. You do, too. But
he couldn't go back, either." He sits up, puts out his cigarette, immediately lights another. "I think I've started my book," he says.

Tony brings Jimmy his drink, and sits down again.

"Yes," says Jimmy, "I believe I've started my book."

The women enter with the food and the wine.

I haven't known Jimmy all of *my* life, but I've known him all of his—a
curious difference, as time goes on. I hardly ever noticed him, until I
started going with Julia. Until then, he'd just been Julia's snot-nosed,
noisy little brother, an absolute drag, and, every once in a while, I'd
have to step over him, politely, or push him aside, politely, or indicate,
politely, that he go fuck himself. I had nothing against him. I just
didn't need him.

While I was going with Julia, I remember him, mainly, coming in
the door, or going out of it: he no longer lived at home. But then, just
the same, he became more real to me: I knew how much he meant to
Julia.

Julia and I were going together in 1957, the year that Arthur went
solo. Julia and I, for reasons that I will have to go into later, didn't last
too long; but Arthur, solo, did. So in 1960 or thereabouts, Arthur was
doing a Civil Rights benefit in a church in the backwoods of Florida;
and his regular pianist was in jail, in Alabama. I went with Arthur on
this trip because I had become a little frightened for him—perhaps
also because, without quite admitting it, I was becoming more involved myself. I had a whole lot of reservations about nonviolent protest, and praying for your enemies, and freedom songs, and all that.
But those white crackers were far from nonviolent. You could hear the
blows and the screams and the prayers from Mississippi to Harlem.
You could catch it on your TV set when you came home. There was

no way—for some people—to act like you didn't know. I say, "some people," and I say it with great bitterness, and even hatred in my heart for, God knows, "some people" were not most people. Most Americans did not give a shit about those black boys and girls and men and women—and some white boys and girls and white men and women—being beaten and murdered, in their name. Most Americans proved themselves to be absolute cowards—that's the truth, and the record bears me out. But I'm running ahead of myself. Some of the kids drove us to the church, because Arthur was determined, and we found Jimmy there, Jimmy had been working in the South for about two years.

Now Julia had told me this, and I also knew that Jimmy played piano: but none of this registered until that moment Arthur and I walked into the church, and found Jimmy sitting there. He was sitting in the kitchen, which was in the church basement. This basement had already been bombed twice. There were sandbags in one corner, and in the hole where one of the windows had been.

Jimmy was sitting on the kitchen table, chewing on a bacon sandwich, wearing a torn green sweater, blue jeans, and sneakers. He was very thin. I didn't recognize him right away, but Arthur did.

Jimmy grinned, and said, "Welcome to the slaughter, children. And don't go nowhere without your comb, your washrag, and your toothbrush—some of these jails have running water." Then he said to Arthur, "I hear your main man's been detained, in the cradle of the Confederacy. I'll play for you, if you want."

"Beautiful," Arthur said. "You want to run through a couple with me, right quick? Just so we'll get a sense of each other."

Jimmy stood up, and finished his sandwich. "At your service," he said, and we walked upstairs, into the church. Jimmy sat down at the piano. A couple of kids gathered around. Two black men stood at the doors, watching the street. It was about two hours before the church service—which was really a protest rally—would begin. Arthur's name hung in banners outside the church. The air was heavy with a tension I was eventually to come to know as well as I know my name.

Jimmy began to play. Arthur waited a little, then he began to sing; he and Jimmy grinned at each other, briefly, as each began to enter the other's beat. A few more kids gathered around the altar. A couple of women, arms folded, stood in the aisle. A telephone rang in the church office; someone immediately picked it up, closing the office door. I joined the two men as the music began to come alive, and stood at the door with them, staring out at the pastoral, apocalyptic streets.

More than a year later, one rainy night in Harlem, we let the rain sort of float us from one bar to another, and we walked and talked, alone on the black-and-silver streets, surrounded by the rain, water dropping from our hair and our eyelashes, from the tips of our noses, and down our backs. Arthur had just come in from London.

No one knows very much about the life of another. This ignorance becomes vivid, if you love another. Love sets the imagination on fire, and, also, eventually, chars the imagination into a harder element: imagination cannot match love, cannot plunge so deep, or range so wide.

Ruth was in the hospital with Tony then, and Arthur and I had had dinner alone. It was raining as we walked out of the restaurant, which was near the Renaissance Theatre, on Seventh Avenue. My apartment, in one of those damn, disastrous housing projects, was behind us, slightly to the east.

Arthur had been very silent during dinner. I watched his face. It was a face I knew and didn't know. He had something on his mind.

We walked out, silently, and found the rain, but we did not start back toward my apartment. We started slowly down the long, loud avenue, long with silence, loud with rain. Cars rocked, proudly amphibious, throwing up buckets of water. People stood in vestibules, in little circles of light, hugged the walls of buildings, splashed furiously through puddles: we walked very slowly. I was wearing a cap, but Arthur was bareheaded, holding a folded newspaper on top of his head. Arthur stopped before Dickie Wells. We looked briefly at each other, and walked in, and sat down at the bar. It was early, that is, it was not yet midnight, and the place was quiet.

The bartender served us, and Arthur looked down into his glass, and then he looked up at me, and he said, "So. We're finally going to work together."

We had decided that, just before he'd gone to London. It was Arthur who insisted. I worked in the advertising department of a black magazine—at least, it said it was black; and the job wasn't bad, but Arthur said that it was turning me into a schizo: and I could see that that might be true.

Arthur was around twenty-six, which means that we had edged into the sixties. Without having yet, as the proverb goes, "made it," Arthur was a tremendous drawing card, absolutely individual, and had reached that curious point through which all memorable careers seem to pass: when you must either go up and over, or down and out.

We were due to sign for his first record album in a matter of days, and this, too, was very much on his mind.

"Are you having second thoughts about us working together?"

He grinned. "You can't get out of it *that* way, baby."

Then again he was silent, and I watched his face.

"When you sing," he said, suddenly, "you can't sing *outside* the song. You've got to *be* the song you sing. You've got to make a confession."

He turned his drink around, and said, in another tone, "Every time I pass that corner, next to the Renaissance, I remember this man who was standing on the corner one day when I came by, and he asked me to go to the store for him. I was about thirteen. He was about thirty or forty, a very rough-looking dude, tall and thin, he wore a hat. He said we had to go to his house to get the money."

Arthur looked at me sideways, with a little grin, a shrug. "He looked like he might give me a nickel, or a dime."

I watched Arthur, and held my breath.

"The house he said he lived in was very close to the corner, and we walked in the hall and started up the stairs. It was funny, I'll never forget it, but the minute we started up those stairs, I knew that man did not live in this house. I knew it. I got scared like I'd never been scared before, but I didn't turn and run, it was like I was hypnotized. I just followed him up those stairs, till we got to the third landing."

I try to see the scene as a minor, adolescent misadventure, as common as dirt. But this is not what Arthur's eyes are saying, nor his voice.

"He said I was a cute boy—something like that—and he touched me on the face, and I just stood there, looking at him. And, while I was looking at him, his eyes got darker, like the sky, you know? and he didn't seem to be looking at me, just like the sky. And it was silent on those stairs, like you could hear silence just growing, like it was going to explode!"

Arthur looked at me and looked away, and took another swallow of his drink.

"He took out *his* cock, and I just stared at the thing pointing at me, and man, you know how we were raised, I did not know *who* to scream for, and then he put his hand on *my* cock and my cock jumped and then I couldn't move at all. I just stood there, waiting, paralyzed, and he opened my pants and took it out, and it got big and I had never seen it that way, it was the first time and so it meant that I must be just like this man, and then he knelt down and took it in his mouth. I thought he was going to bite it off. But, all the time, it kept getting bigger, and I started to cry.

"A door slammed somewhere over our heads, and he stood up, and he put some money in my hand, and he hurried down the steps. I got my pants closed best as I could and I ran home. I mean, I ran all the way. I locked myself in the bathroom, and I looked at the money; it was a quarter and two dimes. I threw them out the window."

He finished his drink. "And I had just started singing."

A shyness I might not have felt with a friend, or a stranger, refused to release my tongue. Nothing so terrible had happened, after all; much worse might have happened. This thought made me ashamed of myself: how do *I* know that? It was not *my* initiation. I am ashamed of myself for another reason; that Arthur never thought to tell his older brother of this violation: he could certainly have told no one else.

But I had been twenty when Arthur was thirteen, far above the childlike concerns of my little brother. It would probably never have occurred to him to look for me, to talk to me. He would have been too frightened, and too ashamed.

"I never forgot that man," Arthur said, slowly, "not so much because of the physical thing—but—"

Arthur stopped, and looked at me, and it was as though I had never before looked into his eyes, or had never before realized how enormous they were, and how deep.

"—it was the way he made me feel about myself. That man made it impossible for me to touch anybody, man or woman, for a long time, and still, he filled me with a terrible curiosity. And, all that time, I was singing, man, I was singing up a storm." Then he stopped laughing. "I've got to live the life I sing about in my song," he said.

He put some money on the bar, and picked up his wet newspaper. "Come on," he said, "let's pub crawl. *I* don't mind getting wet," and he grinned, and propelled me to the door.

We walked out into the rain again, and started down the avenue. We walked slowly, in silence, head down, the only people on the street. Had there been anyone to see us, we would have been a strange sight.

Arthur put his newspaper on his head again, where it began its final disintegration. "If you knew me better, I'm sure you'd say I was a fool, and, if I wasn't your brother, you might laugh at me—but I've had very little experience, and I've always been afraid. And I've stayed busy. And, if you notice, I've kind of stayed away from you. Because

I've always looked up to you, and I love you, and I wouldn't be able to live, man, if I thought you were ashamed of me."

I made a sound like a laugh, a thin, demented sound against the torrent. "Why should I be ashamed of you?"

"Look. You're going to be hanging out with me more and more." We were now beginning to be soaked, we started walking faster, staying close to the walls of buildings; Arthur dropped the sodden newspaper, and we headed for the next bar. "You're going to see my life. I don't want to hide anything from you, brother."

"Why should you hide anything from me?" But my voice sounded hollow, and, yes, I was afraid.

We walked into the bar. This was a bar we no longer knew very well, a poor bar. It can be said that all bars in Harlem are poor, but there are degrees, degrees of visibility; and this bar was poor.

We were very visible, too, as we walked through the bar, and sat down in a booth in the back. The jukebox was going very loud, and so were the people.

Arthur went into the bathroom, to wipe his streaming face, and hair. The barmaid, an elderly woman with a pleasant face, came over to me.

"That the one who sings?"

"Yes." Then, "That's my brother."

"What's his name?"

"Arthur Montana."

"I knew it. That's him. My sister keep talking about him. He got a beautiful voice. You *really* his brother?"

"Why would I say I was, if I wasn't?"

"I don't know why people say a lot of things. You tell him he got a beautiful voice. I heard him at Reverend Larrabee's, me and my sister."

She took the order, and went away. Presently, I heard "—a *gospel* singer? He ain't going save no souls in *here*." Laughter. "He can get wet, just like everybody else," someone said. "And thirsty, too," said another. "Man, didn't nobody say he was no *preacher*." "Let's get him to sing 'Didn't It Rain.' " "You no good sinners," said the barmaid, calmly, "you don't know He's everywhere." More laughter. "Preach it, Minnie!" Dinah and Brook Benton were singing "A Rocking Good Way." "Dinah started out in gospel," somebody said.

Arthur came back, not very much drier—our hair holds the rain—and took off his jacket, and sat down. The barmaid set her tray down on the table. "Give me them wet things," she said, and she took my cap, and coat, and Arthur's jacket, and placed them on a nearby table. "That's better," she said, and poured us our drinks.

"Thank you," Arthur said.

"Don't you let the whiskey ruin that pretty voice," she said, and went back behind the bar.

Arthur stared in her direction, and then stared at me. "You been talking about me?"

"Baby, she heard you sing at Reverend Larrabee's, and she's already told everybody here. She told *me*."

Arthur looked astounded, then—unwillingly—delighted, then thoughtful. He lit a cigarette.

"Don't let them cigarettes wreck that pretty voice," I said.

Arthur grinned, suddenly looking about ten years old, and he said, "Now, don't you do me like that, brother." I remembered teaching him to tie his shoes—his sneakers—years ago, they were brown and white, and I have no idea why I remember that.

"*I'm* not doing it," I said. "It's fame."

"You think I'm going to be famous?"

"Yes," I said, "I do!" and, for the first time, I felt that it was as though a cold wind blew, for an instant, between Arthur and myself: into this void rushed the sound of the jukebox and the voices of the people at the bar.

And Arthur raised his eyes and looked out over the bar, as though he were seeing something for the first time, as though he were hearing a new sound.

I was facing Arthur, my back was to the bar, and so I could not see what he was seeing. Well: there was the gray-haired man, with the yellow teeth, and the foolish grin, who had been standing at the end of the bar as we entered, both hands wrapped around his glass, leaning inward, wearing a torn, black raincoat. Seated on the stool next to him was a heavy black lady, with long, curling, bright red hair, and deep purple lipstick, which made her lips look bruised. She seemed to be more than acquainted with, and to be hoping to escape from, the gray-haired man: his patience, though, was probably as ruthless as his grin. Next to this discontent stood a high yellow dude, in a brown suit, staring into his drink, and ignoring, equally (with an equal effort) the lady of the bruised lips and the tall man standing next to him; who wore a bright mustard jacket, suggesting tweed, and had an unlit pipe, eyeglasses brighter than the wrath of God, a long chin, and heavy rings flashing from compulsive fingers: he tapped his feet in the same way, to no particular music. Two girls and two boys stood next to him, as high as they were weary, playing the jukebox, while waiting for a change in the weather. A fat man stood all alone, nursing a beer. A silent girl sat next to him, wearing a yellow blouse and a long, blue skirt. Two schoolteacher types stood against the wall, chattering and grinning, and very aware of the tall boy in the corduroy pants, who stood alone at the bar, and who seemed to be a friend of the bartender's—the bartender was short, round, and cheerful, with a mustache, and he and the tall boy talked together, whenever the bartender was free. A woman and a man sat silently together, near the window, the rain falling endlessly behind them. The barmaid talked to everyone and saw everything, moved placidly behind the bar, rinsing glasses, checking stock, sometimes sending the bartender into the basement, for this or that. The music played, endlessly, as endlessly as the rain fell. The voices rose and fell like a river, a swollen river, searching the dam. The bottles glittered like malice against the crowded mirror. The cash register clanged, at intervals, like a bell alerting prisoners to judgment, or release. The door kept opening and closing, people entered and people left, but mainly, people entered. The clock on the wall said quarter past two. There was a pencil portrait of Malcolm X beneath it.

Arthur looked back at me.

"Well," he said, "whatever it is—you'll see me through it, won't you? I got nobody but you."

"Oh, come on," I said.

He grinned. I felt that the grin hurt him, and it hurt me. "It's true. You, you've got Ruth, and, now, you've got little Tony, lying up there in his name tag and his diapers—but me, I've only got you." He grinned again, a brighter grin this time. "Don't be upset. My demands are very modest."

"Baby, do you know that you are full of shit?"

"That is no way to talk to a gospel singer."

We both started laughing. "Buy me another drink, you stupid motherfucker; hanging out with you, man, I better get drunk."

"Right. And you—we—have a new life to celebrate."

He looked toward the bar, and, as though she had been waiting for this light from the lighthouse, the barmaid immediately appeared.

"Now I warned you," she said, picking up the glasses, "to be careful about that voice."

"It's all right. I'm with my brother."

She did not exactly smile, but she looked at me again, and then looked back at Arthur. "He the only brother you got?"

"That's right."

Then she looked at me. "Don't you worry about it, then."

We went, eventually, from the poor bar—and the rain kept pouring down—into the after-hours joint, in a cellar, somewhere way west on 118th Street, where everyone knew Arthur. Or, so it seemed to me. This was one of the very last times I was ever to be confused as to who knew Arthur, and who didn't. It was one of the very last times I was ever to allow myself to get drunk when I was out with Arthur. It was the first time I ever watched my brother in a world which was his, not mine. I was drunk that night, and I knew that Arthur was trying to show me something, something which I might not have been able to see if I had not been drunk.

Or, if Tony had not been born two nights before. That joy and wonder and terror and pride surged and danced in me that night, making my life new, making my brother new. It was incredible to me that the first time I had seen him, he had been as helpless and tiny and furious as Tony was now, his eyes as tightly closed, his fists and legs as futile, every inch of him resisting the violence of his meeting with the air.

BOOK TWO

Twelve Gates
to the City

Come on in the Lord's house:
It's going to rain.

TRADITIONAL

"My text, this morning," Julia said, "comes from the Psalms of David. Please turn, with me, to the Thirty-first Psalm, and we will all read together the twenty-first verse."

She was dressed all in white, and standing on a platform which was hidden by the pulpit. This was a special, collapsible platform, constructed by her father, and she looked at him as she stood there, and as he stood up to read. The hidden platform looked like a wooden box, with a rope handle. When her father opened it, with his boyish flourish, the box became a handrail, sometimes painted gold. This contraption, and her father, traveled with Julia everywhere: and made Julia's appearance in the pulpit seem mystical, as though she were being lifted up.

Her mother and father were before her, in the front row, with Jimmy restless between them. They hadn't long arrived from New Orleans, and our mother and father had known Julia's grandmother. We sat right behind them, our mother and father, and Arthur and me, on a Sunday morning. It was weird to have been dragged out to this church to hear a child, who was nine years old, preach the Gospel. Somebody was jiving the public, and I knew it had to be her father and mother, who surely did not look holy to me.

Julia's mother put up the better show, though her hats were flaunting, and her skirts were tight. She had one beautiful ass, and high, tight demanding breasts, and long legs, and she always wore high heels—just to make sure you didn't miss those legs. When she got happy, she would stroke her breasts, and I would watch her thighs and her legs and that ass of hers as she started to shout, and I would get such a hopeless, unregenerate, eighteen-year-old hard-on in the holy place that you could certainly hear this sinner moan.

Her father made very little pretense—he didn't have to, being her father. He was the zoot-suited stud of studs—a mild zoot suit, driving ladies wild wondering what he'd be like wild. He had the cruel, pearly teeth, and the short, black, tickling mustache, and that grin of the sinner man just waiting for the touch which would bring him salvation, and thick, curly, *good* black hair. His eyes were like Mexican eyes, and he seemed, in all things, indolent, waiting for you to come to him.

I was not the only one who would see all this change, but, at that time, Brother Miller had the world in a jug and the stopper in his lean brown hand.

The church was packed, for a child evangelist was, after all, something in the nature of a holy freak-show, and also, something more than that, something which spoke of the promise and the prophecy fulfilled. And this child came from the Deep South, which we, the children, had never seen but which all our parents remembered, with yearning and fear and pain.

She was a small child, darker than her father, with hair coarser than his, hair now mainly covered by the crocheted holy cap. Her father's eyes were bright. Her eyes were dark, flashing, and seemed unbelievably ancient in the tiny, untouched face. Arthur said she was a witch, and could put a spell on you, or else she was a dwarf about a hundred years old, and Brother and Sister Miller had stolen her from Egypt.

She did not sound like a child as she read, and we read behind her—and I still remember feeling very strange, as though I were making, simply by the sound of my voice, some relentless, mysteriously dangerous vow:

"Blessed be the Lord," we read, "for he has shown me his marvelous kindness in a strong city."

Her father sat down—he always stood to read, the congregation sat—and she stared out over us, suddenly very far above us, something like a high priestess, that was true, from some other time and place.

"Amen!" said Julia. "Now that was *David* talking. You all know who David was? David wrote these psalms and I believe they was put to music in the olden times and the people sang and made a joyful noise unto the Lord with the *psalms*. This is David talking, and you know who David was? Well, David went out, one day, looking for this wicked giant, looking for this *big*, terrible looking, *wicked* giant had everybody in the neighborhood scared to death of him, this giant they called Goliath, and little David went out with his slingshot one day, and he *slew* this wicked giant! You all still don't know who David was? David was a shepherd boy, he fed the hungry sheep! I hear some of you saying, Who was this David? tell me more about this David! Well, David was a *King*—you hear them call *King David*, and the multitudes bowed low, oh, yes! I hear somebody asking, who was this David? Well, let me tell you this David had a son, and this son went a-stray, he was running through the forest, trying to hide from the wrath of God, and this son had all this long, beautiful hair, I believe he was mighty *proud* of his hair now, and the Lord just let all that beautiful hair get all tangled up with the vines and the bushes and the thorns from the trees and David's son died there, trying to hide from the wrath of God, and we hear David going down on his knees, crying out loud, crying like a baby, church, I can hear him crying, can you hear him crying now, church? King David humbled on his knees, crying, crying, 'oh, my God, I wish you would have let me die for my son, I wish you would have let me die in my son's place,' oh, hear King David crying, 'my son, my son!' Now you want to know some-

thing more about David? I believe I'll tell you just a little bit more
about King David this morning! The Lord put His hands on David—
out of the house of *David*, comes our Savior, Christ, the Lord!"

Whatever she was doing, she surely wasn't jiving: and that church
seemed just about ready to take off and meet Jesus in the middle of the
air. She couldn't move and pace the pulpit like a grown-up preacher,
because you wouldn't be able to see her once she stepped down off
that box. And yet, she moved as I have seen few people move, her
hands, those eyes, those shoulders, that pulsing neck, and the voice
which could not be issuing from a tiny, nine-year-old girl. For me,
there was something terrifying about it, as terrifying as hearing the
dumb stones speak, or being present at the raising of the dead. For, if
the dead could be awakened, this small child's voice could do it—but
who wants, really, to be present when the dead rise up?

And, while she spoke, the church *Amen'd!* and cried, *Bless your
name!* and *Holy! Holy!* and *Speak, Lord Jesus!*—but, when she paused,
the church paused, and a mighty silence trembled then, a mighty music gathered in the silence, waiting to break, like a storm.

Her mother and father were still, and little Jimmy was still. Arthur
sat straight up, his mouth open, his eyes wide.

"*Now* you all getting an idea who David was? David is the one who
said, 'Blessed be the *Lord:* for He has shown me His marvelous kindness in a *strong* city'! Oh! a *strong* city! David is the one who said, 'The
Lord is my shepherd, I shall not want'! David was a shepherd, and I
believe he was a *good* shepherd, he never let his sheep go *hungry*, amen,
and that's how come he could say, 'I shall not *want*'—not even in this
strong city! Oh, church, I believe he might have had to eat the bread of
affliction sometimes. I believe I can hear him saying, this morning, 'I
will lift mine eyes up to the hills from whence cometh my *help*.' I believe I can hear him saying, this morning, 'Fret not thyself because of
evil-*doers*'—*can* you hear him, church? I hear him saying, 'he that
dwelleth in the secret place of the most *High* shall abide under the
shadow of the *Almighty,*' oh, yes, right here in this strong *city*! I believe
I can see him, looking down the line to *Jesus*, amen, and crying out,

'my God, my God, why hast thou forsaken me?' in this *strong* city! I believe I can see him walking the streets and riding the subways and mopping the *floors,* amen! in this *strong* city, and emptying the garbage pails, and saying 'Yes ma'am' and 'no ma'am'! in this strong city, I believe I hear his babies crying out for bread in this *strong* city, I believe I hear the wicked laughing in this *strong* city, just like Goliath might have been laughing when he saw this little boy with nothing but a slingshot, oh, yes, laughing just before he went to meet his Maker, church, oh, yes, you better not be laughing at God's anointed, ain't going to *be* no laughing in front of the judgment seat. One day—"

My heart thundered, and the church, in silence, thundered.

"—*one day!* we going to wake up in this *strong* city and see the Lord's deliverance! Our children won't be hungry no more! no more! We won't see the old folks all twisted up with the rheumatism, water running down their face—no more! Blessed be the Lord! for His marvelous kindness, in this *strong* city. This strong city. Oh, but I hear another voice, this morning, saying, 'Except the *Lord* watch the city, the watchman watcheth but in vain'! Don't you *hear* that voice, this morning, church? I hear David saying, 'Clap your *hands,* all ye people! clap your *hands!*' I hear David, saying, 'Make a joyful noise unto the lord'! And, now, I believe I can hear one of David's kin-folk, old Brother Joshua, marching around the walls of a *strong* city, blowing his trumpet outside the walls of a strong city, and I hear somebody telling me how the walls of that city come tumbling down. That *strong* city. I hear David, saying, again, 'Lift up your heads, oh, ye gates, and be ye lifted up, ye everlasting doors, and the King of glory shall come in'! I hear somebody singing, *I cried—*!"

My voice answered, and the church answered, "and He delivered me."

"*I cried!*"

"and He delivered me."

"*I cried!*"

"and He delivered—*me.* He delivered: my poor soul."

The floor beneath my feet shook, the very walls seemed to rock, the storm burst in a thunder of hands and feet and the wrath of the piano, the racing—like horses!—of the tambourines, and the people started to shout. Julia stood there, above it, watching, like a high priestess. She had caused this storm, or it had come through her, but she was neither singing nor shouting, and her eyes might have been fixed on Egypt. Her father mounted the pulpit and stood next to her and wiped her brow—and, yes, you could see then, that he loved her—and led her down, out of our sight, to her royal seat up there.

The light in the church seemed very strange to me, and, for the first time, the shouting people scared me. I didn't even think of watching Sister Miller's ass the way I had before. Little Jimmy sat alone in a corner, looking the way I felt—I wanted to get out of there. But I knew that Julia and her parents were coming to our house as soon as service was over and it would just not have been very nice of me to run away. So I sat next to my parents, next to Arthur, and just behind Jimmy, watching the redeemed rejoice.

But the redeemed do not seem so irrevocably redeemed when they are no longer standing in the light of the temple. Brother and Sister Miller came to our house, with their son and daughter: a young couple, merely, she very much in love with him, he very much in love with their daughter. They teased each other, and made a great fuss over Julia—who was a beautiful little girl. What surprised me was that she was a very cheerful little girl. She loved to laugh, especially in her daddy's lap, and her daddy loved to make her laugh. Our mama and daddy—Paul and Florence—fussed over Amy and Julia and Joel, and, to a lesser extent, over Jimmy, who was not cheerful. He was sullen; he was, indeed, left out. Arthur was too old for him, and snubbed him, I was no help, and every time Jimmy's mother spoke to him, he glanced at her murderously, and seemed to want to run. Julia did not appear to have heard of his existence: she had not yet been given the revelation.

If one wishes to be instructed—not that anyone does—concerning the treacherous role that memory plays in a human life, consider how relentlessly the water of memory refuses to break, how it impedes that journey into the air of time. Time: the whisper beneath that word is death. With this unanswerable weight hanging heavier and heavier over one's head, the vision becomes cloudy, nothing is what it seems. The word, *event*, has no meaning, except in a ritual sense: in the sense, that is, of a vow, a bowing down low between the earth of the future and the sky of the past: with joy. You cannot see when you look back: too dark behind me. And the song says, merely, with a stunning matter-of-factness, "There's a light before me. I'm on my way."

How then, can I trust my memory concerning that particular Sunday afternoon? Memory does not serve me, I had nothing to remember then. Julia was a nine-year-old girl; I was eighteen. I did not know that she would leave the pulpit, turn into a whore and then, the mistress of an African chief, in Abidjan. I did not know that we would become lovers, and that she would become one of the pillars holding up my life. I knew nothing about Arthur, who was then eleven, and less about Jimmy, who was then seven, who would become Arthur's last and most devoted lover. Who could know that then? Beneath the face of anyone you ever loved for true—anyone you love, you will always love, love is not at the mercy of time and it does not recognize death, they are strangers to each other—beneath the face of the beloved, however ancient, ruined, and scarred, is the face of the baby your love once was, and will always be, for you. Love serves, then, if memory doesn't, and *passion*, apart from its tense relation to *agony*, labors beneath the shadow of death. Passion is terrifying, it can rock you, change you, bring your head under, as when a wind rises from the bottom of the sea, and you're out there in the craft of your mortality, alone.

But I'm going to have to try to remember. Service broke early, for that church, anyway, and we got to the house around three o'clock.

The churches didn't seem like one church, then—we knew all their distinctions, and tribulations, and their quarrels—but, looking back, they blur into the same church, sometimes changing locations, sometimes changing furniture (never changing pastors). This might have been the church where Arthur would start singing, not too much later, next to the Park Avenue railroad tracks: but maybe I only remember it that way because that was where I first heard Arthur sing in public.

I can be fairly sure of some things. I was eighteen, thirty years ago. The country was between wars, and nobody had quite got his shit together, the killing shit, though everybody was heading in that direction. The pause was useful. Paul played piano in a joint uptown, in what had been Sugar Hill. Mama had a family in The Bronx, and they loved her. I had a job in the garment center, but not pushing a wagon, thank you, I was a shipping clerk. (I can hardly tie a package today, not even Christmas presents; my fingers, at last, rebelled.) I was going to night school, we were hoping to send Arthur to college.

If I was going to night school, then we were living on 135th Street, between Fifth and Lenox. I remember the subway ride. We were worried because we heard that they were going to tear down our building to make room for a housing project.

I remember that we walked from church, because Jimmy had a tantrum, wanting to pee. His mother was terribly embarrassed, but his father laughed and stood beside him while Jimmy peed between two parked cars.

"You feel more like a man now?" his father asked; and Jimmy turned away, and buttoned up. For a moment, I had the feeling that he was about to run across the street and get himself killed. But he took his father's hand and walked beside him.

Amy and Florence were talking about some people in New Orleans. Julia walked between them, suddenly, again, very silent and old. That girl frightened me. Perhaps something in her will always frighten me.

And my father and I walked together, with Arthur between us—ambling down the Sunday afternoon.

When Arthur was with us, between us, as he was that afternoon, our father and I were, somehow, set free, to talk or not to talk: for our subject was palpable, present, both visible, and out of our hands. This unspoken commitment bound us far more certainly than any other declaration of love could have done.

For I can see now that Paul did not want to talk to me directly about the road which had led him to his present—and so precariously perched—piano. That might have frightened me concerning *my* road. But to be concerned about *Arthur's* road did not—directly—engage my future, or—directly—my father's past. This concern, this commitment, was the tacit recognition of our respect for each other as men, and of our love for each other as father and son. For I loved my silent, proud old man—he wasn't old then, he never got old.

And Arthur knew all this, in some other way, though I don't think that he could have known that he knew it. I think he never felt safer than he did when his father and his elder brother were beside him, conferring together, above his head.

We got to the house and climbed the three flights of stairs, Arthur running ahead of us to unlock the door. Paul and Florence, smiling, together, permitted themselves to climb the stairs slowly—Arthur was already in the apartment, and I was in charge of the Millers. My parents climbed the stairs behind me, and I was behind Amy and Joel and Julia and Jimmy. The children's mood had changed.

"You a *story!*" Jimmy whispered, fiercely, to his sister. This was on the landing. Their parents had started climbing the third and last flight of stairs; and I had the feeling that they, too, like my parents behind me, were resting for a moment.

"I'm in the Lord's hands," Julia said calmly.

But she stumbled as she started up the third flight.

Jimmy said with a venom which almost made *me* stumble:

"You lucky you ain't in mine!"

And Jimmy looked at his sister with hatred, as though he wished to push her down the steps, or hurl her over the railing. We all got to the top of the steps, and entered our open door.

Arthur had opened the wrong door, that is, he had opened the door which opened on the small room which led to the kitchen and the bathroom instead of the door which opened on the living room: and the silence was a little heavy as we walked through the two dark bedrooms which led to the front of the apartment. I heard, during that passage, "Now, Jimmy, you be good, you hear me?" and his mother slapped him, hard, twice, across the face. Jimmy didn't make a sound, He ran ahead of my parents and me, into the living room, and stood at the window, looking out.

"Well. Make yourselves at home," Paul said, smiling, and not knowing what else to say, and staring at Jimmy's back.

Florence glanced at Amy briefly, as though she were seeing the past and the future, as though there were something she wanted to tell her—or, perhaps, as though she wanted to strike her—and Amy sat down on the sofa, beside her husband. She didn't look sexy to me now, she didn't even look pretty. She looked like a skinny, scared young thing, not bright, not nice at all. And the dude beside her was suddenly just that, a dude, and he looked frightened, shrunk all inward, as though he were in the hands of the cops in the precinct basement and about to inform on his mother.

It was a kind of frozen moment. Florence walked out of the room. Julia ran and put her head in her father's lap. But both these motions seemed frozen. Arthur moved toward Jimmy, slow and shy, and Paul said, "Hall, take them on down to the ice cream parlor. Dinner won't be ready for a few minutes."

So I was the one who grabbed Jimmy around the neck and pulled him out of the room, and Arthur followed us. We got out of the apartment and Jimmy started to cry and I sat down on the steps and I held him and Arthur stood there. An awful lot began that day, looking back; I *know* that a lot of what happened could *not* have happened, had it not been for that day; and yet, Jimmy hardly remembers it at all. He remembers, and not at all the way I do, that his father let him piss between two parked cars; and I guess that makes sense, too. Lord. Did you say something about being wonderfully and fearfully made?

I walked my two charges around the block, very much the big

brother now, and digging it, and though I knew it might spoil their appetites, bought them ice cream sodas and sat at the counter smoking a cigarette and bullshitting the girl behind the counter. I must say that I loved my brother, Arthur, very much that day because he was being very nice, not forced-and-phony nice but really nice. He was hurt that this snot-nosed kid he'd been snubbing all day had been hurt and was doing all he could to make amends—and had the grace not to seem to be making amends, not to have noticed that anything had gone wrong. He got Jimmy to laugh. I was to forget all this later, but then, later, it was all to come back to me. When I thought they'd laughed enough over secrets they would never entrust to an old man like me, I stood them up and paid the bill and walked them back around the block, to the house. I carried Jimmy piggyback up the stairs and Arthur again ran up the stairs ahead of us, like the advance patrol.

"Why," Amy was saying, as we entered the living room, "when Julia was called—"

"How old was she?" asked Florence.

"I was seven," Julia said. She was sitting on her father's lap, motionless, using him the way the Sphinx uses the plains of Egypt.

Amy sat beside them; she had taken off her hat.

On the long, low table in front of the sofa there was a bottle of Coca-Cola, and one of ginger ale, a plate of cookies, glasses, and a bottle of dry sherry. Amy had been drinking ginger ale, her daughter had been drinking Coke. Paul and Joel were drinking the wine—Paul was keeping Joel company, and he sat on the piano stool with his back to the piano. Florence sat beside him, in the easy chair.

My mother was in her forties, Amy had barely reached thirty— and, yet, facing my mother, she looked dried-out, scared, and old. Above all, scared, and I had never noticed that before. I had never really looked at her before.

As we came in, my mother looked swiftly from Jimmy to Arthur, then to me. I gave her the briefest hint of a nod, and she turned back to Amy.

Arthur and Jimmy took one look, and then went down the hall to the kitchen. I stood by the door.

"Take a seat, son," Paul said. He looked both amused and grim. His voice contained an order. I sat down near the door.

"She came into the room and she looked—oh, I can't tell you—she looked so clean and scrubbed, but scrubbed *inside*—she looked like she had *seen* something—and me, I got so scared, my heart turned over, I thought—I thought, my child is dying.

"I was in the kitchen. It was early in the morning, before she had to get ready for school. Joel had already gone to work. She came right up to me and she reached up and I bent down and she kissed me, and she said, 'I can't go to school today, Mama.' I was afraid to ask her why, but, then, I knew I *had* to ask her and she gave me the most beautiful look I ever saw in all my life, it wasn't a smile, it was just—a *look*—and she said, 'Mama, the Lord has called me to preach.' "

Paul and Joel sipped their sherry at the same time, neither looking at the other; and I felt mightily uneasy, as though I had no business in this room.

"Well, Lord"—and she almost touched her daughter, but she didn't—it was like a gesture of blessing, or the way the hand retreats before flame—"you talk about a troubled *soul*. I did not *believe* that this was *happening*—did not believe it—but it was happening, all right, and there she was, my daughter, who didn't belong to me no more. Then something told me it was a sin not to believe and I put my hands to my face and we went down on our knees together, Julia and me, on that kitchen floor.

"I don't know how long we stayed there. I know I was praying for a sign. Because I love my daughter, and, you know, the devil has many ways to enter. But, at the same time, something told me it was wrong to be praying for a sign. Something kept saying, 'Believe. Only believe.'

"So, I got up off my knees and I said, 'Julia, I'm going to fix your breakfast now' and so I did, and she ate it and I kept watching her, but she didn't seem no different, and, yet, she did."

"How?" asked Florence.

"All I can tell you—it felt like peace had entered. Everywhere."

"Oh, yes," said Julia.

"When I come home from work," said Joel, with his lazy little grin, "I come through the door and it felt like my house had *changed.* I looked *around* me, I wasn't sure I was in my house.

"Then, I heard them in the kitchen, Amy and Julia and little Jimmy, and I hollered out, I'm home! and, I don't know why, I just started to laugh, I felt so good."

"You sure did laugh," said Julia.

"Yes," said Amy, "there was joy all over his face when he come through that kitchen door, and I had never seen him like that before, and I knew that was the sign."

"I hollered out, 'Who's been here since I been gone?' And Julia looked at me for a long time and then she said, 'The Holy Ghost,' and I kind of shivered, I guess, and I sat down."

"Julia preached the very next Sunday, in our church," said Amy. "Joel had to borrow money from his boss so I could make the robe."

"And, then," said Joel, slowly, "a whole new day began for us."

"I reckon so," said Paul carefully, after a moment; and he turned and touched the piano keys lightly.

I caught my mother's glance at Julia. I know I did not move, and, yet, I sat up in my chair.

"I probably shouldn't ask you this now," my mother said, "but, just the same, I'd like to know why you hit little Jimmy so hard. All he was doing, so far as I could see, was that he was acting like a little boy. I got two, so I know something about that." She glanced at Julia again. "We lost our little girl."

Between my birth and Arthur's there had been born a little sister, *my* little sister, Sylvia. She had been born with a kidney ailment and she only lived three years—just long enough for everyone, but, selfishly, especially, me—for she was *my* little sister—to have fallen in love with her. The seven years separating Arthur's birth from mine is almost certainly due to that birth and death.

"Jimmy can get to be pretty obstreperous," Joel said slowly, but Amy interrupted, crying, "Jealous! That's what he is! Jealous of the Lord's anointed! That's a sin, now you know that's a sin, and it scares me—why," and she looked at Joel and Julia briefly, and then back at Florence, "it would be like *me* being jealous."

"But he's just a little boy," said Paul slowly, looking down, strumming the piano keys. "He ain't got to understand all that."

"And whipping him sure ain't going to make him understand," said Florence. "He's still your child, and it ain't the Holy Ghost that's raising him, it's you."

"*She's* your child, too," said Paul, turning now, and looking at Joel, "and I might be speaking out of turn—but I also *might* know something about the Lord's anointed."

"That may be why you're not among them," Julia said.

Amy caught her breath, and muttered, "*Speak, Lord Jesus!*" Florence threw back her head, and laughed. She stood up. "Well—let me go and get dinner on the table." She looked at Amy. "You know I didn't mean no harm."

"My father," said Julia and left his lap and stood in the center of the room, "my father"—in that really terrifying voice, one could not imagine where it came from—"I am to deliver the Word tonight, and we must not break bread in this house." Tears rolled down her face. "You have mocked the Lord's anointed," she said, "and I—I am about My Father's business," and she walked out of the room.

No one moved. The silence, after the sound of that voice, was dreadful. I wanted to laugh, but let me tell the truth about it, too, I was afraid. Paul strummed the piano keys, he sketched *Come by here, Lord, come by here.*

Amy stood up trembling, and moved into her husband's arms. He held her, briefly, staring toward the door. His eyes met mine for a moment, and, very slowly, I stood up, too. Amy moved, and put on her hat. She looked at Florence, Florence looked at her. Paul stood up, abandoning the piano, and then there was silence indeed.

"You're welcome to stay," said Florence. "I can put her to bed. That child's tired. She don't have to work tonight."

"She must go as the Lord leads her," Amy said. She put her arm through her husband's; they moved toward the door. Joel turned for a moment to nod at my father, I had never before seen so helpless a look on the face of any man, though I have seen it since, and then they walked out of the living room, down the hall. We heard them call Jimmy. We heard Arthur unlock the door. Then the door closed behind them. Arthur came running into the room, and, for no reason at all, I grabbed him and held him close to me, and Mama said, "Well, come on, children, I know you must be hungry."

Mama had baked a ham, and biscuits, we had collard greens and yams and rice and gravy—and sweet potato pie, and there was more than enough, since the invited guests had gone. Arthur ate like a pig, and a spoiled one at that, but he meant it when he said that he was sorry Jimmy had had to go.

There were questions I wanted to ask, but not in Arthur's presence. But *he* wanted to ask questions, too—my presence did not inhibit *him*.

"Do she have to go to school? I mean," he added, "because she's a preacher."

"I don't know," Paul said, smiling, "but most of the preachers *I* knew sure had to go to *work*. Of course," he added, after a moment, "they had mouths to feed."

Florence grunted, looked at Arthur, and held her peace.

"How come she's a preacher? what makes her a preacher?"

Paul said, "She says the Lord called her, Arthur."

"What does it mean, Daddy, for the Lord to call you?"

"Your daddy don't know," Florence said. "The Lord didn't call him." She added, under her breath, "Thank the Lord," and Arthur looked, in astonishment, from his mother to his father, and, then, doubtfully, at me.

"Many are called," I said, "few are chosen," and I winked—but no one at the table appeared to find this very funny, and Arthur turned back to his father.

"Could *I* be called?"

"You're called," said Florence. "You're called to eat your dinner and go to bed."

"But it's *early!*"

"Well. Eat, anyway."

And, as quickly as that, Arthur turned his attention from the spiritual to the temporal, hoping to be allowed out of the house for a while, as soon as he had eaten.

"I'm glad that child's mother can't see her," said Florence to Paul—and I could see that this bewildered Arthur, who could not know that Florence was referring to Amy's mother, not to Amy. He decided to stay out of the arena this time, and kept his eyes on his plate. "I never thought that she was exactly overloaded upstairs, but I *did* give her credit for having good sense."

"Her head's not her problem," Paul said shortly.

"No—but what about the boy?"

"*Which* boy?"

"The *little* one," said Florence, "for there *ain't* no hope for the big one."

Arthur coughed, a little boy's cough, and stood, just like the little boy he would no longer have to be the moment he got out of that door and down those steps.

"Mama? Can I go out for a while?"

"Go ahead. But you know what time you supposed to be back."

"Yes, ma'am—Daddy?"

"Don't you be spoiling that child."

But she did nothing to stop Paul from throwing Arthur a quarter, and Arthur said, "Thank you. See you later," and split.

Into the streets he went, where he was soon to meet, or had met already, Peanut, Crunch, and Red.

Peanut had not been christened Peanut, though he had indeed been christened—by his grandmother, whose daughter had died bringing Peanut into the world. Very shortly after this, and, partly because of the grandmother, Peanut's father disappeared. Peanut was never to meet him. Peanut's real name was Alexander Theophilus Brown (I never knew his full name until the search began for his body), and he had been born in Albany, New York, where his grandmother was a hairdresser.

He was about a year older than Arthur—a year, or fifteen months, say; and, since I knew him mainly through Arthur, I cannot say I knew him. My eye followed Arthur's which happens when you care about someone. Still, I'm not Arthur, my eyes are not his eyes. I could not imagine how Peanut got his nickname, for example; later on, I realized that I couldn't imagine it because I wasn't one of the people who gave it to him. But Arthur was—he had been present at the event. Whatever Peanut had done to earn his nickname must have been beautiful—and hilarious—because his buddies pronounced that name with such love and laughter. I don't have a nickname, for example, which probably says a lot about me, but, if I did, only the people who gave it to me would know what I had done to deserve it.

He didn't look like a peanut at all. He was tall, and thin, and kinky-sandy-haired. I would have called him Strawberry, he had that kind of flush beneath the banana-colored skin. His face was long and thin, high cheekbones, long, narrow, amber eyes. In repose, or in that anger which makes silence a dread presence, the face was as closed as some prehistoric mask. Soon, without realizing it, you waited for the delight and the wonder—to say nothing of the relief—of seeing that face open, as when he laughed, or was talking about something that excited him.

He was an orphan, really, who lived with his grandmother, a relentlessly respectable old black lady, who hated all black people and who blamed all black people, especially her grandson, and most vehemently her daughter, for the adversity which had driven her from the heights of Albany into the cauldron of the city. The adversity, real enough, was not at all mysterious, being dictated, merely, by real-estate machinations on the part of the people who owned the land. These machinations forced her to sell her shop at a loss. It was not intended that she get past the labyrinth of laws, banks, and insurance rates and find another location: black people, who have many faults (and who have yet more to discover) are not the authors of this particular devastation. Yet, the old lady, Peanut's grandmother, blamed it all on—us; and matters could not have been helped by the fact that Peanut, standing beside her, was as fair as the morning and she was as black as a shoe. And Peanut had been told that he looked like his mother (or was it his father?). All this must have mightily troubled Peanut's mind, but he was trying to get it together; and he loved his grandmother, who, in her black, bleak, relentless way, loved him. And Peanut never talked about the adversity which had driven them into the city—for it could not have been entirely an adversity for him, he was asthmatic with boredom in Albany—but it certainly had something to do with both his faces.

Anyway, let's say about a year or so after all this, I had a fight on my job with some snot-nosed, red-headed white boy who thought it was fun to call me *"Shine."* And I had been real nice about it, let me tell you. I told him once. I told him twice. The third time—but I was still being nice—I warned him of the agonies of dying of constipation because he wouldn't *have* no ass by the time I got through with it. And when I say I was being nice, I mean that I could see that this brainless Andy Hardy democratic republican had no idea what he was fucking around with, didn't know that he could lose his life. He didn't even mean any harm, he was just having fun the way he'd been taught to have fun. Poor slob, the next time he called me *Shine*—*"Hurry up, Shine, hurry up!"*—I didn't tell him no more. I was on top of the ladder, working loose one of those bolts of cloth which weigh about two tons. You have to be very careful with it. The man on the ladder must lower this bolt of cloth very carefully to the man on the ground. The bolt of cloth is horizontal as you work it loose; it must be lowered vertically into the arms of the man on the ground. The trick is to shift this weight into a vertical position as you work it loose and, since you've got your back turned to the man on the ground, he's got to be ready when you start to slide the cloth down the ladder.

This time, when the child called me *Shine!* I'd just worked the bolt of cloth loose, but he didn't know it. I lifted it, and dropped it, and turned around on the ladder, just in time to see his face, as it missed him. If it had hit him, it would have broken his neck. I'll never forget his eyes—he didn't know what he'd done to make me try to kill him. And, because he didn't know what he'd done, I came off the ladder, and—tried to kill him.

It's a dreadful place to be. I've been there a few times since—hope never to have to go there again. There is a blood-red thunder all around you, a blinding light flashes from time to time, voices roar and cease, roar and cease, you are in the grip of an unknowable agony, it is in your shoulders, your arms, your hands, your breath, an intolerable labor—and, no, it is not at all like approaching an orgasm, an orgasm implying relief, even, sometimes, however desperately, implying the hope of love. Love and death are connected, but not in the place I was that day.

Somebody dragged me off him. The boy was a bloody, bewildered mess. I felt an absolutely intolerable grief and shame. The poor child didn't know. He didn't know. Two lives had nearly been lost, and on those two lives how many others depended? because he didn't know.

I didn't lose my job, miraculously. Though, looking at it coldly, it probably wasn't miraculous at all—I was simply a more valuable worker, and cheaper, than the white boy. I apologized to the child, I was even willing to help him wash up, but they gave me the rest of the day off.

I worked on 39th Street. I walked up Seventh Avenue, intending to go to a movie on 42nd Street, but by the time I got there, I really didn't have the heart to go to a movie and so I just kept walking. Not for the first time, but, then again, maybe *really* for the first time, I wondered, I wondered what I was to do. With my life.

I walked through the city. I just was not able to get into a bus, or a subway. I walked home.

It was about six in the evening. When I got to Harlem, I realized that it had been a nice spring day. It was April.

I heard the piano playing as I got to my floor, and I was happy that Paul was home. I walked in through the door which led to the kitchen. There was no one in that part of the house. I walked through the two bedrooms, to the living room. There were Paul, Peanut, and Arthur; and Peanut was at the piano.

Arthur stood beside Peanut, singing. Paul stood behind them, keeping the beat with one foot; and Peanut was trying to follow the beat.

> *That gospel train is coming*
> *I heard it close at hand*
> *I hear the engines trembling*
> *And rumbling through the land,*

Arthur sang, and *"Now!"* Paul grunted, but Peanut fumbled on the keys.

Paul leaned over him, and struck a chord. "If you do that, *then,* you can get here"—he struck another chord—"home free. And then—hit it, Arthur—*get*—"

> *"On board, little children*—"
> *"Get!"* Paul grunted.
> *"On board, little children*—"
> *"Get!"*
> *"On board, little*—"
> *"Chi-l-dren!"*
> *"There's room*—"

"Come on!"

"—for many a more!"

They all laughed, and Paul said, "You almost made it that time, son. But don't be in a hurry when you play. If you don't let it take the time it takes, then you ain't got no time, you see what I mean?"

Peanut nodded, his forehead vivid with tension, and coated with sweat. He sat, with his hands between his knees, staring at the keyboard. They might have been there all afternoon, or for days; no one had yet noticed that I was in the room.

"You worry too much about the beat. But the beat comes out of the *time*—the space between one note and the next note. And you got to trust the time *you* hear—that's how you play your song."

Peanut turned on the piano stool, and the two boys stared up at Paul, both drenched in the fading sunlight which poured on them through the window. Heavy, black Paul was in profile to me, in silhouette. The two boys looked up at him, in absolute belief and wonder. Peanut's forehead was still tormented.

"Would you give me lessons?" he asked.

Arthur looked at Peanut, and then up at Paul. There was a fascinating collision in his face of jealousy and pride.

"I ain't no teacher," Paul said.

Peanut blushed, and dropped his eyes, and his hands fell between his knees again. "I know," he said, "but—"

Paul said, "If you want to drop by some evening—early, you know, like now—I'll run over the keys with you."

"I sure would appreciate that," said Peanut, "I would sure appreciate that, sir," and he wanted to say more, but didn't know how, and Paul, embarrassed, turned, and saw me. I looked into his eyes, and we smiled. I was so glad to see him, my father, my old man. I thought of the boy who had called me *Shine:* but my father knew about him already, had known him from a long ways off.

"You're home early," my father said.

Arthur and Peanut stared at me, but said nothing.

"It was a rough day," I said, "down yonder in the dungeon. But everything will be all right if you'll just sit down at that piano and play us a little something."

Paul gave me a look, and Peanut moved from the piano stool. Peanut and Arthur stood at the window, and I sat down in the chair by the door. Paul played Duke's "Across the Track Blues." The boys at the window, me in the chair, Paul with his slicked-down hair as the day began to fade, and the Duke, from wherever he was, smiling all over his face.

I don't want to give the impression that I was at all grown up then, because I wasn't, and I'm not sure I'm grown up now. But I'm one of those people who have always had to *seem* to be grown up: this aspect of her husband has probably contributed to Ruth's sense of humor. Like Peanut, I was trying to get it together. I was luckier than Peanut because I had my mother and father, and I had Arthur: but Arthur (I did not know this then) was a double-edged sword.

One's little brother begins his life (you think) within the sturdy gates of one's imagination. He is what you think he is; he is everything that you are not; and he is, though you will never tell him this, much better, more beautiful, and more valuable than you. This is because you are here already, and he has just arrived. You have been used already, and he is newborn. You are dirty, and he is clean. You want the moon for your brother; you have forgotten that you must once have wanted it for yourself. Your life can now be written anew on the empty slate of his: what a burden to give your little brother!

Ah. I saw myself in Arthur. I forgot that we were brothers, and that he could also see himself in me. I might have shriveled and grown old if I could have seen what he was seeing. Well. This is love, just the same, however we warp or weave it. Love forces, at last, this humility: you cannot love if you cannot *be* loved, you cannot see if you cannot be seen.

What was Arthur seeing? I was a fairly good-looking, skinny kid of twenty. With a little light stealing, here and there, I kept myself in fine clothes—fairly fine clothes. I wasn't crazy; didn't, for example, pay down on the car; and then sleep in it. I loved my mother and my father—that helps. I didn't want to be a bad example to Arthur, and that helps. Drugs were flooding the ghetto, and that scared the shit out of me, for Arthur, and so there were a whole lot of things I didn't do and a whole lot of people I told to kiss my ass.

But I was scared. My future dropped before me like a swamp. I clung to night school, I kept my job. I had one girl after another. But if there's no future for you, if fucking doesn't become something more than fucking, then you have to forget it. And then you're worse off than you were before.

Youth must be the worst time in anybody's life. Everything's happening for the first time, which means that sorrow, then, lasts forever. Later, you can see that there was something very beautiful in it. That's because you ain't got to go through it no more.

Still, the weather of some days, the odor of a moment, or the moment you turn the corner, say, into a street which you do not remember, and which yet you will never forget, or seeing a figure leap from a bus, or watching a boy and a girl hand in hand, or, sometimes, seeing a small child smiling, face to the sky, or a tree, or the sky, or a stone, can make you ache, as though no time had passed, with the first time you saw love, the first time love saw you. *The light that's in your eyes/ reminds me of the skies/ that shine above us every day.* The first love disappears, but never goes. That ache becomes reconciliation.

But then—for example, I drank: but young people don't really drink, they swallow, producing instant piss. It's only later that the liquid you pour down your throat backs up.

Ah, then—you walk, you weep, you vomit—you stink; your prick rises up, and you jerk it off (*if thine hand offend thee!*), demons drag you off to sleep, you shudder awake. You shit and shower and shave. You wonder. You get it together, and you make the scene. You tell little brother how everything's cool. He says, for true? And he's watching you.

Here comes Crunch. He was big, the biggest boy in what was to become The Trumpets of Zion quartet. If thunder could be seen, then, I imagine that thunder would look like Crunch; and so would innocence. He owned several plantations of very thick, tangled black hair, a wide nose, which seemed, somehow, both aggressive and abused; heavy lips, a beautiful grin, lots of white teeth, perfectly straight. He was skinny, but powerful, played basketball, and was the boy who made out best with "the ladies": his term.

The term conveyed his bewilderment. Some men, and some women, appear to be born for the purpose of igniting desire: it appears to be their function. It is taken for granted that their intention is to fulfill desire—*your* desire—and that their smile, or their look, is meant to convey this intention.

It is not their intention at all. They have, very probably, barely noticed you, and are too innocent to be able to imagine what you are imagining.

These people are treated with an unbelievable brutality, a brutality made all the more hideous by presenting itself as love. And, in my experience, at least, these people, who are the objects of a lust at once abstract and consuming, rarely know how to defend themselves. They do not know, until too late, that they have any reason to defend themselves. This is because of that invincible innocence: and, less innocent, they would be less attractive—to rouse innocence to an utterly brutal, pounding passion is a fantasy rooted in everybody's nature. It makes the head spin; perhaps it makes the earth spin. What is lacking in every fantasy is that sweat of love which is called *respect.* "*I'm tired,*" Crunch was to say to me, much later, "*of being treated like something hanging on the other edge of a prick.*" For he was King Kong in a jockstrap, poor boy dribbling the ball down the court, striding the avenue, patting children on the head, helping old ladies and blind men to cross the street. He was a beautiful person, manhandled, smashed.

He was the oldest of five children, three girls, two boys. Their fathers came, and went; their mother was, in the main, a barmaid. His name was Jason Hogan, and he had been born in New York City.

Red was his best friend, was, in fact, a distant cousin, and they had grown up together. Crunch called Red his "heart," and he meant it.

A Saturday afternoon. Crunch has the guitar. Paul is at the piano. Peanut, Red, and Arthur stand behind him, Crunch stands to the side.

It is early December. The streets are empty and the air is icy with the threat of Christmas.

They are to make their debut Christmas morning, in *our* church, on Edgecombe Avenue. One of the reasons that we attend this church is because of Paul's following on Sugar Hill. But Paul does not play piano in this church—the church would not approve—except when Arthur sings. He doesn't always play for Arthur, and almost never plays for Arthur in any other church. He didn't carry Arthur around the way Brother Joel Miller carried Julia around. He took a very distant attitude toward Arthur's singing, almost as though it were an adolescent malady his son would have to survive. He was far more available to Peanut, Crunch, and Red than he was to Arthur. This made Arthur jealous, and jealousy made him work—he stayed at that piano, and he listened to everything—so that, if Paul's intention had been to discourage Arthur, his technique boomeranged.

Later on, I understood Paul. I think I may have understood him, though dimly, even then. Paul did not know if Arthur knew *why* he was singing. It was something Arthur had come to all alone, and at the age of thirteen. He had not claimed to be saved. He had not been baptized. (He had been christened at birth, but that is not baptism.) And, yet, he sang—indeed, he sang, and there was something frightening about so deep and unreadable a passion in one so young. Arthur's phrasing was the key—unanswerable; his delivery of the song made you realize that he knew what the song was about.

Your reaction to this passion can destroy the singer. Paul knew this, and Arthur didn't. Paul marshaled the other boys around his menaced son, for he knew why *they* were singing. (The boys thought they knew, too.) He knew they would not sing long—something would get in the way. But if anything got in Arthur's way, Paul would be missing a son.

So, he labored every weekend, my old man with the slicked-down hair, Friday, Saturday, and Sunday evening. It was out of jealousy and curiosity that Arthur joined them, and that's how the quartet got started. Arthur wasn't really anxious to surrender his solo status, he really dug being alone up there. But, on the other hand, it was more of a challenge, and more fun, being up there with the others, and he learned more that way. Paul had painted him into a corner, for he would not work with Arthur without the others: and, teaching the others, he was teaching and guiding his son.

Paul asks, "What do you guys want to start with?"

Crunch strums the guitar, and suggests "When Was Jesus Born?"

"We don't need so much work on that," Arthur says. "We ought to work on 'O, Come All Ye Faithful'—we ain't together on *that*, at all."

"That's true," Peanut says, glumly—being the lead singer on that number.

"Well, I agree," says Crunch quickly. "I just thought that we could use it to loosen up with, you know, get some fire falling—it's *cold*, and 'Come Ye' is a cold song."

"Why you say that, man?" Red asks. "It's slow, but it ain't necessarily *cold*."

"Oh, we going to pump some heat into it, niggers can pump heat into anything—but the song is *cold*—'joyful and triumphant'—I always have a little trouble with that line," and Crunch grins.

"You don't feel joyful and triumphant, son?" Paul asks mildly, and grins, striking the opening chord on the piano. "Well, anyway, if that's the hard one, let's start with that. How we doing it?"

They are in trouble with the long, solemn opening. They are trying to find a way to make it less solemn and more sacred. Arthur finally substitutes a *come on, you all* for *come ye*, which cracks everybody up, and they have to start all over again, but Arthur's invention has helped.

I can't describe it, I wasn't there. It's futile for me to try to describe it: at bottom, perhaps. I really feel that such an attempt is very close to insolence. I have too much respect for the people out of whom the music comes. Well. By the time I got home, that particular Saturday afternoon, they were well into their final number, "Savior, Don't Pass Me By." Arthur sang the lead on this number, and I heard his voice, above all others, as I climbed the stairs.

Paul looked wringing wet, and weary, and his hair was standing up. Now he was following the children, whose voices filled the room: *Savior!*

And then, again, *Savior!*

A pause, then the guitar and the piano, then the soloist, *Savior, don't you pass me by!*

All of the voices, forming a kind of rumbling, witness wailing wall: *Savior. Savior.*

Arthur, alone, eyes closed, meaning every instant of it, beginning high, like a scream, then dropping low, like a whispered prayer, a prayer whispered in a dungeon, *don't you pass me by!*

Whatever I know or don't know, I will never forget the faces I saw that afternoon, as I walked into the room, unnoticed. These were boys, street boys, rough and ugly—in the streets, anyway. They stole, they lied, they fought—they cheated. When they stole, they ran; when they were caught, they lied; when they were beaten, they cursed and cried, they pissed their pants. Yes. I was there. I know. They played handball, football, basketball, boxed, dreamed of becoming champions. They had started to smoke. Some smoked marijuana. Some had gone further than that. They believed that they hated white people, and that's no wonder. They were far from the hard apprehension that they simply could not endure being despised, far from the knowledge that almost everybody is, could not conceive that the world, or, at least, the world we know, could be so tremendously populated by people who despise each other because each despises himself. No. They dreamed of safety—I was dreaming, too. They could not know that they stood in a kind of timeless and universal danger, being, like all men, the Word made flesh. Thus, they imagined that they hated white people because they were not black, and could not imagine that they terrified white people because black people are not white. Their faces and their voices held the promise of the Promised Land; but we never see our faces, the singer rarely hears his song. They had started to fuck: on the flaming, outer rim of love.

Paul stands up, saying, "Well, that's all for now," and takes a handkerchief out of his back pocket and wipes his face.

"What about our encores?" Arthur asks, and Paul, and the others, laugh.

"There going to be three quartets up there," Paul says, "and you all the youngest and the newest, you going on first and you coming off first—*believe* me, you coming down from *there*—and little Sister Julia Miller waiting to preach her sermon, too? You ain't going to be having too much time for encores."

"And," says Crunch, "them Silver Nightingales got their mojo working. We try to do encores, our tonsils liable to pop all over the altar."

"We ought to be ready," Arthur says, "anyway."

He stares at the boys, who stare at him, and then, they all turn, helplessly, toward Paul.

"Don't look at *me*," Paul tells them. "Go on and have your summit meeting and when you got it all together, let me know." He walks to me, and winks. "Come on, buddy, let me buy you a drink."

For I was of age now, and we sometimes hung out a little on Saturday afternoons. Mama often worked late on Saturday because the lady of the family that loved her so much had bridge parties or bingo games or God knows what—orgies, who gives a shit—at her house on Saturdays, the proceeds to go to chairty; and Mama had to stay and clean up.

Paul got his coat, and we started down the stairs, leaving the boys shouting at each other.

Paul let out his breath, and I was about to sympathize with his weariness, but he said, "They're not bad, those little bastards. Maybe something will come of it, after all. One thing," he said. "They *work*. I'll give them that."

And he was smiling as we hit the streets, which were bitter cold, and almost empty. We started down the avenue toward Paul's favorite bar, which is still standing, thank the Lord, one of the few remaining witnesses to my youth.

But I have hardly ever drunk with Arthur in this bar; perhaps because the younger brother can never be a witness to the older brother's youth. These were *my* afternoons, with *my* father.

The cancer of television had not yet attacked every organ of the social body, and so the bar was quiet, with muted conversation, a laugh here and there, the jukebox may have been playing, low. A few of Paul's buddies were there, and, on those afternoons, Paul always said, *"and this is my son, Hall,"* like it was nothing at all. But I could see in his buddies' eyes that they dug he didn't think it was nothing at all. They looked at him with a quickening of love, and a little jealousy. Then they looked at me and I could see, in their eyes, that my father was proud of me. I didn't know why he was proud of me, I didn't know what I'd done to make him proud. But he was, I could see that in the eyes of his friends, and it filled me with a happiness I feel until today. I swore I'd never do anything to make him ashamed. And I don't think I did. I really don't believe I did—thank God, I can say that.

And the moment I say that, I think of Arthur, and I know, if I'm honest, that Arthur didn't think that *he* could say that. I know better, but I would: I knew our father better than he did. That was because my life as a man had begun, my suffering had begun. I had my father to turn to, but Arthur had only me, and I was not enough.

We sat down at a table near the window. Paul took off his hat. His hair was still untidy; in spite of the cold air through which we had passed, his face was still a little damp.

"What are we going to do with your brother?" he asked. "I think he might turn into a real musician—I mean, a real one," he added, "not like me."

I didn't want to pick him up on his *not like me.* I felt a chill go through me, as hard as the streets outside, because I knew he knew that I understood perfectly well what he meant. Paul made his living as a pianist, when he could; when he couldn't, he did other things; but he wasn't talking about making a living.

At the same time, I was far more skeptical than Paul concerning Arthur's being a musician. I knew that Paul knew more about music than Arthur, or than anybody, for planets around: what I didn't see was that it was *this* authority which informed his judgment—*he*, Paul, would know. I really believed that all this was merely a part of Arthur's adolescence, that he would outgrow it, and become a somewhat more predictable creature, but Paul only pretended to believe it, which was probably why his face remained damp and why his hair was standing up.

Paul ordered, and we waited for our drinks in silence, a silence charged, yet peaceful. Our drinks came, and Paul said, "I've been close to music all my life—loved it all my life. But, I swear, I never hoped to see no son of mine turn to music." He laughed, and lifted his glass to me, and sipped his bourbon. "I guess you think I better be glad I'm talking about my son and not my daughter." He stopped laughing, and looked down. He took another sip of bourbon. He sighed what almost sounded like a mortal sigh: *Ah*.

"You're worried," I said. "Why? If he wants to be a musician, a singer—what's wrong with that?"

"Nothing," Paul said, "except it's going to burn him up, burn him every hour that he lives, char the flesh from the bone, man, and leave that for someone to gather up and bury, and"—he finished his bourbon, and looked at me—"that someone is most likely going to be you."

I wanted to laugh, but I didn't laugh. I watched my father's face. He looked into the streets.

"Music don't begin like a song," he said. "Forget all that bullshit you hear. Music can get to *be* a song, but it starts with a cry. That's all. It might be the cry of a newborn baby, or the sound of a hog being slaughtered, or a man when they put the knife to his balls. And that sound is everywhere. People spend their whole lives trying to drown out that sound."

As the kids would say today, Paul was taking me on a far-out trip and I wasn't sure I wanted to make it. But laughter closed her stone gates in my face, I could almost hear the *boom.*

"Oh," said Paul looking at the street—but he might have been looking at a river—"there are other sounds—the sound of water, but that can drive you crazy. It has been *used* to drive people crazy. I bet, if you think about it, you can't think of single *sound* that you can live with. That's why we live with so many—each drowns out the other." He looked down into his empty glass. "I bet you think your old man's crazy."

I started to make a joke, but couldn't, and then I said, "No. I don't think you're crazy."

"If you ever had to think about it—how we get from sound to music—Lord, I don't know—it seems to prove to me that love is in the world—without it—music, I mean—we'd all be running around, with our fangs dripping blood." *He* laughed. He *could.* "Maybe I *am* crazy. But that's why all military music is just cold jerking off. The niggers in New Orleans figured that out, baby, and *didn't* they ramble!"

He was frightening me, suddenly, and he realized it. He ordered another round, and sat staring out of the window again, and I realized, for the first time, how mightily he was troubled.

"What about Arthur?" I asked—lamely, and, without knowing why, dreading the answer.

He was silent for a while. Our drinks came, and still he sat there, leaning on his elbows, looking out of the window.

"I used to run with some girls and boys, when I was young," he said, "and they were beautiful, let me tell you. I won't go into what happened to some of them—some are still around. They were beautiful, like I say. Trouble was, when they weren't singing or playing, didn't nobody know what to do with them. *They* didn't know, either—those that found out—*something*—*when* they weren't singing or playing, well, it took them a while, and they *paid* some dues. God knows they loved, and God knows they hurt, but, look like, they could only do it in public." He grinned, suddenly, a strange, sad grin, which made him look very young, almost as young as Arthur, and there was, swiftly, a resonance of Arthur in his face. This was Arthur's father, too, we were the issue of this man's loins. Now, I felt *my* face beginning to be damp.

"Some, like me, knew what to do and how to do it. It was sweat, but it was no sweat, if you see what I mean—or sweat was all it was. But some did not know, did not *know*, from one note to the next, if they were going to make it. They almost never failed, but they never *knew*. They always looked like a kid who got what he wanted for Christmas, when they left the last notes hanging out there in the air and they came off the stage, or the floor. Lord, they were beautiful. But they damn sure couldn't count to ten, and they couldn't keep house. They loved their kids, but their kids didn't always know it, they didn't always know it, they didn't always remember the wife or the husband or the sweetheart's name: and that didn't mean that they didn't love them. But who's going to be able to figure that out? How you going to believe that somebody loves you, when they way off someplace, getting some wild shit together, and look at you like some bit of dust in the desert, about two thousand miles away? How you going to imagine that, if you leave that person, she going to cry her eyes out, and maybe try to die? No, you see them in the club next Saturday, singing their ass off, and they lift you up, they hit you someplace, inside you, hard, and maybe they even make *you* cry—but— you don't know."

He looked down, and sipped his bourbon, and looked out of the window again. Then he looked at me, looked me directly in the eye.

"You understand me, son?"

"I think I do," I said. "I think I do."

"I think you do," he said. Then, "I had a girl like that, down yonder, when I was about your age, before I met your mama. That's what started me playing. I played for her."

I asked, "What happened to her?"

Paul said, "I don't know. We had a fight, she went away. I tried to find her, but—I never heard from her again."

"Is that why you're talking about Arthur?"

"Yes. No." Then, "Listen. I've been telling you something I *got* to tell you, because time is what time is, man, and I know you love your brother. I *know* that—much better than you do. But I don't want you to think that I married your mother because some wild chick left me. That ain't the case. Lord, if life was that simple, wouldn't be no need for music, nor no need for prayer. I loved the girl, that's true—the way a youngster loves. But don't think I don't love you mother. Don't think I don't love you."

"I might never have been born," I said, smiling, "if she hadn't left you."

"I asked you before," he said, "if you understood me."

"Yes," I said. "And I said yes."

"And—do you?"

"Yes," I said, and I looked at him. "Yes, I do."

He said, after a moment, "I tell you all this because, yes, I *am* talking about Arthur. Lord, it's a mystery." He looked down, looked out, and then looked at me. "Son. Let me tell you one thing. Don't never run from nothing. I swear to you, whatever you run from will come back, one day, armed to the teeth, man, will come back in a shape you don't know *how* to run from, will come back in a shape you *can't* deny!" He swallowed his bourbon. "I look at Arthur, and I think of that girl—that girl I ain't seen since I was twenty-odd. And I have to see that what drove me to her is exactly what brought Arthur here. And I'm going to carry it just as far as I can, but I know, by and by, I'm going to have to leave it with you—my time ain't long."

He scared me so badly that I hardly knew what I was saying: "What the fuck are you talking about—your time ain't long?"

"*I* know what the fuck I'm talking about. A father's time ain't never long, no matter how long it is. That's why"—he raised his glass, and grinned—"I'm taking the liberty of borrowing some of yours."

Then I laughed, it was his grin that did it; I was both terrified and relieved. We touched glasses, and drank, and, at that moment, the streets outside seemed to invade our haven, began resounding in my skull. I looked out of the window. Standing on the corner, their backs to us, waiting for the lights to change, were Peanut, Arthur, Crunch, and Red, still arguing—now, in pantomime. Paul looked up, looked out, and saw them: he smiled, and nodded his head from an unimaginable distance, and with a light in his eyes that I had never seen in anybody's eyes before. Something happened to make the boys laugh. Arthur lunged at Crunch. Crunch grabbed Arthur by the nape of the neck with one hand, and whirled, turning Arthur with him, with the guitar held high above his head. The lights changed, they charged across the street. Crunch seemed to sing like an arrow, lifting tiny Arthur above the ground. Red and Peanut, on either side of them, knew something we didn't know.

On the day before Christmas Eve, I had a whole lot of cash in my pocket from the stuff I had stolen, and sold; and I took a walk through the city.

I had to buy some presents for Paul and Florence, for Arthur, and for my girl friend, a black college graduate welfare worker, Martha: who didn't have a sister named Mary, but who really should have picked up on the gospel line, *tell Martha not to mourn no more.* The child did tend to mourn, and I couldn't blame her: I didn't spend as many hours as she did, for example, in the corridors of Harlem Hospital; wasn't surrounded, as she was, by the stink of blood, the rattle of expiring life, the cool, brutal, high-pitched siren of our indifference: *On Saturday nights, they pick up a torso here, some legs there, over yonder, a head, one eye here, another eye there, some guts draping the garbage can, and they dump everything else they can find into a croker sack and bring it to the hospital and say, sew it up! And, you know? it's hard to believe it, but—sometimes we do. And they walk out in the morning, don't even say thank you.* Yes, the child did tend to mourn, and I couldn't blame her. I wanted her to quit her job, but she wouldn't find another one in a hurry, and I knew I wasn't going to marry her. I didn't want to find myself in a croker sack, and have her sew me up.

Since we were all going to be together at church, on Christmas Day, I also had to find something for Julia and Jimmy and their parents. This was a drag, because I really didn't like the Millers at all. But I had to do it, because I also had to find something for the boys in The Trumpets of Zion. I could not give Arthur a present, and fail to remember them.

So. I walked through the city, my hands in my pockets. It was cold, and I felt it, and yet, I wasn't cold. But there was nothing in the windows I wanted to buy for anyone I loved—and what I saw in the windows that might have suited the Millers would have told them something I knew I didn't have the right to say.

I knew what I wanted for Paul. I had seen it in a window. I hoped I could find again. It was a heavy gray scarf, because Paul sweated at the piano, and didn't always remember to cover up well when he walked out into the street. I was going to buy a bracelet for Florence, a heavy silver bracelet, utterly plain, a closed circle.

Amy and Joel: since that afternoon in our house, I never thought of her ass or her breasts or her legs anymore. I thought of the moment she had slapped her little boy, and the way I had held him on the stairs while he cried, and Arthur's gentle and worried face behind him, and the ice cream parlor, later, and his terrifying sister. These two did not yet exist, you must remember, either for Arthur or for me, as Jimmy or as Julia. They were the strange children of Brother and Sister Miller. Besides, we could tell, though neither of our parents explicitly stated, or burdened us with it, that Paul could not stand Joel, Florence despised Amy. You could almost see her fingers itching to get to Julia's backside, and make her cry for salvation all over again. *Called?* I once heard her say to Paul, while they were sitting in the kitchen, stringing beans, *You let me call her one time. She will know that she's been called!*

And she snapped a string bean, as though it were Amy's or Julia's neck.

But real pain and confusion lay beneath this anger—which anger, in itself, was both true and false. Amy was, after all, the daughter of a woman who had been like a mother to Florence. One day, this woman would come down front and ask Florence about her daughter. Then Florence would no longer be able to hide behind the vague cheerfulness of her letters. She would be forced to drag the mother into a confrontation with the truth. At the same time, she felt that Amy's mother knew the truth, and was counting on Florence either to change that truth, or to protect her from it. This meant that Florence would also be dragged into a confrontation: with the truth concerning the woman who had been like a mother to Florence, but who had, somehow, failed to be a mother to Amy. Who could read such a record? Florence watched her sons, wondering if she had failed already, and watched Paul, sometimes, wondering if they were accomplices in a crime not yet discovered. It was perfectly possible that either one of us might get hung up on, and spend our lives with, someone as pretty and as flaccid as Joel, and—after all—as moving. Julia could not have been foreseen; both women would have been quick to agree about that. But from this, to face a further truth—that, without Julia's notoriety, and her earning power, Brother Joel Miller would long ago have split the scene—was a far colder and more intimidating matter. Joel did not love his wife so much as he loved his daughter because she put bread on the table. It was not an awful lot of bread, but a little can mean a lot, can make the difference: that was why I stole. Florence found herself part of a conspiracy to preserve Joel's ease, his boyhood, a conspiracy headed by a little girl—his daughter: and she found no way out of this closed circle. At another time, in another place, she might have been able to have had the child slaughtered as being possessed of a demon: but not at this time, and not in this place, for Julia spoke in the tongue of fire which was the testimony of the Holy Ghost.

I walked the avenue, in the freezing cold, which somehow did not get to me, looking in the windows. I didn't realize, then, how little choice we are offered by the people responsible for all this bullshit. I knew only that there was very little in those wide open windows that I wanted to take home to anybody. I was downtown, naturally, where the bullshit's cheaper, but bullshit travels well. And everybody seemed avid for it, rushing past me, rushing toward me, bumping me from side to side, like water, but without the friendliness water has when you know you're far from drowning. I sort of rode the water. I saw Paul's scarf, and walked into the store.

There can be a great many advantages to being black; for example, in those years anyway, when you walked into such a store downtown, everybody dropped whatever they were doing and hustled over to serve you at once. If you had any sense, you didn't give them a lecture on how you knew they'd come rushing over to you because they knew you were a penniless thief. No, you smiled, and you smiled at the house dick, idly buffing his fingernails next to the panic button, and let them try to guess where you carried your wallet, if you had one. You took your time, looking intelligent and mightily bored, and, with the humility of the aristocrat, indicated that you'd like to *see*—? With what was not quite a smile, you watched the salesperson nearly strangle on his or her tongue, which had been, most unwisely, about to warn you of the price. With the grace bequeathed you by your ancestors, you pretend not to have noticed how narrowly the salesperson has averted disaster: it is as though you understand how panic can make a person fart, and you indicate that you know the smell won't linger. *Well,* says he, or she, smiling, as taut as a wire, wishing to God the smell of that fart would go away, *we have*—and produces, blindly, a cascade of scarves. You know exactly what you want, but you finger the scarves carefully, doing your best to conceal what is either contempt or despair: you know that this person, who is now anxiously giving you the pedigree of the merchandise, merely works here—you indicate, with a resigned shrug of the shoulder, that you, too, know how hard life can be. And, unable to bear the other's misery a moment longer, you finally say, like a good fellow, *I'll take this one.* Relief floods the face, like sun breaking through the clouds—followed, however, by a swift look at the man who has ceased buffing his nails and who is now intently studying a rack of neckties. He, or she, wraps it. *That'll be*—? you say, touching your heart. *Right over here!* says he or she, and carries you to the cashier—who does not look at you, looks merely at the sales slip. (The rack of neckties has lost the man's interest, now he is looking at hats.) The salesperson lingers, slightly out of orbit; elaborately, you find your wallet, and count out the money. You get your receipt, and your gift-wrapped package. *Merry Christmas!* cries the salesperson, and *A merry Christmas to you!* you say, and you both stagger, in different directions, out of the arena.

I, to a side street off Herald Square, where I bought Florence's bracelet, and the tie clasp for Joel—a tie clasp in the shape of a horse's head—Joel played the numbers. I found a vial of perfume for Amy; and finally decided on a larger, more expensive vial of French perfume for Martha. (It's strange—perhaps—how buying a gift can reveal to you what you really feel about the person for whom you're buying the gift. The revelation can make you warm: it can also chill you, and I was a little chilled by the gift I bought for Martha. She didn't really mean anything to me—that meant I didn't really know her—and, since I slept with her about five or six times a week, that was chilling.)

And, now, I had the children: Arthur, Julia, Jimmy, Peanut, Crunch, and Red. Arthur was fifteen, Julia was thirteen. Jimmy was eleven. Peanut, Crunch, and Red were all a little older, between sixteen and eighteen.

I was not yet burdened down. Paul's scarf and Martha's perfume were in a shopping bag I held in one gloved hand; Amy's perfume and Joel's tie clasp and Florence's bracelet were in my pockets (along with the sales slips). Christmas trees, trussed and unsold, covered the curbs and the gutters. The men who were trying to sell them, shapeless in hoods, hats, gloves, boots, and army-surplus jackets, pranced up and down, beating their hands together. A great, dressed Christmas tree blazed and towered in Herald Square. Smaller trees flickered all around me: Arthur and I, and Paul and Florence, would begin dressing our tree tonight, when I got home. I wondered what Arthur was doing now. I wondered what I would buy him. I wondered—the shape of things to come, my God—if I could buy him anything he needed.

I walked to the Village on that freezing night, on which I felt, just the same, so warm. It wasn't late yet, not quite ten, and all the stores stayed open late tonight, honoring the birthday of the Prince of Peace. And, I suppose, if I really want to get down about it, that they really were—out of the same, blind, self-seeking wonder that forced them to crucify Him. Well. I don't really want to get *that* down about it: *them* is always us, *they* are always we. With that, and a subway token, you can ride from here to glory. A long ride, pilgrim, stopping at doom, despair, confusion, and loss, with a change of trains at Gaza: at the mill, with slaves.

I had a little time, and I thought I deserved a drink, and so I dropped in at a bar I knew: at the mill, with slaves: and squeezed myself onto an empty barstool at the very end of the bar. Then, for the first time, I realized that my body, in fact, was cold, and I was tired. I had been walking a very long time; in fact, I had walked through the city. The bartender was a German refugee named Ludwig, and he served me a double Scotch on the rocks—*On the house!* he cried, and *Merry Christmas!* and, beaming like Santa Claus, moved away, becoming part of the heaving flesh and smoke.

I lit a cigarette, feeling distant and lost. I suddenly saw what I would buy for Arthur: a silver ring for his little finger. I had seen it when I bought Florence's bracelet, but then, I hadn't been sure. Now, I was, but I wasn't sure I'd be able to get it tonight. Okay, one down. Julia. Julia was thirteen: and what did you buy for an adolescent high priestess? I thought at once, *a viper,* but then I thought, *don't be like that,* and laughed to myself, and sipped my drink. I had hardly seen Julia since that afternoon at the house, and I hadn't liked her since that day. I hadn't seen Jimmy at all, naturally, and I wouldn't have been surprised to hear that they'd shipped him off someplace—maybe to his grandmother, for I knew that Florence was worried about that.

Well. Julia. The child didn't wear ornaments, so I couldn't buy her earrings, or any kind of jewelry. I thought of buying her a purse, but I knew I didn't dare do that—her father would have hit me with it. Then, I thought of those tiny little wristwatches girls love, and I knew where I could get one. There couldn't be any harm in that, and if there was, well, fuck it—I was only trying to be nice. I couldn't think of anything for Peanut, Crunch, and Red, but, in any case, all of the rest of my shopping would have to wait until tomorrow. So I was off now, I was free: I'd done my bit for today.

I tried to think I was, but I knew I wasn't. I still had a lot of cash on me, and all these presents, so I couldn't get drunk, I couldn't get laid. I had made out a few times with white chicks, in this bar, but maybe I was growing old fast: I was fascinated, but left untouched; drowned in deep water, but came up thirsty. It must be admitted that I knew absolutely nothing, and was dragged around by the insatiable curiosity of my prick; which was an object of the most compelling curiosity for the little white girls, as well as for their boyfriends, who literally did not know what to make of it. It was more a matter of its color than its size, or perhaps, its color *was* its size. I had lived with it all my life, and knew that it was, roughly, the same color as my ass and my face; and it seemed to be, as I usually was, big enough for whatever it had to do. But they always looked at it as though Napoleon had just dragged it up from Egypt, especially for them, and, though they could make it as hard as stone, they also turned it that cold.

So I finished my drink and got into the wind and took the subway home.

We spent Christmas Eve in the kitchen, eating corn muffins and drinking tea, and placing our presents under the tree in the living room where we drank ginger ale and beer—just Paul and Florence and Arthur and me, very quiet. I had two presents for Arthur, the silver ring for his pinkie, and a black-and-gray striped necktie, for I had got the same necktie for all the boys in the quartet. I had Julia's tiny wristwatch, as hot as hell, and I got a charge out of knowing she'd be wearing stolen goods. Jimmy had been a problem, for I gathered that he manifested a ferocious independence and didn't want to be associated with any of these people, and so I bought him a scarlet turtleneck sweater. I thought he might dig that, there weren't too many like it around then. I didn't know his size, so I bought it large, gambling that he'd grow into it before he wore it out—a gamble I lost.

It was a nice, a quiet Christmas Eve. Paul played, and we all sang a couple of the old ones. I watched Arthur's face, beginning to see something of what Paul saw, but seeing, beyond that, how they resembled each other, how they were father and son. I don't know why that comforted me so, but it did. We went to bed early because Florence was tense about Christmas Day, which we were to spend with the Millers, and Arthur was nervous about singing.

Her eyes had changed: that was the first thing I noticed about Julia that Christmas morning. And she was taller—she was going to be tall. Her father no longer carried that intricate, collapsible platform, and now, Julia strode to the pulpit instead of seeming to be lifted up into it. She was so thin that she seemed, nearly, to be as transparent as a lamp: you could almost see the flame moving as the wind moved, and it made you watch your breath. She was in her gospel heyday, at the summit of her world—but the focus of her eyes had altered, something had happened behind her eyes.

Amy was dressed for Christmas—I almost said, like a Christmas tree—but she was vivid, certainly, in many colors, of which I remember, principally, a kind of silver-blue which looked as though it could electrocute you. She wore high heels, and her long, slender legs were still something to behold, but her skirt was long and full and her blouse beyond reproach. Joel was still the zoot-suited stud of studs, fatigue beginning, perhaps, to undermine the jawline, an embittered bewilderment coming and going in his eyes, but the suit was navy blue, and so was the knitted tie; the shirt was white, the cufflinks gleamed like gold. *A pretty penny!* was the thought that came to me, like a messenger with bad news, and I quickly turned my back on this messenger—who had, however, as I was to discover, been instructed to wait for a reply.

This patient messenger stayed at my side during all that long Christmas Day.

It was a bright Christmas, a silver, stinging air, with the sky above and the pavements below nearly the same color: you couldn't touch the sky, or fall down on it, but the sky looked as hard as the pavement. Arthur was up before me (the reverse of the shape of things to come) and had taken his bath, or maybe two baths, had brushed his teeth, certainly more than once, and shaved, and put on all of *my* cologne before I had opened my eyes. Arthur really didn't have anything to shave, but he didn't like my saying so. I tried to warn him that once he had a beard, he'd have it for the rest of his life and that all he was doing now, by shaving, was stiffening all that peach fuzz into ugly little bumps. He didn't like that, either, especially since it seemed to be true. His hair was a frozen cataract of black-and-silver waves and he was before the mirror, carefully patting down this mess, when I walked into the bathroom.

We looked at each other in the mirror, uncertain, as always, at that point in our lives, as to how well we got along.

I made a violent swipe at his hair, but didn't touch it; he ducked, scowling, and I laughed.

"Merry Christmas," I said, watching that face, which was no longer a child's face and not yet a man's face.

"Merry Christmas yourself," he said and grinned, showing me for an instant, exactly as though he'd known I wanted to see it, the face of the little boy.

"You nicked yourself shaving," I said.

"It's nothing," he said, and yet, gravely concerned, he turned to stare into the mirror again.

He was nearly naked, that is, he was wearing shorts. Standing there like that, with his back to me, staring so gravely into the mirror, it was strange to think how I'd carried him on my shoulders, and had known him when he couldn't walk. His face was always a little sullen when I was around, as though he were warning me to stay out of his business.

I had, of course, no way of knowing what his face was like when I *wasn't* around.

"I got to make myself pretty, too," I said.

"Well, I guess I better let you get to it," he said, grinning. "Take your *time,* man," He started out of the bathroom.

"I won't be a minute," I said.

"Of course not," he said kindly. "Ain't no way in the world you can get that mess together in a *minute.* It's all right, man. We'll wait." He patted my shoulder. "Good luck." And he closed the bathroom door behind him.

I laughed to myself, and almost ran out to grab him, but I was afraid of messing up his hair.

There *is* a tug of wonder in it: here's your father, here's your mother, there's your brother, here *you* are: sitting under the tree, opening your presents. The light falls strangely, or you see it strangely; it is a ceremonial light. There is a hidden terror in it, as you unwrap the gift. The gift will tell you if anybody loves you, if anybody *sees* you—especially your father, your mother, your brother—and the gift will tell you, if you can read it, what *they* see.

My father had bought me a heavy, fleece-lined suede jacket, not quite as dark as chocolate, with deep pockets, and a high collar. It cost so much that I knew he had had to save for it, and had picked it out a while ago. So: he knew about my comings and goings, and he trusted me. I know the tears came to my eyes, but I grinned, and he pulled me into his arms and held me tight for a moment, and I was his little boy again, the firstborn, back where we had started. Then, he pushed me away, and draped the scarf I had given him around his neck. It looked marvelous on him, it really did, it somehow glorified the gray in his hair. Mama had bought me a heavy, black, woolen turtle-neck sweater, and Arthur placed around my neck a silver acorn, hanging on a silver chain. *I sealed magic in it,* he said, *to protect you,* and he hung on my neck for a moment, like my little brother again. He dug the tie, because it went with the dark gray suit his father had bought him and the monogrammed maroon shirt his mother had bought him, and the silver ring on his little finger. Our mother put the silver bracelet on her wrist, and kissed me. Then, with one hand still in my hand, and kneeling under the tree like a little girl, she opened a box and lifted out a small, heavy comb, crescent-shaped, mother-of-pearl.

It looked like you, Arthur said shyly, and our mother, saying nothing, carefully placed it in her thick, black hair. Then she put her hand in my hand again and reached out with her other hand and pulled her baby to her, and held us both close against her, looking up at Paul.

Well! old man, she said, and laughed with tears standing in her eyes, *what* you *got to say?* Paul growled, *Hell, I guess you don't even want to look at that raggedy old fur coat I got you,* and Mama said, *You better not be asking me about where you left your kidskin fur-lined gloves!*

And he *had* found her a fur coat, aided a little, no doubt, by the skill of his friends on Sugar Hill, and she had found for him a beautiful pair of fur-lined gloves, with the help, no doubt, of her family in The Bronx. Mama lifted the coat out of the box, and he helped her put it on. He wore his gloves and his scarf, and he had the cigarette lighter which Arthur had given him in his pocket. I wore my acorn—ah! the shape of things to come!—Mama wore her comb, and no hat; Arthur wore everything that Christmas had brought him, and we walked down the stairs, into the streets, to church.

Everybody was there, the children—who were, really, no longer children—in the front row. Peanut, Crunch, and Red were not children but aching, anxious, peculiarities, awkwardly shaped, itching to be released onto the playing field. Arthur joined them, carrying the three boxes which contained their ties. Then, the four of them sat there, calmly arrogant—this was for the benefit of the other quartets, who formed a solid wall at the back of the church. Julia was already in her royal seat in the pulpit, but, now, her thin face and her burning eyes could be seen all over the church. Her neck faintly throbbed, making me suddenly aware of the small, beginning breasts beneath the long white robe: this child was now able to bring a child into the world.

Jimmy also sat in the front row, but on the other side of the aisle, with his shoulder pressed against the wall as though he hoped to make a hole in it. His face was a marvel of sullen resignation, brightening, briefly, when Arthur entered. But by the time Arthur noticed him, Jimmy was, once again, pressing his shoulder against that wall.

He sat directly in front of his mother and father, and Paul and Florence and I joined Amy and Joel. I cuffed Jimmy lightly on the head, and squeezed that determined shoulder, and was rewarded with a bright, shy grin, like a light, which made me feel how rarely anybody touched him.

We had entered at the very beginning of the service, and the choir, in purple robes, was singing "Mary's on the Road." I listened to the choir. From time to time, I glanced at the back of my mother's head and the milky white comb which glowed there: she and Amy were whispering together. Then the sound of the choir ceased, and the choir sat down, the pastor rose and came to the pulpit, silence fell: and my mother turned from Amy, seeming to look straight at the pulpit, but looking, really, at something else; I saw her face in profile, and it frightened me. She had seen something, something so dreadful that she could not believe it, and I seemed to hear her catch her breath as we rose and bowed our heads and the pastor blessed the congregation.

The first offering was taken up. The pastor—all of those pastors are faceless now, for me, all wearing the same gleaming, going-to-heaven toothpaste—announced the guests who had come to be with us on Christmas morning. Until that moment, I hadn't wondered why Julia had consented to come and preach in *this* church, which was considered, by the sanctified, to be a worldly church. Now I wondered, and I didn't wonder, watching the first offering being carried back up the aisle, in those wicker baskets, to be blessed by the pastor and then to disappear behind the pulpit. Offerings would also be taken up for each of the quartets—freewill offerings—and the baskets were to be seen on the table, placed just below the pulpit, covered with a purple cloth, holding two hymnbooks, and a Bible, and a vase of red-and-white carnations. The congregation was yet more vivid and far more opulent, and their Cadillacs and Buicks were double-parked on the avenue and in the side streets which led, steeply, to this eminence and, as steeply, dropped away.

The quartets came, said the pastor (as though they had issued from his loins that morning) from Philadelphia, Newark, and Brooklyn, and—with a particularly vivid smile, aimed at the boys in the front row—"from just down the street." The congregation made approving sounds, and all of this was considered by Philadelphia, Newark, and Brooklyn to be dirty pool, a below-the-belt blow at their honor and genius, and they leaned back, smiling smug smiles of rage, and straightened their shoulders. The Trumpets of Zion were going on first, and Philadelphia, Newark, and Brooklyn would use what was left of their ass to wipe up the stage, and carry it home. Of course, The Trumpets of Zion had intentions equally crippling, and, if they succeeded, their rivals would be left trying to make themselves heard from the deep hole where the stage had been.

Yet it must be said—and this is a very difficult to convey—this passionate rivalry contained very little hostility; I am not sure that it contained any real hostility at all. Philadelphia, Newark, and Brooklyn were, at bottom, exceedingly curious about their snot-nosed, ignorant little brothers and not at all sorry that they had come along. On the contrary; and something might happen to make them all smile; they all had a lot to learn, and some of that, perhaps, indeed, most of that, they could learn only from each other. It was cold out there, where they hoped to go.

Our boys were announced, along with Paul Montana—"the celebrated pianist, who is a member of this church, and the father of one of the singers of the quartet—the father, in truth, of the quartet you are about to hear." Philadelphia, Newark, and Brooklyn took a black view indeed of this species of dirty pool, though they also seemed to feel that Paul was *their* father, too: they had heard the name, and some of them had heard him play. *Okay,* their rigid shoulders seemed to say, *come on with it now.*

Paul rose and winked at me, and edged out and up to the piano. The boys waited for him, and followed him, with an indescribable respect. Paul had told them that this was the last time he would play for them. *Peanut's your piano player now. And he's good—you think I been wasting my time with Peanut?* But Peanut was terrified of letting down the quartet. He was far more terrified than the others of singing in public, and Paul understood Peanut, and respected this.

So he looked at the boys, and smiled, and sat down at the piano. The boys took their places, bowed, Crunch a little outside, with the guitar—how young they looked up there—looked at each other, began.

Oh, come all ye faithful.

They got through. Peanut's terror was so great that he became impeccable; his voice carried the wonder which must have been present the very first time this song came into the world; that wonder, which is, after all, the anonymous author of the song. They got through. They grinned and bowed, the congregation moaned and shouted, Paul's hair began to stand up, Crunch and Paul opened "When Was Jesus Born?" and Arthur's voice led, and paced, the song. Philadelphia, Newark, and Brooklyn were now enthralled and grinning and clapping their hands, and our boys, after a brief piano-guitar exchange between Paul and Crunch, dropped into a lower key for "No Room at the Inn." Crunch led this song, in his down-home, country boy's voice.

Niggers can sing gospel as no other people can because they aren't singing gospel—if you see what I mean. When a nigger quotes the Gospel, he is not quoting: he is telling you what happened to him today, and what is certainly going to happen to you tomorrow: it may be that it has already happened to you, and that you, poor soul, don't know it. In which case, *Lord have mercy!* Our suffering is our bridge to one another. Everyone must cross this bridge, or die while he still lives—but this is not a political, still less, a popular apprehension. *Oh, there wasn't no room,* sang Crunch, *no room! at the inn!* He was not singing about a road in Egypt two thousand years ago, but about his mama and his daddy and himself, and those streets just outside, brother, just outside of every door, those streets which you and I both walk and which we are going to walk until we meet.

> *Now, when Jesus*
> *was passing by*
> *He heard*
> *a woman cry.*

Arthur's voice, alone, then his witnesses arriving:

> *She said,*
> *Savior! don't you pass me by!*

I looked at my mother, who was watching her son, but who was seeing something else. There was a smile on her lips and there was a darkness in her eyes. She held Amy's hand tightly in hers.

> *If I could but touch*
> *the hem of His garment*
> *I would go,*
> *and prophesy.*

Joel was still. The two women nodded their heads; I heard Amy breathe *Amen!* and *Amen!* breathed my mother, and the song slowly lifted:

Savior!
don't you pass
me by!

Our boys bowed, and Paul bowed with them, and they came on down from there. Philadelphia, Newark, and Brooklyn were jubilant, and dying to outdo them—*and* each other—and anxious to engage in Battles of Song all up and down the nation, and all over the world, until Christmas came again.

Yet in my memory, it was a strange Christmas, with something hard in it, as hard as the earth and sky of that long day. It was a long service, testimonies, offerings—the testimonies short, the offerings long—the pastor's hands and teeth orchestrating each other, the other quartets being brought out at intervals, Paul beside me, sighing, and the heat rising and somewhat submerging Julia's sermon: which, perhaps because of the heat, was short. Men kept ducking into the toilet at the back of the church to pee, or simply, perhaps, to stand up for a moment: and Julia, in my memory, very strange and gaunt that day, blazing with weariness. Why did I think of weariness? I heard it in her voice, and I heard it because I knew she was only thirteen.

Her parents had moved into an apartment not far from the church, and, after a while, we walked there, down a hill—to Edgecombe Avenue, perhaps. Julia walked between her mother and father, as straight as a sorceress, wearing a heavy black coat but with her holy cap still on her head. Arthur and the other boys were behind us, with Philadelphia, Newark, and Brooklyn exchanging battle strategies; sometimes, to illustrate a point, one or more of them would sing a bar or two. I still remember how clear and free their voices sounded, floating over our heads as we descended that hilly street. Paul and Florence walked together, that comb in my mother's hair seeming to soften and dominate the hard silver light. Little Jimmy walked with me, or, to tell the truth, appeared to be willing to let me walk with *him*.

They had moved into a brownstone, of which there are very few left these days, and Julia and her mother climbed the steps together.

Julia was taller than her mother now, especially in her long black coat, and her mother, whose coat was a fashionable, belted dark green, seemed lightly to be leaning on her daughter. Joel stepped ahead of them, into the vestibule, and opened the vestibule's glass-and-wooden door, glass curiously painted, and curtains behind the glass.

I remained below, on the sidewalk, waiting for Arthur and the others to catch up. The other three quartets had left them: Red, Peanut, Crunch, and Arthur came on down the street.

It was not going to be too bad. Red and Peanut and Crunch were really only being polite and keeping Arthur company for a few minutes before going off to have Christmas dinner elsewhere. Arthur and I were trapped, for the Millers had invited the Montanas for Christmas dinner, and Florence had not been able to refuse. But then, after all, it was only between three and four in the afternoon. I was going to pick up Martha, later, at her aunt's house, and Arthur and his men were also going to hook up later. The trick was to get through Christmas dinner without tangling with the holy Christmas bitch.

For none of us liked Julia; we couldn't stand her. We gave the child her due, she could certainly rock a church, but so could Arthur: and, in our world, a world which included the Apollo Theatre, that was not nearly as big a thing as Sister Julia seemed to want to make it. We had seen too many manifestations of the Holy Ghost to be afraid of any of them—the Holy Ghost is a matter of the privacy of the midnight hour—and, in short, we didn't need her, we knew other preachers who were much more fun. Red and Peanut and Crunch would never have accepted an invitation to have "refreshments" at her house had it not been for Arthur.

And Florence had said, "Amy's that woman's daughter. And I got sons. I don't know *where* they might find themselves some cold Christmas Day."

So we entered their apartment, which was on the first floor, and, as I remember, ran the length of the floor; and it may have been two floors, for my memory has Julia disappearing almost as soon as we entered, and disappearing, it seemed to me, upstairs. She disappeared, anyway, for a very long time.

Amy and my mother also disappeared into a room, closing the door behind them—but, unlike Julia, they excused themselves—leaving Joel to do the honors.

So, on this Christmas Day, I looked at Brother Miller. Since it was the first time I had ever seen him in his house, and since I was still, after all, very young, it was almost as though I were looking at him for the first time. I may have felt this because he seemed—somehow—so uneasy in his own house. He seemed more like a guide. But it may also be that the house was so cluttered with such incredible shit that it needed a guide. Paintings of people drowning in sunsets, playing harps; some blue thing on a table which looked like an octopus frozen in orgasm or giving birth—giving birth, as it turned out, to candy, candy being what the writhing tentacles held. Lace covering this, velvet covering that; glass-enclosed cupboards holding I don't know what; lamps like statues; bulbs in the shape of flowers, holy books; hymnbooks; a Bible; a merciless photographic record of the family tree, from toothless smiles to toothless scowls; a Christmas tree which explained why little Jimmy had turned his back on Santa Claus so soon; photographs of Julia everywhere; and posters announcing her appearance. A piano. A pulpit covered with gold cloth, perhaps the same pulpit Brother Miller had carried for so long. I don't believe that all of this could have been in one room, for there were other things, like chairs and tables, and a big dining-room table, and mirrors. There were plants growing in boxes on the windowsills; it was not so much a cluttered as a buried, a secret house. Even the clothes that Brother Joel Miller wore contributed to this airless, hot-house climate, for—they covered him: one did not wish to speculate on his nakedness, or find oneself, in any way whatever, obliged to be a witness to it.

"Well, we'll just make ourselves at home," he said, "until the ladies come back."

He led us through the dining room, where the table was all set, to the big living room which faced the backyard. This room was relatively clear—it was as though someone had simply run out of patience and decided to sit down. Which the boys did at once, side by side, on the sofa. Jimmy sat in a corner by the window.

There was a large table in the center of the room, holding a punch bowl and glasses and dreadful little sweet cakes.

Brother Miller started ladling out the punch, and the boys, politely, sort of stood on line, with their glasses held out. They were in their Christmas best, and they were on their best behavior. Their excessive politeness hid a mocking judgment, but Brother Miller could not have been expected to notice this.

Crunch sipped his punch, delicately, and asked, "Won't Sister Julia be joining us?"

I doubt that Brother Miller knew anything at all about Julia's relationship to her peers, but he looked surprised. "Oh, yes," he said, "she'll be along in just a minute—soon. She likes to meditate right after service." Then, as though he had been reminded of something, he turned toward Jimmy. "Here, boy, don't you want some of this punch?"

Jimmy turned from the window, and I could almost see him trying to decide which course of action would be the least painful—to say no (which was what he wanted to say), and risk a public and humiliating reprimand, or to say yes, and then be trapped in a company in which he was out of place. But Crunch resolved the problem by taking the punch from Brother Miller's hand and carrying it over to Jimmy.

"Merry Christmas, little fellow," Crunch said, and Jimmy said, "Merry Christmas to you," and then, surprisingly, "Merry Christmas, everybody."

I was very grateful for his gravity. It made everybody laugh, and we all wished him a merry Christmas, too.

Then I suddenly wondered if Arthur had thought to buy him a present, or if his present was part of Paul and Florence's present. I had put all of our presents under the tree when we came in, but we wouldn't open them until the women reappeared. But I felt that Jimmy would really have dug having a small ceremony all his own.

"This punch is for the young folks," Brother Miller now said—not noticing how wryly The Trumpets of Zion agreed with this, nor how little they appreciated being called "young"—"but if you gentlemen will just follow me—"

Which we did, of course, having no choice—into the kitchen, which was just beyond this room, to the left.

We could hear the boys' voices, conspiratorial and harsh with humor. They paid no attention to Jimmy, who still stood by the window, holding his glass of punch.

Brother Miller opened the refrigerator—refrigerators were still fairly rare in Harlem then—and took out a bottle and began opening it. "We'll stay in here for a minute," he said, "because little Julia has just never approved of sipping wine." He laughed and got the bottle open and began to pour. "I tell her the Bible says, 'take a little wine for the stomach's sake,' but she says, 'ain't nothing wrong with your stomach!' " He laughed again, and we all wished each other a merry Christmas. Paul and Joel sat down at the kitchen table, and I leaned against the refrigerator, feeling as out of place as Jimmy.

The kitchen smelled, of course, of cooking, but not like our kitchen, which smelled of spice and sweat. Here the odor was heavy and sweet, coming at you in waves, and I was suddenly aware of Brother Joel Miller's odor, which was both sharp and funky sweet.

I heard the boys' voices from the other room:

"—her own sister told me that, man—!"

"—how you get that close to her sister?"

"—you jiving, man—I know them sisters—"

"—in a basement on One hundred and sixteenth Street!"

"For true?"

Laughter. Whispers. Great expectations.

"One reason Julia keeps to herself so much," Joel said, "is that she's worried about her mother. Amy's not been feeling well, lately, and Julia's been fasting and praying—interceding with the Lord, to touch her mother's body."

He said it with a conviction which must have cost him something, for it was not his language at all. I don't know why I suddenly felt sorry for this man whom I didn't like.

"Florence mentioned it to me," Paul said carefully. "What's the trouble seem to be?"

I knew then, for the first time, why Florence felt that she could not refuse this Christmas invitation, and why Paul had not protested. He stared at Joel with a genuine worry, and also as though he were assessing Joel's strength—wondering how the man would bear whatever might come.

His look reminded me, briefly, of the look on my mother's face that morning. Paul and Florence knew, or feared, the same thing.

"We've been to a couple of doctors—but Julia don't believe in doctors—and, look like it's female trouble, brother—one doctor said she might have to have a operation." He looked at Paul, helplessly. "*You* know." He looked, briefly, at me—but I was a man now. Just the same, an old-fashioned reflex caused him to lower his voice. "We kept it quiet—you know—but Amy lost a baby, little over a year ago now. She wanted that baby so bad. And she ain't really never been the same since."

Paul sipped his wine, and Joel sipped his. I stood there, listening to the boys in the other room. From their responses, and the lewd gravity of Crunch's voice, I supposed that he was giving them sexual instruction. I could also guess this from Jimmy's face. He had not moved from the window, and I could see him from where I stood: and he was listening.

"If it's that serious, man," Paul said—he coughed—"I wouldn't depend too much on Julia's fasting and praying. The Lord put doctors here for a purpose."

"Oh, I agree with that, man," Joel said quickly, "and me and Amy made a appointment, just quiet like, to see another doctor just as soon as the holidays is over."

"Why you going to wait that long?" Paul asked; but then we heard Amy and Florence greeting the boys in the other room, and Paul and Joel fell silent, looking at each other.

I watched Amy walk to Jimmy. She rubbed one hand over his head, then bent down and kissed him and took a sip of his punch. He said nothing and made no movement, but his eyes glowed as he looked up at his mother, and she kissed him again.

Then she stood just above him, staring out of the window with him.

Florence came into the kitchen. She said, in a low voice, with no preliminaries, "Joel, you take Amy to see a specialist, you hear me? Don't you be counting ten to do it, and don't you be fooling around with none of Julia's shit about the laying on of hands!"

Joel looked horrified; perhaps he had never before seen a woman so angry.

And Florence repeated, "Yes. I said *shit*, talking about *your* holy daughter, in *your* kitchen, on Christmas Day." She kept her voice low, but with an effort, and her voice was shaking. "You take your wife to a specialist, or *I* will. And I'll teach your daughter something about the laying on of *hands*." She stared at Joel. She said, with sorrow, "You and Amy should have done that a long time ago." Then she leaned down close to his face and whispered, "You goddamn, no-count fool, your wife is *sick*!" She looked at him with a look I had never seen on any face before: if it terrified me, I cannot imagine what it did to Joel. One saw in her face and heard in her voice that she did not want to say it, but she did: "And I'm not *sure* your daughter *wants* her to get well!" Then she watched his face, and her face softened. "Joel. Sometimes people who think they own the kingdom of heaven think they own everything—and every*body* else—too!"

Amy had left Jimmy and started for the kitchen, and I couldn't move, or open my mouth. But Florence straightened, just as Amy entered, and said, in a loud cheerful voice, "If you menfolk hope to eat Christmas dinner, you better get out of this kitchen." She picked up the bottle, and put it in Paul's hands. "You hear me? Now haul it!"

But Joel was in no condition to haul it. His face was wet, he could scarcely rise, his funky sweet odor rose. Amy looked at him and came and put one hand to the side of his face, whispering, "What's the matter, sugar?"

He looked as though he were about to speak, about to weep—about, Paul said much later, to spill the beans all over himself. So Paul said cheerfully, "We'll go for a little walk, he'll be all right," and winked at Amy, and I helped Joel to his feet.

I must say for him that, once on his feet, he straightened, shook his head, and smiled. He said to Amy, "See you in a minute, sugar."

We walked back into the room where the boys were. Peanut, Crunch, and Red were preparing to rise, and leave with us, but I said sharply to Arthur, "Wait here till I come back," and I simply avoided Jimmy's enormous, wondering eyes. Paul put the bottle of wine on the table, and I followed Paul and Joel out of the house. We didn't even bother to put on our coats, and so we made it, quick, to a bar on the corner, saying nothing.

Saying nothing: saying nothing is much to say. Paul and Joel sat near each other. Neither spoke, because neither could: they sat in the whirlwind silence, the silence which one can neither bear, nor bear to break.

And the bar, since this was Christmas Day, was, except for the bartender, empty and silent, seeming to wait.

I wanted to run. I said, as the bartender slouched toward Paul and Joel, "Look. I told the boys to wait till I come back. So, I'll go on to the house and let them go to their Christmas dinner—and—you want me to come back for you?"

"Yes," Paul said. "We don't want to keep your mother and them waiting."

So I went out and back up the street again, and climbed those steps again, and rang the bell.

Amy opened the door for me.

"Why—where's Joel?" she asked, and she sounded terrified, like somebody about to have a fit.

"He's with my father," I said. "They talking. They be back in a minute." I closed the door behind me and walked into the kitchen, Amy walking very slowly behind me. Except for the sounds of cooking, the kitchen, too, was silent. Florence was cutting out biscuits. Julia, dressed in a long, light blue dress, sat at the kitchen table, arms folded, looking, at once, like a high priestess and a sullen girl.

"Where's my father?" she asked me.

"With *my* father," I told her, and walked on into the living room.

"That doesn't tell me where he is!" Julia called behind me.

I walked back into the kitchen. "Your father and my father are sitting in the bar on the corner. You want to see him so bad, you drag your holy ass on down to the corner bar, you hear me, child?"

"Hall," Florence muttered; but she kept on cutting out biscuits; she did not look up.

"Do you know," asked Amy, her eyes suddenly enormous, in a face suddenly grown gaunt, "who you are *talking* to?"

"I know that my mama's doing all the work in your kitchen this Christmas morning," I said, "and I don't care *who* I'm talking to, I don't think that's right."

"My mother's sick," said Julia.

"And you," I said. "What's wrong with you?"

"Told you this was going to happen," Florence grunted to Amy. "*Told* you," and started placing the biscuits in the paper-lined, grease-covered pan.

"I"—Julia began—and stopped. I stood directly in front of her, staring at her, looking her up and down. I made it the most unsanctified look I could manage. I wanted to make her know that her sanctified bullshit didn't reach me, that her daddy wasn't nothing in this world but her clown. The strangest thing was that Amy, standing behind her daughter, eyes blazing out of that blazing face, seemed to hear this message, along with a message I couldn't hear. "Help, Lord Jesus," Amy said, and turned away; while *I* remembered that Julia, after all, was only thirteen years old. I touched her upper arm, she flinched, something altered behind her eyes: I was suddenly frightened, and ashamed.

"I'll go get your father for you," I said, and went back into the living room.

Peanut, Crunch, and Red stared at me—they were sitting on the sofa, hearing, speaking, and seeing no evil. Jimmy and Arthur were at the window, and Jimmy was admiring Arthur's silver ring.

"Okay," I said to the boys. "You're liberated now—let's go," and they grinned and rose. Arthur and Jimmy turned toward us, models of deceit. They had heard everything, of course, everything; but what they had made of what they had heard was not to be revealed to me that day.

Nevertheless there was, in Jimmy's look, as he turned toward me, something trusting and proprietary, and, in Arthur's look, a pride elaborately noncommittal.

"See you, Arthur," said Peanut, Crunch, and Red, and "Merry Christmas, Jimmy!" Crunch ran over and lifted Jimmy off the ground and kissed his forehead. "Don't you worry about a thing," Crunch said, "and you *have* yourself a happy new year, you hear?"

"Yes," said Jimmy, smiling with that incredibly diffident and trusting pleasure to be found only in the face of a child, "you too." And he raised his eyes to Crunch and Arthur, and then turned to us. "Merry Christmas. And happy new year, too."

Julia was standing in the kitchen doorway, arms folded across her breasts. "Look like my brother's mighty popular," she said.

"But so are *you*, Sister Julia," Crunch said quickly. He looked at her, and added, after a brief, charged beat, "We just don't dare express ourselves with *you* the way we express ourselves with *him*." He paused again. "I'm sure you understand, Sister Julia."

She moved her folded arms, embracing herself more tightly, her hands caressed her shoulders. A faint smile touched the corners of her lips, her eyes flashed and darkened. "Of course I do," she said. She smiled again at all of us, but especially at Crunch. "Merry Christmas and happy new year to all of *you*," she said. "Praise the Lord."

"Praise the Lord," the boys said, after a moment, and stumbled through the kitchen to greet and say good night to Amy and Florence.

"I'll be right back," I told Arthur, and walked to the door. Peanut, Crunch, and Red came behind me. I put on my father's Christmas present and I took my father's coat and scarf, and Paul's overcoat, and we all hurried down the steps.

"See you all!" I said. "Merry Christmas! Happy New Year!"

"You too!" they cried. I stood and watched them run in one direction, up the hilly, wintry street. Then, I turned and ran in the opposite direction.

Paul and Joel had not moved at all, and I wondered, for a moment, if they had even spoken. Each had a glass of whiskey before him.

I brought them their coats. I really did not know what to do with myself, whether to go or stay.

"Have a drink," Paul said. "We won't be a minute."

I got myself a drink and wandered to the other end of the bar, looking at the jukebox. I did not want to be there—I didn't want to overhear their conversation. On the other hand, it didn't seem right somehow, to start playing the jukebox. I thought of striking up a conversation with the bartender, but he didn't look like he wanted to talk. He had a dark chocolate, battered face, like an aging prize-fighter, a cigarette burning between his lips, a do-rag on his head, and he was leafing through a magazine.

Just the same, I ventured: "Merry Christmas. Can I buy you a drink?"

He looked up. His eyes, large, dark, and gentle, changed his face completely. It was almost as though the man who looked up was not the man I'd spoken to.

"Merry Christmas yourself," he said. His smile made him look much younger. "Believe I'll have a taste of sherry." He poured it, and raised his glass. "To you," he said. "You live around here?"

"No," I said. "Just Christmas visiting."

He glanced toward Paul and Joel, who were leaning toward each other and speaking in low voices.

"The gray-haired one, he plays piano near here"—and he named the joint—"don't he?"

"Yes," I said. "He's my father."

He smiled. "Ah. You lucky. You still got your father." He sipped his sherry and looked at me gravely. "And you got your mama, too?"

"Yes," I said. "I got my mama, too."

"You the only child?"

"No. I got a brother younger than me."

"How much younger?"

"Seven years. I had a little sister, but she died."

He lit another cigarette. "You lucky, though. My old man split when I was a little fellow, and my mama—well, she give me to *her* mama, you dig?" And he laughed. "So I sort of had to make it best I could. My grandmama passed away last year—so—now, well, I'm all alone on Christmas," and he laughed again.

I didn't know what to say. His laugh, his manner, rejected pity, but: "That's too bad," I said.

"Ah. You got to take it like it comes, right? Anyway, my grandmama was a great old lady. Maybe if it hadn't been for her, I might be dead, or on the needle by now, you know? Who knows. Anyway, my mama and daddy was too young to have a kid—they no more knew what they was doing—!" He looked far beyond me, playing with his glass of sherry.

I heard Paul: "—the Holy Ghost don't change the child's diapers, or teach it how to cross the *street*—!"

I was really beginning to like the bartender. He was considerably older than I was, close to thirty, I judged, but he suddenly made me realize that I had no friends my age. I had never thought of that before, but now, I wondered why.

"Let's have another round," I said. "Hell, it's Christmas."

"Now," he said grinning, "you don't want to show up drunk for Christmas dinner."

"I don't really care," I said, and he and I laughed together again.

I heard Joel: "—I always been a man run and ruled by women, you know that—"

"I don't know *shit*! I know you got a problem in your *house*!"

The bartender poured my drink and his, then looked toward Paul and Joel. "This is on the house. We might as well let the old folks in on the festivities, what do you say?"

And he winked and walked to the end of the bar, and said to Paul, "Me and your son is getting acquainted, sir, and we thought that you might like to join us in a Christmas drink? On the house, sir, if you please."

And he filled their glasses.

Paul looked at the bartender, looked at me, and smiled. "Thank you very much, son," he said, and he and the bartender and Joel touched glasses and I raised mine in their direction. "A very merry Christmas to you, and, if I don't see you before, have a happy new year."

"That goes for me, too," said Joel and turned, raising his glass to me. "And the same to you, Hall!"

I bowed, and sipped my drink. The bartender came back to his place at the bar.

"That your name—Hall?"

"Yeah. What's yours?"

"That's a nice name. My name—my name is Sidney."

"I'm glad to meet you, Sidney."

"I'm glad to meet *you*," he said, and we shook hands.

Paul's voice: "And since when—tell me the truth now—since *when* did *you* start believing in the Holy Ghost?"

"Getting stormy over there," said Sidney.

"Yes," I said. "When was Jesus born?"

"*Today*, you nut," said Sidney, and we both cracked up.

Joel's voice: "—yes, I understand I have a wife and a daughter—"

"*And* you have a son," said Paul.

Sidney was watching my face. "Maybe we should play the jukebox," he said.

"Right away." I walked to the jukebox, and maybe I was drunk—a little drunk—or maybe I was evil, but the first record I played was Nat King Cole's "White Christmas." Sidney was absolutely delighted, laughing so hard that his big, thick, upper lip curled upward toward his nostrils. "You a mess," he said. "And I bet you a liar, too."

For that moment, leaning on the bar, caught in the New York sunlight, which was harsh outside but which was softened here by the curtains at the bar window, his face changing like a fountain of water spinning in the air, his eyes bottomless and bright and flashing, the white teeth in the dark chocolate face hiding and revealing the dark pink tongue, he was incredibly beautiful and I felt myself flow toward him, as I, too, at the jukebox, in my not-quite-chocolate, fleece-lined, three-quarter coat, leaned forward, staring at him, cracking up. It was a moment I was to remember much later, it was to stand me in good stead: the shape of things to come.

But then, I played some of the others, "Silent Night" for example. In my memory, it's Mahalia's voice, though I'm not sure, when I think about it, that Mahalia had started recording then. I came back to the bar, and we quieted down, and my newfound friend and I had another drink together—for the road, for I knew that we had to be leaving soon.

"You be working tonight?" I asked him.

We both looked at the clock behind the bar. It was four thirty. "Well, I get relief from about six to nine, and then, yeah, I come back and work till closing."

"Well, I'll come back later," I said. "Okay? I'll bring my girl with me."

"Beautiful. You a real show-off, ain't you? You got your mama and your papa and a baby brother, *and* a girl."

"Well," I said, "I'm greedy. I'd like to have a friend, too."

He took my hand in his and gripped it hard. "You got it, baby," he said. He let go my hand, and his face changed. "That's just the way it's going to be." He grinned. "What time you coming back?"

"Oh. Around midnight, okay?"

"Cool, Mister Little Cool. Very cool." We shook hands again, and I joined Paul and Joel at the door.

"Good night, son," Paul shouted to Sidney. "Have a real merry one, you hear? God bless." And Joel waved, and I waved.

"God bless *you*," said Sidney, and came to the end of the bar. "You all really made my day, you know that?" And to me, "See you later, baby, be waiting right here. Bye-bye!"

"Bye-bye," I said, and we split.

We walked up the street in silence, until Paul said, "So when did you make the appointment—to take Amy to the doctor?"

"Well, like I tried to tell you, just now—we didn't really make an appointment—we started to, but then, Amy look like she can't make up her mind."

"*She* ain't got to make up her mind. All she got to do is get in a taxi with you and let you take her to the doctor. That's all." He looked at Joel. "Can't you do that?"

"Oh. Sure. But she says she's feeling better. And she looks better. Maybe—"

Paul sighed. "I swear. I ain't never seen nothing like it. You both scared of that child. And you both done let something happen to that child—that ain't supposed to happen—to a child."

"Paul, the Lord can work *miracles* through that child!"

"I know some people who believe in miracles. And I know some who don't. You in the latter category—*I* know what *you* believe in, and it ain't hardly miraculous." We got to the house, and started up the steps. "And the Lord *ain't* going to work *this* miracle"—Paul stopped, grunting, before the door—"I can guarantee you *that*."

Joel had forgotten his keys, and so he rang the bell. Then, as though to give the lie to all Paul's gloomy prophesying, Julia came to the door, as radiant as an archangel, in her lyric, ineffable blue; and it was clear—I saw this for the first time—that she was going to be beautiful.

"Thought you'd never get here," she said, and threw her arms around her father, holding him close.

Like a witness to the miraculous, Amy stood in the hall, beaming, almost as radiant as her daughter. It hadn't registered before, but now, seeing them together, I realized that both the mother and the daughter were dressed in blue, Amy's blue harsher, darker, more electrical.

Paul and I closed the door behind us, and moved on in.

I did not want to be here, I almost asked leave to go, but I didn't. Somehow I knew, and I didn't know why, my father and my mother and my baby brother—yes, and Jimmy, too—needed me to stay.

"We've been with the Lord," said Amy to Joel, "and it was so beautiful, so beautiful—He blessed my soul. I feel like I could walk a hundred miles, and never get tired."

Julia released Joel—he went to Amy. "He said, 'Believe.' Only, 'Believe,' " Amy whispered, her eyes blazing and beautiful in the dim hallway light. She threw back her head and laughed, like a little girl. Julia, arms folded, stood watching her father and mother, with a smile. "Oh!" Amy took Joel's hand. "Come on in the house, sugar. Let us break bread together, and say, 'Blessed be the name of the Lord'!"

And so we walked through the room where the table was set—"*I* set the table," Julia said to me, "This morning"—to the room where Florence sat on the sofa, relaxed, smiling, not yet resigned, the mother-of-pearl comb sitting in her hair, with Arthur's head on her shoulder, and Jimmy's head in her lap.

She looked up as we entered, my mother, and smiled the most beautiful smile I had ever seen. "Ah. Now, everybody's here," she said. "I don't care how many times you walk around the block, don't you never forget how much I love you, you hear? I mean it. I'm blessed."

Gently, she lifted Jimmy's head from her lap, and Arthur moved, and Florence rose. "Let's sit down at the welcome table. Hall, I'm going to ask you to say grace."

Paul was to be proven right: the Lord did not work the miracle, and that day was the last time I saw Amy Miller on her feet. That day marked the beginning of the terrifying end of Julia's ministry, the beginning of the end of Joel, and almost the end of little Jimmy: that silver, stinging Christmas Day.

All I've indicated about Martha is that she tended to mourn, and worked in Harlem Hospital; but there was more to the girl than that; and if I'd been more the man and less the frightened boy in those days, we might really have got something going. So I say now: but I can also see that, in some way, she helped prepare me for love, she helped prepare me for Ruth. She's a part of my life anyway though, forever, even though I haven't seen her since those years and don't know what's become of her.

I didn't know it then, but my life was really controlled by some profound and wordless sense of the role I was to play in Arthur's life. I can't explain that, I won't try; but I know it's true. It was one of the reasons—I realized, when I thought about it—that I had no friends my age. I wasn't free. That's one of the reasons Martha mourned.

When I left the Miller house that night, the pattern of a dreadful future had been established. No one knew that then, though, not even Paul and Florence. Paul and Florence knew just enough to be reduced to hoping against hope that one of the Millers would find the strength to take up arms against their sea of troubles. But, if the Lord works in mysterious ways, nothing is more mysterious than the ways His creatures find to take their burdens to the Lord: and leave them there.

All during the Christmas dinner, there was much talk of the faith that moves mountains, of the glory of the Holy Ghost—relentless, stupefying: in self-defense, I ate like a pig, hoping to stop my ears with food. Joel and Amy were radiant, Julia was serene, Paul and Florence were dumb. I watched Florence's eyes on Jimmy from time to time—not quite resigned, my mother, she yet was calculating as to how, when disaster struck the others, Jimmy might be saved.

She was resigned, now, in any case, to alerting Julia's mother.

And what did I think, feel, I, who am trying to piece together this story, I who am attempting to stammer out this tale? Terrified against my will, hoping to be able to face what I know I scarcely dare to face, myself in all of this, myself, and the self trapped in that brother I so righteously adored. Is adoration a blasphemy or the key to life, to life eternal, our weight in the balance of the grace of God? (*Must Jesus bear the cross alone!*)

I do not know. The Miller family was far from the center of my attention. Arthur was my heart, the apple of my eye. I worried about cops and billy clubs and pushers, jails, rooftops, basements, the river, the morgue: I moved like an advance scout in wicked and hostile territory, my whole life was a strategy and a prayer: I knew I could not live without my brother.

So Joel, Amy, Julia, even little Jimmy, didn't really mean anything to me, didn't trouble, as Martha would have put it, my "smallest" mind. I wasn't horrified, that came much later, when Julia herself told me what she had been doing, and the price she paid, thereafter, for her crime. By that time, horror was mixed with love and pity: it made me see the horrifying underside of adoration.

No. I didn't think, or feel, very much about them at all. Joel and Amy bored me shitless, Julia was a holy freak and a royal pain in the ass; little Jimmy was her cute, snot-nosed little brother. He was the only one I gave a shit about, but that was partly because he was a baby, and I knew Arthur liked him.

Amy's radiance began to falter, near the end of dinner, and Julia and Florence took her upstairs to bed. I sensed a showdown coming, and I left to pick up my girl.

Martha lived on 139th Street and Seventh Avenue, not too far from Harlem Hospital. Her aunt, a very heavy and handsome lady from the islands, "kept an eye out" for her from across the street; and I was picking Martha up at this lady's house.

I heard the beat of the West Indian ballads and of dancing feet as I heavily climbed the stairs. I really had eaten too much, and I simply wanted to lie down somewhere, with the covers over my head, and sleep until I had to get up and go to the bathroom. But Martha would want to dance.

She opened the door for me, dressed in a tight, white blouse, and a flaring dark red skirt, with big, silver hoops dangling from her ears. Her hair was piled high, with a white carnation in it. She looked very, very together, her copper skin bringing to mind the sun.

I really dug her very much, I did, but I was frightened, too. Some small stubborn gulf—my fear?—prevented the communion and commitment which is love.

She danced into my arms, and held me and kissed me.

"Glad you got here, sugar," she said. "Some folks had the nerve to start taking bets."

And she grinned triumphantly and pushed the door shut behind me, and guided me into the small room where coats were piled high on a bed.

"Hey!" some chick yelled behind us. "He's finer than Harry Belafonte!"

"That's right, honey," Martha yelled, "and Harry just called and he said to tell you wait!"

She took off my coat and held it against her face for a moment. "Beautiful," she said. "Real sharp."

"My daddy," I said. I kissed her. I touched my sweater. "My mama." I showed her the silver acorn. "My baby brother."

"I got something for you across the street," she said.

"And I got something for *you*," I said, "in my coat pocket."

She gave me a laughing, speaking look and we walked out of the little room, holding hands, into the larger room which rocked and rang with colors, with music, and which was tight with the odors of spices, perfumes, and flesh.

I knew some of the people in the room, didn't know most of them, but there was certainly no point in attempting introductions. We made our way to the kitchen, where we found Aunt Josephine, who was surrounded by platters of food, and who rather resembled a platter herself. She was piled high like that, was promising and bright like that—it may even be worth pointing out that she had certainly endured a fire. Her color was charcoal brown and she was wearing a lavender satin dress. I don't know how old she was. She grinned, showing her dimples just like a little girl; her hair was no longer charcoal black and yet, it wasn't gray.

"Oh! Here he is! Here's Prince!" she cried. Prince was her nickname for me; I was never to find out why. "Just a minute," she said, disentangling herself from various domestic utensils she had been using. "Merry Christmas." And she put her hands in mine and kissed me on the forehead. I kissed her on the dimple of her left cheek. "Ooh!" she cried. "You go on back to Martha! Martha, you better hurry up and feed and drink this child, you hear me? before he get too *entirely* out of hand."

"I'm not sure I can drink," I said, "and I *know* I can't eat."

"Get this fool out my face," said Aunt Josephine, and poured me an enormous Island punch. She put the glass in my hand and picked up her glass and touched my glass to hers. "And a happy new year, too," she said. "Now Martha, take this child *out* of my presence before I can no longer control *my*self."

She always carried on like that, but she was really a respectable Kingston lady, who had buried between three and four husbands. "Every one of them," she would say, when her rum started getting to her, "died on my hands and died *poor*!" Then she would throw her head back and laugh—a laugh free of any bitterness, at least as far as I could tell.

But they were all, to hear her tell it, underrated fools—fools because they allowed themselves to be so underrated; yet a little finer, just the same, than the clay into which their kinky hard heads had been driven. "I was real proud of so-and-so," she would say, naming one of them. "Even when we didn't have nothing—they beat that man so bad, they busted his kidneys. He couldn't piss but blood." This particular husband—who would appear to have been her favorite, since she talked about him the most—had not been a roustabout tomcat, but a doomed labor organizer. "Then I packed my bags and come up here to my brother." Her brother is Martha's father. "He tried to warn me about up here. I couldn't listen. But, shoot—now I know this white man ain't never going do right. Ain't *in* him."

And takes another swallow of her rum and throws her head back, and laughs.

Martha used to irritate me by leaving—or by seeming to leave—everything to me: she knew perfectly well that I was incapable of any other arrangement. But I pretended to believe, in those years, in a kind of doomed sexual equality as though the man and the woman held the same vision, carried the same load. This pretense simply revealed to Martha how little prepared I was to assume my own burden, that of the man, how little prepared I was to help her be a woman.

Rarely indeed, and there is a reason for this, is a woman, when she fails a man, called a coward. A man can never call a woman a coward: for the same reason, perhaps, that he can never, without a devastating loss of self-esteem, call her a pussy. He can call another *man* a pussy, for reasons also involved with his self-esteem. How women deal with each other men don't, really, until this hour, know.

We danced the dances of the islands, the one far away, and the one on which we struggled.

> *I got sun-shine*
> *on a cloudy day,*

I cannot swear to you that that song was written then, that I had heard the song, then: yet, every time I hear it, I think of Martha, moving so beautifully, so gently, against me and with me, on that long ago Christmas night,

> *and when it's cold outside,*

and I remember, feel again, her tight black breasts against the tight white blouse, feel again, my hands at the waistband of the flaring skirt,

I've got the month of May.

I remember her breath, those lips, and those eyes, eyes holding a depth—or depths—of despair, longing: a terrified blind beauty for which I had no eyes.

What can make me feel this way?
My girl!
Talking about
My girl!

Another girl, later, whatever later means, is, for me, the eyes of "I Want a Sunday Kind of Love."

And I remember Arthur and Jimmy telling me about "Since I Fell for You": how they played and sang it when it looked liked they were falling out, how they played and sang it when they fell back in.

So I, myself, the mighty Hall—who knew everything: who he was: and, certainly, who *you* were, and how to handle it—ah, I, Hall, eventually, inexorably, found himself—and found, I think, is the right word, it must have some connection with the word *foundation*—in that utterly chartless territory in which Huck Finn was lost.

But I did not know anything then. She moved against me and with me; she got my dick hard.

"Let's go," I said.

"Okay, sugar," she said, and moved against and with me again, for one more of the island dances. My dick had started to pray, and she heard it, moving with me and against me—mine: and the music of the islands now drummed louder, signifying, signifying, than all the drums of the signifying world.

It was midnight.

"Come on," I said. "I'll buy you a drink, and I'll take you home."

For I didn't want to break my promise to Sidney, and I knew that we would stay at Martha's house all night.

And I thought Martha might dig this small excursion, just the two of us alone in some funky black bar, on this far-from-white Christmas. It wasn't all that cold. If we walked together like we knew where we were going, it wasn't too far to walk.

So each put an arm around the other's waist, hopping, skipping, and jumping, singing bits of Christmas carols, laughing, talking to each other, fools, wishing everyone who passed a Merry Christmas! We were each capable of a great, childish gusto and merriment which no one else suspected to be in either of us, and which no one else could touch. We were not losers then, mourning Martha and her lugubrious Hall: we were what we had been once, briefly, and were never to become again.

In the bar window now was a small Christmas tree, all tinsel and flashing lights, which I had not noticed there in the afternoon, and these lights and music from the bar spilled out over the pavements. We entered a noisy, greasy, resounding haven, good times rolling like a river, no one, tonight, anxious to be evil with his neighbor. It was an older crowd. They considered Martha and me with paternal-maternal affection as they wished us Merry Christmas!—sometimes throwing their arms around us. Sidney was at the other end, the far end of the bar, showing all his teeth. He had changed his clothers and taken off his do-rag, and he looked much younger, boyish, as he swaggered to the cash register and made it ring.

I called, "Hey, Sidney!" and he turned. His grin deepened, becoming yet more real and far less public, and he motioned us to the far end of the bar. I pressed Martha in before me, and Sidney leaned over the bar, and grabbed my hand.

"Merry Christmas, again, old buddy," he said. "I'm mighty glad you made it." Then, he looked down at Martha. "So this is your girl, huh? *You* lucky so-and-so—*and*-so," and he took Martha's hand in both of his. Martha grinned up at him. I felt that she liked him right away, was, somehow, because of Sidney, seeing me in a new light, and I was absurdly pleased and proud.

"I'm glad to meet you," she said. "I didn't know Hall had any friends."

"Well, he don't have many," Sidney said. "He don't know how to treat them. But now that I see you," and he grinned, "I think there might be some hope for poor Hall after all—did you dig that rhyme?" He turned to me. "I saved you a table in the back." He yelled to someone, "George! Please show my friends to their table, man?" And then to us, "Go on in there, I'll see you in a minute." Then wickedly, to me, "You mind if I give Martha a brotherly, friendly kiss, man?" And he kissed Martha on the forehead; she leaned up, on tiptoe, but could only reach the tip of his nose—we laughed, and George, the waiter, Sidney's buddy, our guide, a kind of off-mahogany color, white-haired, in his fifties, and flat-footed, laughed, too, and nudged me and we followed him to the area behind the jukebox where the tables were set up and there was, indeed, one table, as the small sign proclaimed for all to see, reserved for: *Hall.*

Martha was very moved, I could see that, and I was pleased. It was as though my newfound friend, Sidney, had just given us a Christmas present, like that, for nothing, out of love.

I gave our coats to George, and sat Martha down. The room was bright and black, black, and bright with black people, as jagged and precise as lightning.

"What shall we drink?"

"Well," said Martha helplessly, "I've been drinking punch all night—"

"Oh, well, we can make you a fine punch, ma'am," said George. He looked at me and we both laughed.

"I bet you can," I said. "Okay. For two."

"My pleasure," George said, and plodded back to the bar.

"Well," said Martha, "this is the first time we've been out someplace together in—I don't know how long."

I took both her hands in mine. "You know why? It's because we're both too goddamn serious. You worry too much. I worry too much."

"Why? What do you worry about, Hall?"

And I felt myself retreating, withdrawing, the way a snail gloops back into its shell. I didn't want to retreat. I held on to her hands, and I held her eyes with mine.

I said, "I've got a lot to worry about, Martha. The point is, there's more to life than—worry."

She had met my parents once or twice, seen Arthur once or twice. She knew Paul was a musician—and that was almost all she knew about me.

As far, of course, as I was able, or willing, to tell.

She left her hands in mine, but she dropped her eyes.

"I'm sure there is," she said at last, "only—"

I rubbed her hands between mine. I did not want her to retreat, to withdraw, to withdraw from *me*, even though I had no idea how I could deal with her vulnerability. Yet: "What do *you* worry about, Martha?"

It was, anyway, a real question, which I had not known I was going to ask.

She looked at me and laughed a little laugh. "Oh. My aunt. The hospital. My weight." She laughed again, and I laughed with her. "My life. My future." She looked down again. "My color. My sex." She looked up again. "You," she said, "and me."

I wanted to let go her hand, but I didn't. Now it was my turn to look down. "Here we go," I said. "Look at us, worrying about how much we worry."

She laughed again, and took one hand out of my hand and touched my face. "Don't," she said. "I think I understand."

Silence, then, between us, and the lightning all around us.

"I may be being drafted soon," I said.

"*Oh*, no," she said. "My aunt bought me a shotgun for Christmas, and I'll shoot you in the foot."

George was bearing down on our table like a big-assed bird.

Martha looked around her and said, in a low voice, dry, distant: "Then, you're thinking of spending next Christmas in Korea?"

George arrived with his tray, and I let go her hands. "Something like that," I said.

George set down two of the largest, most exotic-looking glasses I had ever seen—which attracted the attention, indeed, of the people at the next table and must have caused a sensation when he had carried them through the bar.

"Sidney made these himself, special for you," said George. "He say it's full of vitamins. I reckon he know, and you all going to find out," and George gave us a lewd chuckle and lumbered away again.

We raised the heavy glasses in both our hands, and gently, gravely, clinked them together. We looked each other in the eye, a little like children—why did I think of this?—discovering affection, if not love, for the very first time. We sipped the punch, we grinned, but Martha said, "I still believe I'll shoot you in the foot. You don't really *need* ten toes, you know—you can make do with nine. Hell, this city is full of folks ain't got but one or two, I sewed a couple of them on myself." We both laughed, but it wasn't really funny. I didn't want nine toes, I wanted all ten, and I fucking well had no eyes for Korea. I didn't see what right I would have to be there, what right anybody had to send my black ass there. I don't think anybody can really hate his country, I don't think that's possible; but you can certainly despise the road your country travels, and the people they elect to lead them on that road. If I had been a white man, I would have been ashamed, really, to send a black man anywhere to fight for me. But shame is individual, not collective, and, collectively speaking, white people have no shame. They have the shortest memories of any people in the world—which explains, no doubt, why they have no shame.

I said, "Maybe I'll find a way—*not* to spend next Christmas in Korea—and keep my ten toes, too."

"That," said Martha, "would be beautiful. I would dig that, truly."

"Really?"

"Oh, yes, really. For that, I'd steal every cent of Tara's rent money and let it be gone with the wind."

"You crazy, girl, you know that, don't you?"

"What's so crazy about deciding to haul ass out of Georgia? Anyway, you know that I *never* liked Tara—mother *always* loved Scarlett more than she loved me."

We laughed again, and sipped again from our exotic glasses. I thought, *This must be what you feel like when you're happy.*

But we'd never get together the rent for Tara, and, by next Christmas, we might both be gone with the wind. I would almost certainly be in Korea. And what worried me most about that was not what might, then, happen to Martha, but what might happen to my brother.

I wish I could have said that to Martha, then, because I can see, now, that she would certainly have understood it; and some part of our anguish would not have been necessary. I think she understood everything, then, to tell the truth, but *I* didn't, and Martha, so to speak, was not a trespasser and stayed off the grass.

"Let's not worry too much about it now," I said. "It's Christmas now, we have each other now."

Sidney came to the table with all his wavy hair, and sat down, expelling his breath in a tremendously exaggerated sigh. "It's a damn good thing Christmas don't come but once a year. I'm going to have varicose veins by the time the new year gets here." From his tone one could imagine that he was looking forward, gleefully, to this new affliction. He looked, quickly, at both of us. "How you all doing?" He looked at our glasses. "Sure ain't doing much drinking, are you?"

"We were waiting for you," I said.

"Oh, you quick," said Sidney. "You so quick, sometimes I tremble for you."

"It's been a long day for you, then," said Martha.

"The days wouldn't be so bad," said Sidney, grinning, "if you could just cut down on the *nights*. I been here all day, and I left here early this morning—and I didn't go home *then*!"

"Well then, if you get varicose veins," I said, "you won't have nobody but yourself to blame."

Sidney looked at me with a tremendous mocking scorn and pity. "That's right," he said, "who else I'm going to blame? I can see me trying to kick my ass with my crippled foot." He laughed. "You right, Hall, ain't nobody to blame but yourself. I just don't see what difference that makes. I can blame myself for a lot of things. I *do* blame myself for a lot of things. What do that change? It don't change nothing. It don't change *me*. If I could *change* me, I wouldn't have to *blame* me, right? But I don't know how I want to change. My hand might start to tremble while I start the operation, you dig? and I might fuck up everything so bad wouldn't be nobody even left to *blame*. I reckon I might as well keep on blaming Sidney. He's all I got." And he grinned at us, a little drunk, and very winning.

Martha, impulsively, kissed him on the nose. "You're not drinking, either?" she asked.

"Sure, I'm going to drink with you, you know that, you're my *friends*." He looked from Martha to me, his face as bright as a child's face. "Wow! Ain't that something, a Christmas present, and I was so lonely."

Ceremoniously, he kissed Martha on the forehead, and then he kissed me.

George stood above us, smiling.

"You ain't off yet, you know," George said.

"*I* know I'm not off—but I'm off for ten *minutes*. Can't I have my ten minutes?"

"And what you want *with* your ten minutes?"

"Give me my bourbon—"

"And bring me a beer," I said.

For if we were going to hang out, and it seemed likely now that we might be hanging out, I was going to have to shift gears and get off that punch.

George attempted, with small success, a reprimanding scowl, and lumbered back into what was left of Christmas.

But there was, astoundingly, beautifully, a great deal left of Christmas—in Sidney's face, in Martha's: it was the very first time I felt like a Christmas present. This was because they, Sidney and Martha, were themselves Christmas presents for me—Martha's old love, new, Sidney's new love, old—both loves, together, anesthetized me against my fear of love. I threw back my head, and I laughed out loud. Sidney shook those waves, that gleaming mane of his parboiled hair, and Martha grabbed each of us by one hand. Her earrings nearly matched the lightning, there was something inexpressible in it, the fragile moment which lasts forever.

But Sidney's ten minutes were up—oh, in, let's say, fifteen minutes; so then Martha and I decided to move a few blocks down the road to where my father was playing piano. This was partly because of Sidney, who gave Martha the courage to suggest that she would like to see my father again. Sidney promised to meet us there before the place closed, and George promised to have Sidney's ass in the wind, in time.

Paul knew that I was with, as he would cautiously have put it, "some girl," and expected to see me when he saw me. But he hadn't expected to see me tonight, and I had not expected to see my mother, who sat in shadows in a far corner, facing the bar, the mother-of-pearl comb still glorifying her black hair. I saw Florence the moment, though, that Martha and I walked in, and I immediately, instinctively, looked around for Arthur, for Florence would never have left him alone tonight. Arthur was underage, of course, and had no right to be in a bar; but he was also Paul Montana's son, and it was still Christmas.

So there he sat, at a table with his mother, aware that he was too big to be sitting at a table with his mother, and aware also that he was not yet big enough.

Paul was playing as we walked in. Martha and I inched our way through the crowd, and got to the end of the bar, where Arthur and Florence could see us.

Florence saw us at once, but Arthur didn't. His eyes ranged from his father to everyone and everything in the bar. He would see me soon. But for the moment, almost as though I were a spy, as though I sensed this as a moment which would not come soon again, I tensed and tried to make myself little, invisible, as I watched that face, my brother's, the face he had when he did not know I was around.

He had the eyes, the intensity, of a student, a small student on one of the first of his days in school; but it would be a very remarkable elder who would attempt to protect this student. His eyes moved with the splendid, reckless precision of a small bird, an insect with translucent wings, lighting on this, on that, a twig, a stone, a branch, you— and gone, circling, circling back again, gone again: making of air, light, space, and danger, a province, a kingdom—you, rooted to the earth, follow without moving, stare. I could not see what he was seeing. For example, there were people to the left of him, in deeper shadows, whom I could not see at all, whom he regarded from time to time, with a kind of impenetrable pity. From where he sat, he could not see the bar—or he could see only the very end of it. He was facing Paul's piano, and he could see—dimly—the people at the tables behind Paul. He seemed to be watching the people with the intention of defining and conquering the terrain: the way an actor gauges the physical limits, and possibilities, of the space in which he must achieve his performance, or perhaps, simply the way little Julia handled a pulpit. His regard was full of wonder, but it was not naive. At the same time, it was young, and full of trouble. His eyes took in everything, ranged—but his father was the center, his mother was the anchor. Then he saw Martha, whom he recognized immediately, a recognition which troubled him, for he had not seen me. Then he saw me.

It was nice, that recognition. I will always remember it. When he saw Martha, he was afraid that she was cheating on me, that I had been betrayed—that "something" had happened to me. His eyes became electrically dark and alert, as he scanned the space where I should have been. All this took place in a second or two, perhaps less, for something in Martha's face reassured him, and Florence had seen me—then Arthur saw me, and his unguarded child's face opened, and let me know.

Paul sort of doodled on the piano while we made our way to the table, and somehow, got a couple of chairs.

Martha and Florence kissed each other, I held Arthur's head

against my chest for a moment—being mightily careful, just the same, with his hair—and asked Mama, in a stage whisper, how come Skeezix was out tonight, and what she was serving him to drink.

"Well, it's not communion wine, I can tell you *that*," said Mama, and she and Arthur laughed, but it was not a happy laugh. "We'll tell you about it later," Florence said, and touched her hair.

Arthur whispered, "Something awful's going to happen in the house, brother. Something awful. You can feel it."

"We just left a preacher's house," Florence said to Martha, "and Arthur's just surprised at some of the changes you can see in a preacher—from when you see the preacher in the pulpit and when you see him in his *house*!"

Martha grinned at Arthur, openly trying to make friends with him. "I've got a couple of preachers in *my* family. So I think I know what you're talking about."

I didn't feel that she needed, in order to keep on loving me, *that* much help from my baby brother: but I hadn't yet needed to call for help.

"I hope the preachers in your family weren't children," Florence said.

She looked down as she said this, and her face was bitter; without realizing it, she put one hand, lightly, on top of Arthur's hand.

"Chronologically speaking, no," said Martha. "Some of them even vote."

"Don't tell us where," I said, and then, "They just left Brother and Sister Miller's house, you know—where I was—Little Sister Julia's house—"

"Ah, yes," said Martha, "the child prodigy. I've seen her preaching on street corners—I may see her on street corners again one day." She spoke to Arthur and me, of course, since we were there, but the communication was between herself and Florence. Florence and Martha looked each other in the eye, and Florence nodded as Martha said, as though speaking of someone no one knew, "That child's future is tough, you know, because she's already got a past—and *what* a past—and she's going to have to do something about cleaning up that past before she has any future—how old is she now?"

"Thirteen," said Arthur, promptly—and then, "Martha, don't you work in a hospital?"

"Sure do," said Martha. "In Harlem Hospital. Why?"

Arthur looked at Florence. "You see? Mama, listen, that's not far. Why couldn't you and Martha just take a walk with Julia's mother? Maybe tomorrow afternoon? And Martha works in the hospital, she can make an excuse to stop for a minute, and you all go in there and you can get Julia's mother examined—"

"That's called kidnapping," I said. "And there's a law against it."

"Don't discourage him," said Florence. "I'm just about at my wit's end."

Martha asked, "What's wrong with her mother?" She looked briefly at me—I had told her nothing of all this—and then at Florence.

Arthur watched her face, and his mother's face.

Florence said, "She's not young, she's not happy, she lost a baby not long ago."

Silence between the two women: Arthur and I are really out of it.

"How did she lose the baby?"

Florence shrugged.

"Why won't she see a doctor?"

"Her daughter believes in the laying on of hands—the power of the Holy Ghost."

"Her daughter!"

"—is filled with the power of the Holy Ghost," said Florence.

Martha looked at Arthur, then at me, then she looked at Arthur. "I'm not a doctor. I'm just a registered nurse."

"But you *could*—maybe—get her to stop in the hospital?"

"Arthur, we can't tie her down and examine her if she doesn't want to be examined."

(Ah. The good old days. For now, in some parts of the country, a too-fertile black girl, with no husband, needn't consent to be steril-ized.)

"And what about Mr. Miller?" Martha asked Florence.

"Well, let's just say," said Florence, "that he's put just about every-thing in the Lord's hands and goes the way—the Lord leads him."

The two women stared at each other. I don't know why I felt, so suddenly, that something in what my mother had said embittered Martha and hardened her heart against me: that Joel Miller and I had, abruptly, gone under the hammer together.

"Ah," said Martha. "I see."

A silence fell, into which rambled the sound of Paul's piano: "I Cover the Waterfront." Not a Christmas tune, perhaps, but then, there aren't enough of them to last for twenty-four hours.

"I promised to go by there tomorrow, anyway," said Florence care-fully, "and it wouldn't do no harm, really, if you came with me—nothing beats a try but a failure," she added dryly, and took a sip of whatever it was she was drinking.

Arthur had been drinking ginger ale—here in the bar with his mother, anyway: but there had been an interim of a couple of hours, when Paul had come to work, and Florence was still at the Millers' when he had been hanging out with Peanut and Crunch and Red: and he had smoked a couple of joints with his running buddies, I was sure of it. I seemed to recognize in him the resulting combination of ten-sion and ease, warmth and distance, the aura of the private joke—part of his concern for the Millers, for example, had to do with a private joke. But he was also genuinely in earnest. His earnestness could be taken *as* the joke, for, after all, in this as in so many other matters, there was nothing he could do. Or—since the private joke repeats it-self, endlessly inward, like a series of Chinese boxes—there *seemed* to be nothing he could do. In the meantime, he was opening boxes—was soon to sing, for example, at Sister Bessie's funeral. And Arthur's pri-vate joke included me. He wondered if I knew—that he was smoking marijuana, for example—what I would say to him: if I knew. Well. I had resolved to say nothing. I couldn't very well, not yet, light up a joint and smoke it with him. (And *why not?* I sometimes furiously wondered: *you hypocrite*—for I had been doing all the same shit at his age. And I still turned on, when I could, with the buddies I could find—there weren't many. But, no, anyway, no: Arthur was still a kid, I didn't think it was right.)

And I wasn't worried about his smoking, but about where it might lead. Where might anything lead? Arthur's first lay might lead to twenty-seven children, or howling syphilis at the bottom of Bellevue Hospital. This meant that I was worried about his singing: where might that lead? I was sick of myself, goddamn—this meant that I was worried about his height and his weight and his bowel movements and his blood count and his cock and his balls and his pubic hair and his sweat and every hostile or (especially) friendly eye, and every street he crossed, every move he made—didn't I have anything better to do? Lord, *my* Chinese boxes were not funny, made me really sick of myself, and the waitress came then, thank heaven, and we—Martha and I—ordered drinks. If you're that taken up with someone else's life, it means that you're frightened of your own—like missionaries and anthropologists, heavy-hearted, tight-assed creeps—and, yet, it is also true—Chinese boxes!—that we are all, forever, and every day, part of one another.

Then we sat in silence for a while, a curious, charged, interior silence, while Paul played. Now he was playing for us; and Sidney entered, as though summoned by the music, crept over to our table, found a chair, and sat down. I pantomimed, *my mother, my brother*, and Sidney pantomimed his pleasure, and so, the first day of Christmas wound slowly down.

Martha and I woke up late the next day, and there was nothing right between us, nothing. For one thing, she had to jump out of bed right away, because she had promised to meet my mother at Amy Miller's house; and we had always spent our days off, together, in bed. We had fucked hard, hot, and hungry, but we had not made love, something was gone. She came, I came—I made her come, she made me come—but it was as though, at that very moment, locked together, grappling with each other, we were reaching for each other, calling each other across indescribable gorges, with each thrust and spasm resigning ourselves to anguish, each watching the other vanish into an atmosphere at once softer and more treacherous than mist, more relentless than the glare of sun on steel. The ache of our pounding, thrusting bodies sang *nothing to be done, nothing to be done, nothing, nothing, nothing to be done!*

I fell away, at last, then turned back, held her. She turned toward the window. Her dark shape and head against the blinds of the morning, blurred. And I copped out completely, left this body for a while.

"Will you be here when I get back? I want to talk to you."

"Well, sure. Only you don't know exactly what time you'll be making it back."

"Mrs. Miller seems a little unpredictable, that's true—"

"Well, honey, there's also *Mister* Miller, and *Miss* Julia, *and* the little brother—"

"That's your mother's department. All *I* have to do is be charming and efficient—"

"While the menfolk sleep. I know. Don't be bitter. Anyway, baby, believe me, on that scene, the last thing you need is even the *memory* of the odor of some cat's balls."

"Memory. Will you be here? I can shop on the way back."

"You will do no shopping, nor no cooking, neither. I'm taking you out, remember? And if I'm *not* here when you *get* here, I'll *be* here, understand? You won't have time to do no pacing-of-the-floors number."

"You'll probably be asleep."

"If I ever get *back* to sleep, I will. Bye."

She kissed me. I kissed her. Lord, I really dig this girl, what's *wrong*?

I don't want to leave, and I don't know how to stay.

"Later."

"Later—don't worry, now, honey, I'll be here."

"I love you, Hall."

"So do I love you, baby. So do I love you."

And she swung out and I went back to sleep, in Martha's bed, for a while.

For a while: a short while. It was late in the day, the day after Christmas, the second day of Christmas, and the phone began to ring.

Everybody we knew knew about me and Martha, and she wasn't—dare I say the word?—on: *Welfare*. She couldn't be penalized for having a man in her bed, or on the premises, and so, when the phone rang, I always picked it up.

The first call was from Aunt Josephine.

"How's my child?"

"Your child is out, Aunt Josephine—this is Hall—"

"Oh. Prince! What is she doing out, already, and you still there? and I bet you still in bed!"

"That's right, Aunt Josephine—but—"

"Waiting for her to bring home the chitterlings—"

I laughed, and I knew that Aunt Josephine meant no harm, was teasing me, but my laugh was a hollow, exasperated laugh. "Why you so hard on me, Aunt Jo? She and my mother had something to do together today, she was doing my mother a favor—"

"Your *mother*?"

"Yeah. I got a mother."

"Don't jump all salty now!"

"I'm not. But—she was doing—she promised to do my mama a favor, for somebody else, and—I guess they must be at the hospital right now."

The moment I said "hospital," I was stone staring wide awake.

"At the *hospital*?"

"Well—she can explain it to you, Aunt Jo. It was really between her and my mama and—now—well, I'm just waiting for Martha to come home."

Silence. Then, "You two might just as well get married, you know that, don't you? Make life easier for everybody—"

"What makes you think she wants to marry me?"

"Oh, nigger, hush," she said, "and tell my child I called—sure wish *I* could talk to your mama," and Aunt Josephine laughed and hung up.

I hung up, and looked at the phone, and looked around me. I leaned back, and lit a cigarette, and watched, through the cigarette smoke, the vanishing room, which I won't attempt to describe: the incredibly, even heroically, overburdened bedroom of a three-room apartment on the sixth floor of a high-rise tenement. The elevators were useful for a fix or a blowjob, theft, rape, or murder; the roof was ideal for gang-bangs; and the terraces created a picturesque space between the rats, and the garbage, and you.

Oh. I got out of bed, my cigarette burning between my lips—which felt dry, chapped, and bruised—and went to take a piss. While I was still pissing, the phone rang. I hurried it up, and shambled back to the bedroom, feeling like the hunchback of Notre Dame.

This time it was Arthur.

"Hey, Hall?"

"Yeah. How you doing, brother?"

"All right. Hey, Martha told me to call you just in case she was late getting back—they left me here, at the house, to wait for calls, but ain't nobody called me yet, and it's getting late—"

"What happened?"

"I don't know, brother. Mama and Daddy left with your girl friend—Martha—hey, she's real nice, I dig her—and I think Daddy was supposed to deal with Brother Miller, while Martha and Mama got Sister Miller to the hospital—"

"And what about Julia? And Jimmy?"

"I don't know. I guess they must be home. Look. I got to go out. I got a date, I mean, I got a rehearsal."

"Okay. Listen. If anybody calls before you go out, tell them, if I'm not here, I'll be in the bar on the corner of Julia's house—Daddy and Joel Miller and me were there yesterday—just say, Jordan's Cat, that's the name of the bar where Sidney works, Sidney, the cat you met last night, you got that?"

"Yeah. You coming home?"

"Yeah, I'll see you later."

"Okay. Wow. What a scene," and he hung up.

I shaved and showered and got my clothes on. Waiting for the phone to ring, I poured myself a drink. I called my house. There was no answer. I called the hospital several times, getting the busy signal, or no answer. It was six, and night was falling.

I looked at the streets, so far beneath me, nearly empty now: and a belated snow had begun to fall, so vindictively that it was black before it hit the ground.

I dialed the number of Sidney's bar.

"Hello," said Sidney's voice, "Jordan's Cat—"

"Hey, baby, this is Hall. You going to be there for a while?"

"Hey! you sound so—*articulate*—so *early*? Yeah. I'm here. You want to come by?"

"Yeah. I need a friend."

"Hurry up, then, baby, I'm here," said Sidney, and hung up.

The streets, when I descended into them, were bleak with promise. Bleak: not so much with the broken promise, the broken promise having created our style and stamina: bleak with the price of the promise to be kept. This promise rang and rang, through the streets I walked, on the second day of Christmas. It rang in the "do-rag" brothers, and the barber shops, the women, the girls, the children—the lye which cooked the hair had reached the marrow of the bone. And, yet—this is what I find so strange, since my heart was heavy, and I was thinking of my brother and my girl and Korea—something in the poisoned marrow of the bone perpetually calculated and achieved the antidote. How? and how was *I* to do it?

Got to Jordan's Cat, and there was Sidney, with his do-rag off.

The bar seemed nearly as empty, thank God, as it had been the first time I had jumped in there; and that had been—I did not believe this—yesterday? But, yes: Christmas Day was yesterday.

My bewilderment must have shown. I was suddenly glad that I'd shaved and showered, done all those things—but everything showed

anyway, for Sidney said, "You look low, old buddy—what you want
to drink?"

I looked at him, and I put my head in my hands. All of a sudden
something hit me, hit me hard, and I held my head in my hands, and
cried.

Memory is a strange vehicle. Or perhaps, *we* are the vehicle which
carries the increasingly burdensome and mercurial passenger called
memory. *I looked over Jordan.* Oh, yes, but the event, the moment,
engraved in me, which *is* me more surely than my given name is me:
escapes my memory. Memory is mercurial and selective, but passion
welds life and death together, riding outside and making no judgment. *You* are, yourself, the judgment.

Julia remembers Arthur, at Sister Bessie's funeral, singing "What
Are They Doing in Heaven Today?" but Arthur remembers singing
"We Are Our Heavenly Father's Children." I don't know. I know
only that when, before my do-rag brother, I held my head in my
hands and cried, ringing in my head, for some reason, was the song:

> *We have the joy*
> *of this assurance,*
> *our heavenly Father*
> *will always answer prayer:*
> *And He knows*
> *He knows*
> *Just*
> *how*
> *much*
> *we can bear.*

"Come back here," said Sidney, whispering. "Come back here."
He moved, with a beautiful discretion, to the end of the bar, reached
for me, caught me, dragged me to the area behind the jukebox, and, in
that electrifying passage, he never, if memory serves, said a mumbling
word.

I leaned on the table, with water dripping through my fingers. I couldn't stop, and yet, I didn't know why I was crying.

"Take off your coat," Sidney said. "It's hot in here," and he helped me take my coat off, and put a handkerchief in my hand. "I'll be right back," he said, and he left me alone.

I wiped my face and dried my eyes, blew my nose, looked around the back room. I don't know what I was thinking. I could not remember ever being shaken like this before.

I heard people coming into the bar, heard Sidney's heavy, cheerful voice as he served them. I began to feel that I should get on back to Martha's. But I couldn't stay at Martha's, and I certainly couldn't stay here, and now, I couldn't even cry anymore.

Sidney reappeared, carrying a glass of very dark tomato juice.

"This is a double Bloody Mary Molotov," he said looking at me carefully and grinning at the same time, "and she ain't no virgin; she's been around, that's how she met Mr. Molotov. Drink it slow, but drink it. I'll be right back."

A couple came, and took the table in the far corner. He looked like a basketball player, with that kind of raunchy cheerfulness, and she looked like a cheerleader who was also first in her business administration class. They were glowing from the air outside, laughing and being happy together, and they made me feel old.

I sat there for a while. The seven o'clock people were piling in, and Sidney was alone on the bar. His double Bloody Mary Molotov gave you something to cry about, certainly, if you felt you just had to cry, and could probably have disintegrated gallstones, but it made you sit straight up. I wondered what would happen if you drank two. But one, right now, was enough, and Sidney had been beautiful.

I sat there for a while. I knew Sidney wanted me to wait until he could get back to me; I knew he'd understand if I couldn't. Martha would be coming back soon. I wondered what her news would be.

The Miller family, after all, until I had been forced to witness the events of this Christmas, had been distinguished from other families only by the fact that Julia was a child evangelist. But this was not, really, a very great distinction: it did not violate, or even bring into question, any of the reality, or principles, of our lives. If we did not believe, precisely, in the power of the Holy Ghost, the speaking in tongues, the ecstatic possession, the laying on of hands, neither did we doubt it, nor did we know anyone who doubted. We would understand it better by and by—perhaps, on the whole, that was the way we felt about it. If we found some folks ridiculous, we mocked nobody's faith. We may have considered that they themselves constituted a mockery of their faith, but the faith itself was another matter altogether. Each prayed the way he could. We simply took it for granted that everybody prayed—sometime, somewhere.

I didn't feel that Joel Miller, for example, was much of a man, and I know that Paul felt that, maybe we all felt that. But that wasn't because of his faith. It wasn't even really because of his daughter; except in the sense that the father had not been able to correct the daughter; and without that correction, she was not, as she assumed, safe in the arms of Jesus. (Jesus, after all, had other things to do, and couldn't be expected to waste His time taking care of spoiled brats.) No: it was because Joel didn't really seem to believe in anything, not even long enough to fake it. This meant, for us, that he was a man with no prayers in him, no resources—he'd never make it through the storm. Paul found Joel exasperating, but his reaction was not to reject him but to try to lift him up. It was Paul's love for Florence which caused him to attempt to deal with Joel—he was a necessary element in Florence's attempt to deal with Amy: but Florence had no interest in Joel's salvation, nor had she any interest in contesting the power of the Holy Ghost. She wasn't thinking about the Holy Ghost, Who was perfectly all right, she would have said, in His place. But His place was not here. The Holy Ghost had nothing to do with the fact that Joel was too "trifling" to make his ailing wife see a doctor—that was not to be blamed on the Holy Ghost! As for the healing power of the Holy Ghost, well, *all* healing was miraculous, we knew that very well. The hosts of heaven were certainly overworked. It seemed unnecessary and immodest, and in fact, inconsiderate, to call such special and undignified attention to oneself. Lord, others had to do it—just pick up your bed, child, and walk!

But this had to do, too, with Sister Miller's aura of pained and special sanctity because the Lord had shown His favor by giving her an evangelist for a daughter.

So then, sitting there, in my brief, enforced limbo, I thought of Julia in a new way, and I began to be frightened for her.

Joel opened the door for Florence and Martha, and stood there, looking, Martha said later, surprised. He was in his shirt-sleeves, unshaven, and to Martha, he seemed very frail.

"Good evening, Brother Miller," Florence said. "We won't trouble you but for a few seconds. We come to get Amy. She ready, or is she still resting?"

He answered with a slight bow, and a smile, but said nothing. They entered the house, and he closed, then locked, the door. Martha and Florence looked quickly at each other.

"Come on in," said Joel. "Make yourself at home." And he led them to the living room.

There was a heavy constraint in the air, and the house was silent.

"This young lady is from the hospital," Florence said. "Miss Jackson—"

Martha and Joel nodded and smiled at each other, and Joel said, with his little smile, "Can I get you ladies something refreshing?"

Florence looked exasperated, then frightened. "Why, no, Brother Miller," she said. "You just tell Amy we're here, and we'll go on." She looked around, still frightened, not knowing why. "Where's Jimmy? And Julia?"

"Well, I think," Joel said carefully, "that little Jimmy might have gone out to the movies, just a few minutes ago, and Julia—" He paused, and nervously bit his upper lip.

The silence of the house, and Joel's silence, now began to speak to Florence. "Where's Amy?" she asked.

"Well, Julia," Joel said, "she took her mother to a prayer meeting—a new church, somewhere around here, but I don't know the exact address."

"But she made a date to come to the hospital with me and Miss Jackson this afternoon!" Florence shouted.

"Well, you know how Amy is," Joel said. "Looks like everybody knows her better than me. She's always changing her mind—keeps *me* dizzy."

Martha sat stiffly on a straight-backed chair, not knowing where to look. Florence simply stared at Joel.

"How's my buddy, Paul?" Joel asked. "I thought *he* was coming by this afternoon."

There was something unexpectedly moving in the way he said this, as though he really needed Paul. Martha felt as though she were trapped at some secret tribal ritual, and would soon be forced to drink the blood of the sacrifice. She wanted to stand up, and run out of the house.

But Florence, watching Joel, and knowing him better, felt something else—a tepid rage in the man, tepid like water in a saucepan over a low fire on the stove.

She suddenly realized, too, that this tepid rage had always been there, in Joel's style and smile. She noticed it now only because someone had lately turned up the small flame of his humiliation.

"Paul went on to work," Florence said. "He didn't think we'd need him. I guess he was right." She stood up. Martha stood up, too. "Joel, it was right in this room last night that you *made* Amy promise to come and see a doctor with me today!"

"She changed her mind! What can I tell you?"

Florence watched him.

"How long you going to let this go on, Joel?"

He stared stubbornly before him—he wondered, too.

"You don't have any idea where this—*new*—church is?"

"No." Joel sat down on the sofa. "Julia said the Lord raised it up for a purpose—then Amy, she got all excited. Julia wouldn't tell me where the church was—said she didn't trust me to keep a secret." He looked up at Florence, and smiled, a smile Florence had never seen on his face before. "It ain't all milk and honey, living with the Lord's anointed."

"Especially," said Florence, "when it's your daughter, and you ain't never raised your hand to her."

Joel smiled. "She was a real good baby. Wasn't no need. Then—later—" He stood up, and walked to the window. "They might be back soon. You welcome to wait."

"No," said Florence slowly. "They won't be coming back while we're here."

"When all this started," Joel said suddenly, "when Amy lost her baby—we saw doctors then, and everything seemed to be all right. The doctors just told Amy to be careful, and she was supposed to keep coming back for checkups. So I thought she was. Julia didn't know about the baby—she was surprised about that. She took real good care of her mother, and they'd always been so close, I didn't think nothing. I stopped worrying. I'm sure worried now."

"Couldn't you send Amy home to her mother?" Florence asked. She wanted to add *and send Julia to Bellevue?* but she held her peace.

"Amy and her mother get along best at long distance," said Joel.

"Amy. Amy. Every time I ask you a question, you answer me with *Amy.* But *you* the man of the house, Joel."

"This house," said Joel, "was taken over by the Holy Ghost some time ago."

Florence found nothing to say to this, and Martha flashed her a desperate look.

But Florence said finally, as Martha rose, and they began edging toward the hallway, toward the door, "Joel, I'd think about that again, if I was you—the Holy Ghost, I mean. He ain't one of them chumps on the Avenue, ain't got nothing better to do but play with women's minds, and wreck their homes."

Joel followed them into the hall. "What are you telling me?"

Florence turned at the door, and faced him. "I think you know what I'm telling you."

Joel slowly began to unlock the door. The winter air beat against it, then entered the hall as the door swung back.

"Just like that," said Florence. "Just like you opened that door, you take your wife out of your daughter's hands. I'm telling you. The Holy Ghost didn't pay down on that furniture, and the Holy Ghost don't buy your clothes."

She stepped into the air. Joel stared at her, with eyes as black as raisins.

Martha said, "Good-bye, Mr. Miller." She was standing, shivering, on the brownstone steps.

He came briefly back to life, or was reclaimed by his reflexes. He waved one hand, and smiled that smile. "Young lady!" An utterly blind reflex made his eyes travel over the body he did not see and could not want. "I hope we meet again!"

"I'll send Paul over," Florence said. "You say you want to see him. Good night. Tell Amy to call me—if that's all right with the Holy Ghost."

And the two women walked down the dangerously freezing steps into the street. Martha did not hear the door close behind them, but neither she, nor Florence, looked back.

They walked to the corner in silence, stood, waiting, for the light.

"Martha, I'm sorry I made you come out this afternoon for nothing. I truly am."

"That wasn't your fault. But I'm sorry, too, that it was for nothing."

They were standing in front of Jordan's Cat—now they started walking away, not knowing I was in there. Florence was wearing her fur coat and a hat. The mother-of-pearl comb had been wrapped in tissue paper, and hidden at the bottom of a trunk and would not be seen again for a while.

Martha shivered, her hands deep in the pockets of her coat, her head down. Florence looked at her sharply, and stopped walking.

"Here, child, it's cold, don't you let me keep you no longer. You close to home—and is Hall waiting for you?"

"Yes. It's all right. I'll walk you a little ways." Martha looked into Florence's face and smiled, and took her arm. "Come on. I'm not cold. I was just—thinking. What's going to happen to that poor woman? And to *him*. What's the matter with him?"

"He's lazy," said Florence. She smiled. "That might sound funny, but it's true."

They walked in silence through the dark streets, not very crowded now.

"He reminded me a little of my father," Martha said. "He could never make up his mind about anything. It was always my mother who decided. And later on, I heard people saying, 'Well, that's just the way black men *are*—they don't know how to make up their minds.' "

Florence was listening, but not to what Martha was saying. She was listening to Martha.

"Well, that's just not true. And God knows, the last thing a black man needs is for a black woman to feel that way about him."

"I don't know if I feel that way. But I watch the men in the hospital, in the streets—some of these men are pretty awful people, they really are slimy sewer scum, do anything to pay down on the car, to meet the damn car payments—they don't care about women, or men, or nobody. It just seems so *hopeless*. My father used to come home and raise hell in the house because he didn't dare raise hell outside. He just took it out on *us*."

"*What* did he take out on you?" Florence asked.

"*You* know. His job—"

"What was his job?"

"He worked in the post office—he hated it. I guess he hated it, being a nigger all day long. Then, he'd come home and give orders like—King Kong."

Florence laughed, and after a moment, Martha laughed with her.

"I hear you," Florence said. "But there's a little bit more to it than that." They walked in silence for a while. Then, "The only way we can begin to get out of all this shit," Florence said, "is to begin to look at it, like from the very beginning. I mean, in the beginning, when you was a little girl, your daddy was just your daddy—nobody had yet told you anything about *black men*. Then later on, you hear people talking about black men, or what the black man should do, and you start thinking about your daddy, and you think, oh, yes, that's why—he's a black man. And you put him in that cage you just been told about, the cage for black men.

"But ain't nobody else thinking about your daddy. They never heard of him, they don't care about him. But *you* better care. No matter how it might hurt. The world is full of black men, but you only got one daddy. The world is full of black men, but you can only marry *one*—at least, in my day, anyway, you married one at a *time*." She laughed. "You understand what I'm trying to say?"

"I think I do," said Martha, frowning, looking down at the sidewalk, holding on to Florence's arm. "I think I do."

"I don't know what the black man is like," Florence said. "I don't know if I know what my husband's like; I hardly know what my sons are like. But I know they're not the same. If anything should happen to them, I don't know what I'd do. And that's enough to handle, it seems to me." She looked into Martha's face.

"But," said Martha, with a despairing hesitation, "you've *got* them to handle."

Florence laughed. "I got here a little bit before you, daughter. And I didn't say *them*." Then, after a moment, "There's *me* to handle, too. It's not a dead end, daughter. It's a two-way street."

They walked in silence, Martha head down, with her lips pushed out.

"Do you think black women are unfair?" Martha asked. "I mean—to black men?"

"Most of us are unfair, in one way or another, to somebody," Florence said, "and I don't know anything about black women, either."

They passed Harlem Hospital, and turned the corner at 135th Street, toward my house. They walked the block in silence, Martha shivered again, and whistled—a low whistle, close to prayer.

They stopped before the steps of my house. Arthur was not home yet, he was smoking pot with Peanut, Crunch, and Red. Paul was playing piano. I was in Jordan's Cat. Martha looked at Florence, tears standing in her eyes.

"Well. Thank you, lady," Martha said. Then, "No matter what happens, I hope we'll always be friends. You're beautiful." She kissed my mother, moved away. "Good night! Sleep well. You know where to find me if you need me."

"Good night," said Florence. "God bless." She watched Martha hurry down the street. She thought of Amy before Amy had met Joel. She thought of Julia, of Jimmy, of her husband and her sons, climbing the stairs, wondering, trying to compose a letter, knowing that any letter, now, would come too late.

Uncle Sam's greetings came sooner than expected, and I wouldn't let Martha shoot me in the foot. Our last days together in New York were strange, were strangely peaceful. I felt a little cowardly, for something outside of me, outside of us, had forced a decision for which I was not responsible. Well. Martha avoided asking me to marry her, I did not ask her to marry me. We—er, I—had the Korean war as our reason. We both knew—or Martha knew—that this was not the real reason, but oddly enough, this knowledge reconciled us to our last days together. Spring came, and we wandered around New York in a kind of bittersweet luxury of happiness; a luxury we might not have been able to endure had we not known it was fleeting.

Something, in any case, had been decided, and that always brings a certain peace.

Arthur said good-bye to Julia on the church steps the day of Sister Bessie's funeral, and walked out of her life for a while. By the time Amy was buried, in the summertime, he was with The Trumpets of Zion, in Nashville, and I was in Korea.

Jimmy went South with his grandmother. Julia and Joel stayed on in the house. Julia stopped preaching. Someone said they saw her coming out of a movie. Arthur knew that she was seeing Crunch. But Arthur never saw her. Practically speaking, no one saw her, though she was going to a high school in The Bronx and she had a job after school, scrubbing floors, in the same neighborhood. Crunch and Red came on to Korea, but something was wrong with Peanut's eyesight, and he went to Washington to Howard University.

I'll have to backtrack, presently, and go through this in some detail. Now, I'm just trying to get the sequence together in my mind. I was off the scene for much of this. Arthur was my principal (and unreliable) informer. He was just keeping me up-to-date, more or less, about what was happening to him and trying to amuse me with sketches of life in my old stamping ground. All he was really doing then was singing, and he and The Trumpets seemed to be working all the time, and, in holiday seasons and in the summertime, they traveled the road. ATLANTA: *Walked on Peachtree Street today, brother, and all I got to say is they can have the peaches.* And *the trees.* BIRMINGHAM: *I didn't have no banjo but I managed to get out with my knee—not ON my knee. (You only have the right to take out one knee.)* CHARLOTTE: *Peanut got cousins here, but they lighter than Peanut and they didn't dig the rest of us at all, especially Crunch. I think they thought he was too niggerish.* DURHAM: *Red say if this is where they grow tobacco, he going to have to stop smoking.* BOSTON: *Here, when they shit on you, they give you a towel—so you can wipe their ass, I guess.* NEW YORK: *Sure miss you, brother, sure wish you was here. I ain't got nobody to talk to no more.* And: *Mama's fine, she misses you, though, we all do, brother, when is this shit going to stop?* And *Daddy's got a funky piano, you know what I mean? I mean, he's SLY, I'm just beginning to notice how he really puts it down, and I'm in love with Dizzy Gillespie!* and *I don't know if I'll ever really be a singer, brother, what do you think?* and *Look like Julia's wrapped it up, you remember Julia, well, she don't preach no more since her Mama passed. You know, Hall, I wonder if she feels GUILTY, and Brother Joel Miller is hitting the bars (and the chicks) just like a WINO, brother, or a pimp (smile)* and *Red left today, maybe you be seeing him over there, I hope not, sure wish that man would turn your ass loose,* and *I don't see much of Crunch no more, he spends a lot of his time (I think) with Julia. I know he feels sorry for her. Crunch feels sorry for everybody.*

He just can't help it and *Saw Crunch today because he's leaving next week and he figured he had to bring Julia along. I guess Julia's all right but she's so goddamn* skinny *she looks like a fucking razor and she was wearing a whole lot of LIPSTICK. What happened to the Holy Ghost? I think she thinks Crunch is the Holy Ghost now (smile)* and *Somebody say Julia's pregnant and her father wants to whip her ass* and *Crunch left today, he might meet you over there,* and *the way things are going, I might meet you over there,* and *Hall, I know I'm very young and maybe I ask a lot of dumb questions but I hope you don't mind but I have to ask somebody and you're my brother and I love you,* and *Brother Miller whipped Julia's ass real pitiful, and they say she lost her baby and the grandmother came and took her away and maybe Brother Joel going to have to do some time. I don't believe it. I don't believe life can be like that,* and *Happy Birthday, Hall! I sure hope you're here on your next birthday. Or mine. I warn you that I got a birthday coming soon and I want something only YOU can choose from the funky exotic slinky mysterious EAST, your loving brother, Arthur.*

When Julia mounted the stairs to the pulpit on the embattled day of Sister Bessie's funeral, she felt something entering into her and something departing, forever. And she knew it was forever. An unprecedented sweat was on her brow and a new agony in her belly—as she mounted the familiar steps, into a new place altogether.

She placed her Bible on the enormous, open Bible in the pulpit, and looked up, looked out—into a great silence.

The church was strangely packed and tense—it was a wonder where the people came from, for Sister Bessie's friends and relatives were dead, were scattered, few. The nephew was there, with other relatives. The other people were a wonder, especially on a Wednesday or a Thursday afternoon. Arthur was sitting far in the back, alone. Julia's mother was resting; her father sat in the front row.

"Dearly beloved," she said, "we take our text today from the thirty-eighth chapter of Isaiah, the first verse."

She found her father's eyes, and he stood, his open Bible in his hand.

"My father," she said, and helplessly, she smiled. "My *beloved* father, Brother Joel Miller, will read the verse for us."

And Joel read, in a voice which had always amazed her—always, from the very beginning of her ministry, for it did not seem like his voice at all—yet she had heard this voice, sometimes, when he was happy with her mother: Joel read now, happy with his daughter:

In those days was Hezekiah sick unto death. And Isaiah the prophet the son of Amoz came unto him, and said unto him, Thus saith the Lord. Set thine house in order: for thou shalt die, and not live.

Her father looked up at her once, closed his Bible, and sat down.

"Amen!" said Julia. "My text is: set thine house in order."

Then, she paused, frightened, aware, as though for the first time, of the bier at the foot of the altar, and the pastor and the deacon, sitting in the pulpit behind her: the men who had not wanted to be responsible for Sister Bessie's funeral.

"We come together here," said Julia, "because that message just came for one of us, just like it's going to come for *all* of us, each and every one of us one day. She might have had her face turned to the wall, but then, she had to sit up and look around her, and hear the message and we believe, amen! that she called on the Holy Ghost, and she got busy with the Holy Ghost and she started to put her house in order. She didn't have time for trembling, *no*, her trembling days were done, and oh, church, have you ever had to set a house in order? You get up off the bed but you don't make the bed yet, you know you going to have to do that last. Maybe you go into the kitchen, bless God, and you look around you. You look at the stove and it's needing a scrubbing. You go down on your hands and knees, amen, and you get the Old Dutch Cleanser. Oh, yes! And then you start to run the water—and you take out the big brush of *faith* and that little brush of *love* because the big brush scours the stove, children, and that little brush gets into the corners—and you got the water to running, the water of salvation! Pretty soon you see the roaches come crawling out and you scour the walls. And you look at the pots and pans and you put them in the water. And you scrub them and you wash and dry the dishes and you put everything in its place, amen, and you wash down the table and you scrub the floor and look like the windows need a cleaning, too, and you scrub the windows and let the light come pouring in!

"Oh, yes! And all the time you moving around your house, the clock is ticking and *time* is running out. Lord, you hear it in every beat of your heart, and every time you run from one corner to the other, you hear time running *out*! You hear your neighbors dancing and playing music—they not setting their house in order! You hear someone in the street just cursing—cursing God!—he's not setting his house in order! You hear the harlot downstairs with her fornicators!—she's not setting her house in order! You hear the rich man and the poor man, trampling, trampling, trampling down, and you want to run through the streets, crying, 'set thine house in order!' You want to grab the policeman, crying, 'set thine house in order!' You want to grab your mother, your brother, your sister, your father, crying, 'set thine house in order! Set thine house in order! *Set thine house in order, for thou shalt die and not* live!'

"Oh. And the clock, it keeps on ticking. And you ain't got back to the bed to make it up yet—your dying bed. Then maybe there's a mirror on the wall, a mirror you ain't looked in for many a long year. And maybe you say to yourself, 'I better clean that mirror.' And so you walk to that mirror, with time ticking away, and you look in that mirror and you see your face. But you don't see it right, it looks real strange, real far away. And so you start to rub on that mirror and you start to see the face in the mirror and while you rub, you wonder how you are going to face your Maker. 'Lord, Lord, did I hurt somebody?' And the mirror don't answer and time keeps ticking. 'Lord, I'll wash off my makeup'—and time keeps ticking. 'Lord, I'll take the dye out of my hair'—and time keeps ticking. Maybe you got some earrings in your *ears*, and you ain't really seen them since you was a baby and somebody put them in your ears and you say, 'Lord, if these offend You I'll take them off, but help my trembling hands, my blinded eyes, I cannot see.'

"And the Lord say, 'I see what you done with your kitchen. I see what you done with your stove. I see how you scrubbed your floor. I see ain't no roaches in here. I see how you made that windowpane to shine. I see how you scrubbed that mirror because you didn't want Me to be ashamed of you and so we could see each other face to face. You can come into my kingdom with your earrings *on*! I told you to set your house in order, and I see your house in order!'

" 'Now put your hand in my hand, child, and walk with Me to the next room, and let Me make up your dying bed.' "

Then she paused and looked down at Sister Bessie's bier.

"She's walking and talking with the Lord," said Julia, "Our heavenly Father, who sees all the secrets of our heart, who knows all His children, and who promised never to leave us alone. She was born in the time of slavery: and she walked every step of the way with the Lord. Let us remember the text: *Set thine house in order.* And let us all say: *Amen.*"

She bowed her head, and the congregation said, *Amen!* Julia went back to her seat in the pulpit. The pastor rose. The congregation sang. Arthur wondered where Jimmy was—either at school, or in the movies: that was, mainly, how the time was spent.

And after Sister Bessie's coffin was carried out, he walked out on the steps and said good-bye to Julia and walked out of her life for a while.

He watched Julia and her father walk slowly up the block, away from him—for Julia did not go to the cemetery. Her job was done.

That was in the spring. In the summertime, Julia and Joel found themselves alone in the house, a day or two after Amy's funeral.

Jimmy had gone south with his grandmother. Paul and Florence had their two absent sons to worry about. Martha was being consoled by Sidney, though I didn't know this yet.

Julia had not preached since Sister Bessie's funeral. She had not yet begun, as we put it, to "backslide": on the contrary, she was more flamelike, more revered than ever, and this was because of her passionate devotion to her mother. This led her into a fast which very nearly broke her health—no one had ever been seen among us to labor so mightily for the soul of another! In the spring, Amy had been resting: could no longer, that is, rise from her bed, and Julia spent every waking hour at her mother's side. Amy was carried to the hospital—to Harlem Hospital—at the beginning of the summer, but it was already, said Martha, too late. Death enters a face and sits there, in the forehead, the cheekbones, the lips, and inundates, like blood or water, the inside of the eye. The eye seems to have clouded over, but it is also looking straight out, there is fire at the center of the cloud. Julia had become gaunt indeed, but death refused to prefer her over her mother: life, inexorably, sat in Julia's face and her eyes held the furious, driven repentance of the living.

She sat in the hospital all day, and sometimes, all night long. She washed her mother's body; she would have cleaned it with her tongue if she could have. Thus, no one yet considered that she had abandoned her ministry. She was far removed from our concerns, she was striving on holy ground.

And this was true—Florence, with tears in her eyes, confessed it: *She sees the angel, now. Too late. What's done cannot be undone.* And *never thought I'd be weeping for that poor child.* Paul was more laconic, but Julia was, indeed, a child—or was now discovering what it meant to be a child.

Jimmy, however, simply loathed his sister and would not speak to his father, spent all his time in the streets, in the movies, in the parks; began to steal, to smoke, to be fondled and jerked off in subway toilets; and sat on a bench in Harlem Hospital every night, waiting for his sister to let him see his mother.

He never spoke. Martha appointed herself his go-between. When he arrived, and took up his incredible vigil a few feet from the door beyond which he knew his mother lay, Martha would go to Amy's bedside—Amy was behind a screen—and whisper, "Your son is here."

Julia would rise without a word, and so would Joel, if he were pres-

ent. Julia walked straight out, not seeming to see Jimmy, who refused
to see her. Sometimes Joel would wait, but he had no real authority
over his son anymore—even though Jimmy was only around twelve—
and he did not like looking into Jimmy's eyes.

Jimmy would simply sit still until his sister and his father had
passed.

His father might say, "Expect to see you home in a minute," and
Jimmy might react or not react—but in any case, only with his eyes—
and then run to see his mother. Even then, he did not say very
much—except again with his eyes, which seemed to register every
shade that crossed his mother's face—but he answered all her questions, or seemed to: his brave attempt at candor sometimes forcing
him to volunteer distracting information. Amy saw through this, and
teased him, and sometimes looked somber, as though she were struggling to find a way to tell him something. But she *could* tell him something, or she knew he would find it out. She knew that her mother
would be taking him away, out of the hands of her daughter, and her
husband. And she seemed to have nothing, any longer, to say to her
husband: but she had something to say to her daughter.

One afternoon—a Sunday—when Julia was there alone, she tried.

"How's your father doing these days?"

Julia had been sitting on the edge of her mother's bed, looking at
the floor. Now she looked up.

"My father?" She smiled: then her smile made Julia feel that her
face was frozen. Children were told never to make ugly faces, the Devil
might come along and freeze the face into the ugly expression forever.
She tried to unfreeze the face and lose the smile. She said, "He's worried about you, Mama, but other than that, he's fine."

"Oh, shucks," said Amy. "Ain't no need to be worried about me."

She looked down, and played with the thin bedclothes. She looked
at the screen and dropped her voice.

"You going to continue with the Lord's work? you going to keep
on preaching?"

"Why—" said Julia, and looked at her mother. Her throat closed, her mouth became dry—she had, suddenly, nothing to say.

But Amy nodded, as though Julia had answered the question.

"I want you to know one thing," Amy said. "If I didn't know it before, and if don't never find myself able to say it to you again, I found out something about the Lord's will." She smiled. That face, like parchment, stretched, the teeth came jutting out: she held Julia's wrist in one frail and mighty claw. "Trust the Lord's will. When it comes down on you, don't blame the Lord. Just go where He sends you." She leaned back, in all the wretched bedclothes. "Take care of your brother—he's my heart. I used to think he was jealous of you. I was as wrong as wrong could be." She had let go of Julia's wrist; Julia missed her mother's touch. Amy looked up at her. "The truth was just exactly the other way around." She looked up at her daughter now with something very close to hatred, and Julia began to cry.

Amy watched her from her strange, unconquerable, and, somehow, triumphant distance—she did not move to touch her. But she said, as Julia rose and moved, stumbling, shaking, from the bed to the window, "The Lord's going to be taking me away from you soon, and I believe I'm ready to go." She watched Julia's back. "Come back here," she said. "Come over here."

Julia moved back to her mother's side, still weeping. She was blind, and in terror, and utterly alone, held upright by a freezing wind—and her mother's voice came to her out of this wind.

"Save them tears, daughter. You going to need them. Quit fasting and praying for *me*—you don't mean it, and the Lord know it; He ain't never yet accepted a sacrifice that wasn't real. You think the Lord don't see your heart? When *I* see it? *Stop* them tears, and sit down."

Julia sat down on the bed. Amy's hand grasped her wrist again, her hand was as hot as fire, and made the cold wind colder. Through a freezing storm, with fire at the center, she watched her mother's face.

"You start fasting and praying—*today*—for your father, and for *you*. The Lord ain't pleased with you. He going to make you both to know it. How come you think you can fool the Lord? You might done had *me* fooled. But I *wanted* to be fooled! How come you think the Lord don't see? when *I* see!"

And she flung her daughter's hand away from her, it was a curse. She lay back on the bed, and pulled the bedclothes up around her.

"Go home, daughter," she said. "*Run.* Pull the curtains, and fall down on your knees. And don't forget you got a brother. That's how you'll get the Lord's forgiveness."

Then she hid her face from her daughter's eyes, she covered her face—like Hezekiah, she turned her face to the wall.

Julia turned away, walked beyond the screen, through the freezing ward, the freezing hall, down steps like ice, into the blazing Sunday streets.

Tell the wicked daughter, and the prodigal son, they can make it home, if they run!

Never had she avoided her father, or dreaded being alone with him: but now, alone in the house with him, a day or two after Amy's funeral, terror sat in her bowels and rose and fell in her throat.

"Well," he said, "it's just the two of us now."

He had been looking at a photograph of Amy, which he, now, with other mementos, placed in a cardboard box—they had been putting things away.

She had been wearing a bathrobe, with her hair tied up in an old black rag. She had old, gray slippers on her feet, and was so tired she felt faint.

He had been wearing his undershirt and old, blue, dirty workpants. She sat down, suddenly, on the sofa, and he turned and looked at her.

He said gently, "I know how you feel, daughter—think how *I* must feel. But we got to discuss practical matters."

She put her head in her hands and said, "Oh, Daddy, not today."

"I think it's best," he said, as though she had not spoken, "that you get back in the pulpit right away. It's a right long time you ain't been preaching—people keep asking me about you, girl, we got churches lined up for more than a year! And it'll help you get your mind off all this sorrow. You'll see. It's what your mother went away from here praying for—it was her last words to me. She was always so proud of you."

He went into the kitchen and poured himself a small glass of wine, and came back, standing at the window, with his back to her.

"So I'll start setting up dates tomorrow—or this afternoon, maybe, why not? We could start next Sunday, that's not too soon, we could start in Bishop Pritchard's church in Philadelphia, you remember, that's a great *big* tabernacle, what do you think?"

Although Julia always said that she *knew* Sister Bessie's funeral sermon was the last sermon she would ever preach, I really wonder if, until this moment, Julia's conscious mind had made any decision at all concerning her future as an evangelist. I don't doubt that her decision had already, in the inexorable depths, been made: but I think that it was only now that it revealed itself as merciless, unchanging, far beyond the dictates of her will, or her father's ease. It was only now, for that matter, and for the very first time, that she thought of her father's *ease:* it was in his stance, as he stood at the window, his back to her, with his small glass of wine in his hand. The shape of his skull, the curl of his hair, etched themselves into the gray day pounding at the window-pane; and the broad, bony shoulders, the hair and the bone, at the nape of his neck, the thin, dirty undershirt, the hair in his armpits, the broad black belt at his waist, his narrow buttocks, his long, wiry thighs and legs, all bore witness to a mystery she had never considered before, which frightened her. She was suddenly in a room with a stranger: she felt her mother watching, she who had known the stranger's naked body.

Joel turned, and looked at her—with his little smile, a smile she was seeing for the first time. Julia stood up.

"No," she said.

"No? No—*what?*—no?"

Her throat closed, she could not answer.

"No," she said again, and put her hands in her bathrobe pockets. She longed to run to her father; she longed to run out of the room.

It came to her that she was not going to run anywhere, it was too late to run.

"I don't understand you, girl. What are you saying?"

"I'm not going to preach anymore," she said. "Never, never, never anymore."

He put his glass of wine down on the table in front of the sofa.

He smiled again.

"You upset, daughter—you think I don't know how you feel? *I* know how you feel. But you'll get over it. You *have* to get over it. I'm going to go ahead and make those dates, you'll see I'm right. And daughter, you just go upstairs and get some rest—you upset, that's all, and you don't know what you're saying."

"I *do* know what I'm saying!"

But her voice held no conviction, and, to make matters worse, she began to cry.

He moved toward her, and to avoid his touch, she curled up on the sofa, with her back to him, crying. He stroked her back, and the back of her neck. She smelled his armpits, and the wine of his breath.

"Little girl," he said, "we got a lot to do, in a hurry. You go upstairs and get some rest and let me take care of business."

She stood up again, and walked away from him, to the window.

She looked out at the backs of other houses, into a longing and a dread intolerable. She thought, *I'm just fourteen.* She wondered why she thought this. Her father was watching her, and she shivered. *I'm just fourteen. I can't preach anywhere, ever, again.* Why? She did not know why.

"Daddy," she said, "I'm through with preaching. The Holy Ghost has left me."

She felt his furious impatience rising, as he stared at her back, and again she wanted to run out of the room.

"You always told *me*," he said, "that the Holy Ghost don't never leave none of His children alone."

"But you can sin against the Holy Ghost," she said. "You can sin a sin that can't be forgiven."

He was silent.

"Sin?"

Then, again,

"Sin?"

Then,

"What sin you talking about?"

She was silent because she knew she had used the wrong word—at the same time, she was calculating how she might use his swift misunderstanding to her advantage.

He came to her and took her roughly by the shoulder and turned her to face him.

"What sin? what you been doing?"

"It's not," she said, terrified, "a sin of the flesh."

"You been fooling around? One of them boys that come to this house?"

"No."

"*What* sin?"

"Pride."

He laughed. "Go on upstairs. Get some sleep. You'll be all right. You lost your mama, honey, but you still got your daddy. *I* know when you tired and upset."

"You don't understand me—please try to understand me," and she began to cry again, with a quiet helplessness, which caused him to begin to listen—in his way.

"Is it some boy, sugar, got you all turned around? It was bound to happen someday—but I thought *I* was your man," and he laughed, a low, light laugh, holding her by the shoulders.

"No. I just"—and now she wondered, wondered at what she was saying, felt an icy wind blow into her face at the same time that she smelt the wine of his breath again—"I just don't believe it—I don't believe—I don't believe—" And she stared at her father.

"You said you were called to preach—*you* said God called you to preach. *You* don't believe—you made *us* believe!"

"I *did* believe! I *did*! But—now—"

She stared at her father, he stared at her: neither could move.

"And now? Now? Now—*what*?"

She stared into his eyes, it might have been for the first time, she began to tremble, he tightened his hold on her shoulders, she felt herself drowning in his breath.

"If you don't hit them churches, girl, how we going to eat? Tell me that. You know how much money *I* make—you been keeping this house going. You going to turn your father into a beggar now?"

As in the nightmare when a nameless terror approaches and the dreamer cannot move, she stared into her father's eyes.

"You always liked to see me real sharp and pretty—I know you did. What you mean, you don't believe no more? Don't you believe in me?"

"I did it for you," she said—and did not hear herself, did not know what she said.

"Then keep on doing it for me. Ain't but the two of us now."

His arms had tightened on her shoulder. She wanted to put her arms around him, and pull him to her, as she had always done—as she had done when her mother was alive. Then she had been safe.

But he was her father—her father, still. She forced herself to trust him, and she put her arms around him. His arms tightened around her, and his stubble grazed her cheek.

"Just keep on doing it for me," he said. "You keep on believing in *me,* we'll be very happy, we'll live off the fat of the land." He pressed her face into his shoulder, stroked the rag which covered her hair. "Nobody will ever have to know, baby, you'd be surprised; it happens all the time. Love is a beautiful thing, darling; something in every man, I believe, wants to turn his daughter into a woman." She felt his sex stiffen against her, and, somehow, she broke away, for some reason she was terribly aware of the gray window at her back, and the yearning houses. *No place to run. No place to hide.* She knocked over the glass of wine, and the smell of the wine, the scream she could not deliver, nearly burst her brain. She fell on the sofa, and he fell on top of her. Still she could not scream. She knew that something in her had always wanted this, but not this, not this, not this way, she wanted to say, *Please. Please wait,* but he said, in a low, laughing growl, "You and the Holy Ghost been after my ass *awhile;* you wanted me, you got me."

She made one last effort to rise, but he slapped her back; she heard the heavy belt fall to the floor. She knew one thing clearly—she had never wanted this, this rage and hatred. She had always wanted his love. She had, herself, brought about this moment—yes, she had, but not *this* moment. He held her down with one hand while he got one leg out of his dirty blue work pants. She fell into a silence far more real than the silence of the grave. He covered her entirely; she heard, from far away, his moan; he put both hands under her hips, and thrust. Not even when the great grave blood-filled weapon which had given her life came pounding into her was she able to utter a sound. Every thrust of her father's penis seemed to take away the life that it had given, thrust anguish deeper into her, into a place too deep for the sex of any man to reach, into a place it would take her many years to find, a place deeper than the miracle of the womb, deeper, almost, than the love which is salvation.

BOOK THREE

The Gospel Singer

Work: for the night is coming.

TRADITIONAL

In a small town in Tennessee, Peanut and Red and Crunch and Arthur have finished their last number: "Hush, Hush, Somebody's Calling My Name." Crunch is the lead on this song, Arthur the principal backup man. *Oh*, sings Crunch, *you may call for your* mother, *but*, sings Arthur, *your mother won't do you no good*. Peanut is at the piano, Red is moaning: *Oh, my Lord. Oh, my Lord. What shall I do?*

Which is exactly the way they feel.

The last offering had been taken up, and carried off, God knows where. They are anxious to be paid—for they are not always paid—but they mask this terror with their juvenile smiles: smiles more juvenile than they can possibly know, which is why they are not always paid. They have never been South before. They do not really like Nashville, but, at least, it looks like a city. This is a town, about twenty miles from Nashville—not far, unless you have to walk it.

They are in the hands of a Mr. Clarence Webster, a black music teacher, about forty-seven years old, who is their impresario, operating out of Harlem. They realize, incoherently, that he has never been an impresario before, and they also realize, incoherently, that he is yet more frightened down here than they are. This is chilling, for Mr. Webster was born in the South, and knows it better than they do. Yet any white man can make him smile a smile which makes him look like he is holding cold oatmeal—or rather, cold hominy grits, which none of them will ever, if they ever get out of here, eat again—at the bottom of his tongue. Oh, how he smiles! And how proud he is of his boys— dragged out of the streets, by him alone, to their present eminence! They cannot bear being called boys. They cannot bear Mr. Webster, shortly. But they had liked him up North, and he is not, in fact, a bad teacher at all. His attitude with black people is yet more frightening, for he appears to despise them for never having braved the North. They, on the one hand, counter that they have friends and relatives in the North, and, on the other hand, appear to despise him because he lacked the courage to remain in the South.

The boys cannot follow these acrid exchanges, sensing, incoherently, that they are, in some way, at the center of this storm.

The pastor has delivered the benediction, and the boys, the choir, and the congreagation have sung together "God Be with You till We Meet Again."

The elderly ladies, in one way, in their remarkable hats and brooches and heirlooms and with smiles as compelling as the sun, bless the boys for their song; and so do the younger ladies, in quite another way. The pastor, the deacons, the preacher of the morning, the visiting preachers, all in the same melancholy suits, with matching ties and white shirts, are hearty and cheerful and incomparably more distant—presenting the boys with the choice of becoming accomplices, or pariahs.

In Harlem, they knew where they were, and were proud of their accumulating age—they contested each discovery with each other. Here they are confronted with the devastating reality of their youth. Here they begin to suspect, for the first time, that the world has no mercy and that they have no weapons. They have only each other, and may, soon, no longer have that.

They are all, now, descending the steps to the church basement, where the church sisters have set up a feast. At this time in his life, Arthur is always hungry, and his stomach is growling as he keeps on smiling. If he can't keep smiling, he'll moan. A young church sister, Sister Dorothy Green, is walking down the stairs beside him. She is dressed the way she thinks girls in the North are dressed. She's not entirely wrong. Girls in the North *did* dress like that, some time ago.

Arthur, without knowing it, begins to feel historical.

"How do you like our town?" asks Sister Dorothy Green.

Crunch is just behind him, with another sister, prettier, naturally, than Sister Dorothy Green, and appears to be having no trouble at all. They have reached the booming bottom of the stairs, are now in the church basement, wide and deep and—*beautiful* is the word that comes to Arthur's mind—for the light comes in through the basement windows like the immeasurable love of Jesus, blessing all the tables which are draped in white and covered with food for the hungry; and the many warm odors are the proof of safety. No harm can come to anyone here. He looks behind him. Peanut and Red are at the top of the stairs, surrounded by older sisters.

He looks for Clarence Webster, but Webster is already seated at a table, surrounded by sisters and deacons, and is concentrating on the biscuits, the chicken, the rice, the gravy, the yams, the ham, the pineapples, and the applesauce.

He has not answered Sister Dorothy Green's question.

"Why—I don't really know it," he says—foolishly; obviously, he doesn't know it—"I—we—only came in this morning. But it's a pretty town."

"It's prettier than towns in the North, now, isn't it? Tell me the truth."

He has never seen so insistent a smile. He does not, consciously, think it—it does not come to the forefront of his mind—but the smile makes him aware of his virginity, and all the hair of his flesh begins to itch. A little sweat begins at his hairline. He looks for Crunch, who has disappeared. Sister Dorothy Green is leading him, relentlessly, to a table.

Webster is eating, and Arthur loathes him. He is surrounded by sisters and brothers. So are Peanut and Red. As for Crunch, he has probably already split with *his* church sister, and is already making it with her in some other basement.

"I don't really know any northern towns," he says. "I was born in Harlem."

"Well. It's prettier than Harlem. Isn't it?"

"Well, yes," Arthur says, helplessly, after a moment, "it sure is prettier than Harlem. It's *cleaner*"—but he feels like a traitor when he says this.

He begins to resent Sister Dorothy, and looks at her for the first time.

She is not a pretty girl, but she is not a bad-looking girl, either, and she is not very much older than he—between eighteen and nineteen, perhaps. She is the color of gingersnaps, with curly, sandy hair: when he looks at her, he realizes that her eyes are green—like the eyes of Scarlett O'Hara in *Gone With the Wind*. Somehow, and he cannot help it, her eyes, or rather, the color of her eyes, profoundly repels him—starving as he is, he begins to lose his appetite, as the table comes closer and closer. Irrationally, he begins to hate Crunch, whose idea it had been to come here.

He wishes I were there. He wonders (as he wonders every day) if I'm still alive. Then he's glad I'm not there. He'll tell me about it later—if he ever gets out of here, if I'm still alive.

Somehow, this panic lends him a certain force.

Dorothy seats him at a table.

"You sit," she says. "I'll serve you. What do you want?"

"Everything," says Arthur, and looks up at her, and grins.

Somehow, this grin demolishes the distances between them. She grins, too, and her grin is mischievous with promise. She, suddenly, for Arthur, becomes a presence, stepping absolutely out of her curling, straightened, sandy hair, her beige pillbox hat, her beige suit, her green eyes. She puts her handbag down on the table.

"Watch this," she says. "I'll be right back."

"I'm from Harlem," he says. "Remember? I might steal it."

"I dare you," she says, again with that grin. "And anyway, believe me, you will not be stealing very much."

He hears her accent, for the first time, really, for the first time without fear, and begins to like her as she vanishes into a cloud of witnesses.

He looks around him. The church basement is wide and low. I very dimly remember the days in Harlem of Father Divine—when the Father fed the hungry: and let the record show, baby, upon my soul, that he really did do that. (Nobody has since, not one of the grim motherfuckers placed in various offices since then, not one: and let the record also state that, if I didn't love the people I love, I'd think nothing of blowing the unspeakably obscene mediocrities who rule the American State into eternity—and go to meet them there.) Well. Arthur came along later. He has no way of recognizing the wide, low church basement. He does not know what it cost—the blood that bought it, the pain and sweat and danger which built it, the passion which holds it up. He does not know what genius goes into the boiling and baking, the frying and broiling, the scouring—how hard it is to make oneself clean every day, how hard it is to find and prepare the food. He feels only, mysteriously, warm and protected. The voices around him, though the accent is so strange, somehow affirm him. He looks around him. He has never seen any of these people before; and yet, he has, has always known them. He watches Webster. In Harlem, Webster seems very sharp and hip, not old but not young. Here he has no age at all. Dimly, dimly, he begins to suspect something: in all that acrid chatter concerning northern cities and southern towns, of which, indeed, the boys were the center and the intolerably menaced prize, there was a connection as deep as that inarticulate connection between himself and Peanut and Crunch and Red when they sang. It was all in the twinkling of an eye, a beat, a pause, an unspoken question, which got them, carried them, from one moment to the next. He thinks of his father and mother, and he thinks of me. He wonders—now, for the first time, really—how he could possibly live, or have lived, without us: and the wonder brutally reverses itself, for *that* is why we beat him and bathed him and shouted at him and sometimes made him hate us and sometimes made him feel so bad—we love him. We love him. We also wonder how we can possibly live without *him*. He looks around the church basement again, seeing something for the first time. All those sisters, and all that cheerful noise, a warmth, as dangerous as lightning, and as comforting as a stove, fills the space. Laughter rings, gossip abounds: obliterating, for the moment, the endless grief and danger. He sees, but does not see, the swollen ankles, the flat feet, the swift, gnarling fingers, serving the deacons, repudiating the helpless condition, refusing, with a laugh, despair. He watches the faces of the men—more bitter, in an unguarded moment, than the faces of the women, and, at the very same moment, more innocent, more trusting. He wonders, and Dorothy comes back, with

"Everything!" she says triumphantly, and sets his plate before him.

"Ain't you going to eat?" he asks her.

"*I* got to watch my waistline," she says. His look, then, makes her laugh. "I'll nibble a little off your plate—I don't want but a chicken wing. What do you want to drink?"

Her look, then, makes *him* laugh.

"Pepsi-Cola?"

"In just one second, mister," she says and she whirls away again.

He looks around him again. Red and Peanut are at a table far away, with somewhat older sisters. Crunch is nowhere to be seen. He is aware, though the word is not in him, that he has made a conquest—*that chick digs* you, *man*—and that he will be expected to report on it later, the way the others do. But he has never believed their reports: he realizes this for the first time. And he realizes, also for the first time, dimly, that he does not *want* to take Sister Dorothy Green into some dark corner and put his hands up her dress, and then talk about it, later—he does not *want* to do that. He has had his hard-ons, and he's started jerking off—with no object in his mind at all, his mind as blank as a stone. He has a holiness complex—perhaps that is the best way to put it. He is full of wonder. He knows nothing about others: he knows he knows nothing. Love has presented no image yet—no image at all. The man who tried to suck him off that far-off day has dropped to the bottom of a well, deeper than that: that violation, terror, humiliation, is as distant from any idea of love as Kansas from Alaska. Yet a need is growing in him, a tormenting need, with no name, no object. He is beginning to be lonely—we, who love him, are not enough.

For the moment, the song is enough—almost enough: everything, or almost everything, goes into the song.

Still he feels his prick stiffen when Dorothy comes back to the table, bearing her Pepsi-Cola like an offering: and he feels the vanity of the very young male.

She sits, and he smiles.

"How would you like your chicken wing?"

"In my napkin. If you please."

He places the chicken wing, elaborately graceful, into her napkin, and he likes her more and more and wants her less and less. For the very first time, he wonders, with a kind of falling terror, what in the world is wrong with him.

He begins to eat. He watches her breasts, beneath the beige cloth. His prick stiffens a little, twitches, but in a vacuum: he has no real curiosity about those breasts. Her thighs move, and, in his mind's eye, he sees the pubic *V* between her thighs. He would, perhaps, like to go there: but where to go from there? He likes her. She is not a plaything. Dimly, dimly, and with mounting terror, something tells him that he is not for her.

He wishes I were there, so that he could ask me questions; at the very same moment, it is borne in on him that there are, now, some questions that he will never be able to ask anyone. But he smiles at Dorothy, and ferociously, as though to give himself something to do, he begins to eat. He takes a long swallow of his Pepsi-Cola.

"I knew you must be hungry—singing like you do."

"You like the way I sing?"

He is both comfortable and uncomfortable. He likes her. But for the very first time, he wonders what *she* wants, why she likes him, if she does—but he knows that she likes him.

He wonders where Crunch is, and what he is doing, and he feels his prick twitch again and sweat, lightly, breaks out again, on his forehead.

"You sing—right beautiful. Really, you the best of them all."

"Oh, come on. My buddies, they can sing. They older than me. They taught me."

"Well. You sure learned."

He grins at her, with a mouthful of cornbread. "What do you do?"

"Me?" She puts the bones of the chicken wing into her napkin, and folds it. "Next year, when I finish school, I'm going to be a schoolteacher. In elementary school. With real young children, you know? I think I'd like that because I really like children." She grins. "Try to teach them to be wiser than me."

"You going to teach down here?"

"Well. I don't think they going to let me teach up where you come from."

"Why not?"

She laughs, then stops laughing, looking at him. "Do they have any black schools, up yonder, where you come from?"

"What's that got to do with it?"

Dorothy laughs again. "Think about it. Were your teachers white or colored?"

He has never really thought about it. He thinks about it now. "Why—both. I mean"—he thinks about it—"I had—I had *some* colored teachers—"

"How many?"

"Well—not many—"

"Most of them were white?"

"Well—yes—"

"So you've answered your own question."

"You mean—you're going to teach down here because—" He looks at her. She looks at him, with a small, tight smile, and says nothing. He forces a laugh, feeling oddly, and violently ashamed, not knowing why. "You must want to teach real bad."

"Don't you want to sing real bad?"

This time, he cannot manage the laugh. He looks into her proud face. It is the first time he realizes that the face is proud. That is why the face is not pretty. It cannot afford to be pretty. And, though she likes him, and wants him to know that she likes him, she is watching him, too, and holding him outside. He chews something, swallows something. Helplessly, he watches her.

"Don't you?"

"Yes," he says, at last. "I guess I do," and watches her.

"I guess so, too," she says. "That's why you sitting in this basement, trying to figure me out." And she laughs. He likes her very much when she laughs—he laughs with her.

"So," she says soberly, "you on your journey now. And you know, just like I know—if you white, all right, if you brown, you can hang around. But, if you *black—step back, step back, step back!* Singing or teaching, North or South, it don't make no difference. That's the way it is."

Her face, and her voice, now, are bitter indeed, and it strikes him that this is a strange conversation to be having with a strange, perhaps not altogether black girl, in a church basement in a small town, just outside of Nashville.

He wonders what has happened to Crunch. From far away, through the still summer air, he hears the sound of someone sawing wood.

"We can't let that stop us," he says.

"It's put a stop to many. But I don't believe I'll let it stop *me*."

There is silence. Then, "When you all going back?" she asks.

"We going back to Nashville, right after lunch. Then we go to Birmingham."

"You been there before?"

He shakes his head no.

"Every time I go there," she says, "I think about that story in the Bible, I forget just who it was, has to go to this wicked city. The Lord wants to destroy this city, but the prophet asks Him—asks the Lord—if the Lord will spare the city if he can find fifty righteous men. And the Lord says, yes, He'll spare the city if the prophet can find fifty righteous men. But the prophet knows good and well he can't find fifty righteous men and so he asks if the Lord will spare the city if he could find just *one*—just one righteous man. The Lord says, Yes, he'll spare the city if the prophet can find just *one* righteous man. But he knows he won't find one righteous man in Birmingham, although I've never met him. And the Lord hasn't destroyed the city." Then she says, "Be careful. Keep your mouth shut. Don't say no more than you have to—just yes sir and no sir. Them people are just like the herd of swine in the Bible, only there ain't no sea for them to rush down into." She sighs, then she laughs, then she sobers. "If I didn't trust the Lord," she says, "I don't know what I'd do." She grabs him by one wrist. "You be careful, you hear me? You a mighty pretty, *young* colored man. They don't like that. They *kill* boys like you, just for fun, every Saturday night."

She is scaring the shit out of him—it is something in those green eyes. He is not yet afraid of Birmingham, though, God knows, he will be. He is afraid of her. Before his eyes, she has grown old and mad—in her beige pillbox hat, her handsome beige suit.

Call. Call, for your mother. But your mother can't do you no good.

Again he hears, over all the other sounds, through the still summer air, the sound of someone sawing wood. He imagines, insanely, that it might be Crunch, somewhere in the fields outside, just relaxing and using his muscles.

He wants to get out of this basement.

"Can't we take a walk somewhere?" he asks. "Just for a few minutes?"

"If you *got* a few minutes," she says promptly, and rises, as though she had been waiting for this moment.

He rises, too, and looks around him. Webster is deep in conversation with the elders—astoundingly, he is still pushing food into his face. Arthur feels faintly nauseated. Red and Peanut are with some other girls. He can tell that they are dreadfully uncomfortable. No, Crunch is nowhere to be seen. Sister Dorothy Green picks up her handbag, and takes his arm, guiding him toward the steps.

He winks at Red and Peanut.

"Be right back," he says calmly, scared to death.

They walk up the steps, through the empty church, through the doors, into the silent streets of this country town. He looks at the station wagon, which will be carrying them, soon, to Birmingham. Maybe Crunch is in the station wagon.

He has the feeling that he is losing his mind. The streets are bright and empty, stretching into a dreadful future. The houses are low, conspiratorial, trees are everywhere—he has never seen so many trees. He is hanging from any one of them—from every one of them, turned, lightly, from moment to moment, by the still, heavy, ominous air. He can almost feel the rope burning his Adam's apple. He feels the weight of his feet in the air, pulling downward against his snapped neck. A wind blows through his hair, a wind from the glacial mountaintops, the haze, the palpable, wavering summer heat causes the landscape to shiver, to drip like water. He would like to run, forever—where? The sound of someone sawing wood has stopped.

He sees the outhouse at the side of the church. Out of many needs, the physical one being the least pressing, he stops, and says to Dorothy, with a smile, wondering how he is managing to smile, "Will you excuse me just for a moment, Sister?" and he moves his head in the direction of the outhouse.

Maybe Crunch is in the outhouse!

"Why, certainly, brother," she says and smiles, looking away, down those long streets.

He hurries to the whitewashed outhouse, opens the door, and locks himself in. The whitewashed outhouse is scoured, toilet paper hanging by a string. He pees, looking down into the lime-covered depths—there is a bag of lime at the side of the latrine. He would like to shit, actually, if only life were different, but he knows that he cannot possibly manage it here and now, with Sister Dorothy Green waiting, and where would he wash his hands? So he pees, looking at his prick as though it does not belong to him, and wondering where Crunch is. He buttons up. He is alone. He would like to stay alone here, forever, but the smell is beginning to get to him. He opens the door and walks out into the sunlight, smiling, and *Is this life?* he wonders incoherently, *Is it? Is this* my *life?*

Sister Dorothy Green leans against a tree, smiling like a movie star, as he moves toward her.

"Feel better, big boy?" she asks, and, now, he wonders if he likes her at all.

"Much better," he says, and suddenly, against this tree, in the sight of all the world, her arms are around him, and she is in his arms.

Her tongue in his mouth locks his terrified howl within him, and her breasts, against his chest, create a thunder in his skull. Yet there is a terrifying pleasure in it, too, and her hands are everywhere. *Didn't know nobody had so many hands,* he thinks insanely, and that limp bit of flesh which he has just used to pee with suddenly becomes rigid and enormous, and he grinds himself against her. He almost drops his load then and there, in the sunlight, and they pull away from each other, shaking.

But she seems very calm. She touches his cheek with one long, thin hand.

"That was just to let you know that I sure hope you'll come back through here one day." She smiles the loneliest, most avid smile he has ever seen. "I'll sure be here." She straightens her skirt and touches her hat. She takes his hand. "We better go back in."

And, just like that, they walk back into the church, and down the steps, into the basement.

"Crunch, what happened to you this afternoon? Where'd you go?"

"Young lady took me driving in her daddy's automobile."

In fact they had had to leave without Crunch, and the young lady obligingly drove him all the way into Nashville—where they are now, in a rooming house run by some friends of Webster. They are two to a room, Peanut and Red, and Crunch and Arthur. The boys had been so stunned by Crunch's exploit that they hadn't even teased him about it. They had met the young lady, very sharp and cool, and she had had a cup of coffee with them before going back home. And she certainly liked Crunch; she didn't care who knew it.

Arthur doesn't feel like teasing him, either, is just glad he turned up again. And they all react like that down here, to each other's absences. They have never put it into words, they cannot; but each absence is a threat. They never felt this way in New York—they moved all over New York. Here each is afraid that one of the others will get into some terrible trouble before he is seen again, and before anyone can help him. It is the spirit of the people, the eyes which endlessly watch them, eyes which never meet their eyes. Something like lust, something like hatred, seems to hover in the air along the country roads, shifting like mist or steam, but always there, gripping the city streets like fog, making every corner a dangerous corner. They spend more of themselves, each day, than they can possibly afford, they are living beyond their means; they drop into bed each evening, exhausted, into an exhausting sleep. And no one can help them. The people who live here know how to do it—so it seems, anyway—but they cannot teach the secret. The secret can be learned only by watching, by emulating the models, by dangerous trial and possibly mortal error.

He watches Crunch in the other bed, yawning, his hands clasped at the back of his head.

The window next to Crunch's bed gives onto the road—through

the shade and the closed curtain, Arthur senses the trees. Arthur's bed is on the wall, and gives onto the hall and the bathroom and the kitchen.

It is absolutely silent; the heavy, charged, southern silence. It should be peaceful, but it isn't; you wait for the scream which will break the silence, you dread the coming day.

"What time we moving out of here tomorrow, Crunch?"

"I think the old man wants us to be ready to haul ass around six."

"You glad we came down here? I mean, it was really kind of your idea."

Crunch turns on his side, facing Arthur, smiling.

"You want to blame me for something?"

"Oh, come on, man, don't be like that, I'm here, ain't I, and you didn't put no gun to my head, what have I got to blame you for? I just asked you a question."

"Well, look at it this way, Arthur—we working, we making a little bread—a *very* little, I grant you, but we wouldn't be doing no better up in the city—and we learning, at least *I* think we learning—and we ain't starving and we in the fresh air, baby, don't forget that, that's very important—and *some* of us can get fine young ladies to drive us around the town in their daddies' automobiles!"

Arthur throws a pillow at him, and Crunch laughs and throws it back. "So I'm glad I came, yeah." He looks at Arthur with a gentle, rueful smile. "We just drove around, really, that's all—she was showing me sights and monuments. She was real nice. I learned a little bit, today, about down here." He sits up and lights a cigarette, throws the pack and the matches to Arthur. Arthur lights a cigarette, throws the pack and the matches back. "You see, I understand your real question. I can't answer it. This place is a mystery for me, too."

"Does it scare you?"

"*All* mysteries scare me. The only way not to be scared is to be too *dumb* to be scared."

Arthur thinks about this, drawing on his cigarette. They have one dim night-lamp on in the room, and their cigarettes glow a rusty orange against the gloom. They have been speaking in very low voices.

A car passes, swiftly, on the road outside, making a *whishing*, crackling sound, like the roar of a flame.

Then, silence. Crunch sits looking straight ahead, his elbows on his knees, the cigarette held loosely between the fingers of one hand.

"But something in me *comes* from down here," he says, "even though I've never been here. That's a mystery, too, but"—he turns and looks at Arthur—"don't you feel like that, too? Like something's just been waiting here for you, all the time?"

"Yes," Arthur says—but does not know how to say more. Something is turning in him, like the little wheel in the song.

He thinks of Sister Dorothy Green.

"I was with a girl, too, this afternoon," he says, "but she didn't have no *automobile*." And he laughs.

"What *did* she have, then?"

He knows now, that he cannot ever really talk about it. He does not know how—dimly, he feels he has no right.

"I don't know." He looks at Crunch in a genuine helplessness. Crunch watches him gravely. Arthur realizes, for the first time, consciously, that Crunch listens to him, responds to him, takes him seriously—takes him seriously, even though he always makes fun of him. That, perhaps, is as great a mystery as this region, the people of this region. The surface is misleading, is perhaps meant to be misleading, or cannot help but be—the truth is somewhere else, far beneath the surface: like the tenderness, now, at the very bottom of Crunch's eyes, as he watches Arthur.

"I don't know," he repeats. "Pain," he says senselessly. "I felt—her awful pain." He looks over at Crunch. "Do you know what I mean?"

"I think I do," says Crunch gravely. "Yes, I think I do."

"Is that the way it is? I mean—for everybody?"

"Sometimes," says Crunch. "Sometimes. For everybody."

"For you too?"

"Little fellow. You mighty solemn tonight." Then, "Yes. For me too."

He puts out his cigarette.

"Every time I see my mama," he says quietly—so quietly that Arthur's heart leaps, almost in terror. Crunch leans back on the bed, looks over at Arthur. "My mama's a whore, really. I love her, but—that's what she is." He makes a sound between a sob and a grunt. "It's funny—I don't think I'd mind—if *she* didn't. I don't think the other kids would mind—she's our *mama*. She ain't got nothing to be ashamed of—I'm no fool, I know what happened—and the men came and went, but she stayed, she raised us. She did everything she could for us, it ain't her fault the world is like it is."

Arthur holds his breath, hearing the heavy tears at the bottom of Crunch's voice.

"But she's so ashamed, she thinks *we* ashamed—she thinks *I'm* ashamed, for Christ's sake, and I can't get through to her, and I love her."

Now Crunch *is* weeping, a strangling sound, and Arthur cannot move.

"That's why I want to do something, make her happy, buy her some fine clothes, make a lot of money and put it in her hand, treat her like a beautiful woman. She *is* a beautiful woman!"

Now Arthur dares to look and sees the tears rolling, boiling, out of the side of Crunch's eye, into his ear. Crunch's bed shakes gently, he is holding his breath—but this only makes it worse, it is as though he is bleeding inside.

"Crunch, Crunch," he whispers. "Crunch!"

Crunch does not answer, does not seem to hear him. Arthur gets out of bed and crosses the floor and leans on Crunch's bed and puts his arms around him.

"Crunch," he says again. "Please, Crunch. Please, man. Please."

He strokes the wet face, he kisses the tears. "Please, Crunch. You going to make me cry, man."

And this is true: in another moment, his own tears will begin to fall. He does not want to cry. He wants to comfort Crunch, to bring the dark face back to itself, back to him, to hold the shaking body until it ceases to shake.

He takes off his pajama top, and wipes Crunch's face. He holds the cloth at Crunch's nose.

"Blow your nose," he says. "Come on, now."

Crunch weakly blows his nose, then takes the cloth from Arthur and blows his nose again.

He opens his eyes, and looks into Arthur's eyes.

"Thank you," he says, "little fellow."

They cannot stop looking into each other's eyes. They have discovered something. They have discovered how much each cares about the other. Something leaps in Arthur, something like terror leaps in Arthur: something in him sings. He smiles. He whispers, "You all right?"

"I am, now, yes. Thank you." And Crunch smiles.

"You ain't got nothing to thank me for," says Arthur, now feeling very shy, holding the pajama top between his hands.

Crunch looks at him endlessly, very, very gravely, as though he has never seen him before, and Arthur stares at Crunch, blinded by his beauty, by the revelation of his beauty. Deep, deep within him, an absolutely new trembling begins. He does not know if this is happiness, no words are in his mind, but—he has never been so high and lifted up before.

Crunch kisses him on the forehead gravely, then leans up and takes Arthur in his arms. Arthur puts his arms around Crunch. They hold each other, tight, a wonder of joy rising in them like a flood, a wonder of sunlight exploding behind their eyes, everywhere, a great new space opening before them. They need nothing more now, nothing, everything will come, and they know it, everything; they are in each other's arms. They open their eyes at the same moment and look into each other's eyes and laugh.

Crunch kisses Arthur, lightly, on the lips.

"We be alone together soon, okay?"

"Okay."

He has never seen any eyes like Crunch's eyes.

Crunch says gravely, "I love you, you know?"

"I love you," says Arthur. "With all my heart, I love you."

"You and me, then?"

"You and me."

Crunch holds Arthur by the shoulders, then touches his chin lightly with one fist.

"Get some sleep."

"You too."

"Good night."

"Good night."

And Arthur crosses the room, and gets into his bed, holding the pajama top in his arms. Crunch turns out the light, they go to sleep.

They have spent a lot of time alone together, in one way or another: the next morning, they are alone with each other for the first time in their lives. They must hide this secret from all the others—this is strange, and new, and it even hurts a little, for in truth, they would like to rise up, shouting, *Hey, baby, you know what happened?* They cannot shout *hallelujah!* dare not cry *hosanna!*—yet a tremendous, hurting joy wells up from the belly and the loins.

They lay in their separate beds, not daring to look at each other— and also, mysteriously, with no need yet, to look at each other—as the morning light attacked the window shade and crawled across the ceiling, as cars growled by on the road outside, as they listened to Peanut and Red and their hosts, and Webster, in the toilet, in the kitchen, in the hall.

Crunch looked over at Arthur.

"Bathroom's empty. Who goes first?"

"You go," Arthur said, and Crunch rose and draped a towel around his shoulders and bent his long self through the doorway.

Arthur lay still, wishing Crunch had touched him, if only for a second. It really was as though he had never seen Crunch before. He waited helplessly for Crunch to come stooping back through the door; he had never before been afraid of losing him—had never before been afraid of losing anyone, except his father and mother, and me. But our absences had not been at all like the brief absence of Crunch that morning. Arthur waiting in a strange place, a strange bed. He had known that Crunch was tall—now he had abruptly seen, as Crunch bent through the doorway, how *long* he was. He had always liked Crunch's face. Now he had somehow memorized the high cheekbones, like those of an Indian, and how the long, narrow eyes slanted slightly upward and how one eyebrow was always faintly lifted—maybe that was why he almost always looked as though he was about to make fun of you. The nose was long and hooked *like an Indian? Like a Jew?* and two small knobs of bone gleamed faintly on either side of the forehead, just below the hairline. The lips were heavy and full, seemed always ready to smile, or to open in a grin, showing the long, straight, white teeth. The neck and arms and shoulders were powerful. Arthur shifted and turned toward the window. The shade was still drawn, the curtains still closed. Crunch was older than Arthur, but Arthur suddenly saw that Crunch was very, very young. He wanted to take Crunch in his arms and protect him—from the dawn and the road and the cars and the trees outside.

They ate their hominy grits and bacon and eggs, held in their silence, surrounded by the noise. Arthur watched Crunch laughing and joking and making noise; he watched himself laughing and joking and making noise. He made sounds to the host and hostess of the rooming house, and to whoever else, the other roomers, who were there. Webster seemed terribly loud: it was as though Webster, too, were someone he had never seen before. He wondered, for the first time, how old Webster was. He knew the ages of Red and Peanut, but he had never seen them before, either. Peanut's color glowed like peanut butter and honey, and Red's broad, brown, speckled face made Arthur see, as though for the first time, his light brown chocolate eyes. Everything hurt: the napkins and the tablecloth hurt; the black coffee, as the lady poured it, hurt; his smile, when he looked up and said, *Thank you, ma'am,* hurt; the sunlight, relentlessly rising to send them on their way, filling the dining room, crashing in the kitchen among all the pots and pans, thundering in the voices, heard from far away and yet too near, of the cook and the servants—servants?—and the man scouring the pots, hurt, assaulted, began to devastate my brother; and the telephone rang somewhere and someone said, *Excuse me a moment,* and someone else said, *I sure hope you boys enjoy yourselves down here,* and Webster said, *We better make a move,* and Red rose first, and Arthur's heart shook, and then Peanut wiped his lips with the white napkin and smiled, and it hurt; and someone else said, *Bambam, to Birmingham!* and laughter filled the room exactly like the sunlight, and it hurt. And all this time, Crunch had been seated two seats away, laughing and joking and making noise, not looking at him, and yet, and Arthur knew it, entirely concentrated on him, and it hurt. He wanted to run, run, wanted to be with Crunch, somewhere, forever, wanted Crunch to take him in his arms; he did not know what he wanted, the small of his back was wet with terror, *Is this my life?* My *life?* and, to compound this terror, his imagination, like a newly wiped blackboard, held nothing at all, no images at all. Crunch's smell was in his nostrils, the overwhelming image of the hair in his armpits, the basketball player's thighs and ankles, *deep like a river,* Arthur thought, insanely, his arms, his arms; then suddenly, silence dropped on him like a heavy cloud, he looked up, everyone was rising. There was Crunch, on his feet, laughing and joking and making noise, and there was, suddenly, the young lady who had driven all the way back here, this morning, in her father's automobile, to say good-bye to Crunch, and Crunch was holding her lightly in his arms, and it hurt; and Arthur wiped his lips with the white, abrasive, fiery napkin, and rose, and for the first time in his life, the act of rising to his feet made him tremble with anguish, and he shook hands with all the people, and he smiled and he smiled and he heard his voice falling all around his ears from about twenty-seven million miles above his head; his feet, just the same, seemed to be on the ground—though his shoes, suddenly, were too tight, his ankles ached, his toenails seemed to bite into him, suddenly, like the claws of a crab; sweat dripped down inside of his thighs, and Crunch, as though he had known all this all along, looked up, abruptly, looked him directly in his eyes, and said, with a smile which no one else could see—and Arthur saw this, it helped him to move, he had, in truth, been paralyzed—*Come on, little fellow, bam-bam, to Birmingham!* He had one arm around the young lady. With the other arm, he reached out and pulled Arthur to him, he introduced them to each other, Arthur smiled and said the Lord alone knows what, and it hurt, it hurt, it hurt.

They hurried to their room, to pack—they did not have much to pack. Arthur was wet, he was trembling. Crunch locked the door behind them, and stood against the door.

Arthur stood in the center of the room. Crunch watched him.

"What's the matter?"

"Nothing."

He picked up his suitcase, and tried to begin to pack. But he was young, my brother, and he started to cry.

For a second more, Crunch watched him.

"What you crying about?"

"Nothing!"

But he looked up at Crunch with tears spilling down his face; he turned away, and fell on the bed.

Crunch fell on the bed on top of Arthur and turned Arthur to face him and held him in his arms. Crunch wrapped himself around him, arms and legs, held Arthur more tightly than he had ever been held, and kissed him, first like a brother, and then like a lover.

He leaned up, and Arthur opened his eyes.

"What you got to cry about?"

Arthur simply stared at Crunch. He wanted Crunch never to leave him, never to take his arms away.

"Come on, little fellow. We only got a minute. They be knocking on the door in a minute."

Arthur said, terrified, and, at the same time, suddenly at peace, holding on to Crunch, "I'm in love."

Crunch said gravely, after a moment, "That's why you was crying?"

Arthur nodded.

"I don't understand—who you in love with? The young lady? With the automobile?"

Arthur found that he was able to laugh.

"No."

Crunch laughed, too, his belly rumbling against Arthur's belly—in silence: as though their bellies were one.

"With who, then?"

Arthur caught his breath. He watched Crunch's eyes. "With you. I'm in love. With you."

And he caught his breath again. He watched Crunch. Doors began opening down the hall.

"Well—what did I tell you, last night?"

Crunch smiled; then Arthur smiled.

Crunch shook him, lightly.

"Come on—what did I say?"

"You said—you and me."

"What else did I say?"

"You said, you loved me."

"And you don't believe me?"

"I believe you. I—just got scared."

"Why?"

"I've never been in love before," Arthur said—so helplessly that Crunch kissed him again, laughed, kissed him again, and laughed, and stood up.

"Throw them rags in your bag, little fellow—before they come knocking on this door—come on, now."

Arthur rose, and returned to his suitcase.

"I never thought," said Arthur, "that a man could be in love with a man."

Crunch laughed, unlocked and opened the door.

"I never thought about it, neither, love. But I'm sure thinking about it now." He winked, and his whole face changed, holding a kind of mocking, friendly, unabashed desire. "Tell you one thing, you sure ain't got nothing to cry about." He said to Webster, who suddenly appeared in the doorway, "Ready, man, two seconds is all we need." Webster disappeared.

They both closed their suitcases, and Crunch said, in that down-home country-boy preacher's voice, a voice which Arthur was beginning to feel had been meant for his ears alone, it gave him such delight, "We going to be together." He looked down the hall, which was empty, everyone was waiting for them on the porch.

For a second they stood in the doorway, then Crunch touched Arthur's face, lightly. "Come on." He closed their door behind them. They started toward the voices on the porch. Crunch laughed low in his throat, and he whispered, "You think, just because I'm bigger than you that I can't be in love?"

Birmingham *is* a biblical city, in the sense that it awaits the sound of Gabriel's trumpet—mile upon mile upon mile, flat, stretched out, lascivious, the city can suggest no other hope: and the sign of the judgment hangs over the city all day and all night long, in the fiery hills. Arthur thought of Sister Dorothy Green, and wondered why she said, "*Every time* I come to Birmingham." He would certainly never come back here, if he ever got out, and if there was one righteous man here he had to be in an asylum.

They had time to wash and dress, but not to eat—but that was all to the good, Webster explained, for this time their rooming house was next door to a barbecue place, which stayed open all night. They had known that they would miss Paul; they had not known that they would begin to hate Webster. In New York, Webster had seemed to know a lot, and they had trusted him. But down here, they realized that he didn't really know all that much, and they realized this from the music that they heard. They wanted to get close to it, this rough and exquisite sound, not yet known as *funky*—hand out, fall out, try out, get high, and *learn:* there *had* been something, as Crunch said, waiting here for them, all along. In spite of their terror, they were tremendously excited, and their terror, after all, had had nothing to do with black people. They had never known any black people, true, with a house and a lawn, with more than one car, with more than one house for that matter, with *servants;* never been invited for *tea* by a black matron, dressed in a pale blue whispering frock, with hair like Rita Hayworth's; never seen their high-breasted, arrogant daughters, with fingernails which had never rummaged through a garbage can; never encountered such a lofty, irreproachable politeness, such condescension, kindliness, a distance so unquestionably aristocratic; had never shaken hands with the son, blue blazer, open neck white shirt, dark slacks, dark gleaming pumps, a big ring on one finger, *my son is studying law;* never before seen such gleaming sideboards, holding every drink you could imagine; never before shaken hands with a man with a tiepin and a pipe, *our bank president;* never before been smiled down on by *the president of our college.* Peanut and Red and Crunch and Arthur knew that they stank of the ghetto, and had never really been to school, and they knew that a lot of black people they met looked down on them, and that a lot of the sons and daughters were making fun of them, and Peanut's relatives hurt Peanut's feelings— were really very ugly with the boys: but they felt that they could handle that. They didn't really understand it, and yet, they did, and what they didn't understand, they wanted to find out, to *learn.*

But then, here came Webster—sometimes, to their impotent fury, manhandling Crunch's guitar. *He came on,* Arthur told me, later, *like he was Cab Calloway, and we were his Cabettes.* He told everyone how big they were in the North, how he had discovered them, and trained them, made them go to bed early, gave them their cod-liver oil—told everyone listening—college presidents, bank presidents, lawyers, matrons, sons, daughters, servants; told the honeysuckle, wisteria, magnolia; told the long, tall verandas and the somnolent porches, the long, still, flat, country streets; told the fireflies of their punishing schedule, their upcoming dates—in Chicago, in Detroit, in Denver, in Washington and, especially, in New York—and, oh, how hard it was to choose, how he had three phones ringing all the time, saying yes here, saying no there, how his secretaries were tearing their hair,

and soon, he would have to make some kind of decision about England—while the boys stood around him helplessly—fascinated, terrified, humiliated, hating him. They watched the glass in his hand, and
the way, from time to time, he smiled at his hosts—smiled as though
he could buy them and sell them, with a phone call to Pittsburgh.
When the moment came to roll, to get into the station wagon, he always made a joke about the sheriff.

Oh, we know the sheriff, one of the aristocrats might say, *he knows
you've been at our house.*

Good night, one of the boys might say, grimly—with the choked,
despairing politeness of the beleaguered adolescent.

Good night! came back from the shadows, and on went the head-
lights and down the road they went, Webster cursing all the while,
Crunch holding on to his narrowly retrieved guitar.

It was a white city full of black people—they had not thought of
New York this way—and *none but the righteous,* Arthur thought, as
they took their places just below the pulpit, in the Birmingham
church. They were placed so that Peanut, at the piano, could be seen.
Peanut struck the chord, Arthur began the song. Red was to his right
and Crunch to his left, both slightly behind him, as present as heat.

Crunch's guitar began, as Arthur's voice began,

> *Take me to the water*

Crunch moaned,

> *yes! take me to the water!*

He heard Red's witnessing falsetto, but he answered Crunch's
echo,

> *take me to the water*
> *to be*
> *baptized.*

He paused, and closed his eyes, sweat gathered in his hair; he listened to Crunch, then he started again,

> *Take me to the water*
> *yeah!*
> *take me to the water*
> *now!*
> *take me to the water*
> *oh, Lord!*
> *to be*
> *to be?*
> *to be*
> *tell me, now!*
> *to be*
> *to be baptized!*

He paused again, threw back his head to get the sweat out of his eyes, trusting every second of this unprecedented darkness, knowing Crunch and he were moving together, here, now, in the song, to some new place; they had never sung together like this before, his voice in Crunch's sound, Crunch's sound filling his voice,

> *So*
> *I know*
> *none*
> *don't tell me, I know, I know, I know!*

as though Crunch were laughing and crying at the same time

> *but the righteous*
> *so true!*
> *none*
> *don't you leave me now!*
> *but the righteous*

and I hate to see that evening sun go down!
none
amazing grace—!
none but the righteous
yea, little fellow, come on in!
shall see God.

Crunch and he ending together, as though on a single drum. He opened his eyes, bowed his head, stepped back. Red and Peanut looked as though they had been dragged, kicking, through a miracle, but they were smiling, the church was rocking, Crunch and Arthur wiped their brows carefully before they dared look at each other. Peanut struck the chord, *Oh. Oh. Oh. Oh,* and Crunch stepped forward with the guitar, singing, *somebody touched me and,* they sang, *it must have been the hand of the Lord!*

It was a heavy, slow Saturday afternoon in Atlanta, and they were free until Sunday morning. Webster had disappeared early, with many a vivid warning, and they were glad to be on their own; but his warnings remained with them, and the heat was as heavy as the region's molasses. They would have liked to discover the town, and they walked awhile, but they did not dare walk very far. If they got lost, they would have to ask someone for directions, and so they panicked whenever they saw more white faces than black faces. They had been made to know that they were from the North, and that their accents betrayed them and might land them on the chain gang. It happened every day down here, and, the Lord knew, Webster wouldn't be able to help them.

And the city was like a checkerboard. They would walk a block which was all black, then suddenly turn a corner and find themselves surrounded by nothing but white faces. They wanted to run, but, of course, to run meant that the white mob would run after them and they would, then, be lynched. At such moments, they smiled aimlessly, looked in a store window, if there was one, or else elaborately admired the view, slowing their walk to a shuffle. Then, as though the same idea had hit them at the same moment—which it had—they slowly turned and slowly walked back the way they had come. Sometimes they nearly exploded with the terrified laughter they had not dared release until they were again surrounded by black people or back in the rooming house.

So this Saturday afternoon, they returned to the café next to the rooming house. Webster had prepaid their Saturday lunch and dinner. They had a little money in their pockets—not very much, for they had not been paid yet. Webster had all their money. This frightened them, too, but they did not know what to do about it. They had to trust Webster. Wordlessly, though, they trusted Crunch, who was the only one of them who might be able to intimidate Webster.

They sat down in the café, which was nearly empty—they had not yet realized that Southerners move about as little as possible on hot summer afternoons: in general, that is, due to imponderables to which they were reacting, but did not understand—and Peanut and Crunch went to the counter, and brought back four Pepsi-Colas.

"Tell you," said Red. "This trip is starting to fuck with my nerves. Can't wait to get back to Seventh Avenue."

"When you was there," said Arthur, smiling, "you couldn't wait to get away." He lit a cigarette and put the pack on the table. "But I know how you feel."

"We just ain't used to it," Peanut said. "And we don't know nobody. Be different, next time."

"How?" asked Red. "How we going to get to know somebody *next* time? You going to write a letter to the governor?"

Crunch laughed, and picked up the pack of cigarettes, and lit one.

"Well," said Peanut, "if we keep coming back, we *bound* to get to know—*somebody*—"

They all laughed, and, after a moment, Peanut laughed. Crunch said, "Well, *you* know somebody—at least, you *knew* somebody—them cousins of yours in Charlotte—"

Peanut sighed and looked down at the table. "Yeah. I'm sorry about that."

Crunch leaned across the table and clapped Peanut on the shoulder. "What *you* sorry about? *You* can't help it if your cousins are fools."

Peanut is the lightest of us, and Crunch is the darkest, and Peanut's cousins *proved* that they did not like dark meat. They hurt Crunch's feelings, and they reminded Peanut of his bewildering grandmother.

"Oh, little by little, we'll figure out how to move," Red said cheerfully. "I'll find me a swinging chick at one of these church socials and make her be our guide."

"These chicks all looking to get married, man," Crunch said. "And they don't want to marry none of us. What do a bank president's daughter want with—a wandering *troubador*?"

"Oh, hell, Crunch," said Peanut. "Love will find a way."

"Not down here, in the land of cotton," Arthur said, and they laughed.

"Anyway," Crunch said after a moment, "little Arthur's the only one liable to come down here next time."

They all looked at Crunch. "Why?" asked Arthur.

Crunch looked at Arthur. "Where's your brother?"

Arthur said, "My brother?" and stared at Crunch. His heart thundered like an express train, stopped.

"Oh, shit," said Red. "You right."

"Right about what?" Arthur asked. But he knew. He had never thought of it.

"Uncle Sam is saving some people over yonder," Crunch said. "He's making the world safe for democracy again, and he needs some niggers for the latrine detail."

The table became very silent.

"Shit," Red said again.

Arthur said nothing. He did not know what to say. He did not dare look up. He looked at the white marble table, and the brown rings made by the Pepsi-Cola bottles. Then he looked very carefully at the flypaper suspended from the ceiling, with flies sticking, stuck, on the yellow paper. He wondered how many flies there were, and thought of counting them. He was suddenly aware that there was an electric fan whirring nearby—if you put your fingers in the fan, the blades would chop your fingers off. He did not think of me at all—he was not thinking.

"Well, let's not sit here like this," Peanut said shakily. "Let's do something."

Yes, but what? A movie would have been ideal, but then, there was the question of whether black people sat in the balcony, or came in through the back door. None of them knew how it worked down here—they had forgotten to ask, or couldn't remember the answers.

"Hell," Red said, suddenly, "there's a black pool hall on the corner, let's go shoot some pool."

"Okay," Crunch said, and everybody rose except Arthur. They all looked at him.

"Ain't you coming?"

"Look," Arthur said calmly, with a smile, "You all go ahead. I might pick you up later. I got a little headache, I just want to lie down."

Crunch raised that eyebrow at him. "You sure?"

"Yeah, I'm all right. You cats go on, I'll dig you later."

"Okay."

The three of them pranced out into the sun, paused for a moment, laughing, before the great glass window. Arthur waited until they had disappeared. Then he rose slowly, leaning lightly on the table, and walked outside. The sun was like a blow. He looked in the direction the boys had taken—saw them, on the still, far corner, ambling across the street.

Then he turned in the opposite direction. The rooming house was next door, really more like a hotel, a narrow, three-story building. Peanut and Red and Webster were on the ground floor. He and Crunch were on the top floor. He walked into the long, dark, narrow hall, which was absolutely silent, and slowly, shaking, climbed the stairs.

He was covered with cold sweat by the time he reached the top floor, and his hands were shaking so hard he could hardly get the key in the lock, but, at last, the door swung open. Sunlight hammered on the room, and he crossed to the window and pulled down the shade. He ran cold water in the sink, and plunged his face and head under, blindly found the towel, and dried himself. He kicked off his shoes, unpeeled his socks, took off his shirt and trousers, and lay down on Crunch's bed. *Korea.*

He lay there for a long time, numb, as empty as the listening silence, stunned. He lay on his back. The air did not move. He did not move. The sun would not move, the earth, the stars, the moon, the planets, whatever held it all together, the big wheel and the little wheel, and the boulder of his sorrow, which had dropped on him and pinned him to this bed, nothing would move, until he saw Crunch. *Korea.* He fell asleep.

Crunch shook him gently. The room was half dark, not dark yet. Crunch sat on the edge of the bed, looking at him carefully, with that eyebrow raised, half smiling, half frowning.

"You feel better?"

Arthur stared, saying nothing, then he smiled.

"You're back."

"Of course I'm back. You feel better?"

Arthur moved and put his head in Crunch's lap, holding on to him and staring up at him.

The room grew darker. They were alone. Crunch leaned down, and kissed him. Arthur held on to Crunch with all his strength, with all his tears, tears he had not yet begun to shed. Crunch leaned up.

"Let me lock the door," he whispered.

Arthur sat up, and watched Crunch lock the door.

He did it very elaborately, and then turned, grinning, with one finger to his lips.

"We all alone, now, little fellow. Ain't nobody on this floor but us. And it's Saturday night, anyway, *everybody's* out." He grinned, and then his face changed, he stood at the door, looking at Arthur.

"Where's Peanut and Red?"

Arthur was whispering, and Crunch whispered, "I left them in the pool hall. They found some friends."

"They coming back?"

"I told them I was taking you someplace."

He sat down on the bed again, and started taking off his shoes. He looked over at Arthur. "Did I do right?"

"Sure."

"Get under the covers."

Arthur watched as Crunch stripped—Crunch was whistling, low in his throat: and it came to Arthur, with great astonishment, that Crunch was whistling because he was happy—was happy to be here, with Arthur. Arthur watched as Crunch unbuttoned his shirt, watched the long, dark fingers against the buttons and the cloth, watched the cloth fly across the room to land on the other bed, watched as he unbuckled his belt, dropped his trousers, raising one knee then the other, sitting on the bed again to pull the trousers past the big feet, then folding the trousers, and rising to place them on the other bed, pulling off his undershirt, kicking off his shorts, his whole, long, black self padding to the small sink, where he looked, briefly, into the mirror, ran cold water, gargled, his dark body glowing in the darkening room, a miracle of spinal column, neck to buttocks, shoulders and shoulder blades, elbows, wrists, thighs, ankles, a miracle of bone and blood and muscle and flesh and music. Arthur was still wearing his undershirt and his shorts. He hated being naked in front of anyone, even me—perhaps, especially me; I had sometimes given him his bath: but that had been under another condition, for which he had not been responsible, and which he was not compelled to remember. Nakedness had not, then, been a confession, or a vow. Arthur was frightened; then, he wasn't frightened, but he found that he could not move. He could not take off his undershirt. He could not take off his shorts. Crunch turned, and Arthur, in a kind of peaceful terror, watched as the face, and the eyes in that face, and the neck and the chest, and the nipples on the chest, and the ribs and the long flat belly and the belly button and the jungle of hair spinning upward from the long, dark, heavy, swinging sex approached, and Crunch got under the covers, and took Arthur in his arms.

Crunch sighed, a weary, trusting sigh, and put his hands under Arthur's undershirt and pulled it over Arthur's head, and, suddenly, they both laughed, a whispering laugh. Crunch dropped the undershirt on the floor.

"That's called progress," Crunch whispered. "And now," he said, "let's see what we can do down yonder."

He put his hands at Arthur's waist, pulled the shorts down, got them past one foot. Arthur's prick rose.

Crunch stroked it, and grinned. "That's enough progress, for now," he said, but he put his rigid sex against Arthur's, and then they simply lay there, holding on to each other, unable to make another move. They really did not know where another move might carry them. Arthur was afraid in one way, and Crunch in another. It was also as though they had expended so much energy to arrive at this moment that they had to fall out and catch their breath, this moment was almost enough. But it was only a moment: the train was boarded, the engine ready to roll. They held on to each other. This might be the beginning; it might be the beginning of the end. The train was boarded, the engine pulsing, great doors were slamming shut behind them, the train would soon be moving, a journey had begun. They might lose each other on this journey; nothing could be hidden on this journey. They might look at each other, miles from now, when the train stopped at some unimaginable place, and wish never to see each other again. They might be ashamed—they might be debased: they might be forever lost.

Arthur was less frightened than Crunch. He simply held on to Crunch and stroked him and kissed him, for, in the center of his mind's eye, there was Crunch in uniform, Crunch gone, Crunch forever gone, and, now that he had found him, his mind became as still and empty as the winter sky, at the thought of losing him. He held this blankness as far inside him as he held his tears—for, something told him that Crunch could not bear his tears, could not bear anybody's tears. Tears were a weapon you could use against Crunch.

And Crunch—ah, Crunch. He held my brother, falling in love— falling in love with the little fellow. Crunch was older than Arthur, lonelier than Arthur, knew more about himself than Arthur knew. He had never been on this train, true; but he had been landed in some desolate places. He held him closer, falling in love, his prick stiffening, his need rising, his hope rising; the train began to move, Arthur held him closer, and Crunch moved closer, becoming more naked, praying that Arthur would receive his nakedness.

His long self covered Arthur, his tongue licked Arthur's nipples, his armpits, his belly button. He did not dare go further, yet; shaking, he raised himself to Arthur's lips. He took Arthur's sex in his fist.

"Do me like I do you," he whispered. "Little fellow, come on, this is just the beginning," and Arthur, with a kind of miraculous understanding, kissed Crunch's nipples, slid down to kiss his sex, moved up to his lips again. As he felt Crunch pulsing, he pulsed with Crunch, coaxed the pulsing vein at the underside of the organ as Crunch coaxed his, scarcely breathing. Crunch groaned, *little fellow,* groaned again, they seemed to hang for a second in a splintered, blinding air, then Crunch's sperm shot out against Arthur's belly, Arthur's shot against his, it was though each were coming through the other's sex.

They lay in each other's arms.

Crunch looked into his Arthur's eyes.

"Hi."

"Hi, yourself."

Their breathing slowed. Neither wanted to move.

"You think we making progress?"

"I'm with you."

They laughed, holding on to each other, wet with each other.

Crunch asked shyly, "Do you still love me?"

"Maybe we should make some more progress."

Crunch shook with laughter, silently, and Arthur shook with joy, watching him. "Right now?"

"Whenever you ready."

"Oh—come on—!" said Crunch.

"That's what I said."

"You—you something—"

"I love you. I'd do anything for you," said Arthur.

Crunch watched him. "For true?"

"For true."

Crunch held him tighter.

"I want to make love with you—every way possible—I don't care what happens—as long as I can hold you." He watched Arthur's eyes; but he was beginning to feel at peace.

"You want to make progress, *I'll* make progress. We'll make progress together."

Crunch asked, "You and me, then?"

"You and me."

The room was dark. They heard the night outside. They did not want to leave each other's arms.

Crunch asked, "You hungry?"

"No—not now."

"You want to wash up?"

"No. Not yet."

"What you want to do then?"

"Maybe sleep a little—next to you."

"Okay."

They curled into each other, spoon fashion, Arthur cradled by Crunch.

They did not sleep long. Arthur woke up, and peed in the sink, as quietly as possible. He ran the water as quietly as possible. He lifted the shade, and looked out of the window. It was night, he guessed it to be around nine or ten o'clock; there were not as many people in the street as there would have been on a Saturday night in Harlem. Most of the people were already inside some place, or they were on their way, and their voices, and their music, muffled, filled the air, filled the room. He dropped the shade.

Crunch lay as he had left him. One arm was at his side, one arm lay stretched where Arthur had been. His breathing was deep and slow—yet Arthur sensed that Crunch was not entirely lost in sleep. Arthur crawled back into bed, pulling the covers back up. The moment he crawled into bed, Crunch, still sleeping, pulled Arthur into his arms.

And yet, Crunch lay as one helpless. Arthur was incited by this helplessness, the willing helplessness of the body in his arms. He kissed Crunch, who moaned, but did not stir. He ran his hands up and down the long body. He seemed to discover the mystery of geography, of space and time, the lightning flash of tension between one—moment?—one breath and the next breath. The breathing in—the breathing out. The miracle of air, entering, and the chest rose: the miracle of air transformed into the miracle of breath, coming out, into your face, mixed with Pepsi-Cola, hamburgers, mustard, whatever was in the bowels: and the chest fell. He lay in this urgency for a while, terrified, and happy.

He held Crunch closer, running his fingers up and down the barely tactile complex telegraph system of the spine. His hands dared to discover Crunch's beautiful buttocks, his ass, his behind. He stroked the gift between his legs which held the present and the future. Their sex became rigid. Crunch growled, turned on his back, still holding Arthur.

Arthur moved, in Crunch's arms, belly to belly. Pepsi-Cola, mustard, and onions and hamburgers and Crunch's rising prick: Crunch moaned. Arthur knew something that he did not know he knew—he did not know that he knew that Crunch waited for Arthur's lips at his neck, Arthur's tongue at the nipples of his chest. Pepsi-Cola, mustard, hamburgers, ice cream, surrendered to funkier, unknown odors; Crunch moaned again, surrendering, surrendering, as Arthur's tongue descended Crunch's long black self, down to the raging penis. He licked the underside of the penis, feeling it leap, and he licked the balls. He was setting Crunch free—he was giving Crunch what he, somehow, knew that Crunch longed and feared to give him. He took the penis into his mouth, it moved, with the ease of satin, past his lips, into his throat. For a moment, he was terrified: what now? For the organ was hard and huge and throbbing, Crunch's hands came down, but lightly, on Arthur's head, he began to thrust upward, but carefully, into Arthur's mouth.

Arthur understood Crunch's terror—the terror of someone in the water, being carried away from the shore—and this terror, which was his own terror, soon caused him to gasp, to attempt to pull away, at the same time that he held on. His awareness of Crunch's terror helped him to overcome his own. He had never done this before. In the same way that he knew how Crunch feared to be despised—by him—he knew, too, that he, now, feared to be despised by Crunch. *Cocksucker.*

Well. It was Crunch's cock, and so he sucked it; with all the love that was in him, and a moment came when he felt that love being trusted, and returned. A moment came when he felt Crunch pass from a kind of terrified bewilderment into joy. A friendly, a joyful movement, began. *So high, you can't get over him.*

Sweat from Arthur's forehead fell onto Crunch's belly.

So low—and Crunch gasped as Arthur's mouth left his prick standing in the cold, cold air, as Arthur's tongue licked his sacred balls—*you can't get under him.* Arthur rose, again, to Crunch's lips. *So wide. You can't get around him.* It was as though, with this kiss, they were forever bound together. Crunch moaned, in an absolute agony, and Arthur went down again.

"Little fellow. Baby. Love."

You must come in at the door.

He held the prick in his mouth again, sensing, awaiting, the eruption. He, and he alone, had dragged it up from the depths of his lover.

"Oh. Little fellow."

Then, shaking like an earthquake, "Oh, my love. Oh, love."

Atlanta was still. The world was still. Nothing moved in the heavens.

"Oh. Love."

Curious, the taste, as it came, leaping, to the surface: of Crunch's prick, of Arthur's tongue, into Arthur's mouth and throat. He was frightened, but triumphant. He wanted to sing. The taste was volcanic. This taste, the aftertaste, this anguish, and this joy had changed all tastes forever. The bottom of his throat was sore, his lips were weary. Every time he swallowed, from here on, he would think of Crunch, and this thought made him smile as, slowly, now, and in a peculiar joy and panic, he allowed Crunch to pull him up, upward, into his arms.

He dared to look into Crunch's eyes. Crunch's eyes were wet and deep *deep like a river*, and Arthur found that he was smiling *peace like a river*.

Arthur asked Crunch, "All right? do you feel all right?"

Crunch put Arthur's head on his chest, ran one long hand up and down Arthur.

"You're the most beautiful thing ever happened to me, baby," he said. "That's how I feel." Then, "Thank you, Arthur."

"For what?" Arthur asked—teasing, bewildered, triumphant— and safe in Crunch's arms.

"For loving me," Crunch said.

After a moment, he pulled up the covers. They went to sleep, spoon fashion, Arthur cradling Crunch.

Nothing can be hidden; secrets do not exist. They were on the road for ten more days. They were called the "lovebirds," they were called "Romeo and Romeo." They laughed, with their arms around each other sometimes, far too happy to be afraid. For one thing, they were far too young to be afraid. As far as they knew, and as far as they cared, what was happening between them had never before happened in the entire history of the world. Other people had words for whatever it was, too bad, too sad—they were not to be found in that dictionary. They walked in the light of each other's eyes, absolutely unaware of white people or black people, waking up, sometimes, in each other's arms, not knowing what town it was, and not caring: they were called "lovebirds" and "Romeo and Romeo" because they were alone, they were far from other people, they were in danger.

Peanut and Red were happy simply because Crunch and Arthur were happy. They responded to the outward signs: Arthur laughed and talked more and ate more, and Crunch, before their eyes, seemed to become the lord of a vast and beautiful territory. Arthur was his princedom, or, because of Arthur, he began to stride—Crunch was in love. Yes. That is the only way to put it. And Arthur, my brother, Arthur—he was in love, certainly, as irrepressible as a puppy; if Crunch strode on those long legs of his, Arthur seemed to get from one place to another by unpredictable leaps and lunges; but he was far less vulnerable. He did not know this then, he adored Crunch, but time was to reveal to Arthur, and in an unspeakable anguish, the algebra of his life. When, many years later, Crunch was dragged, howling, away from us, with that dreadful space in his mouth where his teeth had been, the sands in Arthur began to shift into that despair which was to kill him. Arthur was stronger than Crunch: it is as simple, as dreadful, and as mysterious as that. Arthur could bear solitude, had been born to it, and could never be surprised by it, however mightily he might be tormented: Crunch feared solitude, and was easily bewildered, he could not love without love. But Arthur could live on stones—he sought love everywhere, but he could live on stones. He could wring nourishment from the silence of stone. He could surrender to Crunch so eagerly, and give all of himself, because not all of himself was his to give. There was, in him, a secret place which could scarcely be entered—*a goddamm echo chamber!*—he was to cry to me much later, where Arthur paced alone.

He did not know this then. He began to be reconciled to this near the end of his life, with his last lover, Jimmy, who was the only person in Arthur's life as strong as he, who loved him more than Arthur ever knew; Jimmy, who trusted Arthur's secret place, who knew he could not live if it were violated, who calculated, coldly, in towns, in planes, in beds, sometimes with Arthur's arms around him, how to keep his lover alive, how to live if his lover was gone.

But then—Arthur knew nothing about death, Peanut and Red knew nothing of love or passion. Crunch and Arthur were funny, and there was a light around them—perhaps, in their differing ways, Peanut and Red smelled a certain freedom, the way a horse smells water. They did not think of Crunch and Arthur as lovers, a condition which they could not, yet, really imagine, but as two cats who had something very deep going for each other: in the same way that Red was Peanut's "heart." That was really all there was to know. All else was a private matter, and it would never have occurred to them to violate this privacy.

But Webster was a very different matter.

"What's going on between you two?" he demanded of Crunch. This was on a Sunday afternoon, on the steps of a church in a Virginia backwater—from here they went to Washington, D.C., and home.

"What's that, sir?" Crunch asked very carefully.

Arthur and Red and Peanut were somewhere behind them. Crunch walked as slowly as possible.

"You hard of hearing?"

"Sometimes, sir. When people don't speak up. Or when they—shout."

They were forced to continue descending the steps.

"The boys," said Webster. "I hear them call you lovebirds. And you and little Arthur, you and him always running off together." He looked at Crunch, who walked slowly, looking at the ground.

"I wouldn't let what the boys say worry me none," Crunch said. "They just fooling around—boys will be boys," he added, and looked into Webster's face.

"I'll ask you again," said Webster. They were now at the bottom of the steps. They were forced to keep moving because of the people behind them, and because they could not afford to seem to be quarreling.

They walked for a few seconds. Crunch did not look behind him, for he knew that Arthur could see *him:* nevertheless, he walked very slowly.

"What was your question, sir?"

Webster looked at Crunch, and Crunch looked at Webster.

"I'm a very understanding guy," Webster said, slowly. "You don't know me."

Crunch said nothing.

"Shall I ask you the question again?"

"Yes. Maybe you better."

"You two"—they stopped, and looked at each other—"what you doing?"

Crunch looked behind him. He signaled Arthur. Arthur signaled back, and started toward him.

Crunch, with his hands in his pockets, turned and looked at Webster, and grinned.

"What do you mean? What do you *think* we doing?"

They kept walking, in the chilly air, and Crunch allowed his guitar to bounce, lightly, on his back.

"I told you—I'm a very understanding guy."

"You so understanding, you want to know what we doing. Why?"

"I might want to do it, too."

Crunch stared at Webster, then said, in a shaking voice, "You don't know what we doing, but you might want to do it, too."

"Why not? Or—I can always make you change rooms."

Crunch stopped. He and Webster looked at each other. Crunch threw back his head and laughed. Carefully, he fingered the shoulder strap of his guitar.

"You ain't going to make no changes, you slimy mother-fucker," he said, cheerfully. "I'll beat your brains out if you try. And I'll tell *everybody* what *you* doing—you don't *know* what *I'm* doing. Anyway, we going home, faggot, and we don't need you no more." He kept his voice low and cheerful, with a slight smile on his face, for the benefit of the people. "Tell you something else—you say a word to a living ass, or you try to lay a hand on Arthur, you won't have no tongue, no hands, and no asshole—you'll find yourself in a mighty sorry condition. We going to finish up down here, real sweet and easy, and then we going home and we don't need you no more, ever. You going to pay us, and we going home. And I *know*—*you* know—that *I* know you going to pay us."

Arthur came loping up, and Crunch laughed and threw one arm around him, the guitar rang, lightly, in the chilly wind.

"Anyway, you *can't* do what we do, brother. You can't sing."

Webster certainly could not imagine what Arthur and Crunch would find themselves doing, an hour or so before they had to jump in the shower and put on their clothes and rush out and face the people— wrestling all around the room, laughing, knowing that the clock was ticking, but so happy that they knew that, somehow, they would be dressed and ready and go out and do their number—so that they could come home, and fall out, and make love again. They were beginning to know each other; the biblical phrase unlocked itself and held them together in a joy as sharp as terror. Crunch lay on his belly for Arthur and pulled Arthur into him, and Arthur lay on his belly for Crunch, and Crunch entered Arthur—it was incredible that it hurt so much, and yet, hurt so little, that so profound an anguish, thrusting so hard, so deep, accomplished such a transformation, *I looked at my hands and they looked new, I looked at my feet and they did, too!* But that is how they sang, really, something like fifteen minutes later, out of the joy of their surrender and deliverance, out of their secret knowledge that each contained the other.

Webster paid the boys, in Washington, ironically meticulous, and with a hostility covered no more effectively—though certainly as vividly—than Adam and Eve imagined themselves to be covered by the poor fig leaves when God came stalking through the garden. He did not, and he clearly regretted this, have anything resembling a flaming sword; and, furthermore, unlike God, he had no way of knowing what the boys might have whispered among themselves concerning his performance as the serpent. He not only lacked the flaming sword, but, what was worse, he had no apple.

Peanut and Red were bewildered. They thought that Webster's manner might have been caused by the fact—the news—that Crunch and Arthur were not coming to New York with them. Crunch had "business," in Washington, some people he had to see: he and Arthur were going to stay in Washington for a day or two, and would be coming home by train.

Webster protested that he had to say something to the child's parents. But Crunch said that he and Arthur had already got our parents' permission, which was true. It had been Crunch's idea, and he was risking a lot: for he was, after all, more than three years older than Arthur, and he could not really know what Webster might say, once in New York. But he knew that Paul and Florence trusted him—he gambled on his love. He felt that no one who loved Arthur could doubt how much Crunch loved him. And he was right about that, I would know.

The shadow of their separation, so soon, the shadow of the army, of Korea, fell more heavily every day, on him and on Arthur. They would have taken almost any risk in order to be alone with each other, for a few more hours.

They would not be alone in New York, not in the same way. Arthur would be with his mother and his father. Crunch had a furnished room, downtown, on Fourteenth Street and Third Avenue, but he would really be with *his* family, and he had, furthermore, another problem: he had to have money for his mother.

But he had to be with Arthur, too, and Arthur did not have to have money for his mother. Arthur was expected to have made some money for *himself*. This came, in a way, to the same thing, but Arthur's margin was wider, it was a bridge he could cross when he got to it.

The shadow of the army was heavy, also, on Peanut and Red, but, in a way, they looked forward to it. Peanut would not be sorry to leave his grandmother, and Red would not be sorry to leave the streets. And Crunch might have looked forward to it, too, had there not been so much holding him—his mother, his brothers, and sisters. And he could quickly have been reconciled even to that, since his mother would have an allotment and the children would not starve—but: there was Arthur. He was in love, for the first time consciously, and as perhaps only the very young can be in love. He fell deeper in love with every hour, he loved Arthur more every day. If he had felt a certain panic, bewilderment, at the realization that he had fallen in love with a male, this panic was as nothing compared to his private apprehension that he was more in love with Arthur than Arthur was with him. Arthur was younger, blazed with wonder, as elusive and unpredictable as a kitten. He would be a full-grown cat when Crunch came back—what they might have longed to endure together each would have been forced to endure alone. They would be changed. Red and Peanut dreaded, and anticipated, the end of their youth, in unimaginable conditions, far from home, but Crunch's youth was ending here, now, where he stood.

The ground floor of the hotel was a drugstore, which seemed to be open around the clock, never empty, never still. It seemed to function as black community headquarters. Later, Arthur was to discover it, at five o'clock in the morning, still open, with a lone black lady, wearing a hat, sitting at the counter, staring down into her coffee, belching her wine, or with a black boy, sitting, stoned, at one of the tables.

Webster, after he had paid the boys, decided to double-check with Paul and Florence, and went into a phone booth. Arthur opened the door of the phone booth, and stood there while Webster talked. He did not ask to speak to his parents. Webster said his good-byes, and hung up.

"Didn't they say it was all right?" Arthur asked.

"Yeah," said Webster irritably. "They said it was all right. I just had to double-check, that's all."

"I understand, sir," Arthur said. "I was just double-checking, myself."

Webster looked at him sharply, but Arthur did not look at Webster, and they walked through the drugstore, onto the sidewalk, where Peanut, Crunch, and Red stood talking, next to the station wagon.

"Is everything all right, then, sir?" Crunch asked cheerfully, of Webster—but the question was directed at Arthur.

Both Arthur and Webster understood this, but only Webster was compelled to reply.

"Everything's all right," said Webster, and got into the car. He leaned out of the window. "Come on now, we ready to roll."

The boys shook hands and held each other's shoulders a moment, all four of them terrified now. Crunch was the first to move—he leaned in the window, saying to Webster, "Drive carefully, man, you got a precious cargo, you hear?"

Red and Peanut got into the station wagon, Red in front, Peanut in back.

"See you in a couple of days!" cried Arthur.

The station wagon moved out into the traffic, the hands of the boys waving outside the windows. Peanut turned all the way around, his face against the back window, his long hand waving in the air.

Crunch and Arthur stood on the sidewalk until the wagon stopped at the first red light. The light changed, and the wagon disappeared.

Crunch turned and looked at Arthur, his hands in his pockets.

"Hey. Little fellow."

"Hey, yourself."

They had a room on the top floor, just under the roof, in this unknown and really somewhat terrifying hotel; it was the end of summer.

"Let's go on up and change," Crunch said, "and maybe try to see this town?"

With his hands in his pockets and that eyebrow raised, and leaning toward the kid, like a tower leans.

"Okay."

They walked back into the drugstore. At the end of the length of the drugstore were doors opening onto the hotel lobby, and the elevator. A jukebox was playing. The counter sold ice cream sodas, Arthur noted, sandwiches, tea, milk, and hot dogs—the counter was too busy, and Crunch and Arthur were moving too fast for Arthur to be able to register it all.

"Hey!" he told Crunch. "We can eat here!"

Crunch was striding to the doors which led to the hotel lobby. He slowed his pace.

"You hungry?"

"No. Not yet. I just wonder how long it stays open."

They walked through the doors, into the hotel lobby. Crunch had kept the hotel key in his pocket, and so they walked straight to the elevators. Crunch had stayed in one or two hotels before this, on his own, but Arthur never had. He was fascinated by everything, and terrified—fascinated by what he took to be space, and splendor, terrified by the noise. All of the faces they passed were black. The sound was black. Dimly, swiftly, from far away, a white face might move into the light, then out of it. The white face might gleam in a distant corridor, opening or closing a door, or be discerned, briefly, behind the wire mesh of a cage. Otherwise the faces were black.

The elevator operator, who took his time arriving, was black.

"How you boys doing?" he asked, with a fine and friendly indifference and Crunch said, "Just fine, sir," and gave him the number of their floor.

"Ah," said the old black man, "you going to the *pent*house. I *know* how you boys doing."

The elevator groaned upward, and, eventually, he stopped it, and opened the doors. "Watch your step," he said. "Good night."

"Thank you, sir," Crunch said. He pushed Arthur out before him. "Could you tell me, sir, how long the drugstore downstairs stays open?"

"It don't never *really* close. But, if you want to eat, hit it before two o'clock in the morning. Later than that, you taking a chance—and not just on the food—"

"Thank you, sir," said Crunch, after a moment. "Good night."

"Good night," said the old one. "Don't let the noise up here bother you." He closed the elevator doors, and the elevator groaned on down.

But now, it was the early afternoon, and there was no noise at all. The walked the silence to their room, and Crunch unlocked the door. They entered the room, the low and stifling room, just under the roof, a room with two short, narrow beds, one window, a small sink with a naked light bulb over it, the only light in the room.

Crunch locked the door behind them, and leaned against the door. He looked at the room.

"I reckon we going be sleeping on the floor," he said.

Then he looked at Arthur. Then he laughed—leaned his head against the door, opened his arms, and laughed out loud. Then he stopped laughing, pulled Arthur into his arms, stroked that face, and kissed it, looking into Arthur's eyes.

"Don't tell me," he said. "I know. I know I'm crazy. I'm crazy about you, I'm where I want to be—okay?"

Arthur murmured, "You sure ask some crazy questions, man. I don't mind sleeping on the floor."

Whoever is born in New York is ill-equipped to deal with any other city: all other cities seem, at best, a mistake, and, at worst, a fraud. No other city is so spitefully incoherent. Whereas other cities flaunt their history—their presumed glory—in vividly placed monuments, squares, parks, plaques, and boulevards, such history as New York has been unable entirely to obliterate is to be found, mainly, in the backwaters of Wall Street, in the goat tracks of Old and West Broadway, in and around Washington Square, and, for the relentless searcher, in grimly inaccessible regions of The Bronx. There are some exceedingly vivid monuments along Riverside Drive, but Riverside Drive, alas for history, is on the western edge of Harlem. No plaque indicates that Harlem was once a Dutch province, with two *d*'s to its name, or that the movie house, on 42nd Street, the New Amsterdam, bears the name the city was given when, again by means of the Dutch, it entered recorded, or acceptable, history. The Dutch lost the city to the English, who, being passionately devoted to a city on their island named York, decided that this was *New* York. The name of the island, an Indian name, Manhattan, was never changed. The conquerors had overlooked something. I always like to think that the spirit of the violated land had whispered, *thus far, but no farther. Manhattan,* the island on which the city rests, is stronger than New York. As time has begun to indicate; as we shall see.

On the other hand, the spiteful incoherence of New York is, at bottom, more bearable than the grotesque pieties of Philadelphia, say, or Boston, or Washington. No one in Philadelphia gives a shit about Benjamin Franklin. No one in Boston gives a shit about Crispus Attucks, or for that so celebrated and overestimated tea party—an event which, clearly, on the basis of the history of the city, was a purely mercantile, exasperated upheaval, involving nothing more noble than self-interest.

What breaks the heart, though, is that self-interest is indispensable to any human endeavor, is the universal human motor, and is noble or ignoble, depending on one's concept of the self. I have said, for example, that I knew I could not live without my brother: can anyone? At the very least, *my* self would have been a very different *self* without him, if indeed, that self would have been able to live at all. I am tipping my hand, I am jumping ahead, but no matter. *Beloved. Beloved. Now, we are the sons of God*—the first song Arthur sang, after they had arrived in New York, and when he knew that Crunch was with Julia, was trying to heal her by the laying on of hands. I'm not joking, children, compassion can be as various and as devastating as the sin of pride.

My brother, turning sixteen then, was alone, and in torment, and in love. He sang, he had to sing, as though music could really accomplish the miracle of making the walls come tumbling down. He sang:

as Julia abandoned her ministry, Arthur began to discover his. But the song which transformed others failed to transform him.

His principal impression of Washington, then, was that it was, itself, the most arrogant and hideous of monuments, designed—this was the general boast—by a Frenchman. Whoever designed it had failed to see the future.

Much later, Arthur returned to Washington, with me, on a civil rights tour. After we left the Lincoln Memorial, Arthur drove us through the city and we stopped for a moment before the desolate hotel in which he and Crunch had lived, under the roof—where, dripping with sweat, they had put their mattresses on the floor, beneath the open window, and, in the still, stale, humid air, made love.

Crunch and Arthur had been in New York about five or six days when Crunch ran into Julia. It was a Saturday, at dusk, on 125th Street. He had just crossed Seventh Avenue, and was heading toward Lenox and the subway. As always on Saturday evenings, the street was full of people, full of good-natured noise; it sounded good-natured, anyway, until and unless you had a reason to listen to it carefully. There were the stores on either side of him, and the bars, the music coming from everywhere. There seemed to be children on this street at almost any hour—running from, or to, a spanking, one hoped. Matrons walked with a stolid authority, rarely looking in the store windows, headed directly toward whatever they were going to buy; their demeanor indicated that they would never buy anything up here, if they could help it. Boys and girls together walked more slowly, pausing to look in the windows—nudging each other, pointing, laughing, walking on—as did the young girls, who were generally noisier, walking in twos and threes. It was warm, and the clothes the people wore made them seem colorful and friendly.

A very handsome, very dark girl, wearing a yellow sweater and bright red slacks, came out of a store entrance, carrying a box; and Crunch slowed his stride a little, and turned his head, giving the girl an admiring look. Thus he bumped into someone, a girl—he was aware only of huge eyes in a gaunt face; and "Excuse me," he said, and kept walking—and then stopped and turned around. The girl had stopped, too, and was staring at him.

It was Julia. Yet it scarcely seemed to be Julia. In the dusk, which was lighted by streetlamps and storewindows and in which people were moving, restlessly and relentlessly, all around him, Crunch almost felt that he was standing in a dream. Julia stood very straight and still—her face opened in the smile he remembered. Yet it did not seem to be Julia.

He moved, and put both hands on her shoulders.

"Sister Julia! How are you, child?"

"I can't complain, Crunch. I'm still alive."

But a short time ago, she would have said, *I praise the Lord for His keeping power,* and it would not have occurred to Crunch to put his hands on her shoulders.

He felt lost. He took his hands away, and put them in his pockets.

"I was mighty sorry," he said, "to hear about your mother."

"Yes," said Julia. "She's gone, and I miss her."

But this isn't Julia! Julia would have said, *Yes. The Lord has taken her home, to be with Him in glory. Blessed be the name of the Lord.* Crunch felt more and more frightened, he did not know why.

"And how's little Jimmy? And—and your father?"

She was all in black; but she seemed, somehow, to be dressed differently than usual. She was wearing high heels. He wondered if she was really wearing a little makeup—he didn't trust his eyes. Her thick, black hair was arranged differently, he could hardly have said how, but it made him aware of her forehead. Her hair seemed to give off a strange, dry, acrid odor, an odor he associated with old age and dying.

But she, suddenly, had no age. Something happened behind her eyes, something unreadable, as he watched her, and she said, "Oh, little Jimmy's been taken out of harm's way, he's down in New Orleans, with his grandmother. And my father"—she smiled, briefly, shrugged, and said—"he's just the same."

"You still at the same place?"

"Yes," said Julia. "Just him and me." She looked at Crunch, her eyes larger and darker than ever. "It would be nice if you could drop by and see us—you, and Arthur and Red and Peanut. How are they?"

Crunch was meeting Arthur on Fourteenth Street. He said, "They're all fine."

"And how did the summer go?"

"It went all right—it went—*good*, I'd say. But now—" He paused. He really hated to talk about it.

"Now what?"

They had moved to the edge of the sidewalk, to be out of the way of the people. The longer they stood there, the more Crunch saw. She was terribly thin. She *was* wearing a little makeup. Her lips trembled a little when she spoke, and so did her voice, and a pulse kept beating on one side of her neck. She was unbelievably unhappy. Her unhappiness was as real as an odor.

He said, "Well, Uncle Sam's inviting us all to a party in Korea, and I expect we'll all be leaving soon—all except Arthur. He's too young. Thank God."

She heard the intensity of his "thank God" and looked at him with a quickened sympathy. He was grateful for this; it eased him a little, almost as though he had made a confession.

But she did not, herself, make any reference to God. She said, "I'd love to see Arthur. He was so nice about singing at Sister Bessie's funeral." Then, lamely, as though catching her breath and holding back panic, "If you all have any time—I know you must be busy but"—she laughed—"you know my father's always happy to offer folks a glass of wine!"

When she laughed, something strange happened between them, almost as though *she* had made a confession.

Crunch grinned, feeling very strangely moved. "Well, I'm going to try to get by to see you, Sister Julia. And you give your father my regards."

"Thank you, Crunch," she said. "Be seeing you."

He had been waiting to hear her say, *Praise the Lord*! but she smiled and waved her hand and turned away. He watched her curiously hesitant progress through the crowd. People turned to look at her—this tall, thin, burning girl, dressed all in black, just out of the madhouse, or on her way.

Crunch watched her, and watched the people watching her, and he almost started to call her back. Call her back to what? He turned, and got to the corner, and ran down the subway steps.

He was of two minds as concerned seeing her again—seeing *who* again? For the girl he had just left was a stranger to him; and there was no reason, really, for him to want to know her; he had certainly never wanted to know her before. Something had happened in her life, but he did not really want to know what had happened. It had nothing to do with him; he was happy as he was. He knew, one day, he would have a girl again, but it would certainly not be *this* girl. He and Arthur were happy now, as they were, and when the time came for Crunch to have a girl again, well, that would be time enough.

He mentioned to Arthur that he had seen Julia, and that she looked strange. Arthur said that this was probably because she had stopped preaching—he knew this from his mother—and no one knew what she was doing with herself.

Florence suspected the truth, but it was only a suspicion, and a most unwilling one at that, and she mentioned it to no one, not even Paul.

But she told Arthur that the girl needed to see people her own age—that, though it was very good of her to devote herself to her widowed father (so Florence put it), it wasn't fair: and so she hoped that Crunch and Arthur would "keep an eye out" for her.

"You and Crunch go on up there and just sort of look around and let me know—*you* know—what it feels like."

Arthur felt somewhat ambivalent about being assigned the role of a spy, even though this role was being given him by his mother.

"Can't Daddy go?"

"Your daddy's not been able to get Joel alone since the funeral. Only times he sees Joel is when he's drunk—and then, he won't look nobody in the eye."

So, late on a Sunday afternoon, Crunch and Arthur climbed the brownstone steps, and rang the Millers' bell.

Brother Joel Miller came to the door.

Crunch had scarcely been able to recognize Julia, something like two weeks before, because she had changed. But Brother Joel Miller was a far greater shock, because he had not changed. He was absolutely recognizable, as though nothing had happened, no time had passed. His hair gleamed, freshly combed; he smelt of after-shave lotion. He had been interrupted while tucking a white shirt into his navy-blue pants. His black pumps gleamed. He had not yet put the cufflinks into the cuffs of his sleeves; the sleeves were rolled, lightly, to just below the elbow. The fingernails had not yet been buffed to their highest sheen.

He stared at them blankly, with a blank hostility.

Arthur said, "Good evening, Brother Miller. Is Julia home?"

He recognized Arthur's voice before he recognized Arthur. When he recognized Arthur, he recognized Crunch. But he remained in the doorway, like someone with his back to the wall.

Then he moved to allow them to enter, covering his face with a smile.

"Good evening, young gentlemen," he said. "Yes, I believe she's home. Come in."

They walked into the dark, still hallway, and followed Brother Miller to the living room.

"She may be sleeping," said Brother Miller. "I'll go wake her up. Excuse me," and he left the room. They heard him climbing the stairs. They looked at each other, and "Damn!" Crunch said. "He didn't even offer us no wine."

But Arthur thought how strange it was that Julia should be at home, sleeping, on a Sunday afternoon, with all those souls outside, waiting to be saved. He remembered the last time he had seen her; he wondered what had happened to her to change her so; he wondered what he would see when she walked into the room. He realized that he did not want to see her.

They heard voices above them, and footsteps. They both sat very still, profoundly uncomfortable, and grateful that the voices were too low for them to be able to understand anything. The low voices contained a disquieting, hostile heat, were not meant to be understood by others.

"We won't stay long," Arthur said. "It's just that I promised my mother."

"Well, I promised, too, little fellow," Crunch said.

"You not mad at me?"

"Mad at you? for what?"

"For messing up your Sunday."

Crunch growled at him, licked his lips, and grinned. "But my Sunday ain't messed up. Yet."

The voices ceased, they heard Brother Miller descending the stairs, he entered the room.

"She'll be with you in a few minutes," he said. He said this as he had always said it: like a privileged person conferring a favor.

Yet, as though some explanation would not compromise either his daughter's dignity, or his own, he added, "Julia took her mother's passing very hard. She wants to get up and go on about her duties, but I have to hold her back and make her rest. I done lost a wife, I don't want to lose a daughter—she's all I got, now." He walked to the kitchen door. "You boys like a little refreshment while you waiting? All I got is a little wine." He grinned at Arthur. "Your mama let you drink wine yet?"

"A little bit, sometimes," Arthur said—which was true enough.

"I reckon you big enough," said Joel, and disappeared into the kitchen. They heard water running in the kitchen, and then Joel reappeared with three glasses and a half bottle of white wine. He poured their glasses, left the bottle on the table in front of the sofa. "To your health," he said, and they sipped the wine, which was thick and sweet. "Julia sure ain't the housekeeper her mother was," said Joel. "Oh course, she ain't really much more than a girl yet, we all tend to forget that, she always been so grown-up." He sat down on the chair facing the sofa. "Julia tells me you all was on the road this summer, singing down South. How'd you all do?"

"Pretty well," Crunch said. He looked at Arthur. "Good, I'd say."

"Yeah," said Arthur. "We did very well."

"Which cities was the best?"

"Nashville, Atlanta—" Crunch said.

"Birmingham, too," said Arthur.

"What about New Orleans?"

"New Orleans was good," said Crunch.

"Reason I asked—little Jimmy's down there with his grand-mother, and Julia wants to see him real bad. That might be just the thing to start her off again—do a string of Southern churches, starting in New Orleans." He sipped his wine, pursed his lips, thinking. "We might do it together—you boys singing, Julia preaching—what do you think? I think we could clean up."

Crunch sighed. "It might be a good idea—but we ain't going to be able to do it."

"Why not?"

"I'm about to be drafted—I'm just waiting for the date—when I have to, you know, say good-bye to you all."

Joel sucked his teeth. "Yeah. The others, too—of course."

"Everybody. Except Arthur."

Joel turned to Arthur. "That's right. Well, what about you and Julia—" but, at this moment, Julia entered the room.

Her head was covered with a green bandanna, and she wore a choc-olate-colored, tight-fitting dress. She carried a small green pocket-book, and wore high-heeled beige shoes. For both Arthur and Crunch, though for different reasons, a total stranger had entered the room. Julia was so thin that the tight-fitting dress could accentuate nothing more than a certain perverse and reckless gallantry: but that was striking and attractive enough. She barely escaped looking like a little girl dressed up in her older sister's clothes. She escaped this by wearing no makeup: her face was ruthlessly, defiantly scrubbed, and she turned it first to her father.

"My Sunday best," she said mockingly, then turned her enormous eyes on Crunch, then Arthur. She went to Arthur and hugged him: involuntarily, he stiffened. "I'm so glad to see you," she said—but he felt that she was speaking to Crunch.

"How are you?" Arthur asked, finally managing to smile. "I'm glad to see you, too."

"I'm fine," she said. "I'm trying." She sat down on the edge of the sofa. "But I'm not allowed to drink yet."

Crunch and Arthur sat down, too, Arthur somewhat more abruptly than Crunch, and Joel said, in a tone that almost made Arthur like him, it held such genuine sorrow, "Girl gets like that sometimes, don't mind her. She's just trying to drive her daddy crazy."

"I am not," said Julia, laughing. "I'm just trying not to drive *myself* crazy." She looked at Arthur again. "How've you been? Tell me something—" and he still felt that she was speaking to Crunch.

She reminded him, abruptly, of Sister Dorothy Green, and he could scarcely catch his breath to answer. *Sister,* he started to say, but the word simply weighed down the edge of his tongue, like a heavy pellet, *Sister Julia.* He said lightly, "You tell *me* something, I ain't got nothing to tell. Crunch already told you—we worked all summer. It was good for us." He was aware of Brother Joel Miller's eyes. "But now, everybody's going to be kind of scattered—so—" He looked down. Pain hit him a terrible blow. He dared touch Crunch's knee with one fist, and the touch made him dizzy. "I'll be all alone," he said. "I guess that's all the something I got to tell you."

"But you and Julia," Joel said. "You make a mighty good team. You ought to think about it, you ain't got to be all alone."

Julia and Arthur looked at each other for the very first time. Neither of them knew anything about the other—for the very first time, they wondered; and Arthur realized that if Julia had changed, so had he changed, so had he changed. He wondered if his change was visible. And then he wondered *what* had changed Julia. He was in love, in love with the man who sat beside him. He knew that this could not be said: but this was what had changed him. What had changed Julia? The death of her mother? But he knew that it could not have been only the death of her mother, it was something yet heavier than that: and he felt Crunch beside him, sniffing down the same path.

Then terror overtook him, like a cloud, like thunder, like the water coming over one's head, and he held his breath, paralyzed, staring at the girl—staring, in a way, into his mirror.

Julia turned to her father and said, "If Arthur wants to try to sing with me, we can do that." She grinned and turned to Arthur. "If your daddy will let us use his piano." She said to Crunch, and to Arthur, and to her father, "I'm not going to preach no more."

A silence fell in the room, a silence as black as her father's eyes.

"Why?" Crunch asked. He had leaned forward, his hands stretched, unconsciously, toward Julia.

"Because," she said, "I'm ignorant. I don't know how to save nobody's soul. I don't know how to save *my* soul!"

"But that's what the preacher says," Crunch said.

"The preacher may *know* it," Julia said, "but he don't say it. Not in the pulpit, he don't—he *can't*! How can you say that to all them souls looking to you for salvation?"

"She'll be all right," Joel said. "She's mighty upset now—she'll be all right."

Julia touched her green bandanna. In the barely controlled trembling of that child's hand, Arthur saw, unwillingly, the terrified intransigence which is the key to beauty. It made her a stranger. It made him want to be her friend. Her anguish made her real. It uncovered her youth. It revealed her age.

She dropped her hand, and grinned at Crunch, and Arthur. "Daddy's right. He's always right—about his daughter. And I love my daddy—I always will. But I'm right, too—about his daughter." Then she looked at her father, she stood up. "These gentlemen going to walk me around the block and buy me a ice cream cone. Don't you tarry too late." She kissed his damp forehead.

Crunch and Arthur stood when Julia stood, and Crunch threw Arthur a worried look—his Sunday might be messed up, after all.

"We won't keep her long," Arthur said quickly. "Me and Crunch got business downtown—but we'll be back to see you real soon!"

"Certainly before I leave here," Crunch said.

Julia had walked the hallway, to the door, and Crunch and Arthur followed her. Joel rose, and walked behind them. "I'll wait here then," he said to Julia, "till you come back."

"All right, Daddy," Julia said. "Suit yourself." She opened the door. Crunch and Julia started down the steps. Arthur, turning to close the door behind them, saw Brother Miller, his shirt-sleeves still rolled, his glass of wine in his hand.

Arthur said, "Good night, Brother Miller," but Joel did not answer.

Arthur closed the door, and started down the steps. Crunch and Julia were standing on the sidewalk, looking up at him, and—Arthur told me later—this was a very strange moment in his life, less than a split second perhaps, but never to be forgotten, a moment occurring outside of time.

He was abruptly aware that he was standing on a height, and, he told me, "They were looking up at me like I had seen something. I hadn't yet started down the steps. She was as skinny as she could be, looking up at me, and Crunch was looking up at me, too. Crunch was lean, but he wasn't skinny—you know, brother, I had held him in my arms, and I knew. And—how I loved him! Maybe that's what happened as I started down those steps. His eyes, and her eyes. Oh. I knew about me and Crunch—I thought I knew. I didn't know. I know I didn't know why they looked at me that way, when I come stumbling down those steps. They looked at me like I was some kind of messenger—of salvation."

His voice, in my memory, drops, then rises—and I, too, can see the children, Crunch and Julia, standing on the sidewalk, looking up at the child—in the busy, funky, end-of-summer streets.

And I am sure that he *did* resemble "some kind of messenger—of salvation." He was certainly that for Crunch. Julia's eyes followed Crunch's eyes, simply, and her need was so great that she saw what Crunch saw—without knowing that she saw it, and with nothing whatever having yet occurred between herself and Crunch. Her eyes followed Crunch's eyes because, otherwise, her eyes were fixed on madness, on despair, on death. She wanted to live. She did not know how she could, or if she could. It seemed to her that she had promised her mother to take care of her brother: *that* was the only reason that she had to live. But it was not enough. She did not see how to get beyond her father to her brother—she needed a human hand to help her lift herself over the chasm. And Crunch was there, with his hand outstretched, although he did not know it. And there was Arthur, too, with his hand outstretched, although he did not know it, because of his love for Crunch.

And Arthur looked, too, at that moment in his life, like archaic, distant portraits of young nobles, princes, Greeks, Turks, Ethiopians, some of the faces in Vandyke: with all that carefully piled, wavy hair, that brow, those eyes and nostrils, those firm and greedy lips, the big, wide, humorous mouth. He caught all the light on the street at that moment, coming down the steps, his eyes looking into Crunch's eyes, his love and his happiness and his sorrow all interwoven and fashioned together and billowing around him like a splendid royal robe. And what he glimpsed, at that moment, in their eyes, as he came down those steps, was a future, greater height, and a longer, slower descent.

Then he was on the sidewalk, beside them. He had trouble looking at Julia because he had trouble recognizing her: she grinned, and he grinned, too. Julia took Crunch by one arm and took Arthur by the other, and they turned and started down the block.

"You don't really have to buy me no ice cream cone," Julia said. "I just wanted to get out of the house for a minute."

"But we ready," said Crunch, "and willing and—*able*, I believe," and he grinned, around Julia's shoulder, at Arthur.

"The train," said Arthur, "is in the station"—feeling very proud.

They reached the corner, and the avenue facing Jordan's Cat. Sidney was not there, he was up at Aunt Josephine's, with Martha.

Crunch, Julia, and Arthur crossed the street, and started down the avenue.

"You all got business downtown," Julia said. "I'll walk you to the subway."

"And, *then*, what you going to do?" Crunch asked.

"Why then," said Julia, "I'll walk back home."

"What you doing with yourself these days?" Crunch asked.

"I guess you could say I'm taking care of my father." Julia laughed, then she coughed. "He took my mother's passing very hard."

"That's only natural," Arthur said—and then, for some reason, wished that he had not spoken.

"Yeah," said Crunch. "But you can't take care of your father forever."

"*You* take care of your mother," Arthur said, and then, again, sharply, wished that he had not spoken.

"We do what we have to do," Julia said.

"But what about *your* life?" Crunch asked.

He sounded both angry and bewildered, and Arthur longed to reach out, and touch him.

"This *is* my life," said Julia. "Right now."

They walked in silence for a while, down the broad, amazing, familiar avenue.

Julia's hand trembled slightly on Arthur's elbow, but it was a firm hand, and she did not stumble. She seemed to know their destination better than he or Crunch knew: it was she who set the pace.

She turned to Crunch. "So," she said, "you're going away from us! Are you glad?"

"I ain't no soldier," Crunch said—and then, after a moment, catching his breath, "No, Julia, I can't hardly say I'm glad."

Julia's high heels seemed to hit the pavement like thunder, but so did Crunch's crepe-soled shoes: Arthur felt a roaring behind his eyebrows, in his skull. The *click-clack* of the narrow high heels and the *sh'm'm* of the crepe soles made the avenue shake beneath him. All the lights of the avenue wavered, he could scarcely see the people, he held himself upright against Julia's hand at his elbow.

"I'd be glad," said Julia, "to get away from here."

"Away," said Crunch, looking straight ahead, "from everyone you love?"

"There's nobody here I love," said Julia, "since my mama died. If I was old enough, I swear, I'd go and get my brother and bring him back here and try to raise him—I don't know—I don't want him down South, all by himself!"

"But he's not all by himself," said Arthur. "He's with his grandmother."

But, as he said this, he remembered that he, after all, had just come back from the South; he remembered Peanut's relatives, in Charlotte; and he knew that neither did he want to leave anyone he loved down South. He could not have left Crunch down South: he would never have been able to sleep again. Sleep? He would not be walking.

As though this terror had been conveyed through his elbow to Julia's hand, her hand tightened.

"He doesn't know his grandmother," Julia said.

Something had been nagging Arthur, and now, he spoke.

"What about your father? Don't tell us, now, that you don't love your father!"

The moment the words were out of his mouth, Arthur wished, again, that he had held his peace. Julia said nothing. They kept walking.

"You see my father," Julia said finally, "don't care how much I may love him, ain't but so much I can do for him. But little Jimmy— that's something else."

Arthur had the impression that she was fighting back tears, and he dared not look at her. She raised her head and said, "Well, here we are, at the subway!" and gestured toward the kiosk as though she invented it.

Then they all stopped, in a silence charged and awkward. Too much had been said, too little revealed—or: too much had been revealed from what little had been said. They did not, any longer, know where they were. Well. They were at the subway station, standing in a light which came from below. Julia walked them to the steps.

"Well, gentlemen," said Julia. "I'm mighty glad I saw you! When we going to see each other again?"

"Before I go away from here," said Crunch. "I promise you."

Arthur, but in a very strange way, was mightily relieved that he and Crunch had maneuvered themselves all the way through Sunday, to *their* Sunday—Crunch's Sunday had not been messed up, after all: the last Sunday they might ever have. But he felt Julia pulling, pulling, against their departure, against their descent of the stairs. He knew that she had nowhere to go, that she would come with them, wherever they were going. If it had not been so nearly their last day together, if they had had time to spare, he and Crunch might have exchanged a brief, secret signal and invited the child to the movies. But—they had no time; too much had been said, too little revealed; or, what had been revealed, much or little, implied a pursuit, the beginning of a journey, which could not be begun at this moment. Yet something had begun, something had been profoundly altered, and Arthur saw this in Crunch's troubled, in Julia's fevered, eyes. "That's one promise he'll keep," Arthur said. "*I* promise you."

"*Can* you? You two as close as that?"

"My heart," said Crunch and Arthur together—each heard the other, looked at each other in wonder, and began to laugh. Julia put her hands on her hips, and laughed with them. "Go on, you two," she said. "Get on down them steps. The both of you—you know?—you remind me of my brother." She sobered without becoming somber. She looked happy, and amused, and Arthur was glad that he and Crunch had made the visit. In her freedom, at that moment, at the top of the stairs, he dimly sensed the beginning of a journey which would forever include Julia. They were little children no longer: they were getting on board the train.

Which they now heard, roaring into the station, beneath them. Arthur and Crunch waved, and Julia waved, Arthur and Crunch ran down the steps.

Julia watched them a moment, then started home. Home was not the place she wanted to go, or to be: but she had no place else to go. She walked slowly because she dreaded getting there. She walked slowly because she was controlled by the attention of the men and the boys on the avenue. She walked with a slow, long-legged stride, lightly swinging her handbag: she was a powerful incitement, and a mystery. She walked as though she did not see the people that she passed, and she didn't—she was burning, burning, and this was why the men and the boys were compelled to watch her pass. It was impossible to know if she were a dressed-up child, or a yearning, burning woman. She had breasts—tiny, pin-pointed, narrow; she had a barely discernible and tantalizing behind. The key, the secret, was in that slow walk, those long legs. Julia sensed, in herself, a power, which, however, and even before she had begun to live! might already have begun to destroy her. She was searching, serching—one may say that she was lost and as only those who have been saved can be lost. She was fourteen, and in Ezekiel's valley, alone: *oh, Lord, can these bones live?* That was the way she walked, although she did not know it, and that was why she tantalized every eye. Her burning created a burning, that was why she walked so slowly. It was the only human attention she had ever had.

And now—she walked the long, broad, familiar, amazing avenue, and got home.

Joel was in his shirt-sleeves, on the sofa.

"You ain't gone out yet?"

"Told you I was going to wait for you, daughter." Then, "Seems like that's all I ever do, these days."

She threw down her handbag—on the sofa, next to him—and waited. She folded her arms over her breasts, as she had sometimes seen her mother fold her arms. She began to pace, as she had sometimes seen her mother pace—looking straight ahead, seeing nothing, exactly like her mother.

I'm just fourteen, she thought. *There's African girls get married at fourteen*. She looked at her father.

She thought of her brother.

"I didn't ask you to wait for me. I don't *want* you to wait for me. What you waiting for me for?"

"You all I got."

It was Sunday night. He would go out. She hoped he would go out and pick up some woman and never come back. He would go out. He would come back drunk. He would fall into her bed, smothering her with his breath; his tears would burn her face. She would endure the touch she dreaded, and to which she had become addicted, feeling like something struggling at the bottom of the sea. Her days and nights were drugged. With all her heart, she wanted to flee—she could not move.

"If I'm all you got," she said, "you in a mighty sorry condition. I ain't got nothing."

"But you in a position to *get* something. And you know you are. Are you just going to sit here and let us be overtaken?"

She had a job scrubbing floors after school, and she gave him almost all the money that she made, which wasn't much. He had had to pawn his favorite pair of cufflinks. She was sitting still, watching everything crumble, and disappear; and yet, she knew she had to move.

"No," she said.

He had hated pawning his cufflinks, which had been a gift from her, and she had felt very sorry for him. She had nothing against him, nothing, either because she did not expect him to be other than he was, or because she was too beaten. She had to move, and yet, she waited. Though she had nothing against him, sometimes, nevertheless, she waited for revenge. Sometimes she hoped his touch would undo the horror of his touch.

"What you going to do, then?"

"Give me time, Daddy."

"Time? The world ain't *got* that kind of time."

She wanted to get to New Orleans, but not as a beggar. She had to arrive with something, with something for Jimmy right away, something to make him trust her.

But she did not want to leave her father with nothing.

He had dried her tears and stroked her and wiped away the blood—she had screamed when she saw the blood. She had wanted to run out of the house, but she had been shivering, trembling, screaming, the wound between her legs would not let her move, her legs would not carry her. She had forced herself to stop screaming because, if not, they would come and take her father away: they had become accomplices.

"I been patient awhile," he said. "Don't make me lose my patience."

"What will you do if you lose your patience?" she asked—and immediately wished that she had said nothing, for the air in the room changed, he stood up, and she was terrified.

"Just don't you make me lose it, that's all," he said. "You won't like it, I guarantee you."

They stared at each other.

"Why you talking to me like that?"

"Because I'm tired of the way you mope around this house, looking like the Book of Job, and looking at me like I was some kind of reptile!"

She sat down in the easy chair, and he come and stood over her, leaning on the arms of the chair.

"What's between you and me happens, happens all the time—this ain't the last time or the first time or the only time. I just ain't being a hypocrite about it—that's all. And you didn't call no cops on your daddy, did you? And you ain't going to, neither. *All* little girls wants their daddy—everybody knows that. I didn't do a damn thing but give you what you wanted. That's why you still here—*I* hear the way you call me Daddy!"

It was true—she became more terrified than ever, and said nothing. She murmured *Daddy* as he pounded into her, as she felt him shoot his semen into her: she was pleased to give him pleasure. His pleasure was overwhelming and terrifying, she could scarcely bear it, his pleasure left her alone in some dreadful place, and yet, something in her was pleased to give him pleasure. With all her heart, she wanted to flee—she could not move. She could not move and yet, she knew she must. Soon it would be too late, she would begin to die.

"Am I telling the truth, or not?"

She stared at him.

"Don't look at me like that! *Am I telling the truth, or not?*"

"I guess so," she said, after a moment.

"You guess so. I *know* so!"

He leaned up, and moved away toward the hall, and his face changed again, becoming gentle and wistful.

"Snap out of it, Julia—for me? Can't you do that for me? We can be real good friends, we can have wonderful times together."

He came back to the chair, and leaned over her, again.

"We love each other, well, let's just love each other. We doing any harm to anybody?"

No, you're just killing me, *that's all,* but she said, "No, Daddy."

"I love you," he said. "You all I got." He kissed her on the forehead—she went numb with the shudder she did not want him to feel. "All right?"

"All right," she said.

He leaned up again, at last, and moved away. "You think about what I said. I'll see you later."

And she listened to him mount the stairs, listened to his footsteps above her head.

Crunch, as good as his word, came by to see her in the late afternoon, three or four days later.

It was a day both bright and sullen, with the gray sky veiling a glaring sun—as she was to remember years and years later, as she remembers now.

Joel was at work on his "little piece of a job," as he put it, and she had just come in from her job in The Bronx, had not been home five minutes: by just that narrow a margin, she barely missed what seemed, then, like salvation.

The bright and sullen day hinted of the coming fall, the coming winter, and Crunch was wearing a gray turtleneck sweater and green corduroy pants.

Her heart lifted up when she opened the door and found him standing on the steps, and she laughed.

"Well, hello there! You all alone?"

"Sure am, Sister Julia. How are you?"

"I'm all right. Come on in. It's kind of a shock to see you without your shadow—people can't get used to it."

They closed the door behind them, and walked into the living room.

"They going to have to get used to it—me and Arthur going to have to get used to it, too. He got a rehearsal someplace and I had to run a errand for my mama, right around the corner—and—so—here I am."

"And I'm glad to see you. Can I get you something? Would you like a glass of wine?"—they both laughed—"or would you prefer beer? That's all we got, I think."

"Beer, please," said Crunch, and sat down while Julia went into the kitchen.

"What you been doing?" she called.

"Working. Waiting. Sure wish I didn't have to go."

She came back with the beer and carefully poured it and handed it to him.

The moment she sat down, an electric current, violent and unexpected, began to flow between them and Crunch carefully crossed his legs and sipped his beer.

"So? What you been doing?" he asked, bewildered, uneasy, and suddenly excited, not quite looking her in the eye.

"Nothing. Staying here with my daddy, and going crazy."

She looked him in the eye more and more insistently—she could not help it—and more and more candidly, moving, now that she was moving, very fast, and frightened to death. Her heart hammered, her breasts rose and fell. She knew that he could not keep his eyes off her breasts. She was wearing a tight white blouse and a black skirt.

"Where's your daddy?"

"He's at work. He won't be back till after dark—he *might* not be back then," and she laughed a laugh which suddenly died, and neither of them, for a moment, could think of anything to say. She stared at Crunch, he stared at her.

"What does your father do?"

"He got a job in some kind of factory—downtown, near Fourteenth Street."

"Oh? I got me a little furnished room down off Fourteenth and Third."

"You do? Oh, Crunch, I sure wish you'd take me with you down there one day!"

He grinned an awkward grin. "You want to see my room?"

"Yes. Yes. I do."

"It ain't nothing to see. It's just a room."

"But it's *your* room. I wish I had a room. I've *got* to get a room somewhere. My father's going to drive me crazy if I don't get out of here!"

"Sister Julia!"

"He is! he is! I don't know what to do!" She shuddered and began to cry and Crunch, in misery, put his beer on the table and clasped his hands together, not daring to touch her.

"I can't tell you," Julia muttered, "I can't tell you, oh, but I got to tell somebody." She beat on her thighs, and stood up. "I need somebody to help me."

"Julia—if there's anything I can do—"

"Take me! Take me! Take me to your room, before it's too late!"

He did not know how to comfort her, he did not know what to say. He did not know what she was talking about, but a great, dreadful, silent suspicion began to gather inside him.

"It can't—it can't," he said stupidly, "be that bad." He stood up and moved toward her. He did not want to touch her, did not dare. He felt a terrible, terrible pity for her, and, at the same time, he wanted to run. "Come," he said. "Sit down," and touched her lightly, turning her toward the sofa. Now she was quiet, but her tears still fell. She sat down. Crunch was trembling; he remained standing.

She looked up at him. "I'm so glad you came," she said. "You don't know how much I need a friend."

"Well, then," he said, smiling, "you got a friend."

"You don't know," she said, "how much I wanted to see you, how many times I've thought of you."

"Of me? Why me?"

"Lying next to my daddy, listening to him snore," she said. "I thought of you, oh, how I wished it was you!"

Her tears began to fall again. He stared at her stupidly, saying nothing.

"Don't look at me like that," she said. "It wasn't my fault, I swear it wasn't my fault, please be my friend."

"Your father—?"

"Don't tell. Don't tell, you hear? It wasn't his fault, either, he can't help it!"

"Your father—?" He felt that he was about to throw up.

"Yes. My father. He says it happens all the time." She looked up at him. "Does it?"

"I wouldn't know," he said—feeling colder and colder.

She looked into his face as though she would never see it again, then rose and moved to the window. He was about to find a way of saying good-bye, of getting out of this house. He watched her frail shoulders, her fragile neck.

"Well. I guess it's all over for me then," she said.

And his heart turned over. He moved, and took her by the shoulders and turned her to face him.

"Don't think like that," he said. "Don't think like that. Nothing's over. It's just beginning—your life is just beginning." He felt her trembling at his words, at his touch, and felt himself begin to tremble with pity and desire, and with fear. He could not catch his breath.

She moved, and buried her face in his chest. He put his arms around her, then she moved again and held him close.

"Oh, Crunch," she whispered. "Please make me well. Please touch me—take me—make me well."

He tried to pull away, with a little smile. He said, "You're just a little girl, Julia."

She looked up at him. "No, I'm not," she said. "Oh, no, I'm not."

She touched her lips to his lips. Slowly, slowly, he pressed her closer to him, he gave her his lips, his tongue—involuntarily, as it were, tentatively: but pity and desire rose, driving, he could not pull back.

"You're sure?"

"Oh, yes, I'm sure, please, I'm sure."

She placed one of his hands on her breasts, her own hands, as though she were blind, stroked his face, discovering it, his back, his buttocks, her hands ran up and down his thighs. She unhooked her skirt and stepped out of it; she ran her hands under his sweater, under his T-shirt, she stroked his skin.

"Your father," he whispered. "Your father—"

"He won't be coming home. He never comes home before night."

He took off his sweater, worried, but, *too late to worry now,* and she stripped herself naked and came, helplessly trusting, back into his arms. He felt at once helpless and helplessly powerful: he could not refuse her. She unbuckled his belt, he let his pants fall to the floor. Her body, now, again as though she were blind, strained against his body, discovering it. He let her have her way, tremendously excited, but frightened, too. He wondered if she really knew what she wanted, he was afraid he would hurt her; but she put her hand on him and looked up at him with eyes which held neither fear, nor the fear of pain. She pulled him down with her to the floor and, very, very, slowly, he entered her—she holding him close, sweating, straining to take it all, as he grew larger and larger, and though still trying to be gentle, thrust harder and harder. She thrust to meet him, with astonishing strength, smiling and calling his name over and over. The sullen daylight beat down on his back, something moved in the body beneath him like waves rising and breaking, she seemed to sing his name. He wanted to whisper a warning about having a baby and thought to pull out, but she held him to her with all her force and he suddenly seemed to have plunged even deeper into her and, soon, it would be too late, too late, he tried to whisper a warning but no words came, only *Julia. Oh Julia.* She murmured his name again with an unbelievable exultation, he pulled up, thrust down again and again, harder and harder and deeper and deeper, she laughing and crying and calling his name and pulling him always deeper into her—almost as though his lunging body would touch and open and drench and heal her soul. He, as it were, prayed with her, longing to give her all that she needed, and yet holding back, the unbelievable delight and agony tormenting, finally, the very tip of his congested sex, boiling there for an eternity, boiling, boiling, he groaned, hiding his face in her neck, and, finally, what seemed like a single drop forced itself out, he was utterly helpless in her arms, and, at last, the wave broke, pounding him full force into her, and she murmured his name, like a song.

He opened his eyes. He began, slowly, to soften inside her. He looked into her eyes which were, now, more peaceful than he had ever seen them, wet, and full of wonder.

"How do you feel?" he asked her.

"Saved," she said, and smiled. "How do *you* feel?"

"Beautiful," he said, and grinned—but he had just thought of Arthur. He raised himself up, and pulled out of her. "Let's get dressed and get out of here. I'm still afraid your father might come home."

She kissed him, then stood up, picking up her clothes. "I won't be a minute," she said. She started for the steps. "There's a bathroom right here, Crunch," and she pointed. "I'll be right down."

She ran, lightly, up the steps.

Crunch pulled up his pants, picked up his sweater and walked to the bathroom, breathing as though he had just run a race, with his knees shaking. He looked into the bathroom mirror as though the face in the mirror could tell him what had happened. Physically, what had happened was more familiar to him than his affair with Arthur—but only physically. And he did not feel, now, as he had so often, the humiliation and revulsion of having been used. He felt exhausted and bewildered—he would have to have it out with Julia. Then he thought of her father and felt a terrible pity for Julia; a pity sharpened by his knowledge that his pity was not his love. Then he wondered if he should tell Arthur. He bowed his head, and washed his face.

Julia stood naked in the upstairs bathroom, and looked at her body and looked at her body and looked at her body and touched it with wonder, and, for the first time, without shame or fear. What her father had stolen from her, Crunch had given back. She was fourteen: suddenly, she was only fourteen.

When she came down, Crunch had helped himself to another beer, and was sitting on the sofa, long legs stretched out before him, arms loosely folded, holding his beer in his right hand, head bent slightly, eyes raised, looking straight ahead. He did not seem to hear her, at first; then he turned and looked at her, and grinned, and gave a long, low whistle.

She was wearing a green halter and green slacks and nondescript loafers and had arranged her hair in a ponytail which was controlled by the green bandanna. Her slacks had pockets; she carried no handbag.

"Do I look all right?"

"I can tell you ain't no preacher."

They both laughed, and he stood up, placing his beer on the table.

"Finish your beer," she said.

He finished his beer in one swallow and put the glass back on the table. She picked it up, carried it to the kitchen and rinsed it, dried it, and put it back in the cupboard. He watched her from the kitchen doorway, his eyebrow cocked, smiling his little smile.

"Ready?"

"Yes. Where we going? You going to take me to see your room?"

"Not today, Julia. I got to stop by Arthur's. You want to come with me?"

"Oh—Arthur. Sure." Then, "Is it all right if I come?"

He laughed. "You've known Arthur just about all your life. What kind of question is that?"

"Oh"—she laughed, looking confused; but this did not dim her radiance. "I just thought, if you wanted to talk—"

"His mama's going to be there, his papa, too, I reckon. We'll talk. Come on."

"Crunch"—she ran to him, and kissed him. "I'm so happy."

He put his hands on her shoulders, and kissed her on the forehead, stepped back. "Come on. Let's hit the streets."

They walked the hallway to the door. "You got your keys?"

"Yes. In my pocket."

She grinned up at him, he opened the door, watching her utterly transformed face. They entered the paradoxical day, and started down the steps. She put her arm in his, as trusting as a baby. He was aware that she had never walked down the streets like this with anyone, in all her life: he was the first. And she was happy, but he was troubled. He was troubled on many levels, unspeakable, inaccessible: on the simplest level, he began to wonder just what kind of freak *he* was, what kind of monster found himself involved with two children, one boy and one girl? For Arthur was not a man yet, and Julia was certainly not a woman. And what was he? He shook his head, forcing the streets to come back into focus. He looked sideways at Julia, who now had both her arms linked around his one arm, and who was looking at the streets, and all the people in the streets, as though she had never seen any of this before.

They waited for a light, then crossed a street. He was aware of one thing only, that Arthur's house was coming closer and closer.

"You know, Julia," he said, "I'm not going to be here long."

She looked up at him, as grave as she had been as a preacher.

"Hush," she said. "I know that."

"Well. But do you know what it means?"

"I know I'm happy—for the first time in my life—"

"Julia! I might have to leave here tomorrow morning!"

"But I'll always," she said, looking up at the covered sky, "have today!" Then, she flew down, as it were, from her glorious height and walked again beside him, matching her step to his; or rather, grateful for her sudden descent, he matched his step to hers.

"I know," she said. "I know. We got—we ain't got no time. I got so many things to tell you—partly about my father—but about so many things—about my mother and Jimmy—and so many things. About me, when I was a preacher and how I always noticed you— oh," and she laughed, "Arthur's older brother, what's his name? Hall—Mister Ha! I always called him." She turned her face to his. "But I just don't want to talk about any of that now—not now. You understand?"

"Yes," he said, finally—then, "But what if I have to leave in the morning?"

"I'll write you," she said. "But anyway—how long we going to stay at Arthur's house? Can't you take me to your room?"

"Julia"—he began to sweat—"no. Not tonight."

"You got another girl?" She laughed. "I know I shouldn't ask you that—that's none of my business."

"It might be," he said, and, suddenly, he laughed. A weight dropped from his shoulders, and yet, dark wonder hovered about his head. "I might have things to tell you, too," he said. "But all right. Not today."

Arthur recognized them from the open window—for Crunch was late—and did not recognize the girl walking beside Crunch, dressed all in green, in slacks, with a bare midriff, and wearing lipstick—he did not recognize Julia at all.

"Here comes Crunch," he said to Florence, "and he's got some girl with him."

Florence came to the window and leaned out. "Why," she cried, "what's wrong with you, boy? That ain't nobody but Julia!" She waved and called, "Hey, you two in green there! Was you fixing to sneak past *my* house?"

"No such thing," Crunch grinned, looking upward. "No such thing, ma'am. We was just asking for directions."

"Look like you got directed right. Julia, how you been, child? You come on up here and let me spank that skinny behind of yours! I declare, the way you been treating me is a *shame*—come on up here now!"

"How'd your rehearsal go, man?" Crunch yelled.

"Not bad, man. Come on in the house, I'll tell you about it."

"Well," said Florence, retreating from the window, "there he is—your heart. And Julia, too. That's beautiful."

It is my impression that the young cannot fool anybody, except those people who wish to be fooled. The young tell you what you want to hear, which is how they learn to despise you, and themselves, and this is also how their youth becomes worthless to them so soon: in any case, Arthur never managed to fool anybody as long as he lived. Now, with his face glowing with a double relief—that Crunch had arrived, that the girl was only, after all, Julia—and facing his mother, our mother would have had to have been a fool not to have known what Crunch and Arthur meant to each other. Indeed, she very probably knew it before they did. It worried her, yes. It worried her the way the identity, the fate, the future of her child always worried a mother. If I had decided to marry a white girl, for example, my mother would have been worried but would never have opposed it. Her concern was that I marry someone I loved, who loved me—if, for that matter, I ever married at all, which was entirely up to me. She was not distressed about Arthur until the word was out on Arthur's ass, and lots of people tried to gang-rape him in indescribable ways—oh, yes, believe me, it's cold out there—and Arthur began to sink beneath the double weight of the judgment without and the judgment within. And, yet, it is true, and Arthur was right when he insisted, *I've got to live the life I sing about in my song:* he meant that he could not afford to live a lie.

Ah. But, then, you've set yourself up for something, inevitably, and this was the nature of Paul's distress, that he saw the day coming but died before the day arrived, when Arthur would cry out, weeping briny tears, *Look! what they done to my song!*

For the rest, a son, or brother, is simply that—a son, or a brother—and you love him, in the shit or out of the shit, and you clean him up if you have to, and you know he's got to go the way his blood beats because that's *your* blood beating in those veins, too.

"Sure hope your father don't tarry too long," Florence said. "Go open the door for them, Arthur, why you standing there like that?"

Florence went into the kitchen, and Arthur went to open the door.

Presently, Julia and Crunch, laughing, huffing and puffing as though they were climbing up the steep side of the mountain, and looking as though they had just had a picnic in Central Park, came up the stairs to the open door, where Arthur stood.

"Girl," Arthur said, grinning, "I didn't recognize you at *all*. I guess you really *have* stopped preaching."

They kissed each other, and Julia said, "You hush. I just *might* be studying a brand-new text."

"Sure looks good on you, girl," Arthur said, and they laughed, and Florence appeared behind Arthur, hands on hips.

"Girl! You want me to beat your behind on the landing or you want to get your behind whipped in this house?"

"Mama Montana, don't beat me *too* hard, I *have* had some hard trials"—but Florence pulled her past Arthur and took Julia in her arms.

Arthur and Crunch were alone for a second, at the door, on the landing. Crunch suddenly pulled the door shut behind Arthur and took him in his arms and kissed him, hard. They held each other a second, pulled away. Crunch opened the door.

"Love you," he whispered. "We'll take a walk later. I got something to tell you."

"Sure." He watched Crunch, vaguely disturbed. "Is everything all right?"

Florence and Julia had gone into the living room; there was no one on the landing. Crunch put one hand on Arthur's shoulder. He said solemnly, "No."

"What's the matter?"

"When I said I love you—I didn't hear you say nothing."

Arthur laughed. "You're crazy, man." Then he took Crunch's face in his hands, and kissed him. "Yes. I love you. With all my heart."

"Then why you standing in the door like that? Look like you don't want me in your house."

"Come on in the house, man. I swear, you the craziest mother-fucker I know."

"I'm going to tell your mama what you said!" Crunch yelled this at the top of his lungs and Arthur collapsed into laughter and slammed the door behind them.

"Will you two stop playing the fool?" Florence cried, "and come on in here? I don't," she said to Julia, "know which of them is worse."

Crunch and Arthur came into the living room, still laughing. Florence and Julia sat on the sofa, side by side.

"What was that you was going to tell me?"

"No, Mama Montana, I don't believe I'll tell you now. I just leave it between Arthur and the Lord."

He sat down in a chair near the window and Arthur sat on the piano stool, still laughing because it seemed that Crunch could not stop laughing. He had no way of knowing that Crunch's laughter came out of both panic and relief. Here was Arthur, he had touched him, nothing had changed between them; *he,* Crunch, had not changed. He knew, at least for the moment, where he was. So he felt that he could handle whatever was coming. He could tell Arthur the truth: he realized, then, that he could tell Julia the truth. He laughed again, briefly, and sobered.

"I'm sorry," he said, "but it's Arthur's fault. He ought to be on television."

Florence looked, briefly at both of them and then turned back to Julia. "So? What *is* your father doing?"

"Oh. He goes to work and he comes home. He don't say much."

She toyed with the bandanna tied around her ponytail, looked first at Crunch, then at Florence. "It's kind of hard to live with someone who don't say much."

"And you—what are you doing?"

"Oh. Trying to take care of my father." Crunch and Florence stared at Julia, Arthur stared at Crunch. Julia looked down. "Going to school. And I got a job on Grand Concourse as a kind of scrub-woman, I guess you'd say," and she laughed, and looked up. Florence grunted. "What I'd really like to do is go to New Orleans and get Jimmy and bring him back up here, with me—but—"

"Jimmy's better off where he is," Florence said. "I don't like to say it, but you know as well as I do that Jimmy and his father ain't never going to get along."

"I know," said Julia. "But I wasn't going to bring him *there*. I want to find another place and take care of him myself."

"But Julia," said Florence, "you ain't but fourteen, you can't take care of your*self*, how you think you going to be able to take care of Jimmy?"

"I promised my mother," Julia said. "I promised my mother I would. She didn't want him to go down South, and she didn't want him nowhere near his daddy, neither." She looked up at Florence, suddenly close to tears, and Florence nodded, not looking at Julia, nodded from a long ways off. "I don't know how I'm going to do it, but I *have* to do it, I promised my mother!"

"Well," said Florence, "we'll talk." She put her hand on Julia's hand. "I think I know how you feel. Why don't you stay here tonight? The change will be good for you, give us time to put our heads to-gether."

"I—I can't." She looked at Florence, looked, quickly, to Crunch: Crunch nodded, very, very gravely. Julia looked back to Florence. "My father—my father—"

"Ain't nothing going to happen to your father."

"He won't know where I am."

"He'll know where you are the minute I pick up a phone and tell him."

"What you going to tell him?"

"That we got to talking and you got tired and I put you to bed."

"He going to wonder what we talked about—"

"Men been wondering what women talk about for ages, honey, ain't no new thing—anyway, all we been talking about is you and little Jimmy."

But she watched the terror and the torment in Julia's face, a terror and torment made vivid by her attempts to hide it.

"Well—there really ain't nothing else *to* talk about—I ain't complaining about him—"

"Well, then," said Florence. "It's settled."

"No," said Julia. "He'll be upset." But she looked at Crunch as she said this, and dropped her eyes. Yet, "He comes in late, too late for you to phone him, you'll be asleep."

"It's now or never," Crunch said. "Mama Montana's right, and you know it."

"And he ain't going to be upset," said Florence. "At least, he won't be no more upset than usual because, if I can't phone him, I'll send Arthur up there, with a note."

"Mama Montana's a mighty good nurse, now," Crunch said, with a cryptic smile, a wink. "And I'll get up here to see you, fast as I can, after work. Maybe we'll walk through the park, or something. I might even buy you a hot dog."

"But I *can't* stay here," said Julia.

"You the granddaughter of my oldest friend," said Florence. "How come you can't stay here?"

"You can't stay up yonder, neither," Crunch said flatly, "you told me that yourself, this afternoon." He lifted that one eyebrow at her. "You forgot already?"

A silence abruptly weighted down the room, a silence like eternity: they heard the streets. Julia stood, abruptly, and walked to the window, her hands in her pockets. The wind briefly billowed the green rag at the back of her head, then let it fall to the nape of her neck.

She turned to Crunch. "No," she said. "I ain't forgot. I'll never forget."

"You can use my bed," said Arthur.

"I was going to make up the couch," said Florence. "Where *you* going to stay?"

"I'll stay with Crunch," said Arthur.

"That's right," said Crunch. "If that's all right with you, Mama Montana."

"Well—run up, and leave a note for Brother Miller."

"Okay. You want me to write the note?"

"No. I'll write it. Don't you two be staying out all night."

The note said,

> *Dear Joel,*
> *Your daughter, Julia, is staying the night with me, so don't worry about her. We'll call you in the morning. Where you been keeping yourself? Both me and Paul would be GLAD TO SEE YOU. May God bless you and keep you.*
> *Florence Montana*

The Miller bell did not answer, so Arthur left the note in the mailbox, with the tip sticking out, and ran down the brownstone steps, to Crunch. Silently, they began walking toward the avenue, toward the subway. The summer day was just beginning to fade. The streets were full, vivid, with people, children, sound—it was as though they were moving through an element which held them up, sustained them, and protected them.

Crunch walked head down, his hands in his pockets, silent. This silence was not exactly uncomfortable, but it was—*new:* Arthur did not know what to make of this silence, or how to break it.

Finally, he said, looking up at Crunch, "You said you had something to tell me."

"I do."

"About Julia?"

"Partly."

He looked at Arthur, and smiled. This smile, too, was new. It came from a new place, a new distance, and it held a new sorrow.

"When you going to tell me?"

"In a minute. Let me think."

"Oh," said Arthur, bewildered, stung. "I'm not trying to rush you, man."

And he looked at the cracks in the sidewalk. They walked down the subway steps in silence, pushed through the turnstiles, waited for the train.

Arthur suddenly felt very young. He wanted to ask, *Do you want to be alone, Crunch? Do you want me to go back home?* But he feared the answer. He felt, as he had sometimes felt with his father, or with me, that he was just a snot-nosed kid, in the way, and the best thing for him to do was to keep quiet.

So he kept quiet as he and Crunch stepped onto the crowded train. Crunch leaned against the door; Arthur stood next to Crunch, still wondering if he should leave. Crunch didn't seem to see him, or to know that he was there. But he knew that if he tried to leave, Crunch would call him back. Crunch would be hurt—it was a game he couldn't play, a risk he couldn't take. He stared at himself in the subway window as the train shook and roared through the tunnel. The people were as silent as people in a dream, numbly submitting to the roar and the movement, each person absolutely, sullenly alone. He would be alone soon, next week, next month, tomorrow, the day after tomorrow—even Crunch's silence would be gone. Then he knew that he could not possibly leave Crunch now, not unless Crunch beat him and pushed him away. But at 42nd Street, when they changed to the shuttle to the east side, Crunch put one arm around him—as though to say that he knew Arthur was there and was glad that he was there. They came out of the subway at Fourteenth Street and started walking east, toward Crunch's room.

The El was still standing then, and so I see them, standing on the corner, waiting for the light, under that monstrous canopy. In the shadow of all that metal, beneath the unspeakable hostility of the inescapable trains—Arthur imagines that a man might climb the stairs to the platform and throw himself under a train, simply to be released from the everlasting roar to get some sleep—Crunch's door, and, all the doors on this avenue, seem furtive, doomed, sordid, choked payment for choked sins. If he were not with Crunch, he would be terrified of the people on this street. He wonders what happened to them, how they got that way—they, who must once have had a mother and father, brother and sister, uncles, aunts, cousins, friends, wives—even, children—who must once have been as young and clean as he and Crunch are now. But, now—they have entered eternity: eternal damnation must look like this.

He wonders if he and Crunch are damned. Perhaps love *is* a sin. But he shakes his head against the thought, and the light changes. They cross the street.

On the corner there is a bar, never silent, never empty. The men in the bar look like soldiers who have barely survived, but hours ago, slaughter; who have seen their buddies hacked limb from limb, have seen them blinded, gutted, castrated; look like men who are carrying bloody souvenirs in their pockets: an ear, an eye, a nose, a penis, a buddy's anklebone. Their dreadful cries seem to be their only proof that they have survived. This hard miracle lives in their fevered and yet lightless eyes, and they have no age. They are all the color of gunmetal, and their sweat causes them to shine like that, and they are all—as far as Arthur can tell—white men. Arthur is young enough to wonder how this can happen to white men; he does not know any white men yet. He does not feel at all vindictive or triumphant; he only feels a kind of falling wonder. In the morning, they will be lying on the sidewalk, drenched in their own piss.

Next to the bar, there is a candy store, still open—candy, chewing gum, newspapers, cigarettes—and the fat owner, always wearing a gray baseball cap, and glasses, sits in the open window, a toothpick between his teeth.

Next to the candy store, beneath three signs, each reading ROOMS, are three narrow doors which seem to be trying to efface themselves by sinking into the hideous walls, and Crunch and Arthur enter the last of these. They were, then, in a narrow hall, facing a steep flight of steps. They began to climb, and a door at the top of the stairs immediately opened and a young black girl in a bathrobe stood there, waiting.

Her hair was uncombed—"nappy"—and the bathrobe was half open, revealing a dirty nightgown and the beginning of her breasts, breasts surprisingly heavy for a girl so thin. And she seemed very young, not much more than a child. Arthur had never seen her before.

"Oh, it's you, Mr. Hogan," she said.

But she had never seen Arthur before, and she stared at him—with wonder and hostility—and then looked back to Crunch.

"He's with me," Crunch said.

Another figure appeared behind her, a heavy-set white man, with iron-gray curly hair, a long, heavy nose, and brutally self-indulgent lips. He put his hand inside the bathrobe, and turned the girl toward him, pushing her toward the open door behind them.

"It's all right," he said. "It's his kid brother. Evening, Mr. Hogan," and they went back into the room, locking the door behind them.

In silence, Crunch and Arthur climbed to Crunch's room, which was on the third floor.

In the split second that the girl and the man had looked at him, Arthur had felt violated, stripped naked, spat on. It was in nothing that was said. It was in the contempt and complicity in the eyes. He had never felt this before, though he had seen the man before. But this time, when the black girl had looked at him, he had immediately wondered what she was doing there: and it was immediately clear to him that *she* did not wonder what *he* was doing there. And what the white man really said, with a lewd grunt, was, He *says* it's his kid brother. And, of course, they would know what was happening, from the sounds, from the sheets—though these were not changed very often. But if Crunch and Arthur could hear others, and they did, every night they spent here, others could also hear them. Then he wanted to run, not from Crunch exactly, but out of this eternity. When Crunch came back, they would find another room, a private place.

But to think of Crunch's return was to think of Crunch's departure, and he put both arms around Crunch's waist and rubbed his forehead against Crunch's back as Crunch unlocked their door.

The room was even uglier than the room in Washington, and smaller, with an old-fashioned, noisy brass bed. There was a table, a chair, a ceiling light, and a sink, and a dim mirror above the sink. The room was on the street, or, more accurately, faced the tracks. The violence of the trains accompanied their ecstasy, and the pinched, glaring faces of the people flying by, through eternity, peopled their dreams.

He had never really disliked the room until now, had never really looked at it. Some nights he and Crunch had lain awake, smoking, the light from their cigarettes the only light, and watched the trains go by, happy to be together and caring for nothing else. Now happiness was leaving, that was all he knew; it was rolling itself up, like a scroll.

Crunch locked the door behind them, and sat down on the bed, and, now, abruptly, it was Arthur's turn to be silent.

Crunch lit a cigarette, and looked over at Arthur, who stood by the door.

"You mad at me?"

Arthur smiled, and shook his head no.

Crunch watched him.

"You coming in, or going out?"

"That's up to you, man."

But Arthur moved from the door, and went to stand by the window, looking out. Now everything was quiet, except the rumble of a train approaching.

"You see something out there you like better than me?"

Arthur turned from the window, and sat down on the floor, at Crunch's knee.

"What's the matter, Crunch? Did I do something?"

Crunch sighed and said, "No, baby." He leaned back and yawned, and took a drag on his cigarette. The downtown train, on the far side of the tracks, came squealing into the station.

"No, baby. *I* did something."

Arthur listened to the train doors opening, the distant murmur of shifting weight. There was a pause, as though silence had made a hole in sound. The train doors thundered closed.

Arthur rested his head against Crunch's knee. Metal squealed against metal, the train pulled out of the station. He heard the uptown train, on their side of the street, approaching.

He knew now, dimly, that he did not really want to know; at the same moment, he realized that he had no choice—he asked: "What did you do?"

"I want to ask you something first, Arthur"—and Crunch sat up, speaking to the back of Arthur's head—"what you going to do when I go away from here?"

"I don't know, Crunch. I don't want to think about it."

"You've *got* to think about it!"

He reached down and turned Arthur's face to his, and his hands were suddenly wet with Arthur's tears. Arthur had not made a sound and his body was not shaking. He turned his face away and leaned the back of his head against Crunch's knee.

"I don't know, Crunch. I'll keep on going to school, naturally, and I'll keep on working with my music—and—I'll wait till you come back."

And suppose I don't *come back?* Crunch wanted to say. But he said, "Arthur, what about?—" The uptown train stopped at the station, seemed nearly, in fact, to have entered the room.

"What about what?"

"Other people."

"What other people?"

"Arthur—have you ever had a girl? No. I guess you haven't."

"What you talking about?"

"It would be good for you—to have a girl."

"Well—I'm sure I will, Crunch—one of these days."

He wiped his face with the back of his hand and turned to look at Crunch.

"Why you talking about that now?"

Crunch looked uneasy, and the uptown train rushed past their window, causing the entire building to shake.

"Maybe I just hope you make love to a girl while I'm gone instead of—"

"A man? Another man?" Arthur looked down at the floor. "I haven't thought about it, Crunch. I haven't thought about it at all. I just love you."

"Well, you can't love me forever, man, you got to grow up, for Christ's sake!" And Crunch rose from the bed and strode to the window, looking out. Arthur watched his back.

"That what you wanted to talk to me about?"

"Yes. No. No."

"Why can't I love you forever? I will anyway."

"Arthur, you just a baby, and sometimes, I swear—!"

"You sorry? You sorry about us?"

"No. No, Arthur, don't take it that way. I just—I just want you to be all right. I want you to be happy. I don't"—he faltered, the streets seemed strangely silent—"I don't want *you* to be sorry."

"Sorry about us? I'll *never* be sorry about us, I swear, no matter what happens."

"I made love to Julia this afternoon."

Crunch sat down, abruptly, on the bed, as though someone had pushed him, and stared at Arthur. His face held fear and pain.

Arthur looked down at the floor again. He asked, "And were you going to bring her here tonight?" Then, looking up, "That why you been so quiet?"

"No. I didn't want to bring her here tonight."

"You can go get her, you know. I don't want you to do nothing you don't want to do, not because of *me,* man—you want me to find a girl now, because *you* found a girl!"

"Arthur, Julia ain't nothing but a child—"

"Then how come you make love to her? Of course, I guess you think *I* ain't nothing but a child!"

"Arthur? will you listen to me? Please? *Please?*"

Arthur stood up and walked back to the window, his hands in his pockets. Crunch could not see his face.

"Arthur?"

"I'm listening."

"Come over here."

Arthur did not move.

"Come over here!"

Arthur moved, and Crunch grabbed him, pulling him down on the bed. Crunch moved so that he was leaning against the headrest, with Arthur in his arms, the back of Arthur's head against Crunch's chest.

"Arthur, please try to listen, and don't get mad at me, and don't jump all evil and proud. I know I can bring a girl down here if I want to, and you can, too, if *you* want to, and I wasn't saying you should get a girl because *I* got a girl. I *don't* have a girl." He paused, and swallowed. He said, "I just have you."

It was impossible to tell, from Arthur's stillness, what was going on in his mind: and Crunch was afraid to turn him so that he could see his face.

"You a beautiful kid, Arthur, you don't know it, and a whole lot of slimy motherfuckers and some of them might look just like me going to be trying to fuck with your ass and you can't blame me if I get worried about it."

"What's that got to do with Julia—and this afternoon?"

"Arthur—people get in trouble and they need help—and, sometimes—you can't say no."

But, Crunch thought, *at least, he's listening:* and he held Arthur a little tighter. Still, he did not know what to say—exactly—he did not know how to say it. He remembered Julia's face, and body, her overwhelming need. He said, "Sometimes a person just needs somebody's arms around them, then anything can happen—one thing leads to another—do you understand me?"

"I think so."

"Do you know I wouldn't hurt you, man, for anything in the world?"

Arthur was silent.

"*Do* you?"

"Yes. But—I don't understand—"

"Look, I can't tell you everything. It ain't for me to tell you. But Julia's in trouble. She's got to get away from her daddy." He paused. "That's why I was glad your mama asked her to stay at your house."

"Crunch—was you fixing to bring her here—if—?"

"No. At least not tonight. I had to talk to *you* first. I wasn't looking to get my brains beat out." He lit a cigarette. "Arthur?"

"Yeah?"

"You listening?"

"Sure."

"I want you to do something for me—do me a favor. Okay?"

"Okay."

"I want you to look out for Julia. Be her friend. Forget about this afternoon. That's just something that happened. That's life. You'll understand it—better—by and by," and Crunch smiled.

"What do you want me to do?"

"Just be her friend. She's got to get away from her daddy."

Arthur moved, and looked up into Crunch's face.

"It's that bad?"

"It's worse than that."

"What does Julia want to do?"

"She told you tonight. She wants to take care of her little brother."

"But she *can't*—she's not old enough!"

Crunch put out his cigarette. His face was bleak as he looked down, and said, "Who knows? She's seen enough already to make her more than old enough."

Arthur was silent. Then, very shyly, "Crunch, do you love Julia? If you do, it's all right. I won't be jealous—"

Crunch grinned. "I bet. That why you was acting so funny a few minutes ago?"

"Oh, I was just surprised—"

"If that's the way you act when you surprised, I damn sure ain't going to be giving you no *surprise* birthday parties!"

"Oh, come on, Crunch—"

"I been thinking about it all day—here we are: she's fourteen. You sixteen. I'm almost twenty. I felt like a old man, a *wicked* old man. But I don't know what else I could have done, except disappear or die. That girl was crying out, Arthur. *Crying.*" He shook his shoulders, remembering the sullen day. He looked down at Arthur. "She don't mean to me what *you* mean to me, and I hope you got that straight in your head now, but she's in trouble and I don't want nothing to happen to her. Be her friend. If she knows she's got you, and your family—that might make a whole lot of difference."

He watched Arthur, realizing that there was peace between them again; and he'd told the truth, without betraying Julia. He leaned back on the bed, pulling Arthur closer.

"But I don't think I want her to be my girl friend," Arthur said.

Crunch laughed. "One thing at a time, son. One thing at a time."

One week later, Crunch was gone—just like that, a great hole opened, and he dropped through it, out of sight.

The summer ended. Day by day, and taking its time, the summer ended. The noises in the street began to change, diminish, voices became fewer, the music sparse. Daily, blocks and blocks of children were spirited away. Grown-ups retreated from the streets, into the houses. Adolescents moved from the sidewalk to the stoop to the hallway to the stairs, and rooftops were abandoned. Such trees as there were allowed their leaves to fall—they fell unnoticed—seeming to promise, not without bitterness, to endure another year. At night, from a distance, the parks and playgrounds seemed inhabited by fireflies, and the night came sooner, inched in closer, fell with a greater weight. The sound of the alarm clock conquered the sound of the tambourine, the houses put on their winter faces. The houses stared down a bitter landscape, seeming, not without bitterness, to have resolved to endure another year.

But, before this time, another year! Crunch might be dead, Crunch might be back: so, this song rang and rang in Arthur's skull as he went about doing whatever he was doing, and he never quite knew what he was doing, though he, somehow, got it done. He walked the tumultuous, resounding streets, streets which were incredibly silent and empty for him—listening for Crunch's footfall beside him, seeing Crunch in the distance, and hurrying to catch up with him, though he knew it was not Crunch, seeing Crunch come toward him—going to school, rehearsing, for a time, with some people he didn't like (he was never, in fact, to sing in a quartet again), working, part-time, as a Western Union messenger, singing, in churches, on the weekends.

> *Faith I am maintaining*
> *I go on, uncomplaining,*
> *But, before this time, another year.*
> *My life may all forsake me,*
> *And death may overtake me,*
> *If I'm with Thee,*
> *I've no need to fear.*

He sensed that Paul and Florence were worried about him. He faced the fact that, for the first time in his life, he had something to hide—he had dreams of Crunch being court-martialed and tortured because he, Arthur, had "talked": and so he mastered a candid surface, stayed in his room only to study, or write letters—with the door open—and, otherwise, remained visible at the piano, his most private place. His second most private place was the movies, but he was never able to remember a single movie he had seen as that summer ended and fall, then winter came.

> *Make my pathway brighter,*
> *Make my burden lighter,*
> *Help me to do good whenever I can.*
> *Let Thy presence thrill me,*
> *Thy Holy Spirit fill me,*
> *And hold me in the hollow*
> *Of Thy hand.*

"That song sure seems to mean a lot to you," Paul said mildly, one Saturday evening. He had been listening to Arthur play for several minutes. Arthur had not realized that his father was in the room.

"Oh—hello, Daddy." He let his fingers drop from the keyboard. "I have to sing it tomorrow night, in Brooklyn."

"You accompany yourself when you sing?"

"Sometimes. Not all the time. Most of the time I follow the church pianist."

"Can they follow *you?*" Paul asked and laughed, and, after a moment, Arthur laughed.

"Sometimes." He looked at his father. "It don't seem to me like I'm that hard to follow—and most of them, really, they play better piano than me."

"Well," Paul said, "you don't really hear yourself. But that's all right—for right now, anyway, that's all right."

They were alone in the house. Florence was out—shopping, or having a drink with Martha.

"You hear from any of the old gang?"

Arthur had a letter from Crunch in his pocket, but it took him a moment to say—trying to look as though it had slipped his mind: "Oh. Yeah, I got a letter from Crunch."

"How is he?"

"He sounds fine. He sends his love."

"He's a fine boy," Paul said, and lit his pipe. He walked to the window. "I reckon you sure miss him, don't you?"

"Yeah," said Arthur glumly, speaking to himself. Then, "I mean, yes sir, I sure do. We—all—had some nice times together."

"How's his family?"

"I believe they're all right, sir."

"Yeah," said Paul. "You latched on to him like he was Hall—like *he* was your big brother."

Arthur felt immediately disloyal. "Why no, sir," he said. "Not exactly." Paul looked at him, and Arthur blushed. "Hall's my *brother*," Arthur said lamely. "Crunch—Crunch—he's my *friend*."

"Just the same, he's older than you, and you always been the *younger* brother and so you needed another *older* brother. Somebody you could trust," and Paul looked at Arthur again. "Ain't nothing wrong with it—the youngest always needs the oldest. Until," he added, after a devastating pause during which he lit his pipe again, "the youngest grows up enough to realize he's his own man and can't keep running to his older brother no more." He paused again, and looked at Arthur. "Especially if he's not really the older brother but just the older *friend*."

"But can't a friend," Arthur dared, "be as important as a brother?"

"He can be *more* important. I'm just saying they're not the same." He sat down in the chair near the window.

"When you get married, for example"—here he paused for another examination of his pipe—"*if* you do, and I hope you do, that woman you marry, she going to have be more important than your mama or your daddy. You ain't going to be living with *us*. You going to be living with *her*, and raising your children with *her*. We can't hold on to you—*we* leaving. We *did* what *we* could. And you can't hold on to us—can't nobody move backward, not far, anyhow. They come to grief." He smiled, but something in the smile frightened Arthur. "And I don't want you to come to grief."

Arthur sensed a warning: he did not want to hear it. To hear it would be to confess. Something in him longed to break his silence, to ask *What's happening to me?* He longed to lay his burden down, and end his tormented wonder. But he could not incriminate, menace Crunch—his "heart": he sat silent, looking down at the keyboard.

"What you thinking about, son?"

"I was thinking about what you said. But," he looked up and smiled, "I don't know what to say about it."

"Well, keep on thinking about it, then. Ain't no harm."

> *Hide me in Thy bosom*
> *Till the storm of life is o'er.*
> *Rock me in the cradle of Thy love?*
> *Feed me, Jesus,*
> *Till I want no more,*
> *And take me to Thy blessed*
> *Home above!*

He was singing for Crunch—to keep Crunch safe, and to bring Crunch back, and he was singing for me, to keep *me* safe and to bring me back: he was singing to hold up the world. There entered his voice then, therefore, a mightily moving, lonely sweetness and the people were transfigured and transfixed: he sang to their love and their worry; he sang to their hope. With his song, and standing before the people, he made his confession at the throne of mercy and knew himself, then, as his voice issued from him, to be redeemed, in the hands of a power greater than any on the earth. His love was his confession, his testimony was his song.

So he gritted through the grinding days and nights, the ferocity of his dreams, his leaping body's ache, the sorrow, like a carpet, at the bottom of his soul. He had no friends anymore, and was unable to imagine himself with friends. Everyone he saw, he saw from very far away, as at the wrong end of a telescope. Their words—sounds—simply spun in the air, utterly meaningless; their words never reached him. He liked his job as messenger because it left him alone for hours in the streets, and demanded nothing more of him than physical energy.

When his job ended, he went to the movies and sat in the dark, letting images and sounds roll over him. He relived, over and over, every instant of his time with Crunch—every song, every gesture, every embrace—until he felt that he was going crazy, began, really, to be afraid that, in another moment, he would begin to howl and be carried off to Bellevue. Sometimes he almost wished that this would happen. But, no—neither Crunch nor I wished to find him in Bellevue. We were suffering, too, after all, and we had a right to expect him to keep the faith. And at such moments, too, he felt that if he were to fail his lover, or his brother, he would then, somehow, have cut the cord binding us to life: if he faltered for an instant, someone, somewhere, on the other side of the world, in that very same instant, would know that love had failed and thus, be enabled to bring us down. At such moments, he shuddered—it is not easy to bear so cosmic a weight— and went back to watching the movie for a while, or rose and walked out into the streets or went home, to the piano.

But sometimes, he simply sat in the movies and let the tears roll down his face, and saw nothing.

And it was hard for him at home, though he did not like to admit this. He wanted, really, to leave home, although he knew that, for the moment, this was neither possible nor just. It was as though, at home, he found himself trapped in a play, acting a role he had played too long.

Paul and Florence *were* worried about him, of course they were. They could not help this, and they could not hide it, and the devices they used to dissemble their concern set his teeth on edge. Their worry was not nearly as specific as Arthur imagined—they were not alarmists. They were not concerned about his attachment to Crunch, which they took as inevitable. Only time could indicate to what extent it was "normal," but normal is a word which has very little utility in a crisis. He had, as far as they could see, no other friends—Peanut was gone, Red was soon to go—but there was nothing they could usefully say, or do, about that; especially since a certain standoffishness was a family trait. Arthur was no worse than I had been at his age, and no worse, certainly, than his father. Yet, they *were* concerned about the nature, the meaning, of his privacy. They did not want to violate it: at the same time, they wanted him to know that they—and life, and love, and the world—were his. They could not break in; he could not break out. They wished that I were home—naturally, for many reasons—though they also wondered what I would be like when I got there. They also realized, though Arthur didn't, that, as he was outgrowing everything and everybody, he would also have outgrown his relationship to *me:* we would have to find a way of finding each other again.

This made mealtime an exercise in grace and tension, sustained by a certain cheerfulness which came, in fact, out of love. But the restless and lonely Arthur needed something his parents could not give him, which no one, in fact, could give him now, not even Crunch—though Arthur did not know this, either. Arthur hid a secret and he hated having anything to hide; he had never had a secret before.

He poured it all into his song, and Paul watched him, and listened, striving to become reconciled.

Julia was the only person Arthur saw. This was partly because of his promise to Crunch. She was the closest thing to Crunch and she was, also, the only person in the world, now, who spoke his language. They knew the same things. And his jealousy had evaporated. There had, literally, not been time for it.

He had given her the key to Crunch's room, and he sometimes met her down there. Then, more than ever, when he entered the room, he had a secret; but this was a secret he could clasp to himself with both pain and joy. Julia did not know, no one in the world knew; only he and Crunch knew what wonders had taken place in this room, this broken-down, filthy, miraculous room! He paced the room sometimes, as Julia talked, remembering: leaned out of the window, looked into the mirror, touched the bed, remembering, remembering, proud, and almost happy. Crunch's odor was still in the bed, in the chair—in the air, and everything Arthur touched Crunch had touched, his fingerprints were still there, Crunch was present in this room! He was almost frightened sometimes, to feel this presence with such power, but he was unbelievably happy, too, and grateful to Julia. Without her need, and Crunch's promise to her, he would never have been able to enter this room again. Perhaps he could see Julia, and nearly no one else, because she shared his secret without knowing that she did.

On a Saturday evening, near the end of summer, he climbed the familiar stairs and knocked on the unusual door.

"Arthur?"

"Yeah."

"Come on in. The door's open."

Julia was wearing a shapeless smock and her hair was tied up and the trash can was full. She had been cleaning the room.

"You shouldn't leave your door unlocked, when you down here by yourself."

"Are you kidding? These locks can't keep nobody out—these *doors* can't keep nobody out. And I don't know *why* I'm trying to clean this room. It can't be done, I must be crazy." She ran water in the sink and soaped her hands and grinned at him. "How you keeping?"

"All right. And you?"

"Okay. All things considered. How was your day?"

"Shitty."

She laughed. "People don't know. We going to the movies?"

"If you want."

"What you want to see?"

"I don't know. I brought a paper, thought I'd leave it up to you."

He doesn't say it, but the truth is that he's already seen everything that's playing.

"I see. You want me to do all the work."

She dried her hands on paper towels which she must have brought with her, and dropped the towels into the trash basket. He sat down on the bed, caressing it, and looked around the room. Julia had brought a plant from uptown and put it in the window, she had washed the windows, and covered the chair with a bright red rag. There were two water glasses on the sink, and she had covered the hideous, rickety night table with another brightly colored rag. That was about the limit of what could be done with the room—the room's only real hope was fire—but it made a difference, and Arthur was very grateful.

"These people giving you any trouble?"

"Oh, that black girl, I believe she's a mental case"—Arthur laughed—"don't laugh. I *do*!—she tried to give me some lip, and I told her again, just like *you* told her and just like Crunch told her, that this was our brother's room and I was going to be responsible for it and keep it clean and all until my brother—*our* brother—got back here. She wanted to know if I was going to *use* the room. I said, Sure I was going to use the room long as I was paying the rent." She paused, and looked at the trash can. "Now, what am I going to do with this? She ain't never going to empty it."

"I'll empty it," Arthur said. "Leave it alone."

"Why don't you go on and empty it now, then? And I'll get out of this smock, and we can go."

"Okay," Arthur said, and picked up the trash can, and walked out of the door. He had to hunt for a garbage can not already overflowing, but he finally managed to empty the trash can. The streets were full, people stumbling or ambling by—no one paid any attention to him at all. He started back up the stairs, whistling.

Julia was combing her hair, was wearing her green slacks, and an old gray sweater.

"Thanks, Arthur." Arthur put the trash can down. "Let's get a hot dog around the corner, okay? I'm hungry."

She locked the door behind them, and put the key in her pocket. As they started down the steps, they heard someone coming up. "Oh, Lord, I bet you that's Blanche," said Julia.

It was the black girl, and they met her on the second story landing. She was, relatively speaking, dressed, in a shapeless skirt pinned with a safety pin, and a blouse swollen by her great breasts. Her dark, narrow

eyes considered them with the aimless and unanswerable hostility
with which she seemed to regard everything and everybody.

"Good evening, Blanche," said Julia.

"You coming back tonight?"

"I might be. I don't know."

Blanche looked at Arthur. This was a different look—unanswerable, but not aimless: contemptuous, triumphant. She knew that Arthur hated her, hated her from his heart; hated her, and feared her
because she knew what Crunch and he were to each other. She had
divined that Julia did not know, and that he did not want her to
know. She knew that he was not Crunch's brother, and Julia was not
his sister.

"*You* coming back?"

"What difference does it make? the rent's paid."

Blanche looked at them from her intimidating distance.

"Yes," she said. "The rent's paid."

She passed them, and continued up the steps.

"Somebody might be coming by, one time, to find out just *how*
the rent gets paid. You mighty young, it seems to me, to be doing what
you doing."

"I don't know what you think I'm doing," Julia said, "but you
look mighty young to *me*, too."

Blanche kept moving up the steps, they continued down. They got
into the streets.

"I *might* be doing anything," Julia said. "They worried about the
law. Shoot. The law don't care. They ought to know that. *Every*thing's
going on down here."

Yeah, Arthur thought, *but we don't know the rules, baby,* but he said
nothing. He was worried about too many things. He was worried
about what Blanche might tell Julia, for he knew that Crunch, in spite
of his intention, had finally said nothing. Crunch might have had the
courage, but certainly had not had the time; Arthur knew that he,
himself, did not have the courage, at least not yet. And he was worried
about Julia being alone down here at night, and Crunch had been

worried, too; the room was in his name, after all, and Julia was a minor. *But,* he had sighed, *we don't have too much choice, man. She's got to get away from her daddy.* Arthur's impression was that Joel Miller was drinking heavily and became uncontrollably dangerous when drunk and that Julia used the room as a haven at those times. This explanation had vaguely dissatisfied him, but it was only now that he was beginning to bring his full attention to bear on it.

"Do you stay here at night, a lot of the time?"

"No." Just before his departure, she had spent one night down here with Crunch, and one afternoon. Arthur did not know this. She was terrified, down here, by herself; but she had been terrified of her father, too. She had sometimes used this room as a refuge, hiding in this room until she was sure that her father had fallen into a drunken sleep.

But she had never managed to sleep alone in this room, it was impossible, though she had tried to steel herself to do it, the way an athlete trains himself to meet a mighty challenge. She had sat all night, with the lights out, huddled at the head, or the foot of the bed, listening to the trains roar by, watching the lights flashing in and out of the room, listening to the streets, to the footsteps on the stairs, the rocking, crashing beds, the muttered, muffled sighs, and curses, the pleas, the commands, the sound of running water. Every time she heard feet climb the stairs, she bowed her head between her knees, and prayed: don't let them unlock this door! Then she longed to run back to her father—at least his touch was familiar, and, when it was over, she would sleep. But it seemed to her, really, that she had not slept since her mother died and would not sleep again until she found her brother.

One night, she had had to go to the bathroom, and she crept out, locking her door behind her. The bathroom was unbelievably filthy, but she was obliged to add her filth to the rest—and leave it there, because the toilet did not flush. When dawn came, she took the subway home. Joel was asleep, fully dressed, on the sofa.

She had wanted to move. She had moved, all right—into an unknown section of hell. She remembered someone saying to her once, *Now, hell, child, you just remember—hell don't have no boundaries.* Then, *But you got to go there to find out.*

Now she and Arthur crossed a street and walked half a block to the hot-dog stand and bought two hot dogs.

"What movie we going to see?"

"I don't care."

"Well—you going to go uptown after, or you going to stay down here?"

"I think I'll go uptown. Don't like the way Blanche looked at me."

"Well—we can see a movie *up*town then," said Arthur, and they started toward the subway.

Yet, just the same, she *had* moved: she had got through those nights. Something had happened; her father knew it, and it frightened him. His fear was no more dependable than anything else about him, she couldn't count on it; but she had seen that he was frightened when she came in on the morning after she had spent the night at our house.

He was just about to leave—she had timed it that way—and was writing her a note. He looked, with elaborate disapproval, at her halter and slacks.

"So, you got kidnapped?" With his little smile.

"Why you saying that? I didn't think you'd mind. They're your old friends."

"They're really your mother's old friends," he said. "Did you all have a good time? Who all was there?"

When he said "your mother's friends," she tensed, as though he had hit her in the belly, or caught her in a lie. Florence had been talking to her about her mother. She had felt that Florence knew much more than she would say: she had longed to break down and tell Florence the truth and beg for her help.

But she felt that it was only she, Julia, who had, somehow, brought herself to this place and only she could get herself past it.

"Just us. We ate, and talked. Mr. Montana came in later." She hesitated. "Crunch and Arthur were there"—she watched his face, but she could see that he did not feel threatened by these boys—"but they had to go somewhere, so it was mostly me and Mama Montana. We had a good visit, she's a nice woman." She paused again, watching him. "They wonder why you never come to see them."

"I didn't hardly ever visit them, daughter. It was your mother."

She realized that he was frightened of any of her "mother's friends" whom she might see outside, who might, as he would have put it, turn her against him.

"That don't stop them from wondering, Daddy."

She could see him calculating, calculating danger.

"Well—we might go visit one evening. I'll do anything to please you, daughter."

He said this with the jaunty, mocking, gallant grin which she had always found so moving, and which moved her now, suddenly, in a very unpleasant way.

"You better get on to work," she said. "Don't, you be late."

"Give us a kiss." This was morning ritual.

She realized that he was standing in the place where she and Crunch had lain the day before. She suddenly felt very sorry for her father. She wondered what had happened to him. She wondered what he wanted.

He came to her, his lips parted, and he covered her breasts with his hands. He whispered, "I missed you last night."

She took his hands away, kissed him, lightly, on the forehead.

"Go on," she said. "You going to be late."

"Well—you going to have to make up for that when I come home." He was being jaunty still, but he was at a loss; he could not find her position. He started for the door. "You all didn't talk about me too much last night, did you?"

"Like I said, Daddy, they just wonder why you never come to see them."

"And what did you tell them?"

"I said you'd been very upset."

"Yeah, you sure got me upset, all right. Don't know what I'm doing half the time." He opened the door. "You going to *be* here now, when I get back?"

He stood in the doorway, with the daylight behind him, around his skull, his curly black hair. His face was in shadow, but she watched the sparkling eyes, the teeth, the anxious, boyish grin.

Soon, just the same, she would be free.

"Go on," she said. "I reckon I'll be here."

He hesitated for yet another moment, then closed the door behind him.

And if I'm not here, she thought, *I'll leave you a note.*

After the movie, they sat down in a coffee shop around 135th and Seventh Avenue, and drank coffee and listened to the jukebox. They had seen William Holden and Gloria Swanson in *Sunset Boulevard.*

"Why did she shoot him?" Julia asked. "If he wanted to go, why didn't she just let him go? That don't make no sense to me at all."

"Well," said Arthur, "I guss she was crazy about the cat—I guess the cat drove her crazy."

"She was crazy, all right. I don't believe in that kind of love. People got a right to their own life."

"It must be wonderful, though," said Arthur, "for someone to love you that much."

"Now *you* sound crazy. To have somebody love you so much you can't even go to the bathroom without them having a fit?"

She sipped her coffee and looked over at the jukebox, where some boys and girls were standing. Some boys and girls were dancing in the streets. She looked back at Arthur, and grinned. "You think it would be wonderful. It would be wonderful, all right—*you'd* be wonderful—inside of a week, you'd be so wonderful you'd be carried away, screaming." She laughed. "Black people ain't made for that kind of nonsense."

"Black people doing it all the time, right on this avenue, girl. Every Saturday night, some chick goes crazy and takes out her razor and starts chopping up her man." He grinned. "You been in the pulpit, you ain't been out here. But—you just stay out here awhile."

She said, after a moment, "It's strange out here, I'll give you that."

"It's dangerous out here, baby."

"Oh, come on. How come you trying to be so grown-up with me? How long *you* been out here?"

"Never mind, sister. Longer than you."

"Well. I sure don't want nobody loving me so much they going to be coming after me with guns and razors."

Arthur grinned. "I don't know, girl. You done lost your salvation and you out of the pulpit and you look mighty fine walking these streets. I'd be careful, if I was you."

"You hush. Anyway, that's way in the future." But as she said this, she thought of Crunch, her face changed, and Arthur laughed.

"It ain't *that* far in the future. I believe you almost ready."

"I got a lot to do before all that." She stirred her coffee, looking both young and old. She looked at the clock on the wall behind the counter. "I got to make some money and get away from here." She looked again, wistfully, at the boys and girls before the jukebox. "I was never young like that," she said.

"You mean—because of the pulpit?"

She shrugged. "I guess. Partly. But—I was just never—*young.*"

"Well—don't you feel younger now?"

She looked at him, and Arthur said quickly, "Well, no, I guess you don't." The reality of her trouble returned to him; he realized that he did not want to understand it.

And he felt, suddenly, sharply, that *she* did not want him to understand it, either. Her swift, girlish, or even boyish manner, and everything she said, were stratagems designed to protect a distance.

Yet she had confided in Crunch. And she was not a virgin anymore; Crunch had held her in his arms. They never talked about it, he rarely thought about it—his imagination simply refused to accept it—and yet, the unspoken love, and the weight of the unknown trouble bound them together and caused them to be friends.

"I guess I better be getting home," she said, and something in the way she said it brought him sharply to attention. It was ten thirty.

"Will your father be home?"

"I hope not. He might be."

Now she looked old; she looked out at the children dancing in the street.

"You can stay at my house," he said.

"Thanks, Arthur," and she smiled. "But I can't *stay* at your house."

"You can, if you want to, you know that, why not?"

"My daddy would shoot me," she said, and she laughed.

"Does he drink a lot—your father?"

"Yes," she said. "Since my mother died. He always drank—a little—but now he drinks a lot."

"That's why you don't want to go home?"

"Well—it's hard—to know what to do when somebody drinking a lot—and you can't talk to him. But I can't just keep *staying* out. I've got to *get* out."

"You don't want to go downtown? I'll ride down with you."

"I'm starting to be afraid of Blanche. That girl is evil. She likely to set everything on fire, she know I'm down there."

He sighed. "I still don't know why you can't come to our house. You could stay there until you figure how to do what you want to do—you want to get to New Orleans—well, Mama could help you find a way to do that."

"Arthur. I can't go to New Orleans like this. My grandmama don't need another mouth to feed. I don't want Jimmy to see me like this."

"Why not? What's wrong with you the way you are?"

She looked down. She said stubbornly, "I got to find a way."

He said nothing—there was nothing he could find to say to her stubborn privacy. Something in her had moved far beyond him. But she had always been beyond him, even as a tiny preacher with those eyes as old as Egypt and that voice which had nothing to do with the time she had spent on earth. It was strange to feel, suddenly, sitting in front of her, that in spite of everything—her manner, her voice, her trouble—Julia had not changed. It was mightily disquieting, a mystery, not a pleasant one, and, while his mind could not turn away from this mystery, neither could his mind grasp it. But he had heard in her voice, when she said, *I got to find a way,* the same inexorable acceptance of the unnameable that he had heard in her voice from the pulpit.

"Hell," he said, mysteriously irritated. "You ain't got to find a way *tonight.*"

"How do you know? There *is* a night coming which won't have no tomorrow."

"Oh, Lord," he said, disguising his tension with a laugh. "You talk like you still in the pulpit."

She said nothing for a long while, and he listened to the sounds from the jukebox. He watched the boys and girls, about their age, older, laughing, talking, seeming to quarrel, moving with and against each other as though they were all bound together by invisible strings, strings which they were both testing and longing to break. Though they were young, they were old, older than he, older than Julia—they seemed to have made their discoveries already. It was this, though, paradoxically, which made them innocent and vulnerable: that they seemed to imagine that there was nothing to discover. They clung to each other, and the jukebox, as though time could never take these away; or as though they had already seen what time could take away and moved and talked and danced now with a kind of belligerent, doomed defiance.

He looked at Julia, who was watching this scene from far away, or who was, perhaps, not watching this scene at all. Her eyes, now, told him nothing.

"We might as well go," she said.

She rose, and he rose with her. He paid the man at the counter, and they walked past the jukebox and the kids at the jukebox, into the streets.

"Which way do you want to go?" he asked.

"I think I better go home," she said. "Maybe I'll come stay at your house tomorrow."

"I'll walk you," he said.

They walked in silence for a while. Then Julia said, "Sometimes, now that I'm out of the pulpit, I feel more *in* the pulpit than I did when I was preaching."

"How come?" he asked.

The streets were dark and very quiet, people standing in pools of light on street corners and on the stoops.

"I don't know," she said. "Maybe I see the people better than I did. Maybe I see myself. When I was preaching, I don't think I knew what I was saying. I didn't know what it meant."

They walked in silence for a while. He did not know what to say.

"But now it comes back to me. I hear myself again—but really, for the first time." She was walking with her hands in her pockets. She said, "I didn't know it was true."

"How could you preach it—if you didn't know it was true?"

"Oh, I *believed* it—but I didn't *know*. And now, maybe, I don't believe it but I'm beginning to *know*." She looked at him and smiled. "I know that sounds crazy."

"Maybe," he said, after a moment. "Maybe not."

"When I preached about how the Lord, He can cause your soul to tremble," she said, "I didn't know that it was true."

"Julia. How did you—?" He did not know how to phrase his question. He had been about to ask, *What made you change?*—but he no longer believed, as he had only a short time ago, that she had changed. This wonder tongue-tied him. It frightened him. And he could not ask *What happened to you?* He was not sure that he could bear the answer even if she could bear to utter it.

The question hung between them in the soft, dark silence.

"Maybe it was the funeral you sang at for me," she said. "What we had to go through to get that poor woman in the ground—or into the kingdom, I don't know. It came to me that *she* was true, even if the rest of us were liars. I don't know."

She was silent for a long time. They crossed a street, approaching her house. She took one hand out of her pocket, holding her keys.

"And then," she said, "my mother"—and she stopped. He said nothing. Her house came closer. "Mama Monta—your mama—says that my mother was a real sweet, pretty, laughing young thing—I never knew her like that. She was just—my mother."

They paused at the bottom of her steps.

"I've kept you out so long," she said. "You want to step in and have a little refreshment for your long walk home? Don't want you dropping by the wayside."

He did not really want to go in, and he was aware that she, too, was double-minded concerning his possible effect on her father. But he remembered his promise to Crunch; perhaps his presence could help, if only for a moment.

"Just for a minute," he said. "I'd like to use the bathroom, please."

"No trouble at all." They climbed the steps, she opened the street door, they walked the dark hall to the Miller apartment.

She unlocked the apartment door, very quietly, switched on the light, and they stepped inside.

Her father's voice came from the living room. "Hey, Julia? Where've you been?"

Arthur felt Julia suck her breath in sharply and, before she could answer and before they could reach the living room, Joel appeared. He was wearing pajamas, carelessly, appallingly open, he was drunk, and he rushed toward Julia.

"I came home early, especially for you! I don't *never* see you no more, *where've you been*?"

"Daddy," Julia said, "just to the movies. With Arthur. Arthur brought me home."

He had seen only Julia. He had not seen Arthur. Julia's words checked him.

He stopped, and looked at Arthur. Arthur had wanted to get to the bathroom, and pee: Joel's look froze his pee inside him, froze everything inside him. He could not have peed, he could not have moved, not if life itself had depended on it. Joel's face was wet, his pretty hair was standing all over his head. When he looked at Arthur, his hair seemed to stand up, a muscle in his jaw throbbed, his mouth fell open, and there seemed to rush into his eyes all the wonder and pain and hatred of a lifetime: Joel's wet lips hanging, his teeth gleaming, the wonder and pain and hatred in his eyes, hatred so powerful that it caused him to shake at the same time that it held him up. His hands shook with anguish to tear out Arthur's throat.

"Who are you? What you doing here with my daughter?" He turned to Julia. "You dragging them in off the streets now?"

"Daddy," said Julia, "this is Arthur. You know him, you know him from when he was little."

"The hell you say! He damn sure ain't little *now*. What you doing, coming in here this time of night, with my daughter? I don't want her fooling around with black scum like you? She got her *daddy* to look out for her!"

Arthur said, "You know me, Brother Miller. You know my whole family—my father and my mother and my brother, Hall. I'm Paul Montana's son."

These credentials, as Joel stood leaning in the passageway, seemed slowly to penetrate his brain. He said, "Paul Montana? The piano player?"

"That's right. I'm his youngest son. Julia and me, we just went to the movies, and I walked her home. That's all."

Joel's lips slowly came together. His eyes changed, cleared, focused—and he saw Arthur. When he saw Arthur, he saw something else—his nakedness. He straightened, tried to close his pajamas. He said to Julia, "You should have said something, daughter."

"You didn't give me time, Daddy."

She was looking at him with pity, and from very far away.

Joel looked at Arthur again, and what Arthur now saw in the eyes was harder to bear than the hatred of a short time before. A short time before—seconds before—the eyes had been alive with hatred, as brilliant and black as coal; now they were lifeless and dead with terror. Seconds before, his voice had shaken the walls and menaced the neighborhood sleep; now his voice was a cracked, dry whisper.

"How's your father?" he managed. "Ain't seen him in a long while—guess that's why I didn't recognize you." He tried to smile. "You have to forgive me, son. These have been some trying days since my wife passed. I ain't over it yet." He looked at Julia, and, strangely, life flickered again in the eyes, and, incredibly, for that second, Arthur was very moved by the man. He looked again at Arthur. "I been almost crazy worrying about my daughter, now that she ain't got no mother." He tried to smile, tried to put it all behind them. "Can't blame a man for trying to protect his only daughter. She's all I got." He turned to Julia. "Take Arthur in the living room, daughter, give him something to drink. I was just getting ready to go to bed." He smiled at Arthur. "No sense in me trying to keep up with you young folks." Astoundingly, abruptly sober, he extended his hand to Arthur. "Forgive me, son. I was just trying to protect my daughter. No hard feelings?"

Arthur shook his hand. "No, sir. No hard feelings."

Joel started up the staircase. "Good night, daughter. See you in the morning."

"Good night, Daddy. Sleep well."

"Good night, Arthur. Say hello to your family for me. Me and Julia be coming to see you soon."

"Good night, Brother Miller."

Joel disappeared up the stairs. They remained where he had left them, like two frightened children—Arthur fighting back a terrifying impulse to crack up with laughter.

"Can I go pee now?" he asked Julia.

They looked at each other a moment and then Julia laughed. They laughed together, low, bewildered, frightened laughter, like children not wishing to be heard laughing. They heard Joel upstairs. Julia said,

"You better, before you cause a real scandal," and they laughed again, until Arthur was afraid he might really pee in his pants. "Hurry up," said Julia. "Go on. I'll see what we got to drink."

By the time he came back, Julia had poured him a beer, and he no longer felt like laughing.

"Girl," he said, sitting beside her on the sofa, and picking up his beer, "what you going to do?"

She said, not looking at him, "Can't say. I mean, I *really* can't say." Then, still not looking at him, her arms folded, "Don't talk to nobody about my daddy, what you saw and heard tonight—I know you won't—I'm going to find a way to do what I have to do." Then she looked at him with a look so candid that he wondered what she knew. "You going to have to do the same thing, one way or another—you know? We all do. Sometimes I think, maybe my daddy, he never found that out—but one thing I can tell you"—and she turned away from him, leaning forward, her hands on her knees, he saw again the great difference—the distance—between her eyes and her father's eyes—"Julia ain't dead. Julia far from dead."

BOOK FOUR

Stepchild

Lead me to the rock
That is higher than I.

SONG

I came home in the fall of the year that Arthur turned eighteen. I think I came home on a Sunday. Arthur met me at the pier. I remember this long, long shed, thousands of people shouting and crying and laughing around me—and the ugly, pinched, white faces of the officials at the pier, who didn't seem at all happy to see so many uniformed black cats home—and then, a kind of space cleared and, from very far away, I saw Arthur kind of loping in my direction. I could tell that he hadn't seen me yet, hadn't picked me out of the khaki-colored tumult. He was taller, and so it seemed to me he'd lost weight. The sun was behind him, throwing his face in shadow. I couldn't make out the expression on his face, but I could feel his apprehension and anticipation. I watched him, maneuvering myself into his path. Something I did, some telltale gesture of mine, no doubt, snagged the corner of his eye, made him turn his head and look directly at me. His whole face opened, he suddenly looked about two years old, and he started running toward me. I dropped my bags, and grabbed him, lifted him off his feet and held him above my head.

"Hey, young lion! How you been?"

I set him down, and we hugged each other. I pulled away, held him by the shoulders to look into his face. He looked like he couldn't stop grinning—guess I looked the same way.

"Hall. Goddamn, it's good to see you."

"It's good to see you, too, baby. You all right? You look kind of skinny."

"Oh, come on, you just don't remember how I look. You *really* look skinny—you lost some weight, man."

"A little. I'll get it back."

"You damn sure will, soon as Mama sees you."

"How *is* Mama? And Daddy?"

"They fine. Mama's been cooking for the last twenty-four hours and ain't satisfied with nothing yet."

We laughed and we picked up my bags and started for the street.

"How was it over there?"

"Just a small police action, son. Had to put them gooks in their places. They worse than the niggers, thinking they got a right to a whole country. Why, even the worst niggers here don't want but a little piece of the country. But we showed them. We put them in their places—six feet under."

He had been watching my face. "It was bad?"

"Oh, yeah, baby, it was filthy. Thought I was going crazy, don't know if I'll ever get clean."

We came into the sunlight, into the street. I had not seen these streets in so long, and I had seen so many other things, that they hit me like a hammer. People adjust to the scale of things around them—cottages, streams, bridges, wells, narrow winding roads—and now I was in a howling wilderness, where everything was out of scale. For a second I wondered how I could ever have lived here, how anyone could live here. I had not heard this noise in so long—incessant, meaningless, reducing everyone to a reflex, just as the towering walls of the buildings forced everyone to look down, into the dogshit at their feet. No one ever looked up, that was certain, except to watch some maddened creature leap from the walls, or to calculate their own leap—yet people lived here, and so had I, and I would: what a wonder. What a marvel.

I was repelled, but fascinated: embittered, but home.

I watched the press of cars and cops around the place. I asked Arthur, "How the fuck we ever going to get out of here?"

"I got a car, man, don't worry. You just stand right there."

He looked from right to left, looking for someone, started across the street, turned back, to stand in front of me.

"You don't know how glad I am to see you, Hall. I missed you. You don't know." Then he started across the street again. "Stay there. I'll be right back."

And he disappeared.

Staying there was not exactly the easiest thing in the world to do. People kept pushing past me as though I were not there, and the cops kept shouting, "Keep moving, please, keep moving!" I moved back a little from the curb, but I really couldn't move very far without being swept back into the building. Women, young and not so young, glowed past me with their loved ones, home safe from the wars; women were there with small children, even with babies in their arms. Yes, papas and mamas and sons were there, and sisters and uncles and aunts and cousins, all of them celebrating their miracle which is homecoming. *Out of the jaws of death*—and, for the moment, it did not matter that they had passed through one danger only to enter another. *Keep moving. Keep moving*—I looked at the cop, he looked at me: something in my look made him look around him, and look away. Cars and cabs piled—parked—three deep, picked up the heroes and their loved ones, and crawled agonizingly into the furious city. Arthur suddenly reappeared, and picked up two of my bags.

"Come on." I picked up my duffel bag and followed him into the chaos of automobiles and people. Arthur opened the trunk of a fairly old blue Pontiac, put the two bags in, took my duffel bag and threw it in, and closed the trunk. He opened the doors.

"You ride in front, so you can see the city—I'm sure you want to see our fair city. Look who I got to be your chauffeur."

He got in back, I got in front. I slammed my door shut, and, for a minute, I didn't recognize my driver—who stared at me with a big grin on his face.

"Goddamn," I said finally, "Peanut!"

"That's right, man. I changed that much?"

We laughed, and hugged each other as best we could, with the steering wheel between us.

I said, "Yes—no, I can't tell, man—yeah, you've changed a little. You put on some weight."

"A little. You didn't, though. Look like you *lost* weight."

"Yeah, I guess I did. I'll get it back."

We started moving. "Lord," said Peanut, "let us get out of this shit and get on home where you can start putting on some weight"—he grinned at me—"and get out of that funky uniform and Arthur can pour us a little taste and we can get to the *grits*."

"How you been, Peanut? What you been doing? I'm sure glad to see you."

"I been busting my nuts in Washington, *dee cee*, the capital of our great land, with some hincty, jive-ass, half-white niggers, trying not to blow my stack, and coming up here for weekends every time I could. I just ran into Arthur by accident, man, yesterday, and"—he grinned—"he pressed me into service." We were turning east, away from the water and the boats and the warfare just behind me, but we were in a bottleneck still. "Patience," said Peanut, watching the traffic and beginning to inch slowly across the avenue. Somebody honked his horn behind us. "Keep farting, motherfucker. You might see some shit."

"You don't like Washington?"

"Well, I'm lucky, let's face it, that the army decided I was half blind and so they didn't send me where they sent *you*. Hallelujah, bless the Lord," and he laughed and moved across the avenue. We started inching along the side street. "But, no, I don't like Washington. I like some of the folks I met there, but—it's a real ugly, racist little town, man. You know that," he said to Arthur. "You and Crunch found that out."

"Yeah," said Arthur. "We found that out, all right."

"I remember," I said. "Arthur wrote me that you all was down there."

"Crunch had some people to see, so he and Arthur stayed on a couple of days. Us, we couldn't wait to get out of there." We stopped, hoping to be able to make the next light. "But it's just been *de*segregated. Say a nigger can go anywhere now, anywhere you please. Ain't that something? Ain't you glad? Now you can eat in the same *room* with them funky white cunts and their ball-less men. I can't hardly wait, myself—but, at the same time, I don't believe I'll try it alone. I'll come up here and get some rough, Harlem cats to test the waters with me." He laughed again, and we made the light.

"You *have* changed," I said.

"Of course. So have you. You was over yonder, I was in Washington. What you see, what you go through, what you see others go through—it changes you, all right. Hey, Arthur, will you light me a cigarette, please?"

Now I know this sounds insane, but that—Peanut's request that Arthur light him a cigarette—came as a shock: a small shock, but a real one. It made me realize how long I'd been gone, how much had happened since I'd been gone. I turned to watch Arthur light the cigarette and hand it to Peanut.

"Would you light one for me, too, please?"

Arthur gave me a quick, bright look, a wink—and lit the cigarette and handed it to me.

"You don't smoke?"

"Sometimes." He lit a cigarette, put the pack back in his pocket. "I don't smoke much. It's not too good for the voice."

We finally got out of the press of traffic, and started up toward our house.

It was a day full of sunshine, a lot of traffic, a lot of people, all moving with what seemed like purpose. Everyone seemed, to my wondering, slowly refocusing eye, exceedingly well dressed. No one looked up, it is true, but then, that was also because they did not expect bombs to come raining down on them from the sky. I had been sent away to help guarantee and perpetuate this indifference. No one, here, knew what was happening anywhere else. Perhaps no one ever knows that, anywhere: wherever *here* may be, it must always happen *here* before it can be perceived to have happened. And then, it is not really perceived, it is simply endured. Out of this endurance come, for the most part, alas, monuments, legends, and lies. People cling to these in order to deny that what happened is always happening; that what happened is not an event skewered and immobilized by time, but a continuing and timeless mirror of ourselves. What happened here, for example, was not stopped at Shiloh, still less at Harper's Ferry: it is happening in our children's lives today. I name the domestic monuments, not because I am being chauvinistic but in my role of Sambo, the tar baby.

It must have been a Sunday—Columbus Circle, with banners on, balloons and horse-drawn carriages, black women pushing baby carriages, young people draped around the base of one of the statues at the entrance to the park, and the park seemed to be full, although the air was brisk—and the mourners on the benches: rigid, silent women, white, sometimes with a book; men as still as cats; and boys as lithe: we inched across the Circle and picked up speed. The houses began to change.

"This place is really becoming Spanish," I said.

"Naturally," said Peanut. "This place was a Spanish queen's idea."

"Watch your language," Arthur said, and we laughed, and I was, suddenly, in spite of everything, apart from everything, happy to be back home.

We reached our block, and began rolling toward the house. Arthur leaned forward and put both arms around my neck. I put one hand on his forearm, and held it tight. The streets were full of people I didn't recognize. But I would soon be seeing faces I remembered, later tonight, tomorrow. I wondered what I was about to find out.

Peanut stopped the car in front of our house. "Arthur," he said, "you take Hall and the bags on up, and I'll park this car someplace and I'll be right with you."

"Okay." We got out, and got the bags. We slammed the trunk shut, and Peanut drove off. Some of the kids on the street looked at me curiously, or rather, looked at the uniform curiously. A black lady whom I didn't know walked by, and said very quietly, "Welcome home." We started climbing the stairs. Paul and Florence stood in the open doorway, and then I was their little boy again, young, younger even than Arthur, that day, because I had been spared.

I didn't want to eat, or do anything, until I had taken off my uniform and had a bath and washed off the stink of battles and barracks, of millions of men. Arthur came in, at the end, to scrub my back and to rinse my hair.

"What you going to do later?" he asked me.

"I don't know. I might not do anything. I'd buy you a drink if you was old enough, but you ain't."

"Depends," said Arthur, carefully pouring water over my head.

"Depends on what?"

"Depends on where you want to buy me a drink."

"So you been breaking the law already?"

"Just a little light lawbreaking. Nothing extravagant."

"Well—I might check out Jordan's Cat."

Arthur, without actually doing so, seemed to sniff ironically, as if to say, *You know damn well you going to check out Jordan's Cat.* He said, "They won't ask me for my draft card in there. And anyway, I can drink ginger ale. You glad to be home?"

"Yeah. Only I don't know what I'm going to *do*—"

"Oh, you'll figure that out, don't worry about it now. I'm sure glad you're home. I missed you, brother."

"I missed you, too, man. Hand me a towel?"

He handed me a towel and I dried my streaming face and hair and stood up.

"See you in a minute, man," Arthur said, and left me alone.

I pulled the plug and the water began to slop in thunder through the pipes. I dried myself, staring into the mirror.

Martha had written me, saying that she had something to talk to me about but didn't want to go into it in a letter. I wondered what it was; I thought I could guess, and I wondered how much I cared. I hadn't, anyway, cared enough to prevent it, whatever it was: we had agreed, tacitly, that we had no claims on each other. That had been fine, before I went away: it was not so fine once I was so far away from home and my imagination began to pulse out great jungle flowers in the garden of what might have been. Close up, you see the person's wrinkles, warts, and pimples; when close to you, the person has innumerable ways of driving you up the wall: but when far from you, these very same imperfections become irreplaceable and beautiful, testifying, after all, to how much each cared about the other. Close up, the person's imperfections matter, but, from far away, you see your own. The question then is not *How did I stand* her? but *How did she stand* me?

Well. I wrapped my towel around me, and walked into the incredible luxury of my own bedroom. If it seemed smaller than before, it also seemed more *mine* than before. It had been scoured, had been put through some changes to be ready for today; all my things were as I had left them. I had the feeling that no one had been allowed to sleep in this room while I had been away, not even Arthur.

And yet, as I started putting on my own clothes, my own underwear, my own socks, I knew that the time had come for me to leave this room, this house, the time had come for me to leave my father's house. I realized that, had it not been for the interruption of the war, I might have left already. I was a certain kind of cat. I needed my own place, my own lair, *my* woman, *my* cubs: I had bounced around enough to begin to realize that. There was no guarantee, of course, that I would get what I needed: but *that* was what I needed. I was not at all like Arthur: I had never before looked that fact so squarely in the face. I did not know what Arthur needed, but I knew that, in order to deal with whatever it was, he needed *me*. And, had it not been for the deep-freeze of the war, my involuntary and dreadful departure, I might, by now, have arrived at another way of "Keeping an eye out" for him: he might, by now, have had two houses instead of one, instead of one brother, other blood relations, claiming him as "uncle."

I was anxious to begin my journey. And now that I was home again, free, my brother was no longer in my way. I felt that I could handle it all—cautious I am, but stubborn, too.

There was laughter in the living room, and music. Peanut and Arthur were playing records of other quartets. Paul was commenting and, from time to time, I heard my mother's laughter, sounding the way she must have sounded as a girl.

I had brought presents for everyone—for everyone, that is, except Peanut—and now, not yet completely dressed, I rummaged around in my luggage for something he might like. I had brought jade earrings for my mother, a marvelously, monstrously carved pipe for Paul, and a three-quarter length black-and-gold dressing gown for Arthur. I had brought something for Martha and Sidney and Aunt Josephine, but all that I could find for Peanut was a large poster of an Oriental battle which I had liked because of the violence of colors and the fragility of the line.

I took all these objects out anyway, and put them on the bed, put on my shirt, put on my shoes, and looked at myself in the mirror as I combed and brushed my hair.

You don't always like what you see in the mirror, but I did that day, since I was home and everything, once again, was up to me. This proves, I imagine, that all you ever really see in your mirror is your state of mind. Leaving that alone: I felt that I, Hall, would be all right, would make no one ashamed of him. At the same time, I was a little afraid to leave the room, to go into the living room, and eventually the streets, and pick up my life again. Behind my face, there was music, the music from the living room. It was a quartet. I heard,

Nicodemus
went to the Lord,
he went to the Lord
by night
He said, Rabbi,
which means Master,
won't you lead me
to the light?
He said, Nicodemus,
let me tell you
like a friend
you must be
born again,
and I never heard
a man
speak like this man!

That sound, the driving sound, always makes me see a black cat, face brilliant and sweating in the sunlight which pours down on his face, pacing, prancing, up a long, high hill. When he stumbles, he does not lean forward; he arches back, using the misstep to pick up the beat. He is surrounded by people urging him up the hill, they are all around him and behind him, but you do not see them. You know, simply, as he does, that they are present. If this sound always makes me think of a black cat, it is because the sound is black. It is black because the people who have betrayed themselves into being white dare not believe that a sound so rude and horrible, so majestic and universal, can possibly issue from them—though it has, and it does; that is how they recognize it, and why they flee from it: and they will hear it in themselves again, when the present delusion is shattered from the earth.

Beneath this sound: Paul's chuckle, Florence's laugh, Peanut and Arthur's deadpan conspiracies, my face—I pick up my presents, and walk into the living room.

"Well, well, well," Peanut said mildly. "Don't look like you going to have any trouble adjusting to civilian life."

"Now, you all leave me alone. You don't know how bad I wanted to get out of that uniform."

"You right. That uniform didn't do nothing for you—didn't bring out the color of your eyes. You see what I mean? But now, with *this* outfit!"

"Peanut, what makes you so jealous?" Florence asked. "And when you *know* the Lord don't like that? My children—and especially my oldest one, *today*—they just naturally sharp, you might just as well go right on ahead and accept it."

"I accept it, Mama Montana, I was just a little dazzled—"

"Ain't no sense in being dazzled, you just go right on ahead and accept it." She laughed. She was a little tipsy, not so much with wine as with happiness—with relief: as though she had been holding her breath all the time I had been gone and could only let it out now.

Paul was another matter. He would probably never again take a really deep breath, but he was a happy man today.

"I brought you all some presents," I said. "But if you keep teasing me, you going to make me so nervous I won't know what I'm doing."

"You want to do that now?" Florence asked. "Or you want to wait till after we eat? I want to get some food in your belly."

"Won't take but a minute." I was nervous, like a child. I concentrated on the packages. "Here," I said to my mother. "This is for you," and I gave her the package—that is, I reached the package to her and then went over to where she sat on the sofa, and kissed her, and "Here," I said to Paul, "this is for you," and I kissed him on the forehead quickly, and "Here, Skeezix, this is for you," and I dropped the big package into Arthur's lap, and "Peanut," I said, "I didn't know I was going to see you today, but I hope you'll like this. All I can say is *I* liked it, that's why I bought it," and I gave him the rolled-up poster and I sat down in the chair by the door.

"After all that," said my father, "before we open the presents, I believe you need a drink."

The table before the sofa was loaded with bottles and trays—peanuts, crackers, ham, cheese—I hadn't even noticed it.

"Look like we having a party," I said.

"You right," Paul said. "We is sure enough having a party. We so glad to see you home, son, don't none of us know how to act. Don't even care if you get drunk—don't care if *I* get a little drunk and you *know* I ain't never said nothing like that to you before. How about a little Jack Daniel's? Or Cutty Sark? Been saving it all for you. As you can see, your mama don't drink"—Florence laughed—"and I don't *hardly* drink and we lock up the bottles when your brother's in the house."

"I'll have a little Cutty," I said. "With some ice."

My father poured it, and handed it to me. We looked each other in the eye for a second—but a very long second: our past, our present, and our future happened in that twinkling of an eye—and we all raised our glasses to each other, and drank.

I do not know why I felt so keenly that this first homecoming was also my first farewell.

A silence fell. The noises from the street came in. The record player had stopped. Paul took out his pipe, examined it with great respect for a moment, put it between his teeth, and waved one hand at me. In my memory, all this occurred in silence. Arthur took out his Oriental robe and put it on, walking up and down the room, like Yul Brynner, and looking into the mirror. But the only full-length mirror was in the dining room, and so he disappeared for a moment. Mama put on her earrings, and Peanut unwrapped his martial scroll.

"Let me put the food on the table," Mama said, and touched her earrings and smiled at me and sashayed into the kitchen.

"That's true enough," Paul said—he was speaking to Peanut—"I can spend the rest of my life and never sit down at a table with white folks—but that ain't really the point."

"Anyway," Peanut asked, "how many niggers in Washington got enough money to go downtown and be desegregated?"

"Oh, some," Paul said. "I wouldn't be surprised if it wasn't quite a number—but you wouldn't like them, either."

"Liking or disliking," Florence said, "has nothing to do with nothing. I remember when you had to change trains in Washington and go to the Jim Crow car—when you wouldn't be allowed in the dining room until all the white folks was through. Well, of course, you don't want to eat with fools like that—but all that's changed. It don't mean I want to eat with white people. It just makes life a little easier—might make my children's lives a little easier. Maybe that's all I want."

"I just don't find it easy to swallow," Peanut said. "These people got the *gall* to claim to be giving us something they didn't never have the right to take away." He took a swallow of his drink—we were at the table, getting some food into our bellies—and said, "It ain't going to make me hold them in no higher esteem, I'll tell you that right now."

"That's not the point, son," Paul said. "It ain't worth talking about. You can't love nobody you can't respect."

I thought of some of the Oriental faces I had seen, and the dry, bitter contempt in their eyes. Some were whores, and some were grandfathers or grandmothers, and some were children. In the case of the old, the contempt might be leavened with pity or, in the case of the children, camouflaged by bewilderment and pain: but the contempt was a constant, at bottom, and bottomless. Not a single white buddy of mine had seen this—but then, they had not seen *me*.

"Well, anyway," Arthur said, "it ought to make things better in the schools."

Peanut grunted. Paul said, "Listen. You all are young. Like it or not, we here now and we can't go nowhere else. I was a kind of half-assed Garveyite when I was young—you would have been, too, had you been young when I was. But you all hardly know who he was, and ain't no white person going to tell you. All I'm saying is, you going to have to do what we've always done, ain't nothing new—take what you have, and make what you want."

He looked around the table, but especially at me.

"We didn't wait for white people to have a change of heart, or change their laws, or anything, in order to be responsible for each other, to love our women, or raise our children. You better not wait, either. They ain't going to change their laws for us—it just ain't in them. They change their laws when their laws make *them* uncomfortable, or when they think they can see some kind of advantage for *them*—we ain't, really, got nothing to do with it."

"If we had *ever*," said Florence, "depended on white folks for *any-*thing, there wouldn't be a black person alive here today."

"Mama," asked Arthur, "you think they can't change?"

She looked down; then she looked at Arthur. "I'm saying you can't depend on it. You've got to depend on yourself." She touched one ear-ring. "Anyway, I'm not really talking about white people. I've known some white people who were beautiful and some black people who were rats." She paused, looking at Arthur again. "Look. When was the last time we sat down at this table and talked about white people? The only reason we talking now is because it looks like they've decided to desegregate this and desegregate that. I hope they do. It might make life a little easier for you and a little better for them. But we're not really talking about *them:* we talking about *us.* Whatever they do, honey, you still got your life to live. I'm glad you don't have to ride in no Jim Crow car, like me and your daddy had to do. But, Jim Crow car or no Jim Crow car, we still had to raise you—it was a good thing they changed the law, but we couldn't wait for that!" Then she turned to Peanut, with a smile. "So you go on down, and test them waters— part of the trouble is, you afraid they just *might* mean it—and then, how you going to look at them, how you going to look at yourself?

But just remember—it don't so much matter what *they* mean to do: it matters what *we* mean to do."

I said—it was partly a question, partly a discovery: "You really mean that, don't you?"

"Of course, I mean that. How you think we sitting at this table? You think me or your daddy waited to get permission from some white man?" She laughed. "Why, honey, they don't give *themselves* permission to do much." She looked very young and happy, her green earrings flashing in the light. "Pass me your brother's plate, Arthur. I ain't going to fatten him for the *slaughter*, but I'll be damned if I don't strengthen him for the battle."

After supper, we went back to the living room. It was still early, the sun had just gone down. The light in the streets was a kind of gray-purple, the streetlights just beginning to be turned on: you could see them way downtown, beyond the park, creeping uptown. It was very quiet, as though everyone had decided to catch their breath at the same time and were doing what we were doing, just sitting around.

I sat at one window, near my father; my mother sat at the other window. Peanut sat at the piano. Arthur sat on a hassock, his head leaning on the sofa. Peanut was humming a song, "Where He Leads Me, I Will Follow." Florence hummed along with him.

"We ain't told you about what happened to Julia," Arthur said. He said it in a strange, dry, distant way, looking up at the ceiling: he said it as though it hurt him.

Florence stopped humming.

"I heard she stopped preaching," Peanut said, "and then dropped out of sight."

"She dropped out of sight, all right," said Florence. "She was *pushed* out of sight."

Paul shifted in his seat, started to speak, held his peace.

"You wrote me about it," I said to Arthur, "some time ago."

"That was some time ago. I didn't write you all of it. All of it hadn't happened—or I didn't know all of it." He lit a cigarette.

"I had just seen her a couple of nights before, down on Fourteenth

Street." He paused. "She had started spending a lot of time down there." He sat up, his hands clasping his knees. "I'm sorry, Mama. I didn't mean to interrupt you."

"That's all right." Then, "I got this phone call, Hall, early one morning, and I didn't recognize the voice, it sounded so *wild* and frightened. The voice kept crying, screaming, Mama Montana! Mama Montana! and I still didn't recognize it. The voice said, Come up here, please, come up here, please, please, I think I'm dying. I said, Who is this? Who is this? and the moment I asked that, I knew who it was, don't know *how*. She said, It's Julia, *Julia*, please come, please come, and she started to crying like I hope you ain't never heard nobody cry. I got into my clothes and ran up there. I took a taxi.

"Time I got there, some neighbors had already got into the apartment because she was crying so, and the door was open. And Hall, I never saw nothing like it, not in all my life. You remember how skinny Julia was? Well, the skinny little thing had been beaten to an inch of her life. Her face, it wasn't no face, it was just a mess of blood and puffed-up flesh. Didn't have no lips, didn't have no eyes—just little dark slits where the eyes was supposed to be. I said, 'Who did this?' I thought somebody had broke in and tried to rob them. And she never answered me, she just kept saying, 'I've lost my baby, I know I've lost my baby.' And I was so turned around, Hall, I couldn't make no sense of what she was saying. Somebody wanted to call the police, but I said, 'No, let me call the ambulance, we got to get this girl to a hospital.' So I called the hospital, and, just lucky I got Martha on the telephone. I wrapped up the child as best I could, in blankets—and the blood came seeping through those blankets, I just knew she was going to bleed to death—and then, for the first time, what she'd been saying about losing a baby made sense, she was bleeding heavy from between her legs. I said again, 'Who did this?' and somebody said, 'Her father. Her father beat her, and he gave her that baby, too.'

"Well, I didn't have time to think—I *couldn't* think on all that, then. The ambulance came and they put her in the ambulance and I got in with her and rode to the hospital. And thank God Martha was there, or we'd *still* be in that hall, answering stupid questions and filling out papers. Martha got rid of all them people and got Julia inside and I sat down on a bench. Everything had happened so fast, wasn't nothing clear in my head.

"But I sat on that bench for a while. And, look like"—she turned away from us, looking out of the window—"a whole lot of my life came back to me while I was sitting on that bench. And I lost a baby, too, one time, didn't nobody know it but me and Paul. But I wasn't a girl, like Julia, I was married, and it was Paul's baby and I'd already had three children." She caught her breath and looked away again. "And I was a young girl a long time ago, somewhere else. It wasn't like some of them young ones sitting on that bench with me, that morning.

"Martha came back, and said that Julia had been beaten pretty bad, but that wasn't the worst—the beating had brought about a miscarriage and Julia was into her third month. They were doing all they could. She might pull through, she might not; she was a mighty frail girl, and she'd lost a lot of blood.

"Then she asked me to get hold of her father, because he was the next to kin.

"She looked me dead in the eye when she said that, like she knew what I was thinking—she was remembering, and I was, too, the time we'd been up there together, before Amy died—and, when she said that, my blood just stopped and froze. I looked at her, but I couldn't answer: I couldn't pronounce his name, I swear I couldn't. Somehow, when Martha asked me that, I knew—for the first time, I *knew!*—that everything I'd been scared to think—was true—that woman had been telling the truth when she said, Her father, he beat her, and he give her that baby, too."

Now it was dark. I could hardly see my mother's face, or anybody's face. The streetlights were on. A dim, deep, soft hum of music and voices came in from the streets.

Paul turned to me. "Your mama wanted me to find Joel," he said, "and so I went looking for him. It took me all day. It took me part of a night. He wasn't on his job. I didn't hardly think he'd be home, knowing him, but I went up there, anyway, and almost got arrested. The cops were still there, and they thought I was him. Well. The place was a mess, I mean it was a slaughterhouse, partly from whatever had gone on there that morning, and partly from the cops—they had turned out the joint, looking for anything but especially for dope. Hall, there was still blood on one of the windows, blood in the sink, blood on the sofa. And I could see that nobody wanted to believe that a man could do this to his *child*. It was more like what might happen if a dude just went crazy and came home and bounced everything he could get his hands on off his *woman*. One of the cops, a black dude, said, 'If this chick's still breathing, she's lucky—must be they just didn't have no room up top for her yet.'

"But all the neighbors swore it was him—that it couldn't have been nobody *but* him. They heard all the noise before he left, and they heard him leave. And then they heard Julia screaming and crying— they was there when your mama came—they swore it was him.

"I didn't want to believe it. Maybe I never thought much of Joel, but I thought more of him than *that*—you just naturally think more of *any* man than that. Especially if you know him, or you think you know him, and you've had drinks with him, and all, and he knows your wife, and your children. And I'm a father, too—no, it was hard for me to believe. But I knew Florence believed it, and she don't believe things easy. It's funny"—he paused, looked at me, looked away, looked down—"I didn't believe it, and yet, I wanted to find that hyena and beat him as bad as he beat Julia and then throw the rest of him into a police station."

"You didn't believe it," Florence said, "but you *knew* it. Just like me."

"Well, I covered Broadway. He used to like to hang out in some of the musician's joints down there. No dice. I went to the Village. No Joel. Came on back up, going to one place, then going to another, doubling back. Went to Jordan's Cat, although I was pretty sure he wouldn't be in there. I went back to his house.

"I sat down on the top step. I guess my brain was kind of in a turmoil. I just sat there. I figured he was going to have to come here, sooner or later, I even rang the bell. There were no cops around and no cop cars, but I figured that one of the neighbors had arranged to call the police station as soon as he showed up. And, I don't know why, I figured Joel was just too dumb to realize that, just like he was too dumb to know what people really felt about him while he was carting little Sister Julia around, and him eating out of her hand. Anyway, I sat there, I was tired.

"But I was going to be late for work, too, so I went on up to the bar where I was playing then, a few blocks past Jordan's Cat, place called The Window Shades, and, wouldn't you know, there he was, sitting at the bar.

"I'll never know, until the day I die, if he knew I was playing piano in that bar and was waiting for me, or if he just happened to crawl in there because it was close to home and he was afraid to go home and afraid to be too far from home. I'll never know. My name was in the window, but, in the state he was in, I doubt that he'd have noticed that.

"He was a mess, too, really, but it hardly showed, unless you looked hard at him. He had some scratches and bruises and his upper lip was swollen—but, if you didn't know, he just looked, really, like he'd been drinking a little too heavy, a little too long.

"He looked at me, and I went over. He said, 'Paul, I'm so glad you came in. I got something to tell you.' I just looked at him. He said, 'Some people broke in the house this morning, they tried to rob us, and I think they hurt Julia.' I still just looked at him. He said, 'You know who I think they were?' He said, 'Paul, I hate to tell you this, but my daughter—Julia'—and then he started to cry—'I think she had a nervous breakdown, since her mama died, she ain't been the same.' He said, 'Paul, I hate to tell you this about my only daughter, but she turned into a prostitute, she been peddling it on the *streets*, man, and one of her pimps broke in this morning and beat her up. My only daughter. Man. Can you believe it? And they want me to testify against her. Now, you know I can't do that. You can't testify against your own flesh and blood, the Bible tells us that's a sin against the Holy Ghost, you can't never be forgiven for *that*.' And he was really crying, real tears was dripping through his fingers, and his shoulders was shaking.

"Well. I didn't know if Joel knew it, but *I* knew that some of the people in that bar lived in his building—the cops would soon have his ass. All my anger left me. He really believed his story. I just left him there, went on to my piano. The cops picked him up that night, or soon after—they didn't pick him up in the bar—but they couldn't hold him." He looked at Florence. "Weren't no eyewitnesses. Julia couldn't talk, and, by the time she *could* talk, she was in New Orleans—her grandmama *hustled* that child out of here."

No one spoke for a long while. I wondered what Florence was thinking—about her old friend, and her friend's daughter, and granddaughter: I sensed that she was trying to find a key to all this in a past which only she remembered. And she was not sure that *she* remembered it now—she was ransacking the past for the details she had overlooked.

"Well," Florence said finally, "she never wanted to say nothing against her father—maybe because it wasn't just *her* father. Anyway," she added, after a moment, "she never did. And I guess we have to respect that."

"It was Crunch's baby," Arthur said. "When Julia could talk, and I went to see her at the hospital, that's what she told me."

I asked, "The grandmama, she didn't bring little Jimmy back with her?"

"Of course not," Florence said. "What for? She left him with some of their relatives down there."

"Poor Jimmy," Arthur said.

"One thing for sure," I said. "She must have damn sure *wanted* it to be Crunch's baby."

Arthur nodded at me, emphatically, his eyes very big and bright, and older than I had ever seen them.

Peanut said, "You mean that Brother Joel Miller was sleeping with his own daughter? I didn't hear *that*!"

"What did *you* hear," Arthur asked, "way down there in Washington?"

"It's a small world." Peanut glanced at Florence, then at Paul. "I heard—she'd been turning tricks—you know, like Brother Miller said—with white men, down on the Bowery, and in the Village, and Brother Miller found out about it and that's why he whipped her—that's why he beat her up."

"Well," said Paul, "look like *his* story's the one that got sold. Anyway, he's still around. You go out tonight, you might run into him. The women still like him."

"How much does Crunch know about this?" I asked Arthur.

"Well—I *think* he knows that Julia was going to have a baby by him, and she lost it." He hesitated. "He had told me about—their *affair*—before he left here." He lit a new cigarette from the coal of an old one, stubbed out the old one in the ashtray on the coffee table. He looked up at me. "Crunch don't say a whole lot in his letters—I was the only one writing him, really, and I don't know what Julia told him. I didn't think it was for *me* to tell him!"

I said, "You're right." Then, "He should be home soon."

Peanut looked at Arthur. "Your heart," said Peanut, and smiled. Then, "Sure wish I had some news from Red. But I really have my doubts, man, that he ever learned to write."

Peanut and Arthur laughed together.

"They both be coming home soon," Arthur said. "Don't worry. We be seeing them any day now."

Paul looked over at Arthur. "Come on and play something for us. Your brother ain't heard your voice in a long time—and, I know, once he hits them streets, he going to be out there for a while—move your behind, Peanut. I don't think Hall ever heard his brother sing and play at the same time."

Peanut moved, and Arthur rose. "Okay, I'll do my best." He grinned at me. "But you just remember, this is a *command* performance—you might just have to grit your teeth and bear it." He sat down at the piano. "For you, brother."

I sat in the window, watching him—space at my back, my arms folded, watching him. He looked down at the keyboard, strummed the keys; it was a different face than I had seen before, and it was a different sound. He turned his face for a second and looked at me, then turned again to the keyboard. His face changed again.

Shine,

looking at me for a second, and at the space behind me, then back down to the keyboard,

on me.

I watched his fingers on the keyboard. His eyes were closed.

Shine
on me.

I watched his face and his hands, as though I had never seen them before, and felt him beginning to drag his song up out of me.

Let the light
from the lighthouse
shine on me.

It was more than strange how the two voices came together, one issuing through his fingers, the other through his throat, both from the same center; and he was the center only because, out of the vast and unmapped geography of himself, he sang, for us, our song. I watched his face, and I really wondered how anybody could bear that.

Let it
shine
on me!
Oh,
let it shine
on me.
I want,

the piano rolling like a river,

the light from the lighthouse,

the voice rising out of our whirlwind, the whirlwind transfiguring Arthur's face,

to shine on me.

He opened his eyes for a moment, as though to check the distance from one place to another, looked down, began again.

I heard the voice of Jesus say,

and out of the space beneath, behind me, I heard a cheerful black lady's voice, a little drunken, calling out to another black lady, and I heard their laughter,

come unto Me,
and rest.

I watched Paul's dark face watching his son's dark face. I did not dare look at my mother, I don't know why. I had the feeling that some people on the street had stopped, listening, but I dared not look behind me, dared not look down.

Lie down,
thou weary one,
lie down
thy head upon my breast.

The noise of the traffic on the streets rang upward. I could see the stoplights on the corner, flashing green, flashing red, and automobiles, with shells like beetles, or dinosaurs, massed together, waiting, or, abruptly liberated, careening off into whatever the future held.

Shine on me,
shine on me,
oh,

the thundering, racing, calling piano now the only voice, then,

let the light,

the piano lower, slower, Arthur's voice rising,

from the lighthouse
shine
on me,

and he stopped, looking toward me, after a moment, smiling.

I had to shake my head to bring him into focus: I hadn't known that my eyes were wet. I knew he wanted me to say something, but I didn't have anything to say. Trying to conquer distance, I came out of the window and, from my distance, I whispered, "I believe I'll buy you a drink. I don't mind breaking the law for a real, honest-to-God law-breaker."

I looked at Paul, and Paul grinned saying many things to me in a split second: "Yes. I believe they might be expecting to see you up the road."

"Who knows I'm home?"

Arthur rose from the piano, he and Peanut looked at each other and slapped palms together, and Paul laughed with them. "Oh," they said, more or less in unison, "just a couple of people, don't you worry about it, they going to *recognize* you, and I do believe they know you're home!"

I looked at my mother.

"Oh, yes, son," said Florence. "I believe the news is out."

Presently, we started rolling toward Jordan's Cat, Peanut, again, at the wheel.

And now, I found that I was really frightened—I felt, to tell the truth, like a coward. I hadn't written Martha, she didn't know I was home (but of course she knew I was home!) and, though I could have, I hadn't called her. I had justified this by telling myself that I didn't need to, or didn't have any right. This utterly threadbare proposition failed to explain why I hadn't written or called Sidney. Perhaps my real intention was to catch them in the act (what act?) thus taking myself off the hook. (But I had made it very clear, before I left, that I had not been hooked.) I could scarcely believe that I could be so base— could see, somewhere, so much, and yet, face so little. Yet here I was, in the ancient, blue Pontiac, rolling toward Jordan's Cat, just like Enoch Arden, ready to confront my friend and my lover with the unanswerable truth of their betrayal of my—after all—indispensable person. I hoped that I would be able to find a style equal, at least, to my paranoia: that the one might cancel out the other.

With another part of my mind, I was horrified by what had happened to Julia, and—though, again, this sounds insane—less horrified by what had happened to Julia than by what might be happening to Arthur. To Arthur, that is, as a result. Arthur, with me, anyway, was exceedingly laconic, all the days of his life. I saw some things—later; when I began to run with him, I saw a lot. Yet, really, when I find myself testifying on Judgment Day, I won't know what I can say I *know* about anybody else's life, including Arthur's: I don't know what I *know* about my own. I put a certain kind of picture together—in time—out of the fragments Arthur let me see, or couldn't hide, or what I divined. If I can say, I think I knew him, it is only because I *do* know that I loved him. But I wasn't in his skin, or in his beds, or in his voice. I saw Crunch, for example, through his eyes, much later, too late: I don't know that I ever saw the Crunch he saw, but I think I saw what Crunch meant to him. (I saw what Arthur meant to Crunch: Arthur didn't.) And, if I saw Jimmy more clearly, that is really because I was finally growing up, and, much more importantly, Julia and I had been lovers long before Jimmy and Arthur made it.

Well. Here we are now, at Jordan's Cat.

I had brought the present for Sidney—a heavy brass ring, in the shape of a serpent, with a scarlet eye—but had not brought Martha's present, telling myself that it was too big to carry, which it wasn't. (It was a heavy, ornate, green silk kimono: I had left it lying on my bed.) But I had wanted to be alone with her when I gave it to her. It didn't seem right to give it to her in public.

As we got out of the car, I realized that I was terribly afraid. I did not know what was about to happen to me.

Arthur was wearing a dark blue suede jacket with a belt. It looked very nice on him, made him look taller, and grown-up. He opened the door, and we went inside.

I think everyone imagines that, when they go away, the scene they have left behind them alters, that their departure leaves a hole in their previous surroundings. The departure may leave a hole in some people's lives, a wound which is invisible; but one's surroundings take as little notice of one's departure as the sea takes of the dead. The scene rolls on, the music keeps playing, no one misses a beat. Children continue, relentlessly, to be conceived; ruthlessly, to be born; and are there when you return, staring at you with their all-seeing eyes—you have not returned; although *they* just got here, it is *you* who have arrived.

Paradoxically, then, this means that every scene is new. That is the only way to play it, though it seemed to me that everything and everyone at Jordan's Cat remained exactly as they had been when I left. The jukebox had not changed position, the tables in the back were still there, it was not the same waitress, but she looked the same. George was nowhere, in evidence, but it was probably his night off. The photographs on the wall behind the bar were still there, the same number of them, and the clock was still ten minutes fast. The jukebox wasn't playing the same tune, certainly, but the beat was still the same. It was crowded, electrical, with voices and laughter—perhaps what had once seemed elegance was, now, a little frayed.

Arthur teased and muscled his way to the bar—a very impressive display of charm and authority—and yelled at Sidney, "Look who we brought to see you!"

Sidney didn't answer at once—he was at the cash register. He rang up the bill, turned to place it on the bar before the customer, and looked straight into my eyes.

I realized that he had seen me when I came in.

He grinned, and tapped Arthur on the cheek—"I saw you sneaking in here!"—and reached out for me and managed to put one hand on the nape of my neck. He held me like that for a moment, looking into my eyes with a smile.

"Welcome home, brother," he said. "You just get in?"

"Yeah. Just today."

"How's the folks? I ain't talking about small fry, here—this young, dumb, full-of-come turkey—how are Papa and Mama Montana?"

"They fine. How are *you?*"

He held me for yet another moment. "I know they mighty happy to see *you.*" Then he let me go. "I'm all right. I'm fine. I'm mighty glad to see you, too, man."

It came to me that something had happened to Sidney—something beautiful: something calm in his eyes, something loving in his smile. His hair was still conked, but—I don't know why—I had the feeling that he was half-hearted about it now, that it wouldn't stay conked long.

"I brought you something," I said.

"Wait. Wait till I buy a drink in the back. What you drinking now?" He looked at Arthur. "You lucky you with your brother, son."

Arthur laughed. "This here's a friend of mine, Peanut. Peanut, this is Sidney."

Sidney and Peanut shook hands, and, again, I felt a kind of peace in Sidney which I had never felt in him before. "I hope," he said, "you know what kind of company you keeping." He began pouring our drinks. "These are the terrible *Montana* brothers, ain't left a woman standing from coast to coast." He scowled, hideously, at Arthur, and poured him a glass of white wine. "This is just for your brother's homecoming. Now go stand in a corner, with your face to the wall." He looked back to me, still with this imitation scowl on his face. "I'll be with you, fast as I can. Hey. You call Martha?"

I said, feeling foolish, "Not yet—" He watched me, smiling. I could think of nothing more to say.

"We love you," he said. "Please call her, she's expecting your call— you need a dime? Here," he said, before I could start searching my pockets, "go on and call her. I'll see you in a minute. You," he said to Arthur, "make yourself useful and take your brother's drink back to the table."

I left the bar and went to the phone booths which were way in the back, near the toilets and the kitchen.

I was out of breath. I felt childish, even base—*vanity* was the word ringing, senselessly, in my mind. I put the coin in the slot, and dialed the number, seeing Arthur and Peanut, guided by the waitress, take a table next to the jukebox. Peanut and Arthur and the waitress appeared to have hit it off, the three of them were cracking up with laughter.

The phone rang twice, three times—then, "Hello?"

I had forgotten the eager little girl pulsing at the bottom of that voice, the voice of a little girl who had, maybe, smoked a little too much, and drunk a little too much—and cried a little too much, too—and who yet believed, at the very bottom of her voice, that something marvelous might happen each time she picked up the telephone.

"Hello yourself. This is: Johnny-I-hardly-knew-you."

She laughed. "Hall. Where are you? Are you home?"

"This afternoon."

"In New York—? Where *are* you?"

"In New York." I cleared my throat. "I'm at Jordan's Cat."

"Oh. So you're with Sidney—"

"*And* my brother, Arthur, and an old friend of ours—"

"Why didn't you call me before?"

"I don't know." Then, thank God, I told the truth. "I was afraid."

"Afraid? Why?" Then, "Oh, never mind. That was a stupid question. But don't be afraid. There's nothing to be afraid of, believe me. I'd love to see you. Can I come over?"

I said, "Yes, I wish you would. I'd love to see you." Then I said, "I brought you a present, but I left it at the house—"

"Don't worry. I'll be right there."

"Okay—Martha?"

"Yes?"

"Forgive me for being so foolish." Then I didn't know what to say—I caught my breath to keep myself from crying.

"You're not foolish. You're *you*—Hall?"

"Yes."

"I'll be right there. Order me—oh, a double daiquiri or something." She laughed. "Oh, and Hall?"

"Yes?"

"Love goes through a lot of changes, but love never dies. You'll see."

"I believe you, mama," I said. "God bless you. In a minute, then," and I hung up.

I hung up, and started getting ready to hang out. Love, which I really knew nothing about yet, had put me through some changes, and yet, was beginning to set me free. What a wonder, what a marvel, yes: but it was strange to feel free and yet wonder what on earth I was to do with my freedom.

I walked past Arthur and Peanut, picking up my drink along the way, and walked to the bar. I signaled Sidney.

"And what can I do for you, sir?"—grinning.

"She wants a double daiquiri, or something like that—on the rocks, maybe, I don't remember."

Sidney laughed. "Got you," he said, and turned away.

It struck me for the first time—consciously—that the world is not overpopulated with those on whom you can, laughingly, and in perfect confidence, turn your back.

I didn't want to rejoin Arthur and Peanut right away. I wanted one says, to think, but that really refers to the need to make some kind of private assessment. I certainly didn't have much time for it, with Peanut and Arthur at the table, Sidney at the bar, and Martha on her way. No: but, sometimes, in order to see in, you find that you must look out and I stalled for time, wandering over to the jukebox. That way, it couldn't seem that I was avoiding anybody. I stood at a slight angle to the box, my drink in one hand, my change in the other. I was looking at the numbers on the jukebox, and I was watching the crowd. I knew, if I decided to, I could get something going. *What* could I get going?

For I was no longer the same person who had been here before.

I watched, for example, the waitress: a pretty girl, light-skinned—a skin somewhat darker than bananas—with dark brown eyes and reddish hair, hair cooked, teased, and tormented into a kind of cotton-candy texture, cut short or piled high; it was exceedingly hard to guess what would happen to this confection in the rain. She had a kind of low-slung behind, not big, but present, and sturdy bowlegs, and she was a good waitress. She could handle herself, the tray, and the floor, and the people. She had had to pay some dues to have arrived at even this brutally limited shadow of authority. She was somebody's daughter certainly, maybe somebody's sister, maybe somebody's woman, victim, or hope, or model, maybe, even, somebody's mother. She had probably not been born in New York. Had she walked all the way here? Why?

Yet, in the state in which I knew I would soon find myself, she would be nothing more than an opportunity, a means of reassurance, or, really, not even that—a means of physical release, a way of dropping my load. Once that had been accomplished, my curiosity about her, my concern, would diminish as inexorably as my softening dick. How did she bear being used like that? For I was really thinking of Martha. And the truth was this: I had not exactly, for reasons of vanity, allowed myself to *hope* to find myself in bed with her tonight, but I had certainly wanted it. And not because she was Martha. I was beginning to see that I had never been terribly concerned with knowing *who* Martha was; on the contrary, I had resisted any such intrusion— then *I* would have had to confess who *I* was. No: I simply wanted to have been with her tonight because it would have been easy, it would have been enormously gratifying still to be wanted after so long, because I had already been there and would not have had to battle for the conquest, because, sometimes, we had been so good together, making love. This memory tiptoed along my spine as I stood there at the jukebox, watching the crowd.

The crowd. It came to me that I could spend my life doing what I was doing right now. The world was full of crowds, waitresses, beds, girls, women, boys, men—maybe, even, full of Marthas. How would I ever know so long as I was determined not to know? I dropped a lot of change in the jukebox, and pressed recklessly, at random, trying to make it seem that I was making choices. But the truth was that I saw absolutely nothing, was, simply, as I hoped, covering myself. And would I spend my life in postures so unmanly, my face at an angle to the music and at an angle to the crowd?

And I had fucked everything I could get my hands on overseas, including two of my drinking buddies. I had been revolted—but this was after, not before, the act. Before the act, when I realized from their eyes what was happening, I had adored being the adored male, and stretched out on it, all boyish muscle and throbbing cock, telling myself, What the hell, it beats jerking off. And I had loved it—the adoration, the warm mouth, the tight ass, the fact that nothing at all was demanded of me except that I shoot my load, which I was very, very happy to do. And I was revolted when it was over, not merely because it really was not for me, but because I had used somebody merely as a receptacle and had allowed myself to be used merely as a thing. I was revolted that my need had driven me, as I considered it, so low: nevertheless, my need had driven me and could drive me there again. And what did a woman feel? I had never asked myself this question before. *Women like it as much as men,* okay, and *a stiff prick has no conscience,* okay again, but that merely justifies a grim indolence. I could spend my whole life in that posture and be found standing at this jukebox when Gabriel's trumpet sounded, at an angle to the music and at an angle to my life.

So then, for the first time, I wondered about love and wondered if I would find in myself the strength to give love, and to take it: to accept my nakedness as sacred, and to hold sacred the nakedness of another. For, without love, pleasure's inventions are soon exhausted. There must be a soul within the body you are holding, a soul which you are striving to meet, a soul which is striving to meet yours.

Then I suspected why death was so terrible, and love so feared— glimpsed an abyss and closed my eyes and shuddered: but I had seen it.

Then, having spent all my change (*I was going to have to get a job!*) I went back to the table and summoned the beautiful and mysterious waitress, and ordered another round.

When she brought the round, I asked her, "Where're you from, child?"

She put her hands on her hips and grinned at me. She had a gap between her two front teeth. It made her face funny instead of merely pretty, the gap was like a bonus.

"Waycross, Georgia," she said. "Now ain't that something?"

We all laughed. Peanut asked, "How'd you get out?"

"You folks up here," she said, "always wondering about how we got *out*. Ain't you never worried about how we going to get *in*? I'm *tired* of being *out*."

"Amen to *that*," said Arthur. "And let the *church* say amen!"

"But I wonder, sometimes," I said, teasing, "how we going to get *over*."

"Oh, we *over*," she said. "We *been* over. You notice how white folks don't never use that word like *we* use it? They afraid of *being* over. And they right. That's how I know we *got* over." She laughed again, all over her mischievous pickaninny's face, and under all that cotton-candy hair. "But sometime soon, I'd still like to make it on *in*."

"Into the kingdom?" Arthur asked this with a smile.

"That one up yonder?—not hardly. I can't *stand* milk and honey, and child, you *know* those folks can't sing." She and Arthur and Peanut laughed together. "And they couldn't get a spare rib or a pork chop together if their *souls* depended on it"—we all laughed again—"and they don't know nothing about chitterlings."

"You're crazy," I said.

"Why, no, I'm not," she said, and looked directly at me, a beautiful, searching, open look. "I just don't see any *reason* to go up yonder with them people who done already drove me *half* crazy down here. And who have drove themselves *completely* crazy." She picked up her tray, and started to move. Someone had called her: her name, I gathered, was *Thomasina*. "So I ain't too much interested in this kingdom down here, neither—I'm coming!" she shouted. "But my grandmama, down in Waycross, she told me, we *got* a kingdom. We just got to move on *in* it—see you in a minute, folks," she said, and went to serve another table.

"Well, *she* don't hardly want to be desegregated," Peanut said. "What's wrong with her?"

"I see," said Sidney, abruptly looming over the table and then sitting down at it, "that you trying to get next to my waitress. But I can tell you right now that she ain't hardly thinking about none of y'all."

"Hands off," said Peanut. "Am I right?"

Sidney grinned, looking quickly at me and then back to Peanut.

"Oh, no," he said. "She don't belong to *me*. I just happen to know that she is *occupied*. Anyway," he added, looking at Arthur with pity and then grinning at Peanut, "she say she don't want no more *children*. You got that, junior?"

Arthur watched him with a small, stubborn smile. "You wait, Sidney. I'm going to surprise the hell out of *your* ass."

"You sure give Arthur a hard time," Peanut said.

"Ain't been doing a thing in the world," said Sidney, "but trying to keep his dumb ass out of trouble while his big brother was away." And he suddenly laughed and grabbed Arthur and kissed him on the forehead. "Now ain't that true? Go on, now, tell the truth and shame the devil."

Arthur grinned, but most unwillingly, weakly resisting Sidney's grasp. "My brother don't never talk to me like that."

"Ah," said Sidney. "That's what's wrong with you. *He* been polite. But *I* will call you a motherfucker and *kick your ass*." He let Arthur go, and turned to me. "That's just because I love you both."

I said, "I guess a lot's been happening since I've been gone."

"Yes," said Sidney, "and then again, no. Depends."

"Depends?"

"Well, yes. It depends partly on what you *want* to happen, partly on what you *afraid* might happen—and *mostly* on what you don't see coming."

I watched him with a smile and took the box with his ring in it out of my pocket and put it on the table. "This is for you, man. I hope you like it."

Arthur and Peanut watched, smiling, as Sidney took the box and held it for a moment between his two big hands.

"If I don't like it—can I trade it in?"

"Go on, man," said Arthur, "and open the box."

Sidney smiled at me, unreadably, as he undid the package and opened the box. He took out the ring and held it for a moment in the center of his palm—"That's *beautiful!*" Arthur said—and then slipped it, finally, on his fourth finger, the scarlet eye gathering force from his dark skin.

He stretched out his arm to admire his hand and looked at me again. "It *is* beautiful," he said. "Thank you, brother." Something seemed to thunder in the air between us for a second, something both troubling and peaceful, and we both smiled. "I'll send Thomasina over with drinks for you people," he said. "I don't drink no more while I'm working."

I had the feeling, from something intense in his eyes, that he wanted to say more, but he stopped and stood up. "I'm going back to work. Listen. You and Martha going to stay here with small fry, or you going to find someplace quiet?"

"I guess," I said, "that we'll find someplace quiet."

"Well. We'll figure it out when she gets here," and he stroked my cheek with his ring hand and went back to the bar.

Arthur was watching me without watching me, and his brow was faintly comic with his effort to conceal worry. I wanted to reassure him, but I couldn't—that would have been jumping the gun. I wondered what he was thinking, what he had seen, what he knew; realized, again, that no one had mentioned Martha to me, and no one had mentioned Sidney. They couldn't: and if they couldn't, they knew that I would soon see why. I felt, now, that I might be in for a fairly rough five minutes. I knew that I didn't know how I was going to handle it, but I didn't feel that it would be worse than that, or more than that. Then something seemed to charge the air at my back and something happened in Arthur's eyes, and I knew that Martha had arrived.

Without turning my head, I could see her, as on that Christmas night we had first come here, leaning up on the bar, on tiptoe, to kiss Sidney on the nose. It seemed to me that I could hear their laughter, the same but not the same, and see their faces: Martha's bright from the chilly wind and Sidney's, a little dulled with fatigue and yet, beautifully heavy with hope. Then it was real to me that time had passed and that, yes, something had been lost.

Or: perhaps *I* had lost something, but something had also been gained. For now, Arthur looked at me with a look he could never have had before—a look warning, apprehensive, amused, and resigned—and said, "Martha's here, brother." It was as though he simply did not want me to be caught unawares: the rest was up to me. And, with that look, he told me not merely what he knew about my immediate situation but also what he had begun to discover about many things in the time I had been gone.

And so, I turned in my seat, making myself ready, not yet daring to stand—not certain that I had the *right* to stand, to make that big a deal out of her arrival: when I had had that right, I hadn't used it—and turned my face to the bar, smiling, as she turned from the bar and started toward us. *She* was smiling, the happiest smile I had ever seen on her, she was wearing a navy blue dress and a tan raincoat, her skin was glowing and her hair a little tousled from the wind. She was a little older, she was exceedingly handsome, and I was very glad to see her. I stood up, and she put her arms around me and I took her in my arms. It was not the same, but it was all right, it was better than all right.

"My God," she said, "you're here at last! We missed you, and we talked about you, I even took up prayer!" She pulled back, with her hands on my shoulders, to look at me. "Well, you sure missed your mother's homecooking, child—*and* mine, and Aunt Josephine's—but, *otherwise*—!"

"No visible scars," I said.

"Ah, but the invisible ones!—we'll get to that, later." She turned to Arthur and Peanut, who were standing. "I'm not sure," she said to Arthur, "that I'm still talking to you, but I'll give you a hug, just for old times' sake. Just because I know it wouldn't be right to beat you up in front of your brother his first day home." She and Arthur laughed, and hugged each other. Arthur said, "I don't know if you've met my friend, Peanut, we used to sing together—"

"Oh"—with a quick look at me—"but I've *heard* of Peanut, believe me." They shook hands. "Sit down, please."

I helped her off with her coat, and sat her down and we simply looked at each other for a moment. Peanut took her coat from me and hung it up. Thomasina appeared with her tray, and began putting our drinks on the table. Sidney had sent me a double Scotch, and Martha's daiquiri, I noticed, had turned out into an old-fashioned. Arthur had been demoted to ginger ale, and Peanut was drinking beer.

"We going to drink up quick," said Arthur, "and leave you two alone. Or we can go to the bar right now."

Martha gave him a look. "Arthur, you just want to hit the streets, don't you be jiving me. You was never worried about leaving us alone before." She raised her glass, first to Peanut, then to Arthur, then to me: "To the one who has come home."

Her face, then, became a face I did not yet know but was to come to know—to meet—in the years stretching before us. It was the face of a woman who had come to a decision, resolutely putting her girlhood behind her, insofar, at least, as she could then know. It was the first time I saw the face of the black girl-woman we would meet all up and down those dusty chain-gang highways, in years to come, for years to come. The face was as intransigent as it was vulnerable, the very definition of nobility—take all *you* have, and give to the poor, but don't bring any of that shit near *me*.

I once was lost, but now I'm found.

I raised my glass: "To being home again, with those I love."

We drank, and Martha and I stared at each other—for what I thought was a very brief moment but it was long enough for both Arthur and Peanut to drain their glasses, and stand up. And they left Martha and I there, alone.

"So," I said. "Where shall we begin?"

"Well," Martha said, after a moment, "first of all, let's forget all about Alice in Wonderland—the end is not in sight and the beginning is a long time ago."

We laughed together, but I did not want to prolong her gallant agony. I watched her face. She was older, yes, but it wasn't really time which had happened in her face—there had not, after all, been that much time—what had happened spoke of lonely, melancholy decision. The price was written in the jawbone and the cheekbone, in the not-quite-false directness and tranquillity of the eye. Not quite false because too hard won: the struggle was more vivid than the victory.

Yet the struggle was itself a kind of victory and only that involuntary depth of love which I knew I did not feel for her could dare attempt distinguish the will from the deed.

I offered her a cigarette, but she waved her hand and smiled no, and we sipped our drinks for a moment.

Everything around us was very quiet suddenly, as though invisible multitudes awaited the outcome of our contest in this arena.

"That letter you didn't write me—was about you and Sidney?"

"Yes. Not exactly. It was about much more than that—but, yes, I wanted to tell you about—me and Sidney."

Martha's eyes, at that moment, were so beautiful and so bright with pain that I could scarcely believe my eyes. I had never seen such nakedness before in the eyes of anyone I loved, or in anyone's eyes. It made me very happy that anyone could look like that, could love like that, and, at the same time, it frightened me, too.

"Well, Martha—why couldn't you write me? About you and Sidney, I mean? I don't have any claim on you. We agreed about that when I left here."

"Yes. You said it, and I agreed. Only—you didn't *really* say it, not in so many words, and so I couldn't really agree."

I watched her, and I thought about that.

"After all—I *had* to think that—one of the reasons you didn't want us to have any claims on each other—was that you thought you might not be coming back. Or that you would be coming back with one leg or no eyes—who knows what you were thinking? But that's what *I* was thinking. And I didn't even know that I was thinking *that*—until—" and she stopped.

"I think we should get out of here," I said. "I'll bring you back, or we can tell Sidney where to meet us."

"That's a good idea," she said, and so we rose and started making our way out of there. We hadn't quite decided where we were going, but we told Sidney that we'd call him.

We went to a very quiet kind of cocktail lounge near 125th Street on Seventh, and sat in a booth way in the back, alone, far from the others. The others were couples a little above our age and station.

The waitress came, and we ordered our drinks. We sat in a charged and friendly silence, listening to Ella Fitzgerald on the jukebox.

"Are you two planning to get married?" I asked.

"I guess so. I hope so." She grinned. "We're much more old-fashioned than you."

I grunted. "You want to bet? I'm just a late starter, that's all."

"Anyway. After you left, I hardly saw Sidney at all. Maybe just instinctively, we avoided each other. I never went into Jordan's Cat, and we never even ran into each other in the street, even though we live in the same neighborhood."

I wanted to tease her a little: "What do you mean—you 'instinctively' avoided each other?"

"Oh, come on, you know damn well what I mean." We both laughed. The waitress came, with our drinks, and peanuts and potato chips. The voice of Ella Fitzgerald gave way to the voice of Pearl Bailey.

"It wasn't all that funny, then," she said carefully. "I didn't know *where* you'd left me—but—you'd left me not liking myself very much."

I said nothing. There was nothing for me to say.

"I didn't want to blame you—and I didn't want to start blaming *men*—so I worked hard, and spent most nights home." She laughed. "Aunt Josephine was *most* upset."

I felt an odd, lonely spasm of regret at her refusal to place the blame, at the same time that I was compelled to respect her. But I also felt, irrationally, that this refusal to place the blame could be seen as a way of demolishing my manhood. Certainly a man looks sharply at a woman who refuses to place the blame on him!

"I didn't really see Sidney until after Julia's father beat her up so bad, and she lost the baby"—she picked up her drink and looked down into it, then looked up at me—"they told you about all that?"

"Oh, yeah. They told me about it."

"When that first day was over—because that shit went on for days, we didn't know whether Julia was going to live or die, and her father was a *revelation*, baby, I never saw anything like it—but I'll tell you about that another day—your mama and I just walked down the road to Jordan's Cat and sat down. Neither of us said a word, nobody said a word, nobody said, Let's have a drink. We just walked to the nearest bar and sat down.

"And you know I wasn't hardly thinking about Sidney. I was thinking about that girl, and her father. And I was sick. Your mama and I were both sick. And we knew already wasn't nothing going to happen to him. They couldn't hold him, they was going to have to let him go."

I watched something enter Martha's face, and it caused a silence in me. My mother, her mother, Julia—at least three women entered Martha's face, all of them appalled by Julia's bloody passage into womanhood. Their eyes were all fixed on something which, perhaps, no man could see. Joel was indeed, for example, as Martha said, a revelation—I would never have used that word: I did not know which, for her, of the seven seals had been broken. Joel appalled the man in me, he made me sick with shame; but I had placed, with speed, so vast a distance between his manhood and my own that he could not threaten me, he had no power over me; and this could not be true for any woman. I could divorce myself from Joel. They could not divorce themselves from Julia. More precisely, perhaps, it wasn't hard for me to protect myself against the possible Joel in me, to blot his presence out completely. But it was not so easy, as I now saw, for Martha to obliterate from her days or from her nights the cord that connected her to the brutally broken virgin.

So we sat in silence for a while. It was getting late, past one A.M. From far away, we heard the voice of Frank Sinatra. I signaled the waitress for another round. She came, with this silence ringing still, and took away our empty glasses, and Martha finally lit a cigarette.

"I don't think Mama Montana and I said more than two words to each other. We just ordered our drinks, and sat there, like zombies. Then Sidney came in, and"—Martha laughed—"it was as though he woke us up. We realized, for the first time, where we were, and we looked at each other as if to say, How did we get here? Like in the fairy tales, you know? when the Prince comes along and he waves his magic wand, and *oo-bop-she-bam!* you're changed!"

And she laughed again, and the waitress came back and set our drinks before us, along with new potato chips, and smiled tolerantly at us, as though she took us for newlyweds, or lovers.

"Sidney was very nice during that whole time, and your mama liked him a lot. And that meant something, I must say"—she leaned forward, gesturing with her newly lit cigarette—"because I trust your mama."

I said, I couldn't help it, "Sure. She treated Sidney like a son." Then I said, "I'm sorry. Go on."

"You should be," she said, refusing to be checked. "After all, you treat him like a brother." She paused, narrowing her eyes, both shrewd and mocking. "Don't you?"

She was calling up my promissory notes. "Yes," I said, "I do."

She was silent for a moment, searching my eyes for something. Then, "We started going out here and there—a movie, a concert, sometimes I'd come and have a drink with him at the end of the bar. Somehow, sitting at the end of that bar at night made me very happy because I knew that he was happy to see me there, just sitting there, even though he was always busy and we couldn't talk much."

"It was sitting at the end of the bar," I said, "that did it." And I was not being mocking. I could see it.

"Yes," she said. She looked down. "He needed me. I made him happy. I made a difference in his life." She looked up, into my eyes. "And that made a difference in *my* life. And—we hadn't yet touched each other, Hall."

She looked around the bar, looking, again, at something I couldn't see.

"And he gave me the courage to begin to think—about you, about you and me. I saw that I had been dreaming. It wasn't because of Korea that you didn't want to marry me—"

"I never said that, Martha. Be fair."

She smiled. "Be fair!" Then, "No. But that was in the background, that was always—unspoken. Anyway," she said. "Remember that I'm not blaming you. For anything."

It was true. It was not true. I watched her eyes. I held my peace. She looked at her watch, and sipped her drink.

"I began to see, anyway, that you would never want to marry me, there would always be something in the way. Well. I began to see that I'd been dreaming—dreaming that when you came home, with all the battles over, and the danger behind, you would feel that you had the *right* to ask me to marry you." She threw back her head, and laughed. "It was a nice dream, though. It kept me going through some rough days. I can tell you. But——"

"The dreamer awoke," I said.

"Yes," she said soberly, after a moment, "the dreamer awoke."

I watched her. I really did not know what I felt, and I decided that I would not try to find out now. I would sort it out later. I had the feeling that something, something very clear, had yet eluded me.

"Is Sidney going to stay on at the bar," I asked, "after you're married?"

"No." Her face changed again, with a warm, wondering, private smile. She touched her drink. "I may never have another drink." She put her cigarette into the ashtray. "I may never smoke another cigarette or"—she looked around the bar—"sit in another place like this again."

I laughed, although I knew I shouldn't have; I laughed because I was frightened. "Are you going to become a Seventh-Day Adventist, or something, or"—I stopped laughing—"or what?"

She was quite untouched by my laughter. She was radiant. "Sidney's studying for us to change our lives—to change the lives of all black people in this country. Especially black *men*, that's the key." She gave me a mocking, affectionate smile. "He might change *you*, too."

Now I was perfectly sober, intent, watching her.

"I know Sidney never told you this, but I know it's all right if I tell you now—he's not hiding it anymore." She paused. "Sidney has a younger brother in prison—did you know that?"

"No," I said, "I didn't." Then, "*My* brother, Sidney, never told me he had another brother."

"Well. He has. And for the past year or so, every time his brother writes, every time Sidney sees his brother, all he can talk about is the Messenger from Allah, about Islam, and how this *truth*, after all these centuries of lies, has helped him clean up his life. And Sidney says it's true—his *brother*, who went to jail for *murder*, is a changed man. But Sidney will tell you, he's been dying to tell you. And I've read some of his brother's letters and they started me thinking in an entirely new direction." She watched my face, and laughed, then sobered. "No, I'm not crazy, but I'll let Sidney explain it to you—he's studying, he spends every spare minute with his Muslim brothers, and it's made him a changed man, too." She paused, and then said proudly, "And if I'm going to be his wife, his helpmeet—well then, I must begin my studies, too."

I simply looked at her. I couldn't take it all in. "This is all new to me. I never heard anything about this."

"But it's not new. It's old. It's thousands of years old. It's just been hidden from us." No doubt, I still looked numb. "Look, the truth about black people has *always* been hidden from us, that's how we got so messed up. But the Messenger of Allah knows the truth."

"And this is a man—a living man?"

"A living *black* man—right here in the United States."

"I think I better have another drink," I said, "quick, and you better have one, too. Sounds like *your* drinking days are almost done."

She laughed. "Why are you so frightened? You look absolutely terrified."

"I *am* terrified. The *truth* is *supposed* to terrify."

I asked the waitress for one more round, and I asked her to make mine a double. Martha watched me from her unassailable distance, with her unswerving love. Then she looked at her watch again.

"I'd better call Sidney. What are we going to do?"

"I'll take you back to the bar, and Sidney and I will make arrangements to discuss this Muslim shit more thoroughly."

"Very well," she said, and took a dime from her purse and went to telephone Sidney.

I walked her up to Jordan's Cat in silence. I didn't want to be silent, but I didn't know what to say: and I didn't want her to talk. I kept thinking about what she had said, and more, the way she had said it; it kept turning and turning in my mind the way a heavy object in the water is pushed and pulled about. It would not sink, it would not stop moving.

So, when I got to the bar, I said to Sidney, "I hear you got something to lay on me, brother."

Sidney gave me the most beautiful smile I had ever seen on the face of any man and said, "I believe I do."

"You want to talk later?"

"You go get some sleep. I'll pick you up at your house around six, okay?"

"Okay."

And so I left them and started for my house. I didn't get there right away, I got drunk but I didn't get laid—I couldn't have, I was watching everything and everyone from too great a distance, I kept hearing Martha's voice and seeing her face—and that was the end of my first day home.

Sidney called me to say he'd meet me at a joint on 110th Street and Lenox Avenue, next to the subway station.

I was alone in my house. Florence, Paul, and Arthur were out. I had the feeling that they were leaving me alone until I got my bearings.

It was a bright fall day, the kind of day, along with some days in winter, that New York is best at, and so I decided to walk—to walk my familiar, and yet unfamiliar streets.

I did not want to think about last night, and Martha, because I knew I didn't understand it yet: and I really didn't know, any longer, how I felt about Sidney. I didn't want to be unfair, and so I kept my mind a blank.

Sidney was standing by the subway station, wearing an old red sweater and old black pants and a cap: and the conk *was* leaving his hair.

We smiled at each other warily. We knew, after all, where we'd been. We didn't know where we were.

He affected a West Indian accent: "Buy you a cup of coffee, mate?"

I laughed. "I'd rather have a beer."

"You show signs, very definite, of being incorrigible—but, as it's you—come on."

We turned our back on the subway and the park, and walked about a block to a loud, raucous bar I had hardly ever entered. It was a bar mainly for whores and their men, and I didn't mind that so much—though this meant that I really had no business there—but I didn't like the cops or the other white men who came in there.

Now, in the late afternoon, it was half empty—perhaps half a dozen young men, some scarcely more than boys, sitting or standing at the bar. A couple of older men were at the tables, discussing the numbers.

Sidney and I sat at the bar. The barman, who was white, greeted Sidney as though he knew him. I didn't like his face. He was young, probably the son of the owner, one of those hip white boys who know that they know niggers, know them so well that they can imitate the nigger's language, and this gives them the right to treat niggers like scum.

He served Sidney a Coke, he served me a beer.

I lit a cigarette and offered Sidney a cigarette, perhaps mainly out of curiosity. Sidney refused.

"You don't smoke anymore?"

"Not for the moment. Time will tell."

I took a swallow of my beer, and jumped in.

"Congratulations about you and Martha," I said, and I offered him my hand.

He grinned, and we shook hands, and I felt better. "I—we—owe it all to you," he said.

"That's a nice thing for you to say, and I appreciate it. But I didn't really have anything to do with it. After all"—I laughed, hoping I wasn't saying the wrong thing—"I wasn't here."

"How was it over there?"

"Man, you know how it was over there. It was bullshit piled high, pressed down, and running over." I sipped my beer. "And lots of spattering blood and guts and brains and whores we treated like shit and V.D. and dysentery and dope." I laughed. "America, the beautiful."

"Well. Look around you, now that you back, and tell me how different is it over here."

I was silent. I looked around me. Past the profile of the boy at the far end of the bar, I looked through the open door, into the street. The sun was traveling westward, that is to say the earth was turning; the sun struck the tops of buildings with a melancholy, departing glare and seemed to shake the topmost windows. I could see, from where I stood, the merciless metal fire escape running down the side of one building, and the entrance to the building, recessed from the street. Some children were playing an impenetrable game, involving both the fire-escape ladder and a ball, in this alley, and on the sidewalk. A bus, filled with black people, moved past slowly, cutting off my view: now I saw only the silhouettes of black people behind the bus windows—just past the profile of the boy at the end of the bar, who had not moved, who seemed to have been struck still, and dumb. The bus moved on. A very sharp hustler, in a sharp white hat, stood at the curb, with two others, less sharp. Three girls walked by, they seemed to be schoolgirls, and the men on the curb watched them. A black woman with a shopping bag walked slowly by, and a patrol car stopped in front of the place. The one in the white hat walked over to the patrol car and stood listening for a moment. Then the patrol car drove off. The boy at the end of the bar still had not moved. His forehead sloped back into a tangle of black hair which had not been combed in days, his nose was long, aquiline, his lips were parted, his eyes were black with wonder. His long hands, on the bar, were absolutely still.

I looked back at Sidney, but found nothing to say. "They have us trapped here," said Sidney, "like rats, because the land belongs to them. Everything belongs to them." He gestured toward the bartender, and said, in a low voice, out of the side of his mouth—something I had never known him to do before—"That devil, and his papa, they own I don't know how many blocks, how much real estate around here, and, between them and the cops, man, and be you a whore or be you a chump looking for a license, you don't turn no tricks, you hear me, if you don't bend over and spread them cheeks. And you better be smiling, and holler thank you!" He finished his Coke. "They got our nuts in a vise, man, and all we can *do* is holler."

I could say nothing. I listened to his voice, and I watched his face—or, really, I could almost say that I listened to his face and watched his voice. I was beginning to hear, or see—to perceive—in another, new, very troubling way. It was as though one of my senses, or possibilities—sight, for example, or motion—had just been denied me, had just been stricken from me, and what remained to me had to do double or triple duty.

"You want another Coke?" I asked.

"No, get me a beer. It's all the same poison."

"Truer words were never spoken," said the friendly barman, the hip white motherfucker, one of those barmen always in earshot. You hope somebody will strangle him one day, and you hope it won't be you.

I watched Sidney's voice because there was a river rolling in it, a deep river, long dammed, about to overthrow everything in the path of the river, including the barman who, now, with a brotherly, conspiratorial wink, placed our beers before us. I heard Sidney's eyes as they thundered behind the barman the entire length of the bar, from a long ways off.

Then Sidney laughed, thank heaven, and my normal senses were returned to me, not quite, however, as they had been.

Then, "Martha told you," Sidney asked, "about my brother?"

I nodded yes.

"He killed a man. I don't blame him. I would have, too."

He sipped his beer, and said nothing more, and I said nothing.

"I wondered, for a long time, how what happened to my brother could have happened. And now I think I know."

He looked beyond me, into the street.

"I used to think *he* was in prison, and I had to get him out. Now I know we *all* in prison, and we got to get *us* out."

I watched him, and I listened.

"They told us God was white, and cut our nuts off, raped our women, slaughtered our children, and got us penned up here, like hogs. And they tell us it's God's will. It *is* God's will—*their* God."

He took a deep swallow of his beer, very calm now.

"It's God's will because they own everything—and they stole everything they own. Their whole history is a lie—ain't a white devil walking who can tell the truth, not one. They even stole God."

I thought to myself, *Good. They can have Him.* But I said nothing. Something was going on, deep inside me, something moving—too deep, too slow, too fast for me to grasp. Something was tormenting me, like the beginning of music, like the void into which one drops to find the word.

Sidney was trying to give me something, or to share something. Whatever it was, I could not possibly give it to Arthur. That may sound strange—and, even now, it sounds strange to me—but that's what I was thinking, if I was thinking at all. Gods who could be stolen and then stolen back did not interest me at all. I wasn't raised to deal in stolen goods. As far as I was concerned, it was all a lie, from top to bottom: and, since we had built it, only we could dare it down. That energy called divine is really human need, translated, and if that God we have created needs patience with us, how much more than patience do we need with God!

Sidney and I walked our streets together until he had to go to work, and I left him at the door of Jordan's Cat. And I knew that I would never see him again, not as I had.

The only person in my life, then, really, was my brother, Arthur—and I accepted this with no complaint, even without astonishment—and time was flying and I had to start working on the building. I did not want to find Arthur standing, one day, in profile to me, at the far end of the bar.

Yes. I started working on the building, Arthur went on the road, and time began to do its number.

I woke up one morning in San Francisco, and I knew that there was something strange about the day, but I couldn't place what it was.

Then I said to myself, with a reluctant wonder, *I'm thirty. I'm thirty years old today.*

I was alone in my hotel room. I had been on the coast for a couple of months, working with the California branch of the advertising agency I worked for in New York. It was a white firm, as need scarcely be said, but, in the sixties, as my countrymen were proud to point out, we blacks were making great strides in fields previously blocked to us.

Thirty. Well. I still had to get out of bed and confront and wash this aging frame. Which didn't feel too decrepit, just the same. In fact, I felt pretty good, and I was even rather pleased that day found me alone. And I didn't feel anything momentous, the need to take stock of my life, or any shit like that. No, I was simply pleased and a little astonished to find myself still among the living, to have lasted this long.

And it was a nice day, and I like San Francisco. I wondered if I could find anyone to have lunch with me. It was a Saturday, so there'd be no one at the office, but I had a couple of numbers in my book.

I got in and out of the shower, got dressed, called room service for coffee. I looked out of my window, seeing, mainly, the tops of tall buildings, but I knew that beneath, below these, were my steeply vertiginous, beloved streets.

The girl came with the coffee and, at the very same moment, the phone rang.

The girl was Oriental, and she left. The phone call, as it turned out, was Faulkner.

Faulkner was blood-related to my boss, precisely to what legal degree I never knew: blood relative of a pirate, a cunning, hard-nosed blond. I loathed him, but I must confess that he frightened me, too—he was only about twenty, and had the moral sense of a crocodile.

"Hall?" That voice, clipped and rushed, remnant of Hollywood films with a British setting, and various private schools.

"Yes? Speaking."

"Something came up, we need you back here."

"Why are *you* calling me?"

"What do you mean, why am I calling you? Listen, I'm Faulkner Grey, I'm part of this firm—"

"I know who you are, and I know you're part of the firm, but you're not my boss. I don't take orders from you."

"Listen, this was just a friendly call to let you know that you're going to be needed on deck back here, why are you jumping down my throat?"

"Because you might be high on something. Because you and I don't have anything to do with each other in the office. Because it's Saturday afternoon—"

"And because you hate my guts, right?"

"I don't think about you one way or the other, Faulkner. I just don't know how to move on your word."

But I rather regretted, just the same, the tone I'd taken. It wasn't smart.

"Do you think I'm calling you because I love your big brown eyes? Do you think I *miss* you, for Christ's sake?"

Could be, I thought, could be. The thought had crossed my mind more than once. The kid damn sure stayed on my case.

And I knew I wasn't being smart, but I couldn't help it: "I certainly miss *you*, darling. What's up?"

"You know, for an intelligent black cat and all, you can be pretty sickening."

"Hush, child. Jealous tantrums will get you nowhere. Is my presence urgently required?"

"If you were smart, you'd get on a plane *today*, so you could be bright-eyed and bushy-tailed early Monday morning."

"On the level? You're not shitting me?"

"No, I'm not shitting you, you bastard," and he hung up.

Junior. You are God's masterpiece, the matchless creep of creeps, and I will never know what I could possibly have done, in any of my previous lives, to deserve you.

Still, he wasn't certifiably insane; if I was a little afraid of him, he was, also, a little afraid of me, and this meant that my presence was required back in New York. Having Faulkner call me was just one more of the little ways they had of letting me know that I might be an intelligent black cat and all, and my people might be making great strides in the kingdom, but I was still a nigger.

And, fuck it, *yes, I am,* and I wasn't going to let these people spoil my birthday, or hurt me or hinder me in any way at all. White people can steal a lot of your time, can steal your whole life, if you let them.

So I figured I would spend the day in San Francisco, and take a flight out in the evening. Time works for you as you head east, and so I thought I might see my parents before my birthday was completely over.

I decided to call them, to give them this news. I didn't know where Arthur was, hadn't seen him in three months. Neither of us lived at home anymore, and Arthur was working all the time. He had still to make, as we say, the "big one," but he got better all the time; he had a faithful, growing audience, mostly black but not entirely; he wasn't making a lot of money but he wasn't starving, either, and he was only, after all, twenty-three. I was proud of him. And we got on well. We loved each other, yes, but that can be a torment. We liked each other, and that was nice.

My mother answered the phone.

"Honey, I was just thinking about you. How you faring out there, with all them cowboys and Indians? Don't get scalped now," and she laughed. "Oh, and happy birthday."

"I'm thirty years old today."

"I know you made thirty, child, I was *there*. Lord, it seems like a dream."

"You proud of me, Mama?" *Have I been a good son?* But I didn't ask that.

"I've always been proud of you. Hush. Your daddy wants to say something to you."

My father got on the phone.

"Happy birthday, son—Hall, I was thinking, now that you beginning to grow up and all, that it's my duty as a *father* to take you aside and give you a little instruction"—here, he coughed elaborately— "about the birds and the bees and such—I think that's a father's duty—"

"The birds and the bees? Aw, shucks, Dad, birds fly and bees sting—is that what you want to tell me?"

"Look like somebody got there ahead of me," he said, and we laughed together. "Can't say I didn't try. When you think you coming this way?"

"Well—that's why I called, really. I'll be coming in sometime tonight." I coughed. "The Board of Directors requires my presence."

"On a *Saturday*? You must be a *big* man on the board."

"Daddy, I know I don't know much about the birds and the bees and such, but how do you spell that? It must be we got a bad connection."

"You got a dirty mind. I'm going to have your mama wash it out with soap. I said *board*, Hall, now pull youself together."

"I'm sorry—no, I've got to be there Monday morning, but I thought I'd come in tonight."

"That'd be mighty nice. Around what time?"

"I don't know yet: Nine, ten, along around that time. I'll call you back, and let you know as soon as I get a flight."

"Well. We'll be here. You know your mama, she going to bake you a cake. You got anybody special you want to see?"

"No. You didn't tell me about the birds and the bees soon enough."

"I knew you was fixing to blame me for something. I didn't tell you to go out there, in all that Indian territory. You ain't *fit* to see nobody."

"I'd like to see my brother, if he's around."

"Man, Arthur is in *Canada*. Tell me he's shaking them up, up there."

"In Canada? *Where* in Canada?"

"All *over* Canada—what?" I heard my mother's voice in the background. "Your mother say, he's in Toronto now, but he's been in Quebec, and everywhere."

"I guess I won't see him, then."

"You'll see him when he *gets* here. You going to be here for a while, ain't you?"

"Yeah. That's true. Well—I'll call you back later, Daddy. Let me go, and take care of business."

"Go with God. We love you."

"I love you, too. Good-bye."

"See you later, son."

And we hung up. I finished my coffee, and descended into the city.

It was the end of spring, you could almost taste the smoke of the coming summer. The streets were crowded with people who seemed to be hurrying toward the summer—I thought of Irwin Shaw's "The Girls in Their Summer Dresses." Their bright summer dresses.

I walked to the corner of my crowded street—I was on the heights of San Francisco—and looked both ways, up and down. There was a cable-car line on the street on which I was standing and a part of me wanted to ride it, just for fun, but another part of me wanted to walk. The street before me simply dropped, dropped as steep, it seemed to me, as a mountain slope, and it ended, I knew, at the wharf. I started down this street, as happy as a kid on a holiday. For a moment, I had nothing to do and nowhere to be.

I also had no one to eat with but this didn't really bother me, either: and I couldn't do anything about it, because I had left my phone book in the hotel, and I wasn't going back for it.

Thirty.

And I had a lobster, all by myself, looking out over the vast, gray crashing water, watching the sun on the water, watching the gulls.

Thirty.

And I was alone, had been for a while, and might be for a while, but it no longer frightened me the way it had. I was discovering something terrifyingly simple: there was absolutely nothing I could do about it. I was discovering this in the way, I suppose, that everybody does, but having tried, endlessly, to do something about it. You attach yourself to someone, or you allow someone to attach themselves to you. This person is not for you, and you, really, are not for that person—and that's it, son. But you try, you both try. The only result of all your trying is to make absolutely real the unconquerable distance between you: to dramatize, in a million ways, the absolutely unalterable truth of this distance. Side by side, and hand in hand, your sunsets, nevertheless, are not occurring in the same universe. It is not merely that the rain falls differently on each of you, for that can be a wonder and a joy: it is that what is rain for the one is not rain for the other. Your elements will not mix, unless one agrees that the elements be pulverized—and the result of that is worse than being alone. The result of that is to become one of the living dead. The most dreadful people I have ever known are those who have been "saved," as they claim, by Christ—they could not possibly be more deluded—those for whom the heavenly telephone is endlessly ringing, always with disastrous messages for everybody else. Or those people who have been cured by their psychiatrists, a cure which has rendered them a little less exciting than oatmeal. I prefer sinners and madmen, who can learn, who can change, who can teach—or people like myself, if I may say so, who are not afraid to eat a lobster alone as they take on their shoulders the monumental weight of thirty years.

Then I walked to the airline office, through my favorite American streets, and bought a ticket.

I was thirty. So I said: "Make that first class, if you please."

No one, as far as I know, has ever tried to describe airports and air travel.

First of all, I am certainly not the only person in the world who, at the very center of his being, is simply numb with terror at the idea of flying at all. I am not grateful for the pilot's announcement that we are now thirty-three thousand feet in the air. I do not want to know that; it is perfectly useless information. I already know that it's a long way down, that this fall will be the mortal fall. I don't think about it, and I don't think I appear to be frightened, and I am *not* frightened, consciously. I can't afford to be frightened consciously. And, of course, I know that automobiles are yet more lethal, that not everyone who steps off the curb manages to get across the street, that the bathtub or the shower can kill, and I know that I smoke and drink too much. Whatever is going to kill me is already moving, is on the road, and I do not know, no more than anyone does, how I will face that last intensity, when everything flames up for the last time and then the flame falters and goes out. I would like it to be swift: yet I know that this moment does not exist in time.

Thousands and thousands of people at the airport, multitudes, multitudes, going where? Everywhere: and, furthermore, Everywhere is numbered. Flight 123 to Dayton, flight 246 to Tucson, Flight 890 to Dallas, Flight 333 to Birmingham, Flight 679 to Denver, Flight

321 to Washington, three-four to Baltimore, five-six to Pick Up Sticks, three-four-five-six-seven, and all good niggers go to heaven.

I was traveling before the days of electronic surveillance, before the hijackers and the terrorists arrived. For the arrival of these people, the people in the seats of power have only themselves to blame. Who, indeed, has hijacked more than England has, for example, or who is more skilled in the uses of terror than my own unhappy country? Yes, I know: nevertheless, children, what goes around comes around, what you send out comes back to you. A terrorist is called that only because he does not have the power of the State behind him—indeed, he has no State, which is why he is a terrorist. The State, at bottom, and when the chips are down, rules by means of a terror made legal—that is how Franco ruled so long, and is the undeniable truth concerning South Africa. No one called the late J. Edgar Hoover a terrorist, though that is precisely what he was: and if anyone wishes, now, in this context, to speak of "civilized" values or "democracy" or "morality," you will pardon this poor nigger if he puts his hand before his mouth, and snickers—if he laughs at you. I have endured your morality for a very long time, am still crawling up out of that dungheap: all that the slave can learn from his master is how to be a slave, and that is not morality.

Leaving that alone: I checked my one bag, picked up my attaché case—great God, a nigger with an attaché case!—took back my validated ticket, and bought a magazine. I had a little time to kill, and so I sat down at the airport bar, a dark bar, and ordered myself a drink.

I looked around me. A black man does not look around him in the same way a white man does: there is a difference. In a way not too unlike the way I have learned to live, more or less, with my fear of flying, I have learned to live in a white world. It may sound banal, or unfriendly, but it must be said: when a black man looks around him, he is looking, after all, at the people who control his social situation, if not his life, at the people his children will encounter, win, lose, or draw, at the people who menace everything and everyone he loves.

And, though this fact controls every single aspect of their lives, the people he sees when he looks around him, either do not know it, or pretend not to know it. Yet they use, and are protected by this power every hour of every day. In the humiliating, dangerous, disastrous, or bloody event, it will make no difference what they know or don't know. All that will matter is what they do, and he knows what they will do: they will kill him, or allow him to die. If one of their number protests this, and attempts to protect him, this white person then becomes not only worse than a nigger, he becomes a traitor—a reproach—and the two, the black and the white, are dispatched together.

It is impossible for a black man, here, not to anticipate, endlessly, disaster at the hands of his countrymen. The result is that he is always looking around him at people who do not know, or dare not know, what he is thinking, people who have been rendered incapable of seeing him. I listen to what white people say and, still more, to what they don't say. I must: my life may depend on what I hear: I cannot afford to be surprised.

This means that, in the generality, everything a white man says to a black man is a confession, though the white man never knows it. Sometimes I sing because I'm happy, true, and sometimes I sing because I'm free: but sometimes I sing because it is so grinding down to spend one's life listening to confessions.

My call was announced, and I paid the man and started for the gate—which turned out to be several miles away. But I got there, and stood on line with the others. We were all, now, in limbo, having surrendered out autonomy with our luggage.

The line was moving though, thank God, and I walked on the plane and took my seat at the window. I opened my magazine, closed it, fastened my seat belt, watched the people as they entered what might prove to be our last vehicle. One never thinks of that when getting into a car, or boarding a train, not even when getting on a boat—though the water is as terrible as the air. Still, one hopes, in the water, to be able to grab something, something floating, which will allow one to hold on to life a little longer—long enough, maybe, to be saved: but there is nothing at all in the air.

I realized these, perhaps, were not the happiest thoughts to be holding while waiting for a takeoff. The people all were seated. There were consultations at the cabin door. Then the girl pulled the door down, and locked it. The plane moved slowly away from the gate.

Slowly at first, then faster, then too fast for the earth. I am always fascinated by that point of no return, when the speed of the plane means fire or air. We rose into the air. The landing gear stowed itself away with a thump. San Francisco careened below us—buildings with flat roofs, buildings with towers, houses, freeways, poles and wires, bridges, and the water—looking as vulnerable as a child's game. Then clouds whispered alongside the plane, then dropped beneath it. San Francisco vanished. Then we were above the clouds, in a blue and golden air, on the great white plains of heaven. We seemed alone up here.

The NO SMOKING sign blinked off, I lit a cigarette. I did not feel like reading my magazine. I looked out of the window, imagining myself an explorer in this dread, silent, utterly limitless space. Then I thought of that incredible army of men and women who had built the cities and towns and houses beneath me, who had crossed this continent on foot, looking up at the clouds for rain, watching the sky for vultures. An incredible moment in the history of our race, but they had lied about the price, and had brought to the savage an unprecedented savagery. The red-skinned tribes were right: the land is not to be bought or sold. The blacks were right: a man is not to be used as a thing. The tom-tom and the smoke signal and the talking drums are true, and the gods are many.

Black models had begun appearing just about everywhere then, and I leafed through my magazine, seeing a black face here, a black face there, advertising the same shit that I was paid to advertise. (I didn't think too much about the implications of my job. I didn't dare. I treated it as a game that I was playing, a necessary game. To have

treated it any other way might have precipitated a nervous breakdown.)

Anyway, the kids were making a quarter, and that might hold off
the holocaust for a time. They smiled, looking sultry, looking boyish,
smoking this and drinking that—as though they had been doing this
all their lives. (And they *had* been doing this all their lives.)

I came to a full-page ad of a lady holding a wineglass. Her thick
black hair was cut short, in bangs, she wore hoop earrings, great circles
which gleamed like gold, and a very tight, low-cut black gown; her
long, large, Egyptian eyes seemed to hold an urgent message: not the
message of the ad, which read (the wineglass was extended) *Try this. It
will make you feel better.*

With a great shock, I realized that I was looking at a photograph of
Julia. It had to be Julia, or her twin, and Julia didn't have a twin. It had
to be Julia, or I was going mad.

I looked at the ad for a long time. I studied it. The girl was thin,
almost to the point of being skinny, but she wasn't flat-chested, and
her legs were long—one leg was visible through a slit in the gown—
and, yes, Julia would look like that now. The pose was sultry, seduc-
tive—she was advertising an aperitif—but there was the very faintest
hint, around the lips, of Julia's tomboy grin. And the eyes—they were
excessively madeup, but there was a lot in those eyes: yes, Julia could
look like that now.

Where the devil was she? We hadn't heard from them in a long
time. Florence's friend, down yonder, had become more and more laconic. We knew that Julia had recovered—with astonishing speed, in
fact, but that was like her. We knew that Jimmy seemed to be all right,
going to school and working. When Crunch returned, he had gone to
visit her, but he had not stayed there long. Officially, even at this
point in time, I knew nothing about Crunch and Arthur, but, perhaps
inevitably, they had broken up: Arthur's life was carrying him far beyond Crunch's orbit. I think that the breakup was devastating for Arthur, but he never spoke about it, and so, neither could I speak.

I think that Crunch did not know how to deal with Arthur, or how to deal with the implications in his life as a man of having a male lover. It would have been simpler if he had simply managed to stop loving him: but, though Billie is right about love being like a faucet and being off, sometimes, when you think it's on, it is also true that, sometimes, the faucet won't turn off.

Crunch was still in New York, working in a school for delinquent boys, and had one girl friend after another. Red was on the needle. Peanut had hit the Civil Rights road.

I had not yet been south. I told myself that I didn't believe in nonviolence, but this objection had long ago become meaningless. Arthur had been, several times, often with Peanut. I didn't want him to go, but I couldn't stop him. I was beginning to realize that it would, finally, be simpler for me to go with him rather than sit in New York, chewing my nails and dreading each television announcement and each phone call. But it was hard for me to get away. So, though I avoided thinking about the implications of my job, I knew, at bottom, that I was about to be forced into painful confrontations, and I was going to have to make some changes.

But my mind went back to Julia. She, who had wanted to get to New Orleans armed to protect and deliver her brother, had instead been carried there, helpless, victim of the father she had so adored—victim of *their* father: I wondered how much Jimmy knew.

Joel had disappeared, for us, anyway. I wondered if he had any contact with his children.

I closed the magazine, and put it in my case.

I got her phone number from the agency—they were looking for her, too. She lived in a loft on East 18th Street, on the top floor. I think I remember three brownstone steps, up from the street, heavy banisters, of some gray, ornately worked metal, double doors leading into the vestibule, mailboxes and doorbells on either side, no intercom.

I rang her bell—JULIA MILLER/JAMES MILLER—and the inside door buzzed open, and I began to climb the stairs.

From way above me: "Hall?"

"It's me, child, just a-huffin' and a-puffin'."

That laugh, from way above me: "Don't you have no heart attack on my stairs, now! Take all the time you *need*, old man!"

"You going to pay for that, Julia, soon as I get up there."

"If I was you, I'd stop talking. You using up the last of your *oxygen*. Just take it *easy*. I'll have a sedative ready for you, by the time *you* get here, and you can fall out on the couch."

She laughed again. I kept climbing. It was six thirty on a Friday evening; I remember that a record player was blowing Miles Davis on one of the floors I passed, there was a faint echo of marijuana on the air. I took the last few steps two at a time.

Her door was open. She stood in the center of the room—a high, long room, with two huge windows behind her. She wore her hair the way she had worn it in the ad, except that she had brushed back or combed back the bangs, and one saw that marvelous forehead. She wore no earrings. She wore a gray frock with a red belt, and stood in the center of the room, in high heels, on those long legs.

"You sound," she said, "like a mountain climber."

And she laughed. Without moving, and with her eyes fixed on mine, she laughed.

No one can describe this. When she laughed, I laughed, too, still standing in her door. I forgot to say, I had flowers—had bought flowers all of a sudden, because I saw them and because I was nervous and I thought she might like them. I held them toward her. I remember only that they were yellow flowers.

I see them still.

And she came toward me, with that tomboy grin, striding on those long legs.

I was so happy to see her—that's what I can't describe. Perhaps I had imagined that I would never see her again, never again in this life.

"Julia. I'm so happy to see you."

She took the flowers, and put her arms around me, and we kissed each other—we kissed each other, in fact, and we both realized this with an unspoken shock as we moved away from each other—for the very first time in our lives.

"I'm happy to see you, too. How've you been?"

Our shock was in her voice, and it was surely in my eyes.

"I'm fine—but *you're* the one! You turned glamorous on us all of a sudden. When you going to Hollywood?"

"You think I turned glamorous?" She laughed, and put the flowers on the table. "Well. I had to do something. Sit down. I'll put these flowers in something, and I'll fix you a drink."

I sat down on the sofa. She disappeared. I looked around me. It was a large, high room, simply, sparsely furnished, but very comfortable. I was in the living room–dining room section of the room—a big, handsome table, the sofa, a couple of easy chairs. There was a grand piano next to a small bar, a TV set, a record player, records piled high on a stool near the record player. The two windows opened on the roof, where there were tables and chairs. The kitchen area—a stove, a sink, a small refrigerator, cupboard, kitchen table, two chairs, were next to these windows. There were two bedrooms opening off this main room, and the bathroom was in a corner, near the front door.

Julia put the flowers in water, and brought the flowers back to the table.

"This is a great place," I said. "And you look marvelous."

"I don't know how," she said, "but I'm glad you think so—I can't get *over* seeing you! It's been so *long*!"

"It's been a while. How long have you been back in the city?"

"Not long, really—about ten days. We just moved in *here* a few days ago. I managed to sublet it through a friend of mine"—she laughed—"in the *business*. Hall, what can I get you to drink? I can't get over you—Mister Young Executive! You look so *smooth*, brother, like you headed for the top!"

"Well, I got to *look* that way, honey, if I don't I'll be kept on the *bottom*, and I don't *like* the bottom."

"I hear you. What do you want to drink?"

"A little Scotch and ice, if that's okay."

"I believe I can do that."

"Can I help? Here, let me help."

I got the ice out of the refrigerator for her, and we put it in a bowl. She poured a Scotch for me, and made a gin-and-tonic for herself. And we sat down on the sofa.

"I hardly," she said, "know where to begin." I offered her a cigarette, and lit it for her. "I've seen your mother and your father and your brother—and—just about everybody—since I've seen you. Of course," and she laughed again, more nervously this time, "we never *did* see much of each other. I was just a little girl, and you didn't like me very much."

What she says is true, but I don't want it to hurt us now.

"Well," I dare to say, "you were a pretty arrogant little girl. I didn't think it was all your fault. But I like you now. Anyway—I don't know—I had to see you."

She is saying that we really don't know each other, and she's right. But she's also been a part of my life for almost half my life, and she's a part of Arthur's life. I begin to feel uncomfortable. I don't know if she knows how much I know about what has happened to her: I can't, for example, talk about her father, or Crunch's baby, not unless she brings it up.

And at the same time that I feel uncomfortable, I am very happy to see her.

So now I can only step out, as the song says, on the promise.

"I'm glad to see you, too," she said. "And maybe I'm just as arrogant, but I'm a little more grown-up."

"Julia—how long has it been since you stopped preaching?"

"Oh—seven years, now. A little more than seven years." She sipped her drink, and looked at me. "Do you believe it?"

"It's hard to believe. What did you do in New Orleans?"

"Hall—the only honest thing I can tell you is that I survived it—how I don't know." She stubbed out her cigarette. "Well. I had

Jimmy. We got to be friends, finally. And then, he was a great help. He was beautiful—he *is* beautiful—"

"He's up here too? He's with you? I saw his name on the mailbox."

"Oh, yes, he's here. He might be walking through the door any minute with his haughty self."

She rose from the sofa, and walked to the record player. She looked at me. "I guess you know how I got down there?"

"I heard a little. Arthur wrote me."

"Your mama didn't tell you?"

"When I came home. But she didn't write me about any of that."

"I guess she didn't know how." She came back to the sofa and sat down, picked up her drink and stared down into it. "I don't know how, either. I thought I'd never"—she halted, still looking down into her drink—"come together again. It had just gone on so long! All that misery. And each time you think you getting up—it knocks you back down." Then she looked up at me with a smile. "But here I am."

"How'd you get to be a model?"

"I was waiting on tables in New Orleans, and I guess I wasn't bad, you know?" She laughed. "Maybe my days in the pulpit helped me to know how to handle people—at least, not to be surprised by them—and then, Jimmy and some of his friends made me some costumes for Mardi Gras, and they were *something*. I mean, they were *really* something. So, some folks from New York came down and photographed me—in these costumes—" she grinned that tomboy grin, threw back her head, and laughed—I watched her pulsing, long, thin neck—"and suddenly, I was on my way. To the Apple. I didn't know shit. I still don't. But I was on my way back here. With Jimmy. And I'd been trying to do that from the time I had to be carried away from here." I watched her long, thin hands on that neck for a moment, she shook her head, as though trying to wake up—"Ah! Would you like another drink?"

"If you do. But remember, I'm taking you to dinner."

"I'd love that. I'll make two very *short* drinks. I was really hoping that Jimmy would get here before we had to leave."

She picked up our glasses, and strode to the bar.

"What's Jimmy doing?"

"Jimmy don't go no place where there's no piano. He'd take his piano to the bathroom with him, if he could. Damn near drove our grandmama around the bend," and she laughed. "That poor lady! She *still* don't know what she did to deserve it all. But," and she brought our drinks to the table and sat down again, on the sofa, "she dealt with it, I'll give her that. Imagine she might be getting some sleep, finally, now that we out of the house." She was silent for a moment—then, "Jimmy's trying to be a musician, but it's rough. Of course. He spends a lot of his time on the road, in the South, playing for Civil Rights benefits, and," sipping her drink, "because of that, of course, he's spent some time in jail. It's a madhouse down there now, and it's going to be worse up here."

"But Jimmy's going to stay in New York now, for a while?"

"Oh, he intends to be here, for a while. But I might come home and find a note saying he's on his way to Birmingham."

I said, after a moment, "He sounds like Arthur."

"Where *is* Arthur?"

"He's somewhere in Canada, singing. I don't know when he's coming back here!"

"I'd like to see him. Your brother—he was very nice to me."

"I can believe it. He's a very nice man, my brother."

Julia giggled. "He's so *serious,* sometimes—he tries to be like you."

I laughed. "Why? Am *I* serious? Or funny?"

"I don't know. But, sometimes, Arthur walks around like you, and it's *funny.*"

I had never thought of that, had certainly never seen it.

"Well—shall we go and eat something? I'm starving."

"All right. Just give me a moment."

And she put down her drink, and disappeared into the bathroom.

I sat there, thinking of many things, including what she had said about Arthur walking around and trying to be like me. I thought that was very funny, and I laughed to myself—why would anybody want to be like me? *I* didn't want to be like me. But there was something distantly chilling in the fact that Julia could so easily make a comparison which I couldn't see at all.

I heard a key turn in the lock, and Jimmy walked through the door. I recognized him at once, of course—the taciturn face, the distant eyes: but this was the first time I recognized him, so to speak, as Julia's brother, saw how they resembled each other—in the cheekbones, the eyes, the impudent lips. Perhaps because Jimmy was a male I looked for his resemblance to his father—but, actually, Julia resembled Joel more than he. Jimmy's eyes were distant because they dared not focus on you? but, when they did, one saw, in the boy's face, the astonished and vulnerable eyes of his mother.

I rose at once as he entered, afraid that he wouldn't recognize me. But he did, at once, with a smile.

"Hey! You must be Hall—right?"

"That's right. You must be Jimmy."

"I guess I didn't change much, then. Julia told me you called. I'm glad to see you. Where's your brother—Arthur?"

"He's in Canada."

"Working?"

"Yeah. He's singing up there."

"Lucky motherfucker."

He was wearing blue jeans and a sweater and sneakers and carrying a battered airline bag. He was fairly husky, though still very much a matter of wristbones, ankles, and kneecaps; his hair was coarser and kinkier than Julia's. He dropped the airline bag near the record player and propelled himself toward the kitchen.

"You all right? Can I get you anything?"

"I'm all right, thanks."

He rummaged in the refrigerator for what turned out to be a beer and came back to the living room. He sat down in one of the easy chairs and I sat back down on the sofa.

"So! You haven't seen my filthy old man around, have you?"

"I haven't *been* around. I just came back from California."

"I doubt he's got the balls to go that far," said Jimmy. He swallowed from his bottle. Then, "I'm not trying to put *you* uptight about it. I just got a couple of things I got to say to him, and I was wondering if you might have come across him—in your travels."

And he smiled. The most terrifying thing about that smile was that it was a real smile, and I suddenly caught a glimpse of what Julia had certainly not foreseen as she began to recover in New Orleans. Whatever Jimmy knew, or didn't know, he *knew*—knew that two women had been violated, by his father: and that made *his* manhood an embattled, a bloodstained thing.

It must have been strange for Julia to have so much desired to be forgiven by her brother, only to be forced to see that it was not *she*, as far as he was concerned, who stood in need of forgiveness. And he who stood in need of forgiveness *could* not be forgiven: it was no longer a human possibility, which made divine forgiveness dubious indeed, if not ignoble: this lesson for the preacher.

Julia came out of the bathroom, more burnished, subtly, than before, and stared down at her brother, one hand on one hip.

"So you got here, I see. You say hello to Hall?"

Jimmy elaborately swallowed some beer, made a rude, farting noise with his lips, she laughed and he laughed, and he said, looking up at his sister with the most brilliant, mocking, loving eyes I had ever seen until that moment in my life, "Why, yes, sister. I said hello to Hall." He turned to me. "Didn't I say hello—what's your name?"

We laughed. Jimmy winked at me, cock of the walk, and Julia came and sat down beside me.

"We going to go and eat something. You want to eat with us?"

"I don't want to interfere, and"—he looked at his sneakers—"I ain't hardly dressed for it. No," and he looked at me, "you all go on. I'll be seeing you. Try to fatten up my sister just a *little* bit." He turned to Julia. His tone changed. "I'm going to work a little bit, a record or two, raid the icebox, and hit the sack. And I got some people to see early in the morning."

And he stood up, forcing me to stand up. He extended his hand.

"I'm glad to see you again. I remember you real well. You was always real nice to me." We shook hands. He pulled Julia up from the sofa, and kissed her on the forehead. "See you later, sister. Try not to stumble over nothing when you come in—because you *know* that makes me *evil*!" He walked us to the door. "You got your keys, child?"

Julia looked in her handbag. "Yes. I've got my keys."

"Well, then. Good night."

He closed the door behind us, and we started down the long, steep steps.

"He's a nice boy," I said.

"Oh, yes," said Julia. "Some things turned out right."

We got to the street. I hailed a cab; for a wonder, it stopped. "I know a nice place in the Village," I said. "You want to try it?"

"I'd love to, sir," she said, and we got into the cab.

I gave the driver the address, and we were off on our first date.

Though that first date was to prove to be a very important date, it resists my memory. It blurs with other dates, weaves itself in and out of my memory, blurs with other occasions. I see Julia's face, that changing face; for a very long time, I could not take my eyes from her face. I saw the face of the child, and the face of the little girl preacher, the faces I had always seen—or never seen—and a new face, or faces, I had never before confronted. Everything she said and did that night was touched, for me, with the miraculous—it was as though she had come back from the dead.

We went to a joint with low lights, on Bleecker, near Tenth, and we had a couple of drinks before dinner. Though what Julia had to tell me was somber, and her situation precarious, she was too proud—or had been through too much—to panic.

They had left New Orleans with very little money, and Julia had only the vague promise of "interviews." But that had had to be enough. Julia had never been happy in New Orleans, had arrived there with too vivid, too mysterious an affliction. She had had an "accident" in New York, as her grandmother told it, seeming to be referring to a traffic accident. But Jimmy had already been there awhile, taken away from his father: who never came to see him. Julia had been living with this father. Now she, too, after her "accident," had had to be taken away from him. The arrival of the boy, Jimmy, had not caused much speculation. But the arrival of the girl, Julia, was something else again. Without knowing why, no one quite believed in her "accident": and why had she, who was, after all, scarcely more than a child, been allowed to stay with a father so little equipped to protect her? It was this brooding, distrustful curiosity that Julia encountered as she began to recover, and this distrust never abated. On the contrary, sometimes before her, sometimes behind, it moved as she moved, it was her shadow.

She was completely out of place in school—which she contrived not to attend for very long—too old, by far, for her peers, too knowing, too removed; and, on the other hand, too weirdly ancient and private for the elders. She exasperated them, she appeared to frighten them, because they could find no way to correct her. And the fact that she had been a child preacher, but was a child preacher no longer— had become a maid, of all work, then a short-order cook, then a waitress, and seemed not to mind the company she was obliged to keep— became a kind of final black mark against her: it was as though she had been marked by the devil.

Julia, in my memory, smiling as she tells me all this, or some of this, sometimes laughing, with those relentless shadows playing on her face.

But, "I don't know, now, how I expected Jimmy to act. I was just a mess when I got there. I hardly remember getting there. It seems like all I wanted to do was sleep," and Julia closed her eyes for a moment. "But every time I started to sleep, I started to dream and the dream was so terrible I tried to wake up and I couldn't. But when I woke up, all I wanted to do was go back to sleep. I didn't want to see—nobody. But especially not Jimmy."

She paused, not looking at me, her arms folded, a cigarette between her long, lean fingers. She sat opposite me, but far away. The candlelight seemed to turn the gray dress silver.

I wanted to ask her—many questions—but I held my peace. At one time, I had thought I knew the answer, but I had not, then, been facing an unknown woman in a Village restaurant. The clarity of the answer diminishes as the intensity of the question rises: as the question fragments itself into many sharp edges.

Yet, "Why not?" I asked.

"He was too young. I didn't want him to know about his father. I didn't want him to know"—she smiled—"anything about me."

"But Julia—how could you keep him from knowing?"

"If I had managed to get down there like I wanted to," she said stubbornly, "with some money, and able to *do* something for him—and I was prepared to turn tricks for *that*, now, that's no lie—well, he wouldn't have had to know it, it wouldn't have had to cross his mind, we could have just moved on from there—leaving Mama and Daddy, yes, and holy Little Sister Julia, too, far behind us." She sipped her drink with a sad smile. "But it wasn't meant to be like that. I got there helpless, and I was helpless for a while."

The waiter came to take our orders. Julia looked up at him, quickly, changing completely in a split second, and, in that split second, I realized that Julia was perfectly aware of her public effect. But her awareness was artless and direct, a little wry, perhaps, but good-natured—the tomboy and the lady exchanging a private wink.

She fussed over the menu for a while, allowing her eyes—far less made up than in the ad—to have their effect, and, finally, settled for chicken cacciatore—"ain't nothing but fricasseed chicken"—and I said I'd have the same, and two more drinks.

"You going to get me drunk," Julia said.

"That's all right. I'll take you home. And we'll see how well *you* manage the stairs."

She laughed. "That place is not the best place for coming home drunk."

"Or for *leaving* drunk. I'd think twice about coming to any of your parties."

"We might be *having* a party soon. Jimmy's got something coming up, and looks like *I'll* be working—at least, I've got appointments all this week."

The waiter came with our drinks, and Julia held out her empty glass, smiling like a little girl. The waiter placed our drinks before us, with a hand not altogether steady, and, in a kind of speechless paroxysm of confusion and delight, smiled back.

I smiled, and lifted my glass. "To you. Something tells me you likely to be working steady."

"Lord, wouldn't that be nice? I damn sure hope so."

She put her drink down. We were silent. In the silence, something gathered—Julia asked, looking at me, "Have you seen my father? does anybody have any news of him?"

"*You* don't? he hasn't written, or anything?"

She shook her head, her great eyes looking into mine as though she were depending on her eyes to communicate something she could never say.

Then, "No. Not in all these years. It's like he's just vanished from the earth."

I said finally, "Well, none of us have seen him—not my mama, not my daddy—nobody's seen him around. *We* figure—he must have left the city."

This city, or this life: *we*, really, didn't care.

Her eyes looked into mine for yet another moment, then she dropped her eyes, and picked up her drink.

"It may sound funny," she said, "and nobody knows everything that happened—except me—but I don't have anything against him. Nothing at all."

"Do you want to see him?"

"I don't think so. I'd just like to know—that he's all right. Somewhere."

I said, "Julia. You're right. I don't know everything that happened. But—from what I know—it seems to me that he might just be—*afraid.*"

She threw back her head. "I *know* he's *afraid*—he's *always* been afraid, that's what's wrong with him." She tapped a cigarette and put it between her lips. I lit it for her. "I hate to think of him dying. Alone, afraid, somewhere." She inhaled, exhaled, blew smoke above my head. She said with a low, muffled passion, "He's not the only guilty party!"

I sipped my drink, and looked at her. I forced myself to pull back, so to speak, and then to look at her and then to say something that I felt had to be said: "Look. Neither are you. And *you* were a child." She looked at me. "I'm sorry, but that's true."

"Children," she said, and looked away from me. "Children know a lot."

"They better. But they're *still* children."

I reached across the table and took one still hand in mine.

"Listen. Children know a lot—okay. But children don't *know* what they know. They just: *testing—testing—testing*—they waiting to find out if anybody's out there." I sensed her resistance: it was in her patiently still, not quite inert hand. "Get one thing straight, baby—a child does not *know,* when he sets a match to the curtains and thinks fire is pretty, and fun, that he's burning down the house, and him with it. You put out the fire and you pick up the child and you whip his ass until he thinks he *is* burning alive. Then he won't think fire is so pretty and he won't do it no more and he might live."

I relaxed my grasp of her hand, and stroked it.

"Maybe I didn't like you so much when you were a child, but I didn't think it was really your fault—I told you that—but your father, Julia, ain't no child. He *is* the guilty party. That's why you ain't heard from him. *You* can't take on his responsibility. How you going to take *on* a responsibility when there wasn't no possible way for you to have *understood* it, or even to know what a responsibility was? And you going to try to assume all that now?"

I let go her hand, and pulled back—the dazzled waiter was approaching with our meal. He set it down in silence. Julia did not look up—said "thank you" from very far away. She picked up her napkin, I picked up mine.

"I understand you. I just don't want to play the innocent, wronged victim—"

"Well. You *are* the innocent, wronged victim. *That's* the truth. Now. Take it from there." I watched her. "You got the balls?"

She had begun nibbling at her chicken—now, she laughed.

"Hall—"

"Don't Hall *me*. I *knew* you as a child."

Something in my tone checked her, made her look directly into my eyes.

"*I* would have whipped your ass so bad, baby, that you would have had trouble getting to the *potty,* let alone trying to preach. Your behind would have been a sermon you listened to for *days.*" I signaled the waiter. "This is our first date, baby. You want some wine with your dinner?"

She dropped her eyes demurely. "I thought you'd *never* ask."

"Keep it up. I might whip your behind before we get out of here— red or white?"

The waiter, more securely intrigued than ever, and more at ease, stood over us.

"Ah! *Red,*" said Julia, and she laughed. "For all *kinds* of reasons!"

I laughed, helplessly, and ordered the wine and we ate in silence for a little while. It may have occurred to me, in that silence, that I was having a ball with my newfound friend. For she was absolutely new to me, although I knew her. Well, I *didn't* know her. I was fascinated by her. I *wanted* to know her.

"So how did you and Jimmy finally work it out?" I asked. "You seem to get along beautifully now."

"Well," she said, with her stunning candor, "I was helpless. I couldn't hide it." She gestured with her fork, aimlessly, then put her fork on her plate and looked at me. "I couldn't play big sister. I couldn't play any of the roles I'd"—and she grimaced, like a child, like a woman—"*played.* I told you, I didn't want Jimmy to know anything about *me*." She picked up her fork again, looked down into her plate. "But he knew—that's part of what I mean when I say, a child knows—I don't disagree with what you just said, but I realized that Jimmy knew a whole lot more than I, or anybody else, told him—*I*, after all, hadn't told!"

Her eyes, when she said this, by some mighty effort of the will, were dry—drier, perhaps, than my own. Our wine came, and our waiter poured it, and Julia picked up her glass.

I watched her, feeling myself being drawn closer to her with every breath I drew.

"I didn't want Jimmy to know anything about me. But I began to see that I was wrong as two left shoes—and, I swear, Hall, that's when I began to get well, I began to stop trying to sleep, I started fighting with my dreams—you know the only question Jimmy ever really asked me?"

She sipped the red wine, and held the glass in both hands for a moment, her elbows on the table.

"He came into the back room where I was, in the bed, and he sat down on the bed and we talked about this and that for a little while—school, his music, white people, black people, shit like that—I was watching his face, and I was a little amused because he's so young and violent—and I was happy because he was talking to me and I had thought he never would—you know what I'm trying to say?"

"Speak on, sister," I said, and I sipped my wine. "I do believe I hear you."

"All of a sudden he asked, 'Did he ever beat you? He ever put his hands on you?' "

She put her wineglass down.

"I didn't know what to say. All I knew was I couldn't lie. All I could say was yes."

She looked at her dinner and picked up her fork and touched it.

"I watched his face. He just looked at me, for what seemed like a long time. Then, he laughed. He said, 'Well, that's two of us, ain't it?' He said, 'Hey, tell you something. I dig having you for a sister. You dig having me for a brother?' And he made a long face, like he knew I'd say no. And I started to laugh and to cry, and I hugged him—

hugged him for the first time in my life. He was laughing and crying, too. He said, 'Well, you better get up out that bed pretty soon, I *need* you out here.' And I started to get well. I *had* to get well. Maybe I thought I didn't want Jimmy to know nothing about *me*—and that really *is* bullshit—but Jimmy made me to know, somewhere, that you can't really hide anything, and anyway, he damn sure needed somebody who knew something about *him*."

She smiled, and made her fork useful for a moment, and got some chicken past her lips.

I watched her—is this an odd thing to say?—very proud of her.

"And—*do* you know something about him? I'm sorry. I don't know why I ask that. I guess I'm not asking *you*."

She said mockingly, "I do believe I hear you, brother. I don't know enough to change him, or to save him. But I know enough to be there. I *must* be there."

"But suppose you get married—you probably *will* get married, one day, you know—and move to Timbuktu?"

"I *am* married, you fool," she said. "And don't talk to me about Timbuktu! What difference does *that* make?"

I laughed out loud. "Child, I don't believe you ever left the pulpit."

She laughed with me. "Well, you know what they say, Hall—"

I loved the way she said my name.

"No. What do they say?"

She raised her wineglass. "You can take the child out of the pulpit—"

I raised mine. We were not quite laughing—smiling, looking at each other, confronting something neither of us could name.

"But," I said, "okay,"—and we touched glasses—I wanted her to say it—"how does the rest of it go?"

We laughed together, the red wine shaking between us.

"Hall, you getting old, your memory's faltering. Soon, you going to have to start worrying about your teeth."

"Come on, you old married lady from Timbuktu—"

We started laughing again.

"Come on, what's the rest of it?"

"And you old enough to have taught it to me."

"Watch it. I don't play that—how does it go?"

"Well, you can't take the pulpit out of *this* child, anyhow, there you satisfied?" and we laughed so hard we spilled a little wine onto the table, and into our chicken.

We went from there to a bar near Sheridan Square. It came to me that I was walking Julia around into and out of places which I had frequented when she was in the pulpit, when she was a child: I could not imagine what she was seeing. But you never can imagine that, when you are trying to see what *you* saw, through someone else's eyes. Neither can the person for whom it is all new—who has not, that is, paid for *this* scene—see what you dimly think you saw. What you saw is in the price you paid, deeper than memory.

Somewhere between Sheridan Square and East 18th Street, Julia and I fell in love.

We walked because, at that time, not many taxi drivers stopped for niggers in New York. At night, you put up your hand and the cab veered toward you; then the driver *saw* you and veered away, like Lot hightailing it out of Sodom. After the third time this happened I was compelled to see that Julia was becoming more and more upset; not about the taxi drivers, but about me. She came into the center of the street where I stood cursing the tailights of a fleeing cab and took my hand and said that we should walk.

She was right. Still, what galled me was that I was not entirely wrong. But—Julia comes from a long line of women who had to sing, *He had a long chain on. Another man done gone.* I put my pride in my pocket, and kept my balls, so to speak, where I could see and touch them, and we started to walk.

It was late, not late—around midnight. It is not a very great distance from Sheridan Square to East 18th Street if two people are walking and talking together. And Julia and I could walk and talk together because we had been through—differently, far from each other—the same things. Neither of us had ever thought of our lives that way—as having been, somehow, always, inexorably connected. We did not really *think* of it now, either, on our walk, as we walked and talked together: and to say that we now *discovered* this makes what I am speaking of far too remote. As we walked, our climates became, imperceptibly, the same climate. This was both warm and terrifying. After all, Julia had been a little girl for me, an exceedingly irritating little girl preacher. I remember both her parents, vanished now in such different ways, and the way she had then treated her little brother. Now here she was, walking and talking beside me, and I knew too much about her to know anything about her at all. I knew only how she made me feel, how she caused a shaking deep within me, caused me for the first time in a long time to dare to wonder about happiness, about joy, to dare, almost, to hope. I didn't want to hope. I didn't know how to stop.

We were walking hand in hand, swinging our hands together gently, like two children—two children we, each, in our different ways, remembered. We turned eastward on 18th Street, on the long, long blocks, dark now, which led to her apartment. We had stopped talking.

Then she said, as we crossed Fourth Avenue, and entered the block which held her building, "Every time I cross here, I think of Crunch, and that room he had on Fourteenth Street. Once we took a walk around here—just before he left. Then, sometimes, I used to walk around here by myself."

Something very swift and subtle, not trembling, not shrinking, occurred in her as she said this, a shifting of the beat: I felt it through her hand and heard it in her voice.

I asked, "When was the last time you saw Crunch?"

"He came to see me in New Orleans. But he didn't really know what had happened. And I couldn't tell him." Then, "Oh, he knew—some things. But he didn't know what happened to *me*—when I lost the baby. I didn't want him to go through life thinking it was *his* baby. That *my* father had kicked *his* baby out of me. It didn't seem fair.

Crunch didn't have nothing to do with it. And," after a silence in which I heard only her high heels on the sidewalk, "I didn't want to use that to make him think he loved me."

I didn't want to use that to make him think he loved me.

Somtimes you hear a person speak the truth and you know that they are speaking the truth. But you also know that they have not heard themselves, do not know what they have said: do not know that they have revealed much more than they have said. This may be why the truth remains, on the whole, so rare. Julia had just told me that she knew she might care more about Crunch than Crunch could ever care about her, and she had also told me how much she loved, or had loved, her father. She had taken it all on; she had taken on too much.

I had tried to tell her something like this in the restaurant. With a certain terror, I began to suspect that I might be forced to try to convey this to her again, armed only with myself. Her father was her stratagem, her sword and shield—how could I, or any man, get past her iron determination not to condemn him? For her only other love was her brother, Jimmy, who was, ironically, an absolutely irreducible element of this determination. I could see, furthermore, that Jimmy certainly agreed with me, was unequivocally on my side. But only Jimmy's death or destruction could bring her father to judgment: and even then, and more than ever, her father's crime would be hers.

I almost said, *Feet, do your stuff,* but I didn't. I held her hand more tightly and looked straight ahead, down the long and empty street. My hope, or dream, of joy and happiness wavered and flickered. It did not go out.

I said, as mildly as I could, "You might not have had to use that, or anything."

She walked a little more slowly. I held on to her hand, refusing to let her stop or drop back. I knew that she was listening, but I couldn't guess what she was hearing.

She said—she sounded young, very young—she sounded scared. "What do you mean?"

"Maybe," I said, "you wouldn't have had to use anything to make him love you. Maybe you weren't listening."

"Oh, Hall. *You* weren't here, you don't know what was happening!"

"You want to bet?"

"Some things—*nobody* knows—who wasn't actually there."

"And sometimes the person who was *actually* there doesn't know, either!—did you ever think of that?"

We walked, in another silence, to her stoop. She moved up one step. I didn't let go her hand. I leaned on the gray, ornately worked metal. She looked down at me with that ancient and utterly vulnerable face, eyes as old as Egypt and as untouched as tomorrow.

A yellow light hung around her, the light from the streetlamps and a dimmer light from the vestibule behind her. Both hope and bewilderment stared out of those eyes.

"What do you mean?"

"I mean what I said, little sister."

She said, "Listen. You can tell when someone loves you."

"Can you?"

Since I wouldn't let go her hand, she couldn't turn away from me, but she turned her face away.

"Can *you*, Julia? Can you?"

She said nothing, kept looking away. She looked down the dark street.

I watched her. I said, "Now, take me, for example—"

Astoundingly, the words, *take me* rang and rang. She turned her head, and looked at me.

I moved up the one step, still holding her hand, and stood beside her. The streets were empty, except for us.

I said, "For example. In my case—"

She tried to smile. "Yes? In your case?"

"What would you do, in my case—to keep from making me think I loved you?"

"Oh. Hall—"

"Don't *Hall* me. What would you *do*?"

"This is the first time you've seen me—since—" She tried to move; I held on. "Hall. Please."

"It's the first time you've seen *me*, too," I said. She looked away. "This is not the first time—*since*—whatever happened. Maybe I don't care what happened. Maybe I think that whatever happened is something you and I can handle. Maybe I think that what *may* happen is more important than what *has* happened. I know this: this is the very first time that you and I have *ever* seen each other."

She wouldn't look at me. She looked down. I put one fist, very gently, under her chin, and tilted her face upward to look into my own. Then I saw in her eyes hope, bewilderment, and fear.

"That's true," she said. "That means that you don't know me."

"I *want* to know you. Don't you want to know *me*?"

She took one hand away, and opened her handbag. "It's late. I've got an early morning."

"Okay. I'll climb the mountain with you."

She opened the front door, and we started up those steep stairs. We walked side by side.

"You're crazy," she said. "You don't know where I've been, what I've done—you don't know *what* I've been."

"Keep talking, mama. You going to have to serve me a drink when we get up yonder."

She giggled. "We'll wake up Jimmy."

"You using up the last of your oxygen, old married lady from Timbuktu."

We laughed together, and reached the first landing. I said, "Jimmy won't mind if we wake him up."

I wanted to take her in my arms but I was afraid—afraid that she would be afraid. We started climbing again. I said, "I don't want you to think that I expected Jimmy to find me there when he wakes up. *This* morning. But you got to think about what I said because I meant what I said. If I can make you happy, and I would dig making you happy, then I'll be a happy man, baby, and Jimmy will be happy, too." She said nothing. We reached her door. I kissed her lightly on the forehead, on the lips. She watched me with those trusting eyes. "Think about it."

She turned and put the key in the lock. I put one hand on her arm.

"Will you think about it?"

She said, so low I could hardly hear her, "Yes. Yes, I will."

"Do you promise?"

Then she turned to me and smiled and kissed me lightly on the lips. "Yes. I promise."

"Then unlock the door, woman, and let's try not to wake up your brother—at least not right away."

She opened the door very quietly, and switched on the light. The wide, long loft was utterly still; but Julia listened for a moment before she threw her handbag on the sofa.

"Ah, Jimmy's home." She grinned. "Sit down. Let's have a drink."

I sat down. I wondered, then I didn't wonder, how she knew Jimmy was home. The first bedroom door was closed: perhaps it would have been open if he were not at home. But it wasn't, on the other hand, a matter of signals, not a code to be deciphered, broken— she knew, simply, that he was home because she would certainly have known if he wasn't. She was behind me, at the bar. I felt, in her curious tranquillity, menaced, as I feared, or confirmed, as I hoped, by my presence, that she knew Jimmy was home because, otherwise, *she* would not be home, would not peacefully be preparing two drinks. It is true that I then heard a faint snore from beyond the closed door of the first bedroom: but I could not possibly have heard this if she had not already known that I might.

It was now a quarter to two in the morning. She came back and handed me my drink, took hers, and sat down on the sofa opposite me.

I looked at her and lifted my glass and she lifted hers.

"Welcome home," she said, and we touched glasses, looking each other in the eye.

And I was suddenly in torment. With no warning, my prick suddenly stretched, thundering upward against my shorts, my trousers, reaching for my navel: reaching for her. This was not at all like the familiar swelling created by the anticipation of a more or less calculated conquest, not at all. I could not remember ever having been so violently shaken before—perhaps I never had been. The past drowned in that moment, it was as though I had no past. It was terror that I felt, a terror both warm and icy. It was not merely that I felt at the mercy of my cock, but that my cock, all of me, was at the mercy of a force unnameable, and why do I say mercy? This force had no mercy. I shifted on the sofa, more unhappy than a boy trying not to wet his pants, and, before I knew it, I had said, "Julia. Julia. Please welcome me home. Please."

It is rare that a cry is heard, and I think we love forever those who hear the cry. Julia looked at me. Even today, until the day I die, in a way that has nothing to do with Ruth, whom I had not yet met (and yet, this moment prepared me for her!) and my children, not yet dreamed of, and Birmingham, and Peanut, and all those other corpses, and Arthur, my God, my God, my God, my God, I remember how Julia looked at me, and set her glass down on the table and stood up.

"Write down your phone number—I *know* you got a phone number, Mr. Young Executive! Is it listed?—so Jimmy will know where to find me and, while you doing that, I'll find a toothbrush." She laughed, then she sat back down and took my hand in hers. "I'm difficult," she said, "but I'm not evil. You and me can stay here together any night but tonight you understand—I don't want Jimmy to *find* out."

She put her hands on my shoulders. Lord. Lord. Lord. I didn't move, but I trembled. Lord. She trusted me.

"I just want to tell him, myself. I think that's fair—okay?"

I said, "Okay."

She started to rise. I didn't know that I was going to do it, but I put one hand on her wrist and pulled her to me. I was then invaded by her odor. She entered me: love is a two-way street. I put my arms around her, she put her arms around me. I had never, never, been held that way, never. I kissed her, or, rather, I sighed myself into her. She held me, then I looked into her eyes.

I said, "If you can find me a piece of paper, mama, I got a pencil."

"I thought," she said, "you'd have a fountain pen by now," and we laughed, I let her go, and she stood up.

I did have a fountain pen. She brought me a piece of paper, and I scribbled my name and address on it. She scribbled above it, *Am with Hall. Love, Julia,* and put the piece of paper in the center of the table, weighing it down with the clock.

She looked at me again, disappeared, and came back with a small overnight bag. I took it from her. She opened the door and turned out the lights and locked the door behind her and we went on down the stairs.

For a wonder, we got a taxi right away, and we went to my place on West End Avenue, in the Seventies.

And, now—now, I find myself before many things I do not want to face. I feel a dread reluctance deep inside me and I would end my story here, if I could. But—what is coming is always, already on the road and cannot be avioded.

Some days after Julia and I had begun, as we now say, to "make it"—and several years before we could face what we meant to each other—Arthur came in from Canada with his nappy-headed self. He had been very successful in Canada, and very happy—one of the reasons that he was so nappy-headed: he hadn't had time to do more than wash and comb his hair. He was now, decidedly, tall, and not only from the paranoid view of the older brother. He was tall and rangy and would remain, for the rest of his days, too thin.

Anyway, he had a pad way downtown on Dey Street, where his practicing didn't bother the neighbors because he didn't have any. When he dropped his bags at his pad and ran a comb through his hair, he called our father and mother, who told him I was back in the city and would probably like to see him. And so he put down the comb with which he had still been combing his hair, and called me.

"Hey! how you doing?"

"If this is a collect call from Canada, operator, would you please reverse the charges?"

"Don't be like that. I'll pay you when I see you."

"And when you counting on seeing me, brother?"

"You want to look at your calendar while I look at *my* calendar? I don't know about *you*, brother, but I'm *booked*."

"About time. What you doing, oh, in the next five minutes? I believe I can steal five minutes because I have *been* booked. I'll steal five minutes for you, you understand, but you going to have to shake your ass."

"Shaking it right now, brother. Here I come." Then, "Love you."

"Love you, too."

"In a minute."

"Right. In a minute."

I hung up, and looked around my pad. I never quite knew what I was doing on West End Avenue, but that's another story. This was a Saturday. Julia and I were not yet living together—that was to come, so much was to come—but we spent a lot of time together. Jimmy had keys to both our doors, and pranced in and out—mainly, as it seemed to me then, in and out of our Frigidaires. All I really remember of Jimmy, then, is sneakers, beer, sandwiches, and ice cream. He was always eating; his legs seemed to grow by the hour. I did not, then, recognize this riot as his happiness. The keys to our houses, which he sometimes threw in the air and caught with one hand were, for him, the keys to the kingdom. He saw his sister as happy and himself as mightily protected. He had her and he had me, and, as to that, I will tell you now, he was absolutely right. But I did not know if Julia and I really had each other. Jimmy could believe that I made his sister happy, and again, as to that, he may have been closer to the truth than I: I couldn't have known that, then. We both had too much to do.

And I loved her. *She* made *me* happy: but I was beginning to be too old to trust the ease sleeping behind that word: *happiness.* I was being forced to see that real love involves real perception and that perception can bring joy, or terror, or death, but it will never abandon you to the dream of happiness. Love is perceiving and perception is anguish.

So I learned, for mighty example, and long before Julia told me, how she had made the money to bring her brother and herself out of New Orleans. *I was looking at ceilings,* she told me, much later—while men pounded themselves into her, less brutally, after all, than her father had, and she picked up the money and took it home and put it aside. She had taken it all on: she had taken on too much. So I had said, and so I was to say again, until my heart was broken: but, in the meantime, there was Jimmy, lying on the sofa, with his sneakers on.

There was, also, Arthur, now, leaning on the doorbell. I buzzed him in. I lived on the fifth floor. I walked to my door, and opened it and stood in the doorway, waiting to see Arthur erupt from the elevator, which was a long way down the hall.

Here he came, presently, loping like a heathen, bright and sharp in a beige gabardine suit. Nappy-headed, grinning, with those eyes, and all those teeth. Seeing him was always new: I always wondered if he still liked me. A childish wonder, true, but not uncommon. His elegance was scarcely at all compromised by his adolescent lope and the fact that he was carrying a large shopping bag.

He got to the door and put the bag in my hand, then kissed me on the cheek.

"Contraband from Canada," he said. "Blazing hot. Close the door, I think I'm being followed."

I closed the door, laughing. "You *are* a fool. You know that?"

"Well. I can't say I haven't been *told.*"

I put the shopping bag on the sofa. He walked around the living room, then stopped and looked at me.

"You look great, I'm glad to see you. What's been happening?"

"Nothing new. Well. A couple of things I'll tell you about. How was Canada? You want a drink?"

"Yeah. I'll have a little taste—here," and he picked up the shopping bag, and we walked into the kitchen. He started unloading the bag. He had brought down cigars, a carton of cigarettes, a tin of ham, and bottles of whiskey and vodka and gin. He put all this on my kitchen table and he was, really, a little like a child who had managed to steal this contraband and bring it all on home.

"Canada was beautiful," he said. He looked at me, with that smile. "Pour us a drink," and he handed me the vodka, "while I go to the bathroom. I'll tell you about it. And then, you got to tell *me* something. You know—we ain't seen each other in a while."

He went to the bathroom. I made drinks for both of us. I heard him singing to himself in the bathroom.

He came back, and we sat down in the two easy chairs near the window. This big window was the nicest thing in the apartment I lived in then. Not much could be seen from this window except the houses across the street, and the street itself, if you sort of leaned up and looked down. Still, one sensed the nearby river and one was aware of the sky and the light changed all the time.

"So—? Tell me about Canada."

"I had the feeling that they hadn't heard anybody like me up there. Of course that's not true, they must have *heard* just about *everybody*. But, look like, they hadn't *seen* anybody like me. They damn sure didn't want to let me go." He smiled. "It was nice."

I watched his face. "What kind of places did you sing in?"

He grinned. "I might be wrong, brother, but I had the feeling that niggers didn't put down roots in Canada the way it happened here." He sipped his vodka, which was straight, over ice. "I might be wrong. You got to remember, there was a whole lot of shit I didn't see, because I was on the road. But—it was different. It was nice, like I say, but it was different." He took another sip of his drink, frowning. "I just didn't see as many of *us*. I didn't see as many churches—their churches are different. I sang in civic centers, you know, and some *white* churches, and"—he laughed—"a football stadium, and, you know?"—his proud astonished eyes now searching mine—"it was full, that stadium was damn near full, there was ump-teen thousand people there, baby, and it was beautiful, I left them rocking to the gospel as I went off, they might have stayed there all night, for all I know." He laughed. "I had to get to my hotel and get some sleep because I was off again in the morning."

He paused again, narrowing his eyes, looking through my window at the buildings across the street. "Maybe that's what I mean when I say I had the feeling that they hadn't seen nobody like me before. They seemed so—*surprised*—you know what I mean? Anyway," and he put his drink down on the table before us, "*I* hadn't seen anybody like *them,* either, and it was something, I think it was good for me, to sing before such a strange audience. They react"—clasping his hands together, looking at me—"in such strange places, it throws you, you don't know where you are. Then—well, you go with it—you *have* to go *with* it—and you find out things." He nodded his head, looking down, like an old man talking to himself. "It was nice. I didn't see a lot of niggers. But I saw some Indians."

"How'd you get along?"

"We got on fine. I had the feeling—you know?—that we were learning something from each other. And some of those cats, man, they know more about what's happening in the States, with Martin Luther King, and Malcolm—man, they knew more than *I* know. I just listened to them, and I'm real glad I was up there."

"Spreading the gospel," I said, and smiled.

He looked at me as though he were afraid that I was making fun of him, but then he saw that I wasn't. "Well, yes," he said finally, "Maybe. But, to tell you the truth, I never thought of it that way before." He frowned and grinned. "I never had to listen to other people *listening* to it before. So, I began to *hear* something because I was listening to them *listen*—does that make sense?" And again, he grinned and frowned, looking into my eyes.

"It makes perfect sense to *me*," I said. "But, really, you've been doing that—listening, I mean—ever since you started singing. You're just beginning to realize it."

He was leaning forward, his hands clasped between his knees. He said, "Daddy always told me that." Then, "And I played piano for myself—accompanied myself—much more than I ever had before, just like Daddy said I would. I had to," and he looked at me with a wonder at once personal and remote, "because, you know, it's another beat they got up yonder. And I can't really find the words for what I'm trying to say—it's like another—*pulse*—the beat inside the beat."

He rose and seemed to prowl, like a hunter, as though whatever was eluding him was certainly quivering somewhere in this room.

"I'd be up there, you know, singing, and the cats behind me would be keeping *time*—but—they couldn't—*anticipate*—you know, when you *leap* from one place to another—they couldn't be with me, I was alone—oh, brother, you've heard it all your life, like me, but I don't know how to say it—the changes some of the old church choirs could ring on 'The Old Rugged Cross,' make you hold your breath and you'd *hold* your breath until they let you know you could let it out—" he turned to me, and grinned, his hands spread wide—"you know, like Billie Holiday and Bessie Smith can just leave a note hanging somewhere while they go across town and take care of business and come back just in time and grab that note and swing out with it to someplace you had no *idea* they were going—and carry you with them, that's when you say *Amen*! and Mahalia can do that, too, and Cleveland, and some of those people I heard down South, and"—he grimaced, and walked to the window, hands on hips—"quiet as it's kept, Miles and Dizzy and Yardbird, *and*"—pointing a triumphant finger at me—"Miss Marian Anderson, baby, people say she can't sing spirituals but she can damn sure make Brahms sound like that's all he wrote." He turned from the window. "I better have another drink," and he grinned. "You must think I'm going crazy."

I picked up his glass. I couldn't help laughing, because of his intensity and because of my love, but then I said, very soberly, "No, brother. I do not think that at all. You sound like you've been working. You sound like you *are* working."

I stood up and I would have started for the kitchen, with both our glasses in my hands, but I was checked, held, by something in his face.

"It's strange to feel," he said, "that you come out of something, and something you can't name, you don't know what it is—something that has never happened anywhere, ever, in the world, before." He grinned, and clapped his hands. "I don't know no *other* people learned to play honky-tonk, whorehouse piano in *church!*" He collapsed, laughing, on the sofa, and I almost dropped the glasses. "And keep both of them going, too, baby, and all the time grinning in Mister Charlie's face." He wiped his eyes. "Wow. And sing a sorrow song so tough, baby, that it leaves sorrow where sorrow is, and gets you where you going." He subsided, looking toward my window. "And *that's* the beat."

I walked into the kitchen with the glasses and poured vodka on the rocks for him and a Scotch on the rocks for me. At the front door, I heard the key turn in the lock.

It was either Julia or Jimmy, and I stood still in the kitchen, waiting.

It was Jimmy. But—I looked at my watch—Julia should be arriving soon.

I heard: "Hey! Arthur! Don't you remember me?"

A beat: "Goddamn. Jimmy—you *live* here?"

"Oh, I hang out here from time to time—I'm glad to see you, man!"

Jimmy had leapt up on Arthur by the time I came out of the kitchen, as friendly and unwieldy as a Great Dane puppy.

Arthur was both astounded and delighted—and somewhat relieved when he finally managed to disentangle himself from Jimmy's arms and legs. He held him by the shoulders and stared into his face.

"Hey, I'm glad to see you, too. When did you get back here?"

"Not long—a month, maybe—"

"Where's Julia?"

"Julia—I thought she was here already."

Arthur turned and looked at me, riding between astonishment and laughter.

I said to Jimmy, "I haven't had time to tell him everything, son.

He just got here, too. Why don't you get whatever you want out of the kitchen and join us?"

Jimmy looked as though he thought he'd done wrong. I handed Arthur his vodka, and laughed, and grabbed Jimmy by one shoulder.

"Don't worry—why you looking like that? Julia's going to be here in a few minutes and, if you put on some decent clothes, I'll take you all out to dinner someplace on one of my credit cards."

"He ain't never said that to *me,*" said Arthur. "I didn't even know about his credit cards." Jimmy laughed. "Come on in the house, man. I just got in from Canada, and I been doing all the talking. But I think I already got everything pretty well figured out." He winked. "I'm delighted you part of the family. I mean that."

Jimmy said, "Man, I am, too," and walked into the kitchen.

Arthur and I sat down again in our easy chairs.

"I'll bring you up-to-date presently," I said—but I felt a strange discomfort.

Arthur lifted his chin and sucked his teeth. "Baby. Don't you worry about it. Wow." Then he laughed. "Life is the toughest motherfucker going."

Jimmy came in with a vodka on the rocks. He suddenly looked very vulnerable, and I watched Arthur watching him.

"I'll have to go home to change my clothes," he said.

"Well. Wait till Julia gets here," I said, "and I'll figure out where we're going to eat and you'll meet us there."

I realized that Arthur also felt a powerful discomfort, and I watched Jimmy watching him.

In my experience—and this is a very awkward way to put it, since I don't really know what the word *experience* means—the strangest people in one's life are the people one has known and loved, still know and will always love. Here, both I and the vocabulary are in trouble, for *strangest* does not imply *stranger.* A stranger is a stranger is a stranger, simply, and you watch the stranger to anticipate his next move. But the people who elicit from you a depth of attention and wonder which we helplessly call love are perpetually making moves which cannot possibly be anticipated. Eventually, you realize that it never occurred to you to anticipate their next move, not only because you couldn't but because you didn't have to: it was not a question of moving on the next move, but simply, of being present. Danger, true, you try to anticipate and you prepare yourself, without knowing it, to stand in the way of death. For the strangest people in the world are those people recognized, beneath one's senses, by one's soul—the people utterly indispensable for one's journey.

So now, sitting before my big West End Avenue apartment window, feeling the discomfort which had entered the room with Jimmy and which had immobilized Arthur, though I did not know what was going to happen, I *did* know that something had happened. I will not say that I looked ahead; clearly, anyway, during all this time, I have been painfully looking backward. But I was glad that Jimmy and Arthur had met at my house, and I was glad that Julia would soon be turning her key in the lock. I was, perhaps defensively, more amused than astonished. Our two little brothers would be compelled to deal with each other and leave the two weary old folks alone.

Jimmy had guts. He said, "Maybe we can work together up yonder, one of these days—I play piano—"

"I play piano, too," said Arthur, more coldly than I had ever heard him sound. "And I ain't going back up yonder for a while. I'm thinking of going south."

"I just came back," said Jimmy promptly. "I'd love to go there with you."

Arthur gave Jimmy a look, which, though it was genuinely exasperated, was also genuinely amazed. He was seeing Jimmy for the first time. He was seeing a stranger who might become a part of his life in quite another way than he had been until now. His nostrils and his upper lip quivered slightly. He could not quite believe that Jimmy was saying so blatantly what he was saying. Arthur was made uncomfortable, too, I could see, by my presence in the room; my presence did not disturb Jimmy at all. Arthur stared at Jimmy helplessly, but he was no longer looking at Julia's kid brother. His eyes darkened—or rather, a light went on, deep behind his eyes, and a most unwilling smile touched his lips.

Jimmy was tranquil, smug, triumphant: he had made Arthur look at him—at *him:* tranquil, triumphant, and smug as he appeared to be, he was also a little frightened, now, of the scrutiny he had so recklessly demanded.

"Well," said Arthur, after a moment. "We'll talk about it." Then, "You sure you want to hang out with an old man like me?"

Jimmy laughed, and I laughed, too—then Arthur laughed.

"You don't look so old to *me*," Jimmy said, and now he had Arthur's full attention. Though, as I say, I knew nothing, officially, about Arthur's life at that moment, I knew more than he thought I knew; or, more accurately, far more than he had told me. I could see how it all made perfect, idyllic sense to Jimmy, who would have a family again, or who would, perhaps, have a family for the first time. He would have Julia and me *and* Arthur, all of us belonging to each other. I could see, too, as Arthur couldn't, that Jimmy had probably had a crush on Arthur all his life.

Then the bell rang, sharply, three times, Julia's sometime signal, and she came on in the house.

Julia sometimes rang the bell, according to Julia, because she didn't want to seem to be spying on me, or risk catching me in my sins: and I accepted this nonsense, as I accepted almost everything from Julia, in those days, with a wry delight.

She was carrying packages, she was dressed in something brown and yellow, she was bareheaded and radiant from the wind outside, and she hadn't gained any weight. I watched her figure very closely in those days because I was hoping to get her pregnant, and so persuade her to marry me.

"My Lord," she said, and put her packages on the table, "we got the whole family here today!" She kissed me briefly, pulled her brother's hair, and ran to Arthur. They held each other a moment, in silence: it was nice to see. "When did *you* get back here?"

"Just today. It's wonderful to see you. How are you?—you *look* wonderful."

"I'm fine—you know your brother's turned me into a fallen woman?" and she left Arthur and came to stand next to me.

Arthur grinned. "He hasn't had a chance to tell me much of anything, I been doing all the talking—but I figured it out—it agrees with both of you."

"He didn't figure it out," said Jimmy proudly, "until he saw *me* come bouncing in here."

"Yeah," said Arthur. "Your brother done got *loud* since *I* last saw him—what you figure on doing with him?"

"We've been running ads in the papers for days," said Julia, "but we can't find nobody to give him to—"

"I understand *that*," said Arthur. "*I'd* sure think twice about it. Wouldn't never get no sleep." He scowled at Jimmy, who grinned, and, in a kind of insolent, delighted panic, lit a cigarette.

"Somebody told me once," he said, "that most people sleep too much."

"Not with *you* around, they don't," said Arthur. He said to Julia, "It would save you a lot of money if you'd let me strangle him right now."

"Ah! Let me have a drink first, and I'll think about it."

"Sit down," I said. "I'm bartender. What do you want?"

"He always asks me that," said Julia. "And he knows I drink gin—have we got any gin?"

"Brought some in from Canada," Arthur said proudly, and they sat down.

I went into the kitchen. I knew what Arthur was worried about, and I wished I could talk to him about it. I wanted to say, *Dig it, man, whatever your life is, it's perfectly all right with me. I just want you to be happy. Can you dig that?* But that's a little hard to say, if your brother hasn't given you an opening. I thought that I would try to make an opening; then I thought that little Jimmy was perfectly capable of spilling all the beans in sight. *He* didn't care who knew what—he trusted his sister more than Arthur trusted me; but then, an older sister is a very different weight, in a man's life, than an older brother. Arthur was worried about another man's judgment; in this case, mine. He was worried about Jimmy's youth. He was frightened, already, though I don't think he knew this, and could certainly not have said it, by Jimmy's speed and single-mindedness: for Jimmy had lit his insolent cigarette on Arthur's *wouldn't never get no sleep* as though he were saying *let's try me, and see.* I laughed a little to myself in the kitchen, as I fixed Julia's drink: unless I missed my guess, Jimmy had Arthur in his sights and wasn't thinking about changing his mind. And, if the weather got rough, Jimmy would turn to me—I could see that coming, too: after all, he had both me and Julia. I would have to tell him the truth, which was that I really felt that it would be a damn good thing for both of them, and a great load off my mind. It would be a great load off Julia's mind, too, and then, maybe, the two weary old folks *could* be left alone. For the fate and the state of her baby brother was in the center of Julia's mind, and there was no way for me not to respect that, for the fate and the state of *my* baby brother was in the center of my mind, too.

Well. I took Julia her drink, and, eventually, we decided where we were going to eat—at Harlem's Red Rooster, though I wasn't sure they took credit cards—and Jimmy bounced out of the house to go downtown and change his clothes, and meet us there.

That left the three of us to have a quiet drink alone, in front of the West End Avenue window. "Lord," said Arthur. "Time is flying so fast. I know, now, we'll never catch up."

"Yes," said Julia, "I was looking at you and thinking of the last time we saw each other—and that room on Fourteenth Street, remember?" And she laughed and then they both laughed. Then, "When was the last time you saw Crunch?"

"I haven't seen Crunch—oh, for a long time now—not since before Christmas."

"And what was he doing?"

They looked at each other. A strange, deep, unconscious sorrow flooded both their faces.

"I don't really know," said Arthur. "He'd been doing a little bit of everything—"

"He was working in a settlement house for a while," I said. "And then I think he was in Philadelphia for a while, and then, I don't know."

"He came to see me in New Orleans," Julia said. "Did you know that?"

Arthur nodded, his eyes big with pain.

"I had the feeling," Julia said, "that something had happened to him in Korea, that something got broken—somehow—"

"Well," said Arthur, "I know he was worried about you—and the baby—" He sipped his drink, and looked down. "I couldn't reach him."

"Yes. But it wasn't just that. Crunch was always worried about *something*. I had the feeling, I keep coming back to it, it's the only way I can put it—that something got broken."

Arthur stared out of the window. "Well. He damn sure wouldn't let nobody touch it—whatever it was." He dared to say, "I tried."

He was holding everything very carefully in, but I knew that he was not very far from tears—he was not very far, after all, from his time with Crunch. But neither Julia, nor I, were supposed to know anything about that. "He was bitter," Arthur said. "I had never known him to be bitter before."

"A lot of us came back from over there bitter," I said. "It was a bitter thing to be part of." I looked at Arthur, who turned to look at me. "It was bitter to see that you were part of a country that didn't give a fuck about you, or anybody else."

"That's true," Arthur said. "I see that." Then, "But you're not bitter."

"I'm not going to let it kill me," I said. "But I'm bitter."

Julia looked at me with a wry, pained pursing of the lips. "You're a little like a loaded gun," she said. "Sometimes—you know," she said to Arthur, "you're afraid to touch it, it might go off." Arthur nodded, watching her. "Like Jimmy, every time he comes back from one of his trips south."

"He told me he'd just come back—he's been working down there?"

"Yes," said Julia. "I don't know how to stop him—but—I guess I wouldn't even if I could."

Then we were silent, watching the evening gather outside my window. I thought of Jimmy, in the subway now, rushing home to get into his glad rags to come rushing back uptown. I knew how Julia trembled for him every time he went south, how she feared the newspapers, the radio, the television set; flinched each time the telephone rang, and trembled even more when it didn't. And, even now, with Jimmy merely riding the subway in New York, not totally at ease; he was surrounded, after all, by a lonely and vindictive and unpredictable people. We were, none of us, ever, totally at ease. Our countrymen gave our children a rough way to go, and it was hard not to hate them for the brutality of their innocence.

"I've got to get there soon," said Arthur slowly. "I've been wanting to get there for a while, but my manager always has other plans."

"Yeah," I said. "Like keeping you alive, for example, so he can keep on paying his rent."

We laughed, and Arthur said, "That's the most bitter thing I ever heard you say, brother."

"I just never wanted to meddle in your business. But I know about managers."

"I always hoped that, maybe, one day, *you* would manage me."

"Me? Are you crazy?"

"No. Daddy hopes so, too."

Arthur said this with that throwaway, wide-eyed cunning which had sometimes made me want to strangle him as a child. He sipped his vodka, looked out of the window, looked at me. I had a cigarette between my lips, and he lit it for me. He said, looking into my eyes, "Not right now—but—later. Soon. I know you got other things to do—can I have another drink? Before you take us out to eat? Big brother?"

Julia laughed, and took his glass and walked into the kitchen.

"Will you think about it?"

"You know fucking well I *got* to think about it—*now!*"

"Don't be bitter," Arthur said.

"That's right," said Julia, returning, and handing Arthur his drink. She kissed me on the cheek. "Lord. You don't know how blessed we *are*—just to be together in this room."

I put my arm around her, and looked at my brother. "That's true. But you're ganging up on me."

Julia and Arthur laughed together. Julia took my glass. "That's right. You being *persecuted*. You need another drink, just before you *really* go around the bend." I laughed, too, watching them: I didn't mind their ganging up on me. Julia said to Arthur, "Watch over your brother while I go and fix my face—he's taking us out, we got to look *correct*." She went back to the kitchen, throwing over her shoulder, "He's not *bitter*, Arthur, he's just damn near paranoiac—he'll be hearing voices pretty soon."

I sat down opposite Arthur. It was dark now, the only light came from the kitchen. But, in a moment, Julia returned and put my glass in my hand, and switched on a lamp. She kissed me on the forehead: *how sweet it is: to be loved by you,* Arthur watching this with a smile, then vanished into the corridor which led to the bathroom and the bedroom. "I won't be a minute!"

I really wanted to follow her. Arthur saw this in my face. We laughed softly together, touched glasses, and drank. Arthur said, "I'm happy to see you happy, brother. And *she's* happy. I think that's a miracle." He grinned. "It strengthens my faith."

I dared to say, "I'd like you to be happy, too, Arthur."

He thrust out his lips in a self-deprecating smile and looked down at his glass, which he held between both hands. Then, looking up at me, "You two going to get married?"

"That's what *I* want. But she's not sure."

He nodded his head slowly, not looking at me, looking within. "Well. I can see that, too. She's *been* through some shit." Then he looked up at me, and smiled. "Well. Patience, brother!"

"Patience, yourself," I said, and I wanted to persist, but I didn't, something told me that this was not the moment.

We finally hauled it on uptown, and I think it was the Red Rooster, a joint I dug a lot in those days, and I associate it with Julia. On the other hand, the Rooster is not too far from where Jordan's Cat used to be, and not too far from where Martha used to live, and I know I avoided that neighborhood for a long time—everything around there hurt me too much. So maybe my memory is playing tricks on me and I associate the Rooster with Julia because we were so happy for a while. Our love was the beginning of my reconciliation with my pain, and, after Julia, I was never afraid to go anywhere again. Maybe I associate Julia with this turf because I had once been happy there and then had been locked out and felt myself lost and Julia gave me back my keys. Who knows? And it doesn't matter. We went to a very groovy Harlem restaurant and had ourselves a ball. I still remember Julia's face, and Arthur's face, and Jimmy's.

One thing I will say, though, now that I think I can, now that I don't get around much anymore: when I realized that Julia and I were not meant to make it together, for reasons inexorably hidden in the cosmos, I entered a void, and, in that void, I discovered that Julia had given me something. She had given me herself, yes, or had given me what was hers to give: but she had given me more than that. Through her, I learned that anguish was necessary, and, however crushing, could be used—that it was there to be used. I sometimes thought that Julia was as wrong as two left shoes, and, in some ways, I still do: but what she saw, she saw, and she never pretended not to have seen it— whatever, indeed, it is that she sees, this ancient child from Egypt! Sometimes I wanted to kill her, and I was very often frightened for her. But, when the chips are down, it is better to be furious with someone you love, or be frightened for someone you love, than be put through the merciless horror of being ashamed of someone you love.

That night, anyway, Jimmy was almost completely unrecogniz-able, mainly because he had not dressed for his sister, or for me, or for the restaurant, and had not given a thought to my credit cards. I had never seen him, as it were, "dressed," and I very much doubt that Julia had: neither of us could have seen, anyway, what Jimmy wanted Arthur to see. God knows what Arthur saw, but even he must have suspected that Jimmy had dressed for him. There he was, then, in a dark gray suit, a beige shirt, a scarlet tie, gleaming brown pumps. His scalp must have been stinging still from the scouring, combing, brushing and greasing of his hair, and his fingernails were very nearly blinding. And, in fact, I realized, as Jimmy hoped Arthur would, realized for the first time (as Jimmy hoped Arthur would) that he was a very beautiful, tremendously moving boy, who might become, with love, with luck, a rare and valuable man. My heart turned over—he, too, after all, had been through some shit—and I hoped, with all my heart, that he would find the love he so needed to give.

He was one of those people who leap on terror as though terror were a dangerous horse, and ride; not quite knowing where they are going, but determined not to be thrown.

Arthur had asked him a question about the South, and Jimmy, rid-ing, was instructing Arthur, and all of us, in the interesting folkways of the region:

"First of all, I thought, Shit, me and my sister been *living* down here. And then I had to realize that I had *not* been living down here. I had been living in Grandma's house because there wasn't no other place to send me. And the second thing I had to realize was that I had not been *born* in Grandma's house, like those kids my age, hitting the waiting rooms and the lunch counters. I had not grown up with that. I didn't see signs, saying WHITE and COLORED—and they so fucking hypocritical and cowardly, those assholes, why can't they say white and black?—till I was past twelve years old—"

He was talking so fast, and becoming, as he talked, so indignant that he had to catch his breath. Julia said mildly, "Take it easy, baby. Eat."

Arthur grinned and touched Jimmy on the cheek. "Don't try to tell it all at once. You got to make sure I understand what you telling me."

Arthur's smile, and his fleeting touch, caused Jimmy, after a moment, to subside and drop his eyes and turn his attention back to his pork chops. Arthur watched him a moment, then turned back to his spare ribs. Julia and I, very much together, looked at each other for a second, and then, for a little while, we ate—except for the jukebox—in silence.

Older brothers, younger brothers—this thought had crossed my mind as I watched Arthur watching Jimmy. It is taken for granted that the younger brother needs the older brother: this need defines the older brother's role, and older brothers remain older brothers all their lives—the proof being that they are always, helplessly, creating, for themselves, an older brother no matter how desperately they may long for one. An older brother is not among their possibilities. But younger brothers also remain younger brothers all their lives, and either seek out older brothers, or flee from them. Loneliness being what it is—and wickedness being what it is—the role of the older brother is the easier role to play: it is easier to seem to correct than to bear being corrected. The older brother's need, whatever it is, can always be justified by what he is able to dictate as being the need of the younger brother.

But what, I had abruptly wondered, watching Arthur watching Jimmy, happens to the younger brother who needs a younger brother to love, and who considers that this need is forbidden?

Jimmy had finished one pork chop, started on his second, and caught his breath.

"What it is, you know," he said to Arthur, "is that you don't believe what you're seeing. That fucks you up, right there. You don't believe these people can be real." He laughed. "It's true. You think they must be part of a fucking circus, or they just escaped from a madhouse—somebody going to come and call for them in a minute, or, you know, they going to turn up the houselights, or *something*."

He laughed again. I watched Julia watching him: her heart.

"Then"—he gestured with those big hands—"you wonder what am I doing here? And I made it a point to *be* here. I walked miles and days to *be* here. And I don't want their slimy coffee and I don't want their fucking greasy hamburger—they can't even cook, I guess they hate food just like they hate everything else, they got no more taste than pigs, man—and then one of them say something like *What you want in here? You know we don't serve you all in here,* and"—he threw back his head, and laughed—"had one motherfucker say to me, *This is a free country! You don't like it, you can go on back to Africa!*"

He laughed, and we laughed with him. Tears streamed down Jimmy's face.

"Then"—sobering—"you start to get scared. It don't come over you all at once. It's slow. It come over you, look like, from your ankle, from your big toe, it creep up the back of your thigh till it reach your behind and your balls get wet. And it's funny, because you were already scared on the way here, but when you walk in, five or six or seven of you, you not scared then. Then—you don't *get* scared, exactly. Just, all of a sudden, you *are* scared. This ain't no vaudeville show, this ain't no circus, ain't nobody coming to take these people nowhere. These people coming to take *you* somewhere. And"—leaning forward to Arthur—"two things, man. You don't want to die, but you waiting. These people really want to kill you. That's hard to believe. You know it, or somebody once told you, or you *thought* you knew it—but now, here they are, and now, they *the only people in the world!* Ain't *nobody* to call on."

He leaned back, lips pursed, forehead wrinkled. He tapped on the table with his fork.

"But the other thing is worse." He looked up, now, at all of us. "Maybe somebody told you once that these people wanted to kill you. Maybe you got some sense of how many of us they already killed. And that's why you there, after all—and you try to hold this in the center of your mind—to force some kind of showdown, to bring an end to the slaughter." He shook himself, a little like a puppy, and sighed.

"But couldn't nobody ever have told you—or you didn't hear it—that *you* would want to kill. Oh"—looking at Julia—"many a time I wanted to kill our father. I even thought, one time, that I wanted to kill my sister," and he grinned. "But—that wasn't really true, you know. That was just—*pain.* But, down yonder—you look into that white face and you look around at them white faces and you want to kill somebody. You want to start killing, and never stop, until you swimming in blood. And then you get scared in another way, all over again. You scared of yourself. You scared of what will happen to your buddies, them sitting beside you, if you don't catch hold of yourself. And then, you see that this ain't no circus, these people are *real,* just like you, because, *now,* you damn near just like *them.* And that makes you feel real cold. If you ever prayed, or *never* prayed, you pray then. Hell is a staining place."

He looked down, looked up—at Arthur. "You still want to go?"

Arthur looked at him for a moment, unreadably. He did not, at that moment, know what to say, nor did Julia, nor did I. Arthur and Jimmy sat facing each other, Julia and I sat facing each other: Arthur could not avoid looking into Jimmy's incredibly trusting eyes. I saw this from an angle. Julia looked down at her plate.

"I might," said Arthur carefully, "consider taking you along as my guide. If you wasn't so fucking undernourished." He tapped Jimmy's plate. "Eat."

"But there's a whole lot more than what I just said—there's something very beautiful, too—some beautiful people, man, the most beautiful people I *ever* saw—!"

Arthur continued to watch him; then he grumbled to Julia, "This child ain't got no respect for his elders. Think my brother got money to throw away on children who pick at their food." Then, to Jimmy, "Eat, baby. We got time to talk."

Jimmy dropped his eyes, and obediently began to eat.

"We going to have a drink," said Arthur, "and when you finished eating, raise your hand."

Jimmy smiled as best he could, with his mouth full of pork chop and his eyes full of Arthur, and nodded. Arthur grinned, and tapped him on the cheek again, and winked at Julia. Julia winked back, and I could see, from that split-second exchange, that she was very grateful to Arthur, for Jimmy had told Arthur more, in an evening, than he had ever told her—or anyone: younger brothers, younger brothers.

The younger brothers put us in a cab, having elected, themselves, to ride the subway. Since they were together, it was almost the first time that Julia and I had said *Good night!* to the younger brother without a small, private, repudiated tremor of anxiety. *Habit*, we called it, silently: but habit is produced by experience.

Our cab rushed past them as they walked slowly down the crowded avenue, Arthur a little taller than Jimmy. They waved, and we waved, and Julia put her head on my shoulder. I pulled her into my arms, held her head against my chest for a moment, and, then, in the speeding, flashing light and darkness, we kissed and kissed each other until I said, "Thank God, Julia, we ain't got to climb no stairs tonight. I'd never make it."

She put her hand on me, and grinned. She said, "Well, if you can manage to get out of the cab, you can lean on me in the elevator. I like it when you lean on me."

Well. But she always seemed surprised, surprised that she filled me so, that there was nothing she had to *do*, to please me. I knew that she would never, consciously or deliberately, do anything to hurt me—or anyone: her dread of inflicting pain was so deep that it could nearly be called an affliction. Nearly, but not quite. I never knew her to hurt anyone but herself, and that is how she broke my heart. But she faced it, and surmounted it, and she gave me the strength to do that, too: and one really cannot ask love to do more than that.

Ah. It is a story I will tell another day. I know I cannot tell it now. Even today, with Ruth, with my children, with time, like thunder, gathering behind us, dark before us, Julia will make a gesture, or throw back her head, and giggle, or lean forward, with a moaning laugh, and I feel a tingling in my thigh, as though some ineffable wound were there, and I see Julia, as we were, so long ago: Julia, stepping naked out of the shower, or Julia's head foaming with shampoo; Julia, not quite certain that she approved of the fact that she shaved her armpits, "But," dryly, "it *is* a competitive business"; wrapping Julia in my bathrobe which immediately became, on her, a tent; creeping under this tent to be with her, like *The Sheik of Araby!* and we would laugh. She would hold my head against her while I nibbled on her breasts, tasted her nipples (someone said that all love is incest), licked her throat, drank at her lips, found her mouth, a swimmer, deep inside me, holding his breath, letting it out, going under, coming up, aware of her astonished, astonishing surrender, aware that I had known her when she had no breasts, trying to lick the secrets out of her pussy, my tongue between her thighs, down those long legs, up again, up, until I covered her entirely, her long fingers on my back, stroking me from the nape of my neck to my ass, my mouth in hers, my mouth in hers, her breath becoming mine, mine hers, her hands on me, her hands on me, her mouth against my chest, my nipples, all the hairs of my body itching, tingling, one by one, her mouth against my navel, against the hairs of my groin, on the tip of my prick, on my balls, her mouth on my prick again, my prick in her mouth, my tongue in her pussy, then, up, up, until I covered her again, my mouth in hers, her mouth in mine, moaning, moaning, those long legs spreading, those thighs holding, that belly rising to meet mine, those fingers on my back, the slow, slow, slow discovery of the wet and seeking warmth inside her, that entry which took so long, there was always more of her, always more of me, I stretched and stretched and thickened, I was always astounded that there could be so much, and she opened, then closed around me, opened and closed, opened and closed, never had anyone held me so, I had never been welcomed with such rejoicing, never, nearly strangling, heard such a laugh come up from me, throbbing and pounding, throbbing and pounding, hearing her cry, hearing her cry my name until that cry was the only sound in the universe, feeling her give and give and give, gasping and grasping, and then, from the soles of my feet, along my thighs, as though dark bells had begun rejoicing, through the crack of my ass and up my spine, electrifying my shoulder blades and the nape of my neck and the top of my head, threatening to close my throat, my breath in hers, my breath in hers, down my chest, tormenting my nipples, my belly, swelling my balls, everything, now, all of me, thundering into that great organ, and, at this moment, not wanting it to end, I always paused, and she would say, *please oh please* but she would also lie still, knowing we couldn't be still long, and we would kiss as though we never expected to kiss again, and, then, without even knowing it, we would be moving, moving, moving, and, always, at the moment I began to come, it always seemed that there was, suddenly, more of Julia and more of me, and more, hard hard hard, and sometimes I was almost frightened, it seemed that the outpouring would never ever end.

Then we would simply lie in each other's arms, in each other's element, each other's time and space, for a long time: and I had never, in my life before, felt such a tremendous safety, or such power to protect. Never before had I felt about another *you are my life my heart my soul.* We sometimes made love on the living room floor, and woke up, in our tent, with the light shining down on us through my big West End Avenue window.

But that night at the Rooster was the last time the four of us were to be together for a while. Arthur did not go south then, his manager had already booked him west—to Seattle, San Francisco, Los Angeles, keeping Arthur, as he thought, out of harm's way. This led to Arthur's break with that manager, and, eventually, I assumed that role—again, another story.

Jimmy went to Birmingham. This was shortly before our countrymen began hearing of Birmingham, and about eighteen months before Peanut and Arthur and I went down: and all of this, for what it's worth, is before the March on Washington.

Shortly before that trip south, Julia had left me to go to Africa—finding herself, for a long time, in, of all weird places, Abidjan—and I wasn't functioning well. The agency had put me, in effect, on sick leave without pay: but I had asked them to do this. And, worried as I was about Arthur, I might not have gone south with him, at least not then, if Julia had not left me. Perhaps he saw me, bumping into walls, cursing out mirrors, drowning in alcohol, picking myself up off my floor in the midnight, crying myself to sleep, yes, crying like a baby, and I don't know if you can call it sleep. I don't know what you can call it. There was nothing I wanted, nor nobody, and nothing I wanted to do. I was aware, the way you hear voices from a long ways off, that my mother, my father, my brother, were worried about me: it was cold to be forced to realize that I knew a lot of people, but I didn't really have any friends, not one, and I was only thirty-two! And, if I didn't have any friends, it was because of something I had *chosen*, it was something I had done, there was no one to blame: and there you go, round and round in the prison of yourself, day in, day out, night-fall, sunrise, day again. Those voices I heard from a long ways off, my father, my mother, my brother—I couldn't really speak, but I didn't want them to be too ashamed of me: those voices forced me to stagger and sometimes damn near crawl across my floor and get to the bath-room and pee, and sit there and force myself to shit and get up and not quite face the mirror, but anyway, shave, and then brush my teeth, and, holding my breath, get into the shower—I always saw Julia there! And, sometimes, using all the strength I had, I would some-times actually shampoo my hair and stand under all that water and cry and cry and cry.

Then, I would get dressed—dressed: she was everywhere, she used to help me dress. This tie, no, she didn't like that tie, this shirt goes better with your skin, she said, my God, Hall, where did you get those socks? Oh, Lord, and wander around that house, those rooms, in and out of that fucking kitchen, Christ, the dishes, fuck the dishes, one shoe in my hand and one shoe on my foot, looking down to make sure they were the same color at least, taking out ice cubes and pouring myself a drink, running an ice cube over my face to stop the tears from flowing, forcing myself to sip the drink instead of smashing the glass against the wall, hearing myself laugh as I got the other shoe on, look-ing into the mirror, dressed, it's all right, you look all right, where has

Hall gone? Then pouring myself another drink and turning on the record player and sitting in front of my window.

All day, sometimes, all night. The phone would ring, it would be my mother, or my father, just calling to say hello, and we'd love to see you, soon as you get the time, or it would be Arthur, long distance, clowning about his life as a gospel singer—delicately suggesting that he could use me out there, if I could find the time.

And I would have to respond, somehow, if only for the exasperating split second, to the unspoken—their respect for my life, and for my pain. I knew that they were not listening, for an instant, to anything I said—which meant that I did not have to say much. They were listening to the tone of my voice, were checking, in effect, my temperature. I didn't want them to start worrying about emergency wards and blood transfusions, after all, I loved them, too, and so I guess I sounded, all things considered, all right.

Yes, we save or damn or lose each other: of this, my soul is a witness. I was under, and nearly helpless, but I was not gone—so those faraway voices insisted, therefore, I was still among the living.

Anyway, Paul and Florence dropped by one evening. Paul had come to take me downtown, to hear a new piano player. Florence just wanted to lie down, she said, and she'd wait till we came back. Paul said that he had a taxi waiting, and so I'd have to hurry, and I did. I was glad to see them, and glad to get out of the house. Paul and I went down to the Village, and the piano player was not bad, in fact, he was very good. My father and I didn't talk much, but we had a very nice time, and I laughed a lot, for the first time, it seemed to me, in the Lord knows when. It was a funny kind of laughter, because it hurt, hurt the way an unused muscle hurts. But Paul liked to see me laugh—why had I never noticed that before?—and I had always loved hanging out with him. I remembered again how proud I had been the first time I realized that he was proud of me. He got me a little drunk, and I knew he was doing it deliberately; he was a kind of honored guest of the house, and people kept coming over to our table, and he was kind of showing off, for me; the young piano player announced his presence, and played a number for him. Paul kept ordering doubles for me, and then, one for the road—which tune, the piano player obligingly played.

Maybe it's not a great song. I'll never know. I was leaning forward, laughing, talking some shit to Paul, when I heard:

> *We're drinking, my friend,*
> *to the end*
> *of a brief episode,*

and I looked at my father and I opened my mouth and I couldn't catch my breath, I felt my father grab one of my hands in his, and that was all, all, I swear to you, that held me in this world, this life, the lights swung, like circus lights, inside and outside my head, I was on some maniacal merry-go-round, and I still couldn't catch my breath or close my mouth, I held on to my father's hand.

> *so,*
> *make it one for my baby,*
> *and one more,*
> *for the road,*

And I closed my mouth, or my mouth closed itself, it hurt my teeth, and when my mouth closed itself and my breath came back, it hurt my chest so, and the tears came pouring down. I just sat there, shaking from head to toe, and I know I didn't make a sound, with water pouring down my face.

> *that long, long road!*

My father didn't stroke my hand, he just held it—held it hard. Then he pushed a handkerchief across the table, near my other hand. I don't know if anybody noticed what was happening. I guess not, I don't know. I hadn't made a sound. Paul never looked around.

I took the handkerchief with my free hand, then took my other hand away from Paul's, and put my face in the handkerchief and wiped my face and blew my nose.

I looked up. Paul was smiling—a strange, sad, proud smile, and his eyes were wet. He was very very cool about it, but his eyes were wet.

He said, "I can't blow your nose for you no more, son." Then, "But you seem to be getting the hang of it."

Then we both laughed—laughed until we almost cried. I said that I wanted revenge—I would buy *him* one for the road. And so I did, and we got out of there sometime long after the joint was closed, and my father took me home, where my mother sat, watching *The Late Late Late Late* Late *Show*. Then they very calmly took their leave, and I crashed.

In the morning, I realized thet my mother had gone over the house with a toothbrush and a fine-tooth comb, scouring, vacuuming, ventilating, exterminating, had hung up all my clothes, and washed all the dishes—meaning: that the rest was up to me.

And so: Peanut and Arthur and I drive south.

In those days, Arthur had no musicians, simply sang behind whatever the local scene offered, or accompanied himself. Peanut was standby, and man Friday, to handle practical details and hold off the mob: for, curiously—though I did not see this then—Peanut was the first to recognize the dimensions, and the potential—to say nothing of the potential danger—of Arthur's popularity. Only he knew, for example, how many churches, deacons, pastors, all over the South, had heard of Arthur, and wanted to see him; only he knew how passionately Arthur's voice was claimed by the students. And this was almost entirely by word of mouth, for Arthur had made no records then. Well, he had appeared on a few, four or five, maybe, with various choirs; but, as these had all been recorded "live," that is to say, had not been recorded in a studio, and as he had been singing with that choir that day or evening anyway; and, as he had not been paid for it, or had been paid something minimal; he had not thought of them as records, it had not occurred to him that his voice carried any further than the given space he happened to occupy at the given moment. Even this is not entirely true, for rumors reached our ears—but they were not real. They were real, however, for Paul, who heard a coming thunder—that is why he wanted me to manage Arthur—and it was certainly real enough for Peanut, who had promised Arthur's presence, and who was de facto manager on this maiden voyage.

I always say Birmingham, because Birmingham, Alabama, was the most wicked and loathsome city I had ever seen in my life. I am not the only nigger, who, dreaming of Birmingham, wakes up in a cold sweat, stifling a scream. But, in fact, our first stop was Richmond, Virginia. Then we were going to Atlanta, Birmingham, and Tallahassee. These places are not exactly garden spots, either, they certainly weren't then—nor are they now; but I was to discover, during this trip, and, later, during so many others, that one would do almost anything to avoid spending an extra night in Birmingham. It sounds insane, perhaps, but, in those years, if one couldn't get as far as Washington, or New York, one breathed a great sigh of relief upon arriving in Atlanta. This is not because Atlanta had seen the light, but because the city simply could not afford public scandals any longer. To give up public lynchings—which had only lately, after all, begun to be looked on as public scandals—was a small price to pay for continued investments and galloping prosperity. And, in any case, life went on as usual—exactly as before—just outside Atlanta, in the Georgia pines.

We traveled by car—instructive: we never did it again. I think Arthur had to find out something, wanted to see for himself, exactly what had changed on these roads since he had traveled them last. Peanut was willing to teach him; Peanut was endlessly willing to see. And they both, for different reasons, in their different fashions, wanted to see what I saw, wanted to see it through my eyes. I think that they felt, obscurely—and I think I understand this—that what I saw, since I was seeing it for the first time, would cause all three of us to see what no single one of us would have been able to see alone.

And, as you travel that road, having crossed the bridge, or got through the tunnel, into and out of blighted New Jersey, getting out of Newark, bypassing Trenton, heading south, to Delaware, Virginia, Maryland, and then, to the unimaginable regions below, you are traveling through history, and at almost exactly the same rate of speed at which that history was created. It is all "new." It is all, already, older than dust. Nothing you pass took longer to throw up, nor will it take longer to pull down, than the moment of your eye's brief and flinching encounter. On the other hand, there is the road, as endless as history, to be endured.

And, on this road, you must stop, from time to time: if history makes demands on flesh, flesh makes demands on history. The demands flesh makes on history are not always easily met: the further down you go, the more vivid this truth becomes.

But no one says anything—what is there to say? And, indeed, we are all very cheerful with each other, and the bright blue day. We stop for gas in, I think, Delaware.

Just the same, I have, without having thought about it, become very aware of colors, am sniffing for attitudes. It is a white station attendant who fills the tank, a pasty-faced blond boy, whose face holds no expression, who seems to have no attitudes of any kind. I get out of the car, I want to pee. Arthur gets out to stretch his legs.

Arthur points out the rest room to me. Peanut is still in the car. Arthur walks up and down. I go to the rest room, pee, and come back.

"I'll be right back," says Arthur, and runs over to the rest room.

Peanut pays the attendant, winks at me, and moves the car into the parking area. He switches off the motor, gets out of the car, locks it. Arthur comes back.

"My turn," says Peanut, and makes it to the rest room.

"You want to get something to eat here, brother?" Arthur asks. "Or—you want to wait?" He grins. "Only—it might be quite a wait."

I know that, in principle, and on the road, public accommodations have been desegregated. But I don't say this.

"It's up to you," I say.

"Well, if you *hungry*, it might be better to eat here, because, you know, otherwise, we might not be able to get nothing to eat until we get where we going—and that's some hours away."

"Well," I say, "we'll let Peanut decide."

Peanut comes strolling back, and we—or rather, I—put the question to him.

"Man," says Peanut, after a moment, "let's just grab a cup of coffee, or a Coke, or something, and get on to where we going." He looks sharply at the car, and we start walking toward the coffee counter. "This place serves dogshit, man, let's go where we can *eat*."

So we get our coffees, and walk back to the car with them. Standing beside the car, we drink our coffees, and smoke our cigarettes. We say very little. All of our attention is beginning to be focused on something else, something concerning which there is absolutely nothing to say. Peanut takes our coffee containers, and, very carefully, drops them into the trash bin.

He looks at Arthur, and grins. "That's the way they do in Canada, right: Everything is *clean*!"

"You get a ticket if you leave anything dirty," says Arthur, and they laugh. We get back into the car, and roll away.

"You want me to drive?" Arthur asks.

"Shit, no. You got to sing tonight."

"Well. You got to play piano."

"That don't involve my voice. But I sure don't want *you* wearing out your New York accent on this man's road. You might never sing again." They both laugh. Then, "No, I'm all right," Peanut says.

It is near dusk, not quite dusk. Arthur is leaning back, humming. We are in Virginia now, approaching our destination—but we are still on the highway—and I say to Peanut, "Man, I'm sorry, but my back teeth are beginning to float. Can we stop for a minute, so I can take a piss?"

Peanut immediately looked into the rearview mirror. The road behind us was almost empty—almost, but not quite; the heavy traffic was on the other side, going north.

"Hold it a minute," Peanut said. "I damn sure can't stop along here."

It was true. There was no margin on the highway, no shoulder, no cover. There were trees, but they were on the far side of a ditch.

"Don't worry about it," I said. "Just stop if you can, when you can."

I leaned back, and looked out of the window, angry at myself, because I knew that my pressing need had been partly produced by my panic. The panic I had been suppressing had transferred itself to my bladder, from which receptacle it could, in principle, oh happy day, be discharged. The sky, the trees, the landscape, flew past. The land was flat: no cover. Then I heard dogs yelping, yowling, barking through this landscape, looking for my ancestors, looking for my grandfather, my grandmother, looking for me. I heard the men breathing, heard their boots, heard the click of the gun, the rifle: looking for me. And there was no cover. The trees were no cover. The ditch was a trap. The horizon was ten thousand miles away. One could never reach it, drop behind it, stride the hostile elements all the way—to Canada? Round and round the tree: no cover. Into the tall grass: no cover. That hill, over yonder: too high, not high enough, no cover. Circle back, no cover; pissing as you run, no cover; the breath and the hair and the odor and the teeth of the dogs, no cover; the eyes and the gun and the blow of the master, no, no cover; and the blood running down, the tears and the snot and the piss and the shit running out, dragged by dogs out of the jaws of dogs, forever and forever and forever, no mercy, and no cover!

We came to a rest area, a wide shoulder off the road, empty. Peanut pulled over, and I jumped out, ran to the farthest tree, and pissed against it. It seemed to take forever, boiling back up at me from the ground, from the tree, but, yes, in a funny way, part of my panic came out with my piss. I was going to have to find a way to deal with both.

I got back into the car, and Peanut, as though he knew exactly what had happened to me, laughed, and said, "You think you ready to hit it now, big brother?"

And I laughed, and said, "Yes, I'm ready."

We got to the home of our hostess, in Richmond; a plain, wooden house, with a gate, on a tree-lined street. A Mrs. Isabel Reed, a dark, plump lady in her forties, a high school teacher who might not have her job much longer. She trusted her students, and they trusted her: this made her, as she said, "doubtful." She laughed as she said this, there being, as she plaintively pointed out, "nothing else for me to do." Her husband was a lawyer, a tall, balding, big-boned man, who said he couldn't wait till they were driven out of town, so he could go back to Zurich and walk around the lake he remembered from his days as a G.I.

It was a nice dinner, though I don't think Arthur ate much—he was never able to eat before a performance—and then, we headed for the church.

The climate of those years is almost forgotten now—well, that is not really true. Who was there, who bore witness, will remember that time forever; but no one wants to hear, now, what they did not dare to face then. Still, some of our children know; some of our children will always know. Out of the plain, wooden house on the tree-lined street, which is a marked house, and we all know it, we get into three cars, all marked, and we all know it, and drive to a marked destination, from which, and we all know it, we may not return.

It is the ordinary black church, Mount Olive or Ebenezer or Shiloh, a proud, stone edifice with a yard and steps, and it is packed. We are really part of a protest meeting, a fund-raising rally, and are associated, then, with Montgomery and Tuskegee and boycotts and bankruptcy and all of the other plagues incomprehensibly being visited on the South. The church is ringed with policemen, in cars, and on motorcycles.

Peanut and the others in the car are old hands at this. Our passenger is one of the supports, one of the stars of the evening: his role, then, though not necessarily simple, is clear. Our roles, too, though not necessarily simple, are equally clear: we must get him in, and get him out. Peanut gets the car as close to the church as possible, and Arthur and I and Mrs. Isabel Reed get out. Peanut drives the car off, to park it, and Mr. Reed stays with Peanut.

Mrs. Reed leads us in, past the two black men standing on the church steps, introducing, hurriedly, my brother and me. They smile, and shake our hands—hurriedly—make some soft, neighborhood joke with Mrs. Reed, and we enter the church. It is only now that I become aware of the music, coming from the choir, but pounding from the walls. Arthur, sharply, catches his breath, and straightens. People are standing in the aisles. Mrs. Reed takes Arthur's hand, Arthur takes mine, and, single file, we walk down the aisle on the left side of the church. She leads us to the first row, leans over, and says something to one of the men in the first row, who immediately rises, and gives me his seat. He goes to stand against the wall. Still holding Arthur by the hand, Mrs. Reed mounts the steps into the pulpit with him. She sits him down, sits down behind him.

The choir is finishing:

> *If you pray right,*
> *heaven*
> *belongs to you,*
> *if you love right,*
> *heaven*
> *belongs to you,*
> *if you live right,*
> *heaven*
> *belongs to you,*
> *oh,*
> *heaven*
> *belongs to you!*

Organ, piano, tambourines, and a drum. I look around for Peanut, which is ridiculous. I would be able, maybe, to see him if I knew exactly where he was sitting, or if he were sitting beside me. I can see Arthur, but only because he's sitting in the pulpit. In any case, Peanut is with Mr. Reed, and Mr. Reed knows where to find us.

Silence, like a tempest, fell when the choir sat down, and Mrs. Reed stood up and came forward. She was too short to stand behind the pulpit—she stood beside it, leaning on it with one hand.

"There's no need," she said with a smile, "to say why we're here tonight. *We* know why we're here, and so do all those motorists outside. They never before been so *quiet* when they come down here to find out how we doing."

She laughed, and the church laughed with her, a good-natured, growling sound.

"We got microphones placed outside the church—and, I guess, they got some microphones placed *inside* the church—and so, I just want to let them all know"—and she raised her voice—"that they are *welcome*. They are *welcome* to hear the truth. The truth can set even the *governor* free. The truth heals *everybody*. Might even cause you to get up off"—she paused, and shook her shoulders, a delicate, loaded pause—"your *motorcycles,* and walk!"

She laughed again, and again, the church responded with that deep, good-natured growl.

"But I'm not here to keep you long. As I say, we know why we're here. We're here raising money to get our children off the chain gang, and out of prison. We're here to let *everybody* know that every human being was born to be free!"

The church roared, she subsided, raising one hand.

"I don't want to get carried away here, tonight. I'm going to ask Reverend Williams to open the service for us, and then, we going to hear some witnesses." She paused, and smiled. "For those of you who don't know him, Reverend Williams is a freedom fighter from over yonder, in Tennessee."

And she turned, extending her hand, and a young white man, with dark blue eyes, and rough, unruly black hair, and a face which appeared to have taken more than its share of punishment, stepped forward. I had not seen him. He had been sitting directly behind the pulpit, and the pulpit blocked my view. I was shocked, but the church wasn't. They seemed to know him. He looked, to me, exactly like one of the cops outside.

But then, as he began to talk, I began to wonder if he was white. I remembered, suddenly, that thousands of black people cross the color line every year; become white Christians without even having to bob their noses, or change their names; they just change neighborhoods. No doubt, for this, they pay another price, a hidden price: but the price the country exacts from them for being white is exactly the price the country pays—for being white—and the price is incoherence.

Reverend Williams was not incoherent, which may be why I wondered if he was white. "I was born on a little farm in Tennessee," he said, revealing that he still had nearly all of his teeth, "and all I remember of the beginning of my life is misery and drudgery. I know a lot of people in this country say that you can work yourself up by your bootstraps. That's a little Marie Antoinette telling the people to eat cake. That's what *she* did, when there weren't no bread in the palace. You can't talk about bootstraps unless you got boots, and, Lord knows, we didn't *have* no boots. I got bunions on the soles of my feet, but I ain't got no corns on my toes. Me and boots were *strangers*—I still feel funny when I pull on my shoes."

The church was silent, causing me to wonder if he were black or white. I realized that the question had never before occurred to me in quite this way.

"We're here," he said, "to get something so simple nobody believes it. To get respect for our labor, respect for each other's lives, and a future for our children. That's all. God bless us all. I'm going back to Tennessee, and see you all soon."

He smiled, and waved, and went back to his seat.

I saw Mr. Reed lead Peanut to the side of the pulpit. Someone found a chair for him. Mr. Reed placed himself against the wall, with his arms folded. Something in his easy alertness made me realize that he, and the other casual men, had every exit and entrance to this church, and the pulpit, under surveillance. They were working.

I wondered about Reverend Williams. I was to wonder about him for many years: I do not mean this particular Reverend Williams, though it might turn out, through some hitherto unpublished FBI report, that I mean him, too.

In those years, one spoke to so many people, so many people spoke to you, one moved through crowds; and there was no way of knowing who you were talking to, who had stopped you, to shake your hand, or to ask your presence at yet another rally. And here, color did not matter at all. There were the people who could not live without causes, who appeared to live entirely by means of famines, floods, and earthquakes; these were mostly white, but by no means always. For me, they were the lame, the halt, the blind, the forbidden, the poor to whom nothing could be given because they had no way of receiving anything, creatures who didn't even have a home in the rock. There were white chicks, like groupies, as we would now say, hitching Freedom Rides because they were mad at Daddy, or were jealous of Mama's new lover, or had just had an abortion, or wanted a big, black dick shoved in them—and okay, why not? All motives are complex, but it's dangerous not to know that. Or white boys with motives yet more impenetrable, trying to exorcise their terror of black men by, at once, instructing and imitating them, and, Lord, the ancient Marxists, whose historical parallels simply had no relevance, and the wealthy liberals who signed checks and appeared at rallies, but who ran for cover when the going got rough and became "bored" with the struggle when the struggle moved north, and, therefore, somewhat closer to their checkbooks.

But these people, on the whole, were part of the price, came with the territory, one understood them and couldn't put them down, and they had, after all, a certain limited value. They were not wicked, or no more wicked than their weakness dictated, and some of them superbly, magnificently, transcended themselves and delivered on a promise they had scarcely been aware of making. They were not so very different, after all, when the chips were down, from myself—I, too, dreamed of safety: it was my luck, and not my desire, that cut the dream short. The really wicked, dangerous people were the informers, the FBI infiltrators, both black and white, who looked and sounded exactly like Reverend Williams. We didn't know who these people were, and could not possibly have known, not until long, long after the damage had been done.

Well. After Reverend Williams, there came others, Mrs. Reed introducing them, as indefatigable as her husband, and far more visible. Nothing new was being said—in a sense; yet it was new for me, because the covered defiance is one force, and it is certainly better not to underestimate that force: but the open defiance is another force, and, while I had seen this force in some individuals, I had never witnessed it collectively. We were, after all, in a small town in the South, not far from John Brown's body: and John Brown, because his views on slavery had been "immoderate," had been hanged by the government of the United States. The "motorists" outside carried guns and clubs and had not been assigned to this place, this evening, for the purpose of protecting our lives. They were there to protect their stolen property, every inch of this land having been stolen: the government of the United States once passed laws protecting my "owners" against theft. Our lives had meant nothing then; our lives meant nothing now. The impulse and the assignment of the motorists was to find an opportunity to hang us—to hang John Brown. They couldn't this evening, or they couldn't yet: this intelligence had been conveyed to them by John Brown's hangmen, the people for whom they worked. But the moment they could, they would; the moment they could, they did. I will tell you about that in a moment, for I watched it. John Brown's body.

In the center of my mind, in a new way entirely, was the danger in which my brother stood—or, more precisely, at this moment, sat. It seemed incredible to me that the simple, smiling, nappy-headed mother could possibly follow John Brown. (*Oh, John! Don't you write no more!*)

I watched Peanut being led to the piano. I had never before realized how tall and heavy he was—perhaps he had not, before, been so
tall and heavy. I watched him shake hands with the church pianist. I
had never before seen his courtesy, a real, a rooted courtesy—style:
this is me. Who are you?

But I realized that this meant that Arthur was about to come on,
and Mrs. Reed stood up.

"We have with us tonight," she said, "a singer from New York. We
been trying to get him down here for the longest while, and"—she
caught her breath, and smiled—"I won't tell you exactly *how* we did
it, but we finally got him down here. It seemed to us, to us who heard
him, that he was—singing about us. He *is* us. He's being accompanied
by"—she looked at a piece of paper she held—"Mr. Alexander T.
Brown. Ladies and gentlemen: Mr. Arthur Montana."

She sat, and Arthur rose, stepping down from the pulpit to join
Peanut at the piano. There was a brief pause, a small rustling in the
church, a cough. Peanut and Arthur looked at each other, Arthur nodded, and Peanut hit the keys.

It was an old song: it sounded, at this moment, and in this place,
older than the oldest trees.

> *Through shady, green pastures,*
> *So rich and so sweet*

There was an indescribable hum of approbation and delight: for,
at this moment and in this place, the song was new, was being made
new.

> *God leads His dear children along.*

I watched my brother with a new wonder, feeling the power of the
people at my back, and all around me. *It seemed to us, to us who heard
him, that he was singing about us.* And so it did, as though a design
long hidden was being revealed. *He is—us.*

Where the flow of cool water
Bathes the weary one's feet

Without a sound, I heard the church sing with him, anticipating, one line, one beat, ahead of him.

God leads His dear children along.

He looked straight out at the people, raising his voice, so that the motorists and the governor could hear:

Some,
through the water

I watched Mrs. Reed's witnessing face, and the faces of the men on the wall. The organ now joined in, and the drum began to bear slow and solemn witness.

Some,
through the flood

The church had still not made a sound: it was as though all their passion were coming through that one voice. And now, it was not only this time and this place. The enormity of the miles behind us began to be as real as the stones of the road on which we had presently set our feet.

Some,
through the fire,
but all
through His blood.

Mrs. Reed nodded her head and tapped one foot, looking down, looking far down.

Some,
through great sorrow!

And she raised her head, looking out. The church had still not made a sound, yet it was filled with thunder.

When God gave a song

If I had been among the motorists, or if I had been the governor, I think I would have been afraid. I might even have fallen on my knees. I was rocked, from the very center of my soul, I was rocked: and still, the people had not made a sound.

In the night season,
and all
the day long.

I felt a vast heaving, a collective exhaling, as though no one had been able to breathe until Arthur had reached the end of the beginning of the song. And now, indeed, I heard the voice of an old woman, saying, as out of the immense, the fiery cloud of the past, *yes, child, sing it,* and Arthur stepped forward, stretching out his arms, inviting the church to bear witness to his testimony:

Have you been through the water?
Have you been through the flood?

And the answer rolled back, not loud, low, coming from the deep, *Yes, Lord!*

Have you been through the fire?

The organ and the drum and the people responded, and the choir now joined Arthur:

Are you washed in His blood?

And that mighty silence fell again, as Arthur paused, threw back his head, throwing his voice out, out, beyond the motorists and the governor, and the blood-stained trees, trees blood-stained forever:

> *Have you been through*
> *great sorrow?*

The organ and the drum, the choir, and the people, Mrs. Reed's face, the faces of the men on the wall, a tremendous exhaling as the song dropped to its close,

> *when God gave a song,*
> *in the night season,*
> *and all*
> *the day long.*

Church-raised people don't applaud as a rule, were raised not to—spectators applaud, but there are no spectators in the church: they let you know by the sound of their voices, with *Hallelujah!* and *Amen!* and *Bless the Lord!* and by the light on their faces. Peanut and Arthur went into their next number,

> *I woke up this morning*
> *with my mind*
> *stayed*
> *on freedom!*

joined by the tambourines, the organ, and the drum, and I looked around me. But I hardly needed to look around me, as the song says, it was all over me, it was deep inside me, a tremendous, pulsing joy and strength.

Hallelu,
Hallelu,
Hallelujah!

And yet, the motorists were still outside, we would have to get past them to get home. One of us, or some of us, might not live through the night: some of us, certainly, would not live through the year. And this was not a matter of one's inevitable mortality, of a man going round taking names: it is one thing to know that you are going to die and something else to know that you may be murdered. We knew that we could hope for neither help nor mercy from the people in whose hands we found ourselves, our co-citizens, some, literally, our blood-kin, flesh of our flesh. Yet the joy and power I felt in myself and all around me was no less real than our danger, had brought us through many hard trials: would be forced to bring us through many more, for many more were coming. And it was something like this I had felt, upon arriving at Mrs. Reed's neat house, on her tree-lined street: I was glad, I was relieved, to be where I belonged. This sounds insane, of course, for I did not know the South, had never been here, did not know Mrs. Reed, or anything about her, had been frightened all the way here, for my brother, for myself, for Peanut—and yet, once I had arrived, I was glad. It was as though something had been waiting here for me, something that I needed. And it was this that Mrs. Reed had meant when she said that Arthur sounded as though he were "singing for us." Arthur had been determined to get here, and, I don't know, I was certain that now, just like me, without being able—or needing—to articulate it, he knew why.

Anyway, here we were, the meeting was breaking up, and we had to get through the motorists and go home. Peanut and Arthur were surrounded, people trying to get them to appear here, or there. Peanut had his notebook out, a green leather notebook, with a clasp; he was taking care of business, synchronizing watches. Arthur was being charming, but I knew he was exhausted, and I wanted to get him home, to Mrs. Reed's. I thought of taking over Peanut's role, but Peanut seemed to be doing all right. Anyway, it was not my role yet, and, let's tell the truth, I was terrified of standing in that relation to Arthur, I was frightened of what he might see in me. And I had just been offered a better job—well, a job that paid more—in the advertising department of a black magazine, and I thought that I might take it. At least, it would get me away from Faulkner, who wasn't going to give me any rest until I beat the living shit out of him. Well. I put all that at the back of my mind. At the moment, I had to get Arthur inside someplace, near a bed.

Most of the cars and motorists had gone when we stepped out of the church. Those who were left gave us a contemptuous once-over, and then elaborately ignored us.

Peanut and Arthur and Mr. Reed walked together, a little ahead of Mrs. Reed and me.

"I don't," Mrs. Reed whispered, "know which is worse—when you see them, or when you don't."

Across the street, one of the motorists, a youngster, leaned, with his arms folded, against his motorcycle. As we passed, he turned his face and spat on the ground at his feet.

I knew enough, already, not to look in his direction. We got in the car, and drove away.

But that puts it too simply. We had all geared ourselves to leave the church and walk into the street. In the street, we did not dawdle. People said their last good-byes quickly, and dispersed. The air was palpable with humiliation, with frustration, with hatred, with fear. The nerves of the men on the motorcycles and those of the men in the cars had been stretched to the breaking point. After all, they had been put through an utterly grueling ordeal, standing outside while the niggers inside sang and speechified and plotted against them—openly—and, sometimes, taunted them. It was best to remove oneself from their sight as quickly as possible—they, literally, could not bear looking at you. Anything could be used as an excuse for violence, if not murder, or one of them might, simply, go mad, and release his pent-up orgasm—for their balls were aching. You could damn near smell it. One walked, therefore, neither slow nor fast, and kept one's eyes focused on some invisible object beyond them. Then, one reached the car, unlocked it, opened it, piled in, locked the doors. No one looked back. One prayed that the motor would start with no trouble, and, when it had, maneuvered very carefully past them, and away. Only then did one let out one's breath, and, even then, no one looked back. If we were being followed, we'd know it soon enough.

There was something in it so ironic, so wasteful. A beautiful night, a beautiful land: I had watched it as we drove here, watched it now, as we drove through it. All the years that we spent in and out of the South, I always wanted to say to those poor white people so busy turning themselves and their children into monsters: Look. It's not *we* who can't forget. *You* can't forget. We don't *spend* all our waking and sleeping hours tormented by your presence. *We* have other things to do: don't *you* have anything else to do? But maybe you don't. Maybe you really don't. Maybe the difference between us is that I never raped your mother, or your sister, or if and when I did, it was out of rage, it was not my way of life. Sometimes I even loved your mother, or your sister, and sometimes they loved me: but I can say that to you. You can't say that to me, you don't know how. You can't remember it, and you can't forget it. You can't forget the black breasts that gave you milk: but you don't dare remember, either. Maybe the difference between us is that it might have been my mother's or my grandmother's breasts you sucked at, and she never taught me to hate you: who can hate a baby? But *you* can: that's why you call me Tar Baby. Maybe the difference between us is that I've never been afraid of the prick you, like all men, carry between their legs and I never arranged picnics so that I could cut it off of you before large, cheering crowds. By the way, what did you do with my prick once you'd cut the black thing off and held it in your hands? You couldn't have bleached it—could you? You couldn't have cut yours off and sewn mine on? Is it standing on your mantelpiece now, in a glass jar, or did you nail it to the wall? Or did you eat it? How did it taste? Was it nourishing? Ah. The cat seems to have your tongue, sir. Tell you one thing: that God you found is a very sick dude. I'd check him out again, if I was you. I think He's laughing at you—I tell you like a friend. He's made it so that you can't see the grass or the trees or the sky or your woman or your brother or your child or me. Because you *don't* see me. Your God has dropped me like a black cloud before your eyes. You make a mistake when you think I want to do anything to harm you. I don't. I really don't. But, even if I did, I don't have to: you, and your God are doing a much better job of harming you than I could begin to dream of. And that means that everything you think you have, and are holding on to, does not belong to you. I always think of the patient Indian. His land was stolen from him, but that does not mean that it belongs to you: he knows that, and you know that. And the Indian has never escaped the land which belongs to him: you *can't* escape anything that belongs to you—but your God has no sense of time. And I know that those who find their lives intolerable are impelled to attempt to destroy everything that lives. But, no matter how hard you try, you will not succeed in drying up the sea and destroying life on earth. Already, here in the North American wilderness, other gods have checked you; now other gods will stop you. Rub your eyes, my brother, and start again. Peace be with you.

Yes, it was something like that I always wanted to say: for after all, human suffering is human suffering. I'll say this: I saw some—not many, but some—white boys and girls and men and women come to freedom on that road, and it was as though they couldn't believe it, that they could actually be, just *be*, that they could step out of the lie and the trap of their history. What I had always wanted to say to them is almost exactly what they said to me, and their being recalled to life was a beautiful thing to behold.

Look at a map, and scare yourself half to death. On the northern edge of Virginia, on the Washington border, catty-corner to Maryland, is Richmond, Virginia. Two-thirds across the map is Birmingham, Alabama, surrounded by Mississippi, Tennessee, and Georgia. Peanut cal-culated that we could drive from Richmond to Durham in about three hours, and from Durham to Charlotte in another three hours. If we left at six in the morning, as we planned, we would be in Charlotte around noon, and we could have lunch there. Then, we would drive from Charlotte to Atlanta, arriving in Atlanta after the sun went down. We would sleep in Atlanta, and the next day we would drive to Birmingham, in time for Arthur's engagement. Arthur's final engage-ment was in Atlanta, the following night. We were going to be forced to spend one night in Birmingham: there was no way around that. From Atlanta, we would drive back to New York, maybe stopping for a day in Washington.

But, to execute all this can be far more frightening than the fright-ening map.

For one thing, Mrs. Reed says firmly, "Don't you *try* to do no de-segregating in Charlotte. Don't you try it. Lord, them white folks in Charlotte just *knew* they had the best niggers in the South. They just *knew* it. And now, they so ashamed, they can't hardly hold their heads up—reckon they might have had to close what *few* hincty restaurants they *did* have."

"Or, if they *do* let you in," said Mr. Reed, "and let one of them aristrocratic colored folk serve you, it *might* be your last supper."

We laughed. We had made it home safely from the church, and were sitting around the Reeds' living room, too wound up to sleep, or even to eat yet, having a few drinks.

Peanut said, "But I got family in Charlotte, and they expecting us for lunch."

Arthur choked on his drink. Peanut looked at him, half grinning, half frowning. "Don't be like that, man. They done *greatly* improved since we was last there."

"You see them often?"

"I can't say I see them *often*." Peanut was blushing. "Only from time to time. They'll be *glad* to have us for lunch. Besides—they know you a celebrity now."

"Yeah. What they mainly know is that we won't be staying for dinner."

Peanut said to us, "Arthur didn't dig my cousins—"

"They didn't dig *us!* they thought we was a bunch of funky niggers."

"Why," said Mr. Reed, "I wouldn't let that upset me. I sure wouldn't let it cut my appetite—*eat* like a funky nigger, that's the way you handle *them* people." We laughed. "Well," he continued, "let's say the cousins feed you. By the time you hit the Georgia state line, the sun will be long gone. You know anyone in Atlanta?"

"Just the people who invited us. But they not expecting us until the next night—not tonight."

Mr. Reed sighed, and looked at his wife. "*We* have friends in Atlanta," Mrs. Reed said.

"You think," asked Mr. Reed, "that they might have room?"

"It's late," she said, "but I just think I'll take a chance on calling them. I'm sure they won't mind." She stood up. "Excuse me a minute," she said, and left the room.

"Listen," said Mr. Reed, "it is *still* a very bad idea to arrive anywhere in the South after the sun goes down. They had to take down some of them signs—didn't look good, we being the leaders of the Free World, and all"—he made a puking sound with his lips—"but they got them in the back room, just waiting." He looked steadily at the three of us. He had our entire attention. "But if you *do* have to arrive after the sun goes down, make sure you got a *destination*. Three northern niggers, with New York license plates on their car, going from door to door, looking for a place to sleep"—he shook his head, and gave a low whistle—"down here, *now?* They got all kinds of things they can pick you up on. And, when they pick you up, they don't hand you a phone, and say, 'Call your lawyer.' Hell, they don't do that up North, neither, but, at least up North, they've *heard* of lawyers and they know a nigger might *have* a lawyer. They don't know nothing like that down here. *They* ain't got no lawyers, how *you* going to have one? You just a symptom of northern interference, come down here to stir up the good darkies—in truth, you much more than that, but that's what they put it on." He smiled. "You boys look tired. Ruby's going to fix you all a bedtime snack and send you off to bed."

"I thought it was bad down here," said Arthur, "when we was here *before*."

Peanut looked very grave.

"And how," he asked, "about stopping on the road—but I guess it just gets worse as you go down—you know—to get gas, and go to the bathroom? I ain't really had no trouble to speak of before, but"—he laughed—"I wasn't going to Alabama."

Mr. Reed sighed. "Well, they got their tricks. They sell you the gas, but the bathroom might be out of order—they got more tricks than I can name, man." He sighed again. "If you alone, it's easier. Sometimes they just sort of grin and bear it and sometimes they real nice, talk to you about the baseball scores, shit like that. Besides, people, most people, ain't really so low that they got to crack one lone nigger's skull—except in times of stress, that is," and he grinned. "But, if you more than one—I don't know, they seem to feel that you come to do something to them—like you the advance patrol of an army." He shook his head. "I don't know. The best thing is not to expect good-will and don't expect bad will. But that wears you out."

I watched him as he stood up and walked to the bar. I suddenly had great respect for him.

"I poured you gentlemen the first drink," he said, "but now, you on your own. Just help yourself." He poured himself a bourbon and ginger ale.

"I'll take you up on that," Arthur said, and joined Mr. Reed at the bar. "Hall, you want anything? Peanut?"

"I'll get it," Peanut said, and I indicated that I was all right.

"Where are you from?" Arthur asked.

"Not too far from where you going. Town called Tuscaloosa." He sipped his drink, and smiled. There was something fearful in that smile. "Whatever you do, don't go there, neither after the sun goes down, nor at high noon, neither." He lit Arthur's cigarette. "You say it was bad when you was down here before. When was you down here?"

"Oh. Six, seven years ago."

Mr. Reed laughed. "Oh, when this shit was just getting started." He paused. "Well, it *is* worse now. You see, then, they didn't *like* those desegregation laws, in schools and such, but they figured they could fuck over that in the courts until the year two thousand. Hell, they knew they could, they had friends in Washington showing them *how* to do it."

Mrs. Reed came back into the room. Mr. Reed paused, and looked at her. His deep-set eyes were larger than, at first glance, they seemed; and, when one realized this, his whole face changed, becoming, at once, more vulnerable and more determined.

"What did they say?" he asked his wife.

Mrs. Reed smiled at Arthur, and then, at all of us. "Well, I explained the situation to them—to our friends—and I explained that this was a *celebrity,* traveling with his accompanist, and his *brother*"— the celebrity laughed, and so did his entourage—"and they said they would be *delighted.*" She moved to the side table, next to the easy chair where she had been sitting, and picked up her drink. "I'm real pleased. Oh—there's just one problem. They've just painted one bedroom, and if the paint's not dry by tomorrow evening, one of the boys may have to sleep on the sofa—the smallest one," and she laughed again.

"Well," said Peanut, "I guess that's where the celebrity is going to have to sleep."

"He *is* the smallest," said Mr. Reed. "Don't hardly seem fair, does it, son?"

"It's a comfortable sofa," said Mrs. Reed. "I slept on it myself, once."

"We're very grateful," I said, "for all your trouble."

"What trouble? I'm just glad it worked out. Makes me feel a little easier in my mind." She finished her drink, and set the glass down. "You all excuse me again, I'm going to fix you all a snack and make up your beds—you all ain't going to get much sleep."

"Well, if we know exactly where we going tomorrow night," said Peanut, "it makes the time thing a little bit easier." He rose. "I believe I will have a refill." He walked to the bar. "Mr. Reed, you had me so scared, I couldn't hardly swallow. I was kind of scared when we was here before, but we was young boys then, traveling with"—he and Arthur looked at each other, laughed, and slapped palms—"a guardian!"

"Whatever happened to that guardian?" I asked.

"I think Crunch threatened to kill him," Arthur said, grinning, "and old Webster kind of crawled back into the woodwork."

"That must be where he is right now," said Peanut. "I know ain't nobody seen him."

"I might as well join you all," I said, and I, too, walked to the bar.

"I'll give you boys the name and address and phone number of our friends," said Mr. Reed. "And a map—I'll draw a map, so you can find them. And you call here, the minute you set out from Charlotte—I won't be here, but Ruby'll be here—and she'll call them and give them a description of your car, and your license plate numbers, and give them an idea of when they should expect you."

I said, "Wow."

"Oh," said Mr. Reed. "The crackers is *hot*. They got *fucked*. They fucked themselves. While they was working out their all deliberate speed bullshit, the people hit the streets. And now, they got the kids in their faces every time they turn around. And they got nobody to negotiate with. And their friends up North can't help them; they scared, too. They know the storm is heading their way. Can't these crackers do nothing *else* but kick ass."

"Or hope it goes away," I said. I poured myself a drink—vodka, because there wasn't any Scotch.

Mr. Reed looked at me. "Yeah. When was the last time *you* hoped something would go away?"

He looked at me. He was not that much older than I, though his manner, and his high forehead made him seem so, at least at first sight. But now, I realized that he was a little younger than his wife, about thirty-eight, or -nine, pushing forty.

I liked him. I would have liked to have got to know him better. He had a long tale to tell. *Tuscaloosa.* And that was another thing about those years: one was always running into people with tremendous life and dignity and charm with real humor, people you would almost certainly not have met under any other circumstances, and you hoped to get to know them better. But it was very nearly impossible. What had brought you together also kept you apart: everyone was too savagely overworked. You met before, during, or after an event, or in the planning stages of an event, you met in strategy meetings, in lawyers' offices, senators' chambers, the homes of friendly Congressmen, the homes of movie stars, in prisons, in remote backwaters you scarcely knew existed (and which you could not *believe* existed, even though you were there), between trains, buses, planes, in and out of cars, at airports, the one on the way to raise money in Cleveland, the other on the way to a remote church in Savannah. Every once in a while, you might meet at a party, fighting against passing out, and going home early. You might share an hour or two in an airplane together. But neither could really concentrate on the other. One's concentration was on the fact that the plane was going to land, and one had another gauntlet to run.

And when the dream was slaughtered, and all that love and labor seemed to have come to nothing, we scattered: it was not a time to compare notes. We had no notes to compare. We knew where we had been, what we had tried to do, who had cracked, gone mad, died, or been murdered around us. We scattered, each into his or her own silence. It was in the astounded eyes of the children that we realized, had to face, how immensely we had been feared, despised, and betrayed. Each had, with speed, to put himself together again as best he could, and begin again. Everything was gone, but the children: children allow no time for tears. Many of us who were on that road then, may now be lost forever, that is true, but not everything is lost: responsibility cannot be lost, it can only be abdicated. If one refuses abdication, one begins again. The dream was repudiated: so be it.

My father said to me, a long time ago, "Son, whatever really gets started never gets stopped. The trouble is," he added thoughtfully, after a moment, "so little ever gets started."

I was far more the pragmatic American then than I am now. Now, watching my children grow, old enough to have some sense of where I've been, having suffered enough to be no longer terrified of suffering, and knowing something of joy, too, I know that we must attempt to be responsible for what we know. Only this action moves us, without fear, into what we do not know, and what we do not know is limitless.

But we had no trouble at all on the road the next day, and it was a very beautiful, bright day. The leaves on the trees were turning, like the changing colors in the sky, and, as the miles increased behind us, our apprehensions dropped, and we were very comfortable with each other. We were comfortable with each other, among other reasons, because, whatever was coming now, we were in it together, and we could not turn back: this sense of having crossed a river brings one a certain peace.

I was driving. Arthur sat beside me. Peanut was stretched out on the backseat.

He had been talking about Red, and how he had first discovered Red was a junkie. It was clear, from his voice, and from Arthur's face, that he had never spoken of this before: there was scarcely anyone else to whom he *could* have spoken.

From Arthur's face, too, I realized that he was thinking of Crunch—Lord, so long ago!—and wishing that he had been able to speak of Crunch the way Peanut spoke of Red.

"You know how close we were. He was my heart, my whole heart. It was like we had always known each other, but we didn't meet, really, until I was about ten, when Grandma brought me to the city. What it was, I didn't have no mama, nor no daddy. I just grew up with my grandma, and I know she did the best she could, but she was just too *old* to be raising a young kid. All she knew how to do was slap me and scold me and she didn't want me to play with the other kids because they wasn't good enough for us, and I'd get my clothes all dirty, and, oh, man"—with a low chuckle, as I kept my eyes on the road, and the trees flew by—"it was awful.

"So what happened, when we moved to the city, I had a friend for the first time in my life. And we were distant cousins, or something, and so Grandma didn't disapprove like she usually did. I think she was relieved, really, that here was some other folks to help her look out for me, and, you know, she wasn't a cruel woman, she was just strict because she was scared, and I think she was happy that I was happy. Anyway, she'd let me stay over at Red's house and his mama got to be like *that* with my grandma, she couldn't *do* no wrong far as my grandma, was concerned, and Red's mama got to be like my mama. And they all treated me like that, like I was one of them, and Red was a little older than me, he could teach me things. Like we used to ride the subway in the summertime, maybe go to Coney Island and lie on the sand and talk about what we was going to do when we got big, and Red taught me to swim. I hadn't ever seen the water. I was scared, but I couldn't be scared in front of him, you know, and so I got to be a pretty good swimmer. And we spent a lot of time running around in Central Park, around the reservoir and the lake and we used to love to watch the horseback riders. They looked so neat, especially the girls, you know, in their little hats and boots and shit, and with that whip, and that horse so proud, just stepping. But the men, they were fine, too, and I wanted to grow up and be one of them men on a horse like that. We didn't never see no black riders, but Red said there were lots of them out West, and, when we got old enough, we'd go out West and buy a ranch and raise horses. Then we'd be rich, and we could send for my grandma, and his mama, and they wouldn't have to work no more."

I couldn't see his face in the rearview mirror because he was leaning too far back, on one side. I glanced at Arthur's face, which wore a cryptic smile.

Peanut gave me that chuckle again.

"Then, maybe as a step in the right direction, we made a couple of shoeshine boxes and started shining shoes, after school, and in the summertime. A whole *lot* of time we didn't *go* to school and I got my butt whipped a whole lot more often than Red did. You see, he could forge his mother's name on the note to the teacher, but he couldn't do nothing with my grandma's signature, my grandma could hardly write. So I'd get the whipping and Red would look all sympathetic and virtuous, like he didn't know why I couldn't be more like him. Man, sometimes I wanted to kill him."

"But you never told on him," Arthur said.

Peanut laughed. "You *know* I didn't. That was all between us."

He was silent for a while. I watched the road, and the road signs, pass: we were going in the right direction, anyway. The Peanut we were hearing was not exactly new, yet we—or, at least, I—had never heard him like this before. He had always been very private—not distant, but not close, either. Now he spoke as though he were looking at something for the very first, and, also, for the very last time: as though he were saying good-bye to Red.

Now he leaned up, and I saw his face for a moment, as he lit a cigarette. Then he leaned back.

"And everything we discovered, we shared. But, I guess it might be truer to say that he was the one who made most of the discoveries, and everything he discovered he used to kind of tyrannize me. I didn't think of it that way though, then, though, and I guess I didn't mind it. Like, for example, one time Red was going to be a boxer, and I was his sparring partner. Then he was going to be a tap dancer, and he got me to go out and steal records for him to dance to. I can still see him dancing around the room, just grinning, those teeth shining, waving his hands like they do in the movies, and he was always smiling in those days, couldn't nothing get him down. Well, you remember, Arthur, he was always like that."

"I remember," Arthur said. But neither of us turned back to look at Peanut. That may or may not be strange. We sensed that, though he was, in a sense, uncovering himself, he did not wish to be seen. He was in that car with us, but he was also somewhere else.

He sat up, and lit another cigarette. This time, he remained seated, his hands between his legs, looking down at the floor. Both Arthur and I now dared to glance at him from time to time, in the rearview mirror. Neither of us ever forgot his face that day. I can only say that it was noble with grief. He was in that car with us, but he was far away, wrestling with an anguish he was articulating for the first time.

"Red was skinny when he got back here, but so was everybody. And he was a little strange, but so was everybody else."

I dared, "You can say *that* again."

Arthur said wryly, "Amen."

"It seemed to me that Red wasn't altogether as happy to see me as I was to see him. But I figured there could be all kinds of reasons for that—maybe he'd left a girl, or a baby, over there, I mean I could see that there could be a whole *lot* of things he might not want to talk about right away, it didn't necessarily have anything to do with me. And I noticed, anyway, that he was like that with everybody—with his mama, and my grandma, with Arthur—with all of us—edgy, like he was trying to get away, like he had something to hide. And that wasn't like Red, he'd *never* tried to hide anything.

"And he didn't seem to want to do anything, and I got the feeling, more and more, that he didn't really want to see me. I'd go over to see him, and he'd be lying on the couch, looking at TV, not saying anything—acting bored, man, like you was intruding on him—or he suddenly had someplace to go, and he was already late, and he'd see me later. And I couldn't figure out what I'd done to make him behave like that with me. But then, too, I had the feeling, deep inside, that he didn't really *want* to behave like that—it was in his eyes, sometimes, a terrible pain, it cut me to pieces to see it—but—I didn't know how to reach him. And so I tried to say, *Well, fuck it,* but I couldn't: I got more and more worried. Something was wrong, somewhere, that was what I felt, and he didn't want nobody to know what it was. Also, I couldn't figure out where the hell he went when he went because none of us ever saw him, none of our friends, none of the people we used to hang out with. I could see his mama getting more and more worried, but she didn't say anything, she didn't know what to say, any more than me. And that was another reason I couldn't just say, *Fuck it*, because she *had* been like a mama to me, I couldn't just turn my back.

"And Red said that he was looking for work, but you can kind of tell when somebody's looking for work. They look worried, they look eager, they look drugged, but they don't come on like Red was coming on. Red would come in the house, his mama told me, around five or six in the morning and fall in bed till evening, sometimes I'd come in the evening to see him and find him fast asleep, just farting and drooling, and that wasn't like Red, at six o'clock in the evening? Shit.

"And he began to look worse and worse. You know, like most of the guys seemed to be shaping up, more or less, rough as it was, but Red just seemed to go down and down. And he didn't laugh no more, he was mean. He didn't have nothing good to say about *nobody*.

"I was there one night, when his mother asked him how his job prospects looked—perfectly simple, ordinary question, I mean she wasn't nagging him, or anything. And he jumped up, scared the shit out of me, and he yelled, 'You want me to peddle my ass to them Jew crackers? That's why black people is where they is today! Always sucking around the fucking Jew! Them bastards had my ass in a vise *one* time and they can't have it no more! You hear me? I'm going to *make* me some money!' and he slammed out the door. And his mama, she sat there and she cried, and if I could have got my hands on Red that night, I'd have cracked his skull.

"I didn't go back there for a few days, because there didn't seem to be anything I could do. There was a heavy weight on my heart. We all know how it is out here, but Red hadn't never talked that way—all that black people–Jew bullshit. Red knew better than that. Shit, I wish it *was* that simple. And, you know, I was living pretty much as I am now, between Washington and New York, and I was doing all right, I had a nice apartment, and a real nice little girl, we was even thinking that maybe we'd tie that knot, but now, all this shit was really beginning to fuck with my mind.

"But, like I said, there was that look in Red's eyes that hurt me, hurt me more and more. It was like a scared, wounded dog. Oh, it hurt me. That's why I was so blind. If it hadn't been Red, had it been some other dude carrying on like that, I'd have realized right away what was going down. But it was Red. He lived in a special place, in my mind, in my heart, and what I saw happening to other people all around us wasn't supposed to happen to Red. Later on, people would ask me, 'Didn't you *know?*' And I had to say, 'No, I didn't know.' And then they would say, 'Well, you just didn't want to know, then.' Well, of course, I didn't *want* to know. But I'm not lying when I say, I didn't *know*.

"But then, his mama told me that she was afraid that Red had stolen the rent menty. And then she asked me if I thought he might have a habit. *Then,* I knew. The moment she asked me that, I knew. A light went on in my brain, so hard it gave me a headache, and I sat down.

"So, I asked Red—just like that. When I asked him, he looked at me as though he was going to kill me, and he turned his back to me. That made me mad, and I went over and turned him around to face me. And then—I'll never forget it—he fell into my arms, crying like a baby, and he showed me his arms. His tracks. I held him tight, like I had sometimes—before—and I said, 'Baby, let me help you. I will do anything, anything, *anything,* to help you.' I held him and held him, I sat him down and held him till he stopped crying.

"He told me he got hooked in Korea, and I told him I understood that. I thought I understood that. He told me how much he hated white people and Jews and all, and I told him I understood *that,* but that was beside the point. It didn't give him the right to steal. It didn't give him the right to hurt the people who loved him. It didn't give him the right to destroy himself. And we talked until morning came. I told him I'd take him somewhere and lock myself in with him till he was straight. He said he didn't want to put me through that, he'd turn himself in for treatment. And he asked me to trust him, and I said I did, I would, and he was as good as his word, he went away and when he came back, he was all right, for a while."

He was silent for a long time, as the trees flew past. Nothing broke the silence. There was only the sound of the tires on the road, the sound of the wind. Arthur's face was very solemn, his eyes very bright: he was in the car with us, but he, too, was someplace else.

"But. Then. His mama's TV set disappeared. An old watch of my grandma's disappeared. He came to see me once, in Washington, and my stereo, and all my clothes disappeared."

His voice was thick with tears, but he was not crying. He lit a cigarette, and leaned back, out of sight.

"That night I spent talking to him, when he asked me to trust him, made my mind go back to a night a long time ago, when he was still being a tap dancer and a boxer and all that, when he was still making all those discoveries, and coming to me with them."

He took a deep drag on his cigarette.

"I was sitting on the roof one night, because that was like our meeting place. If one couldn't find the other no place, we'd look up on the roof, and he came up and found me. I was just lying on my back, with my hands behind my head, looking up at the sky. And he came up and he poked me in the belly button, like we always used to do to each other. I remember it was a summer night, and I was feeling strange and lonely—sad, like you can be at that age, without knowing exactly why. So I poked him back. Usually, then, we started wrestling, but I didn't want us to wrestle on the roof, I was afraid we'd roll off. But he didn't move. He was kneeling next to me, I remember he was wearing a black sweat shirt and dirty white pants. He was grinning, I still see his teeth. He said, 'Hey, I'm nervous. You want to help me relax? I know a great way to relax.' I said, 'Sure.' He said, 'I'll show you how to do it first.' He was still grinning. 'I'll do it for you first, okay? And then you do it for me.' I didn't know what he was talking about, but I always said okay to Red.

"He lay down on his side next to me, and took my dick out. At first, I was scared, because I had just started doing this by myself, and he grinned again, and said, 'Relax, just let it feel good to you, you know I ain't going to hurt you. And then you going to do it for me, I need it, I need it bad.' Then—I thought about doing it for him, and, all of a sudden, I realized that I wanted to. I had never thought about it. So all the time he was working on me, I was thinking about working on him, and it made what he was doing to me more exciting than it had ever been when I did it by myself. He asked me how it felt, and I told him, and I guess I sort of moaned because he picked up speed, I was watching the sky and then I closed my eyes. It was strange to feel so helpless, like there was nothing in the world but his hand on me, and then I shot heavier than I ever had before, it was like straight up in the sky and over my shirt and his hand.

" 'My turn,' he said.

"I put one arm around his shoulder and held him tight, and I took his dick out with the other hand, and I started to work on him. He asked me to do it real slow, because he was so hot already. I loved him so much that night, because, in a way, he'd just taught me something new that I could do for him, that we could do for each other. I started working on him very slow, like he asked me to, watching his dick swell, but what I most remember is his breath next to my ear and his shoulder against mine, and his breathing. And his smell, and the smell of that shirt. He was as trusting as a baby, and I watched the way his legs moved, like all of him was new that night, and that thing got thicker and thicker in my hand until I was almost afraid I couldn't hold it, I had never before realized how it leaps, like an animal, and then I could tell by his breathing that it was time to pump faster and harder, as hard as I could, and so I did, and held him tighter around the shoulder. He started making drowning sounds and he started shaking from top to toe, he turned his whole face into my shoulder, and I held him tighter, as tight as I could, and I watched as his dick shot and shot, against the darkness, against the sky, and I was very happy."

He sat up, and I could see his face in the rearview mirror. His face was wet: again, he lit a cigarette from the coal of the old one.

"You can buy some more clothes, by and by, and another stereo and all that. That's all right. That's not the worst. The worst thing is that you slowly begin to hate, to despise this person, this person that you loved. You hate him because he hates himself. And that's horrible, I swear, to feel your love drip out of you, drop by drop, until you empty of it and there's just a big, hurting hole where that love used to be. And I don't know if anything can ever really fill that hole. It's terrible, but you wish your friend had died. That way, you could have wept for him and put him away and by and by it would be all right, everything would be clean. You wouldn't have that filthy taste of contempt and hatred on your tongue, and you wouldn't have that hurting, empty hole. That hole I got in me right now, that hole which sends burning water and ice-cold water all up and down my spine, every time I think of Red." He stubbed out his cigarette. "My heart."

He leaned back on the seat again, dropping out of sight again, and we drove in silence for a long while.

The lunch in Charlotte was somewhat elaborate, Peanut's cousins having taken Arthur's "celebrity" status more seriously than Peanut had imagined that they would have. They had even invited another couple to be present, to eat with us, and gawk at Arthur. This took some of the weight off Peanut, at least, who was somewhat subdued, and Arthur played the role of the young, boyish, rising celebrity to a smashing fare-thee-well. As for me, I remained steadfastly in the background, the somewhat dull, but watchful and devoted older brother. "No, ma'am," I said to one of the matrons. "I only sing at Christmastime, and in large crowds. That way, my brother doesn't feel threatened."

The matron laughed, rating me, perhaps, as not so dull, after all. And, actually, they were all very nice, they meant to be nice: they were so nice, in fact, that we started out for Atlanta a little later than we should have, Peanut at the wheel.

We filled the tank in Charlotte, and we prayed as we hit the road. Now we were heading for the Deep South: everything, until now, had been a rehearsal.

"Thanks, you guys, for listening to me this morning," Peanut said. "Sometimes, you have to find a way to let it out; don't, you'll explode."

"I'm hip," Arthur said.

Arthur sat next to Peanut. I was in the backseat. I leaned forward and touched Peanut on the cheek, leaned back.

"Where's Red now?" Arthur asked.

"We don't really know. He sees his mama from time to time, but—that's it."

He switched on the radio. This was the time when the country was all upset about Cuba, which, they had discovered, was only ninety miles from Florida, and which was, probably, underhandedly, plotting to inch closer. This was either before or after the missile crisis, I don't remember, but I remember feeling that going to Cuba was a far more attractive idea than descending into the Deep South. One doesn't always prefer the murderous monotony of the devil one knows. However, we were now on our way to Atlanta, traveling, oddly enough, under Mr. Reed's protection: we knew we were expected, and our description had been phoned ahead to certain people in Atlanta. If anything went wrong, and we could not call out, we knew that someone would be calling in. This had a strange effect: it reassured us, and this reassurance, at the same time, made the danger real.

We got to Atlanta late, long after the sun went down, but Mr. Reed's map was clear, and we had no trouble finding his friends—who immediately telephoned the Reeds. We laughed a lot and ate and drank and slept. No one had to sleep on the sofa, because the fresh paint in the freshly painted bedroom had dried.

And we got through Birmingham without a bit of trouble, and, weary and lighthearted, arrived in Atlanta in the late afternoon, with a few hours to spare before Arthur's last engagement on this tour.

The city did not want "incidents": this was absolutely true. It was also true that the citizens bitterly resented that some of the more vivid results of their folkways had come to be regarded as "incidents." They felt that they were being unfairly singled out, were no worse than others, no worse than the interfering North, or the condescending world: and, as to this, if one cannot say they were right, one certainly cannot say that they were wrong. They had missed the point, which was, simply, that they were being made to feel uncomfortable concerning what they took to be reality. This discomfort could, in principle, have afforded them the immense opportunity to reexamine what they took to be reality, and begun to liberate them from their strangling and castrating fears. But, in this, they were thwarted, not only by that lethargy which is produced by panic, but by the obvious truth that neither the spirit nor the perception of the Republic had changed. It was brute circumstance, merely, which had placed them in the foreground of this latest version of the national travesty. The rules of the game had been established during Reconstruction: the blacks would make, or would appear to make, certain gains: then the South and the North would unite to drive them back from the territory gained, or to render the territory worthless. The whites would make, or would appear to make, major concessions—school desegregation, for example, could be considered a major concession. But then, it would prove impossible to implement this concession—the Word would not become flesh, to dwell among us—or the concession would be bypassed, and thus, revealed as worthless. *All deliberate speed*, for example, can, now, twenty-four years later, be taken as referring to the time needed to outwit, contain—and demoralize—the niggers.

Peanut and Arthur walked me around, through some of the streets they had walked, years before, sometimes laughing, sometimes abruptly silent, far away from me, and from each other. They showed me the hotel where they had stayed, and the barbecue joint next to it, and the pool hall on the corner—everything was there as before, seeming, they said, not to have changed at all. But the way they said this betrayed their astonished, and, even, somewhat frightened apprehension that *they* had changed; and perhaps this change, the change in themselves, was the only change of which they could ever be certain. We walked, three abreast, through streets livid with white people, past stores we would not have known how to enter, past restaurants not yet open for us, walked in the limbo of our countrymen.

We stopped in a bar near our lodgings, a friendly black bar, warm as a stove, a haven from the livid streets. We still had a little over an hour before we had to get dressed, and go to the church. Our hosts had invited a few people in, to have drinks with us before the rally, and, while this would be very pleasant, and, hopefully, informative, it would also demand of us something of a performance. So we decided to sneak a carefree drink or two before facing what was coming.

The place wasn't very crowded. We sat at the bar. Peanut wandered off, to play the jukebox.

"How you feeling, brother?" Arthur asked. "You glad you came?"

"I'm not bored, I'll tell you that. Yeah. I'm glad I came. What about you?"

He looked at the bartender, who was busy at the other end of the bar, looked at Peanut at the jukebox. "Yeah. It's strenuous, and it's even—*mysterious*—but I'm glad we came." Then, "It's been good for Peanut—a kind of—catharsis." The bartender came over to us, and we ordered. "*I'm* glad we came, because—if I hadn't come back here, I might never have realized—you know, deep down—how important that first trip was." He was silent for a moment. The bartender served us, I paid him. "I thought I was coming for one reason, and that's true, but—I had almost forgot that I had been here before. Now that I'm here again, I think I know why—why I thought I almost forgot." He raised his glass. "Cheers."

"Cheers."

A chunky, dark kid, wearing a red woolen hat, had cornered Peanut at the jukebox. I couldn't hear him, of course, but Peanut's immobility and the carefully closed blankness of his face made me feel that he was dying to get away.

Presently, he escaped and came back to us, with a strange half-smile on his face. He sat down on a bar stool and picked up his drink, raised his glass briefly, and drank.

Then he said, "Don't look now, but that guy who was talking to me at the jukebox, he was telling me that the Klan had a monster meeting just outside of town last night and has fired up all the people to do something about the niggers before it's too late."

"Ain't nothing new about *that*," Arthur said. "What he tell you that for?"

"Well. I *did* get the feeling that he maybe sees the Klan under his bed at night, but"—he laughed—"he said that they supposed to start getting it on *tonight,* in the streets of Atlanta." He looked toward the street. "Might be turning the corner any minute now."

"Who told *him* all this?" I asked.

"Some niggers who heard them, and saw them, I guess. Like he told me, niggers know everything that's going on, man."

"Well," said Arthur, "if it's true, they'll probably meet us at the church." We all laughed. "So we really ain't got nothing to worry about."

But it was suddenly chilling to think about how many Klan meetings there had been in this neighborhood, chilling to think of the willed results. I had never wondered about this before, but I wondered now: how had *white* people endured it? How *did* they endure it? For, whether or not there had actually been a Klan meeting on the edge of town last night, the Klan was meeting again all over the South, with the intention of striking terror into the hearts of the niggers, and murdering those who refused to be terrified. Not only the Klan: the White Citizens Councils, and the John Birch Society, and representatives of the people so powerful that they were untouchable, like Senator Eastland, for example. White people had embraced and endured this slaughter for generations, and appeared more than willing to perpetuate it for generations to come. It was, when you thought about it, as weird and dreadful as those pictures of *penitentes* howling through the streets, or the wilderness, beating themselves with whips, scouring themselves with thorns—how deeply, how relentlessly, they despised themselves!

Peanut's new friend looked in our direction from time to time, but didn't come over to us. It is true that Peanut offered him no encouragement, but perhaps he also felt that he had done his duty.

I remember that the jukebox was playing that afternoon, over and over, "Don't Let the Sun Catch You Crying," and the voice of Ray Charles rang all along the street, from other jukeboxes, as we walked back to our lodgings. As we neared the house, we saw three white men, two on one side of the street, one on our side of the street, walking toward us. They were casually dressed, did not look official, were not old—men in their forties, perhaps. The one on our side of the street was a dirty blond, with heavy lips, and narrow blue eyes, he wore a brown leather jacket, and khaki pants and scuffed brown pumps. I did not register the other two as clearly, since I did not look directly at them. I had the strangest feeling that we had surprised them, had thwarted something, that they had not expected to see us at this hour. Our car was on the other side of the street, and the two men were walking away from this car. One was large and heavy, not fat but solid, like a bull, with black hair beginning to turn gray. He wore a pinstripe navy-blue suit, a little too tight for him, had a wide mouth and thin lips and eyes like a rodent's eyes. The man next to him was thinner, somewhat younger, with curly black hair and brown eyes, wearing a heavy gray sweater and black corduroy pants. He looked quickly up and down the street before he started toward us, a little behind the heavy man.

We had no choice but to continue walking toward them. I dared not look behind me, but Brown Eyes and I appeared to agree that the street, indeed, was empty.

"Shit," Peanut muttered. "I reckon that kid was telling me the truth."

I said nothing. Arthur said nothing.

The one on our side of the street stopped, and, when we reached him, he said, in a low, gravelly, musical voice, "You boys was visiting us a couple of nights ago, wasn't you?"

I said nothing; we said nothing. I did not know quite what to do with the word *boy*. Neither did Arthur; neither did Peanut. It was ridiculous on my part, certainly, but I suddenly realized that I was the oldest. I was the oldest, and also, I had no function at the rally that night. Arthur and Peanut did, and so, it was more than ever crucial that nothing happen to them. God knows that I didn't want anything to happen to me, either, but, as is the way at such moments, I really did not have an awful lot of room left in which to worry about myself.

So I said, "Yes. We were visiting friends here. Why?"

I had struck the wrong tone—not that there would have been any way to strike the right one. My New York accent had enraged him, and his friends were crossing the street.

"Look. Why don't you northern niggers stay up North?"

"Yeah. Why don't you?" This was the heavy-set man, who now stood next to me. His friend stood next to Peanut.

So, there we were. The street remained empty. Then a woman stepped out on her porch and screamed, *You stop molesting them! You stop molesting them! Come here, peoples! Help! Help!* and, at the same moment, I saw Peanut move, and saw the man next to Peanut go down. I ducked the fist of the man next to me, I realized that Arthur was on the ground, the man's next blow caught me on the side of the head, causing everything to tilt and turn scarlet. I hit him in the gut, I might as well have hit a barrel, but then, *because I had to get Arthur up off the ground!* I jumped up, joining my fists into a hammer, and came down as hard as I could on the top of his skull. We went down together, he and I, but now, I realized that the street was filled with feet, and, voices, and I saw a flicker of fear in the rodent's eyes, and blood came pouring out of his nose. Then, I wanted, more than anything else in this world, to finish the job, to kill him, and my hands, of their own volition, went around his neck, and both my thumbs dug into his Adam's apple. I loved the expression on his darkening face. Somebody pulled me away and up. I saw Arthur, on his feet, leaning on Peanut, blood coming from his lip. And the street was full of black people. The blond had been attacked by a girl carrying a bag full of canned goods, the cans lay scattered all over the ground, and his face was covered with blood. Six or seven black men watched the three white men—who looked, above all, humiliated. One of the black men pulled Rodent Eyes to his feet, and another black man leveled a gun at him.

"What you doing around here?" he asked, in a friendly, concerned voice. "Somebody send for you? Did you lose something around here?"

Rodent Eyes simply stared at him. With a shock, I realized that the man holding the gun was our host.

"Answer me," he said.

Rodent Eyes still said nothing.

"Let them go," said one of the men, "before this spreads all over the city."

For the street was filling up, and the mood was ugly.

"Yeah," said our host, and he tapped Rodent Eyes, not too lightly, on the forehead, with the butt of his gun. "If I see you around here again, you *will* lose something—your life. Go on, get out of here," and he pushed all three of them. Rodent Eyes's friend could not take his eyes from Peanut, Peanut stared at him. Then—and the only warning was the sudden flash of fear in the brown eyes, I will never forget that instant—Peanut, suddenly, uncontrollably, slammed the man across the face with his open palm, four, five, six times, before he was pulled away. The man staggered, but did not fall, and I watched his eyes as he slowly opened them, staring at all of us, and then, at Peanut. The sweat on my back slowly grew ice-cold. This was not a man staring at us, then at Peanut, neither was it an animal. No animal could have been so depthlessly humiliated, and I had never, never seen such hatred. He staggered off, between his friends, and we all watched as they crossed the street and got into an old blue Buick, and drove off. The crowd was silent, knowing that this was not the end.

"Let's get inside," said our host, "before the cops get here. They'll be here in a minute, it's a wonder they ain't here yet." He looked at me, at Arthur, at Peanut. "Come on," and now, he sounded very weary, almost close to tears. We started for the house. "I reckon I really should have held them, and sworn out a complaint. But that would really have been more trouble than it's worth."

He was, at bottom, and this is hard to swallow, absolutely right; just the same, later on, we wished that we had, at least, taken their names. Even though, if one wishes to look the truth in the face, that would not have made any difference, either.

We got to the house, looking rather weird, just as the guests were arriving. Peanut was all right, except that his clothes were a mess—one sleeve had been almost ripped off his jacket, and his shirt was torn. I was all right, except that my clothes were also a mess. Arthur's lip was bleeding, and would probably swell; he would not, I thought, be able to sing tonight. His pants were ripped down the back by his fall, and his jacket would have to be thrown away.

The house had two bathrooms. Peanut went to one, and I went with Arthur to the other.

He turned on the cold water, and put his head under the faucet and washed and washed his face. I had the feeling that he was also weeping, but I could not be certain, and I said nothing. Then, he dried his face and head, and I sat him down on the toilet seat, to examine his lip.

The blow had split his upper lip. It was not serious, but it was certainly painful.

"You won't be able to sing tonight," I said.

"I damn sure *am* going to sing tonight, brother. Now you can make up your mind to that." He tried to grin; the lip was swelling fast. "Go and get me some ice. I'll lie down for about half an hour and keep ice on it, it'll be all right."

"Arthur, you going to split that thing wide open—"

"Will you go and get me some ice? Please? right now?"

He went into the bedroom which we shared, and I went into the kitchen, where my hostess stood with some of her friends, looking helpless and angry.

"May I have some ice, please? For my brother's lip? He claims he's going to sing tonight."

She looked at me as though she scarcely saw me, but moved, automatically, to the refrigerator. "I don't know if he's going to sing tonight. We *might* not leave this house tonight."

She took out the ice, and shook her head, as though to bring everything back into focus. Then she looked at me. She tried to smile.

"Son, you got to forgive me, behaving like this. But we been going through some trying times, down here." She put the ice in a bowl, and picked up a clean dish towel. "Let me have a look at your brother."

I followed her down the hall, into the bedroom. Arthur lay across the bed, his hands over his eyes.

Our hostess—Mrs. Elkins—sat down on the bed.

"Here, young fellow," she said. "Let me look at that."

"It's not serious," Arthur said. "If I just lie still, and keep ice on it, it'll be all right."

Mrs. Elkins looked at the lip carefully, touched it lightly. "Well. Lie still, and keep ice on it, anyway, and we'll see." She packed a dish towel with ice, and wrapped it tight, and handed it to Arthur, who held it against his mouth.

Mrs. Elkins stood up. "It's going to drip," she said. "Let me get you a bath towel so you won't have ice water running down your belly and your back," and she left the room.

"I don't think you're going to be able to sing tonight," I said. "Mrs. Elkins says she doesn't think we can leave the house tonight."

He looked at me, his eyes very big. "It's as bad as that?"

"Well. I don't know. But they *live* down here—*they* should know. And they don't seem—like very excitable people."

Mrs. Elkins came back, with an enormous towel which she wrapped around Arthur's neck and shoulders. "Now. You just lie still. If you want anything, just call. We'll hear you."

"Thank you, Mrs. Elkins. Just let me know when it's time, I'll be all right."

"You just be still."

We joined the others in the living room.

"Pour yourself a drink," said Mr. Elkins. "I know you need one." He turned back to Peanut, who was leaning on the mantelpiece, still gray and shaken, his eyes very dark. "What did he ask you?"

Peanut looked at me. "I was just telling Mr. Elkins what that guy asked us—if we had been in Atlanta two nights ago."

"And—*had* you been?" asked Mrs. Elkins.

"Well—yes," said Peanut. "That was why the question seemed so strange."

I said, "I thought they might just have happened to see us—you know, northern black people seem to be pretty visible down here, they look at you like they think you're carrying a bomb—and the car has New York license plates, and all—"

"But we weren't nowhere near here," said Peanut, "and we didn't walk around town, or visit, or anything, we came in late at night, and we left the next day."

"Where were you staying?" Mr. Elkins asked.

We told him, and Mrs. Elkins shook her head, and she and her husband looked, briefly, at each other.

"No," said Mr. Elkins. "That's nowhere near here."

"Well," said one of the guests, a gray-haired man with a pipe, "them vigilantes, they get around."

The room crackled with a kind of perfunctory laughter, intended mainly, I felt, to reassure Peanut and me. And this was a little frightening.

Mr. Elkins asked, "The people where you stayed—they were expecting you?"

"Well"—Peanut and I looked at each other—I said, "Well, the way it happened was that the people in Richmond had friends here—in Atlanta—and they were worried about where we were going to stay when we got here, because we would be arriving after dark, and so they called their friends in Atlanta and arranged for us to stay with them!"

"They called ahead, and gave their friends the license number of our car, and a description, and when—about when—they could expect us," Peanut said, and silence fell in the room and, for a moment, Mr. and Mrs. Elkins did not look at each other. There were three women and two men in the room, and they all had the same look on their faces, a weary, exasperated fear and sorrow.

"Well," said Mr. Elkins cheerfully, finally, "that's probably it."

Peanut and I waited. The others seemed to know what he was talking about.

"We can't prove it," said Mrs. Elkins carefully, "and I know it might sound like we're all crazy—but a lot of our phones, down here, are tapped."

"We're on the FBI's Most Wanted List," said the man with the pipe. He said this with a proud, bitter smile.

"They're such assholes," said Mr. Elkins. "But I bet you that's what happened."

I asked, "What's the point of tapping your phones?"

"To scare us," said one of the women. "To drive us crazy."

"And so that cracker could harass you," said Mr. Elkins, "and maybe kill you, and, now that he's got our address, too, bomb this house!"

That's hard to believe, I wanted to say, but I said nothing: *was* it hard to believe? I remembered my swift, uncertain impression that the men had been interrupted at something—interrupted at what?—that they had not expected, or desired, to see us. They had not planned the confrontation. Only, when they saw us, they had not been able to control their reflexes. They could not have foreseen, any more than we, that the woman would step out on her porch and scream, that the street would fill up so fast. They could not have guessed, any more than we could have, that Mr. Elkins, one of the pillars of the church, and an apostle of nonviolence, also, nevertheless, kept a gun handy.

Mr. Elkins walked to the window, and stood there, with his back to us, looking out.

"If they come back at all," said Mrs. Elkins, "they won't be coming back till after nightfall." She had forced herself to recover; she was very calm.

"That's just what I'm worried about," said Mr. Elkins. But he turned away from the window.

"Well, now," he said, "what about this rally?"

"Well, now," Mrs. Elkins mimicked suddenly, "what about our *guests?*" She turned to Peanut and me. "In all this excitement, I don't believe I've had the presence of mind to introduce you to *anybody*—"

"Oh, we've made our own introductions, more or less," said one of the women, the youngest. She was copper-colored, Indian-looking, with dark, slanted eyes and silky hair twisted into an elegant bun at the top of her head. She emphasized her Oriental characteristics with long, jade earrings, and a heavy, barbaric-looking bronze bracelet, and she wore several rings on her long, very beautiful fingers. She wore a loose, green dress with a wide brown belt with a savage, gleaming buckle at her narrow waist. "I'm Luana King," she said, "*Miss* Luana King" and she laughed. "I always tell that to the visiting firemen, keep hoping that one of them will carry me out of here."

"You wouldn't know what to do with yourself, away from here," said Mrs. Elkins.

"Oh," said Miss King, and sipped her old-fashioned, "I bet you I'd think of *something.*"

The other two women were Mrs. Rice and Mrs. Graves. Mrs. Rice was quite dark, and, as we say, heavy-set, with a pleasant, kind of pushed-in face, and very bright, intelligent, dark eyes. She was dressed in dark blue, wore a wedding band and a silver brooch, and waved one friendly hand at Peanut and me. Mrs. Graves was thin, and dark, seemed, somehow, disappointed, and "came," as she put it, as though they were parcels, "with Mr. Graves," who was the gray-haired man with the pipe. "I'm sorry about what happened to your brother," she said. "Will he be able to sing tonight?"

"He says yes," I said, "but I say no."

She smiled. "Well. Some of us can be stubborn."

"Yes," said Mr. Elkins. "Now, what about this rally?"

"Herb," said Mrs. Elkins, "one of us *has* to be there."

"Yeah. What about this *house?*"

"Herb, I see no sense at all in your sitting up in this dark house all night long, by yourself, with a gun. And it ain't but *one* gun, you got to remember that, and they *never* come by ones."

"Well, what we going to do then?"

"I think we should just go on like we intended. Sister Beulah, across the street—that's the one who screamed so loud," she explained to Peanut and me—"she can keep an eye on the house, and call the police if she sees anything—funny."

Mr. Elkins sucked his teeth. "Call the police!"

"Well. And *we* ought to call the police, just the same, and report what happened this afternoon, just so it'll be in the record."

"Yeah. I'll do that right away. You know," he said to Mr. Graves, "we going to have to do what we been talking about doing, and arrange to guard each other's houses. Ain't nobody else going to do it for us, now, you can hurry up and believe *that*." He started out of the room. "I'll be ready in a minute," he called back, and we heard him climb the stairs.

Silence fell in the room, an exhausted silence. It was also the silence of people who have more on their minds than they can utter, or than they care, or dare, to utter.

Peanut had not moved from the mantelpiece. I finally, at long last, walked over to the bottles, and poured myself a drink. Then I walked over to Peanut.

"What are we going to do?" he asked.

"I don't know. I really don't see how Arthur can sing."

"Well, if he can't sing—we don't have any reason to stay here."

"You want to leave tonight?"

We looked at each other.

"Yeah—hell, I don't know. I think I'm going crazy." He sipped his drink, and we watched each other. "I wanted to commit murder this afternoon. I mean, I really wanted to *kill*. That's not *me*."

"Well," said Peanut, finally, catching his breath, "maybe we should go and check out Arthur. Then we can decide what we doing."

"I'm not sure," I said, "that anyone is going to allow us to drive at night, out of here, through Georgia. And they might be right."

"I thought of that, too," said Peanut. "Come on. Let's check on Arthur."

"Excuse us," I said to the others—they were seated around Mrs. Elkins, speaking in low tones—"we're going to check on my brother."

We walked the long hall to the bedroom. Arthur lay on his back, his eyes closed, the ice pack held firmly to his mouth. We looked down at him, not knowing whether he was asleep or not. Just as I leaned down, intending to lift the ice pack so that I could see his lip, he opened his eyes.

"Hi. Is it time?"

"I don't know. How do you feel?"

He had handed me the ice pack. Now he touched his upper lip, gingerly, with his tongue.

"How does it look?"

"It's maybe gone down a little. But it's still swollen."

"Turn on the light."

Peanut switched on the light, and Arthur staggered to the mirror above the chifforobe. He peered at himself. The swelling had considerably diminished, but it was still visible, making Arthur look rather like a precociously decadent juvenile delinquent. He smiled, winced, forced himself to smile again.

"I don't think you ought to force it, man," Peanut said.

"Well, maybe I can sort of hum my way through," Arthur said. "Actually, if one of you was to bring me a drink, I might be as good as new."

"Okay," I said. I put down my drink on the night table, and went back to the living room.

"How's he feeling?" Mrs. Elkins asked.

I grinned. "He says he needs a drink."

"Let me go and see about that child." She rose. "You all excuse me a minute," she said to the others. I poured Arthur a healthy vodka on the rocks, and Mrs. Elkins and I walked back to the bedroom together.

Arthur was laughing, though with some difficulty, at something Peanut had said, and Mrs. Elkins walked over to him, firmly took his chin in her hand, and studied his upper lip.

"It's a little better," she said. "But try to sing with your lip like that, it's liable to pop wide open."

"No, it won't. I'll sing quiet songs."

"You got a ways to go yet," she said, "before you start singing *quiet* songs—open your mouth. Wider—does that hurt?"

"A little. But I think I'll be all right."

"It's likely to be worse tomorrow, that's what I'm afraid of. But— all right. I'll explain to the people that you can only sing one or two *quiet* songs. And then you come back here, and put some more ice on that thing, and you go straight to bed, you hear?"

"Yes, ma'am," said Arthur. "Can I have my drink now?"

Mrs. Elkins took the drink from me, and handed it to Arthur. "There. And then you better make yourself presentable and come on out and meet the people, and we'll go on on."

"Okay," Arthur said. "Thanks, Mrs. Elkins."

"Ain't nothing. Start getting ready now," and she hurried off down the hall.

We had been more or less expecting the police to come to the house, but they hadn't by the time we were ready to leave. We did not know whether to take this as a good sign, or a bad sign: a good sign, if it meant that they were wholly ignorant of the matter; a bad sign, if it meant that they already knew all about it, and were hatching other plots. We were running late—there had been two worried telephone calls from the church already—and so it was decided that Mr. Elkins, Peanut, and Arthur, and I would go to the police station in the morning to put the remarkable visit of the three white men on record.

Nothing would come of it, that we knew, but still, it would be best to bring this visit to the official attention of the guardians of the public peace.

We got to the church. This church has so haunted my dreams, so often and for so long, that I have not known, for years now, when I attempt to describe it, whether I am describing the reality, or the dream. I did not know Atlanta then, and do not really know it now, and have never desired or attempted to return to the place we were that night. It seems to me that the church must have been on the outskirts of Atlanta, for I remember the setting as being entirely rural, innocent of sidewalks, asphalt, traffic lights, the sounds and the rush of the city. But this may be, merely, the optical delusion of a native New Yorker, a creature for whom all other cities are bound to seem somewhat rustic. It seems to me that there was a bridge nearby, perhaps a railroad bridge, I am not certain. The church was violent with light: the lights bathed the wide front steps of the church and spilled over the lawn, covering the parked cars and the people walking up the steps, or standing on the church veranda, and whitened the faces of the white policemen, on their motorcycles, or standing beside their cars, and lent a dull sheen to their holsters and the handles of their guns. We approached the church carefully, slowly, idling past the motorcycles and the patrol cars, careful of the people walking on the road. Lights flared in our faces: the lights from another car, a flashlight, the lights from the church. We crawled up the road: there was no possibility of parking anywhere near the church. We crawled past the cemetery across the road from the church, and parked, along with many other cars, in an open field.

We were in two cars. Mr. Elkins and his wife, Peanut, Arthur, and I, were in the first car, and Mr. and Mrs. Graves and Mrs. Rice and Miss King followed close behind us.

Mr. Elkins stopped the car, switched off the lights and the motor, and wiped his face with an enormous red handkerchief. Mr. Graves parked beside us, and we all stepped out, into the surprisingly mild southern air. The sky was an electrical blue-black, and the stars hung low. The trees were great, massed silhouettes on the edge of the field, by the side of the road, seeming to contain the darkness, and to act as a bulwark against it.

We started walking down the road, toward the church, two by two by two. Peanut was just ahead of me, with Miss King, Mr. and Mrs. Elkins walked together, just behind me, and I could faintly hear Arthur, who was walking with the heavy-set Mrs. Rice. I couldn't see him, for he was behind me, but, indeed, I could scarcely see Peanut, who was only a few paces ahead of me—the southern darkness is surprisingly swift and powerful.

I kept my eyes straight ahead, but I was aware of the white faces watching us, the faint, murmuring sounds our passage caused, an occasional rebel laugh. The air became, as we moved closer to the church, almost too thick to breathe. My chest hurt a little; my armpits, the palms of my hands, my forehead and between my legs, were damp. The faces of the afternoon returned to me, and Arthur on the ground, and Rodent Eyes and me, and my hands around his neck. I thought of Peanut's face when he said, *I wanted to kill. That's not* me. I thought, *That's not me, either*, but, deep within, I began to tremble. Music, wave upon wave, rolled from the church and I tried to baptize myself in it. I didn't know the song they were singing, couldn't make out the words, but the violence of the beat began to calm the violence in my heart.

We crossed the lawn and mounted the church steps. The people on the steps greeted us with smiles, with mocking admonitions concerning our tardiness; listened gravely, with a watchful wonder, to Mr. Elkins's laconic account of the reasons for our tardiness; agreed that they would meet, and discuss the matter in depth on the morrow. We entered the church, Mr. and Mrs. Elkins in the lead. And, like Mr. Reed, in Richmond, Mr. Elkins joined other men on the wall. Mrs. Elkins found a seat for me in the front row, and took Arthur and Peanut with her, placing them in camp chairs beside the pulpit. She then entered the pulpit, and vanished from my sight.

My memory of that night is chaotic, kaleidoscopic, at once blurred and vivid. I remember watching Peanut and Arthur, who were sitting one behind the other, facing me, directly in my line of vision. Peanut was sitting behind Arthur, leaned forward from time to time to whisper this or that, or Arthur, would lean back—they were perpetually smiling, but very circumspect. Arthur's slightly swollen lip emphasized the mischievous, impish quality of his face—from time to time, I made faces at them, tried to embarrass them by making them crack up, but they remained impervious and dignified.

There were several speakers, brief, low-keyed, intense, addressing themselves to various aspects of the black community's problems, and possibilities: it was not their fault that precision favored the former. Yet they made the latter real, too, if only by their insistence that the present and future of black people had to be taken in black hands. If, beneath this, thundered the relentless question, *How?* they were not wrong to make us remember that the longest journey begins with a single step. And every black person there could prove this, could prove it in himself, by taking a long look back. Courage is a curious, a many-sided force, and real courage is always allied with the unshakable faith which forces one to go beyond the appearance of things to the essence, the driving force, the key, the wheel in the middle of the wheel.

Mrs. Elkins, true to her word, announced that "our guest singer" had met with a small accident, and had been forbidden—by her—to sing more than one or two "quiet" songs. "But we will get him back down here," she promised, "just as soon as his scars are healed!" She elicited from the church a noisy corroboration, and then introduced "Mr. Arthur Montana. Accompanied by Mr. Alexander T. Brown," and Arthur and Peanut took their positions.

Arthur stepped forward, moving a little away from the piano, and said, "I really am sorry about this accident. If you knew me better, you'd know I don't always look exactly like this. Something happened to my upper lip, and it's a little swollen." He smiled, and grimaced, and there was a murmur of sympathy from the church. "So, when I get to the chorus, I wish you good people would help me out and join me, help me sing the song." He paused, and smiled. "I know all of you know it—it's a real old quiet song."

He stepped back, Peanut hit the keys, and Arthur sang:

Go spread the tidings round,

and a pleased, muffled roar came from the church, and some people began to hum. It was a song I had not heard for years.

Wherever man is found,
Wherever human hearts
And human woes abound
Let every mortal tongue
Proclaim the joyful sound,
The Comforter has come!

He paused, and raised his hands, a welcoming gesture, and the voices of the church rose,

The Comforter has come,
The Comforter has come!
The Holy Ghost from heaven,
The Father's promise given.
Go spread the tidings round,
Wherever
man is found
The Comforter
has come

He stepped back and bowed, and age-old blessings, older than the song, poured over him. I watched him, and I listened to the people, especially the old people, and I watched the faces of the old people, and I watched the faces of the young. Who would dare to say there was no Comforter, even in Georgia, tonight? Even in spite of whatever might happen in the next five minutes.

In the next five minutes, we lost Peanut.

There was a great crowd, friendly confusion, as we moved toward the doors of the church. I was being introduced to people, shaking hands, I felt Arthur's presence nearby. Then we were on the church steps, people were leaving, heading swiftly toward their cars. The motorists and the cyclists watched us, silent and wicked—they were all still there when we came out, not one had left: as far, anyway, as we could tell. We were standing on the church steps—we: we, at this moment, were Mr. and Mrs. Elkins, Arthur, Mrs. Graves, who was saying a last good-bye to Mrs. Elkins and arranging to meet later in the week, and I was saying good night, somewhat elaborately, to Miss King, and thinking about tomorrow and the visit to the police station and then hitting the road out of here. Miss King and Mrs. Graves turned and went down the steps, into the darkness, and then, Mrs. Elkins said, "Why, where is Mr. Brown?"

There were still many people in the church, and we assumed he was behind us. Arthur said, "He left me to go to the bathroom, just a few minutes ago." We didn't think anything, yet. I walked back into the church, anyway, and looked around, but there was no Peanut in sight. I came back out, and I asked, "Where's the bathroom, I'd like to go myself."

"It's a country toilet," said Mr. Elkins. "It's right around there," and he pointed toward the darkness at the left of the church. Then, for the first time, with no warning, a sickness of terror rose up in me, for I could only very dimly make out the shape of a building in the darkness. And, then, in a flash, as though I had communicated it, Mr. Elkins stared toward the outhouse in the darkness, as though he had never seen it before, and, without a word, he and Arthur and I began running toward it. I prayed it would be locked from the inside.

But it wasn't. Arthur got there first, and yanked the door open, yelling, *Peanut! Hey, Peanut!*

There was no answer. The place was empty. There was a kerosene lamp burning low on a shelf above the latrine, and I picked this up, uselessly, and looked around the place. Yes, it was empty. I even held the light above the deep, stinking hole.

"Look," said Arthur. His face was absolutely bloodless, his eyes were black, his lips seemed parched, his voice was as rough as sand.

He was pointing to the floor. I leaned down, and picked up the green notebook with the yellow metal clasp. I knew at once that it was Peanut's, but I opened it anyway, and looked at his name, in his somewhat florid handwriting, handwriting more elaborate and self-conscious than one would have imagined Peanut to be: *Alexander Theophilus Brown,* and his Washington address, and the address of Red's mother in New York.

I looked up at Arthur and Mr. Elkins.

"He was here," I said. I don't know why I said that.

"Yes," said Mr. Elkins. "He was here."

His face was—indescribable: the way a man might look when pinned beneath a boulder.

I remember, no one said anything. We heard human voices, far away.

Mr. Elkins moved to the door of the outhouse, and leaned there for a moment. Arthur moved past him, into the darkness, screaming, *Peanut! Peanut!* at the top of his lungs. I came out of the outhouse, holding the kerosene lamp, looking in the direction Arthur had gone—I could no longer see him. After a moment, I yelled, "Arthur! Come back! Come back!"

The sounds of our voices were beginning to change the sounds of the other voices: they began to respond to the note of alarm, of terror, and some people began moving toward us. I was suddenly certain that Arthur, too, had been swallowed up, and I screamed his name again, again, and again, until I saw him come loping toward me. He looked into my face, and put his hand on my arm—we were both trembling.

From the outhouse door, Mr. Elkins asked, "How long had he been gone before you missed him?"

"I don't know," Arthur said. "Not long—five minutes, maybe, not more than ten."

"He just said he was going to the bathroom?"

"Yes, sir." Then, after a moment, "Of course I didn't know where the bathroom *was*."

Mr. Elkins sighed a mighty sigh, and moved from the door. "Well. Look like, some other folks did." He paused. I sensed him fighting himself, his terror, surprise, and pain, fighting himself upward to a place where he could begin to act. "They couldn't have been waiting for him—must just have seen him run in there." He looked around, helplessly, at the dark wilderness which surrounded us. "We had just about raised the money for an indoor toilet."

I looked up. We were surrounded by people—by black people. They stared at us with a grave, frightened, solemn sympathy, loath to ask the question the answer to which would torment their sleep—the answer might make sleep impossible for many days and nights.

Mrs. Elkins asked, "What's happened, Herb? Where's Mr. Brown?"

"We don't know," said Mr. Elkins.

I said, "We found his notebook in the latrine," and I held it up, as though to prove something, I don't know why.

"Let's look in the church again," she said.

I said, "I already did."

A man's voice said, "There ain't nobody in the church now, sister. The church is empty. I believe it's already been locked up."

As though to prove this, the church lights now went out. A high, triumphant, rebel laugh came from the motorists and the cyclists. They were preparing to move out.

Mrs. Elkins looked toward them with a face which might have been present when bitterness was first distilled.

"Won't do no good, but let's ask them anyhow," she said, and we started across the road, Mr. Elkins in the lead.

We stopped at the first trooper we saw, the nearest one. He stood there with his arms folded, smiling, chewing gum.

His buddies, at some distance, stopped whatever they were doing, and listened—every once in a while, there was a muffled laugh, and, intermittently, that high-pitched rebel squeal of a laugh.

"Officer," said Mr. Elkins, "we're missing one of our party, and we wonder if you might have seen him"—and he described Peanut, very well, under the hideous circumstances, the trooper smiling, and chewing gum the while.

"No. Can't say I seen anybody answering that description."

Laughter, whispers, in the background, a sense of something lewd. The trooper facing us grinned, and licked his lips.

"All I can tell you, he might have found some more attractive company—happens all the time with young black bucks. Go on home, he'll show up in the morning, more dead than alive, probably won't be able to move for a couple of days."

He laughed, and his buddies laughed with him.

I was standing next to Mr. Elkins, and I felt his trembling as I felt my own. It was not fear, or, if it was fear, it was the fear of madness—of suddenly turning into something as total as an earthquake, as vicious as a plague. What would I not have given at that moment to have been able to pierce those bright blue eyes with red-hot needles, clogged the nostrils with boiling tar, poured cement in his asshole, cut his prick off at the tip, hacked off one, and one only, of his feet, and one, only one, of his hands, and then not killed him, no: set him free to wander this wide world until he learned what anguish was! Or, it was fear, yes, it was fear, fear that one word, one gesture, one whispered nuance of mine would set him free to kill my brother, and all the others standing there. I sweated, trembled, sweated, I could not bear that Mr. Elkins say another word to him, I held my peace but could not prevent myself from saying, with the most hideous grin I could manage, the vindictiveness of which must have nearly penetrated even that thick skull, "Well, we surely thanks you for your kindness, Cap'n, believe me, we won't never forget it. Won't *never* forget it, you can believe that. I sure hope I live long enough to see the Lord pour down His blessings on your head." I took Mr. Elkins's arm, and we moved away. "Good night, Cap'n. Good night, all." At least, for a moment, with his mouth open, he hadn't chewed his gum.

We got into the car. "What we do now?" I asked Mr. Elkins.

"We go to the police station," he said. "Lord, why didn't I take those crackers' names?"

"Hush," said Mrs. Elkins. "Don't start that, it ain't going to do no good. Wouldn't have mattered what names they give you. They *got* as many names as Satan."

And we went to the police station, we spent days at the police station. The captain was a little more urbane than his men, but that only made it worse, and it made him worse than his men. We put ads in papers, we ransacked Georgia: but we never saw Peanut again.

That blow, the loss of Peanut, seemed to have the effect of fragmenting each of us where we stood, and, fragmented, we scattered everywhere. His grandmother took the news in silence, but never left her apartment again. Within three months, worn out with waiting for his return, she set out to find him. Red's mother found her lying on the floor of her kitchen, fully dressed, her suitcase packed and standing beside her, her keys in her hand.

Red was nowhere to be found. After the funeral, Red's mother packed up, too, and went back to live among her remaining relatives, in Tennessee. She was not old, just a little past fifty, but, after Peanut's disappearance, her graying hair turned white, her skin turned dry. "I'd like to laugh again, one day," she told me the last time I saw her. "Peanut used to know how to make me laugh." She didn't mention Red, or leave any address for him.

Arthur went west, and then, from Seattle, back to Canada, and then, for the first time, to London, and visited, for the first time, Paris, Geneva, and Rome. His postcards were laconic, and I sensed in him a new note—dry, wary, bitter. *It's lonely as a mother out here,* he wrote, *but maybe that's the best way for it to be. Can't nobody hurt you if they can't get close to you.* But this formula was not entirely satisfactory:

Love must be the rarest, most precious thing on earth, brother, where is it hiding? I knew that he was already being pressured to "branch out" from Gospel, and that he was warily considering this.

In those days, I had no particular feeling about the kind of music Arthur sang. It seemed to me that this was entirely Arthur's affair, and I was not to make certain connections until I saw these connections menaced: perhaps nothing is more elusive than the obvious. Then I was worried about Arthur's private tally sheet, what he made of what time had done to his friends. Red was out of it, he never saw Crunch anymore, Peanut was gone—was almost certainly dead: they had all sung the Lord's song together. Julia was more mine, perhaps, than his, but she was, nevertheless, unanswerably, also his: I received cryptic communications from her, from time to time, from Abidjan, where, it seemed to me, she could not possibly be happy. But I did not dare think too much about her, I kept her outside. I never saw Jimmy. I suppose that he was still on 18th Street, and, every once in a while, I thought of calling him, but I never did.

I left the agency and took the job in the advertising department of the black magazine: and, though my circumstances there were far more agreeable, and I no longer had to deal with the wretched creep Faulkner, it was, really, in essence, the same job, and I knew I was not happy. But I didn't know if my unhappiness was due to the job, or the loss of Julia, or was just, simply, due to me. I felt—unused, therefore, useless, and I felt unwanted, I felt, as the song puts it, so *unnecessary*.

But I, like a multitude of others, got up in the morning and took the subway to work, hacked myself through my working day, even finding small, utterly superficial satisfactions in that day, in the work, and in a kind of provisional camaraderie. I knew that the real reason I got on well with my co-workers was that I was able, but not ambitious, didn't care enough to scheme for advancement, threatened nobody's job. I was marking time, but, on the other hand, time wasn't marking time; time was moving. And, in a few years, if I didn't contrive to rise, I would inexorably descend, and the camaraderie of my co-workers—and my superiors—would be stained with contempt and pity. I knew that I could never bear that, and I would, then, furthermore, be over the hill.

I could never, at bottom, take advertising seriously. I felt it as demeaning. It seemed to me to be really a shell game, based squarely on the sucker principle. One could scarcely respect the people who went for all this okeydoke, who were, indeed, addicted to it. The sense of life with which advertising imbued them—or vice versa—made reality, or the truth of life, unbearable, threatening, and, at last, above all, unreal: they preferred the gaudy image, which they imagined to be under their control. Thus, they entered the voting booth as blindly cheerful and incoherent as they were at the supermarket, reaching out for the "brand" name, the name, that is, which had been most ruthlessly and successfully sold to them. They did not know, and did not dare to know, what was in the package: it had been "guaranteed," and everybody else was buying it. True, there were occasional scandals, moments which might cause one to suspect that the public confidence had been abused: but the noise of scandal was swiftly conquered by the sprightly music of the next commercial. The music of the commercial simply reiterates the incredible glories of this great land, and one learns, through advertising, that it is, therefore, absolutely forbidden to the American people to be gloomy, private, tense, possessed; to stink, even a little, at any time; to grow gray, to wrinkle, to be sexless; to have unsmiling children; to be lusterless of eye, hair, or teeth; to be flabby of breast, belly, or bottom; to be gloomy, to know despair, or to embark on any adventure whatever without the corroboration of the friendly mob. Love, here, demands no down payment, though it must have the Good Housekeeping Seal of Approval, and, though love may be driven from Eden, it is only so that it may "mature" among friendly neighbors. This stupefying ode to purity has pornographic undertones: consider the classic hair-ad which has the portrait of a lady in the foreground and a naked infant in the background. The legend reads, *hair color so natural only her hairdresser knows for sure!* The legend is a dirty street-joke, and has reference to the lady's pubic hair:

but the presence of the baby washes the legend clean. The infant's presence informs us that this is, indeed, a lady, a married one at that, and a mother, and her husband has nothing to fear from her hairdresser—who, probably, furthermore, like all hairdressers, is a faggot. Faggots, of course, never appear in this technicolored bazaar, except as clowns, or as the doomed victims of their hideous lusts, and it goes without saying that here, death shall have no dominion.

Much later, I was to realize that my discomfort was due to the fact that I was operating far, too far, beneath my level; or, in other words, I had more to give than was being demanded and I was being weighed down by the residue. I was also realizing that, though people endlessly fool themselves, they cannot really be fooled: what you really feel shines through you. So, my co-workers, and my superiors, in spite of the camaraderie, sensed my real attitude toward advertising, and, therefore, toward them, and distrusted me—soon, inevitably, they would dislike me. I could not blame them, for, if my attitude toward advertising as concerned the great, white, faceless mass was, at best, ironic, my attitude toward advertising as concerned black people was very painfully ambivalent. I felt that black people had a sense of reality far more solid and arresting than the bubble-gum context in which we operated—though I had days, God knows, when I wondered about this, too.

But who was I, anyway, after all, to *have* an attitude? I was doing the same thing, in the same office, and for the same reason: we had to eat. And we were expected to be aware, too, that the presence of blacks in advertising was a major sociological breakthrough. Was it? for our breakthroughs seemed to occur only on those levels where we were most speedily expendable and most easily manipulated. And a "breakthrough" to what? I was beginning to be wary of these breakthroughs, was not certain that I wanted a lifetime pass to Disneyland. On the other hand, here we were, and you can't have your cake and eat it, too: we would simply have to find a way to use, and survive and transcend this present breakthrough the same way we had survived so many others.

But this is not the best possible attitude for the salesman to take toward the people who buy the stuff he sells.

Arthur called me from Paris, to say that he would be coming home in a few days, and he hoped that I would be able to take time off to go south with him. He had been haunted throughout his journey, everywhere he'd been—I could hear this in his voice, and I, too, was haunted.

"It's not just Peanut," he said, "but all of it, the whole terrible scene. And I just have the feeling that if I don't go back right away, I never *will* go back and—well, I just don't think I want to let it go down like that."

I could see the truth in that, and I told him so. I wasn't sure about getting time off, but I'd begin working on that question right away. I asked him if he wanted me to meet him at the airport.

"No, don't bother. I'll get a cab, and go on home and drop my things. Then I'll call you and we'll take it from there."

I knew he had sung in a club in London, and sat in with some musicians in a club in Paris. "How did it go?"

He laughed. "I don't know, really. I think it went all right, but it was strange." Then, "I dug it, though, I think I'm learning. And I think the people dug it, although"—and he laughed again—"I don't know exactly what it was they *dug*. But they were nice."

"Good, then. See you in a minute."

"Right, brother. Love you."

"Love you, too. Right on."

"*Ciao.*"

"*Ciao, bambino.*"

Arthur hangs up the phone, after talking to me, and walks to the window of his hotel room. This is a long, French window, and it opens on a small stone balcony. He is in a small hotel on the quai St.-Michel, and his room faces the river. He had called me at work, at three P.M., my time: it is nine P.M. for him. He has not yet eaten supper and he has no one to eat with and he has been alone all day but he is not, as he might be, depressed. He had liked walking around Paris alone. It is his first time in France, and he speaks no French, and, yet, strangely, he feels more at ease in Paris than he had felt in London.

He watches the lights in the dark and gleaming water, the orderly procession of lights on the farther bank. It is a chilly night, yet the people walk at a more deliberate pace than is common in New York. In Paris, he feels free to be an outsider, to watch; nothing in Paris really reminds him of home, in spite of the disastrous French attempts to imitate the American scene. These imitations, though, are so blatant that they cannot possibly elicit anything resembling nostalgia, and anyway, he has not been away from home long enough for that. Here he feels free, more free than he has ever been, anywhere; and, though he has yet to realize this consciously, this freedom is very largely due to the fact that he moves in almost total silence. His vocabulary exists almost entirely in his fingers and in his eyes: he is forced to throw himself on the good nature of the French and he will never, luckily, live here long enough to be forced to put this good nature to any test.

And if he cannot speak, neither can others speak to him, and he cannot even eavesdrop. He has no way of understanding what they are saying, therefore, it does not matter what they are saying: in the resulting silence, he drops his guard.

He could never have done this in New York, where all his senses were always alert for danger, or in London, which was exasperating because it spoke a foreign language which sounded, superficially, like his own. But they were saying different things in London, or they were saying the same things in a different way. His efforts to break the code exhausted him.

But nothing is demanded of him in Paris. In Paris, he is practically invisible—practically, free.

He soaps and washes his face, combs his hair, puts a jacket on over his black turtleneck sweater, puts on his overcoat, locks his door behind him, and walks down the two flights of stairs to the tiny, narrow lobby. The concierge, or the night watchman or the owner sits in a cubbyhole not much larger than a closet, all day and all night long.

This cubbyhole is next to a short, L-shaped counter; on the wall behind this counter, the room keys hang on a board. The mail is piled high on a desk in the cubbyhole, and, Arthur has noted (he is not expecting any mail) that being given one's mail demands some patience, the concierge or the watchman or whatever he is, being nearly blind, and unaccustomed to foreign names; indeed, he seems to resent the clear impossibility of pronouncing these barbaric names only slightly less than he resents the fact that his clients get any mail at all. Arthur, not having been guilty of this lapse, or oversight, seems still to be in the guardian's good graces. At any rate, he nods his head as Arthur places his key on the counter, and says, *"Bonsoir, m'sieu,"* as Arthur passes the cubbyhole.

Arthur also nods and smiles, and, helplessly, mimics him—the first step toward learning French: *"Bonsoir, m'sieu."* And he walks into the street.

He is in the student quarter of Paris, has been guided there by some of the people he had worked with at the club in London. In the two days he has been in Paris, he has walked all over the city, from Sacré-Coeur to Notre-Dame, from Notre-Dame to the Eiffel Tower, from the Eiffel Tower to L'Étoile. He has got lost in the side streets running off Pigalle—having been warned not to go wandering along these side streets at night. He has been told that, as long as he can find the Seine, he can find his way home. This has turned out to be true, though the river can sometimes be a discouragingly long ways off. It isn't true that you can't lose the river—you can lose it, all right—but it functions as the North Star, if you can find it, you can be guided by it.

He turns away from the river now, and walks the boulevard St.-Michel until he comes to the boulevard St.-Germain. He walks up St.-Germain toward Odéon and St.-Germain-des-Prés. There is a big pizza place between Odéon and St.-Germain-des-Prés, and, simply because ordering a pizza presents no problems, he walks in and orders a pizza, and a glass of red wine.

And, now, perhaps, he rather regrets his solitude, and wishes he had someone to eat with, someone with whom to share the city. He wishes that I were there, but he needs someone else more than he needs me, he needs a friend. He needs someone to be with, needs someone to be with him.

He thinks of Jimmy. Suddenly, he sees Jimmy's face.

The pizza is hot—there is not much else to be said for it, except that it will keep hunger at bay—and he nibbles on it, and sips his wine, watching the throng on the boulevard.

They seem carefree and happy, in a way that he has never been. My brother is old enough to know—or has seen, at least, enough to suspect—that they cannot be what they seem to him to be. They may be better or worse, happy or less happy, wicked or desperate: they are, in any case, in all cases, other than what his imagination makes of them. There is always more—or less—than one sees: and what one sees is mitigated by ten thousand tricks of light. Arthur, nibbling on his pizza, alone in the alien, splendid capital, tries to make something coherent and bearable out of all that he sees, and doesn't see.

For that, he needs another: in order to see what he fears to see, he must, himself, be seen. He needs to give himself to someone who needs to give himself to Arthur.

He has been tormented by this for a long time now, but he cannot honestly say that he has been confused. Crunch frustrated confusion by thrusting on him an anguish absolutely lucid: so lucid and so total that it would have been nearly a relief to have been able to find a haven in guilt and shame. Yet guilt and shame nag at him, too, when he worries about his father's judgment, or anticipates mine. (He is not worried about his mother's judgment, but is worried about causing her pain.) At bottom, he really feels that his father, and brother, will not love him less for the truth. In a sense, he feels obligated to tell the truth, both for our sakes, and his own. For it is perfectly possible, after all, that it is *his* judgment that he fears and not ours, that he reads *his* judgment in our eyes.

Still, the step from this perception to articulation is not an easy one. He has faltered and turned back many times. And yet, he knows that, when he was happy with Crunch, he was neither guilty nor ashamed. He had felt a purity, a shining, joy, as though he had been, astoundingly, miraculously, blessed, and had feared neither Satan, man, nor God. He had not doubted for a moment that all love was holy. And he really does not doubt it now, but he is very lonely.

And if he walked into these streets outside, right now, and simply looked a way he knew he could look, he need not spend this night alone. He knew that. Sometimes, his encounters had been very, very pleasant, even beautiful; sometimes the encounters had led to friendship, friends who slept together whenever they met, for the pleasure it gave them both, for the ease it brought them. This was not love, but it was very close to love, and easier; but, though it was easier, it was not enough. Both parties recognized this, which was, in a sense, the proof of their friendship: *Ah*, they could say, jokingly, as they were getting dressed again, *we'll always have each other!* Some of these men were married men, with children, whose masculinity had never been questioned by anyone, including, perhaps, above all, themselves: and, indeed, there was no reason to question it. They were living their lives, and their loves.

But these men, though by no means so rare as is generally supposed, nevertheless, were rare: freedom is rare. Sometimes, the encounter was—not so much sordid or demeaning or dangerous, one learned, fairly quickly, where not to go fishing—it was that it was, simply, nothing, nothing made flesh, emptiness in one's bed, in one's arms, in one's heart and soul. One felt that the other had been cheated, and that one had cheated oneself, and, if one continued cheating, love could never come again. Arthur does not know if he can live without love. Neither, on the other hand, can he invent it.

He watches the boulevard. He is practically *on* the boulevard, divided from it merely by a pane of glass. It is like being in the theater, and being, at the same time, a part of the audience and a part of the spectacle. The people on the boulevard can also see *him* as they pass, a strange-looking, wide-eyed black boy, eating a lonely pizza. An American black man—Arthur does not know how he *knows* he is American—with a mustache, and wearing a beret, passes by swiftly, with a Harlem strut, throwing him a wink. Arthur nods, and smiles, but the man is already gone. Two blue-jeaned students, a male and a female, she in a long cape, he in a heavy sweater, pass by, laughing, the girl's cape billowing out behind her. Two North Africans, one quite young, with brilliant eyes, the other not so young, whose eyes are hooded, large, and wary, walk by slowly, deep in conversation—planning a hijacking, perhaps, or, perhaps, simply, a matter which can be almost equally complex, calculating how, and where, to eat and sleep tonight. A policeman walks by slowly, his weighted cape swaying slightly, swinging his club. He stops at the corner, under the light, looking down the boulevard. The clock above the métro station says ten to ten. The lights turn red and the boulevard traffic stops, hordes of people cross the boulevard. One of them is a small, round, brown man, carrying a sketch pad and a shopping bag, and wearing a large knitted hat, of many bright colors. He is remarkable, even a joyous apparition; Arthur cannot imagine where he was born. The shopping bag seems heavy. He pauses at the corner, under the light, near the policeman, and puts the bag down, rubbing his hands together as though to warm them. The policeman looks at him, he looks at the policeman. Suddenly, he throws back his head, and laughs. The policeman, uncertain, bewildered, laughs, too. The small, round, brown man, as though he has scored a victory, picks up his shopping bag and moves on, throwing a brilliant smile at Arthur as he passes. Arthur almost rises to follow him.

A blond woman, probably but not certainly American, walks by, swiftly, purposefully on high heels. She, too, is quite remarkable. Her coat is long and elegant, of some soft, yellow fur. Her hair is fashioned into a bun at the back of her head, her hair pulled up from the nape of the neck. Her eyes are large and dark brown, full of humor and expectation. A tall, thin boy, with curly hair and an upturned nose, dressed too lightly for this weather, runs across the boulevard, barely missing falling under the wheels of the bus he is running to catch. The policeman, exasperated, blows his whistle, but the boy gets to the bus stop and boards the bus. The bus disappears down the boulevard. Another boy, wearing a shapeless gray overcoat too large for him, walks slowly, as in a daze, carrying a violin. Arthur finishes his pizza, orders coffee, sits awhile sipping the coffee and smoking a cigarette, pays the waiter, and joins the boulevard caravan.

He walks up, past the church, on his right, stands a moment before the glass-enclosed terrace of Deux Magots, watching the soundless, somehow glittering people, continues to the Café de Flore, where the terrace is packed. In another mood, he would go in, merely to be consoled by the anonymous body heat, but not tonight. Still, for a moment, he looks over the crowd, noting, prominently, a small woman wearing bangs and an incredible amount of makeup, white on her face, black on her eyes, a thoroughly chilling scarlet on her lips. She holds a tiny Pekingese on her lap, and is smoking a cigarette and drinking coffee. She is looking in his direction—for a moment, it seems that everyone is—and he suddenly very nearly panics, reverting to adolescence, and wondering what he looks like. He looks lonely and vulnerable, that's what he looks like, in his old, navy-blue duffel coat, his black turtleneck sweater, his blue-flannel pants, his scuffed black shoes, that spinning rain forest of nappy black hair, and those big eyes. He looks as though he has just come ashore after six months at sea; and a giant of a man, about thirty, perhaps, with red hair, a square, friendly face, and deep-set, dark brown eyes, looks at him with a kind of friendly amusement, a tiny smile tugging at the corners of his lips.

Arthur turns, and looks across the street. The terrace of Chez Lipp is very nearly empty, and so, he crosses the street, pushes open the terrace doors and takes a table in the corner. There are only three other people on the terrace, a heavy, gray-haired man, smoking a pipe and reading a book, and a middle-aged couple, sitting the length of the terrace away from Arthur, in the opposite corner, against the glass wall.

The waiter comes, and Arthur orders cognac because he has hardly ever tasted it before, and it would be a pity to be in France and not drink it at the source.

He sits there, sipping the cognac, smoking a cigarette, and his mind went back to Crunch.

He was no longer surprised that Crunch remained so vivid for him, after so many years. Crunch had been his first lover, that was reason enough. He did not know if he had been lucky or unlucky in his first love. The question did not make much sense. It could be said that he had been lucky, and Crunch had not been, but the reasons for this were more mysterious than luck. It was only through meeting Jimmy again that he had begun to see how complex the matter might have been for Crunch.

At first, when Crunch had returned, he had felt that it was his concern for Julia, and his torment over the baby, that accounted for his sullen distance, and his unforeseeable rages. He had not wanted to touch Arthur: he said that that was "all over." Arthur had to grow up, and realize what kind of world he was living in. Arthur felt that he knew very well what kind of world he was living in—he intended to have as little to do with it as possible—but he did not see what that had to do with him and Crunch. The world was the world: so fuck the world, who gives a shit what those creeps think?

Ah, but those creeps have the power of life and death, my friend. They can grind your ass to *powder*!

Crunch, all I care about is you and me.

Well, that's not all there is in the world, baby.

Crunch went to New Orleans, and came back, more sullen, more silent, than ever, and with a bright, bewildered pain in his eyes. Arthur spent days down on 14th Street, sitting in a corner, still, watching him, not knowing what to say, or do.

The worst of it was that, while Crunch insisted that it was "all over," Arthur knew that it was *not* all over: not in him, not in Crunch. Crunch wanted to believe that it was all over, for myriad reasons of his own, but he was not able to will passion out of existence. It was in his eyes, every time he looked at Arthur, it was in his lightest touch, it was in his voice, it was in all his contradictions. He would give Arthur, at great length, unanswerable reasons for their not seeing each other, and, then, five minutes later, as though he had said nothing of all that, ask Arthur to run an errand for him, or make a date to see him the next day. And he would actually say, with a small, wistful smile, "Now, you'll *be* there, won't you? Don't keep me waiting."

And, in answer to Arthur's question, "Hell, yes, I love you, that's why I'm trying to beat some sense into your stubborn, hard head. I want you to be *all right,* what's the matter, don't you understand that?"

Arthur did not know how to say that he couldn't be all right, if Crunch wasn't. He waited, numbly, for the tide to turn, for the dam to break, and for Crunch to come back to him.

He never, in all this, blamed Julia, and never felt, in fact, that she had very much to do with it: in this, he was wiser than he knew. The baby, yes, the destroyed fetus weighed much more heavily, but nothing could undo that. Even finding Joel Miller, and beating him to a pulp, would not undo what he had done. Julia would never come to Crunch, *that* was over, certainly. And Arthur was not certain that Crunch really wanted Julia so much as he wanted some unassailable corroboration of his manhood. This, precisely, so far as Crunch was concerned, Arthur could not supply.

He could only, as Crunch saw it, menace his manhood, as he feared he was destroying Arthur's. For, after all, inevitably, the dam *did* break, more than once, during those flame-colored, awful months, nearly drowning them in the flood. And it was Crunch, at the absolute limit of his endurance, no longer able, simply, to contain it, who roughly pulled Arthur into his arms, sobbing and shaking, plowing home. And afterward, he could scarcely dissemble his happiness. It seemed mightily to relieve him to be able to tell Arthur how much he loved him. Yet, at the same time, the shadow lay between them still, the war was not over. Arthur moved between hope and joy and fear and trembling. Eventually, each reconciliation was tinged by the inevitable nightmare of remorse and hostility which would follow it: then, the reconciliation itself became a nightmare. Crunch could say neither yes nor no, and it was Arthur, finally, who crawled away from Crunch, because there was no way, any longer, for them to be together. The dam would break, and break again, but the tide would never turn, and Crunch would never come back to him.

There is still a great, flowing press of people on the boulevard, very close to him, and very far away, leaving him remote and secure in his corner. He looks up, and signals the waiter for another cognac, thinking of Jimmy.

When he and Jimmy had left us, on the night of our dinner at the Red Rooster, Jimmy had suggested a nightcap, and, so they had stopped at a bar Arthur knew, on the Avenue, near 125th Street.

Arthur had gone into mild shock upon the discovery that Julia and I were living together, and were happy, but this was as nothing compared to his astonishment at seeing Jimmy again. This astonishment was compounded by an unbelievable, unforeseen, and, therefore, rather frightening delight: it may be said that it was his joy at seeing Jimmy again that constituted his astonishment.

For he had scarcely ever looked at him before. There had been, after all, virtually nothing *to* look at. Jimmy had been Child Evangelist Julia Miller's sullen, and somewhat scrappy younger brother, who didn't get along too well in the household where everyone was so busy kissing Sister Julia's ass that they only noticed him when he got between them and Sister Julia's butt, and, then, they just pushed him out of the way, and went on smacking. It was assumed, with all that, that he'd certainly turn out "bad," there didn't seem to be any other way he *could* turn out. Arthur, like everyone else, had only a dim idea of where he was, no idea at all of what he was doing, and no one, really, ever expected to see Jimmy again. That we did was due entirely to Julia, as Arthur had very quickly divined, but this did not prepare him for Jimmy. For he found Jimmy funny, brave, and terribly moving. If Jimmy had not been Julia's younger brother—and, perhaps, if Julia and I had not been living together—Arthur might have realized that his reaction to Jimmy, what Jimmy caused him to feel, was not very far from what is called love at first sight: and what is not far from love at first sight probably *is* love at first sight. That, anyway, is the way I always read it.

But Jimmy *was* Julia's younger brother, and something like four years younger than Arthur—perhaps, even, after all, a minor—and, during that first drink, Arthur was busy running the other way. "Look," he had said, finally, when they had ordered their second drink. "You're a beautiful kid, and I dig you, but you don't know what you're saying."

Jimmy lit a cigarette, and stared at him. "Why do you say that?"

"Because it's true. You say you want to hang out with me, get to know me, play piano for me. How do you know all that? You don't know me, you don't know me at all. I might be one weird motherfucker."

"*How* weird?"

Arthur laughed, uneasy, turning his face away, and shifting in his seat. He was happy, and he was miserably uncomfortable. He wished that the boy and he were sitting side by side, instead of face to face—though it was he who had instituted this arrangement—so that he could touch him. He wanted to stroke that face, wanted to kiss him, hold him, and never let him go. The sweat on his back caused his shirt to cling, and become ice-cold, and the temperature sped to his jacket. This was just a kid. He didn't have any right to fuck him up.

It was then that he thought of Crunch.

He turned and faced Jimmy again.

"How weird *are* you? Come on, you might as well tell me, I'm going to find out anyway. You don't know me, you're just getting yourself into more and more trouble."

The waitress came, and set down their drinks.

"Does your sister know about all this?" But Arthur had not meant to ask that question.

"I guess so." He watched Arthur with direct, very candid eyes. "Does your brother know about you?"

"*What* about me?" Arthur countered, laughing. "What do *you* know about me?"

"Just about everything I need to know. You know, you forget. I was watching you when you didn't know I was watching you."

"What do you mean by that? You mean, you've been spying on me?"

"You don't do anything for people to spy on. No, I just mean, when I was a kid, you know, I used to watch you." He sipped his drink. "You were very nice to me."

"I was?"

"Yeah. You used to give me candy sometimes, or a penny—once in a while, when you were rich, a nickel. I remember all that. You gave me movie fare a couple of times. And I remember when you and your brother took me to the ice cream parlor." Then he grinned. "You all didn't like Julia much."

"Well, she was kind of a pain in the ass in those days."

"Yeah. But that wasn't really her fault. Of course, I didn't know that then." He took another sip of his drink. "Hey, if I get drunk, you're going to have to take me home, and carry me up all those steps."

"Then for Christ's sake, don't get drunk, man. How fucking much do you weigh?"

"I was only kidding—not so much. About one hundred and forty—forty-five, somewhere around in there."

Arthur was watching him, a little smile on his face: he couldn't help it. Jimmy was watching him, too, with those astounded, vulnerable eyes, and Arthur realized that Jimmy was never going to be misled by anything Arthur might say. He was not listening to him, he was watching him. And Jimmy asked, "You know what's funny?"

"What's funny?"

"When two people have so much to say to each other that there's almost nothing they *can* say, and they just stare at each other. But that's saying something, too."

"And what do you want to say—when you look at me?"

Jimmy looked down. "I think you know." Then, looking up, "I always hoped I'd see you again. When Julia came, I knew I would—somehow, somewhere, I'd see you. So—I'm real happy to be looking at you, man," and he grinned and nodded. "Real glad."

"And what are you doing? I mean, you going to be hanging around the city, you going back south, or what?"

"I don't know yet. I'd like to say that that depends partly on you, because I meant everything I was saying before. But I'd like to get back south fairly soon."

"I'd like to get there, too. But I think I've got to go west first, from here."

"Well, I told you, I'd dig going with you."

Silence fell between them, and Jimmy stared at him steadily, not smiling, his arms folded.

"You don't think I'm a little old for you?"

Jimmy might have laughed, but he didn't. Later on, when Arthur asked this question, he always cracked up. But now, his arms still folded, he said very calmly, "No. I think you're exactly the right age for me." He paused. "I think I'm exactly the right age for you, too. Since you brought up the question of your age, I *might* say that you seem to be getting a *little* set in your ways—not much, just a little. I'll be good for you. You need somebody to stir you up." He pursed his lips, trying not to smile. "I'll be good for you, I'll keep you stirred up." He nodded gravely, his lips still pursed in that unwilling smile. He handed Arthur a cigarette, lit Arthur's cigarette, and his own, and picked up his drink. "If I seem a little forward, it's only because I know how shy you are."

Arthur laughed, but he was a little frightened, too, his heart was racing, his clothes were suddenly too tight. "You're crazy."

"I'm not crazy. I know what I want." Then, very gravely, "You know, you shouldn't worry about my sister, or your brother. They'll be very happy for us. I know it. My sister will be very happy to trust me with you. And your brother will be very happy to trust *you* with *me*. Believe me. I *know* it."

"*How* do you know it?"

Jimmy looked a little exasperated. "They love us, that's how I know it. You ought to know it, too. You ought to trust it. Then you wouldn't have to go through all those changes about a dirty old man like you fucking up a sweet little boy like me."

Arthur thought of Crunch again, and stared at Jimmy. It was true: he was, perhaps, not as worried about fucking up Jimmy's life as he was about exposing his own.

Jimmy smiled a very beautiful smile. "All right, old man? Listen. The only way you're going to fuck me up is if you don't love me. And, by the way, I've been talking so much, we never got around to that— do you?"

Arthur felt dizzy, as though the kid were dragging him, roughly, up a very steep hill. "Never got around to what?" With Jimmy's brilliant eyes staring into his, he began to get his bearings. Unwillingly, he smiled, beginning to surrender. "Do I what?"

Jimmy whispered, with exaggerated lip movements, "Do you love me?"

Arthur leaned across the table and touched Jimmy on the face for a moment. He whispered, "Yes, you clown, I love you. I've just been playing hard to get."

Jimmy leaned back. "Wow. That was a rough one. I deserve a drink."

"But, then, you'll be drunk and I'll have to carry you up all those stairs."

"Oh, I'll take a piss before we leave here, and I won't hardly weigh nothing at all."

They laughed, and Arthur signaled the waitress. He signaled the waitress out of fear: he felt such a sudden sharp desire to take Jimmy with him out of this place, to be alone with Jimmy, and begin a voyage unlike any he had ever imagined. And this desire caused him to panic. He signaled the waitress, and ordered drinks, in order to give himself time to catch his breath, to steady his hands, to conquer the violence between his legs, the violence of hope in his heart. He had not felt anything so total since his time with Crunch, and then—then—he had been a boy a little younger than Jimmy was now. Nothing in this moment reminded him of anything in his past, least of all of Crunch. He did not even feel, any longer, that he could ever be at all like Crunch, or ever so betray the boy before him: and the word *betray* had never before entered his mind. Still, he was frightened. The boy before him was suddenly sacred, causing Arthur to feel gross, ugly, and clumsy. He wanted them to leave, and get beyond this moment: and he wanted nothing more than this moment. He was urgently seduced by Jimmy's eyes, voice, presence, by the combination in him of vulnerability and power, of innocence and knowledge. He did not know what he would do with it—which means that he did not know what it would do with *him*—and, so presently, he signaled the waitress again.

They were happy, on the other hand, in a way new for them both. Desire and delight transfixed them where they were: and they were certain, after all, that they had all the time in the world.

Then, suddenly, it was closing time. They looked at each other, and, in silence, they walked out into the long, quite silent, not quite dark streets.

"So? you ready to carry me up them stairs, man?"

This, from Jimmy, with a smile at once tentative and daring, eyes at once blazing and opaque.

They were approaching the subway, which, at this moment, in the electrical gloom, could quite truly be considered the valley of decision. And if Arthur now, once more, panicked, it was for reasons both passionate and practical.

For he was being truthful when he said, "I don't want to spend a couple hours with you, and then jump up and run. And I got an early morning."

"Well," Jimmy said, but with reluctance, "I do, too."

"So," said Arthur, "why don't we both just go on and do what we got to do—and then hook up this evening, when we got all the shit behind us—and we can just hang out—and be together?"

He wanted to kiss the boy. He contented himself with touching his face lightly. Yet that light, brief touch seemed to cause each of them to tremble as they stood in the grim light at the top of the subway steps.

Jimmy looked up at him, with those brilliant, astounded, trusting eyes.

"Okay. How shall we—hook up?"

They both laughed. They stood in that brief void between the retreating night and the crouching morning.

"Well," Arthur said, "whoever gets home first, calls the other. Okay? And you meet me down at my place. Okay?"

"Okay." Then, as gravely as a child, "You won't forget?"

Arthur dared, in the void, the silence, the stillness, to put one hand on the nape of Jimmy's neck and held him like that for a moment.

"I won't hardly forget," he said. Then, "Let's go. We got to make tracks."

They walked down the subway steps together: but they did not hook up that evening. Arthur's morning appointment led him to California on that afternoon: he left a message for Jimmy, but he did not see him. When Arthur came back from California, Jimmy was in the South: they failed to make connections. Then there was the storm of Julia's leaving, of which I remember almost nothing. I know that Arthur was in Chicago. Jimmy was exceedingly downcast, partly because of him and Arthur, partly because of Julia and me. His life then seemed to him to be nothing more than a series of ruptures: I know that I was no help to him at all. Which brings us up to the trip south, when Arthur was really hoping to find Jimmy, and when we lost Peanut. Jimmy and Arthur did not meet again for more than two years.

But the truth, beneath all these events, details, circumventions, is that Arthur panicked: he was terrified of confession.

But nothing less than confession is demanded of him. He dreams of Jimmy, and comes, almost, to prefer the dream because dreams appear to be harmless: dreams don't hurt. Dreams don't love, either, which is how we drown. Arthur had to pull himself to a place where he could say to Paul, his father, and to Hall, his brother, and to all the world, and to *his* Maker, *Take me as I am!*

Everyone has now abandoned the terrace Chez Lipp, where he sits, sipping his cognac, and thinking what a thoroughgoing Puritan he is, after all. And he is, indeed. But everyone must be born somewhere, and everyone is born in a context: this context is his inheritance. If he were a Muslim, or a Jew, or an Irish, Spanish, Greek, or Italian Catholic, if he were a Hindu or a Haitian or a Brazilian, an Indian or an African chief, his life might be simpler in some ways and more complex in others; more open in one way, more closed in another. An inheritance is a given: in struggling with this given, one discovers oneself in it—and one could not have been found in any other place!—and, with this discovery, and not before, the possibility of freedom begins.

So my brother is not entirely cast down, in spite of all his cowardice, folly, and rage. He feels, somehow, certain that he will soon see Jimmy again. He senses that something is moving, that he has moved: something is about to happen, something is being changed. He sits still. People are beginning to leave the restaurant.

The red-haired giant whom he has seen seated at the Café de Flore comes to the door of the terrace, smiles, enters, and comes over to him.

"I do not disturb you, I hope?"

The smile is genuine, the eyes very warm and dark.

"Not at all." Arthur gestures: "Won't you sit down?"

"With pleasure," says the redhead. He sits down, looks around, looks at his watch. "But this place is closing very soon." He looks at Arthur, with a smile. "Will you make me the pleasure to offer you a drink in another place I know? It is, oh, less than two minutes from here."

"With pleasure," Arthur says. He finishes his cognac, looks at his bill, and leaves some money on the table. They both rise.

"You are an American," says the redhead. "You have tipped him too much. You will ruin the French economy."

He laughs heartily as he says this, as though the French economy were a thing to be laughed at anyway, and they go into the street.

In the street, he stops and puts out his hand.

"I must present myself. I am Guy Lazar."

They shake hands. "I am Arthur Montana."

"Ah! That is the name of a bar near here—but I think we will not go there." They begin walking. "You are not named for the state of Montana, are you?"

"I certainly hope not," Arthur says, and they laugh.

They turn right, at the immediate corner. There are about half a dozen laughing, unsteady boys and girls, sometimes arabesquing before them, sometimes behind them, sometimes surrounding them. Guy walks with a steady, wide-legged stride, a slightly rolling motion, his hands in his coat pockets. His short, heavy black overcoat is open, his gray scarf is thrown across his neck and one shoulder. The wind ruffles his short, curly red hair, bringing it forward over his brow. He looks straight ahead. They are on a long, wide, dark street. The street grows darker as they move away from the boulevard.

"It is your first time in Paris?"

"Yes. I just got here—oh, a couple of days ago."

"From *Montana*—?"

"Hell, I've never even *seen* Montana. No. From New York, and, then, London, and—now—here."

Guy touches Arthur's elbow lightly, and they cross the street, entering a narrower, darker street. This street is also filled with people— with the moving shapes of people—and music and voices come from the lighted windows and doorways on either side of the street. It is a little like a walk through a bazaar. One might pause at any window, walk through any door, and discuss—oh, many things—while agreeing or disagreeing, as to the quality and the price of the merchandise.

"Ah. And how do you like us?"

"I don't know. You're the first person I've talked to. But I really— *really*—dig Paris."

Guy turns to him with a smile unexpectedly and disarmingly shy. "Good. I shall do all my best, then, for to make you dig—*me.*"

They stop at a door which seems locked, next to windows which seem barred, though muffled sounds of life are coming from within. Guy pushes a doorbell and smiles into Arthur's somewhat anxious face. "It is all right. I assure you, I do not disturb no *one:* it is a private club."

And, indeed, from a slot in the door, an eye peers out. The slot drops back into place—Arthur thinks of the guillotine—and the door buzzes open.

Guy pushes Arthur in before him. They are, then, in a short, narrow vestibule, pale gray or dusty white, facing the high, wide, square entrance to the club—a doorway, really, with the door removed. Some people are seated on the staircase, which is immediately beyond the entrance; to the left, there is a corridor, and another room. To the right, there is a cage, in which a woman sits. It is she who controls the buzzer that opens the door. The person, her indispensable accomplice, who had peeped through the slot and given the signal to the lady in the cage, is a dark-haired youth who is smiling and shaking Guy's hand. Arthur is being inundated, suddenly, by the sound of the French language, and by music—music from home—coming at him from somewhere to his right. He is also drowning in smiles, a tidal wave of smiles: from the youth who now takes his duffel coat and takes Guy's coat and shakes his hand, declaring himself, as Arthur hears it, enchanted, and from the lady in the cage who leans out and kisses Guy on both cheeks and shakes Arthur's hand, declaring herself, as Arthur hears it, ravished, and calling him *M'sieu Montana!* as though she has been looking forward to this meeting for a while. Through all this, Guy is impeccably charming and single-minded, conveying to Arthur, always by means of a slight pressure on his elbow, to keep moving past the smiles and the greetings.

They are, finally, in the club. There are people standing at the bar, seeming to wait, as Arthur senses it, to pounce, and eager males and females smiling from the staircase. Arthur scarcely dares to look into the room on the left, which seems to contain a kitchen: something in all of this, insanely enough, reminds him of Harlem.

Guy looks sharply to the right, where the tables all are full—he smiles and waves, but keeps Arthur to one side of him and does not go near the tables. He gives a signal to the lady in the cage, who responds with all her teeth—including, even, the missing ones, which ache—and he and Arthur, gently displacing the smiling sexes, picking their way through silk and flannel, climb the stairs.

They enter a very large dining room, nearly empty now, and sit down at a table in a corner.

Guy smiles, and says, "I am sorry it was so—*mouvementé*. It is not always like this—never, when I come here alone."

"Well, you know—you maybe just don't notice it, when you're alone."

Arthur is fascinated, is having a ball; is grateful for being exposed to something of Paris—and this *is*, certainly, *something* of Paris; and, for having been shaken out of himself, he is grateful to Guy.

This is more fun, anyway, than his hotel room, more challenging than his lonely walks.

"Well," says Guy, "at least it stays open until all hours. And no one will bother us here."

He takes out a package of Gitanes, and extends the pack to Arthur. Arthur, ruefully, shakes his head.

"I tried one of those the other day. I thought my lungs was trying to come up through the top of my skull." They both laugh. Guy lights his Gitane. "When I come back, maybe. I might have more courage."

"Oh. For a cigarette, it does not matter. You will be coming back—? That would be very nice, it means you like us. When?"

"Oh. I don't know. But I would *like* to come back."

There is silence for a moment. Guy watches him through the smoke of his cigarette.

"If you would *like* to come back, then you *will* come back. And I would like very much to see you again."

Arthur is not really being coy: he isn't, in any case, coy, it isn't one of his attributes. Perhaps he is being reckless, or, possibly, ruthless, because he is not in America. "Me? How come? You don't know me. You just met me."

"Well. It was necessary for me to meet you in order to know that I would like to meet you again."

They watch each other. Arthur wryly nods and smiles, and someone who is apparently the waiter—one of the people who had been sitting on the stairs—arrives with a tray, and clears the table, and waits.

"What would you like to drink?"

"I was drinking cognac. But I think I'd better switch."

He looks at Guy, and, for no reason, they both laugh.

"Certainly. What will you change to?"

"A double vodka. On the rocks."

"Okay. The same."

The waiter disappears. Arthur realizes that the other couples in the dining room have left. It is as though one has given orders that he and Guy should be left alone.

This cannot really be true, and yet, it seems partly true. He doesn't really care. He is curious. He would like to get drunk. He doesn't care what happens tonight. It might be a ball to ball.

It is at this moment, without quite realizing it—or, perhaps, without quite facing it—that he begins to be more and more fascinated by Guy.

A silence falls, and Arthur lights a cigarette—at the same moment, Guy puts his out—and the waiter comes back with their double vodkas.

They raise and touch their glasses, and drink.

"So. Where are you from? Are you from Paris?"

"No. I came late to Paris. I am from a town, no *one* has ever heard of it—near Nantes."

"Where's that?"

"It is north." Guy sips his vodka. *"Very* north."

"What do you do in Paris?"

"I am"—with a smile—"a kind of damned soul—you say that?—I am in *les assurances*—insurance, you call it—"

"Life insurance?"

"No. I am not quite as damned as all that. I have my honor." He looks at Arthur's face, and laughs. "No. Not *life* insurance. Property. Fire. Theft. Those things. I am very good at it. I help people who have money to keep it—is that not a valuable function?"

"Can you help people who *don't* have money to *get* it?"

"Oh. That is much more delicate. And more ambitious. I may ask—what do *you* do?"

He sips his vodka, beginning to feel more and more at ease with his new friend.

"I'm a singer."

"So. I wondered. What do you sing?"

"Gospel."

"Comment?"

Arthur smiles into the intent, wondering brown eyes. "I sing—gospel songs. I'm a gospel singer."

"I understand now. As Mahalia Jackson is—I would love to hear you sing, one day."

"I would love for you to hear me."

A longer silence falls. Music, from far downstairs, seems to be coming up through the floor. Arthur's fingers drum on the table.

"There is a nightclub downstairs, in the cellar. Would you like to dance?"

"No." And he keeps drumming on the table, to the beat.

"You have beautiful fingers. Do you also play piano?"

"Yes. I do," and they smile at each other, a smile which, remarkably, clears the charged air.

Arthur begins to speak about the music, to translate, so to speak, as if he were standing outside. He is a little surprised that he *can* speak this way, of his life, me, the South—he speaks of the trees, but he does not speak of Peanut: Guy's face becomes more and more somber, and he speaks of his days as a soldier in Algeria. Without premeditation, only semiconsciously, they are trying to use all that which might divide them to bring them closer together. Instinct, far more than knowledge, brings them in sight of the danger zone: they hope they can remain outside it. They are speaking as people who have met in a crowded waiting room, on different journeys, speak; wishing that they had met before, hoping that they will meet again, and yet, at the same time, forced to realize that it is only because of their very different journeys that they have met at all. "You got to learn to take the bitter with the sweet!" Arthur suddenly croons, and Guy nods, responding more to Arthur's tone, and the look on his face than to the words: though he understands the conjunction of *bitter* and *sweet*. *"Mais, tu es formidable!"* he says, with a delighted, childlike grin, and Arthur clowns and scats a little more. The waiter reappears, and Guy says, "You will attract an audience. They will all leave *le dancing*." Arthur grins, and they order two more double vodkas.

Then they are alone in the empty room again, more than ever.

"When do you leave Paris?" Guy asks.

Arthur sobers. "I'm not sure. I was thinking of leaving today—tomorrow—I've got to get back."

He has already told Guy that he is going south as soon as he gets back to America.

"You must not leave *today*," says Guy with urgency. "You *cannot*, it is already past three in the morning." To dissemble his intensity, he sips his drink, and lights a cigarette. Then his dark eyes look very candidly into Arthur's. "I am hoping you will spend the day with me—this day, and many days, it would make me very happy." He raises his eyebrows, smiling, and puts one hand on Arthur's hand. *"D'accord?* You will say yes?" His hand is very large, and heavy, very—friendly; it is impossible not to respond to his insistence. Arthur grins, leaning forward, and Guy grins with him. "Please. I will make myself free today, and we will wake up—I will cook you a lunch, I am a very good cook, you know, or we can go out, it does not matter—and *I* will show you Paris, I will show you—*me*—and we will take care of our day, it will be a beautiful day!"

Arthur puts one hand on top of the hand that holds his.

"Then—can I leave tomorrow?"

"We can discuss that tomorrow. All day long."

They both laugh.

"It will be hard to get away."

"Very."

They laugh again, but not as before. Guy's hand tightens on Arthur's, Arthur's hand tightens on Guy's.

"I like you," Arthur says.

"I, too. *Énormément.*"

With those interlocked hands, looking into each other's eyes, each pulls the other closer, and their parted lips meet—thirst slaking thirst. Guy closes his eyes. A trembling begins in Guy which transmits itself to Arthur. Guy opens his eyes and stares into Arthur's eyes, with a kind of helpless, stricken wonder, not unlike a child's delight, and Arthur takes Guy's face between his hands and kisses him again. He is trembling in a kind of paroxysm of liberty. Kissing a stranger in a strange town, and in a strange upper room, and with all the world too busy to notice or to care or to judge, with Mama and Daddy sleeping, and Brother out to work, and God scrutinizing the peaceful fields of New England, his past seems to drop from him like a heavy illusion, he feels it fall to the floor beneath them, he pushes it away with his feet, all, Julia, Crunch, Peanut, Red, Hall, the congregations, the terror of trees and streets, the weight of yesterday, the dread of tomorrow, all, for this instant, falls away, all, but the song—he is as open and naked and questing as the song. He feels Guy tremble with delight, his tremendous, so utterly vulnerable weight shakes the table, and Arthur trembles, too, with love and gratitude: for he knows, too, that all has dropped from him he must pick up again, but not now—now, he and another will lie naked and open, in each other's arms.

They pull back from each other. Neither speaks. Each inhales, faintly, with a delicate, private delight, the other's odor.

"*Ça va?*"

Arthur understands this, more from Guy's eyes than from the words.

He answers, gravely, "*Ça va.*"

"We go?"

"Yes. Where?"

"To my flat. It is not far. Just—*la rue des Saints Pères.*"

"The street of the holy fathers—right?"

Guy grins. "Yes. It is, perhaps, a strange street for me."

"It wouldn't be, if it had a number instead of a name. Anyway—them holy fathers had to be a bitch."

Though they are leaving, neither is yet quite prepared to move. They light each other's cigarettes and lean back, sipping the vodka, catching their breath.

The waiter is back—how long has he been there? But it does not matter. Guy asks him for the bill, and pays him.

They finish their vodka in a very rare silence, set their glasses down, and rise, walking the length of the room to the staircase, which is unencumbered now. The bar is more than half empty, music still pounds upward from the cellar. Those left at the tables are in deep conversation with each other, and have no eyes for them. They get their coats from yet another cheerful lady; Guy tips her, and they walk out into the streets.

The streets are now empty—only, every once in a while, a lone, somehow desolate figure crosses a street, stands motionless on a corner. The streets frighten Arthur. Perhaps they always have. Perhaps they always will. After he and Crunch had broken up, he had wandered many streets at night, terrified and burning. It had been like wandering through hell. He is still terrified that that time will come again, the way someone with an affliction lives in terror of the symptoms which announce a new relapse.

He is calm now, though, and safe, walking beside Guy, in Paris.

They come to a great wall on Guy's long, narrow street, and Guy puts a key in the door in the wall. They are, then, in a great courtyard—Arthur has had no idea that such splendor lay behind such walls, which are all over Paris—and they cross the courtyard to enter an old and massive building. The entrance is wide, with a *loge* on one side, and a broad, curving staircase on the other. They climb the staircase to the first floor, and enter Guy's apartment.

It is old. This is the first note struck in Arthur's consciousness— old and high, with rooms unfolding on rooms, not as though it had been built but as though it had somehow evolved, patiently developing year after year, and century after century. There are great high mirrors and massive chairs, one wall is hung with a tapestry—faded, but celebrating a battle. Arthur makes out horses and hounds, shields, sabers, and suits of armor. Guy takes Arthur's coat, takes off his own, and throws them both on a large sofa, and they leave this *foyer* and go into a larger room, higher and less cluttered, with an immense dark sofa, easy chairs, a massive wooden cabinet, a chandelier—Guy clicks it on with the wall switch—another cabinet with a glass door, holding ornaments and goblets, a long, low table before the sofa, other round tables in corners of the room, two high windows, heavily draped, a door opening onto two corridors, one straight ahead, one to the left. The one straight ahead leads to the kitchen and the pantry, a bathroom, a small bedroom. The corridor to the left leads to Guy's bedroom, his study, his W.C., and his bathroom—Arthur is to discover that these two facilities are (or were) separate in France.

"Wow," he says, wandering around the room, his hands in his pockets, staring at the paintings on the walls.

Guy watches the long, dark figure in the old blue pants, the turtleneck sweater, the scuffed black shoes, with delight. But, "It is old," he says.

"I'm hip it's old. But it's beautiful." He turns to face Guy. "You live here all *alone?*"

"*Hélas.* Yes," says Guy, still smiling.

"Have you *always* lived alone?"

"I had a friend here for a while—a friend from Algeria—but he has gone back to his home." He paces a little, his hands in his pockets;

Arthur realizes that his rolling stride is due to the fact that he is a little bowlegged. "I imagine that he will never come back to France."

"Why not?"

"Well—as you may know—there is some misunderstanding—some difficulties, so I might say—between France and Algeria these days."

Arthur *does* know this—that is, he has read and heard about the Algerian revolt against the French—but he does not *really* know, and, watching Guy's face, does not want to pursue it.

"I see," is all he says, and turns away again.

Guy walks to the wooden cabinet. "Would you like—what do you call it? We say *un bonnet de nuit—enfin*—would you like a *night*-cap—before we wash up and retire?"

Arthur is fascinated by him, yes, but he also likes him more and more. There is something very lonely and vulnerable about him. At the same time, he realizes that this is practically the very first time he has felt so at ease with a white man. But it is only now, seeing Guy in his house, standing, so to speak, among the witnesses to his inheritance, that he thinks of him as *white*. He would not have reacted to Guy in New York as he has reacted to him here, certainly not so quickly. He stares at Guy for a moment. Then, he shakes his head. The truth is, he thinks of Guy as French, someone, therefore, who has nothing to do with New York, or Georgia. He has no learned, or willed response to him because Guy has never existed for him; neither in his imagination, nor in his life, has he ever been threatened by him—that is, by a Frenchman. But he is dimly aware that this may be connected with his reluctance to discuss Algeria. He shakes his head again.

"Are you shaking your head yes?" asks Guy, with a laugh. "Or no?"

He has opened the wooden cabinet and holds the bottle of vodka in his hand.

"Yes," says Arthur. "Don't mind me."

"I will get ice and glasses then."

"Let me come with you?"

"Of course. You are home."

The kitchen is big, and very old-fashioned. It is a kitchen Arthur thinks, that his mother would love. They get the ice out of a refrigerator far from modern, and the glasses out of the cupboard, and return to the living room. Guy pours the vodka, and they sit down on the sofa.

Guy lights a cigarette, and goes to one of the windows and opens the drapes. The dawn, a kind of electrical gray, fills the room.

Guy comes back to the sofa, and picks up his glass from the low table.

"I have sat here many mornings alone, and watched the day come. Sometimes, it is sad, sometimes it is not so sad, but always it is— something awaiting you." He looks at Arthur. "It is so, no? Something waiting, just out there."

"We have a song something like that," Arthur says. "Well, for me, it's just like that. You ever hear of a blues singer named Bessie Smith?"

"Oh, yes. I have many of her records."

"Well, she has a song, goes, *Catch 'em. Don't let them blues in here!*"

Guy laughs, and Arthur laughs, watching him. "Why, yes," says Guy. "It is a little like that."

Then he puts out his cigarette and turns to Arthur, putting one great hand on the nape of Arthur's neck. "I do not feel the blues this morning, though."

Arthur puts down his glass, suddenly feeling as tentative and as powerful as a boy. Tentative, because he is watching, sensing, awaiting Guy, powerful because a depth of desire has been struck in him which will cause both Guy and himself to tremble—powerful, because this desire, dormant for so long, has been awakened by Guy's desire. Again, he feels a kind of thrill of freedom. He and his newfound friend are alone. They have each other to discover; and, for the moment, only each other. He laughs, low in his throat, for pure joy, and Guy laughs with him, and pulls him closer.

Guy is still sleeping when Arthur wakes up, at about three o'clock in the afternoon.

Guy's bedroom opens on his adjoining study, and, in the study, one of the windows has been left slightly open. A small breeze comes through this window, as pleasant and peaceful as the half-light coming through the drapes. Arthur is luxuriously wide awake: wide awake, that is, without wishing to move.

Guy lies on his side, facing Arthur, one arm outstretched toward Arthur. Some faces, in sleep, become tormented, endure hard wrestling matches, undergo great trials: Guy's face was as quiet and defenseless as it must have been when he was three years old. He is snoring slightly, his teeth faintly gleaming through his parted lips. His rough hair is slightly damp and tangled on his forehead. The covers are half off: Arthur watches the faint rise and fall of the hairy chest. He is the spy of the midafternoon: Guy does not see him watching him. The hand at the end of the arm which had been thrown across Arthur twitches slightly, not yet alarmed—but soon, some message will be carried to Guy's brain, waking him up.

Arthur does not disturb the covers, does not touch Guy. He can see all that there is to see—the navel, the darker pubic hair, the labyrinthine sex, the thighs, knees, ankles, the buttocks—all, and much more, all that is not seen, without touching the covers, or disturbing a millimeter of the universe. He will see all this forever, it has become a part of him. When yesterday, last night, shortly before or after the flood, whenever, kissing Guy, he had felt the weight of his past, of his experience, drop from him, so that he could be naked, he had known that he would have to pick it up again. He had not known that it would be heavier, made heavier by a night.

He watches Guy. Anguish translates, it travels well, has as many tongues as vehicles: but desire is among the chief of these, and if desire is not a confession, it can only be a curse. Never, in all of Arthur's life, has anyone been so helpless in his arms, or wanted or needed so much, or given so much. He feels—transformed: in a night, he has grown much older.

He watches Guy, and wishes to protect him. He does not feel that this is ridiculous; or, if it is, he doesn't care. He knows that Guy also wishes to protect him—he does not feel that this is ridiculous, either. It is real to him, for the first time, that this is what lovers do for each other—by daring to be naked, by giving each other the strength to have nothing to hide.

No one can do this alone.

He lights a cigarette, and leans back on the pillow. He looks straight ahead into the vast old study, seeing Guy's desk, and chairs, his lamps, his books, one or two pieces of sculpture; the paintings, some on the wall, some, like scrolls, piled high on a corner; the mail, the ornate North African letter opener, the telephone; the photographs, on the desk, on the walls, some of Guy in uniform, some in North African dress, one photograph of his friend, Mustapha, in a corner above the record player; the records, with a vast selection of Jelly Roll Morton, Bessie Smith, Ma Rainey, Django Reinhardt, Louis Armstrong, Duke Ellington, Billie Holiday, Mahalia Jackson, Ida Cox, Fats Waller—and others, obscure even for him, including some seventy-eights he would love to get his hands on, all tirelessly catalogued and labeled, each in its place.

This apartment, which had seemed so vast last night, he sees, now, as a kind of purgatory; it seems to ring with the quiet and somehow gallant horror of Guy's days and nights.

He looks over at Guy again, Guy has not moved. But his arm moves blindly, and his body lurches closer to Arthur.

Arthur looks straight ahead. His life has grown heavier by a night: for, we are all waiting for him, in America.

He does not feel the romantic schizophrenia. He knows very well that he cannot stay here: that knowledge is as real as the air blowing through this room. But so is the man in the bed as real as that.

Neither does he feel that it is his duty to return—there are a thousand ways of evading a duty. Nor is it a matter of loyalty, a questionable document which can always be torn up, and always, furthermore, for excellent reasons.

He puts out his cigarette: tormented, nevertheless.

He moves quietly out of bed, and, naked, pads to the W.C., and, then, to the enormous bathroom, where he throws water on his face. He looks at his face in the mirror, but one's face, when one searches it in the mirror, reveals nothing at all. He looks tired, triumphant, and sad—as though he has seen more than he wished to see, and is now about to see more than that.

It will be very hard to get away.

Very.

He walks back into the bedroom and stretches out on the bed. He lights another cigarette.

Guy opens his eyes. His smile forces Arthur to smile.

"*Bonjour.*"

Arthur is picking up French very rapidly.

"*Bonjour* yourself."

"*Puis-je avoir une cigarette?*"

"Hey, you remember me? I speak *English.*" But he lights a Gitane, coughs, and hands it to Guy.

"*Pardon*—I am sorry. It is that I am not awake."

Guy puffs on his cigarette, shakes his head, runs his hands through his hair.

Arthur watches him.

"*Pardon.* I must go to the W.C."

And he stumbles out of bed, and pads down the hall. Arthur walks to the study window, and stares out at the chilly day. He has no desire to face it. He feels that, perhaps, he should call his hotel, or, rather, have Guy call; sooner or later, he must call *me;* but not now. He wants to go back to bed. He wants to be with Guy as long as he can be.

So, he is in bed when tall, bowlegged Guy comes shambling back.

Guy puts out his cigarette butt, and crawls into bed beside him. He takes Arthur in his arms.

"You are not hungry?"

"No. Are you?"

"I don't think so." His hands stroke Arthur's back. "Not now."

"Do you think maybe we should call my hotel?"

"We can call later. Or we can go there, if you are worried."

"No. I'm not worried."

As they kiss, as the heat rises between them, as they claim the hours of this afternoon, the coming night, the hours which remain, as Guy's hands and mouth and tongue adore his body, as he gives himself and gives himself to Guy, as they come closer to the impending miracle of mutual surrender, laughing a little, pausing, simply looking at each other, sobbing a little, stroking the rigid, burning sex, drinking in each other's odors, each astounded by the other's color—how many colors a color has! What a labyrinth!—as they descend into quiet places, only slowly, to grow up again, coming closer to the edge, holding back, wanting it never to end, searching each other's eyes, laughing at what each sees there, then, somber, dedicated, like wrestlers, delicately probing, like physicians, testing muscles, experimenting with tastes, comparing discoveries, the one lying still, then the other, each becoming more and more helpless and open to the other, using themselves in defiance of murder, time, language, and continents, history knotted in the balls, hope, glory, and power pounding in the prick, knowing that this suspension cannot last much longer, that each is coming to his own edge, lying quietly in each other's arms, then turning again, this time Arthur's slow entry into Guy, *oh don't move,* the stillness, then, the slow rising and falling, the tremendous conjunction, that sense of mysteries overturned and the sky exploding, something fragile and everlasting being accomplished between two lovers, two men, the gentleness of armpits, nipples, nape, and hair, the unmistakable pounding power of the going-home thrusts *ah oui oh baby,* the last unbelievable burning rigidity, the intolerably prolonged split second before lover finally pours himself into lover, the coming together, the endless fall, the rising into daybreak, weary, spent, at home in each other, there is, yet, a strange, cold pain in everything, and Arthur is thinking, *I wish I could stay. I hope we meet again.*

They go to Arthur's hotel that evening. Arthur pays his bill, for he is moving into Guy's flat. During this brief transaction—Guy has a cab waiting at the door—Arthur can see that the concierge is very impressed by Guy, and a little annoyed with himself for not having suspected that the black American might have had such splendid connections. Arthur has never seen him smile or bow: now he does both, at great length, and with great pleasure. Arthur is not allowed to touch his bags. A creature he has never seen before appears from the cellar and carries them out to the cab.

Ah. The European bewilderment concerning the black American connections is very nearly the root of the problem his presence poses abroad.

Laughing, breathless, a little like children, they deposit Arthur's belongings in Guy's *foyer*, and immediately leave the house. They are going to the movies, then they are going to eat, and Guy has extracted a promise from Arthur: they will not discuss his departure, or make any plans concerning it, until suppertime, tomorrow. They will steal twenty-four hours. What difference can the theft of twenty-four hours mean to eternity? The calendar has so many days to play with: why should the calendar care if we steal one? Arthur knows, now, that eternity is a jealous tyrant, demanding an accounting of every breath, and the calendar a malicious, meticulous bookkeeper pleased to be in the service of eternity—but, never mind, Guy is right, there are moments when one must challenge the tyrant. And tell his clerk to kiss you where the sun don't shine.

So, they leave Arthur's bags in the *foyer*, rush down the stairs and cross the courtyard again, jump into the still waiting taxi, and are carried off to the Champs-Élysées. Or rather, as Guy directs the driver, to L'Étoile. "So, we start at the top," says Guy, "and walk down. That way, you can see it all."

Anyway, Arthur has never seen the Champs-Élysées by night. It is best, of course, to see it for the first time at night, and, if one can manage to be young, that helps. If, in addition to being young, one can also arrange to see if for the first time at night with a lover, one cannot claim to be doing too badly. But, if in addition to being young and seeing the Champs-Élysées for the first time at night with a lover, that lover happens, furthermore, to be French, one is in a rare and exalted category indeed: and might as well take the vow of silence, for if your story is ever believed, it can only poison your relationships.

Nevertheless, at about eight o'clock on this particular Thursday evening, the cab crossed the bridge and left Concorde behind and began rolling up the broad, pompous tree-lined avenue, which seemed to be alive with light. Straight ahead, like the promise of victory, and seeming to be on a height, stood the massive, perhaps somewhat Teutonic, Arc de Triomphe—L'Étoile—under which arch burns the eternal flame for the unknown soldier. There is nothing at all Elysian about the Champs-Élysées; neither does it bring to mind a field. It is a very serious marketplace, both by day and by night. By day, in the spring and the summertime, and some days in the early fall, it can be quite magical, exhilarating, in spite of the piratical prices; and anyway, one can walk on this crowded avenue and still feel quite alone.

Anyway, if one has seen it for the first time at night when one was young, when one was happy, the memory comes back from time to time, and the memory stings, but it causes you to remember that you have not always been unhappy and need not always be.

For Arthur, the shock of discovery and delight is mingled with the certainty of imminent departure. Thus, everything is double-edged. But there is a certain wisdom in Guy's insistence that they not discuss his departure for twenty-four hours. This twenty-four hours is deliberately, consciously stolen—like playing hooky—and so, they are free to make the most of it.

The cab stops at the Place de L'Étoile, and they get out and begin to walk.

Now there is absolutely nothing to see on the Champs-Élysées, especially at night, except other, rather weary and calculating faces, mile upon mile of advertising, shop windows, shop windows, cinemas, and café terraces. But it is all quite magical tonight. Technically, their errand, now, is to decide which film to see, and, after that, where to eat.

Guy says that seeing French movies is a great way of learning French, but concedes that there is really no point in beginning Arthur's education tonight. So they will see an American film, but the marquees they pass are not terribly encouraging. Guy is willing to see a Western, but Arthur is not: "I didn't come all the way to Paris just to see another TV show, man." Guy is partial to Hitchcock, but there is no Hitchcock, and anyway, it begins to be apparent that neither of them is concentrating. They are merely taking a walk. Arthur is fascinated by the men's clothes in the shop windows, and so, they keep stopping, Arthur calculating whether he can buy this, or that, but knowing that he almost certainly can't. There is a raincoat in a window that he particularly admires. Guy agrees to come with him on the morrow—"*before* suppertime?" pleads Arthur—to try it on.

In the meantime, they have covered almost no territory on the famous avenue, and it is beginning to be late to go to the movies. Now they will have to wait until ten, or ten thirty. "Then let me buy you a drink," says Arthur, "and we can discuss it. I'd love to buy my man a drink in a café terrace on the *Champs*."

And, so, they sit down, and order two whiskies.

At the hotel, Arthur had changed his underwear, and put on a white, open-neck shirt and a navy-blue suit and a black gabardine topcoat, with a belt, and changed his socks and shoes. He looks quite elegant, and he is still young enough for this elegance to make him look younger. He is like a winning, questing student, and he is very happy, and this makes him look radiant. Guy smiles every time he looks at him, and calls him *le chanteur sauvage*—the savage singer—and sometimes, "*my* savage singer."

"Keep it up," says Arthur, "you don't know that, where I come from, some *savage* motherfucker would already have done *savaged* you. I'm nice."

They are sitting in a glass-enclosed terrace, watching the people pass by.

"I wonder," says Arthur, "what it would have been like to have been born here."

"Ah," says Guy. "I know one thing—you would feel very differently about it." He searches for his words. "I don't know. I think you might still *love* it. But you would know so very much more about it that it would be a very different kind of love." He nods, wryly, affectionately, at Arthur. "Maybe you would not like it when I joke and call you—*mon chanteur sauvage*. But"—and a kind of torment crosses his face—"I don't know."

"Well," says Arthur carefully, "if you came to New York, it would also be very new for you, right?"

Since neither is certain of the other's language, each is compelled to look the other in the eye when they speak, to make certain that the meaning is getting through.

"Of course, that is true," Guy says.

"And you might love New York—but in a very different way from the way"—he grimaces, looking doubtful—"*I* love New York. *If* I love it. I've never made up my mind." He looks out at the unknown avenue. "I may not know if I love it—well—that's very complicated. But, Lord, I know I can hate it."

"I am certain," Guy says firmly, "that I could never love anything you hate. I would destroy me. I do not know," he continues, searching Arthur's face, "anything about America, and I do not really trust what I hear. But I do not like the Frenchmen I know who like New York— or Florida, or Los Angeles, for that matter. This is just something, you understand, for me. It does not have anything to do with you. I have always felt this way. Oh," and he lights a cigarette, "I do not mean the people who go for ten days, or so, and come back and tell me all about your Radio City or Times Square. *They* always sound as though they are relieved to have escaped with their *lives*."

Arthur throws back his head, and laughs. Guy continues. "No. I mean those people who *really* love it, who take it all seriously, all your shit, and want to be *like* the Americans. Not just because they *work* there." He pauses again. "It's hard for me to explain myself. It is, perhaps, that they take a model which I believe is false, and they want to *be* like that. I work for the Americans, too, of course, and you can say that I am no better than the others, and maybe I am not, I know that. But I do not want to *be* like that, it is like wanting to be German. And, me, I think, it is already much more than enough to be French. Truly."

Arthur watches him. He has understood something, something unexpected, again, mainly from the tone, and, in another way, from Guy's eyes. "How? Enough to be French?"

"To be hypocrites, to be racists—we do not need any models. We are very, very good at it, all by ourselves!" He grinds out his cigarette, immediately lights another. "I am a Frenchman. I have been a French soldier. I know."

Again, Arthur feels almost as though he is eavesdropping: he does not want to pursue this aspect of what he perceives to be Guy's torment. And he has another, deadlier, drier apprehension: if Guy is offering his credentials, he does not want to see them, much less be compelled to examine them.

He thinks about it another way, carefully sipping his whisky, and lighting a cigarette—these gestures are made almost in order to hide his face. If Guy is saying that he does not like being a Frenchman, what would he think of Arthur if Arthur proclaimed that he did not like being a black American? And, indeed, for the very first time, and almost certainly because he is sitting on this unknown avenue, he puts the two words together *black American* and hears, at once, the very crescendo of contradiction and the unanswering and unanswerable thunder and truth of history—which is nothing more and nothing less than the beating of his own heart, his song. In many ways, he does not like being a black American, or being black, or being American, or being Arthur, and, for many millions of people, in his country, and elsewhere—including France—his existence was proof of the unspeakable perversity of history, a flaw in the nature of God. However: here he is, sitting on the Champs-Élysées, with Guy, a Frenchman, a stranger, and a lover, not yet a friend. He does not want to think about it, it will ruin the stolen twenty-four hours, and make his burden, already heavier by a day, much heavier.

He wonders about Guy's Mustapha. He has gone back to Algeria. *He* is going back to America. He does not want to think about it now, he will think about it on the plane, and, swallowing his whisky, he leaps back into the present:

"I suggest," he says, "that we forget about empires past, present, or to come, from Ashanti to Charlemagne to Queen Victoria to Eisenhower, and have another drink and decide where we're going to eat. And then, if there's any music in this town, we can go and hear some music. If not, not. Anyway, we shouldn't hang out too late, right? Get our buns in the house at some reasonable hour, and maybe play a couple of your records and go to bed and make love and go to sleep. How you feel about that, pudding?"

"*Ça va très bien,*" Guy says gravely: but he has been watching Arthur's face, and is aware that Arthur's mood has changed. He is aware, too, that this has something to do with some new assessment Arthur is making as concerns him.

He signals the waiter, and they order their whiskies. Then he looks back at Arthur. He leans forward, one elbow on the table, holding his cigarette, watching Arthur, with a frown.

"I don't know if I make myself clear," he says. "I really would hate for you to misunderstand me."

"So would I," says Arthur, "but"—and he decides to take the plunge, the Puritan in him having announced that the horizontal position will soon be joyless if the vertical position is a lie—"can I tell you something? Well, tell you something, and ask you something?"

"Of course." Guy's square face is tight with concentration, his dark eyes nearly black. He still leans forward on one elbow, the cigarette ash is about to drop.

"Well—first—listen. I just got here, right? Never saw Paris before, never saw London—well, I *had* seen London—but this is not my territory, if I hadn't met you, I'd probably be on a plane by now, or I'd be sitting in my hotel room, jerking off, and I'd be walking the streets, you dig? I wouldn't be sitting here."

The cigarette ash drops, just as the waiter returns. He is elaborately resigned about this misadventure—which Guy has failed to notice—sets down his tray, wipes the table, empties the ashtray, picks up the empty glasses, sets down the full glasses, puts the bill under the ashtray, leaves.

Arthur takes Guy's dead cigarette, and puts it in the ashtray.

"Listen. You were talking about France before, and America, and you mentioned Germany, and you don't want to be like the Americans, and you don't want to be like the Germans, and you don't even want to be like the *French*. Well, I have to ask myself who the fuck *do* you want to be like? Hold it," for Guy has made a gesture. He picks up a cigarette, and Arthur lights it for him. Then he picks up his whisky, and lifts it toward Guy. "Cheers. But listen. All these places may be different. They *are* different for you. Shit, they eat knockwurst in Germany, and pâté in France, and some awful slop in England, and you got different flags and systems and whatnot and you're always at each other's throats and you think that makes you different. But you want me to tell you where you are all *alike*? The *only* subject on which you ain't got *no* disagreement?"

Guy leans back, drawing on his cigarette, watching Arthur with a dry, shrewd pursing of the lips, not quite a smile, with narrowed eyes.

Arthur touches his chest. "Me. You got no disagreement about *me*. I just told you that this is not my territory. I just got here. But I met every single one of *you* motherfuckers *long* before I got here."

He sips his whiskey, watching Guy.

"I met you all in America, working for you. And every single one of you call me nigger, me and my mama and my daddy and my brother and my sister and my daughter and my son. So I don't really give a shit what you think about France or Germany or Switzerland or

England—the differences between you are not important. Whenever you think I'm getting out of hand, you can forget your differences long enough to come and kick my ass. That may not be all I know about you, and I hope that ain't *all* there is *to* you, but, baby, that's what I've learned about you, and that's enough."

He takes another swallow of his whiskey, and lights a cigarette. Now he cannot read Guy's face.

"And—this is all I got to say—I told you I was going to ask you something, this is what I want to ask you—don't you think, on top of all the other shit I got to go through, that I might think it a little *excessive* that I got to give you my sympathy, too? Shit, you still got all the gold and diamonds and all the jet bombers, *and* my ass, and you want to *cry* in my arms, too? Come on, man, there's got to be a limit."

He starts laughing, because Guy has thrown back his head, and is shaking with laughter.

He sits up, drawing on his cigarette, his eyes wet.

He picks up his whiskey, puts it down, finds a handkerchief, and wipes his eyes.

Then he looks at Arthur.

"*Chapeau.* I have never heard it put so before. *Sympathy!*" He laughs again. "I agree, that is somewhat excessive, as you say." He sobers, not without some difficulty. "But yes, sympathy is needed, there is no other hope." He finally manages to take a swallow of his whisky. "I, in fact, do *not* have the jet bombers and so forth, and, after all, if I have *your* ass, you also have mine, which may entitle me to a little *sympathy.*" He sobers again. "But I do not joke. I am paying for something which I do not have and certainly do not want. I do not want a slave, I do not want a colony, I want to be your friend, I want you to look on me as a man like you. That is true, I think you know that. It is true that I am French, and what you say about Europe is true—I can see that. But *I* have never called you nigger, I do not think that it is in me to do so. Of course, you may not believe me. It is perfectly possible that you cannot afford to believe me." He looks down.

"Perhaps so brutal a history can produce only a brute. But I do not believe that, and you do not believe it, either. All history is brutal. I think"—now very earnest, lighting another cigarette, frowning, looking down—"I think that my history has made me a bankrupt in all but the material sense, and will soon make me a bankrupt in that sense, also, and it is not your sympathy, not even your love, which can save me from that mathematic. I am not clinging to my history; my history is clinging to me. My history has told too many lies about too much, has blasphemed what is sacred. I am far from being unaware of that. I *know* why we needed Africa, and it was not merely for the gold and the diamonds! That was the lie we told ourselves: because *we* were civilized." He pauses again, and finishes his whisky. "We had to be. It is a miracle that any one of us can even fart, much less shit." He looks at his glass, wonderingly, then at Arthur. "In spite of all appearance, *cher chanteur sauvage,* you are not the victim. You have been the object of a conspiracy, and the conspiracy has failed."

He watches Arthur with a weary, affectionate smile. "I know, in any case, no matter what you say, that you will never abandon anyone you love. And that is enough." He puts out his cigarette, lights another, a little shy now. "I am drunk enough, just a little, to have one more drink"—he looks at Arthur—"will you join me? And, then, we will go someplace and eat and maybe you will sing for me, later? Out of sympathy." And he laughs a very moving laugh. "Ah. I am glad we talked."

Arthur watches him, and signals for the waiter. "Baby. So am I."

They leave the café, and continue walking down the avenue. Both are beginning to be hungry, and it is beginning to be cold, but they feel, for the moment, a need to walk together. The pretext, though they do not really need one, is that Guy wants to talk a little, to clear his head: the truth is that walking together can induce a very particular silence. There is an important safety in the sound of the other's footfalls, a reassurance in the light touch of the other's shoulder. The profile of the other comes into and out of the light, and each time subtly different, infinities being recorded at a speed outside of time.

One can speak, or not speak, particularly if there is peace between you.

Perhaps, if they had not spoken in the café, they would have leapt into a cab, and hurried to some other public place; would have been compelled to run, that is, instead of being able to walk. Arthur puts up his coat collar, Guy knots his scarf. Each has his hands in his pockets. Guy's bowlegged roll causes his shoulder to touch Arthur's from time to time; from time to time, Guy elaborates this roll a little, deliberately, and he and Arthur glance at each other, smiling.

They do not speak until they reach the large fountain, at an intersection. There is a cab stand in the center of the avenue.

"*Mon cher chanteur,*" says Guy, "we must eat."

They stop, facing each other, under the streetlight.

"Right. Where?"

Guy makes a face, looks around the avenue. "I do not like to eat around here. This is not"—he laughs—"*my* territory."

He looks at Arthur, and laughs, and Arthur laughs.

"Shall we, then, cross the river? We can find a place near home, *d'accord*? And then, perhaps, we shall find some music in *le quartier latin*? That is where you were living," he explains. "I see that you do not remember your old neighborhood at all. Ah! *Les touristes!*"

"Listen, baby. Just get me to some grits, okay? I don't know why all you Frenchmen pick out the coldest-ass street corners to start running down your shit."

"*Ah! comme tu es mal poli! Ils sont tous comme ça, chez toi? Donc, je commence à comprendre enfin ce sacré problème noir!*" He takes Arthur by the arm, laughing, and they cross to the cab stand. "*Saint-Germain-des-Prés,*" Guy tells the driver, and they get into the cab.

Guy presses his hand for a moment, and looks at him. "*Ça va?*"

"I won't lie about it, man," says Arthur. "*Ça va très bien*—my French is improving, right?"

"You are making great progress. If only—" The cab begins speeding toward the Place de la Concorde. The lights spin by, making Arthur remember the lights of a children's carnival, in his childhood, or in his dreams, he does not know. Guy sighs, then grins, and turns to Arthur. "We must not speak of your amazing linguistic gifts before supper, tomorrow night. But it would be a pity to let them go to waste."

"I imagine," says Arthur, "that we're going to have a pretty late supper."

"It is possible," says Guy, "especially since I am the cook."

Arthur watches the immense column of the Place de la Concorde come closer, as icy as some relic watched over only by the moon. Perhaps it does not belong here; just as it is strange to name a place where the guillotine once stood. *Concorde.*

But history may be the most mystical of all our endeavors, and Arthur turns his mind away from the monument exactly as the cab turns, and begins to cross the river.

They eat in some crowded, cheerful, friendly place, somewhere in the shadows of the rue Monsieur-le-Prince. They are at a corner table, in what must have been a Chinese, or, in any case, Oriental restaurant, because waiters keep coming with dishes. The seem to eat for hours, and, since they are happy, everyone around them seems to be celebrating something. They drink a lot of wine: waiters keep coming with bottles. They talk—or Arthur talks: into Guy's square, flushed, and laughing face, Guy's hand always seeming to be poised above yet another covered dish. Arthur shovels it all in, and so does Guy, it is as though they are connected by invisible threads, choreographed from the depthless center, as though the calendar has been corrected by eternity, and eternity is smiling.

Yes. My brother was happy. I wish I had been there. I am glad that I could not have been there. He could not have seen, if I had been there (though I could have seen it—of course) that he was happy because he made Guy happy. He has never known himself to make anyone happy before.

He does not really know this, now: yet, here it is, before him, Guy's radiant face, Guy, with those deep-set brown eyes, that just-beginning-to-be-weathered brow, that rough, red, curly hair. Above all, the delight in those eyes when they look at Arthur.

It must have been a Chinese—or an Oriental—restaurant, for they drink tea, finally, after all the exotic dishes have been cleared away. The restaurant, abruptly, is less crowded, but it is not late. Arthur looks at his watch, and it is just a little past midnight.

Guy is watching him.

He picks up Arthur's pack of cigarettes, lights one, and hands it to Arthur. Arthur takes it, and they watch each other.

There is a look in Guy's eyes which Arthur is beginning to know. There is an anguish in those eyes, at the bottom of those eyes, like something living, and determined to live, in the depths of a dungeon, having been hurled there: which knows, and wants you to know that it knows, what happened: something which refuses reconciliation. This is also the look at the very bottom of Arthur's eyes, though Arthur does not know this, and, of course, has never seen it: in his own eyes, that is.

Guy sees in Arthur what Arthur would not dream of looking for in Guy. The stubborn anguish Guy sees in Arthur corroborates Guy's reality, may be said, even, to give him the right to live; it begins to divest him of his irksome privilege, his blinding color, and welcomes him, so to speak, into the human race. Thus, he can, he hopes, he imagines, meet Arthur on Arthur's ground, and anyway, Guy cannot do this, not yet, and Arthur knows it. It is not because he cannot know Arthur's ground, but because he does not know his own. Guy and Arthur may be equally lonely, but guy is far more isolated. Arthur is far more a stranger for Guy than Guy can be for Arthur; at least, in principle, and as a result of history. Arthur does not need Guy's suffering to corroborate his own reality, or Guy's. Those realities, simply, are not in question, and, as for being welcomed into the human race, that was long ago accomplished, by iron and fire.

Guy has said that his history is clinging to him, but what he means is that he has no acceptable access to that history: it cannot feed him, it can only diminish him. In any case, it must all be reexamined and overhauled before it can possibly be used, and this examination will take the rest of Guy's life. Guy, like many another, like Arthur, like you and me, in fact, would rather spend his life without wrestling with history.

For this is also Arthur's torment, although the terms are so unutterably different.

To overhaul a history, or to attempt to redeem it—which effort may or may not justify it—is not at all the same thing as the descent one must make in order to excavate a history. To be forced to excavate a history is, also, to repudiate the concept of history, and the vocabulary in which history is written; for the written history is, and must be, merely the vocabulary of power, and power is history's most seductively attired false witness.

And yet, the attempt, more, the necessity, to excavate a history, to find out the truth about oneself! is motivated by the need to have the power to force others to recognize your presence, your right to be here. The disputed passage will remain disputed so long as you do not have the authority of the right-of-way—so long, that is, as your passage can be disputed: the document promising safe passage can always be revoked. Power clears the passage, swiftly: but the paradox, here, is that power, rooted in history, is also, the mockery and the repudiation of history. The power to define the other seals one's definition of oneself—who, then, in such a fearful mathematic, to use Guy's term, is trapped?

Perhaps, then, after all, we have no idea of what history is: or are in flight from the demon we have summoned. Perhaps history is not to be found in our mirrors, but in our repudiations: perhaps, the other is ourselves. History may be a great deal more than the quicksand which swallows others, and which has not yet swallowed us: history may be attempting to vomit us up, and spew us out: history may be tired. Death, itself, which swallows everyone, is beginning to be weary—of history, in fact: for death has no history.

Our history is each other. That is our only guide. One thing is absolutely certain: one can repudiate, or despise, no one's history without repudiating and despising one's own. Perhaps that is what the gospel singer is singing.

For presently, Guy and Arthur leave the restaurant, which is, somewhere, forever, in the shadows of the rue Monsieur-le-Prince, and they walk, in the chilly winds, and along various byways, and along the quai St.-Michel, looking down at the river and across to the other shore, and enter, finally, the rue de la Huchette: which translates, Arthur told me, as "the street of the fishing cat." (He seemed to feel that the street had been named for him.)

It is Guy's idea, for he knows, as Arthur does not, that there are several jazz joints—"*Dee*-xie-land," according to Guy—along this street. They enter one of them, purely at random, pulled in by the music. There is an American trio playing, and an old blues singer from Memphis, Sonny Carr, is sitting in.

The place is not very large, is very crowded, and the trio—two young blacks, and one young white, piano, bass, and slide trombone—are playing. All of the tables are occupied. Guy takes their coats to the *vestiare*, and they stand at the bar, which is also very crowded.

It is a fairly young crowd, and somewhat more varied than would be likely to be found in any other quarter of Paris: young French students, and students not so young, children from the Netherlands, from Germany, from England, Americans, black and white, black Africans, and children from North Africa.

The last two groups are the people who intrigue and intimidate Arthur most. He feels a great need to reach them, but does not know how; does not know, for that matter, if they want to be reached, and, in any case, he does not speak French. He does not know if he likes them or not, and this is because he is so terrified of *not* liking them. In this, he does not see how American, how Western, how *white* he is being, which is to say, and in the most subtle sense of the word, how racist: for why *should* he like them, after all, to say nothing of *how*? Nobody *likes* great crowds of people, unless he intends to use them, and some of the people who make up such a marked mob are perfectly aware of this. Earlier, Arthur had hoped not to be forced to examine Guy's credentials, but now, he is somewhat worried about his own. If he doesn't know what he thinks of *them*, he certainly doesn't know what they think of *him*, and *he* is not a crowd.

But the ancient blues singer, a weary and triumphant mountain of a man, is sitting quietly—or, more precisely, quietly towering—at the end of the bar, and he and two or three of the young Africans seem to be having a fine time together.

The old blues singer is as black as the black Africans, or very nearly, and much darker, of course, than the North Africans. Though this observation is somewhat too swift; it is necessary to revise the optic through which one sees what has come to be called color. The children from the Netherlands, from Germany, from England, for example, are all, more or less, the same color, and this would not even have been a question, had Arthur found them in New York, or in Boston. In the harsh, democratic light of these metropolises, they would have been the same color, whether they liked it or not. But, truthfully, if one really looks at them, though they are, anonymously, the same color, they are not, intimately, the same shade. Different histories, and different hazards, are written just beneath the skin, these histories and hazards accounting for the subtleties of shade. Some descend from the Viking by way of Constantinople, some from the Turk by way of Vienna, some from the Jew by way of Turkey, some from Turkey by way of the Spanish Jew, some from the Portuguese by way of New England: and all from a history, if that is the word we want, which predates what is known as Europe. And these subtleties are in their eyes—if one wished, ruthlessly, to pursue the matter, in their names. They are, therefore, not only what their history has made of them, they are also what they make of their history. And what brings them here? So far from the Druid forest? To listen to a trio, piano, bass, and slide trombone, from, after all, let's face it, the Lord alone knows where. One will not find the answer in the colors of their skins.

And this is also true of the venerable blues singer, and the Africans who surround him. In New York or in Boston, they would, of course, all be the same color, being seen, necessarily, through the optic of power and guilt—being seen, necessarily indeed, as objects. But here, in this beleaguered capital, and not as far from home as Arthur is, no matter which way he turns, which body of water he faces, or which overland journey, their shades are more vivid than their color. Their shades are mute testimony to a journey which the Netherlands, for example, deny. It is impossible to know what future can be made out of an alabaster past so resounding, and an ebony past so maligned, but some key may be found in the palette which experiments with colors in order to discover shades, which mixes shades in order to arrive at a color, or color, which, by the time one has arrived at it, and by means of this process, always bears an arbitrary and provisional name. Shades cannot be fixed; color is, eternally, at the mercy of the light.

Sonny Carr's hair is pepper-and-salt, and still very thick; his teeth are still bad news for a pork chop. Arthur has heard of him all of his life, and scarcely dares imagine how old he must be.

Paul has spoken of him, had known him in the South, many years ago, and briefly: but Sonny Carr had been a man when his father had still been a boy. And he has not really worked in the United States for very nearly as long as Arthur has been on earth.

Here he is, now. Arthur dare not imagine what drove him here, what his connections are, or have been. He appears to be treated with a mocking, respectful affection. Arthur sees this in the face of the young men, and in the old man's face: though he does not really think of him as an old man, there is something in the face too present, too joyous, and too generous. But they are not really talking, for the trio is playing. Sonny Carr growls encouragement to the trio from time to time, and the trio responds with the faintest suggestion of a mocking flourish—but always responds—and this is almost precisely the rapport between the blues singer and the Africans: easy, tense, and precise.

Arthur wonders about all this, and Guy touches his elbow. "What will you drink?"

For the barmaid is standing before them, a tall, thin, dark-haired girl, with high cheekbones and enormous dark eyes, and a genuine smile.

"*Bonsoir, m'sieu,*" she says.

"*Bonsoir, mam'selle.*" He looks at her, at Guy, feeling a little embarrassed, he does not know why. "I'll have a whiskey," he says, "with ice."

"*Bon. Et vous, m'sieu?*" This, to Guy.

"The same," says Guy.

"*Bien.*" She goes to the end of the bar, suddenly, apparently having been summoned by Sonny Carr. She leans toward him, while he whispers something to her. She nods, smiles, and pours their drinks, returns.

She puts their drinks on the bar, before them. When Guy attempts to pay, she puts up one hand, in refusal. "Later." She turns away, with a laugh. "Do not go. You will understand, later." She addresses something she sees in Guy's face. "*Attends. Que ça reste entre nous.*"

"*Je n'ai pas tort, dis?*"

She shrugs. "*Ah!*" And laughs, and begins serving other customers.

Arthur asks, "What was that about?"

"I really cannot tell you," Guy says, and lifts his whiskey. "Cheers. *Sacré chanteur sauvage.*"

Arthur studies his face. Guy looks somewhat stunned, but very pleased.

The trio finishes with a genuine flourish—it must be admitted that Arthur has not really been listening to them, has been plunged into his own version of a tale of two cities: but has been horribly aware of the black pianist, who reminds him of Peanut, and the slide trombonist, who reminds him of Crunch, and, in some way, of me. And he shakes his head against all these terrors, and sips his drink.

Guy touches his elbow. "We will now hear Sonny Carr."

For the slide trombonist, riding the applause, has taken the microphone, and, wiping his brow with a willed and florid handkerchief—a handkerchief with a history—and smiling, says, "Ladies and gentlemen, *mesdames et messieurs,* I cannot tell you how honored I am to be able to stand here and present one of the greatest blues artists of all time—*mesdames, messieurs, notre père et notre ami, le grand*—Sonny Carr!"

And he steps back, and Sonny Carr steps up.

There is a curious and subtle difference in him when he takes his place before the microphone. He does not, in the first place, seem to know what the microphone is doing there: it is clear that the microphone is a trivial and dubious instrument and he is willing to put up with it, if it acts right. In the second place, he seems to grow, not so much taller as, in every way, immense, as though he is threatening the roof and the walls. He grins, and one sees the dimple in one cheek, which cannot have changed very much since he was young, and a wonder in his eyes. He says nothing. He looks around him once, at the musicians, and snaps his fingers, and, at the same moment, begins:

> *Water-boy,*
> *now, tell me*
> *where you hiding?*
> *If you don't a-come,*
> *I'm going to tell your mammy,*

sounding cajoling, tender, stern and weary—thirsty, for he really needs that drink of water, then he smiles, seeming to look straight down the bar, at Arthur,

> *you jack of diamonds,*
> *you jack of diamonds,*
> *I know you of old, boy,*
> *yes, I know you of old!*

He shifts, without pause, into

> *See, see rider,*
> *See what you done done,*

and then, triumphantly,

> *Take this hammer,*
> *carry it to the captain.*
> *Tell him I'm gone, boys,*
> *tell him I'm gone.*

And ending like that, something like the blow of a hammer, with the trombone supplying the vast and hostile landscape, and the bass and the piano supplying the rigors of days and nights. The place explodes with applause, and Sonny Carr stands there, and bows his head.

It is, suddenly, a mighty gesture. Arthur has seen this gesture all his life, and yet, has never seen it before.

It is a gesture as far beyond humility as it is beyond pride. Sonny bows his head before what his audience supposes to be his past, and his condition. He bows his head before their profound gratitude that this past, and this condition, are his, and not theirs. He bows his head before their silent wonder that he can be so highly esteemed as a performer and treated so viciously as a man: whenever, and wherever, he is esteemed to be one. He hears, in their applause, a kind of silent wonder, inarticulate lamentations. They might, for example, be willing to give "anything" to sing like that, but fear that they haven't "anything" to give: but, far more crucially, do not suspect that it is not a matter of being "willing." It is a matter of embracing one's only life, even though this life so often seems to be, merely, one's doom. And it is, in a way, though not "merely." But to refuse the doom of one's only life is to be trapped outside all nourishment; their wonder, then, is mixed with, and their lamentations defined by, that paralyzing envy from which what we call "racism" derives so much of its energy. Racism is a word which describes one of the results—perhaps the principal result—of our estrangement from our beginnings, from the universal source.

And the applause functions, then, in part, to pacify, narcotize, the resulting violent and inescapable discomfort.

Sonny brings the applause to an end by raising one hand, and saying, with a smile, "*Merci, messieurs-dames.* Good evening, ladies and gentlemen. I think we might have a surprise for you a little bit later. Don't go 'way."

He looks at the trio, and they bounce into an old, good-natured ballad Paul sometimes sang for Arthur, when Arthur was little, "Get Along Home, Cindy, Cindy," and they made something very cheerful and bawdy out of it. Arthur assumes that the crowd can certainly not understand Sonny's down-home, sexual cross-references—Cindy, in Sonny's version, is quite a prodigy, but he, somehow, forces himself to match her—but they appear to follow him with no effort at all. They are following his eyes, and his voice, of course, and he telegraphs, and comments on, each joyous convolution. Arthur wonders what he would feel like before this audience.

The trombone's moan cuts off the applause, a warning, urgent, insistent sound. The bass and the piano have melancholy news, and Sonny begins to spell it out:

> *Ever since Miss Susan Johnson*
> *lost her Jockey, Lee,*

Guy grabs his elbow.

"That is *my* song!" he whispers. "It is Bessie Smith. Never have I heard anyone else sing it before!"

> *There has been much excitement,*
> *more to be*

Very dry, an announcement, suggesting, furthermore, that there is nothing new about it. Yet, he has the entire room waiting for the news.

> *You can hear her moanin'*
> *night and morn.*
> *Wonder where*
> *my Easy Rider's gone?*

This is quite another girl than Cindy; or it is Cindy, later. Sonny is merely telling the tale. It is, furthermore, an exceedingly laconic tale, and Arthur wonders what the present audience can make of it. The room is absolutely silent, as though everyone held his breath, waiting for the message to be delivered.

> *All day, the phone rings,*
> *but it's not for me.*

Arthur looks around the tense, silent room, and he wonders; wonders what they are hearing, indeed; but, beyond that, wonders. The voice does not falter in the telling of the tale: the three musicians supply the literally unutterable truth. A world is being created around this laconic event, an event, which, without commenting on itself, steadily becomes more terrible. An anonymous runaway, and his pacing, waiting woman, somewhere in the American Deep South, when? Right now, if one is to judge from the silence on the faces, and in the room, and the runaway, or the woman, may walk in from the streets at any moment.

For,

> *He's gone where*
> *the Southern*
> *"cross"*
> *the Yellow Dog.*

All possibilities open, or all possibilities closed. The question is left hanging until it is submerged by applause.

The applause is tremendous, but it is time, says the trombonist, that they take a break.

Guy and Arthur look at each other. Guy shakes his head, smiling. *"Il est formidable."* He purses his lips, smiling, and nods his head. *"Merde."* He looks over Arthur's shoulder, and his face changes.

Arthur turns, and sees Sonny Carr walking down the bar, and he comes straight to Arthur.

Arthur realizes that Guy had known that this moment was coming.

"Maybe I'm mistaken," says Sonny Carr to Arthur, "but if two and two and two make four, I believe I can call your name. Just tell me yes or no: is your name Arthur? Your *first* name?"

"Yes, sir," Arthur says.

"And your father's name is—Paul?"

"Yes, sir." Arthur cannot help smiling. He does not know what is happening to him.

"And you just come in from London?"

"Yes, sir."

"Tell you how I know. I got friends in London, told me about a young dude come through, singing gospel, name of—I'll recognize the name, now, you give it to me—now, what is it? Wisconsin? Oklahoma? Ohio? Indian name, I believe—not Chattanooga?"

They are both laughing, and Guy is laughing, and so is the barmaid. The trio, and everyone else in the bar, are immobilized.

"No, sir. The name is Montana."

"Knew it was somewhere around there. How's your father?"

"He's fine. He used to talk to me about you, when I was little."

"Oh. I used to talk to him—when *he* was little." He smiles, and takes Arthur's hand in his. "Will you sing a little for us? Come on." Then he pauses, very delicately—Lord, the humility, the depthless courtesy, with which experience recognizes youth!—and looks at Guy. "Good evening, sir. *Bonsoir,* and God bless you. I'm going to try to kidnap him for a little while, but I ain't going to take him far. He'll be right where you can see him." He smiles and extends his hand.

Guy takes his hand, smiling. "I am most honored to meet you. I am Guy Lazar."

"I'm glad to meet you, too. Come on up here, and have a drink with us." He throws an arm around Arthur, and signals Guy, and the three of them walk back to the end of the bar.

So he is to meet the Africans, and the North Africans, after all. He is keenly aware that he is, visibly, with Guy. He wonders how the North Africans, especially, will take this.

It occurs to him that he is now in a position not entirely unlike that of a white person in the States, worried about how his white friends will look at his black friend—well: worried, too, about how his white friends will look at *him*.

He cannot pursue this dizzying speculation. They are being introduced.

He need not have worried. He has entered Sonny Carr's orbit with Sonny's arm around him, Sonny has sought him out, and claimed him. This makes him special and makes Guy special, at least for this moment, tonight.

They shake hands, all around. There is, perhaps, the very slightest stiffening and exaggeration of courtesy in the North African reception of Guy, but it passes swiftly, like a faintly acrid odor on the air. Sonny announces what the barmaid already knows, that Guy and Arthur are his guests—they have been his guests since they entered—and that Arthur is the son of an old friend of his, from way back yonder, and that Arthur will sing. So he meets the trio. The white bass player is from Chicago, the trombonist from Oakland, the piano player from Syracuse. And, after the first few stiff, shy seconds, they begin to talk to each other, Guy and two of the North Africans entering into a discussion which sounds—or, rather, perhaps, looks—guarded, friendly, and intense.

The trio establishes, above and beside them, a fine, rocking beat into which Arthur can enter at will. Sonny announces him as the "surprise" he had promised earlier. Arthur steps onto the bandstand.

Sonny, sitting on his bar stool, towers over Guy, who stands beside him. The faces of the Africans, and the North Africans, burn in the dim light, like statues in a cave. And the faces beyond this circle, beyond the circle nearest Arthur, are both vivid and shapeless, a kind of breathing, waiting sea.

Arthur moves with the beat for a moment, his shoulders back, as I have seen him move while dancing. But his mind has gone blank: he cannot think of the words to a single song. He looks at Sonny, and Sonny sees this in his face, and laughs.

"Sing 'Daniel'!" he cries.

Still not certain of the words, Arthur opens his mouth, and the words come out!

> *Daniel*
> *saw the stone*
> *that was hewed*
> *out the mountain,*

and everything comes together, he and the trio and the beat, Sonny's black face and Guy's white face, and all the other faces.

> *Daniel*
> *saw the stone*
> *that was rolled*
> *into Babylon.*

It is all right. Sonny is clapping his hands: *"Well, let's have a little church in here!"* Guy's face is burning. The other, darker faces meet him with the intensity and the beauty of the beat he rides, and the faces beyond this circle seem to come forward with a mute appeal.

> *Jesus is the stone*
> *that was hewed out the mountain,*
> *tearing down*
> *the kingdom of this world!*

The applause washes over him, like the sound of a crumbling wall. The crowd refuses to let him go. Finally, Arthur and Sonny sing together,

> *Oh, when I come*
> *to the end of my journey,*

and Sonny looks into Arthur's eyes, as they sing,

> *weary of life,*
> *and the battle is won.*

Arthur hears the great, gallant weariness of someone making himself ready for the last, or the first, great test. Now standing next to Arthur, at once towering over him and leaning on him, one arm on Arthur's shoulder, Sonny does not look, or seem, but *is* his age. It is almost certain that he will never see Arthur again. He will surely never see Paul again: but he is standing here, singing with Paul's son.

> *Carrying the staff,*
> *and the cross of redemption.*

Yes, Sonny Carr is old. For Arthur, he is unimaginably old. Standing next to him, Arthur can feel, as they sing together, the faint, uncontrollable tremor in the hand on his shoulder, the rasp at the bottom of his voice. His breath is slightly acrid from the years of women and whiskey and smoke; of wandering, rejection, silence, and sound; of wandering, of going under and rising up; of tears, and rage, and laughter and lust and tenderness. Arthur cannot imagine what lies be-

fore Sonny now. Does the road open, or does it close? Does he look
back, wishing to turn back? What does he remember?

He remembered my father, Arthur thinks, from when my father
was young. And that's how he recognized me.

But he is too young, by far, for these speculations. So far from trying to detach himself from memory, he is only beginning to acquire
one. Anguish is still, for him, a new and dreadful country, he has yet
to pitch his tent, and contest the weather there. Nor does he know
whether the road before him is open, or closed. *Oh, yes,* Sonny growls,
I know, and Arthur sings with him, the last lines of the last song they
sang together that night,

> *I'm pleased with what you've done,*
> *and your race has been run*
> *and I've brought you the key*
> *and I've got your key here with me*
> *and I praise God, I have another building,*
> *not made with hands!*

Guy and Arthur spend the night with Sonny and his friends, ending up having breakfast in Sonny's apartment, which is in a courtyard
off Pigalle. They get home long after the sun is up, and sleep till suppertime.

Then, there is, of course, their late, prolonged, and quiet suppertime. This is Friday night, and they agree that Arthur will leave on
Sunday night.

"Paris will be empty without you," says Guy, lying on the sofa, his
head in Arthur's lap. "I will miss you, *mon cher chanteur sauvage.* But
even if I were a million times more unhappy than I am, I could not be
sorry to have met you. It has meant very much to me, it has"—he
smiles up at Arthur—"given me the hope to live again."

"It's been beautiful for me, too," Arthur says. Then, "Let's not
spend the weekend saying good-bye. You know, shit, let's have a ball.
Like, let's go and price that raincoat tomorrow, for example, and let's

say good-bye at the airport, just like that. Because you'll see me again, baby, don't worry about it."

Guy grimaces. "Do not forget to send me tickets when you open at L'Olympia. That is where Josephine Baker, all the great ones, Trenet, Piaf, Montand—they all have sung there." Arthur grunts. "No, I am not kidding. You will surely sing there, one day."

Guy takes him to the airport on Sunday, and kisses him good-bye at the barrier. Arthur is wearing the raincoat he so admired, which Guy has insisted on buying for him. "That way, whenever it rains, you will surely think of me. Perhaps, there will be a deluge in America. That would please me very much."

He watches Arthur's back while Arthur gets his passport stamped. Then Arthur turns, one last time, and waves. Guy waves back. He feels tears gathering behind his eyes. Arthur's long, lean, loping figure disappears up the ramp.

Julia had flown from Abidjan to Paris the day before, and arrived in New York, on another flight, on that same Sunday. She had warned no one of her arrival except Jimmy, but Jimmy was in the South.

BOOK FIVE

❧

The Gates of Hell

It's me, it's me,
It's me, oh, Lord,
Standing in the need of prayer.

TRADITIONAL

I know my robe's going to fit me
   well
I tried it on at the gates of hell.

TRADITIONAL

YOU HAVE SENSED my fatigue and my panic, certainly, if you have followed me until now, and you can guess how terrified I am to be approaching the end of my story. It was not meant to be my story, though it is far more my story than I would have thought, or might have wished. I have wondered, more than once, why I started it, but— I know why. It is a love song to my brother. It is an attempt to face both love and death.

I have been very frightened, for: I have had to try to strip myself naked. One does not like what one sees then, and one is afraid of what others will see: and do. To challenge one's deepest, most nameless fears, is, also, to challenge the heavens. It is to drag yourself, and everyone and everything and *everyone* you love, to the attention of the fiercest of the gods: who may not forgive your impertinence, who may not spare you. All that I can offer in extenuation of my boldness is my love.

Today is Sunday, and I am alone in the house. Winter is in the air.

It was raining earlier, but now, the sun is out. A couple of hours ago, I watched Ruth and Tony and Odessa pile into the car, to drive to the city. Ruth is taking them to a matinee of *The Wiz.*

I was supposed to go, but, at the last moment, I asked Odessa to invite one of her girl friends. (I could not make the same suggestion to Tony, not out of even vaguely Puritanical motives, but, simply, to keep peace in the family. Odessa is persuaded that her brother is a sexist, and, considering my age, has her doubts about me. So. I'll make it up to Tony.)

I decided not to go, because, early this morning, Jimmy called, and said he'd like to see me, if I was free today. He's been busy, and I've been busy, and we haven't seen a lot of each other, and I know he's been working on his book. And he said that Julia had suggested that we come by for a drink.

The day proposed to me, in short, though somewhat more grueling than the matinee, was, equally, more urgent. Still, I feel a little guilty about not being with Ruth, and the children. But I have something, yet, to work out. I am not reconciled.

You would think that, at my age, I would be. But an age means absolutely nothing until it is *your* age, and then, you don't know what your age means. It doesn't mean any of the things you imagined it might mean. It doesn't mean that you are any wiser or any better or any different and it doesn't mean that you can easily become reconciled or that you can become reconciled at all.

Still, children are the beacon on this dark plain. They intimate what you must do, and dare: else, *they* never will be reconciled. I am their only key to their uncle, the vessel which contains, for them, his legacy. Only I can read this document for them. No more than I have dared to cheat in all that I have tried to say so far, do I dare cheat them.

Tony and Odessa: God knows what they are making of all this. I can see myself in them, for I know what we, the elders, made of all this. I can see what we were, and what we have become, and it really all happened in the twinkling of an eye. Not one of us saw our futures coming: we lived ourselves into our present, unimaginable states, until, abruptly, without ever having achieved a future, we were trying to decipher our past. Which is all right, too, I guess, on condition that one does not consider the past a matter for tears, recriminations, regrets. I am what I am, and what I have become. I wouldn't do it over if I could, and, if I could, if I had to do it over, I wouldn't know how. The very idea causes the spirit within me to grow faint with fatigue. No. Thank you: I do not forget that fire burns, that water overwhelms, rolls, and drags you under, that madness awaits in the valley, the mirror, and on the mountaintop. I have no regrets, I have no complaints: furthermore, I know very well that there is no complaint department. *I* will carry on from here, thank you. My hand is on the Gospel plow, and I wouldn't take nothing for my journey now.

But the children do not yet, of course, see themselves in us, are as imprisoned in their futures as we are in our pasts.

Jimmy's low-slung Triumph enters the driveway, and Jimmy steps out into the chilling, sunny, Sunday air. I watch him from the window. He is bare-headed, wearing a green military jacket and brown corduroy slacks, a black sweater. He takes a large paper bag out of the car.

As he reaches it, I open the door.

Jimmy gives me his quick, surprised grin. "Howdy, brother of mine. How you making it?"

"How *you* doing? I'm hanging in."

"That's better," he concedes, "than hanging up. I'm trying to hang in there, too." He puts the paper bag on the kitchen table. "I brought some beer, and stuff. So—the family's gone with *The Wiz?*"

"That's right. Without the old man."

He gives me a consoling pat on the shoulder. "Don't despair. It's a big hit, you'll get a chance to see it."

"Thanks." Jimmy takes off his jacket, and goes into the living room. "What time is it?"

"Close to four."

"What time is Julia expecting us?"

"Oh. When we get there. We can call."

"Are you hungry? You want a drink, or what?"

"I don't know. It's early. Let me have a beer."

"You want a glass?"

"No."

I go into the living room with two cans of beer. Jimmy is standing near the piano.

"Some days, I don't know if I'm trying to write a book, or trying to write a symphony." He takes the beer, and sits down on the sofa.

I sit down in the big chair facing him. "How's it going?"

"I don't know. It's kicking my ass, though, I'll tell you that."

I smile, and watch his face. He looks very, as we say these days, together; lean, single-minded, calm. Calm may not be quite the word: his stillness is the stillness of someone paying absolute attention, of someone quietly paying his dues. "I wanted to see you, but now, I can hardly say why. Well. You know what I mean. But maybe I just wanted to be able to check out my sense of reality. Because, memory, man, when you start fucking around with memory, that can be a bitch."

He takes a swallow of his beer, and smiles at me. "It's true. I was trying to remember the very first time I saw Arthur. Of course, that's bullshit, what difference does it make? But it was like a game I was playing with myself. It seemed to me, when we were running together, that he'd always been there, like I'd known him all my life." He looks at me. "But that doesn't jibe with the fact that I always felt that he'd made a great difference in my life." He rises, and goes to his jacket, and takes out his cigarettes, lights one, sits down again, handing me the pack. He lights my cigarette for me. "It's almost like—everything that happened to me *before* Arthur—didn't happen," and he pauses, frowns. "I think I understand that—but—they *did* happen, that's why he made such a difference." He laughs. "You see what I mean."

"Yes. But the first time you saw Arthur must have been at church."

"I know—like I know the first time I ever saw *you* was at church. But those churches all run together. I've blurred them all together. For me, church was mainly Julia—well, Julia, and my mother—I hated when Sunday came. It just meant that everybody was going to be all up on top of Julia, and pissing on me, and I think I must just have slept through all that. I hardly remember Arthur in the church. I remember"—this with a surprising shyness, and sipping his beer—"when you took us to the ice cream parlor. I thought we almost got to be friends that day, Arthur and me. Damn, I sure wanted a friend. But, no. He kept me waiting for a while."

"Why did you wait?"

"Oh, come on. Who knows?" Then, he laughs. "Well. It wasn't like I had so many other things to do."

He leans back on the sofa. "I think I knew something, somewhere. Like, you know, I hated Julia, but, at the same time, I knew something else."

"Well. Julia was in your way."

"Man, I always felt that nobody wanted to hang out with *me* because I had this *freak* of a holy sister!"

We both laugh. Then Jimmy says abruptly, "But Julia felt that, too, though—all that shit, back there, has a lot to do with Julia, until today. And—tell you something else—if it hadn't been for Julia, I might never have seen Arthur again." He looks up at me, looking very much as he had, years ago, when everything was beginning. "I'm not making any sense, am I?—just going around in circles."

Arthur had come back into his life after everything else had gone out of it—his mother and his father, and, for a very long time, his sister. I thought I could see why Jimmy's memory drew a blank. Furthermore, there was the church before Arthur, and the church after Arthur. And the church after Arthur—the church in which Jimmy functioned, at first without Arthur, and, then, briefly, with him—was in the apocalyptic South, on a battlefield. There was more than enough reason for the memory to stammer.

Jimmy sets his beer down on the coffee table, and walks to the piano. He stares at it for a while, then sits down. He lifts up the cover, and touches the keys. He looks over at me. "I found it hard to touch a piano for a while." He plays a chord. "But playing all over, like I did—that helped me."

Then he shakes his head, leaves the piano, and comes and stands in the middle of the room. "Look. I've been keeping to myself, you know, just working, making it on home, watching TV, if I don't get home too late, not seeing nobody. And I woke up this morning, all of a sudden, around four or five o'clock, and I thought to myself, Damn, baby, you're only thirty-seven, you're supposed to be living, you are *supposed* to have a *life*. And you're still fucking around here, in sack-cloth and ashes. What is *wrong* with you?" He puts his hands in his pockets, takes them out, looks at his hands. "I didn't know it took so long, because I know he's"—but he has to catch his breath before he can say the word—"dead. And I know he loved me, and doesn't want me to suffer, he wants me to live. I know. But I just don't seem to have any interest in—anything, really—and I just cannot imagine having an interest in any *body*. It's like my life stopped, too, in London. I still wish I'd gone with him." He stops. "That's what I can't get out of my mind, it's like that's almost all I remember, and that's so fucking stupid, and it's *wrong*!" He stops, smiles, looks at me, tears standing in his eyes. "I didn't come here to have a tantrum all over your nice clean carpet."

"Have a tantrum. I don't mind. I don't mind for *me*, that is. But you're still feeling guilty, and that *is* stupid—you don't have anything to feel guilty about."

Arthur had been singing on the Paris music-hall stage. He and Jimmy had had a fight in Paris, and that was why Arthur had left for London without him. But Jimmy had planned to pick him up in London, and travel with him back to the United States.

Arthur had been very difficult those last months. I remembered very well. He had been difficult with *me*. He frightened me. I had begun to realize that he hated what he was doing. He did not know how to stop, and I did not know how to stop him. Jimmy had tried to stop him by threatening to leave, to cease being his accompanist. And, in fact, he had not played for Arthur that last night in Paris, and this is what torments him still.

But Arthur, who had always been able to drink, had begun to drink with a difference, and he had discovered drugs—nothing more than hashish, Jimmy hoped, but he didn't know: cocaine, and heroin, were also floating around, and there were some very creepy people in the world which had begun to encircle Arthur. And Jimmy had had to deal with all that. He lived with my brother. I didn't. And, if love and fear sometimes caused Jimmy to blow his stack, who can blame him? Arthur often made *me* blow *my* stack, too, but then, I repeat, I wasn't living with him.

"That's true," Jimmy says. "I *know* that. But how long will it be before I *believe* it?" He blows his nose, and goes back to the piano.

"Would you," I ask carefully, "like a *real* drink now? Or do you want to wait until we get to Julia's?"

"I'll have it now," he says cheerfully, "if you'll join me. Light on the usual, heavy on the rocks."

I go into the kitchen to do this. Jimmy begins improvising on the piano, around "Here Comes the Sun," blending it with "Oh Happy Day," and threatening, generally, to work himself up into a fine camp-meeting frenzy. It sounds very clear and beautiful, in my empty house, on this chilly, sunlit Sunday.

I find the glasses and ice cubes, run water over the ice, and the music, somehow, blends with the feel of the cold, running water, the feel of the ice cubes, and the many lights the light strikes from them, and the light on my hands. I pour the dark, honey-colored whiskey into glasses like kaleidoscopes, as chords crash in the living room, and I realize that Jimmy is praying, is praying as hard as he knows how.

I stand for a moment, then, at the kitchen window, watching the trees, and the yard, and the quiet street beyond, listening to a sound which remains, in essence, strange and menacing for this place.

I come back into the room, and Jimmy finishes, elaborately, resoundingly, and stands up, and takes his glass.

"Cheers," we both say, and sit down. We talk of other things, work, money, politics, color—music, finally, for Jimmy says suddenly, "It might really turn into a symphony. It might not be a book."

I decide not to go, after all, to Julia's with him, for, now, the sun is going down, and my tribe will be leaving the city, heading home, and I feel that I should be with them.

When Arthur arrived from Paris, on that far-off Sunday, he had taken a taxi across the Williamsburg Bridge straight to his loft on Dey Street, and then, he had called me from there. I had not been in when he first called; he got me later, and we saw each other that night, and, more or less, figured out our next trip south.

Arthur had started to call Jimmy, then decided to put it off. He had been afraid. Yet, he knew, somehow, that he was certain, now, to see him.

Julia had, finally, come through Customs at about the time Arthur arrived at his loft, and had gone straight to the flat on 18th Street.

New York seemed very strange, after the landscape to which she had chained herself for so long. She felt dizzy with space, awkward with freedom: she wondered if she could ever live here again. Jimmy's note, which was several weeks old, did not surprise her. She thought of calling me, then decided to get her bearings first: and she was not sure that she had the right to call me. There were many things she wanted, indeed, needed, to talk about with someone; but, apart from us, the Montanas, that is, and her brother, she really had no friends here.

She had made two friends in Abidjan, both women, one very old, and they had not wanted her to leave, to return to her mysteriously barbaric country. But she had felt herself beginning to shrivel in the French West African outpost. If she had wanted to find another definition of what it meant to be a woman, and especially a black woman, well, then, she had found it: but it did not appear to be a role that she could play.

Now, she did not exist, on two continents.

She had set down her bags, read Jimmy's note, then gone into the bathroom, and run a bath as hot as she could bear it. Then she had undressed swiftly, as though discarding all evidence of her voyage. She had looked into the mirror. The African sun had darkened her skin and coarsened her hair: and she liked that. But she did not know—yet—what she had gained, or lost. She felt that she had gained—something—something for which she had, as yet, no words. Perhaps she had come home in order to make an assessment which could be made nowhere else.

She had filled the tub with bath salts, and stepped into the tub, sinking into the heat, gratefully, scrubbing herself with a rough sponge, scrubbing her hair as though she meant to tear something from her skull, her brain, scrubbing her body as though to wash it of sin. And she had actually thought that, her movements made her think that; perhaps, indeed, that was what she had always thought. She had lain still for a while, resting in the water, as still as leaves on ponds she had seen in the airless noon. She had touched her body, her loins: not even Africa had been able to make her fertile.

Then she had rubbed her body with her oils and perfumes, some of her fatigue subsiding into a kind of luxurious, lonely languor. But her loneliness was very particular, and it seemed that it would never end. And her beauty accused her.

She had put on her long, gray robe, and gone into the living room, and poured herself a drink. She had lit a cigarette, sitting in vigil over her life.

Arthur had come back to America with the intention of going south, and he began preparing for his journey at once. I hadn't, yet, done everything necessary to free myself to go with him. One reason was that I was weary of compromise, and was considering burning my bridges. And the other reason was that I had just met Ruth. These reasons—with hindsight, one may say, of course—were to prove to be the very same reason: but, at the time I am speaking of, I was feeling my way.

But we managed to get it all together. It wasn't easy for me, and it wasn't easy for Arthur: and it turned out to be my first rehearsal as Arthur's manager.

Arthur was not a star then, had no money except the money he made on the road. Also, a crucial matter which Ruth was the first to point out to me, he had virtually no clothes. Arthur thought of himself as dressed, when, in fact, he was merely covered, and, if asked, would have said that he loved to "dress." But, in fact, as distinguished from his moving delusion, he lived, mainly, in old shirts, slacks, sweaters, and shit-kickers, went shopping only when he could no longer possibly avoid it, or when he saw something in a window, went in, bought it, and walked out: this always made him feel so tremendously virtuous that whatever he had bought would have worn out long before Arthur realized that it was time to go "shopping" again. As he was the very last person in the world to have been forced to live his life in a goldfish bowl, he was, of all voyagers, the least capable of packing a suitcase. His idea of packing was to throw everything he saw into a suitcase and close it, and rush to the next plane—he never thought of opening the closets, or the drawers. Thus, throughout what we call the "civilized" world, and even beyond its borders, there is an appalling chain of Arthur's watches, charm bracelets, rings, lockets, combs, brushes, socks, shorts, shirts, ties, tiepins, cufflinks, jackets, trousers, shoes, wallets, address books, records, photographs, books, awards, appeals, fan mail, invitations, oil paintings, watercolors, notes, and scrolls, letters unanswered and letters unfinished.

To reproach him for this was utterly useless: one had to learn to take these aspects of Arthur into account when dealing with him.

Of course, our first problem was money—the walking-up-and-down and shopping money, sometimes known as "front" money: the money which pays for the "front." We called it cash; we had, of course, no credit. There had been no record offers worth considering. All this was about to change, but we didn't know that, then.

There was no money in the South, and managers are in business to make money. A minority of performers in any area become "stars," but those who are not stars work enough, nevertheless, to keep various functionaries in bread-and-butter money. Arthur couldn't be booked into the Copacabana or Vegas, but he was valuable on the college circuit; his reputation was growing in rather unexpected places. San Francisco-Oakland, for example, Seattle, Philadelphia, New York, of course, sections of New Jersey, Boston—and, for some reason, Vancouver, Toronto, Montreal, and London. These were the places his agency wanted to book him, naturally. Anyway, they *couldn't* book him—*they* couldn't—into places like Savannah, Tallahassee, New Orleans, Birmingham, Memphis, and so forth. They wouldn't have known how to get him out of the hands of the sheriff, or off the chain gang, or out of prison. They didn't want him to get hurt, and this concern came, very often, out of genuine affection. But they also didn't want him, certainly not at the very beginning of his "promising" career, to be too closely associated with what was, after all, an exceedingly controversial, and, finally, unpopular cause. Furthermore, as J. Edgar's demise has permitted my innocent countrymen to discover, exceedingly brutal pressures could be brought to bear on all kinds of persons, and corporations, and in all kinds of ways. Arthur, himself, was not yet that visible, but some of his handlers were.

Anyway, the money in the South, then, was needed for bail-bond money, fees, and food. One was not, according to Arthur, supposed to carry anything out of the South, except one's person, if possible: and I agreed with him.

This meant that Arthur had to pay for the southern road by—going on the road. While his managers were busy booking him into places where he could pick up some change, I was busy booking him into places where he couldn't: Arthur's booking in Vancouver, for example, would pay for our journey to Jackson, Mississippi.

It was marvelous for me. I loved it. It was something I wanted to do: and I discovered that I *could* do it. Anyway, I had to, I was the synchronizer of the watches.

Let us say that Arthur, working his way down from Vancouver, has dates in Seattle, and Boston. From Boston, he is to pick me up in New York, and fly to various points south.

And Montreal, let us say, having heard that Arthur has been a sensation in Vancouver, wants Arthur on a day when I know he must be in Tuskegee.

"I'm sorry, it's not possible," I say, into the breathing phone. "Mr. Montana is booked for that day—in fact, for that entire week—"

"Booked? Booked where?"

"In colleges and churches in the South, sir."

"Oh. May I ask—who am I speaking to?"

"My name is Hall."

"Well—Mr. Hall—"

I learned one thing at once. They always felt that the bottom difficulty was money, and they always raised the price. So, naturally, later, I began at the highest price last quoted, and, then, sometimes, doubled it, feeling my way.

I found out. But that's another story. Arthur found out, too, in a way, but never in the way that I did, and that's because he had another assignment. I began to understand our connecting conditions. This was partly through Ruth, who worked with me during this first rehearsal, and who should have won several Oscars for her performances on the phone.

Time out, while I tell you how I met Ruth:

One of the black organizations—still called Negro, in those years—was throwing a party, either in victory or lamentation, I don't remember, somewhere in midtown Manhattan. I had to be there, because of my job. Arthur had said that he'd try to be there, but he never showed. When I think about it, I can say only that the pulse of the party was neither victory nor lamentation, neither moaning nor tambourines. The real pulse, at many speeds, was, simply, resolution.

There was much fire-baptized and shining hair. The Afro was, then, just around the corner—the far corner, that is; having, as of now, very lately, disappeared around the nearest one. There were many hats, some designed, apparently, by architects: neither the bu-

bu nor the dashiki had yet appeared, demanding to be addressed in Swahili. Oh, the brothers and the sister were "heavy," but, mainly, they were wearily resolute. If they flaunted such a vast amount of surface, it was to make certain that anyone misled by the surface would crash through the ice, and drown. Their note of resolution was countered by their knowledge that they, themselves, were tiptoeing, slipping, or striding, inches over an icy grave. But they had been, after all, through the fire.

The brothers were, by far, less dazzling, mute, one might almost say, covered by the decent, self-effacing, missionary cloth. Whereas the ladies wore hair, they had eyes.

There I was, anyway, one of the brothers, his life wedged tightly up his ass, utilizing, like a shield, the obligatory glass, and smiling the obligatory smile. The party was in a townhouse, a house on the East Side, a house like the houses in Henry James. The host was a descendant, bore the name, of one of the country's most terrifying, lethal financiers, one of the century's most renowned plunderers, hailed from sea to shining sea. Well. He hoped to purchase something out of all our desperate, surface splendor. He was a nice man, a very sincere man. I talked to him as long as I could, insofar as I could, but that wasn't long. My sphincter muscle was tiring: I had to escape with my life. He couldn't help but look, poor man, as though he'd been trapped in some resounding slave-auction, on the auctioneer's day off.

I walked down a flight of stairs, intending to ease my way out of here—Arthur wasn't coming. I was at the head of a second flight of stairs when someone stopped me, someone I knew vaguely, someone, let us say, from a rival firm, another kind of pirate, an adventurer in the antipoverty bullshit type.

He was black, though not, I hope, like me—in fact, he was gingerbread-colored—and I grinned at him as he grinned at me. His name, which I always thought was unfortunate, was Roy Furlong. Some of us described him as, *for me, but not for long!*

"How you doing?"

"You see me standing here. How about you?"

"Beautiful." He whispered, I can't imagine why, the FBI knew everything already. "Getting some bucks for my theater, man."

"Oh? Crazy. Where's your theater?"

"Ain't no big thing, you understand—just my loft down on the East Side—off the Bowery. Got the kids making sets out of old bedsheets, and mops, and raggedy blankets. We spray them with paint, you know—even got somebody's mama's old washing board!" He laughed, his fox-face leaning in toward me.

"Beautiful," I said.

"I been looking for your brother—somebody said he was going to be here tonight. Is he here?"

"I don't think so. I haven't seen him."

"If you ain't seen him, he ain't here. Tell you what I'd like him to do—come on down, and give them kids a kick in the ass—sing them a little gospel, let them know where they come from."

I thought, *Wow.* "Those kids come from all kinds of places," I said. "Like Catholic parishes and Russian synagogues and Chinese temples—"

"That's just the point, man—one song from Arthur, and they'll shake all that shit together." He lowered his voice. "And it'd be great publicity for the school—you know, we let a couple of the black brothers in the media in on it, you dig, and *they'll* cover it, and it would be great publicity for your brother, too." He smiled, very pleased with himself. "Everybody gets a little taste."

I might now have made the really ridiculous error of pointing out that it didn't seem to me that the children were going to be given very much of a "taste"—had opened my mouth to frame the words, when a heavy-set girl, wearing a tan cape, and a hat which looked like a demented Chinese pagoda, appeared out of the confusion around us, and tapped Roy on the shoulder.

"You told me it had a money-back guarantee," she said, "and it *didn't.*" She pursed her lips. "Now I don't have to tell you what I *could* do to your ass."

"Ruth, honey!" Roy cried, throwing his arms around her, and kissing her—partly, I felt, to shut her up, in case she was not really joking. "You been here all night? I didn't see you!"

"I've been skulking corners, listening to you peddle your wares. I am wired for sound, all the way to my teeth—you just wait, Mr. Furlong, until I turn in my report!"

Roy said, "You wouldn't do nothing to hurt me, sugar, I know that." He turned to me, with some relief. "Have you two met? This is Ruth Granger, we used to work together a while back. Ruth, this is Hall Montana."

We shook hands. I liked the feel of her hand in mine. "I'm glad to meet you, Mr. Montana. Have you known this medicine man long?"

"We run into each other at parties," I said.

"Ah. *Fund*-raising parties. Of course," she said, and grinned at Roy.

Roy laughed, and raised his hands, helplessly. "I don't know why you so down on me, mama. I declare. What can I do to please you?" and he looked at me in what he thought was mock-despair. "I see you're not drinking. Can I get you a drink?"

I said, "*I* will get the lady a drink. We will leave you here, to plot and scheme some *other* way of getting back into the lady's good graces." I grinned at Ruth. "*May* I?"

She was also carrying a rather menacing shoulder bag, which she now shifted to the opposite shoulder, so that she could take my arm: she was accoutered, definitely, for any improbability. "I think you have found the perfect solution," she said, and smiled sweetly at Roy. "Good night, Mr. Furlong!" and we moved back into the crowd.

I hadn't meant to do this, had really meant to go. But, once I had seen Ruth's face, under that absurd and winning hat, and been exposed to all her preposterous paraphernalia—well, my mood changed, I was no longer that anxious to be alone. I liked her. She was funny. She was direct. I did not dream of attempting to imagine her history. When she laughed, she looked exactly like a calculating, ten-year-old shoeshine boy. She was heavy-set, but she wasn't fat—a big-boned chick—and, ordering all that solidity, at the center, was a hurt and courageous little girl. I sensed all this, in the way one senses things. I liked her.

It's strange, but when a man likes a woman from the git-go, he tends not to think of her as a woman: this comes later, if it comes at all. In the beginning, he is simply relieved that he is not being forced into attempting a conquest. He is relieved to be released from his role. Much later, he may realize that he has been released from a delusion which menaced both the woman and himself. And a woman then becomes a much more various and beautiful creation than she has been before.

If Ruth's exterior was elaborate, not to say strong-willed, her tastes were simple. She was not longing for a Brandy Alexander, for example, or a sticky sweet Manhattan, or something preciously French, or Russian, but took what we were, finally, able to get, two Dewars on the rocks. Then, we made our way back to the staircase where we had met. Ruth put her shoulder bag on the floor, and sat down on the top step.

I don't know why we hadn't, already, simply decided to leave the place, but I think we both felt, in our different fashions, that this might have been, disastrously, to risk moving too fast: curious to observe how we act on what we don't yet know that we know.

I sat down on the step below her, my back leaning against the iron grille of the balustrade.

"I'm glad to meet you," I said, "but I really can't resist asking you—how, and where—did you get that hat?"

She laughed, and touched the remarkable thing. "You remember Hattie McDaniel, she played Mammy in *Gone With the Wind*?"

"Yes."

"Well, you remember, somebody finally gives her something— scarlet petticoats, no less—"

"I think it was actually Clark Gable who gave them to her—I really don't *dare* think—but anyway, she *shows* them to Clark Gable—stop *laughing*—"

"I can't—and—?"

She touched her hat again. "We all have our different ways of seeking approval. With Gable, I admit, I blew it, but there'll be others. I just want them to see how well it becomes me—what they gave me."

I am sure that I had begun to look somewhat alarmed, for she laughed, and said, "No. It's just a fun, insane hat. It's got something to do with what these people call serendipity. I bought it on an *especially* rainy afternoon, and I wear it when I'm in a certain mood."

"What mood is that?"

"Oh. When I want them to see the hat before they see me."

"But that doesn't work. The moment I saw the hat, I wanted to see *you.*"

"That means that you are abnormal, and, possibly, dangerous—you suspect the possibility of cause and effect."

We both laughed loud enough for people to turn and look at us.

"Where are you from, child?"

"Mississippi delta. Been up South awhile."

"How do you know Roy Furlong?"

"Is there any way *not* to know him?" She grinned, and sipped her drink. "I used to be private secretary to"—she named a black actress-singer, who had died about a year before—"and she got roped into one of his 'benefits,' and I had to curse him out a couple of times."

She reached behind her, and rummaged in her shoulder bag, and found a pack of cigarettes. She offered me a cigarette, lit mine, lit hers. She put the cigarettes back in the bag. "We aren't what you would call intimate friends."

"I gathered that."

"That wasn't hard, I hope. In spite of the hat."

"No. *Because* of the hat."

She laughed. "Thank God. Now, I won't have to wear it for at least a month."

We had both finished our drinks. I said, "Why don't we get out of here? If you're not in a hurry, I'd like to buy you a nightcap someplace. Okay?"

"Okay," she said, and rose, stealing a glance at her watch as she did so. I took both our empty glasses, and left them on one of the tables near the head of the stairs. She shouldered her bag, and we went down the stairs, smiling and nodding at various points and people, hoping not to be intercepted either by Furlong, or our host: who were almost certainly, however, by now, busily exchanging fantasies, reveling in each other. We got into the wind. Ruth had her car, and so we drove to Small's Paradise, and sat there, drinking and talking until about two or three in the morning, comparing the Indian-stained Africas in which each of us had first seen the light of day. Ruth had then lived on Riverside Drive in the nineties, which meant that we were practically neighbors, and she drove me home, dropping me at my door. We were going to see each other for lunch, in the next couple of days. I remember watching her drive away before I turned into my building, and wondering why I felt so wearily peaceful, so tremendously at ease.

We went south, as scheduled, into a punishing climate. I do not mean, now, merely the seasonal climate, or the climate of my heart, or Arthur's. I mean something harder than that, harder to define. It was the climate created by something riding on the wind. It was as though the landscape awaited the scalding purification of the latter rain— the ruthless and liberating definition. This was in the faces, the voices, the accents, in the horror of what could not be said.

We flew from city to city, but drove from town to town, walked many a dusty road, crossed endless railroad tracks, walked under many an underpass, saw endless depots, warehouses, scrap heaps, houses abandoned on the edge of town, tough weeds threatening wood and stone, passed many a quiet evening veranda, entered many a church and hovel, saw many and many a child. We both realized, at once, wordlessly, that we were still searching for vanished Peanut, for light, reddish-colored Alexander Theophilus Brown. He was absent from every room we entered, threatened to appear at every corner, whispered in the rising and the setting sun. We didn't speak of him— we couldn't; we couldn't say to each other that we had entered a state like madness. We lived in pain and terror, unrelenting, walked in the shadow of death, and the shadow of death was in every eye. It was in the eyes of the men and women willing and anxious to accomplish our destruction, and in the eyes of the black people who were watching us, and watching the eyes which watched us. No one ever spoke of this, any more than my brother and I ever spoke of Peanut. Yet everything referred to—all that could not be said.

It could not be said that kinsman was facing kinsman, but it was nothing less than that: father slaughtering son, brother castrating brother, mother betraying lover, sister denying sister—kissing cousins chaining kissing cousins, tracking them down with dogs, gutting them like cattle, as they had sold them like cattle. Said: it could not be whispered. Whispered: it could not be dreamed. Dreamed: it could not be confessed. Not all of the sheriff's children are white, this knowledge was in every eye. Not all of my mother's children are black. This knowledge, which is the same knowledge, was also in every eye, but with a difference.

This difference is the difference between flight and confrontation. Or, if I may stoop to borrow from a lexicon stupefying in its absolute and desperately sincere dishonesty, it is the difference between being black, or white. The words seem infantile and weightless in such a context, words absurdly trivial to account for so lethal a storm: but I have had to stoop, as I told you, and borrow from a book I did not, thank heaven, write. For, these were the only two words uttered, all that could be said, all that could be heard riding on the southern wind. If I could scarcely believe my ears, if it diminished me to see that we could be so basely craven, yet, I had to hear it, for I was traveling with my brother, and we trembled for our lives. For them, we were black, and that was all there was to it. Oh, I might like to laugh, and perhaps my life was dear to me, perhaps my fingers were capable of field-stripping a rifle, or playing a violin, perhaps I loved my wife, my son, or my daughter, or my brother, perhaps I, too, like all men, knew that I was born to die. None of this mattered, none of this contributed the faintest hair's-breadth to the balance, for I was black. If I could not conveniently die, or decently smile, gratefully labor, then I should be carried to a place of execution, the dogs to feast on my sex; fire, air, wind, water, and, at last, the earth, my bones: it came to that, for me and mine, and in my own country, which I loved so much, and which I helped to build.

I watched the eyes of the black men and women, watching the eyes watching us. The eyes held pity and scorn, and a distant amusement—and calculation, for, after all, surrender was not a possibility. You may be blind, the eyes seemed to say, but *I* can see, and I see *you*. It is hardly possible that I have been here with you, for so long, and have endured so much at your hands, and yet, have loved you so much, and washed your naked body so often, spanked your children into what they were able to grasp of maturity (for *you* were not a model!) watched you when you thought you were safe (and, therefore, had no use for me) opened my door to you when the web of safety broke and sent you crashing down (and what other door would have opened? Your friends are all like you) walked to the graveyard with you, and to the christening, Lord, on the mountain, in the valley, trumpets, trombones, and melancholy, leading you to rock your soul in that one more river, do you now suppose that this density of passionate connection has turned me into nothing more than a peculiar mirror, reflecting only what you want to see? What do I care, if you are white? *Be* white: I do not have to prove my color. I wouldn't be compelled to see *your* color, if you were not so anxious to prove it. Why? And to me, of all people.—But I know why. You are afraid that you have been here with me too long, and are not really white anymore. That's probably true, but you were never really white in the first place. Nobody is. Nobody has, even, ever *wanted* to be white, unless they are afraid of being black. But being black is nothing to be afraid of. I knew that before I met you, and I have learned it again, through you.

Perhaps being white is not a conceivable condition, but a terrifying fantasy, a moral choice. Certainly, the punishing climate through which Arthur and I were walking resembled nothing so much as a terrified fantasy, and was the result, incontestably, of a moral choice.

By the time we got to Florida, we had lost weight, were running low on money, and had lost the pianist, a Harlem boy named Scott, to the chain gang. This was in Montgomery, Alabama, an angular town so white that it seems dead, like a bone bleaching in the desert. There are towns like that, towns with colors that stay in the mind: Jerusalem, for example, really *is* golden, as the sun drops behind those weary, sacred hills. As the sun leaves Montgomery, one is reminded of nothing so much as the smokeless, fiery, alabaster gates of hell.

Scott was a loudmouthed Harlem boy of about twenty-two, ill-equipped for nonviolence, but willing to try it, kidnapped, in Montgomery—I refuse to use the legal word, "arrested"—for spitting on the sidewalk, and, as it turned out, having no money in his pockets. The charge was vagrancy, and, for good measure, due to his loud-mouthed, disorderly conduct, and he was sentenced to ninety days. This was at dusk, while we were sitting in the hotel room, waiting for him. We went on to the church, the ministers began calling the police, we got through a quite indescribable night: and didn't find out what had happened to Scott until late the next afternoon. By that time, he was on the chain gang.

A great deal can happen to a man in ninety days, and this is why Scott was not escorted back to the hotel, where he was registered, and where we had the cash to prove that he was not a vagrant. As for the disorderly conduct charge, running off at the mouth a little when accosted by strangers, in or out of uniform, is one of the American's most sacred attributes. When kidnapped for spitting in the gutter of the alabaster city, Scott said nothing that America has not been applauding for generations, whenever it was said by, for example, John Wayne, or, for that matter, J. Edgar Hoover. Nothing succeeds like success.

We had to raise the bail-bond money, an arbitrary, but far from trifling sum. Arthur wired his agency, and their lawyer—it was the first time I realized that *we* didn't have a lawyer—and I wired the magazine, and their lawyer. We hoped that we had intimidated the authorities enough to prevent Scott from following Peanut. But we couldn't depend on that, either in or out of Dixie, down South, or up South. *We* had to raise the money, and come back with it in our pockets and hand it to the judge and pick up Scott and limp back north, somehow. For the first time, Arthur would have to pocket his southern honorarium: we couldn't miss, or cancel, a single date, and so we got to Florida.

We were not unaware, although it could not be said, that kidnapping Scott was a way of menacing Arthur. They were brandishing the popular sign, still waiting, patiently, in various closets, to be brought back into daylight: *Nigger, read this and run. If you can't read, run anyhow!*

They, too, remembered Peanut. They didn't want us to forget him.

And so we arrived at the basement of that church, in the backwoods of Florida, where a Jimmy so thin I hardly recognized him was sitting on a table, wearing an old torn sweater, and eating a sandwich.

I didn't recognize him, because, for the first time, he reminded me of Julia: and I had just met Ruth. I know it sounds ridiculous, but it was something like that, as though, when I saw him, I blinked my eyes against a sudden, too strong light.

"Welcome to the slaughter, children!"

And we followed him upstairs, into the main body of the church. He sat down at the piano, and Arthur began to sing, and so they began, at last, their time together.

"You think you might be ready to carry me up them stairs now, man?"

"Yes. I think I might be ready."

"You sure kept me waiting."

"I didn't mean to. I couldn't help it."

"I was calling you a whole gang of motherfuckers, man."

"I guess you were."

"Didn't you think about me? Naw—you didn't think about me."

"Oh, yes. I did."

"What did you think? Did you think I'd just be waiting—like a chump?"

"I—just hoped you'd be glad to see me. I couldn't think any further than that."

"Were you glad to see *me?*"

"You *know* I was glad to see you."

"How'd it go in London?"

"Okay."

"How was Paris? what did you do there?"

"Oh—walked around. Saw some monuments."

"Like what?"

"Oh—the Arch of Triumph."

"It's beautiful, right?"

"Very beautiful. But I wasn't there long."

"We'll go there together?"

"If you want."

"Oh. You are so full of shit, man."

"I was only kidding. I wasn't planning to go without you."

"You better not. I been waiting, man, a long time, for you."

And Jimmy turns toward Arthur, who pulls him into his arms. They are in Jimmy's bed, at the back of the house where Jimmy stays. It is about two o'clock in the morning.

The house is very quiet, as are the streets outside. Jimmy and Arthur are very quiet, too, very peaceful; it is as though each has, finally, come home.

They had been intensely, incredibly aware of each other in the church, but had spoken very little. They had been surrounded, they were busy, Arthur was tense, worried, and exhausted. Behind him was the image of Scott on the chain gang, and, before him, the question of his performance at the rally. There would not be time to eat, or to change. He had known, sensed, that, somehow, he would soon see Jimmy, and had been longing to see him. But he had also been afraid to see him, and it seemed vindictive on the part of fate to have arranged for them to meet under such grueling circumstances, at this moment, and in this place.

Nevertheless, imperceptibly, the atmosphere between them began to ease as they dealt with the music. Each sensed the other, swiftly and precisely: it was, suddenly, quite amazing to realize that they had never before worked together. Without having had an instant to mention the past, they found themselves becoming comrades in the present, and the music, indeed, had already begun to move them into the future: if they could play this way together, they would certainly be fools to lose each other now!

So their anticipation, however reluctantly, increased. Perhaps they were richer than they had thought.

We liberated, without, on the whole, recuperating, Scott, and limped back into New York, and Julia called me. She had just seen Jimmy, who, both weary and exultant, had arrived to put his bags down; and Arthur arrived very shortly afterward, to pick Jimmy up. So there were the four of us reunited, though I was not present: and the moment the two younger brothers left her loft, Julia got me on the phone.

It was a Saturday, late afternoon, early evening. I was alone, playing records, and kind of half reading, and thinking of tomorrow, when I would be seeing Ruth. (I had called her. She was going to try to get out of a previous dinner date, and have dinner with me.)

She was to call me back. In the long meanwhile, I was free. I knew that I would not be seeing Arthur or Jimmy tonight. I had no duties of any kind, except to Hall. I had decided that I would not go out. I would telephone for a Chinese dinner, take a shower, and watch television. And I had taken off my shoes and socks and trousers, preparing to go into the shower, when the phone rang.

I was sure it was Ruth. I pad-padded happily over to the phone, and picked up the receiver, looking out at still, cold West End Avenue, absently scratching my belly button, and my balls.

"Hello! What's the verdict?"

One should never, never do that: never anticipate the voice at the other end, never assume you know to whom you are speaking. The voice I heard sliced me as cleanly as a razor. The sweat suddenly dripping from my armpits slid down my body as smoothly, as crucially, as my blood would have run down, had I been slit from armpit to thigh. "Hall—?"

I knew her name, and I wanted to call her name, but I couldn't. For some reason, I grabbed my dick. The houses across the street seemed, with a hostile attention, to tilt toward me.

"It's Julia."

"I know. How are you, child?"

"Oh. The verdict isn't in yet."

"That wasn't meant for you," I said, now feeling very awkward indeed, and wishing that I had said something else, at the very same moment that she laughed, and said, "Oh, I know it wasn't for me. How are you, Hall?"

"I've been worse. I've been better."

My dick began to stiffen under my hand. This frightened me, and made me angry at Julia. Then, insanely, it made me angry at Ruth.

"I'd like to see you, Hall."

I'd like to see you, too. "Sure. When?"

"Well, I just saw your long-lost brother, along with *my* little long-lost brother, and so I know you must be tired—"

"I'm not *that* tired. When did you get back?"

"Oh, around the time that Arthur got back, I guess. But I didn't know where any of *you* were."

"Well, the Lord knows, child, we didn't know where *you* were."

Stop calling her child. *It's none of your business where she's been, or was.*

I began to be frightened. I ached more and more. I had come to the phone anticipating Ruth. My prick was heavy, getting hard, and I did not know if this ache was hope, or memory, nor could I, any longer, tell the difference.

"Well. You always warned me that I might find myself in Timbuktu."

"Girl, even Timbuktu has got to have post offices, and telegraph and telephone wires."

"Well"—and she laughed—"that's one of the strange things about Timbuktu. Sometimes, it looks like they do. Then when you look again, they don't."

"That sounds a little like you and me."

"Not really. I hear you. But—not really."

There was a silence. I ached, as helpless, now, as only a grown man can be.

"Do you want to see me tonight?"

I wanted her to say yes. I wanted her to say no. I wanted to get in, or get out.

"No—not tonight. Tomorrow?"

"I—I think I'm tied up for dinner—tomorrow night—"

I started to say, *But maybe I can break it,* but I didn't.

"What about lunch?"

"That would be cool."

"Well—shall we arrange it now, or shall I call you in the morning?"

"We can arrange it now."

"Okay. Why don't we meet—oh, on the steps of Carnegie Hall, at one thirty? Then we'll decide where to go from there."

"All right."

"Good-bye, Hall. Have a good night—get some sleep."

"Yes—Julia?"

"Yes—?"

"I'll be very glad to see you. It was beautiful, hearing your voice."

She seemed to catch her breath. Then, "I think I may have begun to learn something—in Timbuktu. But you're the only person I can tell. You're the only person who might know."

My ache began to subside, and, yet, began to rise, into another, sweeter, more inexorable sorrow.

"Thank you for that. I'll be listening."

"Good night, Hall. Till tomorrow."

"Good night—Julia?"

"Yes?"

"I'll always love you, you know. I mean"—I held my breath, I dropped my dick—"no matter what."

"I think I've always known that. Anyway, I know it now. I'll always love you, too." She laughed, and it was a laugh low in her throat, but, astoundingly free of bitterness. "No matter what. Until tomorrow, then."

"Until tomorrow."

And she hung up, then I hung up. I stripped naked, and took my shower, free, until tomorrow.

Tomorrow was a bright, cold Sunday, with a coldness and brightness peculiar to New York. The sky remains metallic, but raises itself up to where the sky should be: the buildings concede your right to be here, and give you elbowroom. And I walked down West End Avenue, wearing a black Russian fur hat, I remember, and the serious, distinguished, winter garb which Russian fur hats demand, feeling perhaps, within my difficult ease, a leashed panic, but trying to be ready for whatever this tomorrow—as the song says—would bring.

And turned east on 59th Street, walking those long blocks to Columbus Circle, which was filled with the New York Sunday innocence—that is to say, with people who scarcely knew where they were, or why: and crossed the Circle, and continued down to 57th Street, turning east again toward Carnegie Hall, with my heart beginning to hammer, and the brow beneath—within—the band of my Russian hat beginning to be hot and cold and wet.

And waited for the light at Seventh Avenue, a long night, watching the people milling about in front of Carnegie Hall, watching the people on the steps, looking at the unchanging red light, watching the cars speed by, the taxis, and a horse-drawn carriage turned onto the avenue from the Plaza Hotel, a man and a woman and a little girl sat in it, and this carriage clumped down Seventh Avenue, and passed me, crossing 57th Street, and the light changed.

I crossed the avenue. But I was still on the wrong side of the street.

It had not occurred to me that I could have crossed the street while I was waiting to cross the avenue. I watched the posters outside Carnegie Hall; apparently, there was a concert there, this afternoon. There were many people on the steps. I looked at my watch. It was twenty-five minutes to two. It could not really be said that I was late. The light changed, and I crossed the street.

She was standing on the top step, near the series of doors farthest from the avenue. She was wearing a gray, belted, cloth coat, with a high collar. She was wearing black, high-heeled boots. She was wearing a stylish black turban, which covered her ears. She had her hands in her pockets.

She did not seem to be waiting for anyone, was not anxiously watching the streets. She stood at a kind of three-quarter angle to me, watching the people coming in and out of the doors, or watching nothing—it was impossible to tell what she was watching—and standing perfectly still, as though she were certain of being found.

I stood at the bottom of the steps for a second, watching her. Then I started up the steps. She turned her head, and saw me.

Welcome is indescribable—rare: it cannot be imitated. When Julia turned her head, and saw me, I knew—I *knew*—that, though I did not mean to her what I had hoped to mean, I meant more to her than I would ever be able to imagine. I surrendered myself to her welcome. Whatever anguish she had caused me I felt being blown away from me by the faint wind around my head and shoulders as I climbed the steps.

Then, I stood next to her, holding both her small, cold, ungloved hands. *Drink to me only with thine eyes*—that riciculous song suddenly made sense to me. *And I will pledge with mine.* Then I took her in my arms, and we kissed each other, like brother and sister.

"How are you?—old, *un*married lady, late of Timbuktu?"

"I'm fine, I'm so happy to see you."

"Me too."

Then, we just looked at each other.

"You hungry?"

"I think I must be starving."

"Where shall we eat?"

"Do you have a lot of money?"

We laughed. I said, "Enough for a Sunday afternoon."

"Well, I broke into Jimmy's piggy bank. Let's go next door. They used to know me there."

"Oh?"

"Part of the glory of being a model. But I never wanted to bug you with that side of it. Come on. It's cold, to be fighting these streets."

"At your service, child."

And so we walked down the steps, and entered the Russian Tea Room. We hadn't chosen a bad hour, in spite of the fact that it was Sunday. The people heading for a matinee were paying their checks and leaving, and the evening people would not be arriving for a while.

And it was true that they knew her here. It was "Miss Miller" this, and "Miss Miller" that, all the way from the checkroom to our table. But I had the feeling that they really liked her, that she had given them some reason to respect her, that they respected each other.

We sat down, facing each other.

"You're famous, child."

"Others might not put it so nicely, but, yes"—she grinned—"I've had my day."

"I have a feeling—your day is just beginning."

For that was the way she looked. There is a moment in a man's life, a woman's life, when all, all that *is* the person seems to come together for the first time, when all of the warring, disparate elements—the chin, the nose, the eyebrow, the set of the head, the look in the eye—form, for the first time, a coherent composition. Julia was beginning to look like Julia.

It is true that, as a child preacher, she had been quite unforgettable; but she had looked like no one then, she had simply been the disquieting illustration of a mystery. She had been unforgettable precisely because, at that moment, as a child and as a preacher, she had not belonged to herself, nor had the remotest idea who she was. She had then been at the mercy of a force she had had no way of understanding. That was why I, for example, had wished to be able to turn my eyes away from the inevitable spectacle of her dreadful fall from grace, had hoped not to be present, still less summoned, at the hour her trumpet sounded.

Now something *had* happened to her, that was unmistakable, and, out of what she had begun to create herself. I am sure that Julia did not put it that way to Julia: but I was welcome because she trusted what she saw in my eyes.

"Well. Where shall we begin?"

"Oh. I don't know. I've just come back. I don't know where I am. I'm not sure I know where I've been."

"Africa?"

"Maybe. I'll tell you one thing: the people running around saying they *discovered* Africa are all completely mad." She laughed, that holy-roller urchin's laugh. "I think Africa might have discovered *them*—to drive them mad—but—ain't *nobody* ever discovered Africa."

The waitress came, and took our drink orders, inquiring as to Miss Miller's health, and treating me with the deference due Miss Miller's escort.

"How long were you there—I mean," and I laughed, "wherever you were?"

"Oh. Since I last saw you. About two years. But—putting it that way doesn't really make any sense—you know what I mean? It was some *other* kind of time."

I watched her. "No. I don't know what you mean. *What* do you mean?"

"Well—look. I was in a city called Abidjan. They call it a city. And it's on the west coast of Africa. But *it's* not really in Africa—Africa is in *it*, and driving it crazy." Watching my face, she laughed again, and said, "Yes. I think it drove *me* a little crazy, too."

"I never really understood," I said carefully, "what you were doing there—why you went—"

She looked down. Then she picked up my pack of cigarettes, and lit one. "Well. Let's say I thought it might be more cool—and more fair—to lay some questions on Africa that I didn't want to lay on you." She looked down again. "You're not history."

"I concede that. But—you've lost me." She gave me a look. "As concerns the particular detail, I mean. You'll never *lose* me."

"It's hard," she said, "to tell the truth. Partly because you don't know it. Partly because you're afraid—"

"Afraid that you *do* know it—?"

I don't know why her face made me put it to her that way. Perhaps I was reading my mind.

The waitress came with our Bloody Marys, and we ordered something to eat.

Julia raised her glass, and I raised mine, and we bowed to each other.

"Do you know why," she asked, "a Bloody Mary is called a Bloody Mary? Instead of, for example"—we both laughed—"a Bloody Virginia, for example? Or a Bloody Julia?"

Luckily, the Russian Tea Room was fairly sparsely populated at that moment, or we might have been asked to leave. As it was, heads turned, wondering what had so cracked us up.

"No," I said finally. "And I don't want to find out."

"Well," she said, "that means that you *do* know why." She sipped her Bloody Mary. "That's part of what I began to learn—in Timbuktu." She put out her cigarette. "That's why no one has ever discovered Africa. They don't dare."

She picked up another ciagrette, looking at once very young and very weary. I picked up my lighter, and lit her cigarette: a reflex, created, partly, by the surroundings. I knew that she didn't really want another cigarette. But she inhaled, and blew the smoke, carefully, above my head.

It is astounding to behold—endure—a beauty to which you are forever and inexorably connected, and which will never, never, never belong, submit, to you. It shakes one mightily to confront the vulnerability before which stone and steel give way.

For the girl before me longed to belong to someone. It was the depth of her longing which altered the nature of the transaction, which demolished the expected, the habitual terms. She had been frightened too deeply to be easily frightened again, had endured possession long before dreaming of love. This gave her, cruelly, an intimidating freedom: who would dare attempt to possess her?

This, too, she had begun to learn during her curious pilgrimage. "He was a very nice man. I never learned enough, you know, about *his* world. Maybe I never will. But, you know, he came up through the church schools, and was sent to France, and Switzerland, to study. I met him at some U.N. function. I was there, you know, with all my glamor on. He seemed to look through all that, straight on down to me. I had the feeling that he could never be fooled.

"And he was so *black*. Not just *physically* black—he was that, too, but *really* black, black in a way I'd never encountered. He was old enough to be my father—and—I guess—that made him beautiful in my eyes."

She broke a hard roll, carefully, as she said this, and swallowed a mouthful of her beef Stroganoff. I watched her, not knowing what to say: she was not, for example, confessing to an act of infidelity.

"He was married, of course, and had children my age, in school. A girl, and a boy—there were younger children I met later, over there. But the boy and the girl were very nice to me. I don't know what I expected, but I hadn't expected that. They seemed amused, too, as though I were one of the packages their father loved to bring home from his travels. I had the feeling that they were telling me not to worry about *them—they* were used to it."

She laughed and sipped her wine, looking around the restaurant. I was beginning to be more and more fascinated by a story which included me, and which, yet, held me outside.

"He wanted me to come with him, to Africa. I said, I couldn't—he told me I was lying, I was dreaming. There was nothing holding me here."

Again she paused, and looked at me—not exactly as though she feared she might be hurting me: she acknowledged this likelihood with a wry pursing of the lips. She looked at me as though she wondered if I understood, or could help her understand. Her story locked me out at the same time that it locked me in—with her. She was talking to me about something which was happening to *us*.

This was the strangest and most grueling sign of respect anyone had given me, in all my life.

"And, so, I had to think about it. *I* knew what was holding me here."

She reached out, and put one hand in mine, for a moment.

"I would have liked to be able to have said—to myself—that it was you. But I would have been lying—to myself, and to you, and I love you too much for that."

She dropped my hand, and nibbled at her rice. The restaurant was full, but not yet inundated, we had, for the moment, a haven.

"I said before—you're not history. You couldn't undo it. I couldn't lay it on you. Sometimes, you walk out of one trap, into another. I think I thought that *he* was history. Because he reminded me of my father. And because he was black, black in a way my father never was." And she smiled. "Perhaps I thought that *he* could undo it."

She took off her turban, abruptly, and dropped it on her seat, beside her. I saw her coarse, beautiful, half-Spanish, half-kinky hair. She had piled it all up, under the turban, knotted in a bun at the top of her head. So one saw the fine lines in her high forehead, and around her eyes. She was beginning to look like Julia: the price she would pay was beginning to show.

"Anyway—finally—I went on over there."

She paused, and picked up her wineglass, looking at me over the wine.

"There were lots of things I wanted to say to you then, but I couldn't. I wanted to ask you to take care of everything over here—while I tried to find out what I had to find out—over there." Then she smiled. It was a smile that made me know that she was a part of me, forever; and, precisely because she was a part of me, she was part of a mystery I would never unlock.

"I couldn't say anything to you, really, because we were hurting too much. But I knew that you would do it, anyway. I knew"—and she sipped her wine—"that you had your brother, and you knew that I had mine. So I wasn't afraid."

She put her wineglass down.

"I said I wouldn't go unless I had a way of making a living over there. I said I wasn't cut out to be nobody's concubine." She laughed, it was the most unexpected sound, it rang through the place, and people turned, and smiled. "Of course, there are any number of ways of being a concubine—as he knew, and as I was about to find out."

She looked down at the table as though she were looking into a well, looking for something which she had, mistakenly, dropped into the bottom of a well. "He knew the one thing I didn't really know—he knew how much I trusted him."

I looked around the restaurant, wishing, really, to flee, and not *from* Julia—*with* her; and this made me wonder about all my relationships, until this moment, and to come. I chewed on whatever it was, a chicken Kiev, I think, and looked around me at a setting which was, abruptly, hideously, brutally foreign.

But no more foreign, really, than any setting becomes the moment one is compelled to examine, decipher, and make demands of it: no more foreign, certainly, than the European outposts jutting, like rotting teeth, out of the jaws of West Africa. If teeth rot, it is because their host, the body, gives them nearly no nourishment. The explicit or exotic European outposts of North America do not, for the moment, appear to lack vitamins, and yet, they do bring uneasily to mind the notion of a mystery imposed on a dilemma: details ripped from their context manifest a sinister and relentless incoherence. All of the details of the room in which we sat once were part of a life elsewhere, but certainly not, as far as the senses are able to report, here.

"I had a position working for one of the airlines. I have to call it a position, because it damn sure wasn't a job, I was sort of in charge of the VIPs who didn't speak French." She laughed. "They didn't speak much English, either, but I got by on guesswork, and flattery. And I actually learned some Dutch, French, and German, and, who knows, it may all come in handy one day.

"But my friend, there, once I was there, began to be more and more important to me. *He* understood something. He was the only person who did—well, the only *male*. But, in the beginning, I didn't know any women at all.

"A black girl in Africa, who wasn't *born* in Africa, and who has never *seen* Africa, is a very strange creature for herself, and for everyone who meets her. I don't know which comes first, or which *is* worse. They don't know who they are meeting. *You* don't know who they are meeting, either—you may have thought you did, but now, you know you don't—and you don't know why *they* are either. You may have thought you did, but you don't. You don't know a damn thing about any single day they've spent on earth. You go through the village, or the villages, but you don't really see them—Hollywood threw acid in both your eyes before you were seven years old. You're blind, *that's* the first thing you realize is that you're blind. Later you begin to see—something. And, then, you begin to see why you couldn't see. But, at first—damn, you know more about the Mississippi cracker, even though you hate him and you know he hates you. And then"—looking up at me, with those eyes—"you see how people try to hold on to what they know, no matter how ugly it is. It's better," and she laughed, "than nothing!"

She finished her Stroganoff, wiped her lips carefully with her napkin, and picked up her wine.

"But maybe what's been happening to you all your life will keep happening to you in Africa, too—why not? Every thing *has* happened there already, you just weren't present. Like, you don't know what tribe produced you, and you don't even know what that means, but the people watching you, in Africa, *they* know. They don't even have to think about it—they *know*. And are they remembering what they last did to you, or what you last did to them?

"The old man, my friend, didn't think that any of that would matter very much, in Africa, in what he called the 'long' future. But he expects me to live to about a hundred, and that's in what I guess he could call the 'short' future. So—I began to see that I would not be able to understand anything that *anyone* was saying to me unless I began to hear—to trust—another language." She frowned and smiled, her forehead as tense as music. "But you cannot *hear* another language, unless you've heard it already. And you certainly didn't *want* to hear it, the first time!"

I looked around the place again. The evening people were beginning to arrive. They had dressed to be seen, they were dressed to be "out." I don't know why, but, almost for the first time, or for the first time so sharply, I found their procession moving. They all seemed, vaguely, like refugees. Many of them *were* refugees, or had so begun their lives in America. In one way, they were certainly more at home in America than Julia or I could claim to be; and yet, in another way, in a way that Julia and I were not, they were homeless. I wondered how much this had to do with what one remembered of home, with how much one could carry out, or with how much had to be left behind. And left behind, after all, how, and in what hands, or even, come to think of it, where? Does anyone dare remember? Is it possible? If she had not been stricken still and dumb by her last sight of the flaming city, perhaps Lot's wife could tell us—perhaps, indeed, she does. But memory cannot be a pillar of salt, standing watch over a dead sea: we need a new vocabulary.

Julia, too, looked over at the people, couples, families, being led to their tables. It was a Sunday, and it seemed to me, therefore, that family was more in evidence than usual. Grandmothers, plump, with brooches on the ample bosoms, hair rinsed silver or blue, made up with a discretion which, yet, owed something to television, and their daughters, or daughters-in-law, smooth, polished to a high gloss, hair artfully free, and tumbling. The winter air had stung the skin, quite beautifully, to life, and their eyes glowed with the pleasures of safety.

The men were proprietary, with a muted Sunday cheerfulness, but seemed to be very proud of their families, very solicitous of their children. I had once envied these people, or so I had thought. I didn't anymore, but it was nice to watch them in a setting in which we did not seem to menace each other. They, also, glanced casually at Julia and me, seeming to feel a similar ease and relief.

I watched a grandmother, a delicately boned lady, with auburn-and-silver hair, cut short. She was wearing a copper-colored two-piece suit, very smart, an emerald brooch, and matching earrings. She had to have been extremely beautiful when young, with that kind of fragile, breathless, wide-eyed beauty one associates, for some reason, with Vienna. On one hand, she wore a wedding ring; the other hand was bare. There was no one at the table who could have been her husband; she was with her daughter, or her son, and her grandchildren.

Well, suddenly I saw her, as she might have been, years ago, in, let us say, Vienna; saw the nervous, bony hands, the wide mouth, the big, dark eyes the simple, tasteful outfit she would have been wearing then—somewhere in Vienna, in an office, in a room, in a restaurant. I could not hear what she was saying, but her eyes conveyed her inability to believe that she had been marked for death, and was now about to be carried away, to die. I could not hear what she was saying because no one could hear what she was saying. Her jewelry was taken from her, and thrown into a box. Someone who did not look unkind stripped her of her simple, tasteful outfit, and took her shoes. Then someone signaled, pushed, or pulled her, and she took her place in line, and followed everybody—the way one follows the airport guide, not too unlike the way one follows the waitress of the table. With the whole world refusing to listen, or to watch, she arrived, naked, at Golgotha.

She did not remember it. Perhaps the wedding band remembered, flashing briefly now, as she reached across the table to ruffle one of her grandchild's hair. Perhaps dreams were her testimony, perhaps terrors were her proof, perhaps one eyelid twitched violently at certain subway stops, and she took long baths because she was unable to step under a shower: this proves the deep and endless effect of the event, but may or may not be due to what we call memory.

I wonder, more and more, about what we call memory. The burden—the role—of memory is to clarify the event, to make it useful, even, to make it bearable. But memory is, also, what the imagination makes, or has made, of the event, and, the more dreadful the event, the more likely it is that the memory will distort, or efface it. It is, thus, perfectly possible—indeed, it is common—to act on the genuine results of the event, at the same time that the memory manufactures quite another one, an event totally unrelated to the visible and uncontrollable effects in one's life. This may be why we appear to learn absolutely nothing from experience, or may, in other words, account for our incoherence: memory does not require that we reconstitute the event, but that we justify it.

This cannot be done by memory, but by looking toward tomorrow, and so, to undo the horror, we repeat it.

This is, perhaps, why I so often thought of safety when I watched these so lately baptized Americans, and why I thought of them as homeless. They *had* to believe in safety, who on earth could blame them? But I knew that they were *not* safe: if I was not safe in my country, if no viable social contract had been made, or honored, with *me,* then no one could be safe here. I may not believe that safety exists anywhere, but it certainly cannot exist among such dishonorable people. They did not want to hear this—now that *they* were the Americans, I was the stranger—I couldn't blame them, and I held my peace. Still, I had to wonder what their memory made of their ordeal: which could never have so mercilessly overtaken them, had they not believed themselves to be safe. So it was true, after all, however odd and brutal: I knew there was no hiding place down here; *they* were homeless, I was home.

I looked over at Julia.

"How does it feel to be back?"

She pursed her lips, looking very somber. "I'm glad to be back.

But—that's the same question they asked me over there. And they weren't wrong."

I watched her. Again, she seemed to be staring into the bottom of a well.

"I mean, it wasn't a bullshit, my-African-sister kind of thing. The ones who came on like that just despised you, and wanted to find a way to use you. No. The question was serious. There was something true in it, though I still don't know how to put it into words. It comes out of a place, anyway, without words, somewhere where the question *is* the answer."

She looked up at me, as though she were wondering if she made any sense. I didn't know, yet; she did, and she didn't. She did, that is, if *she* did: I was all attuned to her.

Something she saw in my face made her smile. "Well, I'm trying to get it together, brother. The diaspora didn't happen in a day." We both laughed. "But I mean—we've been raised to think that a question is one thing, and the answer is another—and we always say, *the* answer. But it may not be like that." She smiled. "Just think of all the people you watch going through their whole lives looking for the answer, waiting for the answer—and never dealing with the question. So—I really just had to accept the question as saying something tremendous about—*me*."

She stopped, still smiling, and toyed with the cigarettes on the table. Our waitress came, and we ordered dessert—chocolate mousse for Julia, Russian cream for me—and coffee. It was past four o'clock. My date with Ruth was at seven thirty.

And I suddenly wondered what I would tell Ruth about this afternoon; wondered, for the first time, what I would tell her about Julia. Julia, for the first time, was someone I would have to try to clarify to another.

And I looked at her as though I were already trying to form the words in my mind, or as though I were about to say good-bye. But I had already said good-bye to Julia, and I realized, abruptly, and absolutely, that I was never going to say good-bye to her again, nor she to me. We had done that, and it hadn't been any fun at all, and we'd never, thank heaven, have to go through that again. We had accepted our terms, or perhaps, we had dictated them; it made no difference now. Too much joined us for us ever to be pulled apart: our love was here to stay.

And I hummed a bar or two of that song, in fact, while Julia looked at me, ironically, her chin resting on one fist.

"There," she said, "that's a very good example—of the question being the answer, I mean."

I had to laugh. "Get away from me, old obeah woman."

"It's the way I was raised," she said, and we laughed together.

Our dessert came, and we ate, for a while, in silence. Then Julia said, looking down, "He told me that I was barren, that childbirth takes many forms, that regret is a kind of abortion, that sorrow is the only key to joy." She looked up. "I don't know. But he gave me something to think about—maybe he gave me a *way* to think about it. He made me begin to look forward, instead of looking back."

She looked down again. "And—I wanted to see you—because—somehow—I feel differently. I'm not *happy*, but—I'm not tormented, as I was. I wanted you to know. You deserve to know. And there's no one else I could tell. Oh," and she looked up at me again, "one day, I'll tell you other things. It was a nightmare for me, I didn't know *who* I was. But that was very important—to know I didn't know. It was strange to be looked on, not merely as yourself, but as part of something other, older, vaster. I hated it. But now that I'm back here, among all these people, who think that everything begins, and ends, with them, it all begins to make: sense." She shook her head, laughed, looked up. "I don't know what that word *sense* means anymore, but I'm learning to trust what I don't know." She leaned over, surprising me, and took my hand. "Maybe that's all I wanted to tell you. So you'd be at ease in your mind about me, and be free."

I took her hand in both of mine. I know that we looked like lovers, and it was beautiful to realize that, in truth, at last, we were.

"Thank you for that," I said. "But what I'm mainly going to do with my freedom is watch over those I love."

"That's a two-way street," she said. She watched me for a moment. "You've been somewhere, too."

We left the place around six. I managed to find a taxi, and I put her in it, and I walked home, scarcely believing that I could be so happy, or so free. Nothing, after all, had been lost. We were going to live.

It is very largely because of Jimmy that Arthur became: a star.

That is a somewhat curious statement, and relates to what was to become a part of Jimmy's agony: but I must let the statement stand.

I do not at all agree with Jimmy's assessment of his responsibility, and Jimmy will be forced to agree with me as his agony subsides. I watched it happen, after all, without quite knowing what I was watching, but one thing was very clear to me: Jimmy made Arthur happy. There is no other way to put it. I saw my brother happy, for the first time in our lives. When someone you love is happy, you have been given a great gift; you are the honored guest at a rare celebration. If you are burdened, the joy of your brother lightens your burden, if you are crawling on your belly, his joy brings you to your feet. It's true: my soul is a witness. After days, or weeks, of despair, and inertia, you are given the force to go out and contend for the rent money, and to get your watch out of the pawnshop. The happiness of someone you love proves that life is possible. Your own horrors, whatever they may be, must simply await your return from the celebration—there can be no question of your taking them with you. And there they sit, indeed, in your room, when you return, looking baleful and neglected, and you realize that some horrors need *you* far more than you need them, and, mercilessly, you begin to clean house.

But in truth, I, too, then, was very happy, not only because I had Ruth, but because I had not lost Julia. These two truths were related: I might not have been free, for Ruth, or anyone, if Julia had been lost. And I might never have known why I wasn't free, might never, consciously, have made the connection: it was only when the cloud lifted, when I saw Julia again, that I realized how dense the cloud had been, how long I had been wandering. Oh, I had responsibilities, commitments, a privacy of pride (or a pride of privacy) and a relatively stong will. These are not trivial attributes, but I know what they can, and cannot do. They can help you to put on your armor, and teach you how to wear it, but they cannot help you to take it off. Something itches, something burns, something, finally, fatally, begins to stink. And when you begin to be engulfed by your own odor, you dare not let anyone near you, and your life becomes a matter of ritual and evasion. It is true that I had Arthur, but Arthur was a grown-ass man— my brother, not my ward—and if I could not, so to speak, buy my own ticket to the concert, he would soon have no choice but to have me locked out of the hall: I was not *his* ward, either.

So my West End Avenue apartment was a kind of joyful tabernacle that winter, as my thirty-second year began to end, as my thirty-third year, incredibly, beautifully, blew trumpets in the distance.

Julia was seldom there. She was working all the time. Her absence, somewhat to her surprise, had had the effect of increasing her value; she was in at the very beginning of a kind of high-fashion African craze. Her journey had also given her another, more haunting quality, and, according to Jimmy, Broadway, Hollywood, and television producers were on the phone, and Julia had actually read a few scripts: after which, again according to Jimmy, "Julia thinks modeling is about as low as she wants to sink." To some extent—indeed, to a very important extent—I could guess Julia's state from Jimmy's, for his eye was always on *that* sparrow, and, more than that, Jimmy always trusted me. Just as he knew that I knew he loved my brother, he knew I loved his sister.

And I could gauge, yet more vividly, Arthur's state from Jimmy's. When I was thirty-two, Arthur was twenty-five, and Jimmy was twenty-one. Twenty-one is a cunning, carnivorous, but far from devious age. Neither Arthur nor Jimmy could ever really hide anything, nor did they ever, it must be said, when the chips were down, try: but

Arthur was far more veiled, especially, of course, in his relation to Jimmy, around me. I thought Arthur was very funny—downright, as the old folks would say, "cute." Here came Jimmy, bouncing in, in the canvas shit-kickers which had replaced the sneakers, wearing Arthur's duffel coat, blue jeans, and a sweater, glowing like a planet, kissing Ruth, whom he called "Mother Mattie," throwing his arms around me, and heading, of course, for the kitchen, rubbing his hands, and complaining about the cold, and yelling behind him, "Hey, old gospel warrior, you ain't had nothing to eat all day! What you want me to fix you?"

This to Arthur, who, very soberly, has more or less limped in behind him, doing his best to look exasperated, and dissembling the pleasure he cannot hide by throwing his smile at Ruth, or me—we always caught it—and then, frowning, under the necessity of answering Jimmy's yell, in the utterly doomed hope of shutting him up before he reveals *all* the secrets of the château, "I didn't hear you ask Hall for permission to go into his icebox, man!"

Jimmy (at the door of the kitchen, bottle of Scotch in one hand, loaf of bread in the other): Would you like a ham or fried chicken or spare rib sandwich? You got to eat something, baby. Your brother don't want you to starve. (To me) Do you?

Me: Certainly not.

Jimmy: I'll fix you a drink first. You want Scotch or vodka? (To me) Where's your vodka?

Me: In the cabinet, under the sink—*you* know.

Jimmy: Oh. Yeah. (To Arthur) Which is it?

Ruth: You fix the drinks, Jimmy. I'll fix the food.

Jimmy: Okay, Mother Mattie. (To Arthur) Which is it?

Arthur (ceasing to struggle): Scotch. Double. Rocks. (Under his breath): Motherfucker.

Ruth goes into the kitchen, and Arthur looks at me—a very moving look, a mocking scowl, a question, an irrepressible joy. And I laugh.

After a moment, Arthur laughs, too. "Ah. What you going to do?"

"Eat. Drink. And, baby, be happy."

And he looks at me again, more than ever my baby brother, and I dare to say, "I love you. Don't forget it. And, whatever makes you happy, that's what you supposed to do, and whoever makes you happy, that's where you supposed to be."

He looks at me again, and something seems to fall from him. Then, "Okay. I love you, too."

Then Jimmy comes out of the kitchen, with Arthur's drink, and hands it to him, and there is something very moving in the way he does this. It is probably impossible to describe it. Every gesture any human being makes is loaded, is a confession, is a revelation: nothing can be hidden, but there is so much that we do not want to see, do not dare to see. The boy had poured the stiff drink Arthur ordered into what I knew he considered to be a special glass, in fact, Arthur's glass: a square, heavy glass, with a wide silver band. He did not kneel as he handed Arthur his drink, as, for example, a Greek or an Elizabethan page might have done, but he was compelled to lean forward, and, unconsciously, he bowed. I was aware of this, perhaps, only because I was watching Jimmy's face, and I saw how his eyes searched Arthur's: his devotion was in his eyes, and that was why he seemed to bow. It was mocking, wry, niggerish, salty, but it was love, and Arthur, as he took the glass, looked into Jimmy's eyes, and seemed to kiss him, on the lips, and on the brow. And both were very happy. Arthur raised his glass to Jimmy, then to his lips, and Jimmy moved away, back into the kitchen. We heard his voice, and Ruth's, and their laughter.

Jimmy and Arthur spent all their time together, really, either at 18th Street—"Man, we finally made it up all them *stairs!*" Jimmy once irrepressibly crowed to Ruth and me while Arthur scowled, and blushed—or at the Dey Street loft, where they also worked, practiced, rehearsed, around the clock. It was beautiful to watch them; freedom is an extraordinary spectacle. It was a tremendous moment in all our lives, I remember it, until this hour, as the turning point: and Tony was conceived then. And when I say that it was largely because of Jimmy that Arthur became: a star: I do not mean that this possibility had entered either of their minds. Each learned, working, enormous things from the other, but they were far from calculating a public conquest: at that moment, indeed, it was not only the farthest thing from their minds, but would have been, had they thought of it, a trap to be avoided. People who think that they wish to become famous have no idea how the process works: fame cannot be summoned; it strikes, like a hammer, and the trick, thereafter, is to stand up under what has seemed to be a mortal blow. No, they were happy, they were working, they were learning to trust the unanswerable truth that each was indispensable to the other—should they lose each other, each would have to learn to live all over again—and, if I say that it was largely due to Jimmy that Arthur became *The Soul Emperor! Mr. Arthur Montana!* I mean that Jimmy's presence in Arthur's life, Jimmy's love, altered Arthur's estimate of himself, gave him a joy and a freedom he had never known before, invested him with a kind of incandescent wonder, and he carried this light on stage with him, he moved his body differently since he knew that he was loved, loved, and, therefore, knew himself to be both bound and free, and this miracle, the unending wonder of this unending new day, filled his voice with multitudes, summoned, from catacombs unnameable, whosoever will.

Arthur's first hit record, for example, was more than a year in the future, but here is, partly, how it came about:

In the Florida church, on that far-off afternoon, when Jimmy had first played for Arthur, Arthur, after two, or three, improvisations, had thought that they would stop and that we would all go back down to the church basement, where we would wash our faces and change our shirts, if we had shirts to change into. We might have just enough time to drive somewhere, for a quick drink.

So he stopped, and turned toward Jimmy to indicate a break; but Jimmy, very deliberately, with great impertinence, and looking Arthur straight in the eye, banged out the opening of "Just a Closer Walk with Thee."

Arthur caught his breath, and nearly cracked up, but had no choice but to follow Jimmy's lead:

Grant it, Jesus,
if You please.
Daily, walking, close to Thee.
let it be,
dear Lord,
let it be.

I had no idea, then, of course, how direct, and, as it were, sacrilegious, Jimmy was being—considering the uses to which we put the temple of the Holy Ghost, sacrilegious is a very strange word—but, however that may be, his call was very direct and moving, and brought from Arthur a response which seemed to ring out over those apocalyptic streets, and caused me, and the two men standing at the church door with me, to look back and see where that sound was coming from.

This song became for them, then, theirs, a sacrament, a stone marking a moment on their road: the point of no return, when they confessed to each other, astounded, terrified, but having no choice, in the hearing of men, and in the sight of God.

Arthur was never to have another accompanist like Jimmy, and Jimmy was never to have another singer like Arthur. This is a mystery to which one must, simply, say Amen: it will never be deciphered. One has seen dancers, for example, quite extraordinary alone, or with whatever partner—and then one sees the two dancers together, who seem to have been created to be together, from the moment the earth was formed. Together, they accomplish mysteries which neither could dream of confronting alone, and their defiance of space and death lifts us, also, shivering and shining, up into the middle of the air.

Arthur and Jimmy were like that. I have rarely heard, or seen, a freedom like that, when they played and sang together. It had something to do with their youth, of course, it had something to do with the way they looked, it had something to do with their vows, with their relation to each other: but it was more, much more than that. It was a wonder, a marvel—a mystery: I call it holy. It caused me to see, in any case, that we are all limited, and, mostly, misshapen instruments, and yet, if we can, simultaneously, confront and surrender, extraordinary fingers can string from us the response to our mortality.

They worked their behinds off, for example, on this old number, but, by the time they hit the last note, it was true for everyone who could hear, and, even, I swear, for those who could only feel vibrations:

> *I can tell the world,*
> *about this!*
> *I can tell the nations,*
> *I'm blessed!*
> *Tell them what Jesus,*
> *He has done!*
> *Tell them*
> *the Comforter has come,*
> *and He brought*
> *joy, joy, joy,*
> *unto my soul!*

So there we were after all, the four of us, reunited, Julia, Jimmy, Arthur, me, bound together, as it now turned out, for life, and with the addition of Ruth, who arrived, simply, and transformed the space which had been waiting for her.

Arthur and Jimmy are in the Dey Street loft, working on "Lift Him Up," which is one of the numbers they are doing for Christmas, at one of the great Harlem tabernacles.

I rarely visited Arthur's Dey Street pad, not because I didn't like it, or didn't feel welcome there, but because it was so much more his workshop than it was his home. That's, suddenly, a chilling way to put it; I don't think I put it to myself that way, then. If I say, I hardly remember what it looked like, that's because of all the time I had to spend down there, putting things in crates and boxes, closing Arthur's eyes.

It was on the top floor of a three- or four-story building. The inferior stories were occupied by various small businesses, visibly and swiftly entering bankruptcy, if one were to judge from the faces one sometimes saw. All day long, throughout the building, motors whined and rumbled, so that the building always seemed to be purring, like some great cat. After five or six o'clock, the purring ceased, the building, and the entire neighborhood, became silent and empty. Virtually no one lived down here. This was perfect for Arthur, who could experiment as loudly as he wished all night, and indeed, for that matter, all day. His music scarcely troubled the steady industrial roar.

It was marvelously retired and peaceful on Saturday afternoons; and this is a Saturday.

Oh,
the world is hungry
for the living bread.

Arthur sings this in a low voice, standing at the window, watching the shuttered windows of the luncheonette across the street. In front of it lean two winos, white, sharing a bottle, seeming not to care about the cold, though the frayed jacket of the one and the torn, black raincoat of the other afford them absolutely no protection. Wretchedness does not, so far as Arthur has been able to tell, appear to have the power to transcend race, or, more accurately, habit: white winos travel, in the main, with whites, and blacks with blacks. They appear to be utterly oblivious to everything and everyone outside their world, are aware of others only as a means to another bottle. They are a great mystery for Arthur, he wonders what hit them so hard, so soon—for many of them are young, their youth seems tentative and frozen beneath the shining sweat and grime.

The loft stretches the entire length of the top floor, half-heartedly divided by a clothesline with a sheet draped over it. Behind this sheet is the bed: a king-size mattress on a wooden frame, close to the floor, covered, in the daytime, with a heavy dark-blue blanket, and many loud pillows. There is the bathroom, and the rudiments of a kitchen lean against the far, blank wall.

Lift the Savior up,
for men to see.

In the front of the loft are Arthur's piano, records, tape recording apparatus, sheet music, books; all more or less contained, or controlled, by a system of wooden cabinets. There is a sofa, chairs, a big table. On the walls, photographs: Paul, Florence, Arthur, me; Arthur, with some of his friends, or co-workers; Julia; and, now, of course, Jimmy; an indifferent painting or two; and posters, like theatrical posters, announcing Arthur, announcing others.

Jimmy, wearing an old green jump suit, is sitting at the piano, fooling around, but also, listening to Arthur. Arthur is in blue jeans, a sweater, and sandals, and is walking up and down, combing his hair.

Trust Him,
and do not doubt
the words that He said:
I'll draw all men
unto Me!

And Arthur goes behind the sheet, to the bathroom, to check on his hair, and to get rid of the comb.

Jimmy continues his investigations, very peacefully, with Arthur's tempo ringing in his head. Arthur's tempo is the meaning of the song, Arthur's tempo, and the key he and Jimmy strike together. Or the song is revealed as it is delivered, and by the manner in which it is delivered. Sometimes Jimmy responds to Arthur's line—his call—by repeating it precisely, sometimes he questions or laments, sometimes he responds from close by, and, sometimes, from far away. Sometimes they both feel imprisoned by the song, leaping to go further than the song, or Arthur's tempo, allow: then they sweat hardest, learn most. There is always a beat beneath the beat, another music beneath the music, and beyond.

Arthur comes back, his hair looking, as it should, extremely combed, and they go to work: not only on "Lift Him Up," but on the other two numbers they are scheduled to sing for Christmas, which is, now, a little more than a week away. For a wonder, the phone does not ring, all the afternoon long, as they rehearse, call and respond, call and respond. This sound rings through the canyon of the darkening, deserted street, as night comes down.

> *And, if I,*
> *be lifted,*
> *up, from the earth,*
> *I will draw all men*
> *unto Me!*

Around seven thirty, eight o'clock, Jimmy throws up his hands, yawns, and disappears behind the sheet, to go to the bathroom. Arthur also yawns, somewhat astonished by the hour—he has been on his feet all afternoon—walks to the window, peers through the pane into the empty street, then lights a cigarette, and throws himself on his back, on the sofa.

Jimmy returns with a beer and a Scotch. He hands the whiskey to Arthur, then sits down on the floor, the back of his head against Arthur's knee.

He reaches for Arthur's cigarette, uses it to light his own, then hands Arthur's cigarette back to him.

"So—man—how you feel?"

"I feel like we moving. But sometimes, I don't know—I'm not sure—I know where."

Jimmy drags on his cigarette. "Yeah. Sometimes I feel that."

Arthur pulls himself up, putting his feet on the floor, and leans forward, holding his drink between both hands.

"But I don't mind feeling that," says Arthur. "In fact, I dig that. It's a little scary. But maybe, that's what I've been looking for."

"You ever think," asks Jimmy, "of branching out from gospel?—you know, blues, ballads, all the other music you got in you."

Arthur says, after a moment, "I've thought about it. People ask me that all the time."

"No kidding. But—I'm not people."

"Touché. But: gospel's my home."

Arthur says this haltingly, with wonder, as though he is translating the words as he speaks.

"Oh, come on, baby, you left home a long time ago, you ain't nothing but a gypsy—you made *me* leave my happy home." Then, he turns his head, laughing to look into Arthur's face—he was caught himself by surprise. "Hey, dig. For example. We could do something *great* and *that*."

Arthur sips his whiskey, and looks at Jimmy, from a very great height.

"You. Are. Sick. Two cats, two *black* cats, and we supposed to be the noble motherfucking phallic savage, doing *that* number? Why don't we do 'What Did You See in Her?' "

They both crack up, but Jimmy is persistent.

"Man, I am not suggesting that we turn ourselves into a freak show, and try to conquer the freak market. I've had my day in that market, that zoo, you didn't get back here, believe me, a moment too soon."

He rubs his cheek against Arthur's knee for a second, then straightens, and sips his beer.

"But we could get away with 'Since I Fell for You.' You won't be singing it *to* me—it's not a Nelson Eddy–Jeanette MacDonald toothpaste ad"—they both crack up again—"it's a recollection, a barroom confession, you'll be singing to all the other people out there, and I'll just be bearing witness. Hey—listen—"

He rises, and goes to the piano. The chord he strikes echoes his introduction to "Just a Closer Walk": for a moment, Arthur, sitting still on the sofa, is not certain he knows where Jimmy is heading. Then, the melody resolves itself, comes to the fore. Arthur moans it, sitting on the sofa—he sings the last lines:

> *I guess I'll never see the light*
> *I get the blues most every night,*
> *since I fell for you.*

Arthur's last note is Jimmy's last note, something like the last note struck on a drum: the piano makes no comment. But the last note continues to gather in the strangely summoned silence.

Jimmy turns on the piano bench, grinning at Arthur.

"That wasn't too bad. We could get that together."

"Only," says Arthur, after a moment, "I don't *get* the blues—since I fell for you."

"Oh, shit," says Jimmy, "I never thought of that," and walks back to the sofa and takes Arthur in his arms.

After a moment, Arthur puts his hands on Jimmy's shoulders, pushing him up, in order to look into his eyes.

"When you talk about the song, man, what you really mean—is—you don't want to be consoled—you don't want"—he laughs, but it is a very dry laugh—"no consolation."

"Maybe," Jimmy says, and he laughs, too, "I can't get none."

"If you can't get none," Arthur says, "you don't want none."

"That's never true," says Jimmy, and looks at Arthur, and takes him in his arms again.

And this time, Arthur holds Jimmy as though one of them is about to die. He holds on, holds on, he does not want to hurt the boy, does not really want Jimmy to feel, to bear, his weight, to endure his odors, to drown in his tears. Yet for no reason that he knows, as he holds on to Jimmy, he begins to weep great, scalding, salty tears, tears deeper than tears produced by pride, humiliation, tears deeper than any vocabulary. He does not know why he is weeping. He is astounded by the force of his tears, astounded that he cannot stop, amazed that he can weep at all, and in the arms of a boy: for Arthur, too, is the elder brother.

Jimmy curls his green, jump-suited body around Arthur's arms and legs, puts his face against Arthur's salty face, his fingers uncomb Arthur's hair, he says nothing, just holds on.

Slowly, Arthur's body ceases to shake, but he does not relax his hold on Jimmy. For a very long moment, they do not move at all. The canyon is absolutely still: proving that there can be peace in the valley.

Then Arthur looks up into Jimmy's face.

"Hey."

"Howdy."

"It were mighty nice of you to take me in."

"Weren't a fit night out there, for man, nor mule."

"What'd you do with my mule?"

"He over yonder. Fast asleep."

"You sure?"

"Well—last time I *looked*"—and they laugh, laugh, now, as hard as Arthur cried, and in the tremendous luxury of their private space, free, on each other, to stretch out.

"You hungry?"

They laugh again.

"Come on. Be serious."

But they keep laughing.

Yes. But what is Arthur doing, lying on his back, on the floor of the basement of that London pub?

I have tried, every which-a-way, not to go there, and yet, I haven't tried as hard as Arthur tried, Arthur, who simply, finally, saw it coming, saw that he couldn't avoid it, had been running toward it too long, had been alone too long, didn't trust, really, any other condition. Jimmy came too late.

But if I say that, I've got, equally, to consider the possibility that Jimmy came too soon, was a part of his landscape, if not a part of his life, from the very beginning of that life. According to Arthur, he never noticed Jimmy when they were children; but he noticed him enough to be nice to him, on that far-off Sunday afternoon, when his mother slapped him. He noticed him enough for Jimmy to know that he was noticed; and who knows how that helped Jimmy through his valley? Which, furthermore, certainly, called him down too soon. Or too early, or too late. I don't know. I'm left with what I don't know.

It would simplify matters, perhaps, if I could say that we don't know what we don't want to know: but I, we, are not that simple. We know. Almost everything we do is designed to protect us from what we know: consider the uses to which we put the troublesome past tense of the verb.

So if I say, I'm left with what I don't know, I could, equally, be saying, with tears in my eyes, I *knew!* But, Lord, how I hoped I didn't know—how I hoped my hand could hold up the sky!

Well. Let us go back to the loft. There they are, on the sofa still, they are not laughing now. They are very quiet, in each other's arms, and Dey Street is absolutely silent. Arthur or Jimmy has drawn the black monk's-cloth blinds. The only light in the room is the light around the piano, and the very faint light, filtering through the bed-sheet, from the kitchen.

Jimmy asks, "You hungry?"

Looking down into Arthur's face, relentlessly uncombing his hair, allowing all of his weight to rest on Arthur.

"I'm starving—now that I think of it."

"You want to go out?"

"*You* want to go out?"

Jimmy shifts his weight, pushing both of them deeper into the sofa, rubs his cheek against Arthur's, murmuring, "I asked you first."

"Shit. Do *we have* to go out?"

Jimmy laughs, one hand tangled in the hair at the nape of Arthur's neck. "No. We got eggs and pork chops, some leftover red beans and rice, and a chicken wing." He leans up. "Bread, a little stale, but I can heat it up, you know. Some beer, a little whiskey. I mean—we don't have to go *out*, not unless you just *want* to go out." He grins. "I can *get* it together, now."

"You want me to help you?"

"I'll nibble on the chicken wing, that's all the help I'll need. I'll let you set the table."

They both laugh.

Then they both look over at the table, which is piled high with the debris of the afternoon's work.

"Maybe," says Arthur, "I'll let *you* set the table, while I get into the pots."

"Or," says Jimmy, "we can eat in the kitchen, and leave all that where it is, until tomorrow—it's all going to end up there tomorrow, anyway."

He kissed Arthur lightly, leans up, stands up, pulling on his jump suit.

"Just lie easy till I call you, baby." He picks up Arthur's glass. "I'll freshen your drink."

And he disappears behind the bedsheet.

Arthur remains, in the dim light, on his back, on the sofa, in the loft in which, in fact, he has always lived alone. He had hoped, for a long time, that Crunch would come to visit him, even, perhaps, come to stay. Then he had begun to see that Crunch would never do this, that he could not: neither come to visit, nor come to stay. This was not because Crunch did not love him, but for a more terrible reason.

It cannot be said that he is listening, but he *hears* Jimmy, humming in the kitchen: somewhere, that is, behind the halfhearted partition. The melody eludes him, comes and goes, like a headache, but he knows that he has always known it.

Jimmy comes back with a fresh drink. Arthur sits up, putting his feet on the floor, and Jimmy puts his drink in his hands. Wordless, humming, he disappears again.

Arthur sits staring at the black monk's-cloth-covered windows.

There is a sound in the street, someone shouting, or singing, from far away. A car door slams, this brief, brutal blow ringing through the canyon.

Arthur rises, walks to the window, and looks through the blinds. The street is as empty as it has always been, and as silent. Well, some brutally isolated figure seems to shuffle, slowly, around the near corner, our of view; not so very far away, tourists are beginning to clamor, at the Fulton Fish Market. Chinatown is within walking distance. He knows: he has walked the distance often enough.

He scratches his chest, he sips his drink, and wonders if he knows enough to know that he is happy.

For he *is* happy, even though he feels, obscurely, that happiness is not his right, that he has no right to be happy. He does not know *why* he has no right to be happy, and this is why he thinks of Crunch. He was happy, once, with Crunch, as Jimmy is happy, now, with him— the tune Jimmy is humming, in his fashion, is "Didn't It Rain," and he has, apparently, cut up some onions to go with the pork chops on the fire.

Arthur knows, too, furthermore, that he is not Crunch, any more than he is Jimmy, or that Jimmy is the other younger, Arthur, and that Julia cannot be a threat to their love: perhaps: insofar as he knows now, or can know now. Love takes many forms and faces, and Julia, so far as Arthur can see, loves Jimmy, and no one else.

I could have told him that the truth was rougher than that, but time, distance, speech, and ourselves, are as real, as unanswerable, as love.

Arthur, nevertheless, is astounded by his happiness. It is as though someone, by mistake, gave him a wallet containing a fortune, thinking to do him a service, persuaded that they had seen him drop it. The wallet does not belong to him: but it is in his hands now, and the friendly stranger has vanished around the wintry corner. There is no one on the street to whom he can explain his dilemma, no one, certainly, to whom he can give the wallet: indeed, he cannot stand here very much, longer, like a fool, holding the wallet in his hands. He will become an occasion of sin, in others. Whether he deserves it or not, he is happy, and what can he do with the money but spend it?

He thinks of Crunch, perhaps, because—this is not the way he puts it to himself, but it is something like this wonder which holds him at the window—he has never thought of joy as being a potential of the air one breathes, or of happiness as being as simple, for example, as the light in Jimmy's eyes when Jimmy looks at him, or Jimmy's utterly irreplaceable walk, or the two indentations just above Jimmy's buttocks, placed there, obviously, for Arthur's thumbs, and for no other reason—what other reason could there possibly be? Jimmy's teeth, and Jimmy's grin, his many odors—which are so many signals—his stormy and sometimes weather: clouds lifting, clouds gathering, stars, planets, milky ways, moons like craters, craters like moons, the sun, daybreak, nightfall, the rising and dropping of the sea, the dialogue of planets—all, within the narrow frame of a twenty-one-year-old boy, who, furthermore, wants the world to know that he belongs to Arthur. As, indeed, he does: Arthur has enough sense to know that he cannot drop the wallet in the gutter, cannot, as others might put it, drop the money and run.

And yet—the wallet will, one day, be empty, the money spent, God knows where. Happiness goes.

Ah, thinks Arthur, standing at the window, listening to the pork chops, the onions, and Jimmy, but to *have* it!—if only for just one time! And he smiles—scratches his chest, sips his drink, and smiles. And anyway, something in him knows that something, nevertheless, something, however the deal goes down, something, as the disaster of your happiness strikes the sewers, like the last note of a song, or the look in your mama's or your daddy's eyes, something, something, remains forever, and changes the air we breathe.

Happiness is humiliating, terrifying: what is one to do later? It has to become later before one sees that the question is vain, before one ceases to ask this question, but one is always afraid that later will be too late. Too late: so Arthur, now, stands at the window, knowing perfectly well that, in a moment, he will go behind the halfhearted partition, grab Jimmy by those two dimples just above his ass, growl, and bite, into the nape of his neck, sniffing the hair there, just like a cat, cup both his hands under Jimmy's prick, and grind Jimmy's behind against his own prick, playfully, while Jimmy protests—playfully— and lets the onions burn while he turns and takes Arthur in his arms: too late. The pork chops, too, may burn, unless Jimmy, as he often does, exhibits great presence of mind, and turns down the one flame, while both calming, and surrendering to the other: *Motherfucker. Ain't you heard about* food? *You skinnier than that mule Abraham Lincoln promised us. Your brother see you now, he'd have my ass. Sit down and eat. I ain't going nowhere. Without you. And you damn sure ain't going no place without me, unless you going on stumps. Or crutches. And I ain't going to buy you no crutches.*

Jimmy laughs, and Arthur laughs: bewildered by his happiness, and, quiet as he hopes to keep it, terrified. He cannot believe that Jimmy loves him, cannot imagine what there is in him to love.

Ah. What is he doing on the floor in a basement of that historical city? That city built on the principle that he would have the grace to live, and, certainly, to die, somewhere outside the gates?

Perhaps I must now do what I have most feared to do: surrender my brother to Jimmy, give Jimmy's piano the ultimate solo: which must also now, be taken as the bridge.

So: Arthur walks through the halfhearted partition, *and, man, he bites me on the neck.* He starts fooling around with me. I don't mind that, in fact, I dig that, but my hands are all slippery with grease and onions, and I can't move for a minute.

He turns me around and he kisses me, long enough for the chops to start burning. So I push him away, and I try to laugh, and I turn the pork chops over. I can feel him watching me. I'm happy, but I'm scared, too. I don't know why. Well. I do know why, in a way. Those eyes, your brother's eyes, are asking something of me which no one has ever asked before, something, maybe, which no one will ever ask again. You hope you can answer the question you see. You hope you can give what is asked of you. It's the most important thing in the world, the *only* thing in the world, to be able to do that. What you *can* do hardly matters, if you can't do that.

Now, sometimes, when I try to talk about Arthur, I feel like a freak. And, for whatever it's worth, I guess I *am* a freak. But, dig it, baby, when I held your brother in my arms, when he had his arms around me, I didn't feel like a freak then. Even when people started talking about us, the way they did, you remember, I really did not give a shit. I was only hurt because Arthur was hurt. But I will tell Great God Almighty, baby: I was in love with *your* brother.

It's only since he left us, and I've been so alone and so unhappy, that all the other *moral* shit, what the world calls moral, started fucking with my mind. Like, why are you like this instead of like that? Well, how the fuck am I supposed to know? I know this: the question wouldn't even come up if I wasn't so alone, and so scared, wouldn't come up, I mean, in my own mind. I'm scared, and I'd like to be safe, and nobody likes being despised. And, quiet as it's kept, you can't bear for anyone you love to be despised. I can't break faith with Arthur, I can't ride and hide away somewhere, and treat my love, and let the world treat my lover, like shit. I really cannot do that. And the world doesn't have any morality. Look at the world. What the world calls morality is nothing but the dream of safety. That's how the world gets to be so fucking moral. The only way to know that you are safe is to see somebody else in danger—otherwise you can't be sure you're safe.

Look. I've been walking up and down my room, up and down my room, walking these streets, and driving these roads. And I miss my buddy, my lover, your brother, like there ain't no language for it. So then you listen to the world, and you hear *that* consolation—ah! everybody knows I'm Jimmy Miller, and everybody knows I was tight with the late, great, Arthur Montana. Don't none of these mothers know shit, man. They don't know. They cannot *afford* to know. In the Book of Job, Job calls these cats "miserable comforters," and Job was right. They want you to believe that it's "psychological"—that *we* are *psychological.* What a crock of shit. If that was true, how could we sing, how could we know that the music comes from us, *we* build our bridge into eternity, *we* are the song we sing?

Jimmy's voice stops, then starts again:

The song does not belong to the singer. The singer is found by the song. Ain't no singer, anywhere, ever *made up* a song—that is not possible. He *hears* something. I really believe, at the bottom of *my* balls, baby, that something hears *him*, something says, come here! and jumps on him just exactly like you jump on a piano or a sax or a violin or a drum and you make it sing the song you hear: and you love it, and you take care of it, better than you take care of yourself, can you dig it? but you don't have no mercy on it. You can't have mercy! That sound you hear, that sound you try to pitch with the *utmost* precision—and did you hear me? Wow!—is the sound of millions and millions and, who knows, now, listening, where life is, where is death?

I know. Maybe I sound this way because I can't tease your brother no more, or look him in the eye, can't watch him walk on stage, or into a room, will never, never, never again, grease his ashy elbows, and his spiky knees, never, again, have to find a way to tell him you really don't hardly have no buns, man, and, so, you can't buy these pants, because they make you look like you don't have no ass. He was such a tired, black Puritan, your brother. He'd turn, and look at me, you know, like he was Ezekiel, or Saint Paul, or Isaiah—those desert cats didn't have no ass, either, and they didn't have no Jimmy to go down on them.

Sometimes I thought he hated me for the way—the ways, all the ways, I loved him. I couldn't hide it, where was I to hide it? Every inch of Arthur was sacred to me.

And I mean: sacred.

I will testify that, to all the gods of the desert, and, when they have choked my throat with sand, the song that I have heard and learned to trust, my friend, at your brother's knee, will still be ringing.

And will bring water back to the desert, that's what the song is supposed to do, and that's what *my soul is a witness* is about.

Think about where you would have had to go, to put those five unrelated words together, and make of the connection, a song.

Well. The sermon does not belong to the preacher. He, too, is a kind of talking drum. The man who tells the story isn't *making up* a story. He's listening to us, and can only give back, to us, what he hears: from us.

Like, it's absolute bullshit, you know, when they are defending how they make their money—which is, also, exactly how they betray their children, and how their children are lost: when people are defending how they fuck, and get fucked, without kisses, and even without Vaseline: they are compelled to tell the people only what the people wish to hear.

Dig it: that means that they are better than the people to whom they tell nothing but lies.

So, now, *you* have become a liar, and everybody returns the favor you did them—sends back the elevator, as the French would put it— and tells you only what *you* want to hear.

Arthur got hurt, trapped, lost, somewhere in there. I had to deal with some of his old friends, lovers, leeches, from Paris to London to Amsterdam, to Copenhagen: all Arthur wanted was for the people who had *made* the music, from God knows who, to Satchmo, Mr. Jelly-Lord, Bessie, Mahalia, Miles, Ray, Trane, his *daddy*, and *you*, too, mother-fucker, *you!* It was only when he got scared about what *they might think of what he'd done to their song—our* song—that he really started to be uptight about our love.

That wasn't no easy scene, our love, but we *did* hang in there, baby, for almost fourteen years.

Arthur: is leaning on the bar of the London pub, alone. The pub is fairly crowded.

He is the only black person there, but gives off a reassuring accent: and everyone is distantly polite to their baffling, unpredicted, but indisputably American cousin.

Facing him, in the wall facing him, on the other side of the bar, is a small, brown, wooden service door, a door which swings, lightly, but remarkably, each time one of the staff enters, or exits, to accomplish this or that. He has been fascinated by the door, or has been thoughtlessly mesmerized by the door, for more than an hour: and, during this time—he does not realize this—he has moved only to lift his glass, or to order another whiskey, or to light his cigarette. He does not realize how his long, black, silent immobility immobilizes the patrons of the London pub: who, whether or not they know it, are not accustomed to being ignored. To be ignored involves waiting to be recognized, or, as they might, once, have wistfully put it, discovered.

Jimmy is now thirty-five years old, Arthur is thirty-nine: and Jimmy and Arthur have, indeed, spent fourteen years together. I agree that this does not seem possible: but with or without our agreement, time passes, just like that.

Boy,
you sure took
me
for
one big ride.

He had sung that, as an encore, on the Paris music hall stage, for Jimmy, who had not been there. He had played his own piano, he had not, after all, been bad, not as far, in any case, as his audience had been able to hear. He had been drunk, stoned, in a state of fury and anguish and panic, and had certainly not, as far as he had heard himself, been good.

He had been certain that Jimmy was ashamed of him, and should have been ashamed of him, and that that was the reason that Jimmy had not been there.

Yet the people—that void beyond him—roared. He was imprisoned, blinded, by the light, and had completely lost the sense of humor which had been his key to

boy,
don't get too lost
in all I say.

He had always handled it as a funky, light, blues-ballad; now, last night, he couldn't handle it at all, managing to get through it without entirely losing the beat—that is to say, the meaning—standing up, and bowing, and getting the fuck off that stage, pouring out saltwater, a flood of saltwater, from his eyes and his prick, in the toilet.

but, at the time,
I, really,
felt that way.

Now, he does not know what he feels, and a tremendous weight seems to gather, in his chest, and between his shoulder blades.

He wonders what I, his brother, Hall: what I think of him, really. He wonders if Paul, his father, is dead, in the grave, because he was ashamed of his son. And, at the very same moment that he knows that he knows better, he also knows that he does not know, will never be released from the judgment, or the terror, in his own eyes. For he knows that it is he, and only he, who so relentlessly demands the judgment, assembles the paraphernalia of the Judgment Day, selects the judges, demands that the trumpet sound. He wants to state his case, and be released from the judgment: but he can be released from the judgment only by dropping the case.

Lord knows,
I've got to stop believing
in all your lies,

but anguish is real, and has massive consequences. It is true that our judgment flatters the world's indifference, and makes of us accomplices to our doom: but to apprehend this, and change it, demands a larger apprehension of our song.

For, in fact, at this moment in Arthur's life, Jimmy has packed his bags, in the Paris hotel, has wearily, sternly, dried his weeping eyes, has called the desk to wake him in the morning and to have a cab ready to take him to the airport, where he will take the plane for London. He regrets the lover's quarrel of the night before, but now, intends merely to get back to his lover and travel with him to New York: and the book he opens, after he has poured himself a drink and stretched out on the bed, is not Lamentations. He is a little worried, true, but one is always worried by the conundrums of the space to be conquered in order to be joined with the conundrum of one's lover. He has not the remotest thought of judgment, judges, or trumpets. In fact, to tell the truth, Jimmy simply misses Arthur, and wants Arthur in his arms; gets a mild hard-on, and shifts his weight in bed, still reading. He is reading, as one always does at such moments, something by Agatha Christie, and will have got to the end of it before realizing that he has read it before: Jimmy claims that he has read, in his life, exactly one Agatha Christie novel, but that he has read it about eighty-seven times.

And Ruth and I are waiting for them in New York, Ruth deciding what to feed them, Julia, who will do the actual shopping, writing down these decisions as Ruth delivers them over the phone. I just want to get some sleep before the two voyaging monsters come in, because I certainly won't get much sleep once they *have* come in, and the kids—more accurately, Tony: Odessa is too young—wondering what their uncles will have brought them.

Arthur leans on the bar. He has begun to be aware that others in the pub are aware of him. He is aware, that is, suddenly, of his notoriety, of himself as a famous singer, standing, drinking alone, in some obscure London pub. In fact, it may or may not be obscure, he doesn't know. He simply wandered in, sometime ago.

He walked from Piccadilly, and now, he knows where he is. He is not far from his hotel.

He is aware of his notoriety in another way: a pair of Irish eyes—he is certain that they are Irish—are staring at him, have been staring at him, from a table in a far corner of the room.

It cannot be said—tonight—that Arthur is tempted by, or is able to respond to, the astoundingly open confession, or the hope, or the plea, in those eyes. On another night, yes, in this city, or in other cities, yes: but promises can be made with the body as sacred as those made in speech, and Arthur has, according to Arthur, defaulted too often on these promises. So he straightens his shoulders, seeing himself, or, rather, his attire. We do not change very much, really, and so Arthur is wearing black boots, old black corduroy trousers, a gray turtleneck sweater, and a pea jacket. And his thinning hair is just beginning to be sprinkled with salt.

He has a moment of panic as he straightens, for he has one of the bad habits of a star, or at least, of a star so beleaguered and improbable, which is to wander about with no identification and no cash.

Both delicately and courageously, he plunges into his pea jacket, relieved to discover his wallet, passport, traveler's checks, and, the Lord alone knows how, some English pounds.

The fact of the English pounds is due, entirely, he realizes, to Jimmy, and he smiles as he takes a five-pound note out of his wallet.

He is aware of the unsmiling Irish eyes at the far corner of the room, is aware of the other eyes on him, and he wants to get away from here, suddenly, away from these people, these eyes, this death. For, it *is* death, the human need to which one can find no way of responding, the need incapable of recognizing itself.

And then, again, something hits him, lightly, in the chest, and between the shoulder blades. He leans, lightly, on the bar, holding on to his five-pound note. He thinks that it must be gas, indigestion, he will go to the toilet, as soon as he pays his bill.

He pays his bill, but his hands are shaking, he puts his change in his pockets just any old way, and crosses the room. The toilet is at the far end of the room, through a narrow door, and down a flight of steps.

The journey across the room is the longest journey he has ever forced himself to make. He starts down the steps, and the steps rise up, striking him in the chest again, pounding between his shoulder blades, throwing him down on his back, staring down at him from the ceiling, just above his head.

I had a dream the other night. Jimmy and Julia and Arthur and me were standing on a country porch. It was raining, but we were sheltered from the rain. It fell before us, like a curtain. We could see outside this curtain, but nobody could see us.

It was as though we had all been sitting in the house, talking, or playing cards, or playing music, and someone had said, *Oh, children! Come, look here! Look, over yonder!*

And so, in my dream, Julia, who has been sitting in the house, writing a poem, puts the poem in the belt at her waist—a heavy belt, I remember it from somewhere, but I don't have time to ask her anything—and Jimmy, who has been cutting Arthur's hair with some big, cruel, golden scissors, and Arthur, who has been sort of weaving the hair as it falls to the floor into something he wants to give Jimmy, and me, I, Hall, who seems to have been chopping wood, so that we can have a fire tonight, all go running to the porch. I have the feeling that it might have been Paul's voice, but it might have been Ruth's voice: she is somewhere in this dream, either holding my elbow, a little bit behind me, or talking to Florence.

But Florence is in the rain pouring down on the road, just beyond this country porch. She is, at first, the only person I see, and I see her because of the mother-of-pearl comb in her hair: which calls the rain, flashing on the comb, like lightning flashes, or the pillar of cloud, by day. Amy is helping her to hold up Martha, and, just behind her, Sidney and Joel are trying to help each other up the blinding road.

I hold Tony on my shoulders; his hands cling to my hair. Odessa clings to my knee.

Ruth's finger strokes my back.

Arthur moves, to stand beside me.

"Shall we tell them? What's up the road?"

From the torrent of the road, Florence gives a warning, exasperated look: *Oho, oho.*

Paul flashes the magic silver locket my brother gave to me, and is covered by the rain. *Oho—oho.*

I turn, and look at Arthur.

We hear the rain, just beyond us: the rain pours down.

"Brother. I'm going away, to leave you."

Oho—oho

"Let's go inside," says Jimmy.

Oho—oho

Then, everyone is laughing. I have made a fire. We have fed the children, and the children are in bed. We are all drenched from the rain, even though I don't remember that we ever left the porch. The fire begins to dry us, at the same time that it makes us know how wet we are. And Arthur repeats his question.

"Shall we tell them? What's up the road?"

The question torments me, like a song I once heard Arthur sing, and can't now, in my dream, for the life of me, remember.

"I wish," says Jimmy, busy with the brilliant scissors at Arthur's rain forest of Senegalese hair, while Arthur's fingers are busy with whatever garment it is that he is weaving for Jimmy, "that you'd just let the rain do whatever the rain is doing."

"Oho—*oho*," says Julia.

> *Hurry down,*
> *sushine,*
> *see what tomorrow brings.*

I never heard Arthur sing this song. He turns his head, and watches me.

> The sun went down,
> Tomorrow brought us
> rain.

Then I do remember, in my dream, the beginning of a song I used to love to hear Arthur sing, *Oh, my loving brother, when the world's on fire, don't you want God's bosom to be your pillow?* and I say to him, in my dream, No, they'll find out what's up the road, ain't nothing up the road but us, man, and then I wake up, and my pillow is wet with tears.